Zimbabwe (ruins) ∴

Sofala

R H O D E S I A

Florence Ruth Schur

March—1981

Limpopo River

M O Ç A M B I

Phalaborwa

T r a n s v a a l

Mosega

Pretoria   Waterval-Boven

Johannesburg   Vrymeer   Venloo   Lourenço Marques

Chrissie Meer

Vaal River   SWAZI
                                        LAND

Veg Kop

Blood River   Umfolozi R.

ange   Kerkenberg   Spion
                              × Kop   Tugela R.   Dingane's Kraal
S t a t e
                          Blaauwkrantz
loemfontein

aba Nchu

A   LESOTHO

                          Durban (Port Natal)

D R A K E N S B E R G   N a t a l

I N D I A N   O C E A N

at Fish R.

Grahamstown

ay

The Nations of South Africa and Surrounding Lands

Jean Paul Tremblay

Volume 1

THE
COVENANT
Volume 1
James A. Michener

Random House New York

Chapter drawings in the style
of Bushmen art by Lois Lowenstein

Cartography by Jean Paul Tremblay

Drawing of baobab by Carole Lowenstein

Manufactured in the United States of America

Note

Mr. Errol L. Uys, a distinguished South African editor and journalist now living in the United States, was exceedingly helpful in the preparation of this manuscript. With a rare understanding of his birthplace and its people, he was able to clarify historical and social factors which an outsider might misinterpret, to correct verbal usage, and to verify data difficult to check. Working together for two years, we read the finished manuscript together seven times, twice aloud, a most demanding task. I thank him for his assistance.

JAMES A. MICHENER
St. Michaels, Md.
Christmas 1979

Acknowledgments

On my latest visit to South Africa, I was treated with invariable courtesy, and when it became known that I intended writing about the country, my phone rang daily with offers of assistance, erudite information and untrammeled discussion. When I returned to my hotel at night people waited to discuss points with me, and others offered me trips to places I would not otherwise have seen. This was true of all sectors of the society: black, Coloured, Indian, Afrikaner and English. The number of those to whom I am indebted reaches the hundreds; the following were especially helpful:

General: Philip C. Bateman, a free-lance writer with commendable books to his credit, spent seven weeks guiding me through his country on my hard-research trip. We traveled about five thousand miles, during which he introduced me to most of the experts cited below. I could not have done my work without his informed and congenial guidance.

Diamonds: John Wooldridge, Barry Hawthorne, Alex Hall, George Louw, Dr. Louis Murray of De Beers. Peter van Blommestein took me deep into the mines. I was unusually privileged to spend a morning with Lou Botes, a lonely old-time digger still operating in the Kimberley area, and to share an afternoon with J. S. Mills at his modern operation. Historian Derek Schaeffer was of great assistance, and Jack Young spent a day explaining how diamonds are moved through the market. Dr. John Gurney, head of Kimberlite Research Unit, University of Cape Town, checked details most helpfully. Dr. John A. Van Couvering, American Museum of Natural History, brought recent theories to my attention.

Early Man: Professor Philip Tobias allowed me to spend a day with him at one of his archaeological sites, and Alun Hughes showed me fossils of the great finds. Dr. C. K. Brain, director of the Transvaal Museum, was most helpful. Professor Nikolaas van der Merwe, head of Archaeology at the University of Cape Town, organized an extensive field trip in conjunction with his associate Janette Deacon and others. At the Africana Museum, Johannesburg, Mrs. L. J. De Wet and Hilary Bruce assisted me regarding San (Bushman) materials. Johannes Oberholzer, director of the National Museum, Bloemfontein, spent long hours sharing his conclusions.

Zimbabwe: Curator Peter Wright spent two days instructing me in the intricacies of the monument. Professor Tom Huffman, head of Archaeology of Witwatersrand University, was invaluable in explaining concepts.

Cape Settlement: Dr. Anna Böeseken, the nation's foremost woman scholar, was most helpful both in verbal instruction and in her remarkable printed materials. Numerous Dutch and Indonesian officials instructed me as to operations in Java. Officials of the government of Malaya helped me regarding Malacca. Peter Klein, Rotterdam, offered expert help on the V.O.C. James Klosser and Arthur Doble took me on an extensive field trip of Table Mountain. Dr. I. Norwich showed me his collection of early maps. Christine Van Zyl took me on a tour of Groot Constantia and the Koopmans de Wet Museum. Victor de Kock, former chief archivist, helped. Professor Eric Axelson, distinguished expert on early history, provided numerous insights.

Huguenots: Mrs. Elizabeth le Roux of Fransch Hoek and Dr. Jan P. van Doorn of Den Haag helped with summarizing data. Jan Walta spent three days showing me the Huguenot memorials in Amsterdam. The proprietors of two historical vineyards, Mr. and Mrs. Nico Myburgh of Meerlust, and Mr. and Mrs. Nicolas Krone of Twee Jonge Gezellen, Tulbagh, were unusually hospitable and informative. Professor M. Boucher, Department of History, University of South Africa, provided comment which helped.

Trekboers: Gwen Fagan organized a memorable trek to Church Street, Tulbagh (Land van Waveren). Colin Cochrane spent a day re-creating the old glories of Swellendam. Dr. Jan Knappert, London School of Oriental Studies, gave me valuable perspectives. Dr. D. J. van Zyl, head of History, University of Stellenbosch, offered valued criticism.

Mfecane: Dr. Peter Becker was generous with his time and insights. In 1971 I met with various Zulu leaders during an extensive tour of Zululand.

Great Trek: Professor C. F. J. Muller, leading expert, shared his ideas generously. Dr. Willem Punt, Sheila Henderson, Professor

Jack Gledhill, Grahamstown, who is writing a biography of Piet Retief, discussed details.

Salisbury and Old Sarum: Mrs. J. Llewellyn-Lloyd, Surrey.

Oriel College: Donald Grubin, a student of that college.

Afrikaners: P. J. Wassenaar; Professor Geoffrey Opland; Brand Fourie. Martin Spring was especially kind in discussing his book on South African–United States confrontation; Colin Legum; Harry Oppenheimer; The Honorable John Vorster, who spent an hour with me in forthright discussion; Jan Marais, member of Parliament, who entertained me socially and intellectually. Dr. Albert Hertzog spent a long evening sharing his views.

The English: Dr. Eily Gledhill, Grahamstown, took me on an extended field trip to sites of the Xhosa wars. Professor Guy Butler, Rhodes University, was unusually keen. Dr. Mooneen Buys of the De Beers staff discussed her doctoral thesis with me while curators of the Rhodes material provided insights, records and photographs. Professor P. H. Kapp, head of History, Rand Afrikaans University, checked the missionary section.

Black Life: I made continuous effort to meet with and understand black spokesmen. Some, like Bloke Modisane the writer, were in exile in London. Others, like the gifted social analyst Ben Magubane, of the University of Connecticut, were pursuing their careers outside South Africa; I spent three days with Magubane and he commented sharply on the Shaka chapter. Sheena Duncan was most helpful. Credo Mutwa showed me his witch doctor's establishment. Justice A. R. 'Jaap' Jacobs of Northern Cape District advised me. I spent five different days in Soweto, three under government supervision, two at night on my own. During these visits I met with many black leaders, those supporting government policies and those who were determined to end them.

Indian Community: I was able to visit various sites at which Indian merchants were being removed from areas reserved for whites. In Durban, I met with leaders of the Indian community to discuss these measures. Also A. R. Koor, Fordsburg.

Coloured Communities: My contacts were frequent, especially in Cape Town, where Brian Rees and Paul Andrews showed me squatter areas, in which I visited shacks and held discussions.

Boer War: Fiona Barbour, ethnologist at the Alexander McGregor Memorial Museum, Kimberley, analyzed the battlefields; Benjamin and Eileen Christopher conducted a two-day inspection of Spion Kop, Blaauwkrantz and the historical riches of Ladysmith; Major Philip Erskine, Stellenbosch, showed me his extraordinary collection of relics, including much material on General Buller.

Concentration Camps: Mrs. Johanna Christina Mulder, who survived the Standerton Camp, was wonderfully helpful; Johan Loock of the University of the Orange Free State provided much useful information.

Banning: In London, I spent an afternoon with Father Cosmos Desmond, who had just finished a protracted spell of banning. In 1971 I met with four banned persons, two white and two black. In 1978 I spent a morning with Reverend Beyers Naudé.

Sports: Morné du Plessis, major rugby star was most helpful; Louis Wessels, editor of a major sports magazine; Dawie de Villiers, famous Springbok captain (1971); Gary Player, with whom I had an extensive discussion in America.

Mining: I am especially indebted to Norman Kern, who spent a day showing me the deepest levels of the gold mines at Welkom.

Animals: Graeme Innes gave me three days of personal touring in Kruger National Park; Nick Steele showed me Hluhluwe and arranged for me to visit Umfolozi. Ken Tindley, a South African naturalist in charge of Gorongoza in Moçambique, allowed me to work with him for a week. John Owen and Miles Turner gave me unequaled aerial tours of Serengeti.

Vrymeer: I am particularly indebted to A. A. 'Tony' Rajchrt, who allowed me to inspect in great detail his farm at Chrissiesmeer, its operation, its chain of lakes and herd of blesbok.

Various scholars honored me by consenting to read chapters which impinged on their fields of specialization. I sought their harshest criticism and welcomed their suggestions. Where error was identified, I made corrections, but where interpretation was concerned, I sometimes ignored advice. No error which remains can be charged to anyone but me.

For each chapter, I consulted most of the available historical studies and found a wealth of material. Some of it substantiated what I wrote; some contested it. Since many biographers of Cecil Rhodes gloss over or suppress his embarrassment with the Princess Radziwill, I was left with only three accounts: two brief statements by two of his young men, and one excellent full-scale treatment by Brian Roberts: *Cecil Rhodes and the Princess*.

I wrote the brief segment in Chapter XIV concerning Cambridge University two years before the unmasking of Sir Anthony Blunt as the notorious 'fourth man.' My own inquiries had led me to his trail, or to that of someone exactly like him.

Contents

This is a novel and to construe it as anything else would be an error. The settings, the characters and most of the incidents are fictional. Trianon, De Kraal, Venloo, Vrymeer and Vwarda do not exist. The Nxumalo, Van Doorn, De Groot and Saltwood families do not exist. A few real characters do appear briefly—Van Riebeeck, Shaka, Cecil Rhodes, Oom Paul Kruger and Sir Redvers Buller, for example—and things said of them relate to recorded history. The Battle of Spion Kop is faithfully summarized, as are the principal events of the Great Trek. Great Zimbabwe is accurately presented in light of recent judgments. All incidents in the chapter on apartheid are offered from the research of the author alone and are vouched for by him.

The Covenant comes to its end as of December 1979 and therefore can take no account of subsequent events, such as the independence of Zimbabwe and the extended rioting that is taking place in South Africa as these pages are being proofread. It is believed that the narrative prepares the reader for these happenings and others that will follow.

It has been impossible to avoid certain labels once popularly accepted but now deemed pejorative: Bushman (instead of San or Khoisan); Hottentot (instead of Khoi-khoi); native, Kaffir and Bantu (instead of black). Coloured is capitalized because in South Africa it designates a legal classification.

THE COVENANT

Volume 1

I. Prologue

IT was the silent time before dawn, along the shores of what had been one of the most beautiful lakes in southern Africa. For almost a decade now little rain had fallen; the earth had baked; the water had lowered and become increasingly brackish.

The hippopotamus, lying with only her nostrils exposed, knew intuitively that she must soon quit this place and move her baby to some other body of water, but where and in what direction, she could not decipher.

The herd of zebra that came regularly to the lake edged their way down the bare, shelving sides and drank with reluctance the fetid water. One male, stubbornly moving away from the others, pawed at the hard earth, seeking to find a sweeter spring, but there was none.

Two female lions, who had been hunting fruitlessly all night, spotted the individualistic zebra and by arcane signals indicated that this was the one they would tackle when the herd left the lake. For the present they did nothing but wait in the dry and yellow grass.

Finally there was a noise. The sun was still some moments from the horizon when a rhinoceros, looking in its grotesque armor much the same as it had for the past three million years, rumbled down to the water and began rooting in the soft mud, searching for roots and drinking noisily through its little mouth.

When the sun was about to creep over the two conical hills that marked the eastern end of the lake, a herd of eland came to drink—big, majestic antelopes that moved with rare grace, and when they appeared, a little brown man who had been watching through the night, hidden in deep grass, whispered a prayer of thanks: 'If the eland come, there is still hope. If that rhinoceros stays, we can still eat.'

Gumsto was typical of his clan, four feet ten inches high, yellowish brown in color, thin and extremely wrinkled. Indeed, there were few areas of his body that did not contain deep indentations, and sometimes within a square inch twelve lines would run up and down, with eight or nine crisscrossing them. His face looked like the map of a very old watershed, marked by the trails of a thousand animals, and when he smiled, showing small white teeth, these wrinkles cut deeper into his countenance, making him look as if he were well past ninety. He was forty-three and his wrinkles had been with him since the age of twenty-two; they were the mark of his people.

The clan for which he was responsible numbered twenty-five; more would prove too difficult to feed; fewer, too vulnerable to attacks from animals. His consisted of himself as leader, his tough old wife Kharu, their sixteen-year-old son Gao, plus assorted males and females of all ages and all possible relationships. The safety of this clan was his obsession, but at times he could be diverted. When he looked up to greet the sun, as he did each morning, for it was the life-giver, he saw the two rounded hills, exactly like a woman's breasts, and he thought not of the safety of his clan but of Naoka.

She was seventeen, widowed when the rhinoceros now drinking at the lake killed her hunter husband. Soon she would be eligible to take a new mate, and Gumsto looked on her with longing. He realized that his wife was aware of his passion, but he had a variety of plans for circumventing her opposition. Naoka had to be his. It was only reasonable, for he was the leader.

His attention was deflected by a thunder of hooves. Zebra lookouts had spotted the two lions and had sounded retreat. Like a swarm of beautifully colored birds, the black-and-white animals scrambled up the dusty bank of the lake and headed for safety.

But the male who had seen fit to wander off, dissociating himself from the herd, now lost its protection, and the lionesses, obedient to plan, cut him off from the others. There was a wild chase, a leap onto the rear quarters of the zebra, a piteous scream, a raking claw across the windpipe. The handsome animal rolled in the dust, the lions holding fast.

Gumsto, watching every movement in the attack, muttered, 'That's what happens when you leave the clan.'

He remained immobile as seven other lions moved in to share the kill, attended by a score of hyenas who would wait for the bones, which they would crush with their enormous jaws to salvage the marrow. Aloft, a flight of vultures gathered for their share when the others were gone, and as these predators and scavengers went about their business, Gumsto proceeded with his.

His immediate responsibility was to feed his clan, and this day he would mount an attack on that rhinoceros, kill it or be killed by it, then gorge his people with one gigantic meal and move them off to some better site. As he reached these basic decisions, his small brown face was wreathed in a contented smile, for he was an optimist: There will be a better location.

Leaving the dying lake, he went to the living area of his clan, which consisted of absolutely nothing except a halting place beneath low trees. The terrain of each family was outlined by sticks and a few piled rocks, but there were no huts, no walls, no lean-tos, no paths, no shelter except grass rudely thrown across a framework of interlocked saplings. And each family's area contained only enough space for members to lie in hollows scooped out for their hips. The few possessions had been meticulously selected during centuries of wandering and were essential and tenderly prized: loincloths and skin cloaks for all, bows and arrows for the men, body powders and small adornments for the women.

Gumsto's family kept its shelter at the base of a tree, and when he had taken his position with his back against the trunk, he announced firmly, 'Antelope are leaving. Water too foul to drink. We must leave.'

Instantly old Kharu leaped to her feet and started striding about the small area, and since each of the other stick-lined habitations was close, everyone could hear her grumbling protests: 'We need more ostrich eggs. We dare not leave before Gao has killed his antelope.' On and on she ranted, a harridan of thirty-two with a horribly wrinkled face and a complaining voice. She was only four feet seven, but she exerted great influence, and when her tirade ended she threw herself upon the ground not eight inches from her husband and cried, 'It would be madness to leave.'

Gumsto, gratified that her complaint had been so moderate, turned his attention to the men in the other areas, and they, too, were so close that he could address them from his tree: 'Let us kill that rhinoceros, feed ourselves, and start for the new waters.'

'Where will we find them?'

Gumsto shrugged and pointed to the horizon.

'How many nights?'

'Who knows?'

'We know the desert continues for many nights,' a fearful man said. 'We've seen that.'

'Others have crossed it,' Gumsto said quickly. 'We know that, too.'

'But beyond? What then?'

'Who knows?'

The imprecision of his answers alarmed him as well as the others, and he might have drawn back from this great venture had he not chanced to see Naoka lolling in the dust behind the thin line of sticks that marked her quarters. She was a marvelous girl, smooth of skin and decked with beads cut from the thick shell of the ostrich egg. Her face radiated the joy of a fine young animal, and obviously she wanted a husband to replace the one the rhinoceros had killed. Aware that Gumsto was staring at her

in his hungry way, she smiled and nodded slightly as if to say, 'Let's go.'
And he nodded back as if to reply, 'What delight to share the dangers
with you.'

It was remarkable that a girl as nubile as Naoka was available for a
new marriage; a clan might operate together for thirty years without such
an accident, because it was the custom of this tribe for a girl to marry
when she was seven and her husband nineteen or twenty, for then trouble
was avoided. It was a fine system, for the husband could rear his wife in
ways he preferred; when she entered puberty to become a real wife, she
would be properly disciplined, knowing what things angered or pleased
her man. And he, having been forced to practice restraint while his wife
was still a child—ostracism if he molested her sexually prior to her second
period—acquired that self-control without which no man could ever become a good huntsman.

There were weaknesses in the system. Since the husband had to be
much older than the wife, there was in any group a surplus of old widows
whose men had died at the hunt or been killed by falls when searching
tall trees for honey. These elderly women were welcome to stay with the
band as long as they could function; when they could no longer chew or
keep up with the march, they would be placed in the shade of some bush,
given a bone with meat clinging to it, and one ostrich egg, and there they
died in dignity as the clan moved on.

Useless old widows were therefore common, but beautiful young ones
like Naoka were a precious rarity, and Gumsto calculated that if he could
somehow placate old Kharu, he stood a reasonable chance of gaining
Naoka as his second wife. But he realized that he must move with some
caution, because Kharu had spotted his intentions, and he was aware that
his son was also eying the beautiful girl, as were the other men.

So as he leaned against the tree, his right foot cradled in the cavity
above his left knee, he took stock of himself. He was a normal, good-looking man, rather taller than others in his group. He was compact, angular
of shoulder and slim of hip, as the desert required. His teeth were good,
and although he was deeply wrinkled, his eyes were powerful, unstained
by rheum or brown. Best of all, he was the master-tracker. From a distance
of miles he could discern the herd of antelope blending with the sand and
find the one that was going to lag, so that it could be detached and struck
with an arrow.

He possessed an inner sense which enabled him to think like an animal, to anticipate where the antelope would run or where the great rhinoceros was hiding. By looking at a track days old and noticing the manner in which the sand had drifted, he could almost detect the life history
of the animal. When fifteen tracks jumbled together, he could identify the
one made by the creature he sought and trace it through the medley.

Night fell, and a woman responsible for tending the fire placed her
branches with delicate attention, enough wood to produce a flare to warn

away predators, not too much to waste fuel. The swift, sure blackness of the savanna lowered upon the camp, and the twenty-five little brown people curled up under their antelope cloaks, their hips nestled in the little hollows. Two hyenas, always on the prowl, uttered their maniacal laughs at the edge of darkness, then moved on to some less-guarded spot. A lion roared in the distance and then another, and Gumsto, planning his exodus, thought not of these great beasts but of Naoka, sleeping alone not a dozen lengths away.

His plan had two parts: ignore old Kharu's bleating but involve her always more deeply in the exodus so that she would have no alternative but to support it; and lead his hunters on the trail of that rhinoceros for one last meal. In some ways it was easier to handle the rhinoceros than Kharu, for at dawn she had six new objections, delivered in a whining voice, but despite her irritating manner her cautions were, as Gumsto had to concede, substantial.

'Where will we find ostriches, tell me that,' she railed. 'And where can we find enough beetles?'

Glaring at her ugly face, Gumsto showed the love and respect he felt for this old companion. Chucking her on the cheek, he said, 'It's your task to find the ostriches and the beetles. You always do.' And he was off to muster his men.

Each hunter reported naked, except for a quiver of slender arrows, a bow, and a meager loincloth to which could be attached a precious receptacle in which he kept his lethal arrow tips—but only when the rhinoceros was sighted. Few hunters have ever sallied forth with such equipment to do battle with so monstrous a beast.

'From the next rise we may see him,' Gumsto reassured his men, but when he followed the spoor up the hill, they saw nothing. For two days, eating mere scraps and drinking almost no water, they pressed eastward, and then on the third day, as Gumsto felt certain they must, they saw far in the distance the dark and menacing form of the rhino.

The men sucked in their breath with pleasure and fear as Gumsto sat on his heels to study the characteristics of their enemy: 'He favors his left foreleg. See, he moves it carefully to avoid pressure. He stops to rest it. Now he runs to test it. He slows again. We shall attack from that corner.'

On the next day the little hunters overtook the rhino, and Gumsto was right: the huge animal did favor his left front leg.

Deftly he positioned his men so that no matter where the beast turned, someone would have a reasonable target, and when all were ready he signaled for them to prepare their arrows, and now a cultural miracle took place, for over the centuries the clan had developed a weapon of extraordinary complexity and effectiveness. Their arrow was like no other; it consisted of three separate but interlocking parts. The first was a slight shaft, slotted at one end to fit the bowstring. The secret of the arrow was the second part, an extremely delicate shaft, fitted at each end with a collar of sinew which could be tightened. Into one collar slipped the larger shaft; into the other went a small ostrich bone, very sharp and highly polished, onto which old Kharu's deadly poison had been smeared.

When assembled, the arrow was so frail that of itself it could scarcely have killed a small bird, yet so cleverly engineered that if properly used, it could cause the death of an elephant. It represented a triumph of human ingenuity; any being who had the intellect to devise this arrow could in time contrive ways to build a skyscraper or an airplane.

When the final tip was in place—handled with extreme care, for if it accidentally scratched a man, he would die—Gumsto used hand signs to direct his hunters to close in, but as they did so he detected one last avenue down which the rhino might escape if it saw the hunters. Ordinarily he would have placed one of his practiced men at that spot, but they were required elsewhere, so perforce he turned to his son, and with deep apprehension said, 'Keep him from running this way.'

He prayed that Gao would perform well, but he had doubts. The boy was going to become a fine hunter; of that there was no doubt. But he was slow in mastering the tricks, and occasionally Gumsto had the horrifying thought: What if he never learns? Who, then, will lead this clan? Who will keep the children alive on the long marches?

Gumsto had been right to be apprehensive, for when the rhinoceros became aware of the hunters, it galloped with great fury right at Gao, who proved quite powerless to turn the beast aside. With a contemptuous snort it broke through the circle of hunters and galloped free.

The men were not hesitant to condemn Gao for his lack of bravery, since they were hungry and the escaped rhino could have fed the entire clan, and Gumsto was appalled, not at his son's poor performance in this particular hunt, but at the grave danger his clan faced. Twice recently he had sensed his age—a shortness of breath and a weakness at unexpected moments—and the safety of his people weighed heavily upon him. The inadequacy of his son reflected on him, and he was ashamed.

In sore irritation he abandoned the rhinoceros and concentrated on a herd of little springbok. Assuming full control of his men, he brought them to a spot from which they could take good aim at two animals, but neither was hit. Then Gumsto himself stalked another and lodged his arrow in the lower part of the beast's neck.

Nothing visible happened, for the arrow's weight was quite inadequate to kill the beast; all it accomplished was to deposit the tip beneath the tough outer skin, where the poison would be free to disseminate. And now the excellence of this arrow manifested itself, for the springbok, feeling the slight sting, found a tree against which to rub, and had the arrow been of one piece, it would have been dislodged. Instead, it came apart at one of the collars, allowing the shaft to fall free while the poisoned tip worked its way ever deeper into the wound.

The springbok did not die immediately, for the effect of the poisoned arrow was debilitating rather than cataclysmic, and this meant that the men would have to track their doomed prey for most of that day. During the first hours the springbok scarcely knew it was in trouble; it merely felt an itching, but as the poison slowly took effect, strength ebbed and dizziness set in.

At dusk Gumsto predicted, 'Soon he goes down,' and he was right, for now the springbok could scarcely function. Even when it saw the hunters approach, it was powerless to leap aside. It gasped, staggered, and took refuge beside a tree, against which it leaned. Pitifully it called to its vanished companions, then its knees began to crumble and all was confusion as the little men ran up with stones.

The butchering was a meticulous affair, for Gumsto had to calculate exactly how much of the poisoned meat to toss aside; not even the hyenas would eat that. The first concern of the hunters was to save the blood; to them any liquid was precious. The liver and gizzard were ripped out and eaten on the spot, but the chunks of meat were taboo until taken back to camp and ritually apportioned so that every member of the clan could have a share.

Gumsto could not be proud of his accomplishment. Instead of bringing home a huge rhinoceros, he had produced only a small springbok; his people were going to go hungry, but what was worse was that at the tracking only he had foreseen which way the animals were going to move, and this was ominous. Since the clan knew nothing of agriculture or husbandry, it lived only on such meat as their poisoned arrows killed, and if those arrows were not used properly, their diet would be confined to marginal foods: tubers, bulbs, melons, rodents, snakes and such grubs as the women might find. This band had better develop a master-hunter quickly.

Normally, the son of a leader acquired his father's skills, but with Gao this had not happened, and Gumsto suspected that the deficiency was his: *I should not have allowed him to drift into peculiar ways.*

He remembered his son's behavior at their first big hunt together; when other lads were hacking up the carcass, Gao was preoccupied with cutting off the tips of the horns, and Gumsto realized then that there might be trouble ahead.

'You're collecting them to hold colors?' he asked.

'Yes. I need seven.'

'Gao, our clan has always had some man like you, showing us the spirits of the animals we seek. Every band has, and we treasure the work they do. But this should come after you've learned to track and kill, not before.'

Wherever the San people had traveled during the preceding two thousand years, they had left behind on rocks and in caves a record of their passage: great leaping animals crossing the sky with brave men pursuing them, and much of the good luck the San hunters had enjoyed stemmed from their careful attention to the spirits of the animals.

But before prayers, before obeisance to the animal spirits, before anything else on earth, the band must eat, and for a lad of sixteen to be delinquent in the skills of obtaining food was worrisome.

And then a shameful thought crept up on Gumsto: If Gao turns out to be a proficient hunter, he will be entitled to Naoka. As long as he remains the way he is, I face no trouble from that quarter. That exquisite woman was reserved for a real man, a master-hunter, and he himself was the only one available.

So when the meager portions of meat were distributed, he asked his wife airily, 'Have you talked with the widow Kusha about her daughter?'

'Why should I?' Kharu growled.

'Because Gao needs a wife.'

'Let him find one.' Kharu was the daughter of a famous hunter and took nonsense from no one.

'What's he to do?'

Kharu had had enough. Rushing at her husband, she shouted for all to hear, 'It's your job, worthless! You haven't taught him to hunt. And no man can claim a wife till he's killed his antelope.'

Gumsto weighed carefully what to say next. He was not truly frightened of his tough old wife, but he was attentive, and he was not sure how he ought to broach this delicate matter of moving Naoka into his ménage.

How beautiful she was! A tall girl, almost four feet nine, she was exquisite as she lay in the dust, her white teeth showing against her lovely brown complexion. To see her flawless skin close to Kharu's innumerable wrinkles was to witness a miracle, and it was impossible to believe that this golden girl could ever become like that old crone. Naoka was precious, a resonant human being at the apex of her attractiveness, with the voice of a whispering antelope and the litheness of a gazelle. Desperately Gumsto wanted her.

'I was thinking of Naoka,' he said carefully.

'Fine girl,' Kharu said. 'Gao could marry her if he knew how to hunt.'

'I wasn't thinking of Gao.'

He was not allowed to finish his line of reasoning, for Kharu shouted across the narrow space, 'Naoka! Come here!'

Idly, and with the provocative lassitude of a young girl who knows herself to be desirable, Naoka rolled from the hip on which she had been resting, adjusted her bracelets, looked to where Kharu waited, rose slowly, and delicately brushed the dust from her body, taking special care with her breasts, which glowed in the sun. Picking her way carefully, she stepped the few feet into Kharu's quarters.

'Good wishes,' she said as if completing a journey of miles.

'Are you still grieving?' Kharu asked.

'No.' The girl spoke with lovely intonation, each word suggesting others that might have been said. 'No, Kharu, dearest friend, I'm just living.' And she squatted on her haunches, knees and thighs tightly flexed, her bottom just off the ground.

'That's a poor life, Naoka dear. That's why I called.'

'Why?' Her face was a placid mask of innocence.

'Because I want to help you find a husband.'

Disdainfully the girl waved her right arm, indicating the bleak settlement: 'And where do you expect to find me a husband?'

'My son Gao needs a wife.'

'Has he spoken to Kusha? She has a baby daughter.'

'I wasn't really thinking of Kusha . . . or her daughter.'

'No?' the girl asked softly, smiling at Gumsto in a way to make him dizzy.

'I've been thinking of you,' Kharu said, adding quickly, 'Now if you married Gao . . .'

'Me?' the girl said in what seemed astonishment. Appealing to Gumsto, she added, 'I'd never be the proper wife for Gao, would I?'

'And why not?' Kharu demanded, rising.

'Because I'm like you, Kharu,' the girl said quietly. 'The daughter of a great hunter. And I was the wife of a hunter, not quite as good as Gumsto.' She flashed a look of power at the little man, then added, 'I could never marry Gao. A man who has not yet killed his eland.'

For this terrible dismissal she had chosen a freighted word: *eland*. The clan coexisted with the antelope, finding in them their physical and spiritual needs. They divided the breed into some twenty categories, each its own distinguished unit with its own terrain and individual habits. Any hunter ignorant of the variations of the antelope was ignorant of life.

There were the elegant little klipspringers, not much larger than a big bird; the small impala with black stripes marking their rumps; and the graceful springbok that could leap as if they had wings. There were the duiker, red and short-horned, and a universe of middle-sized animals: steenbok, gemsbok, blesbok and bushbuck, each with a different type of horn, each with its distinctive coloring.

These prolific animals of the middle range the hunters stalked incessantly; they provided much food. But there were four larger antelope that fascinated the little men, for one of these animals would feed a clan: the bearded wildebeest that trampled the savanna in their millions; the lyre-horned nyala; the huge kudu with its wildly twisting horns and white stripes; and rarest of all, the glorious sable with its enormous back-curved horns, so enchanting that hunters sometimes stood transfixed when they chanced to see one. Beast of beauty, animal of wonder, the sable appeared only rarely, as an apparition, and men at their campfires would often recall where and when they had seen their first. Not often was a sable killed, for the gods had given them perceptiveness beyond normal; they kept to the darker groves and rarely appeared at exposed watering holes.

That left the animal which the hunters treasured above all others: the giant eland, taller than a man, a remarkable beast with horns that twisted three or four times from forehead to tip, a tuft of black hair between the horns, a massive dewlap, and a distinctive white stripe separating forequarters from the bulk of the body. To the hunters this stately animal provided food to the body, courage to the heart and meaning to the soul. An eland was walking proof that gods existed, for who else could have contrived such a perfect animal? It gave structure to San life, for to catch it, men had to be clever and well organized. It served also as spiritual summary to a people lacking cathedrals and choirs; its movements epitomized the universe and formed a measuring rod for human behavior. The eland was not seen as a god, but rather as proof that gods existed, and when, after the hunt, the meat of its body was apportioned, all who ate shared its quintessence, a belief in no way unusual; thousands of years after the death of Gumsto, other religions would arise in which the ritual of eating of a god's body would confer benediction.

So Naoka, faithful to the traditions of her people, could laugh at old Kharu and reject the idea of a marriage with Gao: 'Let him prove himself. Let him kill his eland.'

It was now obvious to Kharu that unless she made it possible for her son Gao to qualify as a hunter, and thus marry Naoka, that young woman was going to steal Gumsto, who showed himself pathetically eager for the theft. It became advisable for the old woman to encourage hunts, but to do this she must ensure an abundant supply of poison for the arrows. That had always been her responsibility, and she was prepared to find a new supply now.

Like her husband, she was deeply worried about the safe continuance of her clan, and she saw that to protect it she must instruct other women in the collecting of poisons, but none had demonstrated any special skill. Clearly, Naoka was the one on whom the clan must depend in the future, and it was Kharu's job to induct her, regardless of the fear in which she held her.

'Come,' she muttered one morning, 'we must replenish the poison.' And the two women, so ill-matched and so suspicious of each other, set forth upon their search.

They walked nearly half a day toward the north, two women alone on the savanna with always the chance of encountering a lion or a rhinoceros, but driven by the necessity of finding that substance which alone would enable the band to survive. So far they had found nothing.

'What we're looking for is beetles,' old Kharu said as they searched the arid land, 'but only the ones with two white dots.' In fact, they were not looking for adult beetles, only for their larvae, and always of that special breed with the white specks and, Kharu claimed, an extra pair of legs.

It was impossible to explain how, over a period of more than ten thousand years, the women and their ancestors had isolated this little creature which alone among beetles was capable of producing a poison of remorseless virulence. How had such a discovery been made? No one remembered, it had occurred so very long ago. But when men can neither read nor write, when they have nothing external to distract their minds, they can spend their lives in minute observation, and if they have thousands of years in which to accumulate folk wisdom, it can become in time wisdom of a very high order. Such people discover plants which supply subtle drugs, and ores which yield metals, and signs in the sky directing the planting of crops, and laws governing the tides. Gumsto's San people had had time to study the larvae of a thousand different insects, finding at last the only one that produced a deadly poison. Old Kharu was the repository of this ancient lore, and now she was initiating young Naoka.

'There he is!' she cried, delighted at having tracked down her prey, and with Naoka at her side, watching attentively, she lay prone, her face a few inches from earth: 'Always look for the tiny marks he leaves. They point to his hiding place below.' And with her grubbing stick she dug out the harmless larva. Later, when it had been dried in the sun, pulverized and mixed with gummy substances obtained from shrubs, it would convert into one of the most venomous toxins mankind would discover, slow-acting but inevitably fatal.

'Now my son can kill his eland,' Kharu said, but Naoka smiled.

Only two tasks remained before the imperiled clan was free to embark upon its heroic journey: Gumsto must lead his men to kill a ritual eland to ensure survival; and his wife must seek out the ostriches. Gumsto attacked his problem first.

On the night before the hunt began, he sat by the fire and told his men, 'I have sometimes followed an eland for three days, hit him with my arrow, then tracked him for two more. And when I stood over his fallen body, beautiful and slain, tears sprang from my eyes, even though I had tasted no water for three days.'

The effect of this statement was ruined when Kharu growled, 'We're not interested in what you did. What are you going to do this time? To help your son kill his eland?' Gumsto, staring lasciviously at Naoka, ignored the question, and was profoundly excited when the girl winked at him, but on the hunt his desire to find an inheritor of his skills drove him to work with Gao as never before.

'In tracking, you notice everything, Gao. This touch here means that the animal leans slightly to the right.'

'Is it an eland?'

'No, but it is a large antelope. If we came upon it, we'd be satisfied.'

'But in your heart,' Gao said, 'you would want it to be an eland?'

Gumsto did not reply, and on the fifth day he spotted an eland spoor, and the great chase was on. Avidly he and his men trailed a herd of some two dozen animals, and at last they spotted them. Gumsto explained to his son which of the animals was the most likely target, and with caution they moved in.

The delicate arrows flew. Gumsto's struck. The eland rubbed itself against a tree, and the poison collected by Kharu and Naoka began to exert its subtle effect. One day, two days, then a moonless night settled over the savanna and in darkness the great beast made a last effort to escape, pushing its anguished legs up a small hill, slowly, slowly, with the little men always following, never rushing their attack, for they were confident.

At dawn the eland swayed from side to side, no longer in control of its movements. The fine horns were powerless; the head lowered; and a violent sickness attacked its innards. He coughed to clear himself of this undefined pain, then tried to gallop off.

The animal stumbled, recovered, and got to the top of a sandy rise, turning there to face his pursuers. When he saw Gumsto charging at him with a club, he leaped forward to repel this challenge, but all parts of his body failed at once, and he fell in a heap. But still he endeavored to protect himself, lashing out with his hooves.

And so he lay, fighting with phantoms and with the shadows of little men, defending himself until the last moment when rocks began smashing down upon his face and he rolled in the dust.

With intense passion Gumsto wished to utter some cry that would express his religious joy in slaying this noble beast, but his throat was parched and he could do nothing but reach down and touch the fallen eland. As he did so he saw that Gao had tears for the death of this creature, and with a wild leap he caught his son's hands and danced with him beside the eland.

'You were the good hunter today!' Gumsto shouted, inviting the other men to join, and they did, in celebration of the eland and Gao's honest participation. As they danced, one man who stood aside began a song of praise for this eland who had defended himself so gallantly:

'Head down, dewlap astray, dark eyes bleeding,
Sun on the rise, night forgotten and the glades . . .
    He stands, he stands.
Hot sand at the hooves, dark pain in the side,
Sun at the peak, morning forgotten and the lakes . . .
    He stands, he stands.

> Dark head, white line along the flanks, sharp horns,
> Soul of a dying world, eyes that pierce my soul . . .
>> He falls, he falls.
> And I am left with the falling of the sun.'

While the other women dried strips of eland to take on the perilous journey, Kharu attended to the ostriches, and with Naoka at her side to learn this element of survival, she walked far south to where the huge birds sometimes nested. She was not concerned with the birds themselves, for they were barely edible; what she sought were their eggs, especially old ones that had not hatched and were dried in the sun.

When they had collected a score, their contents long since evaporated, they wrapped them carefully in the cassocks they wore, slung them over their shoulders, and returned to camp, where the men were much relieved to see their success.

'We're almost ready to leave,' Kharu said, as if she had satisfied herself with omens, but before the clan dare move, she and Naoka must attend to the eggs. They carried them to the edge of the brackish water, and there, with a sharp stone awl, she made a neat hole in the end of each egg. Then Naoka submerged it in the lake, allowing it to fill. When all the eggs contained water, however poor, Kharu studied them for leakage and instructed Naoka in plugging the holes with wads of twisted grass: 'These will keep the clan alive through two risings of the new moon.'

When the time came to assemble the travelers, Gao was missing, and a young hunter said, 'He's up there.'

High on the rear face of the hill, in a kind of cave, they found Gao standing by a fire. About his hips hung a rhinoceros-skin belt, from which dangled seven antelope tips containing his colors. On a sloping rock he had engraved with a series of puncturing dots his evocation of the dark rhinoceros which had escaped because of his carelessness. With purity of line he boldly indicated the head with one sweep from mouth to horn, using another unbroken line to show the huge bulk of the animal, horn to tail. It was in the representation of the hindquarters, however, that he was most effective, for with one swift stroke he indicated both the form of the ham and its motion in running. The front legs, thundering across the veld, he again indicated in one sweep of line, and the colors he used to show the animal in its swift movement through the grass vibrated against the heavy color of the rock.

Run through the grass, dark beast! Gallop over the unconquered savanna, horns high! For a thousand years and then ten thousand run free, head level with the earth, feet pumping power, line and color in perfect harmony. Even Gumsto, looking at the completed animal, had to admit that his son had transmuted the moment of defeat when the rhinoceros broke free into a glowing record of what had otherwise been a disappointing day, and he was personally proud when a singer chanted:

> 'Earth trembling, sky thundering, heart catapulting,
> He breaks free, earth thundering,
> And my joy gallops with him . . .'

But he controlled his enthusiasm by warning his son, 'You caught him with your paints. Now you must catch him with your arrows.'

Why did the San, these Bushmen—as they would be called later—take so much trouble to depict the animals they killed for food? Was it to release the soul of the beast so that it might breed again? Or was it expiation of the guilt of killing? Or an evocation of animal-as-god? It is impossible to say; all we know is that in thousands of spots throughout southern Africa these hunters did paint their animals with a love that would never be exceeded. Anyone who saw Gao's rhinoceros would feel his heart skip with pleasure, for this was an animal that throbbed with life. It represented one of the purest expressions of art that man would achieve, and it came in the waking hours of human civilization. It was a product of man at his most unsullied, when artistic expression of the highest order was as natural and as necessary as hunting.

But Gumsto's theory on the matter must also be taken seriously. He asked each of his hunters to stand by the fire and look at the rhino over the left shoulder: 'It's bound to bring us good luck.' He knew that art contained a much-needed talismanic power.

In the 1980s experts from other continents would hear of this rhinoceros and come to stand in awe at the competence of the artist who had created it. One critic, familiar with Lascaux and Altamira, would say in his report:

> This splendid rhinoceros, painted by some unknown Bushman, is as fine a work of art as anything being done in the world today. Fortunately, someone built a fire in the cave, so we can carbon-date it to 13,000 B.P.E. (Before the Present Era), which makes us wonder at the excellent technical quality of the pigments, which seem much better than the ones we use today. But the excellence of this work lies in the power with which the animal is depicted. He is real. He flees real hunters whom we do not see. His head is held high in the joy of victory. But there is more. This is an evocation of all animals as seen by a man who loved them, and with this wild and joyous rhinoceros we gallop into worlds we might otherwise not have known.

* * *

Since the San could never know when they might kill another animal, when they did get one they gorged outrageously—eat, sleep, eat, fall in a stupor, eat some more—after which an amazing transformation occurred: the deep wrinkles that marred their bodies began to disappear; their skins became soft and rounded once more; and even old women of thirty-two like Kharu filled out and became beautiful, as they had been years before. Gumsto, seeing her thus, thought: She's beautiful the way I remember her. But then he saw Naoka lying insolently in the sun and he had thoughts that were more pertinent: But Naoka's going to look beautiful tomorrow, too.

After the eland was consumed, Gumsto said, 'In the morning we start,' and all that night he stood beside the lake that had comforted his people. He watched the animals come and go and was pleased when the zebra and the antelope stayed close together, each to its own clan, all members obedient to one general discipline which enabled them to survive attacks by the prowling lions.

At dawn, as if to send the travelers on their way, a host of pink flamingos rose from the far end of the lake and flew in drifting arcs across the sky, turning at the other end and doubling back in lovely involuted curves. Back and forth they flew some twenty times, like the shuttle in a loom weaving a cloth of pink and gold. Often they dipped low as if about to land, only to sweep suddenly upward to form gracious designs in their tapestry, the bright pink circles on their wings spilling through the air in vivid color, their long red legs trailing aft, their white necks extended fore. As Gumsto watched them, they circled for the last time, then headed north. They, too, were abandoning this lake.

When the file formed up, twenty-five persons one behind the other, Gumsto was not in the lead. That spot was taken by old Kharu, who carried a digging stick and about her shoulders a skin garment in whose flowing cape she had wrapped four ostrich eggs filled with water. Each of the other women carried the same supply, with little girls caring for only two.

She was in command because the clan was heading due west for five days to a spot where, two years before, Kharu had buried an emergency nest of nine eggs against the day when stragglers reached there exhausted. Since they were leaving this area, she wanted to recover those eggs and take them with her.

As they moved into land where few lakes or springs existed, she became the spiritual leader, for she knew the curious places where dew-water might be hiding. Or striding along earth so parched that water might never have existed there, she would spy a tendril so brown and withered that it must be dead, but when with her digging stick she traced it far underground, she would find attached to the vine a globular-root which, when dragged to the surface and compressed, yielded good water.

She enforced one inviolable rule: 'Do not use the ostrich eggs.' She was in charge of the water, and would allow no one to touch it. 'Dig for the roots. Drink them.' The ostrich eggs must be reserved for those frightening days when there were no roots.

Gumsto's clan did not inhabit this vast area alone. There were other San tribes hidden away in the savanna, and often they would meet as their journeys crisscrossed, and sometimes a woman from one clan would leave to marry a hunter from another, or children whose parents had died would be adopted from group to group. And in these chance meetings Gumsto's people would hear of other bands less fortunate: 'They went into the desert without enough water and were seen no more.'

It was Kharu's responsibility to see that this did not happen to her people, and often as they walked she would pass many trees without stopping, then notice one with a slightly different look, and when she went to that tree she would find trapped in the fork where branch met trunk a cache of sweet water.

Best of all, she would sometimes walk ahead for two or three days, her ostrich eggs bouncing behind, convinced that water lay hidden somewhere —her eyes sweeping from one horizon to the other. Then, stopping for the others to catch up with her, and in obedience to some signal they could not detect, she would indicate with her digging stick that all must head in this direction, and when they attained a slight rise they would see a far bank covered with vines bearing tsama melons, speckled, smaller than a man's head and filled with loose pulp from which extraordinary amounts of water could be extracted.

A tsama melon, Gumsto decided, was among the most beautiful objects in the world, almost as lovely as Naoka. He had been watching the girl, and was impressed by the manner in which she listened to Kharu's instructions in the rules for survival; at the end of this journey the girl was going to be competent to lead her own band across deserts, and Gumsto intended sharing that leadership with her.

'I am still thinking about Naoka,' he told Kharu one night.

'I think about her, too,' the old woman said.

'You do?'

'She will soon be ready to lead this clan. But she must have a husband, a young one, and if we can't find her one, we should give her to some other clan, for she is going to be a strong woman.'

Gumsto was about to say that he had seen enough of strong women, but Kharu interrupted: 'There are the thorn bushes!' and when she ran to them and uncovered the nine hidden ostrich eggs, she found the water still sweet. Sighing with gratitude, she said, 'Now we can enter the desert.'

Gumsto spent that night beset by two nagging problems: he could not understand how old Kharu could frustrate every plan he devised for taking Naoka to be his extra wife; and he could not cease staring hungrily at that beautiful girl. It was tantalizing to see her, smooth-skinned and lovely in the moonlight, with dust upon her long legs, lying so near to him and yet untouchable.

But as the long night passed, he had to admit that on one basic fact, Kharu was right. If she could instruct Naoka, a girl she disliked, in the principles of survival, he was obligated to speed his son's induction into manhood, and if in so doing, he qualified Gao to marry Naoka, that was a small price to pay for the safety of the clan. So he began investigating the terrain, looking for locations where eland might be grazing.

It was he who now walked at the head of the file, for the clan was penetrating land they had not touched before, and quick decisions were often necessary. They were a curious lot as they walked bravely into the arid lands, with four peculiarities that would astonish all who came in contact with them later.

Their hair did not grow like that of other people; it appeared in little twisted tufts, separated one from the other by considerable space of empty scalp.

The women had buttocks of enormous size, some projecting so far backward that they could be used by babies to ride upon. *Steatopygia* this phenomenon would be called (suet buttocks), and it was so pronounced that alien observers frequently doubted the evidence of their own eyes.

Their language was unique, for in addition to the hundred or so distinctive sounds from which the world's languages were constructed—the *ich* of German for example, or the *ñ* of Spanish, the San added five unique click sounds formed with lip, tongue and palate. One click sounded like a noisy kiss, one like a signal to a horse, one a clearing of the throat. Thus Gumsto used the normal complement of consonants and vowels, plus the five clicks, making his speech an explosive chatter unrivaled in the world.

The male penis was perpetually in a state of erection. When the first observers reported this to an incredulous world, explorers rushed to confirm the miraculous condition, and one French scientist said, 'They are always at the ready, like a well-trained unit of infantry.'

When they were far into the desert, their search for food became so imperative that they could not make much forward progress, but even so, their drift toward the west and south was irreversible, and as the moons changed they passed deeper and deeper into the desert. It was not an endless sweep of white sand, such as the desert of northern Africa would become in historic periods; it was a rolling, brutal mix of isolated rock sentinels, thorn bush clinging to the red sun-bleached surface, little animals scurrying about at night, larger antelope and their predators moving by day in ceaseless search for water, but never seen. To venture forth upon this cruel expanse of blazing noontimes and bitterly cold nights even if one had adequate food and water would be daring; to try to cross it as these Bushmen were doing was heroic.

One afternoon Kharu, always casting about with hungry eyes, leaped in the air like a gazelle, shouted 'Oooooooooo!' and sped across the desert like an antelope with torn and dirty coat. She had spied a tortoise, and when she captured it, with the band cheering, she looked up in wrinkled triumph, her tiny hands holding the delicacy above her head. A fire was quickly started from the rapid friction of two sticks, and when the coals were hottest the tortoise was pitched upon them, upside down, and there it sizzled, sending its precious aroma through the clan.

The steam popped its shell apart, and when it cooled Kharu apportioned its meat and juices, not much more than a smear to each of the twenty-five, and an extra dab to Kusha, who was pregnant, and although the amount each received was scarcely enough to chew, it had a wondrous effect, for it reminded the small people of what food was like. It could not possibly have satiated anyone, but it sustained everyone.

The problem of water was equally acute, for in the desert none was found in the tree forks, and often there were no trees. Tsama melons, which could survive almost anywhere, were sparse and shriveled in this terrain. The wanderers had been forced to draw upon the ostrich eggs until there were only nine left, but Kharu knew from past adventures that this water must be kept for the last extremity, and they were far from that. With her stick she dug for roots that might contain a tiny bit of liquid and allowed her people to chew on these until their mouths were wet. She sought any shrub that might have trapped an accumulation of dew, and always she looked for indications that some deep-hidden trickle was moving beneath the rocky sand.

When she located such a spot she dug as deeply as she could with her hands, then pushed a long reed beneath the surface. If she guessed right, she could painfully suck out small amounts of water, drop by drop, and take them into her mouth but not drink them. Along another reed, which she held in the corner of her lips, she let the water trickle down into an ostrich egg, from which her threatened companions would later drink.

When two days passed with no water at all, it was obvious that she must begin to draw upon the nine eggs, and in accordance with ancient tradition she drew first upon the seven carried by others, reserving hers for what were called 'the dying days.' Each noon, when the sun was hottest, she moved among her people, encouraging them: 'We will find water soon,' and she would refuse them a ration, but in the late afternoon, when they had survived the worst, she would order an egg to be passed, not to drink, but for a wetting of the lips, and as the water diminished a mysterious phenomenon overtook the women who carried the eggs. As long as the eggs were full and heavy they constituted a burden pulling down on the women's shoulders; but even with this weight, they moved with light steps, knowing that they carried the safety of all; but when the water was drunk, making the eggs no longer a burden, the women walked painfully, their shoulders hungry for the lost weight, their minds always brooding upon their inability to be of further service because of their empty shells.

Kharu, feeling the consoling heaviness of her eggs, knew that as long as she could retain them, the clan could live, but the afternoon came when she, too, had to broach one of them, the next to last, and when the journey resumed she could detect the difference in weight, and the terror began.

As the senior woman she had another obligation not to be avoided: it came when Kusha went into labor, forcing the band to halt in a barren stretch of sand. It was the custom for pregnant women about to deliver to move apart from the others, seeking some gully or tree-protected glade, and here, unaided, to bring forth the newborn, and Kusha did this, but after a while she summoned Kharu, and the withered old woman went behind the hillock to find that Kusha had delivered twins, a boy and a girl.

She knew instantly what she must do. Placing the tiny female at Kusha's breast, she took the male aside and with her digging stick prepared a shallow grave. With gentleness she placed the boy in it, and hardened her heart when he began to cry. Quickly she smothered the babe by throwing down earth to refill the hole, for although children were needed to keep the clan vital, twins were omens of bad luck, and when a choice as painful as this became obligatory, it was always the male that was sacrificed. Even one extra infant, during a desert crossing, would consume water that might prove critical.

Kharu, having discharged her obligations, now demanded that Gumsto fulfill his: 'We must take even the boldest steps to secure water and meat. And you must allow Gao to do the killing, for he cannot lead this clan without a wife.'

Gumsto nodded. He had used every stratagem to delay this moment, but now he was satisfied that his son must ready himself for command: 'It's difficult to think of him leading the hunters. Or Naoka gathering beetles.'

Kharu smiled at him. 'You're an old man now. It's time you gave up your foolish dreams.' She moved close to him and took his hand. 'We never suffered in this clan when you were leader. Now teach Gao to be like you.'

He took his son aside and said grimly, 'We are close to perishing unless we have the courage to take daring steps. Those hills to the west, I'm sure they hold eland and water. But they also hold lions. Are you ready?' When Gao nodded, Gumsto led the file west, with everyone surviving precariously on sips of water from Kharu's final egg.

As they headed for the ridge of hills they were kept under observation: far in the blazing sky, wheeling endlessly to mark anything that moved across the desert, a flight of vultures watched the tiny band impassively. That these forlorn stragglers would accomplish their salvation seemed most improbable, and the vultures waited, patterning the sky with impatience. Hyenas stirred in various parts of the desert, for if the vultures remained aloft, some living thing must be about to perish, and the scavengers moved close, certain that some older person would soon fall behind.

This time they were cheated by old Kharu, her wrinkles so deep that not even dust could penetrate. It was she who apportioned the last water from her final egg and who then strode ahead, determined to keep her people moving forward, and it was she, not her husband, who first saw the eland exactly where he had predicted.

It was a frustrating hunt. Near death from thirst and hunger, the little band watched impotently as the eland moved majestically out of one trap after another; the combined skills of Gumsto and his son were neutralized by the cleverness of the animals. On the second night the fatigued men heard an ominous roaring, and for a long time no one spoke, but finally Gao, who understood animals, uttered the fateful words: 'We must use the lions.'

This strategy was usually avoided, for it entailed so much danger that none of the hunters wished to employ it, but old Kharu, who was watching her clan disintegrate, desperately wanted to encourage the men. She knew that in matters of hunting, decisions must always be left to them; nevertheless, when no one supported her son, she broke ancient tradition by thrusting herself into the midst of the hunters and saying firmly, 'Gao is right. We shall die if we don't use the lions.'

Gumsto looked at his weather-beaten old woman with pride, knowing the courage required for her to intrude upon this meeting. 'Tomorrow we will use the lions,' he said.

This tactic, used only in extremity, would require the united effort of all, even the children, and the probability was great that one or several would lose their lives, but when the continuance of the band was at stake, there was no alternative.

'We go,' Gumsto said quietly, and his little people spread themselves into a half-moon, creeping toward the eland. Gao left the group to ascertain exactly where the lions dozed, and when he signaled their position, Gumsto and another hunter started to move noisily, so that the eland would hear them and edge away. As planned, the big animals did see them, did become nervous, and did run off, directly into the claws of the tawny beasts. A female lion grasped the throat of the biggest eland, bit into its neck, and brought it down.

Now came the time for audacity and precise execution. Gumsto and Gao kept their people in hiding, each person quietly grasping clubs and rocks for the heroic moment. They watched the lions feeding, and the lips of even the bravest grew dry; the hearts of the women beat faster in contemplation of what they must now do; and children who had never previously participated in a hunt knew that they must succeed or perish.

'Now!' Gumsto cried, and with a sudden rush, everyone surged forward, shouting madly, brandishing clubs and hurling rocks to drive the lions from their kill.

It was a most perilous maneuver, for the lions could easily have slain any one or two or three of the San, but to have so many rushing at them and with so much confusion bewildered the beasts, and they started to mill about. It was at this point that Gumsto sprang directly at the principal lions, beating them about the face with his club.

He had volunteered for this suicidal mission because the continuance of his band was more important than the continuance of his life, but at the moment when all hung in the balance—one man against the lions—he was saved by the sudden appearance of Gao at his side, roaring and thrashing, and forcing the snarling lions to withdraw.

But when the eland was taken by the San, with a dozen hyenas chuckling in anticipation, it was neither Gumsto nor Gao who assumed charge, but Kharu, rummaging with bloody hands through the exposed entrails until she found the most precious portion of the carcass, the rumen, that preliminary stomach of all animals called ruminants. When she felt how heavy it was, her old face broke into smiles, for it was here that the dead eland had collected grass for later digestion, and with it a large amount of water to make the grass soft.

Ripping open the rumen, Kharu squeezed the grassy accumulation, expelling enough liquid to fill her eggs, and in a peculiar way this liquid was better than water, for it was astringent, and bitter, and cleansing, and when she doled out a few drops to all, their thirst was assuaged. On this miraculous fluid the band would survive.

At the end of their joyous feasting, the exhausted gluttons lay about the carcass in stupor, their bellies extended; when they revived, Kharu made her speech: 'Since Gao found the eland, and since he drove away the lions, let us proclaim him a hunter and award him a wife. Naoka, step forward.'

One man, a considerable hunter himself, protested justifiably that since Gao had not actually slain the eland, he did not qualify, and there was consternation. But Kharu nudged her husband forcefully, and Gumsto stepped forward. Taking his son by the hand, he stood before the clan and said proudly, 'A lion is just as important as an eland. And this boy drove away four lions that were about to kill me. He is a hunter.' And with emotions that almost tore him apart, he passed his son's hand into that of Naoka.

'Ah-wee!' Kharu cried, leaping into the air. 'We shall dance.' And when the calabash sounded, and hands beat out the rhythm, the little people swirled in joy, celebrating their victory over the lions and the satisfying news that soon Naoka and Gao would have children to perpetuate the clan. Round and round they went, shouting old words and stomping to

raise a sanctifying dust. All night they danced, dropping at times from exhaustion, but even from their fallen positions they continued to shout
oracular words. Other antelope would be caught; other wells would be
found for replenishing the eggs; children would grow to manhood; and
their wandering would never cease. They were hunter-gatherers, the people with no home, no fixed responsibilities except the conservation of food
and water against the day of peril, and when the allotted moons had come
and gone, the dancers would go, too, and others would cross these barren
wastes and dance their dances through the long nights.

Gumsto, watching the celebrants, thought: Kharu was right, as usual.
The young to the young. The old to the old. Everything has its rules. And
when he saw his wife dancing vigorously with the women, he leaped up
and joined the men. Kharu, watching him, noticed that he limped
slightly, but she said nothing.

The festivities had to be brief, for the clan must move on to safer
areas, but in the moving, Kharu saw something else that disturbed her:
Gumsto was beginning to lag, surrendering his accustomed position in the
van to Gao, and when this had occurred several times, she spoke to him.

'Are you grieving over Naoka? You know she merited a younger husband.'

'It's my leg.'

'What?' The simplicity of her question hid the terror she felt, for a
damaged leg was about the worst thing that could happen on a journey.

'When we charged the lions . . .'

'They clawed you?'

'Yes.'

'Oh, Gumsto!' she wailed. 'And I sent you on that mission.'

'You came, too. The lions could have got you.' He sat on a rock while
Kharu explored the sore, and from the manner in which he winced when
she touched certain nerves she knew that it was in sad condition. 'In two
days we'll look again,' she said, but when he walked with a sideways limp,
dragging his left leg, she knew that neither two days nor twenty would
heal his hurt. And she noticed that aloft three vultures followed him with
the same relentless attention he had exercised when tracking a wounded
antelope.

Whenever the clan moved onward, she stayed close to him, and once
when the pain surged with great force and he bit his lip to prevent tears
from showing, she led him to a resting spot, and there they remembered
the days when he had taken his eland to her father, that great hunter, and
asked for Kharu in marriage.

'You were seven,' Gumsto said, 'and already you knew all things.'

'My mother mastered the desert.'

'You were a good child.'

'I was proud of you. Taller, stronger than the husbands of the other
girls.'

'Kharu, they were good days, in those lands around the lake.'

'But the water grew stale. The water always grows stale.'

'The rhinoceros, the herds of wildebeest, the zebras.' He recounted his triumphs from the days when his band ate well.

'You were as knowing as my father,' she conceded. Then she helped him rejoin the band as it moved south, and when it became apparent that he could never again lead the hunt, she told Gao, 'Now you must find the meat.'

Gumsto's accident produced an unforeseen result that both pleased and perplexed him. When the band halted eight days, both to replenish their ostrich eggs and give him time to recover, Gao quickly left the camp to find a large slab of smooth stone, on which he worked with furious energy during all daylight hours. From his resting place Gumsto could see his son, and guessed that he was creating a memorial to some important animal, but later, when Kharu helped him to the rock, he was unprepared for the wonder that was revealed.

Across a broad expanse Gao had formed not one eland but thirty-three, each as well composed as any he had previously drawn, but done with such fury that they exploded across their stony savanna. They leaped and quivered and exulted and rushed at unseen targets, a medley of horn and hoof that would astonish the world when it was discovered.

But there was a deficiency, and Gumsto noticed it immediately: 'You haven't colored them carefully.'

He was right. Gao had worked so feverishly to record this epic before his band moved on, that in the end he had simply splashed colors here and there, attempting to finish some of the creatures, satisfied with merely indicating the hue of others. The result was a confusion of movement and color, though it did give the massive composition a curious balance and a sense of real eland chasing across the timeless rock.

But why had the boy been so careless? Time was pressing, but he could have pleaded for two extra days. Pigments were also precious, and perhaps he realized he might not have enough to show each of the thirty-three properly, but he could have enlisted some hunter to help him find more.

There were a dozen other reasonable explanations for the wild coloring, but none approached the truth: Gao had created the eland in this arbitrary manner because at the height of his powers, when his senses were ablaze, he had experienced a revelation which showed that it was not the faithful laying down of color within the confines of his composition that would best indicate the reality of an eland, but a wild splashing that would catch the spirit of the sacred animals. It was an accident, the kind of accident that inspired artists contrive, and Gao could not explain it to his father.

Gumsto did not like the carelessness, not at all, for he deemed it an insolence to the eland, whose colors should be thus and so, as all men knew, but as he was about to complain he saw in the lower right-hand corner of the mural his son's depiction of a San hunter, a man awed by the eland but facing them with his frail arrow, and he saw that this little fellow was himself. This was a summary of his life, the recollection of all the eland he had slain to assure his people survival and meaning, and he was silent.

Three times he asked his son to carry him back so that he might study it, and live again with the animals that had meant so much, and whenever he saw himself so small at the lower corner he felt that Gao was right. This was the manner of life, that a man live forever with the major concerns, not with the grubs hiding under the bark of the thorn tree. To be on the savanna with a tiny arrow tip, and it the difference between death and life, and to throw oneself among the mightiest of the antelope, not the klipspringer and the duiker, and to fight them as they came, that was the nature of man—and it was his son who had shown him this truth.

When the others realized that Gumsto's days were almost finished, for he was now forty-five, a very old age for these people, they knew that the day was approaching when they could wait for him no longer, and one afternoon they watched indulgently as he crawled from his area into the one occupied by Gao and Naoka, where the young bride lolled in the sand. 'I wanted you for my wife,' he told her. She smiled. 'We could have . . .'

'It's better this way,' she said without moving. 'Gao is young and you're an old man now.'

'No more hunting,' he said.

'How good that your son learned.'

'Indeed,' the old man agreed. He had an infinity of things he wished to say to this splendid girl with the unwrinkled face, but she seemed uninterested, yet when he started to crawl back to his own area she smiled at him in her ravishing way and said, 'I would have liked you for my husband, Gumsto. You were a man.' She sighed. 'But my father was a man, too, and one day Gao will be as great a hunter as either of you.' She sighed again. 'It's always for the best.'

Everyone in the tribe knew that the decision had to be made. Gumsto lagged so constantly that he was becoming an impediment, and this could not be tolerated. For two more days old Kharu served as his crutch, allowing him to lean upon her while she leaned on her digging stick, two old people striving to keep up, and on the third day, when it seemed that he must be left behind, Kharu was surprised to find Naoka coming back to urge Gumsto along.

'Let him lean on me,' the girl said as she assumed the greater burden, and in the heat of the day, when Kharu herself began to falter, Naoka alone carried him along. At dusk, when the others were well ahead, Gumsto told his two women, 'This is the last night.' Naoka nodded and left the old couple by a thorn tree.

In the morning Kharu overtook the others, asking for a filled ostrich egg and a bone with some meat on it. These were provided by Gao, but it was Naoka who carried them back to where Gumsto sat propped against the thorn. 'We bring you farewell,' the girl said, and it was from her smooth hands that he took his final supplies.

'We must leave now,' Kharu said, and if she was crying, Gumsto could not detect it, for her tears fell into such deep wrinkles that they quickly became invisible. Gumsto leaned back exhausted, able to show no interest in the meat or the water, and after a while Naoka knelt down, touched him on the forehead, and departed.

'You must catch up,' Gumsto warned the woman he had tended since the age of seven.

Kharu rested upon her digging stick, reflected for a moment on the days they had spent together, then pushed the bone nearer to him and strode off.

For just a moment Gumsto looked up at the gathering vultures, but then his eyes lowered to follow the disappearing file, and as he watched it move toward better land he felt content. Gao was a hunter. Naoka was learning where the beetles hid, and the luscious tubers. With Kharu to guide them for a while, they would do well. The clan was twenty-five again, the right number: he was gone, but Kusha's baby restored the balance. The clan had survived bad days, and now as it disappeared he wished it well. His last thoughts, before the predators moved in, were of that zebra: He had insisted on moving away from his clan, and the lions had got him.

Kharu, walking with determination, soon passed Naoka, then overtook the main portion of the file, and assumed at last her place in the lead. There, with her stick to aid her, she led her band not due west, as it had been heading recently, but more to the southwest, as if she knew by some immortal instinct that there lay the Cape—with its endless supply of good water and wandering animals and wild vines that produced succulent things that could be gathered.

II. Zimbabwe

IN the year 1453 after Christ, the effective history of South Africa began by actions occurring at a most unlikely spot. At Cape St. Vincent, on the extreme southwestern tip of Europe, a monkish prince of Portugal in his fifty-ninth year sat in his monastery on the bleak promontory of Sagres and contemplated the tragedy that had overtaken his world. He would be known to history as Prince Henry the Navigator, which was preposterous in that he had never mastered navigation nor sailed in one of his ships with an explorer who had.

His genius was vision. At a time when his narrow world was circumscribed by fear and ignorance, those handmaidens of despair, he looked far beyond the confines of Europe, imagining worlds that awaited his discovery, and although he had studied carefully the reports of Marco Polo and knew that civilizations existed in the far Orient, he was convinced that until white men from Europe, baptized into Christianity, had stepped upon a piece of land, it remained for all reasonable purposes undiscovered, heathen and condemned.

His target was Africa. Twice he had visited this dark and brooding continent which lay so close to Portugal, once in grand victory at Ceuta when he was twenty-one, once in shameful defeat at Tangier when he was forty-three, and it fascinated him. From much study he had deduced that his ships, each flying a flag blazoned with the red cross of Jesus Christ, could sail southward along the western coast of Africa, turn a corner at the southern tip and sail up the eastern coast to the riches of India, China and mysterious Japan. Obstinately he had pursued this goal for forty years and would continue until his death seven years hence, but he would fail.

His defeat was Africa. No matter how forcefully he goaded his captains, they never accomplished much. They did rediscover the Madeira Islands in 1418, but it took sixteen more years before they passed a cape jutting out from the Sahara. They did round Cape Blanco in 1443, and one of Henry's ships had ventured a little farther south, but there the matter rested. The great hump of Africa was not yet rounded, and by the time Henry would die in 1460 very little would be completed; the notable voyages of Bartholomeu Dias and Vasco da Gama would not be made till long after the Navigator was gone.

His triumph was Africa. For although he was permitted by God to witness none of the success of which he dreamed, it was his dreams that sent the caravels south, and if he never saw a shred of merchandise from India or China coming home in his ships, he did fix Africa in the Renaissance mind, and he did spur its exploration and its conversion to Christianity. It was this latter goal that was of major importance, for he lived a monastic life, eschewing the grandeurs of the court and the intrigues which might have made him king, satisfied in his servitude to God. Of course, as a youth he had fathered an illegitimate daughter and later he did rampage as a soldier, but the main burden of his life was the Christianizing of Africa, and that was why the year 1453 brought him such grief.

The Muslims, those dreadful and perpetual enemies of Christ, had swarmed into Constantinople, lugging their ships across land to break the defenses, and this outpost, which had long protected Christianity from the infidel, had fallen. Since all Europe could now be invaded by the followers of Muhammad, it was more urgent than ever that a way be found around Africa to circumvent the menace, and it was this problem which preoccupied Henry as he studied his maps and laid his plans for new explorations.

What did he know of Africa? He had assembled most of the material available at that time, plus the rumors and the excited speculations of sea captains and travelers. He knew that millennia ago the Egyptians had ventured down the east coast for great distances, and he had talked with sailors who had touched Arab ports in that region. He had often read that amazing statement in Herodotus about a supposed ship which had set south from the Red Sea with the sun rising on its left and had sailed so far that one day the sun rose on its right; this ship had presumably circumnavigated the entire continent, but Herodotus added that he did not believe the story. Most enchanting were the repeated passages in the Old Testament referring to the immense stores of gold that Ophir, somewhere in Africa, provided:

> . . . and they went with the servants of Solomon to Ophir, and took thence four hundred and fifty talents of gold, and brought them to King Solomon.

Kings' daughters were among thy honourable women: upon thy right hand did stand the queen in gold of Ophir.

I will make a man more precious than fine gold; even a man than the golden wedge of Ophir.

The happy phrase, 'the golden wedge of Ophir,' sang in Henry's mind, urging him to visualize the vast mines from which the Queen of Sheba had brought her gifts to Solomon. But there were other verses that haunted him: King Solomon built a navy at Ezion-geber; his ships conducted voyages lasting three years, returning home with cargoes of gold and silver, ivory and apes and peacocks; and once King Jehoshaphat assembled a vast fleet to bring back the gold of Ophir 'but they went not; for the ships were broken at Ezion-geber.'

It was all so factual—the fleets, the voyages, the gold. 'And where was this Ezion-geber?' Prince Henry asked his sages. 'It was the city we know as Elath,' they replied, 'lying at a northern tip of the Red Sea.' When Henry consulted his maps it was clear that the Biblical ships must have gone south to Africa; there was no way by which they could have entered the Mediterranean. So somewhere along the east coast of Africa lay this golden wedge of Ophir, immeasurably rich and doubtless steeped in heathenism. To salvage it became a Christian duty.

And now, in 1453, the obligation was trebled, for with Constantinople in Muslim hands and the profitable trade routes to the East permanently cut, it was imperative that Africa be saved for Christianity so that ships could sail around it directly to India and China. Then the soldiers of Jesus Christ could capture Ophir from the Muslims and turn its gold to civilized purposes. But where was Ophir?

While Prince Henry brooded and plotted at Sagres, constantly goading his reluctant captains to seek the Cape which he knew must mark the southern tip of Africa, events at a small lake in that region were taking an interesting turn. To the undistinguished village of mud-and-thatch rondavels that huddled along the southern edge of this lake, a gang of noisy children came shouting, 'He comes! Old Seeker comes again!' And all the black inhabitants came out to greet the old man who dreamed.

When the file of newcomers reached the edge of the village it stopped to allow the Old Seeker time to arrange his clothing and take from a bag carried by one of his servants an iron staff topped by a handsome spread of ostrich feathers. Bearing this nobly in his left hand, he moved two steps forward, then prostrated himself, and from this position called, 'Great Chief, I bid you good morning!'

From the mass of villagers a man in his fifties stepped forward and nodded: 'Old Seeker, I bid you good morning.'

'Great Chief, did you sleep well?'

'If you slept well, I slept well.'

'I slept well, Great Chief.' Both the chief and his villagers must have sensed the irony in those words, for he was by no accounting a great chief, but protocol demanded that he be called such, especially when the man coming into the village sought advantages.

'You may rise,' the chief said, whereupon the Old Seeker stood erect, grasped his iron staff with one hand, placed his other upon the wrist, and rested his powder-gray head on both.

'What do you come seeking this time?' the chief asked, and evasively the old fellow replied, 'The goodness of the soil, the secrets of the earth.'

The chief nodded ceremoniously, and the formal greetings ended. 'How was the journey south?' he asked.

The old man handed his staff to a servant and said in a whisper, 'Each year, more difficult. I am tired. This is my last trip to your territories.'

Chief Ngalo burst into laughter, for the old man had made this threat three years ago and four years before that. He was a genial, conniving old rascal who had once served as overseer of mines in a great kingdom to the north and who now traveled far beyond his ruler's lands searching for additional mines, observing remote settlements, and probing always for new trade links. He was an ambassador-at-large, an explorer, a seeker.

'Why do you come to my poor village?' Chief Ngalo asked. 'You know we have no mines.'

'I come on a much different mission, dear friend. Salt.'

'If we had salt,' Ngalo said, 'we could trade with the world.'

The old man sighed. He had expected to be disappointed, but his people did need salt. However, they had other needs, some of them mysterious. 'What I could use,' he said confidentially, 'is rhinoceros horns. Not less than sixteen.' They were required, he explained, by older men who wished to marry young wives: 'They need assurance that they will not disappoint in bed.'

'But your king is a young man,' the chief said. 'Why does he need the horn?'

'Not he! For the rich old men with slanted eyes who live in a far country.'

From the tree under which they took their rest, the two men looked down at the lake, and Ngalo said, 'Tonight you will see many animals come to that water. Buffalo, lions, hippos, giraffes and antelope like the stars.' The Old Seeker nodded, and Ngalo added, 'But you will never see a rhino. Where can we possibly find sixteen horns?'

The old fellow reflected on this question and replied, 'In this life man is assigned difficult tasks. How to find a good wife. How to find sixteen horns. It is his task to find them.'

Chief Ngalo smiled. It was pleasurable to be with this old man. Always when he wanted something badly, he devised sententious and moral justifications. 'Mankind does not want sixteen rhinoceros horns,' he chided. 'You want them.'

'I am mankind.'

The chief could not resist such blandishments, but neither could he comply. 'Look, dear friend. We have no rhinos, but we have something much better.' Clapping for an aide, he cried, 'Tell Nxumalo to fetch the heavy earth!' And in a moment a boy of sixteen appeared, smiling, bearing three roughly rectangular ingots made from some kind of metal. Placing them on the ground before his father, he started to depart, but the Old Seeker asked, 'Do you understand what you have brought me, son?'

'Iron from Phalaborwa,' the boy said promptly. 'When my father's people went there to barter for these, I went with them. I saw the place where men worked the earth like ants. They had done so, they told me, for as long as anyone alive could remember, and many generations before that.'

'What did you trade?' the old man asked.

'Cloth. The cloth we weave.'

The Old Seeker smiled to indicate his pleasure that this lad should know the provenance of things, but once he had done so, he frowned. 'If I had wanted iron from the mines at Phalaborwa, I would have gone directly there. Thaba!' he shouted. 'Bring me the staff!' And when his servant ran up, bearing the carefully wrapped iron staff, the old man uncovered it and thrust it at the boy.

'That's real iron. From our mines south of Zimbabwe. We have all we need,' and contemptuously he pushed aside Nxumalo's rude ingots. Then he drew out from inside his robe a small oval object such as Nxumalo had never seen before. It was a shimmering yellow that glistened when light fell upon it, and it was suspended from a chain, each careful link of which was made of the same substance. When the old man thrust it suddenly upon him, Nxumalo found that it was surprisingly heavy.

'What is it?' he asked.

'Amulet.' There came a long pause. 'From Persia.' Another pregnant halting, then: 'Gold.'

'What is gold?' the boy asked.

'Now, there's a question!' the old man said, sitting back on his haunches and staring at the lake. 'For forty travels of the moon through the stars it was my job to find gold, and like you, I never knew what it was. It's death at the bottom of a deep pit. It's fire engulfing the iron containers when the smithy melts the ore. It's men sitting day after day, hammering out these links. But do you know what it is most of all?'

Nxumalo shook his head, liking the feel of the heavy metal. 'In the end it's a mystery, son. It's magic, because it lures men from lands you never heard of to come to our shores, to ford our rivers, to climb our mountains, to come a journey of many moons to Zimbabwe to get our gold.' Gently, almost lovingly, he retrieved the amulet and placed the chain about his neck, hiding the golden pendant beneath his cotton robe.

That was the beginning of his attempt to persuade Nxumalo: 'What you must do, son, is find eight rhinos and take their horns, then follow my trail to Zimbabwe . . .'

'What is Zimbabwe?' the boy asked one evening.

'How sad,' the old man said with unfeigned regret. 'Not one person in this village has ever seen Zimbabwe!'

'What is it?'

'Towers and soaring walls.' He paused and pointed to the low stone wall that surrounded the cattle kraal and said in an awed voice, 'Walls ten, twenty times higher than that. Buildings that reach to the sky.' A group of elders shook their heads in disbelief and clucked among themselves, but the Old Seeker ignored them. 'Our king, lord of a thousand villages bigger than yours, the great one the spirits talk to, he lives in a kraal surrounded by walls higher than trees.' He placed his hand on Nxumalo's arm and said, 'Until you've seen Zimbabwe, you live in darkness.'

Whenever he spoke like this, telling the boy of the grandness of the city from which he came, he reverted to the problem of the rhinoceros horns and the necessity of bringing them to the city, but one morning as he spoke with Nxumalo and his father he said abruptly, 'Ngalo, dear friend of many searchings, today I leave you to look for the Ridge-of-White-Waters, and I want Nxumalo to lead me.'

'He knows the way,' Ngalo said, pointing directly west to where the prominent ridge lay. It was a four-day journey which entailed some dangers, but the path was a pleasant one. 'Why do you wish to go?'

'In my day, Ngalo, I have sought many things. Women, high office, the path to Sofala, the king's good wishes. But the best thing I ever sought was gold. And I am convinced that in your terrain, there must be gold somewhere.' Contemptuously he dismissed the iron ingots that remained under the tree. Addressing only Nxumalo, he said, 'Iron gives temporary power. It can be made into spearheads and clubs. But gold gives permanent power. It can be fashioned into dreams, and men will come a long way to satisfy their dreams.'

On the third day of their journey west, after they had passed many small villages which the old man seemed to know, it became apparent to Nxumalo that the Seeker knew very well where the Ridge-of-White-Waters lay and that he had insisted on having companionship only because he wanted to convince Nxumalo of something. That night, as they were resting at the edge of a miserable kraal, the old man spied the boy standing alone, in his eyes a mixture of sadness and anticipation as he stared toward the empty lands to the south.

'What is it, young friend?'

'It is my brother, mfundisi,' he said, using a term of respect. 'Last year he left for the south, and I must go too, when it is time.' It was a custom

that he must honor: the oldest brother always succeeded to the chieftainship, while the younger brothers moved to the frontier and started
their own villages. And this had been done since these blacks came down
from the north, centuries ago.

'No, no!' the Old Seeker protested. 'Find me the rhinoceros horn.
Bring it to me in Zimbabwe.'

'Why should I do so?'

The old man took the boy's hands and said, 'If one like you, a boy of
deep promise, does not test himself in the city, he spends his life where?
In some wretched village like this.'

On the fourth day such discussions halted temporarily, for the Old
Seeker's troop was attacked by a band of little brown men who swarmed
like pestilential flies determined to repel an invader. When their slim
arrows began buzzing, Nxumalo shouted, 'Beware! Poison!' and he led the
Old Seeker to safety inside a ring of porters whose shields repelled the
arrows.

The fight continued for about an hour, with the little men shouting
battle orders in a preposterous series of clicking sounds, but gradually the
taller, more powerful blacks herded them away, and they retreated into
the savanna, still uttering their clicks.

'Aiee!' Nxumalo shouted with exasperation as the little fellows disappeared. 'Why do they attack us like jackals?'

Old Seeker, who had worked with the small people in the north, said
calmly, 'Because we're crossing hunting grounds they claim as their own.'

'Jackals!' the boy snorted, but he knew the old man was right.

On the morning of the fifth day, as planned, the file of men reached
the Ridge-of-White-Waters, which later settlers would call Witwatersrand,
where the Old Seeker hoped to find evidence that gold existed, but the
more carefully he explored the region—a handsome one, with prominent
hillocks from which Nxumalo could see for miles—the more disappointed
he became. Here the telltale signs, which in the lands about Zimbabwe indicated gold, were missing; there was no gold, and it became obvious that
the exploration had been fruitless, but on the evening of their last day of
tramping the hills the Old Seeker discovered what he was looking for. It
was an ant hill, eleven feet high, and he rushed to it, breaking it apart
with a long stick and fumbling through the fine-grained soil.

'What are you looking for?' Nxumalo asked, and the old man said,
'Gold. These ants dig down two hundred feet to build their tunnels. If
there's gold here, they bring flecks to the surface.'

At this site there were none, and reluctantly the Old Seeker had to
admit that he had taken this long journey to no avail: 'I didn't come to see
your father. I didn't come for rhino horn. Son, when you have a multitude
of targets, always aim for the one of merit. I came seeking gold, and I'm
convinced there's gold here.'

'But you didn't find it.'

'I had the joy of hunting. Son, have you listened to what I've been telling you these days?' He led Nxumalo some distance from the spot where his bearers waited, and as he looked out over the vast bleakness visible from the fruitless ridge he said, 'It isn't even gold I seek. It's what gold can achieve. To Zimbabwe come men from all across the world. They bring us gifts you cannot imagine. Four times I went down the trails to Sofala. Twice I sailed upon the dhows to mighty Kilwa. I saw things no man could ever forget. When you seek, you find things you did not anticipate.'

'What are you seeking?' Nxumalo asked.

The old man had no answer.

The task of collecting sixteen rhinoceros horns was proving much more complex than Nxumalo anticipated when he accepted the challenge, and after the Old Seeker had departed to visit other tribes who might or might not know of gold mines, the boy approached his father: 'I want to track down the rhinos.'

'So the old talker poisoned you?'

Nxumalo looked down at his feet, unwilling to admit that he had been entrapped by blandishments and singing words. 'Like the iron,' his father said. 'You went, and you dug for iron, and you found it. And when you came home with ingots . . . they didn't mean very much, not really.'

'I want to see the city,' Nxumalo said.

'And you shall. And when you come home you'll tell me, "It didn't matter very much."'

Those of Nxumalo's brothers who remained at the kraal wished him well in his quest for the rhinoceros horns but showed no interest in joining him. The tribe was essentially sedentary, with fixed villages, sturdy wattled huts and a settled agriculture. The women knew how to cultivate fields, the men how to manage cattle and tend the fat-tailed sheep. One brother directed the metalworkers who provided tools for the region and another was gaining a reputation in the district as a herbalist and diviner.

But it was Nxumalo who championed the ancient arts of hunting and tracking in the wild, and because of this he seemed the more regal figure, the young man who best preserved the historical merits of the tribe. He was the only one with much chance of tracking down eight rhinoceroses and delivering the sixteen aphrodisiac horns to Zimbabwe, so on a warm summer morning he and six helpers moved eastward toward the heavily wooded area leading to the sea.

He was an imposing lad, not yet full height but taller than most men, and the principal characteristic that struck those who saw him for the first time was power: his arms and legs were well-muscled and his torso much broader than his hips. His face was large and placid, as if he knew no anger, and when he smiled all his features participated and his shoulders moved forward, creating the impression that his entire body was enjoying whatever sensation had evoked the smile; and when his lips parted, his white teeth punctuated the grin. It was obvious that when he reached the age of eighteen he would be able to marry whom he pleased, for he was not only the chief's son but also a young prince among men.

He was so totally different from the small brown hunters who had once inhabited this area that he seemed unrelated to them, and in a way he was. Earliest man, Australopithecus, had once flourished over a large part of Africa, and as he developed into modern man, one branch settled close to the equator, where the sun placed a premium on black skin, which adjusted to its punishing rays; no primitive tribe of pale-white complexion could have prospered long in those blazing regions which produced Nxumalo's people, just as his heavily pigmented skin would have been at a severe disadvantage in the cold north, where the sun's parsimonious rays had to be carefully hoarded.

Slowly, over many centuries, Nxumalo's black ancestors, herding cattle before them and carrying seeds in their skin bags and baskets, had migrated southward, reaching the lake about four centuries after the birth of Christ. They arrived not as conquering heroes but as women and men seeking pasturage and safe enclaves; some had continued southward, but Nxumalo's tribe had fancied the encompassing hills about the lake.

As they lingered they came into contact with the small brown people, and gradually these had been pushed south or into the mountain ranges to the east. From these places the insatiable little hunters raided the kraals of Nxumalo's people, and there had to be confrontations. Some did live in peace with the invaders, trading the spoils of their hunt for tools and sanctuary, but thousands of others were turned into serfs or put to work at the mines. Association continued over centuries, and occasionally at Nxumalo's kraal some woman of his tribe would have enormous buttocks, signaling her inheritance from the small people. There were fierce clashes between the two groups but never a pitched battle; had there been, the end result might have been more humane, because as things turned out, the little brown people were being quietly smothered.

It was an able group that had moved south in this black migration: skilled artisans knew the secrets of smelting copper and making fine tools and weapons tipped with iron. In certain villages women wove cloth, sometimes intermixing threads of copper. And every family owned earthenware pots designed and crafted by clever women and fired in kilns in the ground.

Their language bore no resemblance to that of the small people. A few tribes, moving south along the shores of the eastern ocean, would pick up the click sounds, but Nxumalo's people had acquired none. Their speech was pure, with an extensive vocabulary capable of expressing abstract thought and a lively aptitude for tribal remembrance.

Two special attributes set these tribes ahead of any predecessors: they had developed sophisticated systems of government, in which a chief provided civil rule and a spirit-medium religious guidance; and they had mastered their environment, so that cattle herding, agriculture and the establishment of permanent villages became practical. And there was one more significant addition: over the vast area trade flourished, so that communities could socialize; Chief Ngalo's people could easily import iron ingots from the great mines at Phalaborwa, one hundred and seventy miles away, and then send fabricated spearheads to villages that lay two hundred miles southwest, beyond the Ridge-of-White-Waters.

In other words, when Nxumalo set forth to find the rhinoceros horns that would carry him to Zimbabwe, he was the inheritor of a substantial culture, which he intended, even at his early age, to augment and protect. He knew that when his father died, his older brother would inherit the chieftainship, at which time he himself would take a wife and move farther west to establish a frontier village of his own, and this prospect pleased him. His impending excursion to Zimbabwe was an exploration, not a removal.

On the sixth day of their march, after passing great herds of buffalo and wildebeest, Nxumalo told his companions, 'There must be rhinos among those trees,' but when they reached the area where the savanna gave way to real forest, they found nothing, and an older man suggested, 'I've never seen rhinos where the trees were so many,' and he pointed back toward the sparser savanna.

Nxumalo was about to rebuke the man, for he had once been with hunters who had found their rhino in heavy woods, but he restrained himself and asked, 'You found rhinos back there?'

'We did.'

'Then let's look there.' And when they did, they saw unmistakable signs of the mighty beast. But these blacks were not Bushmen, and the mastery the brown people had shown in tracking animals was little known; it was obvious that rhinos had been here, but where they had gone, the hunters could not determine. They hunted, therefore, in a hit-or-miss way, moving about in large circles and with such noise that a Bushman would have been shocked. But they were fortunate, and in time they came upon a black, pointed-snout rhino with two massive horns, one behind the other.

Killing so formidable a beast required both skill and courage. The former would be contributed by the six huntsmen with iron-tipped spears, the latter by Nxumalo as leader of the expedition. Placing his men along the route he intended the animal to follow, he moved quietly into position somewhat ahead of the beast, leaped suddenly from the grass and exposed himself to the startled animal, which, with instant impulse to destroy, lunged madly at the boy like some enormous juggernaut launched upon an undeviating course.

Horns low to impale, little legs pumping, snout ablaze and throat uttering deep growls, the rhinoceros charged with enormous power, while the boy ran backward with beautiful deftness. It was a moment no hunter could forget, that grand relationship of beast and man, when a single mistake on the part of the latter meant immediate death. And since the animal could run much faster than the boy, it was obvious that the latter must be killed unless some other force intervened, and this occurred just when it seemed that the powerful horns must catch the lad, for then the six hunters rose up and thrust their spears to turn the animal aside.

Four of the iron-tipped spears found their mark, and the great beast began to thrash at the low bushes in his path, forgetting the boy and wheeling to face his new adversaries, one of whom was stooping to recover his weapon. With a wild charge the beast bore down upon the man, who leaped aside, abandoning his spear, which the rhinoceros broke into many pieces. Then Nxumalo closed in with an axe, taking a mighty swipe at the beast's back legs. As he did so, another man thrust his spear with great force into the animal's neck.

The battle was not over, but its outcome was certain, and instead of trailing the damaged beast for days, as the Bushmen would have done, these determined men, with their superior weapons, closed in and brought him down with stabs and thrusts and tormentings. The great black beast tried to defend himself, kicking and goring, but in the end the seven men were too persistent, and he died.

'Two of our horns,' Nxumalo said as his men hacked the precious item from the carcass. They were curious, these horns, not horn at all but heavily compacted masses of hair, and their presence doomed this magnificent animal to near-extinction, for silly old men in distant China believed that rhinoceros horn, properly administered in powder form, restored virility, and China in these days was rich enough to search the world for horn. Nxumalo's men, so prudent in so many ways, cut from this dead rhinoceros only the two horns, cached them beneath a tree blazed with many cuts, and abandoned the ton or more of choice meat as they set out to find their next quarry.

They killed three additional rhinos on this hunt, driving them into pits lined with jagged stakes. The eight horns they carried back to the village, leaving the carcasses to the vultures, hyenas and ants, and in each of the killings young Nxumalo had run in the shadow of those piercing horns and those thundering feet. 'He is a skilled huntsman,' the men told the chief. 'He can do anything.' And when the boy heard this report he smiled, and his handsome black body glistened as he leaned forward to show his appreciation.

In almost no respect did Nxumalo's village resemble the dwelling place of the little brown men which had preceded it: now there were substantial rondavels instead of open space on the ground, and carefully nurtured grains and vegetables instead of chance gatherings; now there was a fixed community. But in one regard life was much the same: women and men wore almost no clothes.

So it was remarkable that one of the principal industries of the village was the weaving of cotton cloth, and when young Nxumalo returned with his eight rhinoceros horns, to be hailed a hero, it was natural that he take notice of one of the girls who sat in a low grass-roofed building by the lake, throwing their shuttles and shifting their looms.

Often as they spun their cotton they would pause to watch the animals grazing on the far side of the lake, and if a zebra kicked its heels or a gazelle danced in the air, the girls would applaud. And if a troop of elephants chanced to move in, or a flight of cranes, there would be cries of pleasure and not much would be accomplished.

Among the weavers was Zeolani, fifteen years old and daughter of the man who knew how to make copper wire from ingots brought south from the Limpopo River. From bits and pieces left over from the consignment, her father had made her the seven slim bracelets she wore upon her left wrist, so that when she threw the shuttle in her weaving she created soft music, which pleased her and set her apart from the others.

The work was not onerous; nothing that the tribe did demanded sustained effort, and there were long periods when the girls spent most of their days in idleness. Zeolani used these times to slip back to the looms and weave for herself cloth made of second-grade cotton adorned with bits of copper taken from her father's hoard. This cloth was not pure white, like that woven for trading; it was a honeyed tan, well-attuned to her blackness, and when its copper flecks caught the sun, the cloth seemed to dance.

Of it she made herself a skirt, the first seen in this village, and when she wrapped it about her slim waist and pirouetted by the lake, her dark breasts gleaming in the sunlight, she made herself a girl apart.

'They say you were brave at the hunt,' she said to Nxumalo as she danced by when he lingered at the silent weaving shelter.

'Rhinos are hard to find.'

'And hard to kill?' As she posed this question, she swung away from him, aware that as her skirt flared outward it showed to fine advantage.

'The others did the killing,' he said, entranced by her gentle movements.

'I kept watching to the east,' she said. 'I was afraid.'

He reached for her hand, and they sat looking across the lake at the desultory animals who wandered down for a midday drink: a few antelope, two or three zebra, and that was all. 'At dusk,' he said, 'that shore will swarm.'

'Look!' she cried as a lazy hippopotamus half rose from the waters, jawed mightily, then submerged.

'I wish the strangers in far lands wanted hippo teeth instead of rhino horns,' Nxumalo said. 'Much easier to do.' Zeolani said nothing, and after a while he touched her skirt, and then, almost as if he were driven to speak, he blurted out: 'When I am gone I'll remember this cloth.'

'It's true, then? You've decided to go?'

'Yes.'

'The old man talked and talked . . . and you believed him?'

'I'll go. I'll see the city. And I'll come back.'

Taking her by the hands, he said fervently, 'When I traveled with the Old Seeker we came upon a fine land and I thought, "We'll leave the lake to my brothers . . . to tend their cattle and their fields. Zeolani and I will find a few good hunters and we . . ."'

She did not coyly repeat the *we*, for she knew well what Nxumalo had been thinking, because she, too, had contemplated moving away from this village and starting a new one with her hunter-husband. Instead of speaking, she took his hand, drew it close to her naked breast, and whispered, 'I shall wait for you, Nxumalo.'

After the next hunt, in which Nxumalo brought down four more rhinos, the young lovers found many opportunities to discuss their uncertain future. 'Can't I go to Zimbabwe with you?' Zeolani asked.

'So far! The way uncertain. No, no.'

They decided upon a course fraught with danger, but their love had matured at such a dizzy speed that they were eager to risk the penalties. At Zeolani's signaling they wandered by different routes into the savanna east of the village to a spot hidden by the two small hills shaped like a woman's breasts, and there they made love repeatedly, even though it could mean the end of his trip to Zimbabwe if she became pregnant. If word of such condition circulated, the tribe would condemn her for having known a man without sanction and everyone would know who the man must have been, and they would be severely punished.

There, between the hills, they kept their trysts, and fortune was with them, for there was no pregnancy. Instead, there developed a deepening love, and as the day approached when Nxumalo must march north with the tribute, their last meetings assumed a mournful cast that could not be dispelled.

'I will walk behind you,' the girl said, 'and come into Zimbabwe as if by accident.'

'No, it's man's work,' said this boy of sixteen.

'I will wait for you. You are the only one I will ever live with.'

They went boldly to one of the hills south of the village and looked west toward the spot that Nxumalo had chosen many months ago. 'It lies far beyond. There's a small stream and many antelope. When I was sleeping there I heard a rustle, so I opened one eye. It could have been an enemy. What do you suppose it was?'

'Baboons?'

'Four sable antelope. Their horns were wider than this,' and when he extended his arms to their maximum, Zeolani slipped into them and they embraced for the last time. Tears came to her eyes as her slim fingers traced the muscles in his arm.

'We were intended,' she said. 'By every sign we were intended.' And she counted the omens that should have brought them together, and each knew that never in this life could another mate be found so inevitably right.

'I shall wait for you,' the girl said, and with this childish and futile promise ringing in his ears, Nxumalo set forth.

It was a journey any young man would want to make, five hundred miles due north across the heart of Africa, crossing wide rivers, sharing the pathway with animals innumerable, and heading for a city known only in legend or the garbled reports of the Old Seeker. Sixteen men would accompany their young leader, and since only the guide Sibisi had made the first part of this trip before, the others were at least as excited as Nxumalo.

He was surprised at how lightly the men were burdened; on one of his hunting trips his helpers would carry three times the weight, but Sibisi explained, 'Much safer if travel light. Use the first days to tighten muscles. Enjoy the freedom and make yourselves strong, because on the twenty-seventh day . . .' He dropped his voice ominously. 'Then we reach the Field of Granite.'

The loading would have been simpler if the rhinoceros horns could have been reduced to powder and adjusted to the men's other cargo, but this was forbidden. The horns had to be intact upon delivery at Sofala to the waiting dhows that would carry them thus to China, so that apothecaries could be assured they were getting true horn and not some admixture of dust to make the packages larger.

The file set forth at dawn on a clear autumn day, when the swollen rivers of spring and summer had receded and when animals born earlier in the year were large enough to be eaten. Sibisi set a pace that would not tire the men at the beginning, but would enable them to cover about twenty miles each day. For two weeks they would travel through savanna much as they had known at home, with no conspicuous or unusual features.

Two men who carried nothing proved invaluable, for it was they who ranged ahead, providing meat for the travelers. 'I want you to eat a lot and grow strong,' Sibisi said, 'because when we reach the Field of Granite we must be at our best.'

On the morning of the sixth day the march speeded considerably, and the file covered at least twenty-five miles a day until they approached the first notable site on their journey. 'Ahead lies the gorge,' Sibisi said, and he regaled the novices with accounts of this spectacular place: 'The river hesitates, looks at the wall of rock, then leaps forward shouting, "It can be done!" And mysteriously it picks its way through the red cliffs.'

Sibisi added, 'Mind your steps. You're not clever like the river.'

The gorge was so extremely narrow, only a few yards across, that the river rushed through with tremendous force, its turbulence well suited to the towering red flanks. The transit required the better part of a day, the porters following a precipitous footpath that clung to the eastern edge of the river and carried them at times down into the river itself. At the mid-point of the gorge the tops of the walls seemed to close in, so that the sky was obliterated, and here birds of great variety and color flashed through, playing a game of missing the cliffs as they darted about.

'Insects,' Sibisi said, showing the others how the turbulence of the water created air currents that tossed insects aloft, where birds awaited, and for a while as Nxumalo paused to absorb the wonder of this place—a river piercing a wall of rock—he felt that his journey could have no finer moment, but he was wrong. The true grandeur of this trip lay ahead, for as the travelers came out of the gorge they entered upon a place of wonder.

The land opened out like the vast ears of an elephant, and across it trees of the most outlandish nature scattered. 'They're upside down!' Nxumalo cried, rushing to a massive thing much thicker than any he had previously known. It was fifteen feet through the center, with bark soft and shaggy like the skin of an old dog; when he pressed against it, his thumb sank deep within. But what was truly remarkable were the branches, for this mighty tree reaching sixty feet into the air carried only tiny twigs resembling the roots of some frail plant, ripped out of its soil and stuck back in, upside down.

'It is upside down,' Sibisi agreed. 'The gods did it.'

'Why?'

'They made this excellent tree. Perfect in every respect. Big branches like an ordinary tree. But it was lazy, and when they came back to gather fruit, they found nothing. So in anger they ripped it out of the ground and jammed it back in, upside down, as you can see.'

When Nxumalo laughed at the sight of this monstrosity, Sibisi gripped his arm. 'No ridicule. Many men owe their lives to this tree, for when you are perishing from thirst you come here, puncture the bark, and out will drip a little water.' Nor was it only water the baobab gave, for its leaves could be boiled and eaten, its seeds sucked or ground to make a tingling drink, and its spongy wood stripped and woven into rope.

It was a tree that festooned the landscape, its great pillars of thick glossy bark and tangled branches spreading far into the sky. Wherever he looked north of the gorge, there stood these trees, as if to cry, 'We are sentinels of a new land. You are coming onto the earth we guard.'

And it was a new land. The savanna sprouted different grasses, and there were different birds and different small animals running between the rocks. But in the distance there were always the same large animals: elephant and eland and galloping zebra. They were the permanent gods that accompanied men when they journeyed north, and at night when they lit their campfire, Nxumalo could hear the lions prowling near, lured by the smell of human beings but repelled by their flames, and in the distance the soft grumbling of the hyenas. It was as if a man traveling across the savanna carried with him a garland of beasts, beautiful and wild and useful. Nxumalo, peering into the darkness, could sometimes see their eyes reflecting the flames, and he was always surprised at how close they came; on nights when it was his turn to keep the fire alive, he would allow it to die perilously low, and in the near-darkness he would see the lions moving closer, closer, their eyes not far from his, their soft and lovely forms clearly discernible. Then, with a low cry, he would poke the embers and throw on more wood, and they would quietly withdraw, perplexed by this untoward behavior but still fascinated by the wavering flames.

On the morning of the seventeenth day Nxumalo saw two phenomena that he would always remember; they were as strange to him as the upside-down baobab trees, and they were premonitory, for much of his life from this time on would be spent grappling with these mysteries.

From a hill three days north of the gorge he looked down to see his first mighty river, the Limpopo, roaring through the countryside with a heavy burden of floodwaters collected far upstream and a heavier burden of mud. The waters swirled and twisted, and to cross them was quite impossible, but Sibisi said, 'They'll subside. Two days we can walk across.' He could not have said this in spring, but he knew that this untimely flooding must have originated in some single storm and would soon abate.

In the waiting period Nxumalo inspected the second phenomenon, the vast copper deposits just south of the Limpopo, where he was surprised to see women, some as young as Zeolani, whose lives were spent grabbing at rock and hauling it lump by lump up rickety ladders to furnaces whose acrid fumes contaminated the air and shortened the lives of those who were forced to breathe them.

The tribe in charge of the mines had accumulated large bundles of copper wire, which Nxumalo agreed to have his men transport to Zimbabwe, and now the two who had been carrying nothing were pressed into service. Even Nxumalo, whose burden had been light, took four measures of the wire, since the miners paid well for this service.

'We've always traded our copper with Zimbabwe,' the mine overseer said, 'and when you reach the city you'll see why.' His words excited Nxumalo, and he was tempted to ask for more details, but he kept silent, preferring to find out for himself what lay at journey's end.

When the Limpopo subsided and its red-rock bottom was fordable, the seventeen men resumed the exciting part of their march, for now they were in the heart of a savanna so vast that it dwarfed any they had known before. Distances were tremendous, a rolling sea of euphorbia trees, baobabs and flat-topped thorn bushes, crowded with great animals and alluring birds. For endless miles the plains extended, rolling and swelling when small hills intervened, and cut by rivers with no name.

At the end of the first day's march from the Limpopo they came upon the farthest southern outpost of the kingdom of Zimbabwe, and Nxumalo could barely mask his disappointment. There was a kraal, to be sure, and it was surrounded by a stone wall, but it was not the soaring construction that Old Seeker had promised. 'It's larger than my father's wall,' Nxumalo said quietly, 'but I expected something that high.' And he pointed to a tree of modest size.

One of the herders attached to the outpost said, 'Patience, young boy. This is not the city.' When he saw Nxumalo's skepticism he led him along a path to a spot from which a valley could be seen. 'Now will you believe the greatness of Zimbabwe?' And for as far as his eye could travel, Nxumalo saw a vast herd of cattle moving between the hills. 'The king's smallest herd,' the man said. Nxumalo, who had been reared in a society where a man's status was determined by his cattle, realized that the King of Zimbabwe must be a man of extraordinary power.

When Sibisi and the outpost headman settled down with their gourds of beer, Nxumalo, uninformed on the topics they discussed, wandered off, to find something that quite bewitched him: one of the herdsmen, with little to do day after day, had caught a baby eland to rear as a pet. It was now full grown, heavier than one of Nxumalo's father's cows and with twisted horns twice as long and dangerous, but it was like a baby, pampered and running after its mother, in this case the herdsman, who ordered it about as if it were his fractious son.

The eland loved to play, and Nxumalo spent most of one day knocking about with it, pushing against its forehead, wrestling with its horns and avoiding its quick feet when the animal sought to neutralize the boy's cleverness. When the file moved north the eland walked with Nxumalo for a long time, its handsome flanks shining white in the morning sun. Then its master whistled, called its name, and the big animal stopped in the path, looked forward to his new friend and backward to its home, then stamped its forefeet in disgust and trotted back. Nxumalo stood transfixed in the bush, staring at the disappearing animal and wishing that he could take such a congenial beast with him, when the eland stopped, turned, and for a long spell stared back at the boy. They stayed thus for several minutes, consuming the space that separated them, then the animal tossed its head, flashed its fine horns, and disappeared.

Nxumalo now carried only two bundles of wire, for Sibisi had said quietly, 'I'll take the others. You must prepare yourself for the Field of Granite.' In the middle of the plains, blue on the far horizon, rose a line of mountains, and marking the pathway to them stood a chain of ant hills, some as high as trees, others lower but as big across as a baobab. They were reddish in color and hard as rock where the rains had moistened them prior to their baking by the sun.

On the twenty-ninth day as they neared Zimbabwe they saw ahead of them two mighty granite domes surrounded by many-spired euphorbias, and as they walked, bringing the domes ever closer, Sibisi pointed to the west, where a gigantic granite outcropping looked exactly like some monstrous elephant resting with its forelegs tucked under him. 'He guards the rock we seek,' Sibisi said, and the men moved more quickly to reach this vital stage in their progress.

Between the twin domes and the sleeping elephant lay a large field of granite boulders, big and round, like eggs half buried in the earth. Nxumalo had often seen boulders that resembled these, but never of such magnificent size and certainly none that had their peculiar quality. For all of them were exfoliating, as if they wished to create building blocks from which splendid structures could be made; they formed a quarry in which nine-tenths of the work was done by nature, where man had to do only the final sizing and the portage.

The rounded domes, fifty and sixty feet high, had been laid down a billion years ago in layers, and now the action of rain and sun and changing temperature had begun to peel away the layers. They were like gigantic onions made of rock, whose segments were being exposed and lifted away. The result was unbelievable: extensive slabs of choice granite, a uniform six inches thick, were thrown down year after year. Men collecting them could cut them into strips the width of a building block and many yards long. When other men cut these strips into ten-inch lengths, some of the best and strongest bricks ever devised would result.

There was only one drawback to this operation: the Field of Granite lay in the south; the site where the bricks were needed was five miles to the north. To solve this problem the king had long ago decreed a simple rule: no man or woman traveling north to Zimbabwe was permitted to pass this field without picking up at least three building blocks and lugging them to the capital. Strong men, like Sibisi's, were expected to carry eight, and even couriers like Nxumalo, son of a chief, had to bring three. If their other burdens were too great, they must be laid aside, for no man could move north without his stone bricks.

Masons working at the site tied the stones in packages of four, binding them with lianas found in the forest, and these were waiting for the southerners as they arrived. When the masons found that a chief's son was in the train, they prepared a bundle of only three bricks for him, and with this new burden he set off.

At first the stones were not oppressive, but as the hours passed, the men groaned, particularly those who had already been burdened with the copper. That night four men had to share the watch, tending the fire and fighting exhaustion, and when Nxumalo stood guard, he was so tired he forgot the animals and watched only the stars that marked the slow passage of his watch.

At dawn the punished men climbed the last hill, and at its crest they received a reward which made the drudgery acceptable, for there in a gracious valley, beside a marsh, stood the city of Zimbabwe, grand in a manner no one from Nxumalo's tribe could have imagined. There stood the mighty edifices built of rock, pile after glorious pile of gray-green granite rising from the valley floor.

'Look!' Sibisi cried in awe. 'That must be where the king worships!' And Nxumalo looked to the north where a hill of real size was crowned by a citadel whose rough stone walls shone in the morning sunlight. The men from the little village stood in silence, gaping at the wonder of the place. From a thousand huts in the shade of the mighty walls and parapets the workers of the city were greeting the dawn of a new day.

'This is Zimbabwe,' Nxumalo said, wiping his eyes, and no one spoke.

No group of visitors from beyond the Limpopo could expect to enter any of the handsome stone enclosures, so after dutifully depositing the rhino horns with the authorities, Nxumalo and his men were led to the section of the city occupied by the common people, and there they rested for fifteen days before starting their return journey. On the day of departure Nxumalo left his lodgings with a sense of sadness, for he had enjoyed this city and its manifold offerings, but as he reached the area where his men assembled, he felt his arm taken by a firm hand.

'Nxumalo, son of Ngalo,' a voice said, 'this is to be your home.' It was the Old Seeker, come to rescue the boy in whose future he had taken such a deep interest. 'You are to work on the walls.'

'But I am the son of a chief!'

'Since when does the smallest calf run with the bulls?'

Nxumalo did not reply, for he was learning that this old man was far more than a dreamy wanderer exploring the Ridge-of-White-Waters. In Zimbabwe he was a full-fledged councillor at the king's court, and now he told his young protégé, 'In Zimbabwe you do not force your way, Nxumalo. Our walls are built by the finest men in the city. They will not tolerate fools at their side. Satisfy them, and you will gain entrance.' And he pointed to the stone towers in the valley and the walls of the mountaintop citadel.

Zimbabwe in the year 1454 was certainly no duplicate of a European city like Ghent or Bordeaux. Its architecture was much ruder; it contained no Gothic cathedral; and its palace was infinitely simpler. Although its principal ritual and royal centers were made of stone, its houses were of clay-and-thatch construction. No one in the city could read; the history of the place was not written; there was no nationwide system of coinage; and society was less complex by many degrees than that in Europe.

It was, however, a thoughtfully organized, thriving community with a brilliant business capacity, evidenced by the teeming marketplace to which a network of producers and traders gravitated. A mild, healthful place with a fine water supply, it enjoyed the most advanced amenities of that day, right down to an ingenious system of drains. It had a particularized work force and a government which had been more stable than most of those in Europe. But even as it stood supreme over this heartland of southern Africa, dangerous undercurrents threatened the continuance of the place, for it was stretching its control and resources to the limit at a time when other regional forces were in movement, and no one could predict how much longer this great capital would continue to prosper.

It was into this center of grandeur and uncertainty that Nxumalo was projected, and as he labored on the wall, tapping into place rocks like those he had transported, he watched all things.

He saw how a constant stream of porters arrived from the compass points, each man bearing whatever valuable goods his district contributed to the capital, and he began to detect the variations that marked the different regions. There were, for example, noticeable shades of blackness among the men: those from the north, where the great rivers flowed, being darker; those from the west, where there had been more of the little brown people to mate with, being shaded toward brown. And one tribe from the east sent men who were conspicuously taller than the others, but all seemed capable.

They spoke in various tongues, too, when they were among themselves, but the variations in language were not great, and all could manage the speech of Zimbabwe, with amusing dialect differences betraying the fact that some were of the swamps and others from the empty plains. It was the residents of the city who attracted Nxumalo's principal notice, for they moved with an assurance that he had previously seen only in his father. They were in general a handsome people, but among them moved a cadre of officials who were outstanding. Usually taller than their fellows, they wore uniforms made of the most expensive imported cloth into which had been woven strands of gold and silver; they were never seen carrying anything except staffs indicating their office, and even these they did not use as walking sticks but rather as formal badges. Ordinary people moved aside when they approached, and one of these officials came each day to inspect the work being done by the stonemasons.

He was a considerate man who wanted to like the work for which he was responsible; only rarely did he order any section torn down and rebuilt, and one day when he was standing over Nxumalo, pecking at the young man's work with his staff, he suddenly burst into laughter, and no one knew why. 'We should get him to do the heavy work,' he said with a wave of his staff, indicating a baboon shuffling along on its hind legs and front knuckles, stopping to root in the ground near the post of the chief stonemason, who had found the creature abandoned at birth.

The inspector watched the tame baboon for some moments, then tapped Nxumalo with his staff: 'Your job will be to train him.' Chuckling at his joke, he moved along to inspect another part of the wall.

Having identified Nxumalo among the temporary sojourners who came great distances to labor at the walls before returning to their homes, this inspector formed the habit of asking him each day, 'Well, how are we progressing with the baboon?' then laughing generously. One day he asked, 'Aren't you the chieftain's son?' When Nxumalo nodded, he said, 'Old Seeker wants to see you. He says it's time,' and he ordered Nxumalo to lay down the board on which he had been carrying adobe.

The boy was about to descend when he saw a sight below which staggered him, for moving toward the marketplace came two men of astonishing appearance. They were not black! Like the cloth that Zeolani bleached in the sun, the skin of these men was not black at all, but a pale honey-tan, almost white, and they were dressed in flowing robes even whiter than their skins, with filament protection for their heads.

He was still staring when Old Seeker came up, bustling with importance. 'What's the matter, son?' he asked, and when he saw the strangers whose appearance had so shocked Nxumalo he laughed. 'Arabs. Come up from the sea.' And taking Nxumalo by the arm, he teased: 'If we follow them, you can waste the fortune you've been earning on the walls.'

Nxumalo and his mentor fell in behind the two white men as the latter proceeded regally toward the marketplace, followed by thirty black slaves who had carried their trade goods up from the seacoast. Wherever the procession appeared it was hailed with shouts, and hundreds of city residents trailed along behind to watch the strangers halt at a compound, where they were greeted effusively by a short, rotund black who dominated the market.

'What wonderful treasures I've put aside for you,' the round man cried as the Arabs moved forward to greet him. He was about to disclose more, intimating that as in the past, he had secreted a private hoard of goods to be exchanged for his personal gain, but at sight of Old Seeker his voice lost its animation, for the old man was a court official who sat in judgment on such illegal trading. Punishment was lifetime banishment, so the little merchant, much deflated, ended lamely, 'I'm sure you've brought many good things.'

'I'm sure the king will be pleased with our gifts,' the taller Arab said.

Mention of this august and mysterious figure caused Nxumalo to tremble, for in the months he'd been here, only twice had he glimpsed the king and even then not properly, for it was law that when the great lord of Zimbabwe passed, all must fall upon the ground and avert their eyes.

'It's wise of you to double your gifts,' Old Seeker told the Arabs as he watched them put aside the goods they intended to present the king. 'Last season your gifts were scarcely fit for this fat one here.' And he noticed the signs of worry that crossed the short man's face.

When the Arabs had their gifts prepared, Old Seeker surprised Nxumalo by handing him the iron staff of office: 'This day, son, you shall enter the great place with me.'

The young man who had so valiantly defied the rhinos looked as if he would faint, but the old man placed a reassuring hand on his shoulder: 'It's time for the grandeur I promised you, Nxumalo, son of Ngalo.'

There were no guards at the narrow northern entrance to the Grand Enclosure, for no mortal would dare cross that threshold unless eligible to do so. Since it was the custom for councillors to sponsor young men of promise, Old Seeker had been granted permission to introduce the able young fellow from the south.

They all halted just outside the entrance, for here the slaves must deliver their burdens to the court attendants. The Arabs themselves were not permitted more than three paces inside the austere walls, but as the visitors stood at attention Old Seeker moved forward to lead them into a smaller walled-in section of the enclosure.

'We shall wait here,' the old man said. 'We must follow every order with care.' To Nxumalo he whispered, 'Do what I do.'

The boy said nothing, for he was awed by what was being revealed. He had labored on walls such as these which surrounded him but had never guessed the grandeur they hid. The area subtended by the sturdy granite encirclement seemed to stretch to the heavens, and indeed it did, for no attempt had been made to cover the walls or the rooms with a roof.

A group of elder councillors filed into the meeting place and stood to one side. Then came three spirit-mediums attached to the king's person; they squatted against a wall and seemed to disapprove of everything. When an imposing figure in a blue robe appeared from within, Nxumalo assumed this must be the king and started to fall upon his knees, but Old Seeker restrained him.

'Lo, he comes!' the figure cried, and from all present the exciting message was repeated: 'Lo, he comes!'

This was a signal for everyone, and especially the Arabs, to sink to the smooth mud-packed floor. Nxumalo went down quickly, forehead pressed against the hard surface, eyes squeezed shut, and knees tightly pressed to still his trembling.

He was still in that position when he heard laughter, but he dared not move.

The first gust was followed by a chorus of laughter. Everyone in the reception area seemed to be roaring, and then he heard a quiet voice saying, 'Come, little bird, onto your legs.'

It was a kindly voice, and seemed to be directed at him. A sharp nudge from Old Seeker caused him to look up, and he found himself staring directly into the thin handsome face of the king, who looked down at him and laughed again.

Instantly everyone else in the area did likewise, and from outside the walls came the sound of hundreds laughing, for it was a law in Zimbabwe that whatever the king did had to be imitated by everyone in the city. A laugh, a cough, a clearing of the throat—all had to be repeated.

Pleased with the laughter, the king indicated that the Arabs might rise, and as they did, Nxumalo noticed that whereas all those in attendance on the king wore expensive cloth woven with metals, he wore stark-white cotton, completely unadorned. Also, he moved with kingly grace and never timidly like the others.

When he reached the Arabs he nodded and spoke easily with them, inquiring about their journey up from the sea and asking them to share any intelligence they might have acquired concerning troubles to the north. He was interested to learn that traders from Sofala no longer deemed it profitable to risk travel into that agitated area, and he listened attentively as the Arabs reported the staggering victory their people had enjoyed at a place called Constantinople, but he could make little of the information except to observe that the Arabs seemed to think that this strengthened their hand in dealings with him.

'And now the gifts!' the tall Arab said, whereupon he and his companion unwrapped their bundles, one after another, gracefully turning back the cloth bindings until the treasures were revealed: 'This celadon, Mighty One, was brought to us by a ship from China. Observe its delicate green coloring, its exquisite shape.' The dazzling ceramics were from Java, to which gold would be sent. The fabrics, finer than anyone in Zimbabwe could weave or imagine, came from Persia; the filigreed silver from Arabia; the heavy glazed pottery from Egypt; the low tables of ebony from Zanzibar; and the exciting metalware from India.

At the end of the presentation the Old Seeker leaned toward the king, heard his wishes, and told the Arabs, 'The Mighty One is pleased. You may now trade in the marketplace.' They bowed respectfully and backed off, and Nxumalo started to follow them, assuming that his visit to Zimbabwe had ended; soon he would be on his way back to his village.

But the king had other plans for this promising lad, and as Nxumalo moved off, a regal command halted him: 'Stay. They tell me you work well. We need you here.' Old Seeker could not mask his joy at this recognition of his protégé, but Nxumalo showed that he was bewildered. Did the king's command mean that he would never again see his brothers or Zeolani at her spinning?

It was the king who answered that unspoken question: 'Show the young man these buildings. Then find him a suitable place to stay.' With that he strode away while Old Seeker and a score of others fell in the dust to honor his passing.

'Well!' the old man cried as he brushed himself off. 'Honors like this come to only a few, believe me.'

'What does it mean?'

'That you're to live here now . . . to become one of us.'

'But Zeolani . . .'

The old man ignored this question that had no honorable answer. 'You'll see things which ordinary mortals . . .' His eyes glowed as if the triumph were his, and with fast, busy steps he started Nxumalo on their tour of the Grand Enclosure.

They entered a narrow passageway parallel to the high outer wall, and Nxumalo feared it might never end, so long and sweeping was it, but finally it opened into a courtyard so grand that he and the old man intuitively fell to their knees. They were in the presence of a mighty royal scepter, unlike any symbol of majesty seen in Africa before or after. It was a soaring conical tower, eighteen feet in diameter at its base, thirty feet high and tapering sharply as it rose. At the top it was adorned by a chevron pattern built into the stone, and as a whole it represented the majesty of the king. On a raised platform next to the tower stood a collection of handsome unadorned monoliths, each symbolizing some achievement of the king and his forebears.

'Beyond lie the king's chambers,' Old Seeker said. 'His wives and children live there, and no man may enter.' Then briskly he moved toward the exit, beckoning Nxumalo to follow him. 'We must see what the Arabs are accomplishing in the marketplace.'

When they rejoined the traders, Nxumalo studied the two strangers in disbelief, keeping as close to them as possible, watching all they did. Their hands were white and their ankles, and he supposed that if he could see their skin below the exposed neckline, it would be white too. Their voices were deep, displaying an accent unlike any used by workmen from distant regions. But what impressed Nxumalo most was that they exhibited a self-assurance as proud as that of the king's councillors; these were men of importance, men accustomed to command, and when they lounged in the courtyard of the depot, as they did now, waiting for the exchange of goods, it was they who determined what should happen next.

'Spread the gold here, where the light falls,' the taller man directed, and when attendants brought in the precious packages and began to turn back the corners of the cloth, everyone showed excitement except the two Arabs. They expected the gold to be of high quality; they expected a copious amount.

'Look at this!' the round man cried, his voice rising. And from the packages emerged a score of ingots of pure gold, wrenched from mines a hundred miles away, and rings carefully fashioned, and pendants for officials, and a great plaque with a rhinoceros rampant.

'By the way,' the chief Arab interrupted, pushing the gold aside. 'Did you get the rhinoceros horn?'

'We did,' the round man said, clapping his hands, whereupon servants brought in three large bundles. When opened, they produced an accumulation of three dozen horns, which excited the cupidity of the Arabs, who hefted them approvingly.

'Very good. Really, very good.' Rupturing the exchange of pleasantries, the principal Arab barked at one of his waiting slaves, 'See that these are handled properly,' and from the way all treated the horns, it was obvious that they were of great value.

'And what else?' the Arabs asked.

There followed a small parade of Zimbabwe men bringing to the Arabs a treasure of ivory tusks, copper wire and artifacts carved from soapstone. With each new disclosure the Arabs nodded and ordered the goods moved outside for packing by their own men. Then the leader coughed and said evenly, 'And now you will want to see what we bring you?'

'Indeed,' the round man said, his voice betraying his eagerness. He then did a strange thing. Taking Nxumalo by the hand, he introduced him to the Arabs, saying, 'This is the young fellow who brought you the best horns.'

Nxumalo felt the white man's hand touch his, and he was face-to-face with the stranger. He felt the man's hand press into his shoulder and heard the words spoken with heavy accent: 'You bring excellent horns. They will be well received in China.'

Proudly, as if they owned the goods, the slaves undid the bales, producing fine silks from India and thousands of small glass beads—red, translucent blue, green, golden-yellow and purple. These would be sewn into intricate patterns to enhance garments, necklaces and other finery. The Arabs were pleased to obtain gold, which they would use to adorn their women; the blacks were just as gratified to get these beads for the adornment of theirs. So far as utility was concerned, it was a just exchange.

The Arabs also brought a collection of special items for bartering with vassal chiefs, and among these was a small metal disk on which an elephant and a tiger had been carved. This came from Nepal and was not worth much, so the Arab leader tossed it in his hand, judged it, and threw it to Nxumalo: 'For the fine horns you brought us.' This disk, with its filigree chain, would be sent south to where Zeolani waited, and fifty years later when she died it would be buried with her, and five hundred years later it would be found by archaeologists, who would report:

> Indubitably this disk was made in Nepal, for several like it have been found in India. It can be dated accurately to 1390. Furthermore, the tiger which shows so plainly never existed in Africa. But how it reached a remote hill east of Pretoria passes explanation. Probably some English explorer whose family had connections with India carried it with him during an examination of the region and lost it. As for the fanciful suggestion that the disk might have reached some central site like Zimbabwe as an article of trade in the 1390–1450 period and then drifted mysteriously to where we found it, that is clearly preposterous.

* * *

The mines of Zimbabwe were scattered across an immense territory, Zambezi to Limpopo north to south, seashore to desert east to west, and it became Nxumalo's job to visit each mine to assure maximum production. Gold, iron and copper had to flow in to Zimbabwe and lesser marketplaces throughout the kingdom so that the Arabs would continue to find it profitable to pursue their trade. His work was not arduous, for when he reached a mine, all he did was check the accumulated metal; rarely did he descend into an actual mine, for they were small and dangerous affairs with but one responsibility: to send up enough ore to keep the furnaces operating, and how this was achieved was not his concern.

But one morning at the end of a journey two hundred miles west of the city he came upon a gold mine where production seemed to have ceased, and he demanded to know what slothful thing had happened. 'The workers died, and I can find no others,' the overseer said plaintively.

'I saw many women . . .'

'But not little ones.'

'If the mine's so small, get girls. We must have gold.'

'But girls can't do the work. Only the little brown people . . .'

In some irritation Nxumalo said, 'I'll look for myself,' but when he saw the entrance to the mine he realized that he could not climb into that crevice. Since he insisted upon knowing how the production of a mine could be so abruptly terminated, he ordered the overseer to summon men who would widen the entrance, breaking away enough rock to permit his descent.

When he lowered himself to the working level, holding a torch above his head, he saw what the overseer meant: there at the face of the gold-bearing rock lay seven small brown figures, dead so long that their bodies were desiccated, tiny shreds of their former being. Four men, two women and a child had died, one after the other over a period of months or even years, and when the last was gone, no further ore had been sent aloft.

He remained in the mine for a long time, endeavoring to visualize the lives of these seven little people. Because the mine was so cramped, only they could work it, forced one time into the narrow opening, condemned thereafter to live underground for as long as they survived, eating whatever was thrown down to them, burying their dead in a pile beside the rock, living and dying in perpetual darkness.

Nxumalo remembered what Old Seeker had said about the wandering bands of small brown people with their poisoned darts. 'Jackals,' he himself had termed them. Prior to visiting this mine he had never before seen them rounded up and enslaved, and certainly the councillors at Zimbabwe would not have sanctioned it, but on this far frontier, out of all touch with the capital, any mine overseer could act as a law unto himself.

'How long do they survive?' Nxumalo asked when he climbed out.

'Four, five years.'

'The children?'

'If the old folk live long enough, the children learn to mine. One family, maybe fifteen, eighteen years.'

'And if the old ones die too soon?'

'The children die with them.'

'What do you propose doing about the mine?'

'Our men are out hunting for some new brown workers. If they find any, we'll be able to mine again.'

'Will you find them?'

'Hunting them is dangerous. They use poisoned arrows, you know.'

'Put your own women to work down there. That's how we do it at other mines.'

'Our women prefer the sun and the fields,' the overseer replied, and in conspiratorial whispers he added, 'You're a man, Nxumalo. You know what fat beauties are for.'

'You opened the entrance for me to go down. A little more, and they can squeeze in.'

'What use could we men have of them if they came home exhausted from laboring underground? Tell me that.'

'When you have the hunger for them, let them rest a day or two.'

'I tell you, sir, our women would refuse to work as miners. You must bring me people from outside.'

Sternly Nxumalo said, 'I shall return next season, and I will expect to see this mine operating at capacity. We must have gold.'

This ultimatum would be met, for as Nxumalo marched back toward Zimbabwe, the mine overseer, who loved his five fat wives, was relieved to see a band of his warriors returning from the desert with nine small brown people. They would fit nicely into the mine; they would eat what was tossed down to them; and never again would they see daylight.

As Nxumalo visited the distant mines he often recalled that moment when he first saw the Limpopo and when he first climbed down into a mine: It was a premonition. I spend my life crossing rivers and descending shafts. Wherever he traveled through the vast domains of Zimbabwe he came upon the old treasured mines, and in time learned how to predict where new ones might be found, and although nine out of his ten guesses proved barren, that tenth repaid all efforts. Each new find, each old mine that increased its output enhanced his reputation.

Although he had made himself familiar with thousands of square miles of the kingdom, there remained one place he had not visited: the citadel atop the Hill of Spirits at Zimbabwe itself, but now as he returned from his latest trip he was summoned to the king's residence to deliver his report in person to the ruler and his councillors. He was guarded about what he said concerning the enslavement of the small brown people at that frontier mine, but he spoke boldly of the problems in the north, and when he finished, the senior councillor indicated that the king wished to speak with him alone.

After the assembly left, this councillor led Nxumalo through a maze of passages to the inner court, where, in a small roofless enclosure, he waited for his private audience. Soon the king appeared in his austere white robes, hastened directly to Nxumalo and said, 'Son of Ngalo from the lands my people do not know, I have never seen you at the citadel.'

'To go so high is not permitted, sir.'

'It is permitted,' the king said. 'Let us go there now and ask the spirits.' And under palm umbrellas the king and his inspector of mines walked down the main passageway through the city, past the area where the joiners and the masons dwelt, past the site where workmen brought stones for the walls. It seemed a lifetime since Nxumalo had helped repair those walls, and it was like a dream to be walking beneath them with the king himself.

They moved swiftly along the royal path that led to the rock-encircled citadel, and now the way became little more than a track, four feet across, but twice each day forty women swept it so that not a blade of grass or a pebble marred its surface. To attain the steep trail that led up to the summit, they had to pass the pits from which women dug wet clay used for plastering walls; and as the king went by, they all bowed their heads against the moist ground, but he ignored them.

The winding path climbed through a grove of trees, then traversed bare, rocky slopes, and reached at last an extremely narrow passageway between boulders. The king betrayed that he was out of breath, and although Nxumalo was well trained because of his distant journeys, he deemed it prudent to make believe that his chest heaved too, lest he appear disrespectful. At last they broke into a free and level space, and Nxumalo saw a grandeur he had not even vaguely anticipated when staring at the citadel from below.

He was in the midst of a great assembly of walls and courtyards twined among the immense granite boulders which gave the place its magnificence; those massive rocks determined where the walls must run, where the gracefully molded huts could stand. Rulers came from far distances to negotiate with the king, and so long as the meetings were held down below in the city, these foreign rulers, often as rich as the king, were apt to be slightly contemptuous of his soft-spoken arguments, but once they had been forced to climb that difficult path to see the citadel, they had to acknowledge that they were dealing with a true monarch.

Nxumalo was startled by the vivid colors that decorated the walls, the sculptures that marked the parapets and the symbolism that abounded. But what interested him most were the little furnaces at which metallurgists worked the gold ingots he sent from his mines, and he watched

with admiration as they fashioned delicate jewelry by processes so secret
they were never spoken of outside the citadel.

Despite his interest in the gold, Nxumalo was led away to the eastern
flank of the citadel, and again he walked with that inner fear that had
marked his first meeting with the king, for he knew that he was heading
for the quarters of the great Mhondoro, the one through whom the spirits
spoke and the ancestors ruled. By accident he caught a glimpse of the
king's face and saw that he, too, had assumed a solemn mien.

The Mhondoro's enclosure seemed deserted when Nxumalo entered,
but soon a shadowy figure could be seen moving in the dark recesses of a
hut that filled one corner of the area. The main feature was a platform,
waist-high, from which rose four soapstone pedestals, each topped by a
sculptured bird which appeared to hover above the sacred place. Another
wall contained a lower platform on which stood a collection of monoliths
and other sacred objects of great beauty. Each related to some climactic experience of the race, so that in this enclosure stood the full history and
mythology of Zimbabwe, a meaningful record of the past that could be
read by the Mhondoro and his king as easily as European monks unraveled the writings of their historians.

The king was permitted by custom to walk to the meeting platform,
but Nxumalo had to crawl on his knees, and as he did so he saw that
when the discussions began he would be sitting among skull-like carvings,
clay animals decorated with ostrich feathers, elaborate collections of medicated beads and pebbles, and tangled clumps of precious herbs. But no single item arrested his attention like the crocodile six feet long, carved from
hard wood in such reality that it seemed capable of devouring the holy
man; when Nxumalo took his seat beside this monster, he found that its
scales were made from hundreds of wafer-thin gold plates that moved and
glistened when he disturbed the air.

Now from the interior of his hut the Mhondoro appeared, wearing a
yellow cloak and a headdress of animal furs. It was the king who paid
homage: 'I see you, Mhondoro of my fathers.'

'I see you, Powerful King.'

'This is the one who was sent,' the king said.

The Mhondoro indicated that Nxumalo must keep his gaze forward,
lest his eyes fall upon the symbols of kings long dead and anger their
spirits, who would be watching. The young man scarcely dared breathe,
but at last the Mhondoro addressed him: 'What news from the mines?'

'The gold from the west declines.'

'It used to be copious.'

'It still is, to the north, but our men are afraid to go there.'

'Trouble, trouble,' the spirit-medium said, and he turned to the king,
speaking softly of the problems overtaking their city.

Nxumalo appreciated their concern, for at times on his recent journeys
he had felt as if the entire Zimbabwe hegemony were held together by

frail threads of dissolving interests. He sensed the restlessness and suspected that certain provincial chiefs were entertaining ideas of independence, but he was afraid to mention these fears in the presence of the city's two most powerful men. There were other irritations too: wood, grazing rights, the lack of salt. And there was even talk that the Arabs might open their own trade links in areas beyond Zimbabwe's control.

The painful afternoon passed, and when fires appeared in the city below, the Mhondoro began chanting in a dreamy voice: 'Generations ago our brave forebears erected this citadel. Mhlanga, son of Notape, son of Chuda . . .' He recited genealogies back to the year 1250 when Zimbabwe's walls were first erected. 'It was the king's great-grandfather who caused that big tower down there to be built, not long ago, and it grieves my heart to think that one day we may have to give this noble place back to the vines and the trees.'

In the silence that followed, Nxumalo became aware that he was supposed to respond: 'Why would you say that, Revered One?'

'Because the land is worn out. Because our spirits flag. Because others are rising in the north. Because I see strange ships coming to Sofala.'

It was in that solemn moment that Nxumalo first glimpsed the fact that his destiny might be to remain always in Zimbabwe, helping it to survive, but even as he framed this thought he looked at these two men sitting beneath the beautiful carved birds and he could not conceive that these leaders and this city could be in actual danger.

When he accompanied the king down from the citadel, servants with flares led the way and stayed with them on their progress through the city. Out of deference to the king, Nxumalo volunteered to attend him to the gateway of the royal enclosure, but the king halted midway in the city and said, 'It's time you visited the Old Seeker.'

'I see him often, sir.'

'But tonight, I believe, he has special messages.' So Nxumalo broke away and went to his mentor's house beyond the marketplace, and there he found that the old man did indeed have special information: 'Son of Ngalo, it's time you took the next cargo of gold and rhino horns to Sofala.'

This was a journey of importance which only the most trusted citizens were permitted to undertake. It required courage to descend the steep paths lined with leopards and lions; it required sound health to survive the pestilential swamps; and it required sound judgment to protect one's property against the Arabs who bartered there.

'The Arabs who climb the mountain trails to visit Zimbabwe have to be good men,' the wise old fellow warned. 'But those who slip into a seaport and remain there, they can be ugly.'

'How do I protect myself?'

'Integrity is a good shield.' He paused. 'Did I ever come armed to your father's kraal? Couldn't he have killed me in a moment if he wished? Why didn't he? Because he knew that if he killed a man of honor, he'd soon have on his hands men with none. And then the whole thing falls apart.'

'You know, I'm sure, that my father used to laugh at your stories. The miracles you spoke of, the lies.'

'A man cannot travel great distances without developing ideas. And now I have one of the very best to bring before you.'

He clapped his hands, and when the servant appeared, he gave a signal. Soon the curtains that closed off the living quarters parted and a young girl of fourteen, black as rubbed ebony and radiant, came dutifully into the room. Lowering her eyes, she stood inanimate, like one of the carved statues the Arabs had presented to the king; she was being presented to Nxumalo, the king's inspector of mines, and after a long time she raised her eyes and looked into his.

'My granddaughter,' the old man said.

The two young people continued gazing at each other as the Old Seeker confessed: 'From the first day I saw you at the lake, Nxumalo, I knew you were intended for this girl. Everything I did thereafter was calculated to bring you here for her to see. The rhino horns? I had all I needed waiting in the warehouse. You were the treasure I sought.'

Because of the pain that comes with all living, Nxumalo could not speak. He was acutely aware of this girl's beauty, but he could also remember Zeolani and his promise to her. Finally he blurted out: 'Treasured Father, I am betrothed to Zeolani.'

The old man took a deep breath and said, 'Young men make promises, and they go off to build their fortunes, and the antelope at the lake see them no more. My granddaughter's name is Hlenga. Show him the garden, Hlenga.'

It was in 1458 that Nxumalo assembled a file of sixty-seven porters for the perilous journey to the coast. The route to Sofala was horrendous, with swamps, fever-ridden flats, precipitous descents and swollen rivers barring the way. As he listened to accounts of the journey from men who had made earlier trips, he comprehended what Old Seeker had meant when he said, 'A wise man goes to Sofala only once.' And yet Arab traders appeared at Zimbabwe regularly, and they had to traverse that formidable route.

This contradiction was resolved by the Old Seeker: 'The Arabs have no problems. They start from Sofala with fifty carriers and arrive here with thirty.'

'How is it they're always the ones that arrive?'

'White men protect themselves,' the old councillor said. 'I went down with the father of the man who gave you that disk. At every river he said, "You go first and see how deep it is." So at one crossing I said, "This time you go first," and he said, "It's your task to go. It's my task to protect the gold." '

Nxumalo laughed. 'That's what one of our mine overseers says when tossing a catch of little brown men down the shaft: "It's your task to go down there. It's my task to guard the gold when you send it up." '

'One more thing, Nxumalo. Arabs in a caravan will be your staunchest friends. Share their food with you, their sleeping places. But when you reach Sofala, be aware. Never go aboard ship with an Arab.'

Nxumalo coughed in some embarrassment. 'Tell me, Old Seeker, what is a ship? The king spoke of it and I was ashamed to ask.'

'A rondavel that moves across the water.' While the young man contemplated this improbability, the old man added, 'Because if you step aboard his ship, the Arab will sell you as a slave and you will sit chained to a bench and never see your friends again.'

This almost casual mention of friends saddened Nxumalo, for the friend he cherished most was Zeolani, and the possibility of never seeing her again distressed him. At the same time he recognized that all things happening in Zimbabwe were conspiring to prevent him from ever returning to his village, and he supposed that if he succeeded with the forthcoming expedition to Sofala, his position at Zimbabwe would be enhanced. Yet memories of Zeolani and their impassioned love-making behind the twin hills haunted him, and he longed to see her. 'I want to return home,' he said resolutely, but Old Seeker laughed.

'You're like all young men in the world. Remembering a lovely girl who is far away while being tormented by another just as lovely, who is close at hand . . . like Hlenga.'

'On your next trip to my village . . .'

'I doubt I shall ever wander so far again.'

'You will. You're like me. You love baobabs and lions prowling your camp at night.'

The old man laughed again. 'Perhaps I am like you. But you're like me. You love rivers that must be forded and paths through dark forests. I never went back, and neither will you.'

On the morrow, with a kiss from Hlenga on his lips, this young man, twenty-one years old, set forth with his porters to deliver a collection of gold, ivory tusks and other trading goods to the waiting ships, and so heavy was the burden that progress under any circumstances would have been tedious; through the forests and swamps which separated them from the sea it was punishing. Nxumalo, as personal representative of the king, headed the file, but he was guided by a man who had made the difficult traverse once before. They covered only ten miles a day, because they were so often forced by turbulent rivers or steep declivities to abandon established trails. They were tormented by insects and had to keep watch against snakes, but they were never short of water or food, for rain was plentiful and animals abounded.

At the end of the sixth day everyone had subsided into a kind of grudging resignation; hour after hour would pass with no speech, no relief from the heat, the sweat and the muddy footing. It was travel at its worst, infinitely more demanding than a trip of many miles through the western savanna or southward into baobab country. This was liana land, where vines hung down from every tree, tormenting and ensnaring, where one could rarely move unimpeded for ten feet in any direction.

But always there lay ahead the fascinating lure of Sofala, with its ships, and Chinese strangers, and the glories of India and Persia. Like a tantalizing magnet it drew the men on, and at night, when the insects were at their worst, the men would talk in whispers of women who frequented the port and of Arabs who stole any black who tried to visit with these women. The travelers had an imperfect understanding of the slave trade; they knew that men of foreign cast traveled the Zambezi capturing any who strayed, but these invaders had never dared invade Zimbabwe and risk a disruption of the gold supply, so their habits were not known. Nor did the murmuring blacks have any concept of where they might be taken if they were captured; Arabia they knew only for its carvings, India for its silks.

When the great escarpments were descended and the level lowlands reached, the travelers still had more than a hundred miles of swampy flat country with swollen rivers to negotiate, and again progress was minimal. It was now that young Nxumalo asserted his leadership, dismissing his guide to the rear and forcing his men into areas they preferred to avoid. He had come upon a well-marked trail which must lead to the sea, and as his men straggled behind, unable to keep the pace he was setting with his lighter burden, they began to meet other porters coming home from Sofala or were overtaken by swifter-moving files heading for the port, and a lively excitement spread through the group.

'We must not step inside a ship,' the guide repeated on the last night, 'and all bargaining is to be done by Nxumalo, for he knows what the king requires.'

'We will wait,' Nxumalo said, 'until the Arabs make us good offers, and they must be better than what they offer us at home, for this time we have done the hauling, not they.' He was prepared to linger at Sofala for months, selling his goods carefully and obtaining only those things his community most needed.

'What we really seek,' he reminded them, 'is salt.' Even his gold bars would be bartered if he could find the proper amount of salt.

When his porters took up their burdens next morning, passers-by confirmed that Sofala would be reached by noon, and they quickened their pace; and when salt could be smelled in the air, they began to run until the man in the lead shouted, 'Sofala! Sofala!' and all clustered about him to stare at the port and the great sea beyond. In awe one man whispered, 'That is a river no man can cross.'

The bustling seaport did not disappoint, for it contained features which astonished; the sheds in which the Arabs conducted their business were of a size the Zimbabwe men had never imagined, and the dhows that rolled in the tides of the Indian Ocean were an amazement. The men were delighted with the orderliness of the shore, where casuarina trees intermingled with palms and where the waves ran up to touch the feet and then ran back. How immense the sea was! When the men saw children swimming they were enchanted and sought to run into the water themselves, except that Nxumalo, himself perplexed by this multitude of new experiences, forbade it. He felt that he must face one problem at a time, and the first that he encountered proved how correct he was in moving prudently, for when he inquired about a market for his goods, and traders heard that he had twoscore elephant tusks, everyone doing business with China, where ivory was appreciated, wanted to acquire them, and he was made some dazzling offers, but since he had not intended selling immediately, he resisted. He did allow himself to be taken to an Arab ship, which, however, he refused to board; from the wharf he could see inside, and there, chained to benches, sat a dozen men of varied ages, doing nothing, making hardly a movement.

'Who are they?' he asked, and the trader explained that these men helped move the ship.

'How long do they wait like that?'

'Until they die,' the trader said, and when Nxumalo winced, he added, 'They were captured in war. This is their fate.' They were, Nxumalo reflected, much like the small brown men who were thrown down mines to work until they died. They, too, were captured in war; that, too, was their fate.

Wherever he moved in Sofala he saw things that bewildered, but constantly he was enticed by the dhows, those floating rondavels whose passage across the sea he could not comprehend but whose magic was apparent. One afternoon as he stared at a three-masted vessel with tall sails he saw to his delight that the white man who seemed to be in charge was the same tall Arab who had traded at Zimbabwe.

'Ho!' he shouted, and when the Arab turned slowly to identify the disturbance, Nxumalo shouted in Zimbabwe language, 'It's me. The one you gave the disk.' The Arab moved to the railing, peered at the young black, and said finally, 'Of course! The man with the gold mines.'

For some hours they stood on the wharf, talking, and the Arab said, 'You should carry your goods to my brother at Kilwa. He'll appreciate them.'

'Where is the trail to this Kilwa?'

The Arab laughed, the first time Nxumalo had seen him do so. 'There is no trail. It couldn't cross the rivers and swamps. To walk would require more than a year.'

'Then why tell me to go?'

'You don't march your men along a trail. You sail . . . in a dhow.'

Nxumalo instantly recognized this as a trick to enslave him, but he also knew that he yearned achingly to know what a dhow was like, and where China lay, and who wove silk. So after a night's tormented judging he sought the Arab and said simply, 'I shall deposit all my goods here, with my servants. I'll sail with you to Kilwa, and if your brother really wants my gold . . .'

'He'll be hungry for your ivory.'

'He can have it, if he brings me back here to get it.'

It was arranged, but when his men heard of his daring they protested. They, too, had seen the slaves chained to the benches and they predicted that this would be his fate, but he wanted to believe the Arab trader; even more, he wanted to see Kilwa and discover the nature of shipping.

Toward the end of 1458 he boarded the dhow at Sofala for the eleven-hundred-mile passage to Kilwa, and when the lateen sails were raised and the vessel felt the wind he experienced the joy that young men know when they set forth upon the oceans. The rolling of the dhow, the leaping of the dolphins that followed the wake, and the glorious settings of the sun behind the coast of Africa enchanted him, and when after many days the sailors cried, 'Kilwa, the golden mosque!' he ran forward to catch his first sight of that notable harbor to which ships came from all cities of the eastern world.

He was overwhelmed by the varied craft that came to Kilwa, by the towering reach of the masts and the variety of men who climbed them. He found the Arab equally moved, and as the dhow crept through the harbor to find a mooring place, the trader pointed to the shore where buildings of stone glittered and he said with deep feeling, 'My grandfather's grandfather's father. We lived in Arabia then, and he sailed his trading dhow to Kilwa. On that beach he would spread his wares. What wonderful beads and cloths he brought. Then he and all his men would retire to his boat, and when the beach was empty of our people, the black-skinned traders would come down to inspect the goods, and after a long while they would leave little piles of gold and ivory. Then they would retire, and my father would go ashore and judge the offer, and if it was miserly he would touch nothing, but return to his dhow. So the men would come again and add to their offer, and after many exchanges, without a word being spoken, the trade would be consummated. Look at Kilwa now!'

Nxumalo succumbed to its spell, and for nine days did not even bother to barter his treasures. When he visited the mosque, lately rebuilt and one of the noblest in Africa, he thought: That tower they call the minaret. It resembles the tower I worked on at Zimbabwe. But ours was built much differently. Perhaps someone like me came here to Kilwa, and saw this fine city and went home to do his building.

He visited all the ships then in harbor and the trading points on the mainland, and after a while he began to comprehend the intricate world in which black men and yellow and honey-tan like the Arabs met and traded to mutual advantage, each having something precious to the others. Because he had gold and ivory, he could deal on a basis of equality with Egyptians and Arabians and Persians and Indians and the soft, quick people from Java.

He would have sailed with any of them to the far side of the sea; he would have been a willing passenger on any ship going anywhere; but in the end he arranged for the Arab's brother to sail him back to Sofala for his entire cache of goods. He might have bargained for a slightly more advantageous trade with other merchants, but to do so would have been undignified for an officer of the court of Zimbabwe.

It was a long, drifting trip back to Sofala, and during such a protracted voyage anything might have happened, but the passage was calm and uneventful, with Nxumalo talking at great length with the Arab traders and learning from them of the vast changes occurring in the world. The significance of Constantinople was explained; although he knew nothing of the name, he deduced that the Arabs must now enjoy an enormous advantage. What was of greater interest were tales the Arabs told of changes along the Zambezi: 'Many villages have new masters. Salt has been discovered and tribes are on the move.'

When their ship neared the mouth of that great river the captain pointed out the little trading post of Chinde, and Nxumalo began to recite the melodious names of this enchanted coast: Sofala, Chinde, Quelimane, Moçambique, Zanzibar, Mombasa. And the sailors told him of the distant ports with which they dealt: Jidda, Calicut, Mogadiscio, Malacca.

While these narcotic names infected him with their sweet poison he stayed on deck and watched the moon tiptoe across the waves of an ocean he still could not comprehend, and grudgingly he admitted that he was so enamored of this new world—the towers of Zimbabwe, his register of mines across the country, the fleet of ships at Kilwa and Sofala, the grand mystery of the ocean—he could never again be satisfied with his father's village and its naked men plotting to snare a rhinoceros. His commitment lay with the city, not to any grandiose concept of its destiny but to the honorable task of doing better whatever limited assignment he was given. He would supervise his mines with extra attention and trade their gold to maximum advantage. He would work to strengthen Zimbabwe and help it maintain itself against the new hegemonies forming along the Zambezi. To undertake such tasks would mean that he could never go south to claim Zeolani, and as night faded, the moon sinking into the western sea seemed like the slow vanishing of that beautiful girl. At the moment when the golden disk plunged into the waves it looked much like the Nepalese disk he had sent her, and he could think only of their love-making and of the sorrow that would never completely leave him.

At dawn he sought his Arab mentor and said, 'I must buy one special thing . . . to send south . . . to a girl in my village.'

'You will not take it to her yourself?'

'Never.'

'Then make it something precious, for long remembrance,' and the Arab put before him a selection of items, and from them Nxumalo started to choose his gift, but as he looked past the trinkets he saw the slaves, chained forever to their benches, and he was in confusion.

When Nxumalo led his porters back to Zimbabwe at the close of 1459, he brought with him goods from distant lands and much intelligence regarding developments on the Zambezi, where Sena and Tete were becoming important trading towns. He brought rumors of areas farther up the river where salt was available and the land not exhausted. And he secreted in his bundle a jade necklace from China, which he sent south with the Old Seeker on the trip which that fellow again averred was his last.

For many days he met in the citadel with the king and the Mhondoro, discussing the Zambezi developments. He reported on all that the Arabs had told him, and he started an impassioned description of what steps must be taken to protect and augment Zimbabwe, but he did not get far, because the king cut him short with an astonishing statement: 'We have decided to abandon this city.'

Nxumalo gasped. 'But it's a noble city,' he pleaded. 'Even better than Kilwa.'

'It was. It is. But it can no longer be.' The king was adamant in his decision that Great Zimbabwe, as it was called then and forever, must be surrendered to the jungle, since further occupancy was impractical.

As he reiterated this doleful verdict the three men looked down upon the fairest city south of Egypt, a subtle combination of granite-walled enclosures and adobe rondavels, a city in which eleven thousand workers enjoyed a good and differentiated life. It was a place of constant peace, of great enrichment for the few and modest well-being for all; its faults were that it had spent its energy searching for gold, its resultant income on ostentation. It had ignored clear signs that the press of people in the capital city had impaired the environment; the delicate balance between man and nature which had endured for so long was upset. Its economic stability and assured gold had pleased distant Arabs and Indian princes, but as its natural resources dwindled, its existence was doomed. Those long lines of slaves carrying in precious goods had done nothing to nourish the real city, so at the very apex of its glory it had to be abandoned.

On no one did the decision fall with harsher force than on Nxumalo, for on the dhow that night he had committed himself to the perpetuation of this city, yet on the day he returned to put his promise into action he was informed that the city would no longer exist. For two weeks he was disconsolate, and then it occurred to him that a worthy man dedicates himself not to one particular thing which attracts him, but to all tasks; and he vowed that when the time came to move this city to its new site, he would devote all his powers to that endeavor and, with Hlenga's help, make the new city superior to the old.

It is difficult, five hundred years after the event, to describe in words the precise quality of thought available to the men who made this decision to abandon Zimbabwe, but because the act was so crucial in the history of southern Africa, an attempt must be made without inflating or denigrating reality. The king was no Charlemagne; he was unaware of libraries and monetary systems, yet he had an uncanny sense of how to keep a sprawling empire functional, and if he knew nothing about armies or military policy, it was only because he kept his nation at peace during a long reign. He spoke only one language, which had never been written, and he had no court painter to depict his likeness for foreign princes, yet he knew how to keep Zimbabwe beautiful; the additions he made to both the lower city and the citadel were commendable. He was a ruler.

The Mhondoro was certainly no Thomas Aquinas speculating upon the nature of God and man; indeed, he was sometimes little more than a shaman propitiating dubious spirits that might otherwise destroy the city. But if he lacked a comprehensive theology like Christianity or Islam with which to console his people, he did have remarkable skill in banishing their grosser fears, controlling their wilder passions, and lending them the assurances they needed to keep working. He was a priest.

The condition of Nxumalo was more puzzling. Offspring of a minimal society, child of a family with extremely limited horizons, he had been allowed adventures which lured him always toward larger concepts. He was one of those wonderful realists who can add a tentative two to a problematic three and come up with a solid five. He saw Zimbabwe exactly as it was, a city fighting for its life in a rapidly changing world, but he also saw in his imagination the cities of India and China, and he guessed that they were struggling too. He realized that if there existed something as magnificent as an ocean, there could be no reasonable limit to the wonders its shores might contain. He could not read or write; he could not express himself in scholastic phrases; he knew nothing of Giotto, who was dead, or Botticelli, who was living, but from the first moment he saw those carved birds adorning the citadel he knew they were art and never some accidental thing from the marketplace. He was a pragmatist.

Any one of these three, or all as a group, could have learned to function in any society then existing, given time and proper instruction. The king certainly was as able as the Aztec rulers of Mexico or the Incas of Peru and markedly superior to the confused brothers of Prince Henry, who ruled Portugal abominably; had the Mhondoro been a cardinal at Rome, he would have known how to protect himself at the Vatican as it then operated; and if Nxumalo with his insatiable curiosity had ever had a chance to captain a ship, he would have outdistanced Prince Henry's reluctant navigators. These three might be called savages, but they should never be called uncivilized.

Yet this is precisely what Henry the Navigator did call them as he lay dying in his lonely monastery on the forlorn headland of Europe. He sat propped in bed, surrounded by a lifetime of books and documents, striving to devise some stratagem that would speed his captains in their attempt to turn the southern tip of Africa and 'discover and civilize' places like Sofala and Kilwa. It required an arrogant mind to consider these great entrepôts 'undiscovered' merely because no white Christian had yet traveled up the eastern coast of Africa, whereas thousands upon thousands of dark Arabs had traveled down it, and had been doing so for a thousand years.

These were the closing weeks of 1460, while Zimbabwe still functioned as the capital of a vast but loosely ruled hegemony, with its royal compounds decorated by celadons from China, but Prince Henry could say to his assembled captains, 'Our mighty task is to bring civilization to the dark shores of Africa.' He added, 'That the gold mines of Ophir should be occupied by savage blacks is repugnant, but that their gold should fall into the hands of those who worship Muhammad is intolerable.'

So in the final days of his life, while Nxumalo and his king wrestled with sophisticated problems of management, Prince Henry challenged his captains to round Africa. Two generations of these men would die before anyone breasted the Cape, but Henry approached death convinced that the discovery of Ophir was close at hand. 'My books assure me,' he told his sailors, 'that Ophir was built by those Phoenicians who later built Carthage. It is very ancient, long before the days of Solomon.' He took real consolation in this belief, and when a captain said, 'I have been told it was built by Egyptians,' he snorted, 'Never! Perhaps Old Testament Jews drifting down from Elath, or maybe powerful builders from Sidon or Arabia.' Not in his worst fever could he imagine that blacks had built an Ophir, and worked its mines and shipped its gold to all parts of Asia.

And even had he survived long enough to see one of his captains reach Sofala, and if that man had sent an expedition inland to Zimbabwe, and if he had reported upon the city, its towers gleaming in the sun, its carved birds silent upon their parapets—and all managed by blacks—he might have refused to accept the facts, for in his thinking, blacks capable of running a nation did not exist.

There were dark-skinned Muslims who threatened the Christian world, and yellow Chinese of whom Marco Polo had written so engagingly, and soft-brown Javanese who traded with all, but there were no blacks other than the unspeakable savages his captains had met on the western coast of Africa.

'The only people with whom we contend,' he told his captains, 'are the Muslims who endanger our world. So you must speed south, and turn the

headland which I know is there, and then sail north toward the lands our
Saviour knew. We shall confront the infidel and win a world for Christ,
and your soldiers shall enjoy the gold of Ophir.'

Prince Henry was sixty-six years old that November, a worn-out man
and one of the supreme contradictions in history. He had sailed practically
nowhere, but had provided a fortune to his captains, threatening to bank-
rupt his brother's kingdom, in his rugged belief that the entire world
could be navigated, that Ophir lay where the Bible intimated, and that if
only he could get his ships to India and China, his priests could Christianize the world.

Henry of Portugal was an explorer *sans égal,* for he was goaded onward solely by what he read in books, and from them he deduced all his
great perceptions. How sad that his captains, in his lifetime, did not indeed reach Sofala, so that he could have read their reports of a thriving
Zimbabwe. Had he seen proof of this black civilization, it might have
shaken his preconceptions, for he was, above all, a man of probity. And if
the few remaining stragglers in the area had accepted Christianity, he
would have found a respectable place for them in his cosmogony. But his
people had neither reached Zimbabwe nor envisioned its existence.

Even sadder was the fact that after Vasco da Gama did finally reach
Sofala in 1498, the Portuguese considered such ports merely as targets for
looting, gateways to vaster riches inland. By 1512, fifty-two years after
Prince Henry's death, Portuguese traders were beginning a brisk business
with the chiefdoms that had grown up in the shadow of Great Zimbabwe,
and one priest composed a long report of his dealings with a representative
from one settlement who had come down to Sofala leading sixty blacks
bearing cargoes of gold and ivory and copper, just as the Bible had predicted:

> His name, Nxumalo, third chief of a city I was not privileged to see
> but on which I interrogated him closely. He was very old, very
> black, with hair of purest white. He talked like a young man and
> wore no adornment or badge of office except an iron staff topped by
> feathers. He seemed able to speak many languages and talked ea-
> gerly with all, but when I asked him if his city was the ancient
> Ophir, he smiled evasively. I knew he was trying to mislead me, so I
> persisted, and he said through our Arab interpreter, 'Others have
> asked me that.' Nothing more, so I pressed him, and he said, 'Our
> city had towers, but they were of stone.' I told him he was lying,
> that our Bible avers that Ophir was made of gold, and he took me
> by the arm and said quietly, in perfect Portuguese, which startled
> me, 'We had gold too, but it came from mines far from the city, and
> it was difficult to obtain, and now the mines have run dry.' I noticed
> that he had all his teeth.

III. A Hedge
of Bitter Almond

THERE was no close parallel to the miraculous thing that happened at the Cape called Good Hope.

In 1488 Captain Bartholomeu Dias in a Portuguese caravel rounded this Cape, which he considered to be the southernmost point of Africa, and he proposed going all the way to India, but like other captains before and after, he found his crew afraid and was forced by their near-mutiny to turn back.

In 1497 Captain Vasco da Gama landed near the Cape, remaining eight days and establishing contact with large numbers of small brown people who spoke with clicks.

In the ensuing century the Portuguese penetrated to the far reaches of the Indian Ocean: Sofala of the gold dust, Kilwa the splendid entrepôt, Aden and its shrouded figures, Hormuz with the metaled jewelry of Persia, Calicut offering the silks of India, and Trincomalee with the rare cinnamon of Ceylon. It was a world of wonder and riches which the Portuguese dominated in all respects, shipping its spices back to Europe to be sold at enormous profit and leaving at the outposts priests to Christianize and functionaries to rule.

As early as 1511 one of the greatest Portuguese adventurers, Afonso de Albuquerque, ventured out of the Indian Ocean, establishing at Malacca a great fort that would serve as the keystone to Portuguese holdings. Whoever controlled Malacca had access to those magical islands that lay east of Java like a chain of jewels; these were the fabled Spice Islands, and their riches lay in fee to Portugal.

During the entire sixteenth century this small seafaring nation transported untold wealth from the area, making irrelevant the fact that Muslims controlled Constantinople. Profit was now made not from tedious overland camel routes but from seaborne traffic. However, it was not this explosive wealth which led to the miracle.

In the opening years of the seventeenth century two other very small European nations decided to seize by force their share of the Portuguese monopoly. In 1600 England chartered its East India Company, known in history as John Company, which quickly gained a solid foothold in India. Two years later the Dutch launched their counterpart, Vereenigde Oostindische Compagnie (United East India Company), to be known as Jan Compagnie, which operated with stubborn troops and very stubborn traders.

The eastern seas became a vast battleground, with every Catholic priest a forward agent of Portugal, every Protestant predikant a defender of Dutch interests. Nor was it merely a commercial-religious rivalry; real warfare was involved. Three hideous times—1604, 1607, 1608—mammoth Dutch fleets strove to capture the dominating Portuguese fortress on Moçambique Island, and the sieges should have ended in easy victory, because the island was small, 3,200 yards long, 320 yards wide, and defended by as few as sixty Portuguese soldiers against whom the Dutch could land nearly two thousand.

But the defenders were Portuguese, some of the toughest human beings on earth. Once when there was little hope that the few could resist the many, the Portuguese mounted a sortie, swept out of their fortress walls and slew the attackers. The Portuguese commander taunted: 'The company defending this fort is a cat that cannot be handled without gloves.' During one of the sieges, when all seemed lost, the Portuguese proposed that the affair be settled by fifty Dutch soldiers fighting a pitched battle against twenty-five Portuguese, 'a balance honoring the character of the contesting armies.'

The Dutch tried fire, trenching, towers, secret assaults and overpowering numbers, but never did they penetrate those fortress walls. How different the history of South Africa might have been had the Portuguese defenders been one shade less valiant. If in 1605 the sixty had surrendered to the two thousand, by 1985 the strategic ports of Moçambique would probably rest in the hands of the descendants of the Dutch; all lands south of the Zambezi River could have been under their rule, and in the ensuing history South Africa would have been the focus, not Java. But never could the Dutch mount that final push which would have carried them to great victory in Africa.

In these years, when a Portuguese soldier disembarked from one of his nation's ships to take up duty within a fort at Moçambique or at Malacca, on the straits near Java, he could expect during his tour of duty three sieges in which he would eat grass and drink urine. Some of the most courageous resistances in world history were contributed by these Portuguese defenders.

One salient fact differentiated the colonizing efforts of the three European nations: the manner in which the effort related to the central government. The Portuguese operation was a confused amalgam of patriotism, Catholicism and profit; the government at Lisbon decided what should be done, the church ruled the minds of those who did it. When the English chartered their East India Company they intended it to be free of governmental interference, but quickly saw that this was impossible, because unless John Company behaved in a generally moral way, the good name of the nation was impugned; thus there was constant vacillation between commercial freedom and moral control. The Dutch had no such scruples. Their charter was handed to businessmen whose stated purpose was the making of profit on their investment, preferably forty percent a year, and neither the government nor the church had the right to intrude on their conduct. Any predikant who sailed in a ship belonging to Jan Compagnie was promptly informed that the Compagnie would determine what his religious duties were and how they would be discharged.

It was soon apparent that three such radically different approaches would have to collide, and soon the English were battling the Dutch for control of Java, while the Dutch stabbed at Portugal for control of Malacca, and all three fought Spain for control of the Spice Islands. Yet ships of these battling nations constantly passed the Cape of Good Hope, often resting there for weeks at a time, with little effective effort to occupy this crucial spot or arm it as a base from which to raid enemy commerce. It is inconceivable that these maritime nations should have rounded the Cape on their way to war and passed it again on their return without ever halting to establish a base. It is even more difficult to believe that hundreds of merchant ships bearing millions of guilders' and cruzados' worth of spices should have been allowed to navigate these difficult waters without confrontation of some kind. But that was the case. In two hundred years of the most concentrated commercial rivalry in Asia and war in Europe, there was only one instance in which a ship was sunk at the Cape by enemy action.

The explanation, as in the case of many an apparent inconsistency, rested in geography. A Portuguese ship setting out from Lisbon made a long run southwest to the Cape Verde Islands, replenished there and sailed almost to the coast of Brazil before steering southeast to round the Cape for the welcoming anchorage at Moçambique Island, from which it headed east to Goa and Malacca. Dutch and English ships also passed the Cape Verdes, but realizing that the Portuguese would not welcome them, continued south to the crucial island of St. Helena, which they jointly commanded, and once they cleared that haven, it was a brisk run to India. From there the English could head for entrepôts in the Spice Islands while the Dutch could anchor at their tenuous foothold in Java. There was really no reason why anyone need interrupt his journey at the Cape.

So from 1488, when Dias 'discovered' it, to 1652—a period of one hun-

dred and sixty-four years climactic in world history—this marvelous headland, dominating the trade routes and capable of supplying all the fresh
food and water required by shipping, lay neglected. Any seafaring nation
in the world could have claimed it; none did, because it was not seen as
vital to their purposes.

Although it was unclaimed, it was not untouched. In this empty period one hundred and fifty-three known expeditions actually landed at the
Cape, and since many consisted of multiple ships, sometimes ten or
twelve, it can be said with certainty that on the average at least one major
ship a year stopped, often staying for extended periods. In 1580 Sir
Francis Drake, heading home at the end of his circumnavigation with a
fortune in cloves, caused to be written in his log:

> From Java we sailed for the Cape of Good Hope. We ranne hard
> aboard the Cape, finding the report of the Portugals to be most false,
> who affirme that it is the most dangerous Cape of the world, never
> without intolerable storms and present dangers to travallers, which
> come neare the same. This Cape is a most stately thing, and the
> fairest we saw in the whole circumference of the earth.

In 1601 when Sir James Lancaster arrived with a small fleet—an appalling
two hundred and nine days out of London—one hundred and five men
were dead of scurvy, with the rest too weak to man the sails. There was
one exception; in General Lancaster's own ship the men were in good
shape:

> And the reason why the Generals men stood better in health than
> the men of other ships was this; he brought to sea with him certaine
> bottles of the Juice of Limons, which hee gave to each one, as long
> as it would last, three spoonfuls every day . . .

Lancaster kept his men ashore forty-six days, plus five more at anchor in
the roads, and during this time he was astonished at the level of society he
encountered among the little brown men who occupied the land:

> We bought of them a thousand Sheepe and two and fortie Oxen;
> and might have bought more if we would. These Oxen are full as
> bigge as ours and the sheepe many of them much bigger, fat and
> sweet and (to our thinking) much better than our sheepe in Eng-
> land . . . Their speech they clocke with their tongues in such sort,
> that in seven weeks which wee remained heere in this place, the
> sharpest wit among us could not learne one word of their language;
> and yet the people would soone understand any signe wee made to
> them . . . While that wee stayed heere in this baye we had so royall

refreshing that all our men recovered their health and strength, onely foure or five excepted.

Year after year the ships stopped by, the sailors lived ashore, and the clerks wrote accounts of what transpired, so that there exists a rather better record of the unoccupied Cape than of other areas that were settled by unlettered troops. The character of the little brown people with their clicking tongue is especially well laid out—'they speak from the throat and seem to sob and sigh'—so that scholars throughout Europe had ample knowledge of the Cape long before substantial interest was shown by their governments. Indeed, one enterprising London editor compiled a four-volume book dealing largely with travels past the Cape, *Purchas his Pilgrimes*, and entered unknowingly into literary history as the principal source for *The Rime of the Ancient Mariner*.

Two engaging traditions endeared the Cape to sailors. It became the custom that whenever the navigator sensed that he was nearing the Cape, he would alert the crew, whereupon all ordinary seamen would strain to see who could first cry out: 'Table Mountain!' After his sighting was verified, the captain ceremoniously handed him a silver coin, and all hands, officers and men alike, stood at the railing to see once more this extraordinary mountain.

It was not a peak; as if some giant carpenter had planed it down, its top seemed as flat as a palace floor, and not a small floor, either, but a vast one. Its sides were steep and it possessed a peculiarity that never ceased to amaze: at frequent intervals, on a cloudless day when the tabletop showed clear, a sudden wind sweeping north from the Antarctic would throw a cloud of dense fog, and even as one watched, this fog would spread out, obliterating Table Mountain. 'The devil throwing his tablecloth,' men would say later, and the mountain would be hidden, with the hem of the cloth tumbling down the sides.

The second tradition was that of the post-office stone. As early as 1501 the captain of a Portuguese vessel passing the Cape came ashore with a letter of instructions to aid future travelers, and after wrapping it in pitched canvas, he placed it under a prominent rock on whose surface he scratched a notice that something of importance lay beneath. Thus the tradition started, and in all succeeding years captains would stop at the Cape, search for post-office stones, pick up letters which might have been left a decade earlier, and deliver them either to Europe or to Java. In 1615 Captain Walter Peyton, in the *Expedition* at the head of a small fleet, found post-office stones with letters deposited by different ships: *James, Globe, Advice, Attendant*. Each told of dangers passed, of hopes ahead.

There are few reports of letters ever having been destroyed by enemies. A ship would plow through the Indian Ocean for a year, fighting at port after port, but when it passed the Cape and posted its letters beneath some rock, they became inviolate, and the very soldiers who had fought this ship would, if they landed for refreshing, lift those letters reverently and carry them toward their destination, often dispatching them on a route that would take them through two or three intervening countries.

What was the miracle of the Cape? That no seafaring nation wanted it.

On New Year's Day 1637 a grizzled mariner of Plymouth, England, reached a major decision. Captain Nicholas Saltwood, aged forty-four and a veteran of the northern seas, told his wife, 'Henrietta, I've decided to risk our savings and buy the *Acorn*.' Forthwith he led her to The Hoe, the town's waterfront, and resting there in the exact spot occupied by Sir Francis Drake's ship in July of 1588, when he waited for the Spanish Armada to come up the Channel, stood a small two-masted ship of one hundred and eighty-three tons.

'It will be dangerous,' he confided. 'Four years absent in the Spice Islands and God knows where. But if we don't venture now . . .'

'If you buy the ship, how will you acquire your trade goods?'

'On our character,' Saltwood said, and once the *Acorn* was his, he and his wife circulated among the merchants of Plymouth, offering them shares in his bold adventure. From them he wanted no money, only the goods on which he proposed to make his fortune and theirs. On February 3, the day he had hoped to sail, he had a ship well laden.

'And if the sheriff abides his word,' he told his wife, 'we'll take even more,' and they went together to the ironmonger's, and as before, their surety was their appearance and their reputation. They were sturdy people and honest: 'Matthew, I want your lad to keep watch on my foremast. If I raise a blue flag, rush me these nineteen boxes. I'll pay silver for seven. You contribute the dozen, and if the voyage fails, you've lost all. But it will not fail.'

At the door of the mongery he kissed his wife farewell: 'It would not be proper for you to deal with the sheriff. I believe he'll come. You watch for the blue flag, too.' And he was gone.

Three bells had sounded when a cart from Plymouth prison hove into sight, bearing ten manacled men guarded by four marching soldiers and a very stout sheriff, who, when he reached the wharf, called out, 'Captain Saltwood, be you prepared?'

When Saltwood came to the railing the sheriff produced a legal paper, which he passed along for one of his soldiers to read, since he could not: 'Ship *Acorn*, Captain Saltwood. Do you agree to carry these men condemned to death to some proper spot in the southern seas where they are to be thrown ashore to establish a colony to the honor of King Charles of England?'

'I do,' Saltwood replied. 'And now may I ask you, has the passage money been voted?'

'It has,' the fat sheriff said, and as he stepped aboard the *Acorn* he counted out the five pieces of silver for each of the condemned men. 'Now the delivery. Captain Saltwood, I want you to appreciate the rogues you're getting.' And as the manacled prisoners came awkwardly aboard, chains dangling, the soldier read out their crimes: 'He stole a horse. A cutpurse. He committed murder, twice. He robbed a church. He ate another man's apples. He stole a cloak . . .' Each man had been sentenced to death, but at the solicitation of Captain Saltwood, who needed their passage money, execution had been stayed.

'Have you granted them equipment to found their colony?' Saltwood asked.

'Throw them ashore,' the sheriff said. 'If they survive, it's to the honor of the king. If they perish, what's lost?' With that the four soldiers climbed into the cart and pulled the wheezing sheriff in behind them.

'Run up the blue pennant,' Saltwood told his mate, and when it fluttered in the breeze the ironmonger hurried down to the ship with his nineteen crates of tools badly needed in the distant islands.

As soon as the *Acorn* stood out from harbor, Saltwood ordered his carpenter to strike off the manacles, and when the convicts were freed he assembled them before the mast: 'During this trip I hold the power of life and death. If you work, you eat and are assured of justice. If you plot against this ship, you feed the sharks.' But as he was about to dismiss the unfortunates, he realized that they must be bewildered by what might happen to them, and he said reassuringly, 'If you conduct yourselves well, I shall seek the most clement coast in all the seas. And when the moment comes to disembark, I shall provide you with such equipment for survival as we can spare.'

'Where?' one of the men asked.

'Only God knows,' Saltwood said, and for the next ninety days the *Acorn* sailed slowly southward through seas it had never traversed before, and the heavens showed stars which none had ever seen. The prisoners worked and partook of such food as the regular crew received, but always Saltwood kept his pistols ready, his defenses against mutiny prepared.

On the ninety-first day out, the *Acorn* sighted St. Helena, where the condemned men prayed to be set ashore, but a congenial port like this was not the intended destination, so the convicts were kept under close guard while the ship was provisioned, and after four restful days the *Acorn* headed south.

On May 23, in rough weather, the little ship, barely visible against the massiveness of Africa, stood off the sandy beach north of Table Mountain, for it was here that Captain Saltwood proposed to cast his convicts ashore. But before he did so, he gave them a selection of implements from one of the crates of tools, and his men contributed food and spare clothes for the apprehensive settlers.

'Be of good cheer,' Saltwood advised the convicts. 'Select one of your group to serve as leader, that you may subdue the land quickly.'

'Won't you sail closer to the shore?' one of the men asked.

'This coast looks dangerous,' Saltwood said, 'but you shall have this little boat.'

As the convicts climbed down into the frail craft he called, 'Establish a
good colony so that your children may prosper under the English flag.'

'Where will we find women?' the impertinent murderer called.

'Men always find women,' Captain Saltwood cried, and he watched as
the criminals manned the oars and rowed ineffectively toward the shore.
When a tall wave came, they could not negotiate it; the boat capsized and
all were drowned. Captain Saltwood shook his head: 'They had their
chance.' And he watched with real regret as his boat shattered on the in-
hospitable beach.

But this voyage of the *Acorn* was not remembered for its loss of the
ten convicts, because such accidents were commonplace and barely reported in London. When the stormy seas subsided, men from the ship
went ashore at the Cape proper, and one of the first things they did was
check the area for post-office stones; they found five, each with its parcel of
letters, some intended for Amsterdam, some for Java. The former were
rewrapped in canvas and put back under one stone; the latter were taken
aboard for delivery in the far Far East. Under a special stone engraved
with the *Acorn's* name, the mate deposited a letter to London detailing the
successful passage via St. Helena but ignoring the loss of the ten prisoners.

The shore party was about to embark for the long trip to Java when a
group of seven little brown men appeared from the east, led by a vivacious
young man in his twenties. He offered to trade sheep, which he indicated
by cleverly imitating those animals, if the sailors would provide him with
lengths of iron and brass, which again he indicated so that even the
dullest sailor could catch his meaning.

They asked him his name, and he tried to say Horda, but since this
required three click sounds they could make nothing of it, and the mate
said, 'Jack! That's a good name!' And it was under this name that he was
taken aboard the *Acorn* and introduced to Captain Saltwood, who said,
'We need men to replace the convicts. Show him to a bunk for'ard.'

He was naked except for a loincloth made of jackal skin, and a small
pouch tied about his waist; in it he carried a few precious items, including
an ivory bracelet and a crude stone knife. What amazed the sailors were
the click sounds he made when talking. 'God's word,' one sailor reported
to another, 'he farts through his teeth.'

Within a week of watching the sailmaker ply his awls and needles,
Jack had fashioned himself a pair of trousers, which he wore during the
remainder of the long voyage. He also made a pair of sandals, a hat and a
loose-fitting shirt, and it was in this garb that he stood by the railing of the
Acorn when Captain Saltwood led his little ship gingerly into the Portuguese harbor at Sofala.

'You were daring to enter here,' a Portuguese merchant said. 'Had you been Dutch, we would have sunk you.'

'I come to trade for the gold of Ophir,' Saltwood said, whereupon the Portuguese burst into disrespectful laughter.

'Everyone comes for that. There is none. I don't believe there ever was.'

'What do you trade?'

'Where do you head?'

'Malacca. The Spice Islands.'

'Oh, now!' the trader said. 'We accept you here, but anyone who tries to enter the Spice Island trade . . . they'll burn your ship at Malacca.' Then he snapped his fingers. 'But if you're brave, and really want to trade, I have something most precious that the Chinese long for.'

'Bring it forth,' Saltwood said, and with obvious pride the Portuguese produced fourteen curious, dark, pyramidal objects about nine inches square on the base. 'What can they be?'

'Rhinoceros horn.'

'Yes! Yes!' In the pages of his ship's log, on which he had prepared his notes for this great adventure, he had noted that rhinoceros horn might profitably be carried to any ports where Chinese came. 'Where would I trade them?' he asked.

'Java. The Chinese frequent Java.'

So a bargain was struck, after which the Portuguese said, 'A warning. The horns must be delivered as they are. Not powdered, for the old men who yearn to marry young girls must see that the horn is real, or it won't work.'

'Does it really work?' Saltwood asked.

'I don't need it yet,' the Portuguese said.

Wherever the *Acorn* anchored, Jack studied the habits of the people, marveling at their variety and how markedly they differed from the English sailors with whom he was now familiar and whose language he spoke effectively. At stately Kilwa he noticed the blackness of the natives' skins; at Calicut he saw men halfway in darkness between himself and his shipmates; at resplendent Goa, where all ships stopped, he marveled at the temples.

He gained great respect for Captain Saltwood, who not only owned the *Acorn* but ran it with sagacity and daring. For one dreamy day after another the little vessel would drift through softly heaving seas, then head purposefully for some harbor none of the crew had heard of before, and there Saltwood would move quietly ashore, and talk and listen, and after a day of cautious judgment would signal to his men, and they would bring to the marketplace their bales of goods, unwrapping them delicately to impress the buyers. And always at the end of the trading, Saltwood would have some new product to fill his holds.

Like all the little brown people, Jack loved to sing, and in the evening when the sailors idled their time in chantey, his soft clear voice, echoing like some pure bell, joined in. They liked this; they taught him their favorite songs; and often they called for him to sing alone, and he would stand as they lolled, a little fellow four feet ten, his slanted eyes squeezed shut, his face a vast smile as he chanted songs composed in Plymouth or Bristol. Then he felt himself to be a member of the crew.

But there was another tradition, and this one he disliked. From time to time the English sailors would cry, 'Take down your pants!' and when he refused, they would untie the cord that held up the trousers he had sewn and pull them down, and they would gather round in astonishment, for he had only one testicle. When they questioned him about this, he explained, 'Too many people. Too few food.'

'What's that got to do with your missing stone?' a Plymouth man asked.

'Every boy baby, they cut one off.'

'What's that got to do with food?' The Plymouth man gagged. 'My God, you don't . . .'

'So when we grow up, find a wife, we must never have twins.'

Again and again when the voyage grew dull the sailors cried, 'Jack, take down your pants!' and one sultry afternoon in the Indian Ocean they brought down Captain Saltwood. 'You'll be astonished!' they said admiringly as they sought the little fellow, but when they found him and stood him on a barrel and cried, 'Jack, down with your pants!' he refused, grabbing himself about the middle to protect the cord that tied his trousers.

'Jack!' the men cried with some irritation. 'Captain Saltwood wants to see.'

But Jack had had enough. Stubbornly, his little face showing clenched teeth, he refused to lower his pants, and when two burly sailors came at him he fought them off, shouting, 'You not drop your pants!' And there he stood on the barrel, resisting, until Saltwood said quietly, 'He's right, men. Let him be.'

And from that day he never again dropped his drawers, and his self-stubbornness had an unforeseen aftermath: he had been the sailors' toy, now he became their friend.

The part of the journey he liked best came when the *Acorn* slipped past the great Portuguese fort at Malacca and wandered far to the east among the islands of the spice trade; there he saw for the first time cloth woven with gold and the metalwork of the islands. It was a world whose riches he could not evaluate but whose worth he had to acknowledge because of the respectful manner in which his friends handled these treasures.

'Pepper! That's what brings money,' the sailors told him, and when they crushed the small black corns to release the aromatic smell, he sneezed and was enchanted.

'Nutmeg, mace, cinnamon!' the sailors repeated as the heavy bags were heaved aboard. 'Turmeric, cardamom, cassia!' they continued, but it was the cloves that captivated him, and even though guards were posted over this precious stuff, he succeeded in stealing a few to crack between his teeth and keep against the bottom of his tongue, where they burned, emitting a pleasant aroma. For some days he moved about the ship blowing his cloved breath on the sailors until they started calling him Smelly Jack.

How magnificent the East was! When the *Acorn* completed its barter, Captain Saltwood issued the welcome command: 'We head for Java and the Chinese who await our horns.' And for many days the little ship sailed along the coast of Java with sailors at the rail to marvel at this dreamswept island where mountains rose to touch the clouds and jungle crept down to dip its fingers in the sea.

Captain Saltwood found no time to enjoy these sights, for he was preoccupied with two serious problems: he had traded so masterfully that his ship now contained a fortune of real magnitude and must be protected from pirates; but the fortune could not be realized unless he got his ship safely past the fort at Malacca, across the seas, around the Cape of Good Hope, through the storms of the equator, and home to Plymouth. It was with these apprehensions that he anchored in the roadstead off Java and was rowed ashore to bargain with the Chinese merchants who might want his rhinoceros horns.

While the *Acorn* lay at anchor, waiting until the next fleet formed for the journey to Europe, Jack had an opportunity to explore the trading center that the Dutch had established on Java. He lounged by the waterside, learning to identify the varied craft that worked these Asian waters: carracks with their bristling guns, swift flutes from Holland, the amazing proas from the islands—by shifting the location of their mast, they could sail in either direction with equal speed—and best of all, the towering East Indiamen.

It was while watching one of these monsters unload that he became aware of a tall, thin Dutchman who seemed always to preempt the best cargo for his warehouse, which stood close to the harbor. Traders called him Mijnheer van Doorn, and he seemed a most austere person, overly conscious of his position, even though he could not have been more than twenty-three. Jack was awed by his stiff dignity and spoke to him in broken English, which Van Doorn as a trader had to know.

'Where you from?' the Dutchman asked, looking down as if from a great and sovereign height.

'Many days.'

'You're not black. You're not yellow. Where?'

'Setting sun.'

The interrogation was so unsatisfactory that Van Doorn summoned a sailor from the *Acorn* and asked, 'Where's this fellow from?' and the man replied, 'Picked him up at the Cape of Good Hope.'

'Hmmmm!' Van Doorn stepped back, looked down his long nose at the little fellow, and said, 'The Cape, is it a fine place?' Jack, understanding nothing of this, laughed and was about to retreat when he spotted a white person about his own size, a boy of thirteen whom Van Doorn treated affectionately.

'Your boy?' Jack asked.

'My brother,' Van Doorn replied, and for the last two months that Captain Saltwood idled off Java, Jack and this white lad played together. They were of equal size and equal mental development, each striving to understand the complex world of Batavia. They formed an attractive pair, a thin little brown man with bandy legs, a stout Dutch lad with blond hair and wide shoulders, and they could be seen together in each of the quarters allocated to the different nationalities: Malay, Indian, Arab, Balinese, and the small area in which the industrious Chinese purchased almost anything offered for sale, but only at the prices they set.

One day young Van Doorn explained that Dutch children had two names; his other one was Willem. 'What's yours?' he asked.

'Horda,' his playmate said with a blizzard of click sounds. 'And his name?' he asked, pointing to the older Van Doorn.

'Karel.' And while Jack was repeating the two names, Willem produced his surprise. Having noticed that Jack owned only the clothes he wore, he had procured from the Compagnie warehouse an additional pair of trousers and a shirt, but when Jack put them on he looked ridiculous, for they had been cut to fit stout Dutchmen, not dwarfish brown persons.

'I can sew,' Jack said reassuringly, but after the clothes were altered he reflected that aboard the *Acorn* whenever one man gave another something, the recipient was supposed to give something in return, and he very much wanted to give Willem van Doorn a gift, but he could not imagine what. Then he remembered the ivory bracelet hidden in his pouch, but when he handed it to Willem it was too small to fit his stout wrist. It was dour Karel who solved the problem. Taking a silver chain from the Compagnie stock, he fastened the ivory circle to it, then hung the chain about Willem's neck, where the combination of silver, ivory and the lad's fair complexion made a fine show.

That night Captain Saltwood, richer than he had ever dreamed because of the trade he made on the rhino horns, informed his crew that since no other ships were preparing to depart for home, the *Acorn* had no alternative but to make a run up the Straits of Malacca to join with some English fleet forming in India. 'It will be a grave adventure,' he warned his men, and they spent that night preparing their muskets and pikes.

At dawn Jack wanted to slip ashore to say farewell to his Dutch friend, but Captain Saltwood would not permit this, for he wished no interference from Dutch authorities and intended sailing without their knowledge or approval. So Jack stood at the railing of the *Acorn*, looking vainly for his companion. Willem knew nothing of the departure, but toward eleven a Dutch sailor ran into the Compagnie warehouse, shouting,

'The English ship is sailing!' and Willem, fingering his ivory gift, stood by the water's edge watching the ship and its little brown fellow disappear.

It required two weeks for the *Acorn* to transit Java waters, sail along the coast of Sumatra and past the myriad islands that made this sea a wonderland of beauty as well as fortune, but in time the sailors could see that land was beginning to encroach on each side of the ship, and they knew they were headed directly into the critical part of their voyage. To port lay Sumatra, a nest of pirates. To starboard stood the massive fortress of Malacca, impervious to sieges, with nearly seventy major guns on its battlements. And fore and aft would be the pestilential little boats filled with daring men trying to board and steal the prize.

The fight, if it came, would be even, for the *Acorn* was manned by men of Plymouth, grandsons of those doughty fellows who with Drake had routed the ships of King Philip's Armada. They did not intend to be boarded or sunk.

It was Captain Saltwood's strategy to remain hidden behind one of the many islands to satisfy himself that there was adequate wind, and then to run the gauntlet at night when the Portuguese might be inattentive, and this plan would have succeeded except that some Malay sailor, lounging on the northern shore, saw the attempted passage and sounded an alarm.

It was midnight when the battle began, great guns flashing from the fort, small boats darting out in an attempt to set fire to the English ship, larger boats trying to ram and board. Jack understood what was happening and knew from conversation with the sailors what tortures he and the others might expect if their ship was taken, but he was not prepared for the violent heroism of his English mates. They fought like demons, firing their pistols, thrusting and stabbing with their pikes.

Dawn found them safely past the looming fortress, with only a few small craft still trying to impede them; like a bristling beetle ignoring ants, the *Acorn* swayed ahead, its sailors shooting and jabbing at their attackers, and before long, pulled away. The dangerous passage was completed.

In India, Captain Saltwood faced a major disappointment: no English fleet would sail this year. So once more he went on alone, a daring man carrying with him enough wealth to found a family and perhaps even acquire a residence in some cathedral town. Getting home became an obsession, and he sailed the *Acorn* accordingly.

At Ceylon, pirates tried to board; off Goa, Portuguese adventurers had to be repulsed. South of Hormuz the Plymouth men ran into real danger, and at Moçambique two crazed carracks lumbered out to give chase on the remote chance that they might take a prize, but when the *Acorn* sailed serenely on, they abandoned the pursuit. Finally Sofala was passed to starboard, with Captain Saltwood saluting the unseen merchant who had sold him the rhinoceros horn. The southern coast of Africa guided them westward, and the morning came when a sailor shouted, 'I see Table Mountain!' and Captain Saltwood himself handed him the silver coin, saying, 'We're one step nearer home.'

When the bay was reached and the longboat prepared, Jack said farewell to his accidental friends, standing on tiptoe to embrace them. Once ashore, he walked slowly inland, pausing now and again to look back at the ship whose victories and tribulations he had shared for nearly four years. But the moment came when the next hill must close him off forever from the *Acorn*, and when he passed this and began to see familiar rocks and the spoor of animals he had always known, a strange thing occurred. He began divesting himself of the sailor's uniform he had worn these many months. Off came the shirt, the carefully sewn trousers, the leather shoes. He did not throw them away, nor the extra raiment given him by the young Dutch boy at Java, but tied them carefully into a little bundle, which knocked reassuringly against his leg as he walked homeward.

When he reached his village he was sucking a clove stolen at Java, and when his old friends poured out to greet him, he breathed a strange odor upon them, and undid his bundle to display what he carried, and to each he gave a clove in remembrance of the many times during the past four years that he had thought of them.

By 1640 the grim-faced Dutchmen who proposed to rule the East from Java had endured enough: 'Those damned Portuguese at Malacca must be destroyed.' In stinging reports to the Lords XVII, the businessmen who controlled the East Indies Company from their dark offices in Amsterdam, they had complained: 'The Catholic fiends in Malacca have sunk our ships for the last time. We are prepared to besiege their fortress for seven years if necessary.'

The Lords XVII might have rejected this daring proposal had not a gentleman, whose grandfather was burned at the stake while trying to protect Dutch Protestantism from the fury of Spain's Duke of Alva, argued passionately: 'Our fortunes teeter in the balance. Malacca must be destroyed.' His oratory carried, and plans to crush the Portuguese had been approved, not by the Dutch government but by Jan Compagnie. The hard-headed citizens of Holland knew in what kind of hands responsibility should be placed. Merchants with something to protect would know how to protect it.

When authorization reached Java the local Dutchmen responded enthusiastically. Funds were made available. New ships were built. Javanese natives in sarongs were taught to handle tasks afloat. And of equal importance, ambassadors were dispatched to large and petty kingdoms to assure them that when the Dutch moved against Malacca their interest was not territorial: 'We intend to take no land belonging to others. But we must stop the Portuguese piracy.'

Among the ambassadors chosen for this ticklish task was Karel van

Doorn, now twenty-five and with a solid reputation as a loyal Compagnie servant. He was severe, honest, humorless, and gifted with an understanding of finance and the profitable management of Compagnie slaves.

Such promotions as Karel had achieved were due principally to his mother, the stalwart widow of an official who had been killed while endeavoring to extend Compagnie holdings in the Spice Islands. He had been a man of enormous energy; by arrogance, bluff, courage and expropriation he had protected the Compagnie; by chicanery, theft, falsification and diversion he had at the same time built up his own clandestine trading interests—a thing severely forbidden—and in so doing, had accumulated a considerable wealth which he had been trying vainly to smuggle back to Holland when he died. His widow, Hendrickje, now found herself with a growing fortune which she could spend only in Java.

Fortunately, she flourished in the tropics, and as soon as the Dutch destroyed the Javanese city of Jacatra and began building opposite its ruins their own capital, Batavia, she appropriated one of the choicest locations on the Tijgergracht (Tiger Canal) and there built herself a mansion. Curiously, it could have stood unnoticed on any street in Amsterdam, for it was done in massive Dutch style, with heavy stone walls and red-tiled roof protecting it from snows which never came. Thick partitions separated the rooms, which were illuminated by very small windows, and wherever a breeze might have entered, some heavy piece of furniture shut it out.

The only concession indicating that this massive house stood in the tropics was a garden of surpassing beauty, filled with the glorious flowers of Java and punctuated with handsome statuary imported from China. In this garden, to the sound of the tinkling gamelan comprised of eleven musicians, many decisions regarding Dutch fortunes in the East were reached.

Mevrouw van Doorn, a voluptuous blonde who might have been painted by Frans Hals, who did paint her mother, had arrived in 1618 when that notable administrator Jan Pieterszoon Coen was running affairs in his harsh, capable style, and she had quickly endeared herself to him, supporting him eagerly no matter what he did. She heard him warn the populace that acts of immorality among servants must cease, and when one of her maids became pregnant she herself dragged the frightened girl to Coen's headquarters and was present in the square when the girl was beheaded. The young man involved was also sharply reprimanded.

Two obsessions controlled her life: business and religion. It had been she who goaded her husband into setting up his illegal private businesses, one after another. It had been she who supervised those operations, earning a profit of sixty percent a year when the Lords XVII could make only forty. And it had been she who sequestered the stolen funds when they reached Batavia. Indeed, her husband's estate was now so complicated that she dared not risk returning to Holland lest it fall in chaos. As she reported to her younger sister in Haarlem:

> I often think of coming home to live with you in our house on the canal, but I dread those cold winters. Besides, I am kept prisoner here supervising the sixty-nine slaves who work for me. By Haarlem standards I know this sounds a lot, but it really isn't. When I go about Batavia, attending my affairs, eight slaves accompany me to assure that coaches, umbrellas and footwear are available. Seven girls tend my clothes, six watch over my retiring room. I need six cooks, nine serving men, eleven members for my orchestra, twelve to tend the grounds and ten for general services. So you see, I am kept quite busy.

Her devotion to religion contained no shred of insincerity, nor should it, considering her family history. Her grandfather, Joost van Valkenborch, had been executed by the Spaniards in 1568 when the great Count Egmont went to his death; both patriots had given their lives in defense of Holland and Calvinism. Her father, too, had died fighting the Spanish Catholics; Willem van Valkenborch had established the first Calvinist assembly in Haarlem, a clandestine affair whose members knew they would perish if caught. One of her first memories was of secret night worship when her father spoke eloquently of God and the nature of man. Religion was more real to her than the stars over Java, more encompassing than the canals that served Batavia.

Before her husband died they had shared the pleasure of receiving from the Lords XVII a Protestant Bible printed in Dutch, a massive affair published in 1630 by Henrick Laurentsz of Amsterdam, and together they had read in their own language the glowing stories that had sustained her father and grandfather in their martyrdoms. Despite all the wealth her husband had left her, she held her chief treasure to be this Bible; it was the light that ruled her life.

Her next treasures were her two sons, who lived with her and whose fortunes she supervised so carefully, nudging the local directors whenever she thought Karel merited an advancement. It was she who had proposed him for the embassy to governments neighboring on Malacca, and when the trip was in preparation it was she who suggested that young Willem go along so as to witness the vast extent of the Compagnie's trading interests.

'He's only fifteen,' Karel protested.

'Proper time to learn what ships and battles are,' his mother snapped, and on a very hot afternoon when flies buzzed in stifled air, members of the diplomatic mission were briefed by high officials of the Compagnie, who sat like gargoyles in the white-walled council chamber, nodding gravely as an old man who had been fighting the Portuguese for three decades spoke portentously: 'A solemn moment approaches. We're about to crush Malacca.'

Karel leaned forward. 'Assault the fortress?'

The old man, clenching his fists and dreaming of long-gone defeats, ignored him. 'In 1606 we tried to capture that damned place and failed. In 1608 we tried again, and 1623. In 1626 and '27 I myself led the landing parties. We got to the walls but were driven back. During the last four years we've tried to blockade the Straits, starve them out, and always they've laughed at us. Now,' he shouted, banging his frail hand on the table, 'we destroy them.'

'How soon do we sail?'

'Immediately.'

When Karel showed disappointment at missing the siege, where promotions might come quickly, the old man said, 'You'll be back for fighting. We may not attack for at least a year. And remember what your job is. To assure all our neighbors that when we capture Malacca we shall seek no territory for ourselves.'

Another officer said sententiously, 'All we insist upon is trading rights. We'll take the fort but leave the land.'

And then a very large man with a voice that rumbled from much preaching added, 'Explain to them all that if they do business with us, it's only business. An honest deal for all. We will not try to Christianize them, the way the Portuguese have done with their oppressive Catholicism. Mark my words, Van Doorn, your strongest weapon could be religion. Tell them to watch our deportment when we capture Malacca.'

'If we capture it,' someone corrected.

'No!' a dozen voices cried. 'Dr. Steyn is right. When we capture it.'

The minister coughed and continued: 'When we occupy Malacca, nothing is changed. The sultan continues in power, freed of Portuguese influence. Muhammad continues as their God, freed of pressure from the Catholics. The Chinese, Arabians, Persians, Ceylonese, English—and even the Portuguese traders themselves—anyone with a business in Malacca will continue to own it and operate it as he wishes. All we seek is the right to trade, for all men. Tell the rulers that.'

In four days of concentrated argument this point was hammered until Van Doorn understood better than most of the Lords XVII back in Amsterdam what the practical politics of Jan Compagnie were. The Lords, representing all regions and aspects of Dutch life, had to be cautious, aware that whatever they promulgated enjoyed the force of law; indeed, their decisions were stronger than ordinary law because from them there was no appeal. But the governors in the field, who needed two years to send a query and receive an answer, had to be daring. On their own they could declare war, appropriate an island, or conduct negotiations with a foreign power. The governor-general in Java could order the execution of anyone, slave or free, English or Chinese: 'For stealing property belonging to the Compagnie, he shall be dragged to the port of Batavia and keel-hauled three times beneath the largest vessel. If still living, he shall be burned and his ashes scattered.'

The governor-general, accustomed to exercising these powers, glared at Karel and said, 'We expect you to convince the nations that they have no reason to oppose us when we make our attack.'

'I shall,' Van Doorn assured him.

There was at this time riding at the port of Batavia a trading ship heavily laden with goods for China, Cambodia and the Dutch entrepôt on Formosa, and free space for the stowing of such spices and metals as might be picked up in the course of a long journey. To this ship Karel, his brother Willem and their sixteen servants reported. Because of the importance of this mission, the captain had vacated his cabin and assigned it to the brothers, and there, surrounded by books and charts, they started the long voyage to the ancient ports of the East, sailing through waters that Marco Polo had known, past islands that would not be touched by white men for another century.

Wherever they stopped, they assured local leaders that the Dutch had no designs upon their territory, and that Java expected neutrality when the attack came on Malacca. 'Won't these people warn the Portuguese?' Willem asked.

'The Portuguese know. We've been attacking Malacca every ten years. Surely they expect us.'

'Won't they build their defenses?'

'Of course. They're doing it right now.'

'Then why didn't we attack right now?' the boy asked.

'Next year will be just as good. Our job now is to pacify allies.' But later, when the Dutch were dining alone, Karel was inspired to raise his glass to the sailors and soldiers who would participate in the siege: 'To that brave man amongst us who could well be the governor of Malacca before this year is out!' And all the Dutchmen drank in silence, imagining the possibilities: in their army a man did not have to be a nobleman to become an admiral or a governor.

By late April 1640, when the Van Doorns returned to Batavia with assurances that no neighbors would interfere with operations in the Straits of Malacca, and when a fleet of war vessels had been assembled, Governor-General van Diemen decided that the time was proper for the major thrust.

'Karel,' he told the returning ambassador, 'you're to accompany the fleet. Take charge as soon as the fortress is secured.'

'Looting?'

'It will be a long, dangerous fight, Karel. Allow the men three days to capture what they will. Then establish order. After that, no one is to be touched, Muslim or Christian.'

'The sultan?'

'Protect him, by all means. The soldiers will probably loot his palaces and take some of his women. But let him know that he survives with our blessing . . . and only because of our blessing. He'll prove our strongest ally.'

When the sails of the fleet were raised, they covered the sea like a sheath of white lace, and spies rushed overland to launch small boats in which they would scurry to Malacca to inform the Portuguese that the next siege was under way. It required thirteen days for the straggling fleet to reach the Straits south of the fortress, and when young Willem van Doorn looked up at the mighty battlements, thirty feet high, twenty-six feet thick, he gasped, 'No one could break them down.'

He was right to be apprehensive, for the fortress was much greater now than when the Dutch had first assaulted it. Five large churches stood within the walls, two hospitals, granaries, many deep wells, accommodation for four thousand fighting men. The town outside contained twenty thousand people, the harbor and the river more than a thousand small boats. From five towers sixty-nine major cannon controlled all approaches, and most important, the battlements were commanded by a man who had withstood other sieges and who was determined to outlast this one.

For five long and terrible months he succeeded. Two thousand of his people starved to death, then two thousand more, and finally another three. But he exacted a fearful toll on the Dutch assailants; more than a thousand highly trained men died in their attempt to approach these mighty walls.

They did achieve a limited success: by heroic measures they wrestled their cannon ashore, protected them with abutments, and proceeded methodically to knock large holes in the fortifications. Now all that was required was for foot soldiers to charge through the holes and the fort would be theirs, because deserters assured them: 'The Portuguese are eating rats and chewing upon the hides of horses.'

But to reach the holes, the Dutch would have to wade up to their armpits through malarial swamps, then swim turbulent streams while Portuguese on the walls shot at them, and this they were hesitant to do. So a kind of waiting war developed, during which yachts were dispatched regularly to Java seeking reinforcements and advice; in December, Willem van Doorn sailed on one of them, bearing messages:

> Our predikant Johannes Schotanus was an excellent man while the first fighting was under way, but in this waiting period he is again proving most difficult and has had to be suspended. We are sorry, for he possesses wonderful gifts. His teachings are exemplary, if only he would practice them. He could accomplish so much if he stayed sober, but we must not let him act as predikant after we capture Malacca because he would disgrace the Compagnie by his wild insobriety.

In the sixth month of the siege young Willem returned to the fleet in a large ship, bringing fresh supplies, much gunpowder and instructions that the fortress must now be taken. So on a Sunday night in January 1641 every able-bodied Dutchman moved ashore, forded the swamps, and made a predawn attack, driving the Portuguese from the openings in the walls by means of a furious barrage of hand grenades. By ten that morning the keystone of Portugal's empire in the East had fallen.

One of the most enthusiastic victors was Willem, who found that he did not fear gunfire or towering walls. Indeed, he was more resolute than his older brother and much more willing to press forward whether others accompanied him or not. He was among the first into the city, cheering wildly as cannon were drawn inside, lined up, and pointed down the narrow thoroughfares. Ball after ball, huge spheres of solid iron, leaped from the muzzles of the cannon, wreaking fearful destruction. Willem applauded the fires that raged and was in the forefront of those greedy soldiers who rampaged through the treasure-laden buildings that escaped the blaze.

It was a bloody triumph, but as soon as the looting was brought under control, the Dutch behaved with their customary magnanimity: the Portuguese commander was saluted for his bravery and given a ship in which he could transport his family, his slaves and his possessions to whatever haven he chose; the gallant captains who had defended the towers were permitted to accompany him with all they owned; and when an unsuspecting Portuguese merchant ship sailed into the channel laden with cloth from India, it was encouraged to dock, on the principle that since the islands under Dutch control produced little surplus cloth, trade with Portuguese India must not only be permitted but encouraged.

And so the vast Eastern empire started by Magellan and Albuquerque dissolved. Only the village of Macao would be retained on the threshold of China, a part of tiny Timor in the waters north of Australia, the minute enclave of Goa in India, and the savage hinterland behind Moçambique Island—these were the remnants. All the rest was gone: Ceylon, Malacca, Java, the important Spice Islands. A man's heart could break at the loss of such glorious lands.

While the fires still smoldered, the victors reported to the Compagnie managers in Batavia: 'Noble, Valiant, Wise, and Honorable Gentlemen, Malacca has fallen and will henceforth be considered private territory and a dominion of the Dutch East India Compagnie.' Now the eastern world was secured and time was ripe for the Dutch to think seriously about establishing a safe resting point between Amsterdam and Batavia where sailors could recover from scurvy. Logic dictated that it be located at the Cape of Good Hope, but its founding had nothing to do with logic. It was sheer accident.

*　*　*

Batavia! This tiny enclave on the northwest coast of Java, this glorious capital of a vast and loosely held empire, had been named after the Batavi, those fierce, sullen men encountered by the early Roman emperors in the marshes that would subsequently become Holland.

It would always be a contradictory place, a walled fortress town perched on the edge of a jungle, totally Netherlandish in disposition, appearance and custom; but at the same time a garden-filled tropical escape from Holland, festooned with lovely flowers and strange fruits in great abundance. It was a heavenly place, a deadly place, and many Dutchmen who came here were dead within ten years, struck down by indolence, gluttony and drunkenness. It was in this period that Compagnie men, returning to Batavia from forced stints in the outlying Spice Islands, conceived the feast that would always be associated with Java.

It could be observed at its best in the spacious dining room of Hendrickje van Doorn, where fifteen or twenty guests would assemble to the playing of her musicians. Javanese slaves in sarongs would pass huge platters of delicately steamed white rice, nothing more, and each guest would form a small mountain on his plate. Then the first group of waiters would retire, and after an expectant pause Mevrouw would sound a tinkling Chinese bell, and from the kitchen out in the garden would appear a chain of sixteen serving men, some of the gardeners having been called to assist. Each carried in his open palms held waist-high two dishes, making a total of thirty-two: chicken bits, lamb cuttings, dried fish, steamed fish, eight rare condiments, ten fruits, nuts, raisins, vegetables and half a dozen tasty items that no one could identify.

As the sixteen servants passed along the table, each guest heaped edibles around his rice until the plate resembled a volcano rising high above the sea. But this was not all, for when these servants retired, others appeared with flagons of translucent gin, from which copious draughts were poured. Thus reinforced, the diners started on their meal, calling back the thirty-two little dishes from time to time lest the plate appear empty. This was 'the sixteen-boy rice table of Java,' and it accounted in some measure for the fact that many men and women who had lived rather circumscribed lives in Calvinistic Holland were reluctant to go home, once they knew Batavia.

Nevertheless, twice each year Dutch merchant ships trading throughout the East convened at Batavia in preparation for the long journey back to Amsterdam; each fleet would be at sea for half a year, rolling and dipping with the long swells of the Indian Ocean, sailing close-hauled into the storms of the Atlantic. On occasion a third of the fleet would be lost, but whenever a ship seemed doomed, it would hoist a panic flag, whereupon others would cluster around, wait for clearing weather, and transfer its cargo into their holds, and in this way the precious spices continued their homeward journey.

The first fleet sailed around Christmas; the second, waiting just long enough to obtain the monsoon cargoes from Japan and China. The holiday sailing was especially popular with the Java Dutch, for just about this time of year they began to be homesick for the wintry canals, and to see the great fleet waiting at anchor was a sore temptation. In 1646 there was no exception; an immense fleet gathered off Batavia under the command of an admiral, and on the morning of December 22 it hoisted sail.

At the last minute three ships whose smaller size and trimmer rigging would enable them to move more swiftly than the others were detached and ordered to wait for three weeks to serve as the after-fleet to carry important last-minute messages and any Compagnie officials who wished to depart after the Christmas celebrations. *Haerlem, Schiedam* and *Olifant* were the ships, and they tied up so that their sailors could roister ashore, and large fights broke out because sailors from the first two ships, which bore honorable names, began to tease those from the *Olifant*, Dutch for *elephant*.

Christmas that year was a noisy time, but at the spacious home of Mevrouw van Doorn it exhibited a lovely Dutch grace. Her musicians were dressed in batiks from Jokjakarta, her serving men in sarongs from Bali. There was dancing, and long harangues from minor officials serving in the Spice Islands, but as the day wore on, with enormous quantities of food being consumed and gallons of beer and arrack, the governor-general found occasion to take Mevrouw van Doorn aside to give her advice concerning her sons.

'They both should sail with the after-fleet,' he said quietly as his assistants snored away their beer and vittles.

'Deprive me of my staunchest support?' she asked, directing the slaves with the fans how best to move the air.

'Your sons are no more staunch in their support of you than I,' the governor said, bowing in his chair. When she acknowledged the compliment, he continued: 'Karel was born in Holland, and this is a permanent advantage. But he has never served there and the Lords XVII are not acquainted with his talents.'

'Karel will prosper wherever he's put,' his mother said sharply. 'He needs no special attention from Amsterdam.'

'True, an admirable son, sure to reach positions of significance.' Dropping his voice, he reached for her hand. 'Positions of eminence, as I did under similar circumstances.'

'Jan Pieterszoon Coen often told us that you were one of the greatest. And you know that Karel is of your stamp.'

'But remember the counsel of prudent men where authority is concerned: "One must stand close enough to the fire to be warmed, but not so close that he is burned." Karel really must be seen in Compagnie headquarters. There is no alternative, Hendrickje.'

For some moments she reflected on this advice and knew it to be sound. Jan Compagnie was a curious beast, seventeen all-powerful men who did not know the East at firsthand, making decisions that influenced half the world. She would never want her sons to be members of that tight, mean-spirited gang of plotters, but she did want them to achieve positions in Java and Ceylon which only the Lords XVII could disburse. It really was time for Karel to put in an appearance. 'But Willem?' she asked softly, betraying her love for this tousle-headed lad. 'He's too young. Truly, he should stay with me.'

The governor laughed heavily. 'Hendrickje, you astonish me. This lad has been to Formosa, Cambodia. He fought valiantly at Malacca. He's a man, not a boy.' Then he grew serious, asking the servants to withdraw. 'Let us keep the fan-boys. They speak no Dutch.'

'Hendrickje, for Karel to be seen in Amsterdam is policy. For Willem to report there is survival. His entire future life may depend on this.'

'What can you mean?'

'What you know better than I. Few boys born outside Holland can ever hope to attain a position of power within the Compagnie. And especially no boy born in Java.'

Mevrouw van Doorn rose impetuously, ordered the fan-boys to leave the room, and paced back and forth. 'Outrageous!' she cried. 'My husband and I came here in the worst days. We helped burn Jacatra and build this new Batavia. And now you tell me that because our son was born while we were here . . .'

'I do not tell you, Hendrickje. The Compagnie tells you. Any boy born in Java suffers a dreadful stigma.'

He did not continue, for there was no need. No matter how angry Mevrouw van Doorn became over this tactless reminder that her son Willem suffered a disadvantage which might prove fatal in Compagnie politics, she knew he was right, for Dutch settlement in the East produced contradictions which simply could not be resolved. The Dutch were honest Calvinists who took their religion seriously, and the drowsy rooms in Batavia contained many persons whose forefathers had died protecting their religion. They were the spawn of heroes, prepared to die again if Calvinism were threatened.

But they were a paradoxical lot. They believed that God in His mercy separated the saved from the damned, and were convinced that the Dutch were saved, not all of them, but most. They firmly believed in sobriety, yet drank themselves into a stupor five days out of seven. They believed in strict sexual deportment, much stricter than the Portuguese or English; they spoke of it; they read those passages in the Bible which condemned lewd living; and their predikants roared at them from the pulpit. They did believe in chastity.

And there was the difficulty. For they were also a lusty lot; few men in Europe had a quicker eye for a flashing skirt than the Dutch of Amsterdam. They rousted and stormed through brothels, chasing girls brought from Brazil and Bali and from God knows where; but always they did this after protestations of virtue and before prayers of contrition. Few men have ever behaved so lustily between episodes of protective devotion.

In Java the problem was trebly difficult, for to it came the most virile young men of Holland to serve five to ten years, but with them came no Dutch women, or few, and these of the worst sort. Hendrickje van Doorn had written to at least a hundred young women in Haarlem and Amsterdam, begging them to come out as wives to these splendid young men who were making their fortunes, but she attracted not one: 'The voyage is too long. I shall never see my mother again. The climate is too hot. It is a land of savages.' A hundred marriageable girls could recite a hundred good reasons for not going to Java, which meant that the young men would have to work there without wives until such time as they could go home with their wealth.

Without wives, but not without women. The girls of Java were some of the most attractive in the world—slim, shy, whispering beauties who created the impression of knowing far more about love than they admitted. The girls of Bali were even more seductive, while the wonderful women of China were strong and able as well as beautiful. It was a Dutchman of stalwart character who could listen to his predikant in church on Sunday and keep away from the glorious women of the compounds during the next six nights.

The Lords XVII and their subordinates were tough-minded businessmen out to make a fast profit, but there arose occasions when they had to turn to other issues, and none was more vexing than this problem of the mixing of races. As the directors agonized over miscegenation, two opposing schools of thought emerged: the enlightened ones who saw considerable merit in encouraging their employees to marry women of the East, thus forming a permanent settlement; and the narrow ones who foresaw the degeneration of their own race. The puritan view prevailed, though in practice it meant little whenever a lonely man needed the warmth of a concubine or slave.

The debate would rage for centuries, not only in Java but in other Dutch settlements. At one stage intermarriage was advocated to the extent of offering Compagnie employees a cash bonus if they married local girls and settled permanently; but, bedeviled by conflicting philosophies, the directors were never able to find a satisfactory solution. While they searched their souls for just answers, an endless number of illegitimate children appeared.

Of course, the most delectable local women would have nothing to do with the invaders; many were Muslim and would rather die than convert or carry the child of a kaffir, an unbeliever, as they termed the Dutch. Thousands of others, less committed or concerned, slept with their masters, and the more liberal Dutchmen welcomed the new brown offspring as an enchanting addition, since the parental combination of handsome Dutch blond of clear white skin and slim Javanese women with orchid complexion produced clever half-caste boys and irresistible girls.

But such sentiments were rare. Most Dutchmen who ruled the tropics were convinced that the races must be kept apart, lest the superior intelligence of those from Europe be contaminated. That sentiment was used by one of the Lords XVII, who fulminated against half-castes:

> 'These piebald gentry are the children of the devil, the spews of sinful lust, and they have no place in our society. The men are not to be employed as scribes and the women must not be allowed to marry our employees. They are a disgraceful accident of whom we cannot be proud and against whom we must protect ourselves.'

The Lords XVII, many of them sons of clergymen, found much delight in exploring the ramifications of this subject, always pointing out that half-castes were a condemnation of orderly rule. They were not unaware that the bulk of those who went to the East were thrown into a society in which they need scarcely lift a finger, and certainly not to labor as they had done in Holland. Such men corrupt easily. Still, the directors consoled themselves with the belief that it was not the laziness of their employees but the lasciviousness of the women with whom they came in contact that threatened Holland's sons.

For this reason, the Lords were always cooperative if a young man in their employ wished to go home to find himself an honest Dutch wife. The men did go home; they proposed to the young women of Amsterdam; and they were, of course, refused. So the young men came back to Java alone, the supply of half-castes multiplied, and Java acquired a malodorous reputation which increased the difficulty of finding wives for the men. The most condemnatory reports were submitted by investigators dispatched from Holland to check upon conduct:

> Java is a moral sink, the white women often being worse than the men. They spend whole days in lechery or idleness, eating themselves into insensibility, drinking to excess, consorting with the lowest of the islands, and accomplishing nothing. I know of three wives who in Holland would be exemplary church members who do nothing from one week to the next but eat, fornicate with strangers, and complain about their slaves, of whom they have an abundance.

Small wonder that the Lords XVII established the iron-clad principle that no position of leadership could be held by a man born in the islands. Such men would lack the moral fiber automatically obtained during an education in Holland; their judgment would be sullied by their contact with the Javanese, their force corroded by the deleterious effects of the East.

'There is one escape for a boy like Willem,' the governor said, calling for the fan-boys again, since the air was becoming oppressive. 'If he goes home now, before contact with Asian women, and if he enters the university at Leiden, he may cleanse himself of his Javanese birth. If he remains here, he condemns himself to third- or even fourth-level positions.'

Disheartened, Mevrouw van Doorn sank into a chair. She was only fifty-one and wanted to keep her sons with her in the big house with the multitude of servants, but she appreciated the dangers of which the governor was speaking. Karel's progress might be impeded if he did not get back to Holland, but Willem would be disqualified for any advancement. She must send her sons home.

'The after-fleet will sail in January,' the governor said. 'I can find them two passages on the *Haerlem.*' When she hesitated, he added, 'God knows, Hendrickje, there's a dark future for them in Java. At best, marrying some local girl of dubious reputation. At worst, sinking into the gutter.'

She sighed, rose and went to the doorway to contemplate the flowers in her garden, and said, 'Arrange for them to go,' and with that she abruptly turned all her attention to her New Year's festival. It would be free and open, like the ones her husband had offered Compagnie people when he was alive, with everyone invited.

She began by borrowing musicians from homes of her friends, and smiled approvingly as the brown-skinned slaves carried their bronze gamelans and bamboo drums into the various rooms where dancing would occur. Then she enrolled cooks from these same houses, until she had more than forty servants in and about the kitchens. The walls she decorated with her own fabrics, hanging them in great festoons until the colors danced. Twenty-four turbaned footmen attended the carriages, and an equal number of women watched after the guests when they entered the halls.

The celebrations lasted three days, and were especially vivacious in that many of the leaders of Batavian society had departed on the Christmas fleet, so that those who remained felt obligated to show extra enthusiasm to replace that which had been lost. People ate and drank till they were near senseless, then slept sprawled on beds and floors until the soft music awakened them so that they could sing and dance and eat themselves into another stupor. At times some amorous woman, having dreamed of this party for weeks, or one whose husband had left on the fleet, would catch a stout burgher as he was about to go to bed, and she would join him in one of the smaller rooms, often retaining the fan-boy to keep the humidity lowered.

Mevrouw van Doorn's two sons watched the New Year's celebrations with detached interest; stern Karel had observed the carryings-on in previous years and judged them to be the inevitable release of spirits by people who were far from home and sentenced to live among natives they did not respect. He had no wife as yet, nor any intention of finding one for the present, and whenever some lady far in drink wanted to drag him into a corner, he smiled wanly and moved away. In previous years young Willem had usually been kept away from the rowdier celebrations, but now that he was both a practiced ambassador and a front-line soldier, to do so any longer would be incongruous, so he wandered among the guests, listened to the music and watched with unusual attention the prettier slave girls.

'It's time he should go,' his mother conceded as she saw him follow one serving girl into the kitchens, and when the party was over, and the borrowed musicians had returned to their accustomed places, she ordered her carriage with its six attendants and rode down the streets of Batavia to the Compagnie headquarters.

'I should like the two passages on the *Haerlem,*' she said crisply, and the documents were handed over.

Since the three swift vessels would not depart until the seventeenth of January, overtaking the main fleet somewhere in the vicinity of St. Helena, where fresh stores would be taken aboard, the brothers had two full weeks of farewells. Young Willem spent his in visiting numerous friends, but Karel reported each day to the Compagnie offices, mastering details of that year's intended sales and purchases. He took note of the various fleets that would sail east and north, and of the captains who would command them; at times, as he studied the complex operations, he felt that he was sitting like a spider at the heart of a web, controlling the destinies of half a world. There were now no Portuguese in Malacca; those Straits were Dutch. There were no other Europeans at Nagasaki, either; Japan was now exclusively a Dutch concession. English vessels still stopped at their little entrepôt but were no longer allowed in the Spice Islands; and even the occasional French merchantman, its sails ragged from the long voyage out, had to obey regulations set down by the Dutch.

'We rule the seas,' he exclaimed one morning when the full power of Jan Compagnie was revealed.

'No,' an older man cautioned. 'The English are beginning to rule India. And the Portuguese still control Macao and the China trade.'

'Let them have the tea and ginger,' Karel conceded, 'so long as we keep the spices.'

When the brothers approached the three ships, they could smell the spices from a considerable distance, for the holds were crammed with last-minute sacks and bundles from the eastern islands; the ships moved in a splendid ambience, reeking of fortunes and the promise of gold. They were taking the heart of Asia to the center of Europe, and each ship represented a greater wealth than many small nations would handle in an entire year. Jan Compagnie controlled Java, and Java controlled the seas.

On the fourth day, after the little ships had passed through Sunda Strait, a vigorous storm arose, with visibility almost nonexistent. Great winds raged for three days, and when the low clouds lifted, the *Haerlem* was alone. The captain fired cannons, listened for replies, and when none came, followed the basic rule of navigation: 'If separated, proceed to the point of rendezvous.' Without further apprehension as to the fate of the *Schiedam* and *Olifant,* he headed for St. Helena and the body of the fleet.

It would take more than two months to negotiate this distance, and as the *Haerlem* sailed westward, sunrise at her back, sunset glowing ahead, spars creaking and sails filled by reassuring winds, the brothers speculated as to what might have happened to their sister ships. 'They're good captains,' Karel said. 'I know them, and they know the oceans. They're out there somewhere, because if we survived, so did they.'

'Will we see them?' Willem asked, peering always toward the horizon, as if on this vast sea three tiny ships might accidentally converge.

'Not likely. They may have rushed ahead. They may have lagged. We'll see them at St. Helena.'

'You think they're afloat?'

'I'm sure of it.'

On the long reach, it became apparent that the Van Doorn brothers were heading for Holland with conflicting motivations. For Karel, who had been born there and who vaguely remembered both his mother's home in Haarlem and his father's in Amsterdam, it was merely a return to the seats of power where he must establish himself with the Lords XVII against the day when he would become governor-general of Java. For Willem it was quite another matter. He was afraid of Holland, not because he knew anything adverse about it but because he loved the East so much. Those days with the little brown man, wandering through the various quarters and meeting traders from all nations, had enchanted him, while the languorous trip to Formosa had awakened him to the magnitude of his birthland. He was not old enough to comprehend the limitations he suffered as a Java-born Dutchman, and he simply refused to believe that a man born in Amsterdam was inherently superior to one born in Batavia.

When he questioned Karel about this, his austere brother frowned. 'The Java Dutch are mainly scum. Would you even dream of marrying a girl from one of those families?' This perplexed young Willem, for not only had he dreamed of marrying the Van der Kamp girl; he had also dreamed quite actively of marrying the little Balinese who served as his mother's maid.

Next morning, for reasons he could not have explained, he rummaged in his gear, found Jack's ivory bracelet still attached to its silver chain, and defiantly placed it about his neck. When Karel saw this he said sharply, 'Take that silly thing off. You look like a Javanese.'

'That's how I want to look,' and from then on, the bracelet was rarely absent.

In the middle of March unfavorable winds were encountered, and although the crew remained remarkably healthy, the captain grew apprehensive about his water supply and announced that he was planning to stop at the Cape of Good Hope, where fresh water would surely be available and bartering cattle with the little brown people a possibility.

During the reddish sunset Willem remained aloft, savoring his first glimpse of the famous rock, and even after the sun had sunk beneath the cold Atlantic, the curve of earth allowed its rays to illuminate the great flat area, and he noticed that the sailors relaxed, for they considered the Cape the halfway point, not in days, for the run to Amsterdam would be long and tedious, but in spirit, for the alien quality of the spice lands was behind them. The Indian Ocean had been traversed; the homeward passage through the Atlantic lay ahead.

At dawn on March 25 Willem did not see Table Mountain, for as so often happened in these cold waters a wind has risen, bringing clouds but no rain; the flat summit was obliterated. But then the wind abated, and toward noon the lookout shouted, 'Ship ahoy!' and there, nestled at the far end of the bay, rode a little merchant vessel. The chief mate and a few oarsmen were dispatched in the skiff to ascertain who she was, but as they drew away, the weather closed in, a stout wind from the southeast forcing the *Haerlem*'s captain to make sail close-hauled. The other ship became lost to sight as the wind freshened to storm level, pushing the *Haerlem* toward shore.

At this point it was still in no real danger, but now the wind veered crazily, so that sails which had been trimmed to hold the ship offshore became instruments for driving it on. 'Cut the spritsail!' shouted the captain, but it was too late; fresh blasts caught the sails and drove the little ship hard aground. When the captain tried to swing it around, hoping that other gusts would blow it loose, rolling seas came thundering in. Timbers shivered. Masts creaked. Sails that had been cut loose whipped through the air. And when night fell, the *Haerlem* was hopelessly wrecked and would probably break apart before morning.

'Anchor chain has parted!' a watchman's alarm pierced the night, and the Van Doorn brothers expected the ship to go down. The captain ordered four cannon shots to be fired, trusting that this would alert the other ship to the peril, but the message was not understood. 'By the grace of God, our only Helper,' as the captain wrote in his log, 'the power of the waves abated. We were not ripped apart. And when dawn broke we saw that while our position was hopeless, we were close enough to shore to save those aboard.' In the misty morning the skiff returned to report that the ship in the roads was the *Olifant*, so a longboat was lowered and made for the beach, but the *Haerlem*'s men watched with dismay as the boat foundered in the pounding surf, drowning one sailor who could not swim.

'We must get ashore!' Karel shouted to the captain.

'There is no way,' the captain replied, but Karel judged that if he could lash two barrels together, they would float him ashore, and it was on this rig that Karel and Willem van Doorn landed at the Cape of Good Hope.

The following days were a nightmare. Led by the Van Doorns, the crew of the *Olifant* tried three different times to reach the sinking *Haerlem*, but always the surf pounded their longboat so that they had to retreat. Fortunately, two English merchantmen sailed into the bay, homeward bound from Java, and with daring seamanship a boat from the *Haerlem* succeeded in reaching them with a request for help. To the surprise of the Dutch, the English crew agreed to aid in transferring the smaller items of cargo to the *Olifant*, and for some days they labored at this as if they were in the pay of Amsterdam: '. . . a hundred sockels of mace, eighty-two barrels of raw camphor, eighty bales of choice cinnamon, not wet, and five large boxes of Japanese coats decorated in gold and silver.' And when this arduous work was completed the English captains offered to carry forty of the *Haerlem*'s crew to St. Helena, where they could join the main Dutch fleet on its way to Amsterdam.

But before these good Samaritans sailed, Willem was given a task which he would often recall. 'Fetch all letters from the post-office stones,' he was told, and when he started to ask what a post-office stone was, an officer shouted, 'Get on with it.'

Ashore, he asked some older hands what he must do, and they explained the system and designated two young sailors to protect him as he roamed the beach, even to the foot of Table Mountain, looking for any large stones which might have been engraved by passing crews. Some covered nothing, but most had under them small packets of letters, wrapped in various ways for protection, and when he held these frail documents in his hands he tried to visualize the cities to which the letters were directed: Delft, Lisbon, Bristol, Nagasaki. The names were like echoes of all he had heard on the voyage so far, the sacred names of sailors' memories. One letter, addressed to a woman in Madrid, had lain beneath its rock for seven years, and as he stared at it he wondered if she would still be living when it now arrived, or if she would remember the man who had posted it.

He brought nineteen letters back to the English ships, but six were addressed to Java and other islands to the east. Gravely, as part of the ritual of the sea, the English mate accepted responsibility for seeing that the thirteen European letters were forwarded, after which Willem took the others ashore for reposting under a conspicuous rock.

When the English ships departed, the Dutch had time to survey their situation, and it was forbidding. It was impossible in this remote spot to make the gear that would have been required to refloat the *Haerlem*. It had to be abandoned. But its lower holds still contained such enormous wealth that neither the *Olifant*, nor the *Schiedam* if it put into Table Bay, could possibly convey it all back to Holland. A temporary fortress of some kind must be built ashore; the remaining cargo must then be taken to it;

and a cadre of men must remain behind to protect the treasure while the bulk of the crew sailed home in the *Olifant*.

Almost immediately the work began, and the foundations for the fort had scarcely been outlined when the work party heard cannon fire, and into the roadstead came the *Schiedam*. Though marred by the disastrous grounding of the *Haerlem*, it was a joyous reunion of the three crews, and soon so many sailors were working to construct the fort that the captain had to say, 'Clear most of them out. They're getting in each other's way.'

Now came the exhausting task of rafting the bulk of the *Haerlem*'s cargo ashore, and with speed lest the battered ship break apart. The Van Doorns worked on deck, supervising the winches that hauled precious bales aloft, and when three sailors were sent to the lower hold to shovel loose peppercorns into bags, Karel directed: 'You're not to leave a single bag down there. It's precious.'

But soon the men hurried aloft, gasping, and when Karel demanded why they had left their posts, they pointed below and said, 'Impossible.'

But since rich stores lay beneath the deck, Karel leaped down into the hold; the sailors had been right. Salt water, leaking into the pepper, had begun a fermentation so powerful that a deadly gas was being released. Choking and clutching at his throat, Karel tried to get back on deck, but his feet slipped on the oily peppercorns, and he fell, knocking his head against a bulkhead.

He would have been asphyxiated had not young Willem seen him fall. Without hesitating, the boy leaped down, shouting for help as he went. Ropes were lowered and the limp body of Karel was hoisted aloft. Willem, with a handkerchief pressed over his face, climbed out, his eyes smarting and his lungs aflame.

For some time he stood by the railing, trying to vomit, but poor Karel lay stretched on the deck, quite inert. Finally the brothers recovered, and Willem would never forget how Karel reacted. It was as if he had been personally assaulted by the pepper, his honor impugned, for with a burst of vitality, his eyes still watering, he went back to the rim of the hold, still not satisfied that the exudations were too powerful to be sustained by any sailor.

'Tear off the other hatches!' he bellowed, and when this accomplished little, for the hold was large and the cargo tightly packed, he ordered holes to be chopped in the upper deck. This, too, proved useless, so in a towering rage he shouted for a ship's cannon to be moved into position so that it could shoot down into the hold and out the sides of the ship.

'Fire!' he shouted, and a cannonball ripped away five feet of the hull, allowing fresh air into the hold.

'Swing the cannon!' he cried, and from a different angle another shot blasted a tremendous hole in the other side. Three more shots were fired, enabling the gas to escape, and when the hold was cleared, Karel was first down to salvage the precious pepper.

By April 1 the situation was under control. Work was progressing on the mud-walled fort, and a well sixty feet deep dug by the enterprising men was producing fresh water. Transfer of the cargo from the wreck was proceeding so smoothly that the leaders of the three ships could gather on the *Schiedam* to formulate final plans.

The captain gave it as his opinion that the *Olifant* and *Schiedam* should sail for the fatherland, taking with them as many of the *Haerlem*'s crew as possible. He asked what this number would be, but Karel interrupted by saying that the major consideration must be the salvage of the cargo, and that before any sailors were sent home, a determination must be made as to how many would be needed to man the fort until the next homebound fleet arrived. The captain acceded to this sensible recommendation, and the council decided that sixty or seventy men, if well led by a capable officer, could protect the pepper and cinnamon during that time.

The council members looked at Karel, hoping that he would volunteer to stay behind and guard the cargo, but he realized that his opportunity waited in Holland, and he did not propose endangering it by a protracted absence at the Cape. So it was agreed that two tough marine officers would remain at the fort with a cadre of sixty while the Van Doorn brothers would hurry to St. Helena, where they would catch a fast trading vessel direct to Amsterdam. But on April 12, when the *Olifant* and *Schiedam* departed, young Willem van Doorn stayed onshore: 'I feel I'm needed at the fort.' It was the kind of self-confident statement old fighting men could respect, so they concurred. 'Hold the fort!' they called as the two little ships sailed off, leaving history's first group of Dutchmen alone at the Cape.

Only twelve days later, at the end of April when the finest days of autumn came, Willem surprised the fort commanders by announcing, 'I'd like to be the first to climb Table Mountain,' and when permission was granted he enlisted two friends. They marched briskly toward the glowing mountain, some dozen miles to the south, and when they stood at its foot Willem cried, 'We don't stop till we reach up there.'

It was a punishing climb, and often the young men came to precipices which they had to circumvent, but at last they reached that broad, gracious plateau which forms the crest of this mountain, and from it they could survey their empire.

To the south lay nothing but the icebound pole. To the west were the empty Atlantic and the New World territories owned by Spain. To the north they saw nothing but wind-swept dunes stretching beyond the power of the eye. But to the east they saw inviting meadows, and the rise of hills, and then the reach of mountains, and then more and more and more, on to a horizon they could only imagine. In silence the three sailors studied the land as it basked in the autumn sun, and often they wheeled about to see the lonely seas across which winds could howl for a thousand miles. But always their eyes returned to those tempting green valleys in the east, those beckoning mountains.

But looking eastward, they ignored the clouds which had formed almost instantaneously over the ocean to the west, and when they turned to descend the mountain, the devil threw his tablecloth and any movement became perilous.

'What can we do?' his companions asked Willem, and he replied with common sense, 'Shiver till dawn.' They knew that this would result in anxiety at the fort, but they had no alternative, and when the sun finally rose, dispelling the fog, they marveled anew at the paradise which awaited in the east.

From the first days of isolation the sailors had been aware of little brown men who occupied the Cape. They were a pitiful lot, 'barely human,' one scribe wrote, 'dirty, thieving and existing miserably on such shell fish as they could trap.' They were given the name Strandloopers (beach rangers), and to the sailors' dismay, they had nothing of value to trade but wanted everything they saw. It was a poor relationship, marked by many scuffles and some deaths.

But on June 1, when the marooned men concluded that they had seen everything worth seeing in their temporary home—rhinos feeding in the swales, hippos in the streams, lions prowling at night, and antelope untold —an incident occurred, so bizarre that everyone who later wrote his report of the wreck commented upon it:

> On this day at about two in the afternoon we were approached from the east by a group of some twenty little brown men much different from the pathetic ones we called Strandloopers. They were taller. Their loincloths were cleaner. They moved without fear, and what joyed us most, they led before them a herd of sheep with the most enormous tails we have ever seen. We called them Huttentuts from their manner of stuttering with strange click sounds and got quickly to work trying to trade with them. They were quite willing to give us their sheep for bits of brass, which they cherish.

> And then the most amazing thing happened. From their ranks stepped a man about thirty years old, quick and intelligent of manner, and God's word, he was dressed in the full uniform of an English sailor, shoes included. What was most remarkable, he spoke good English without any click sounds. Since none of us knew this language, I went running for Willem van Doorn, who had learned it at Java, and when he left the fort, knowing that a Huttentut had come who spoke English, he asked me, 'Could it be?' and when he saw the little man in the sailor's uniform he broke into a run, shout-

ing, 'Jack! Jack!' and they embraced many times and fingered the ivory bracelet that we had seen on Van Doorn's chain. Then they danced a jig of happiness and stood apart talking in a language we did not know of things we had not seen.

Actually, among the Hottentots with whom the Dutch did business during their year as castaways, there were three who had sailed in English ships: Jack, who had been to Java; a man named Herry, who had sailed to the Spice Islands; and Coree, who had actually lived in London for a while. But it was with Jack that these Dutchmen conducted their trade.

This meant that Willem was often with the Hottentots when there was bartering, and as before, he and Jack made a striking pair: Jack seemed even smaller when standing among big Dutchmen, and Willem, now full-grown at twenty-two, towered over his little friend, but they moved everywhere along the bay, hunting and fishing together. Toward mid-July, Jack proposed that Van Doorn accompany him to the village where the sheep-raising Hottentots lived. The fortress commander suspected a trick, but Willem, remembering the responsible manner in which the little fellow had conducted himself at Java, begged for permission.

'You could be killed,' the commander warned.

'I think not,' and with that simple affirmation, young Van Doorn became the first Dutchman to venture eastward toward those beckoning mountains.

It was a journey of about thirty miles through land that gave signs of promising fertility. He passed areas where villages had once stood and learned from Jack that here the land had been grazed flat by cattle. 'You have cattle?' the Dutchman asked, indicating with his hands that he meant something bigger than sheep.

'Yes.' Jack laughed, using his forefingers to form horns at his temples, then bellowing like a bull.

'You must bring them to the fort!' Willem cried in excitement.

'No, no!' Jack said firmly. 'We don't trade . . .' He explained that this was winter, when the cows were carrying their young, and that it was forbidden to trade or eat cattle before summer. But when they reached his village, and Willem saw the sleek animals, his mouth watered; he intended reporting this miracle to the fort as soon as he returned.

His stay at the village was a revelation. The Hottentots were infinitely lower in the scale of civilization than the Javanese, or the wealthy merchants of the Spice Islands, and to compare them with the organized Chinese was ridiculous. But they were equally far removed from the primitive Strandloopers who foraged at the beach, for they had orderly systems for raising sheep and cows and they lived in substantial kraals. True, they were mostly naked, but their food was of high quality.

Living among the little people for five days encouraged Willem to think that perhaps a permanent settlement might be practical, with Dutch farmers growing the vegetables required by the passing fleets of the Compagnie and subsisting on the sheep and cattle raised by the Hottentots; this possibility he discussed with Jack.

'You grow more cattle, maybe?'

'No. We have plenty.'

'But if we wanted to trade? You give us many cattle?'

'No. We have just enough.'

'But if we needed them? You saw the English ship. Poor food. No meat.'

'Then English grow sheep. English grow cattle.'

He got nowhere with the Hottentots, but when he returned to the fort and told the officers of the wealth lying inland, they grew hungry for beef and organized an expedition to capture some of the cattle. Van Doorn argued that to do this might embitter relations with the brown people, but the other sailors agreed with the officers: if cattle existed out there toward the hills, they should be eaten.

The argument was resolved in early August when Jack led some fifty Hottentots to the fort, bringing not only sheep but also three fine bullocks which they found they could spare. 'See,' Van Doorn said when the deal was completed, 'we've won our point without warfare,' but when the officers commanded Jack to deliver cattle on a regular basis, he demurred.

'Not enough.'

The officers thought he meant that the goods they had offered were not enough and tried to explain that with the wreck of the *Haerlem* they had lost their normal trade goods and had only spices and precious fabrics at the fort. Jack looked at them askance, as if he could not decipher what they were saying, so one of the officers procured a boat, and with six Hottentots and Van Doorn, went out to the disintegrating hulk to let the little men see for themselves, and to pick up any stray bits of material they might want in trade for their cattle.

It was a futile trip. All that remained aboard the creaking wreck were the heavy guns and anchors and the broken woodwork, and these had no appeal to the Hottentots, who had been taught by Coree after his return from London, 'Wood nothing, brass everything.' The brass had long since vanished.

But as the others climbed back into the boat, Willem chanced to find a hidden drawer containing an item of inestimable value. Hearing the officer coming down the gangway to hail him, he slammed the drawer shut and followed the Hottentots ashore.

That night when others were asleep he told the watch, 'I want to inspect the *Haerlem* again,' and silently he rowed out to the ship, which had now settled nine feet into the sand. Fastening his line to a stud, he climbed aboard, going quickly to the captain's quarters, where he opened the drawer. And there it was, with thick brass corner fittings and center clasps.

Carefully opening the brass locks, he turned back the cover and saw the extraordinary words: 'Biblia: The Holy Scripture translated into Dutch. Henrick Laurentsz, Bookseller, Amsterdam, 1630.' This was a printing of the very Bible his mother had cherished and he knew it would be most improper to allow a book so sacred to sink at sea, so covering it with his shirt, he carried it back to the fort, where he hid it among his few possessions. Occasionally in the days ahead, when no one was watching, he gingerly opened his Bible, reading here and there from the sacred Word. It was his book, and at the New Year he borrowed a pen and wrote on the first line of the page reserved for family records: 'Willem van Doorn, his book, 1 January, 1648.'

The Dutch sailors at Table Bay were not forgotten. During the twelve months they stayed, nearly a hundred Dutch ships engaged in the Java trade passed back and forth between Amsterdam and Batavia, standing far out to sea as they rounded the Cape. Some English ships actually sailed into the bay, offering help as needed, and in August three Compagnie ships anchored near the fort, providing mail, information and tools.

The captain of the *Tiger*, leader of the flotilla, caused Willem serious trouble, because on the evening prior to his departure for Java, he announced at the fort that any sailors who wished to return to that island for an additional tour of duty were welcome, and three volunteered. 'We sail at noon tomorrow,' the captain said, and all that night Willem wrestled with the problem. Intuitively, with a force he would always remember in later years, he shied away from going on to Holland, a land he did not know and to which he felt no attachment. But if he failed to join the *Tiger*, right now, the next fleet would be Europe bound, and he might never see Java again.

Toward midnight he woke the fort commander and said, 'Sir, my whole heart pulls me toward Java.'

'And mine,' the officer responded, and with swift phrases he explained how any man of character who had once seen the Spice Islands would never want to work elsewhere: 'It's a man's world. It's a world of blazing sunsets. Java, Formosa! My God, I'll die if I don't get back.'

'My mother argued—'

'Son, if I weren't commander of this fort, I'd ship aboard the *Tiger* like that!' And he snapped his fingers.

'My mother says that no Dutchman has a chance with Jan Compagnie if he's born in Java—unless he gets back home for education and proper church training.'

'Well, now!' the commander said in the dim candlelight. 'Well, now, Mevrouw van Doorn is the smartest woman in the islands, and if she says . . .' In some irritation he banged his fist on the table, causing the candle to flicker. 'She's right, goddamnit, she's right. Jan Compagnie has no respect but for Amsterdam trading gentlemen. I'm from Groningen and might just as well be cattle.' Mention of this word diverted him, and he gave Willem no more guidance, for in the darkness he intended to send a troop of gunners out to fetch those Hottentot cattle.

When dawn illuminated Table Mountain, young Willem van Doorn made his decision: the *Tiger* would sail without him; he would obey his mother's orders and sail on to Holland with the March fleet—but as the *Tiger* was about to hoist anchor he set up a great shouting, 'Captain! Captain!' until the commander thought he had changed his mind and now wished passage to Java.

Not at all. He was running to the post-office stone under which he had buried the six letters addressed to Java. Puffing, he ran to the *Tiger's* longboat, and the documents were on their way.

When the ship pulled away he felt little regret, for as it went he had the curious sensation that he was intended for neither Amsterdam nor Batavia: What I'd like is to stay here. To see what's behind those mountains. That night he read long in his Bible, the sweet Dutch phrases burning themselves into his memory:

> And Moses sent them to spy out the land of Canaan, and said unto them . . . go up into the mountain and see the land . . . and the people that dwelleth therein, whether they be strong or weak, few or many; and what the land is that they dwell in, whether it be good or bad . . .

And as he studied other texts dealing with the reactions of the Israelites to the new land into which they had been ordered to move, he felt himself to be of that exploring group; he had gone up into the mountain to spy out the land; he had journeyed inland to see how the people lived and whether the land was good or barren. It was ordained that he should be part of that majestic land beyond the mountains; and when three days later the swift little flute *Noordmunster* left to overtake the two slower vessels bound for Java, he saw it go with no regret. But how he might manage to stay at the Cape he did not know, for the Dutch were determined to abandon it as soon as a homeward fleet arrived.

In the empty days that followed, Van Doorn occupied himself with routine life at the fort. On a field nearby he shot a rhinoceros. In a stream inland he shot a hippo. He went aboard the English ship *Sun* to deliver mail, which the captain would forward from London, then helped two sick Dutch sailors aboard for the long trip home. Of great interest, he headed a hunting party to nearby Robben Island, where the men shot some two hundred penguins; he himself found the flesh of these birds much too fishy, but the others averred that it tasted better than the bacon of Holland. And twice he led parties that climbed Table Mountain.

Only one unusual event occurred during these quiet days. One after-noon, at about dusk, a small group of Hottentots approached the fort from the east, leading cattle, and when the sailors saw the fresh meat coming their way—animals much larger than those at home—they cheered, but the trading was not going to be easy, because Jack was in charge, and in bro-ken English, said, 'Not sell. We live in fort. With you.'

The officers could not believe that these savages were actually propos-ing that they move into the fort, and when Willem insisted that this was precisely what Jack was suggesting, they broke into laughter. 'We can't have wild men living with us. You tell them to leave the cattle and go.'

But Jack had a broader vision, which he tried to explain to the Dutch-men: 'You need us. We work. We grow cattle for you. We make vegeta-bles. You give us cloth . . . brass . . . all we need. We work together.'

It was the first proposal, seriously made, that natives and whites work together to develop this marvelous tip of the continent; Jack knew how this might be accomplished, but was brusquely repelled: 'Tell him to leave those damned cattle and begone!'

Van Doorn alone, among the white men, understood what was being suggested, and he had the courage to argue with his officers: 'He says we could work together.'

'Together?' the officers exploded, as if with one voice they spoke for all of Holland. 'What could they do to help us?' And one of them pointed grandiloquently to the Dutch guns, the ladders, the wooden boxes and other accouterments of a superior culture.

Van Doorn suggested, 'Sir, they could help us raise cattle.'

'Tell them we wish only to deal with them for the beasts.'

But when the officers proposed to start the bartering, they found that Jack and his little people refused to trade: 'We come. Live with you. Help you. We give you these cattle. Many more. But no more trade.'

This was incomprehensible, that a band of primitives should be lay-ing down terms, and the officers would tolerate no such nonsense. At Banda Island east of Java when the sultan opposed them over the matter of cloves, the entire population of fifteen thousand had been slaughtered. When the Lords XVII heard of this they demurred, but old Jan Pieters-zoon Coen had explained firmly, in letters which reached Amsterdam four years after the event: 'In Holland you suggest what we should do. In Java we do what's necessary.' When the sultan on another island refused to co-operate, he and ten thousand of his people were forcibly resettled on Am-boyna. If the Compagnie did not tolerate opposition from Spice Islanders, who, after all, were semi-civilized even if they did follow Muhammad, it was certainly not going to allow these primitives to dictate trading terms.

'Take the cattle,' the officers said, but at this, young Van Doorn had to protest: 'In the villages beyond the hills are many Hottentots. If we start trouble . . .'

'He's starting the trouble. Tell him to take his damned cattle, and if he ever comes back here, he'll be shot. Get out!'

The officers would permit no further negotiation, and the Hottentots were dismissed. Slowly, sadly, they herded their fat cattle and started back across the flats, unable to comprehend why their sensible proposal had been rejected.

Willem saw Jack again under pitiful conditions. A group of six sailors applied for permission to hunt the area well north of the fort for eight or nine days, and since barter with the Hottentots was no longer possible and meat was needed, they were encouraged to see if they could find a hippopotamus or a rhinoceros, both of which provided excellent eating. Because the land they were exploring was more arid than that to the south and east, they had to go far, so that they were absent much longer than intended, and when they returned, there were only five.

'We were attacked by Hottentots, and Van Loon was killed by a poisoned arrow.' They had the arrow, a remarkable thing made in three sections bound together by tight collars of sinew, and so made that when the poisoned tip entered the body, the rest broke away, making it impossible to pull out the projectile.

'We cut it out,' the men explained. 'And he lived for three days, always getting weaker till he died.'

The officers were outraged and swore revenge on the Hottentots, but Van Doorn recalled something Jack had told him during his stay at the village: 'We don't ever hunt north. The San . . . that's their land.' That's all he could remember; it had been a warning which he had overlooked, and now his companion was dead.

He suggested that he go east to discuss this tragedy with Jack, and although the officers ridiculed the idea at first, upon reflection they saw that it would be unwise to engage in open warfare with the little brown men if the latter enjoyed superior numbers and a weapon so frightening. So they gave consent, and with two armed companions Van Doorn set out to talk with Jack, taking the arrow with him.

As soon as the Hottentots saw it they showed their fear: 'San. The little ones who live in bush. You must never go their land.' They showed how the arrow worked and explained that they themselves were terrified of these little men who had no cattle, no sheep, no kraals: 'They are terrible enemies if we go their land. If we stay our land, they let us alone.'

It was amusing to Willem to hear the Hottentots speak of this vague enemy as 'the little ones,' but Jack convinced him that the San were truly much smaller: 'We keep our cattle toward the ocean. More difficult for little ones to creep in.'

And so open warfare between the Hottentots and the Dutch was avoided. One of the men drafted a report to Amsterdam, explaining that the Cape was uninhabitable, worth positively nothing and incapable of providing the supplies the Compagnie fleets required:

> Much better we continue to provision at St. Helena. There is no reason why any future Compagnie ship should enter this danger-ous Bay, especially since three separate enemies threaten any estab-lishment, the Strandloopers, the Hottentots and these little savages who live in the bush with their poisoned arrows.

At the moment this man was composing such a report, an officer was walk-ing through the fortress gardens and noticing that with the seeds rescued from the wreck of the *Haerlem* his special group of gardening men had been able to grow pumpkins, watermelons, cabbages, carrots, radishes, tur-nips, onions, garlic, while his butchers were passing along to the cooks good supplies of eland, steenbok, hippopotamus, penguins from Robben Island and sheep they had stolen from the Hottentot meadows.

In January the sailors at the fort observed one of the great mysteries of the sea. On 16 September 1647, two splendid Compagnie ships had set sail from Holland, intending to make the long journey to Java and back. This could require as much as two years, counting the time that might be spent on side trips to the Spice Islands or Japan. The *White Dove* was a small, swift flute, economically handled by a crew of only forty-eight and cap-tained by a man who believed that cleanliness and the avoidance of scurvy were just as important as good navigation. When he arrived at the Cape for provisioning, all his men were healthy, thanks to lemon juice and pick-led cabbage, and he was eager to continue his passage to Java.

He told the personnel at the fort that the Lords XVII had them in mind and thanked them especially for their rescue of the peppercorns, which would be of immense value when they finally reached Amsterdam.

'Thanks are appreciated,' the fortress officer growled, 'but when do we get away from here?'

'The Christmas fleet out of Batavia,' the captain said. 'It's sure to pick you up.' He asked if any sailors wished to return with him to Java; none did, but his invitation rankled in Willem's mind.

It was not like before. He did not oscillate between Holland and Java. His whole attention was directed to a more specific question: What could he do now to best ensure his return to this Cape? He was finding that it contained all the attraction of Java, all the responsibility of Holland, plus the solid reality of a new continent to be mastered. It was a challenge of such magnitude that his heart beat like a drum when he visualized what it would be like to establish a post here, to organize a working agreement with the Hottentots, to explore the world of the murderous little San, and most of all, to move eastward beyond the dark blue hills he had seen from

the top of Table Mountain. Nowhere could he serve Amsterdam and Batavia more effectively than here.

He found no solution to his problem and was in deep confusion when
the *White Dove* prepared to sail, for he could not judge whether he ought
to go with her or not. His attention was diverted when that ship's sister,
the towering East Indiaman *Princesse Royale*, limped into the bay. She
was a new ship, grand and imposing, with a poop deck like a castle, and
instead of the *White Dove*'s complement of forty-nine, she carried three
hundred and sixty-eight. Her captain was a no-nonsense veteran who
scorned lemon juice and kegs of sauerkraut: 'I captain a great ship and see
her through the storms.' As a consequence, twenty-six of his people were
already dead, another seventy were deathly ill, and the tropical half of the
voyage still loomed.

When the two captains met with the fortress officers, Willem could see
clearly how dissimilar they were: A man who runs a big, pompous ship
has to be big and pompous. A man who captains a swift little flute can
afford to be alert and eager. He was not surprised next morning when the
White Dove hauled anchor early, as if it wished to avoid further contact
with the poorly run *Princesse Royale*, nor was he surprised when he
found that the *White Dove* had taken with it a healthy portion of the
available fresh vegetables and fresh meat. After sixty-eight steaming-hot
days the flute would land in Java without having lost a man.

When Willem loaded provisions aboard the *Princesse Royale* he was
appalled to find that more than ninety passengers lay in their filthy beds,
too weak to walk ashore. Many were obviously close to death, and he saw
for himself the difference between the management of the two ships.
They had sailed from the same port, on the same day, staffed by officers of
comparable background, and they had traversed the same seas in the same
temperature. Yet one was healthful, the other a charnel house whose
major deaths lay ahead. But when he asked the men at the fort about this,
they said, 'It's God's will.'

He thought much about God in these days of perplexity, and secretly
went to the brassbound Bible, trying like his forefathers to ascertain what
God wished him to do. And one night by a flickering candle he read a
passage which electrified him, for in it God ordered his chosen people to
undertake a specific mission:

> And I will establish my covenant between me and thee . . . And I
> will give unto thee, and unto thy seed after thee, the land wherein
> thou art a stranger, all the land of Canaan, for an everlasting pos-
> session . . .

God was offering this new land in covenant to his chosen people, and the
manner in which a few ardent Dutchmen had been able to withstand for
generations the whole power of Spain proved that they were chosen.

Willem was convinced that soon the Lords XVII in Amsterdam must recognize the obligation that God was placing upon them. Then they would manfully occupy the Cape, as He intended—and where would they find the cadres to do the job? In Java, of course, where men who understood these waters worked. He would hurry back to Java on the *Princesse Royale* to be ready when the call came.

When he informed his officers of this decision, the man from Groningen applauded: 'Just what I'd do,' but he would have been incredulous had he known why Willem was doing it.

On the night before sailing, Van Doorn sat in his quarters, wondering how to safeguard his large Bible. If he took it aboard ship, it would be recognized as Compagnie property and confiscated; this he would not tolerate, for he felt in some mystical way that he had saved the Bible for some grand purpose and that it was dictating his present behavior. So toward morning, when the fort was quiet, he carried it away, and as he walked through the fading darkness he remembered the post-office stones, where messages of grave importance were deposited, but a moment's reflection warned him that whereas tightly wrapped and sealed letters might survive in such dampness, a book like this Bible would not. Then he recalled that on one of his climbs of Table Mountain he had come upon a series of caves, not deep, and although the mountain was distant, he set out briskly for it, carrying his treasure, and before midnight, with the moon as guide, he found the cave and hid the canvas-wrapped Bible well in the rear, under a cairn of stones. He was convinced that it would be his lodestone, drawing him back. At noon, when the *Princesse Royale* sailed, he was a passenger.

It was a voyage into the bowels of hell. Before the Cape was cleared, sailors were tossing dead bodies overboard, and not a day passed without the quaking death of someone suddenly attacked by fever. When Willem first saw the mouth of a woman struck down by scurvy—her gums swollen so grossly that no teeth could be seen—he was aghast; he had crossed this sea in the *Haerlem* without such affliction and he did not yet fully understand why this ship should be so stricken.

As it limped down the Straits of Malacca, two and three bodies each day were thrown overboard, and when Van Doorn wanted, in his exuberance, to explain how the Dutch had captured the Portuguese fort that had once blocked these waters, he found no one well enough to listen; the great Indiaman creaked and wallowed in the sea, with more than a hundred and thirty dead and many of the survivors so afflicted that the sweats of Java would kill them within a few months.

When the charnel ship reached the roadstead at Batavia, there waited the little *White Dove,* washed and ready for a further trip to Formosa. The two captains met briefly: 'How was it?' 'As always.' 'When do you return to Holland?' 'Whenever they say.' On the return trip the *Princesse Royale* would lose one hundred and fifteen.

* * *

Mevrouw van Doorn was not pleased to learn that her younger son had returned to Java. She suspected that some deficiency in character had driven him to scurry back to an easy land he knew rather than risk his chances in the wintry intellectual climate of Holland, and she feared that this might be the first fatal step in his ultimate degeneration.

Willem had anticipated his mother's apprehensions but feared he might sound fatuous if he spread before her his real motivations: a vision from a mountaintop; a friendship with a little savage; a dictate from a buried Bible. Keeping his counsel to himself, he plunged into the solitary job of drafting a long report to his superiors in Batavia, in hopes that they would forward it to the Lords XVII.

In it he made his sober estimation of what the Dutch might achieve if they were to establish a base at the Cape of Good Hope. *A Cautious Calculation* he titled it, and in it he reconstructed all he had witnessed during his months as a castaway, informing the merchants in charge of the Compagnie of the potential riches in this new land:

> Three separate vessels gave us seeds, two from Holland, one from England, and every seed we planted produced good vegetables, some bigger than those we see from home. Sailors who know many countries said, 'This is the sweetest food I have ever eaten.' On my trip to the native village I saw melons, grapelike climbers and other fruits.

He compiled meticulous lists of what had flourished in the Compagnie gardens, how many cattle the Hottentots had, and what kinds of birds could be shot on Robben Island. It was a catalogue of value and should have been an encouragement to anyone contemplating the establishment of a provisioning base, but suspicious readers were apt to linger most carefully over those passages in which he detailed the life of the Hottentots:

> They go quite naked with a little piece of skin about their privities. To gain protection for their bodies they smear themselves with a mixture of cow dung and sand, increasing it month after month until they can be smelled for great distances. Men dress their hair with sheep dung, allowing it to harden stiff as a board. The women commonly put the guts of wild beasts when dry around their legs and these serve as an adornment.

He provided the Compagnie with a careful distinction between the Strandloopers, a degenerate group of scavenging outcasts, the Hottentots, who were herders, and the Bushmen, who lived without cattle in the interior.

He calculated how many ships could take on fresh vegetables if the

Compagnie established a place to grow them at the Cape, and then showed that if they could stabilize relations with the Hottentots, they might also obtain almost unlimited supplies of fresh meat. He advised abandoning the stop at St. Helena, with the sensible caution that if the Dutch did not peaceably withdraw, the English would in time throw them out.

It was a masterful calculation, prudent in all important matters, and it accomplished nothing. Officials at Batavia felt that a spot so distant was no concern of theirs, while the Lords XVII deemed it impudent for a man little more than a sailor to involve himself in such matters. So far as he could see, nothing happened.

But a word once written will often accidentally find a life that no one anticipates; it lies folded in a drawer and is forgotten, except that sometimes at moments unexpected someone will ask, during a discussion, 'Isn't that what Van Doorn said some years ago?' The passage from *A Cautious Calculation* which kept reviving in two cities half a world apart concerned ships:

> How is it that two ships of comparable quality throughout, manned by men of equal health and training, can sail from Amsterdam to Batavia and one arrives with all men ready for work in Java while the other comes into port with one-third of its crew so stricken that they must die within a year from our fevers and another third already buried at sea? There are no such things as good-luck ships and bad-luck ships. There are only fresh food, rest, clean quarters and whatever it is that fights scurvy. A halt of three weeks at the Cape of Good Hope, with fresh vegetables, lemon trees, and meat from the Hottentots would save the Compagnie a thousand lives a year.

Many of the Lords XVII felt that it was not their duty to worry about the health of sailors, and one said, 'When the baker bakes a pie, some crust falls to the floor.' He was applauded by those other Lords who had rebuked a subordinate in Java for sending two ships of Compagnie food to starving field hands in Ceylon: 'It is not our responsibility to feed the weaklings of the world.'

But to other members of the ruling body, Van Doorn's comments on the Cape reverberated, and from time to time these men brought the matter of excessive death to the attention of their fellows. One estimated that it cost the Compagnie a goodly three hundred guilders to land a man at Batavia, and that if he did not work at least five years, that cost could never be recovered, and there the debate ended, with no action taken.

Mevrouw van Doorn watched with dismay as her younger son slipped into the dull routine of a lesser clerk at the disposal of less able young men who had been trained in Holland. Willem's brightness dimmed and his shoulders began to droop. He often wore a girlish chain about his neck with an ivory circle dangling from it, and what was most painful of all, he was beginning to drift into the orbit of the few Dutch widows who stayed on at Batavia, but without the family fortunes that Mevrouw had when she decided to remain. They were a fat, sorry lot, 'sea elephants ridden by any bull that wished,' and it would not be long before Willem would be coming to inform her that he proposed taking one or the other to wife. After that, nothing could be salvaged.

And then one day in 1652 as Mevrouw van Doorn, white-haired and plump, arranged for her New Year's celebration, the startling news reached Batavia that a refreshment station had been started at the Cape of Good Hope under the command of Jan van Riebeeck. It was a matter of debate as to which part of this news was more sensational, the station itself or its proposed manager, but as Hendrickje said loudly, to the delight of her audience, 'If a man isn't clever enough to steal from the Compagnie, he won't be clever enough to steal for it.'

Willem van Doorn was in the garden when his mother said this, but he caught the name Van Riebeeck and asked as he came through the doors, 'Van Riebeeck? I met him. What about him?'

'He's been chosen to head a new settlement at Good Hope.'

Willem, twenty-seven and already flaccid, just stood in the doorway, framed in spring flowers, and his hands began to tremble, for the long dry period of his life was over. After he gained control he began to ask many questions regarding how he might win an assignment to the Cape, when an aide to the governor-general called him aside: 'Van Doorn, we've been asked to send the new settlement a few of our experienced men. To help them get started.' And Willem was about to volunteer when the aide said, 'Younger men, of course, and the council wondered if you could recommend some men for the lower echelons. For the higher, we'll do the choosing.'

And so Willem van Doorn, no longer considered young enough for an adventurous post, busied himself with selecting the first contingent of Batavia men to serve at the Cape, and it was a sorry task because none of the men wanted to leave the luxury of Java for that windblown wilderness.

The fleet sailed and Willem was left behind; his essay was kept in chests, both in Amsterdam and Batavia; and the man who as much as any had spurred the establishment of this new station was barred from joining it. The months passed, and Willem ran down to each incoming fleet to inquire as to affairs at the Cape, and then one day a message reached the council that Commander van Riebeeck was wondering if he might have permission to obtain a few slaves from Java for his personal use in growing vegetables, and the same aide who had dashed Willem's hopes previously now offered a dazzling proposal: 'Van Riebeeck's buying a few slaves for the Cape. And since you drafted that report . . . I mean, since you know the land there, we thought you might be the man to handle this courtesy.'

Willem bowed, then bowed again. 'I would be honored to have such confidence placed in me.' And when the aide was gone, he dashed to see his mother, shouting, 'I'm going to the Cape.'

'When?' she asked quietly.

'With the Christmas fleet.'

'So soon!' She had longed for the day when her son would announce that he was returning to Holland, 'to save himself,' as she put it, and was distraught that he was sentencing himself to a place even more demeaning than Java. Now he would never attain a Compagnie position, and only God knew what might happen to him. But even the Cape was better than lingering here in Java and marrying some local slut. So be it.

On the eve of departure she sat with him in her spacious reception room and said, 'When you think of me, I'll be here in this house. I'll never sell it. If I went back to Holland, I'd be tormented by memories of my musicians playing in the garden.'

She seemed so completely the epitome of those Dutch stalwarts who controlled the world—Java, Brazil, Manhattan Island, Formosa—that Willem knew she needed no cosseting from him, but when she took down her Dutch Bible and said, 'I memorized passages at night when it was death at Spanish hands to own a Bible,' he was overcome with love and confided: 'When our ship was breaking apart I crept back and found this great Bible abandoned to the sea. And when I saw that it was the same as yours, I knew I had been sent to save it, and that if I showed it to anyone, it would be taken from me. So I buried it in a cave, and it calls me to return.'

'I've never heard a better reason to sail anywhere,' his mother said, and when the Christmas fleet departed, on December 20, she was at the wharf to bid him farewell. That night, back in her big house, she began her preparations for what she termed 'the feast of the dying year.' She borrowed the musicians, supervised the roasting of the pigs, and nodded approvingly when servants dragged in the liquor. As the year ebbed she and her Dutch equals roared old songs and wassailed and fell in stupors and slept them off. Java would always be Queen of the East and Batavia her golden capital.

The council had agreed that Van Riebeeck's slaves must come not from Java, whose natives were intractable, but from Malacca, where the gentler Malayans adjusted more easily to servitude, so when the fleet transited the Straits, Willem's ship put in to that fine harbor and he went ashore to inform the commandant of the fort that four slaves were to be delivered, whereupon a sergeant and three men went off to the forests back of town, returning shortly with two brown-skinned men and two women. Before nightfall Willem's ship had overtaken the fleet, and the long journey to the Cape was under way.

One of the slaves was a girl named Ateh, seventeen years old and beautiful in the tawny manner of most Malayan women. She pouted when the sailors confined her and the others in a caged-off section below-decks, and she protested when food was thrown at them. She demanded water for washing, and the sailors heard her commanding the others to behave. And at some point in each day, no matter how dismal it had been, she broke into song, whispering words she had learned as a child in her sunlit village. They were songs of little consequence, the ramblings of children and young women in love, but she made the dark hold more acceptable when she sang.

By the time the journey was half over, this girl Ateh was so well known that even the captain had to take notice of her, and it was he who gave her the name by which she would later be known: 'Ateh is pagan. If you're going to sing in a Christian church, you've got to have a Christian name.' Thumbing through his Bible, and keeping to the Old Testament, as the Dutch usually did, he came upon that lyrical passage in Judges which seemed predestined for this singing girl: 'Awake, awake, Deborah: awake, awake, utter a song . . .'

'Prophetic!' he said, closing the book reverently. 'That shall be her name—Deborah,' and henceforth she was so called.

Since it was Willem's responsibility to deliver the slaves, and since he wished to keep them alive if possible, it being usual in these waters that thirty percent died on any passage, he was often belowdecks to satisfy himself that they were properly cared for, and this threw him always into consultation with Deborah. Before he came down the ladder, she would be huddled in a corner reviling the ill fortune that had brought her there, but when she saw him coming she would move forward to the bars of the cage and begin to sing. She would feign surprise at his arrival and halt her song in mid-note, looking at him shyly, with her face hidden.

Since the fleet had now entered that part of the Indian Ocean where temperatures were highest, the penned slaves were beginning to suffer. Food, water and air were all lacking, and one midday, when the heat was greatest, Willem saw that Deborah was lying on the deck, near to prostration, and on his own recognizance he unlocked the gate that enclosed the slaves and carried the girl out to where the air was freer, kneeling over her as she slowly revived.

He was amazed at how slight her body was; and as she lay in shadows her wonderfully placid face with its high cheekbones and softly molded eyelids captivated him, and he stayed with her for a long time. When she revived he found that she could speak the native language of Java, with its curious tradition of forming plurals by speaking the singular twice. If *sate* was the word for the bamboo-skewered bits of lamb roasted and served with peanut sauce, then two of the delicacies were not *sates*, as in many languages, but *sate-sate*; to hear natives speaking rapidly gave the impression of lovely soft voices stuttering, and Willem began to cherish the sound of Deborah's voice, whether she sang or spoke.

On most days he arranged some excuse for releasing her from the cage, a partiality which angered both the Dutch seamen and the other slaves. One evening, when the time came for her freedom to end, he suggested that she not go back into the cage but remain with him, and through the long, humid night, when stars danced at the tip of the mast, they stayed together, and after that adventure everyone knew they had become lovers.

This posed no great problem, for scores of Dutchmen working in Java had mistresses; there was even a ritual for handling their bastard offspring, and no great harm was done. But the captain had been commissioned by Mevrouw van Doorn to look after her son, and when he saw the young Dutchman becoming serious about the little slave girl he felt obligated to warn him as a father might, and one morning when sailors reported: 'Mijnheer van Doorn kept the little Malaccan in his quarters again,' the older man summoned Willem to his cabin, where he sat in a large wicker chair behind a table on which rested another of those large Dutch Bibles bound in brass.

'Mister Willem, I've been informed that your head has been twisted by the little Malaccan!'

'Not twisted, sir, I hope.'

'And you've been acting toward her as if she were your wife.'

'I trust not, sir.'

'Your mother put your safekeeping in my hands, Mister Willem, and as your father, I deem it proper to ask if you've been reading the Book of Genesis?'

'I know the Book, sir.'

'But have you read it recently?' the captain asked, and with this he threw open the heavy book to a page marked with a spray of palm leaf, and from the twenty-fourth chapter he read the thundering oath which Abraham imposed when his son Isaac hungered for a wife:

'And I will make thee swear by the Lord, the God of heaven, and the God of the earth, that thou shalt not take a wife . . . of the daughters of the Canaanites . . . but thou shalt go unto my country, and to my kindred, and take a wife . . .'

Slowly the captain turned the pages till he came to the next passage marked by a frond. Placing his two hands over the pages, he said ominously, 'And when Isaac was an old man, having obeyed his father Abraham, what did he say when his son Jacob wanted a wife?' Dramatically he lifted his hands and with a stubby finger pointed to the revealing verse:

And Isaac called Jacob, and blessed him, and charged him, and said unto him, Neemt geene vrowe van de dochteren Canaans.

Willem, seeing the words spelled out so strictly, felt constrained to assure the captain that he meant nothing serious with the Malaccan girl, but the older man was not to be diverted: 'It's always been the problem in Java and it will soon become the problem at the Cape. Where can a Dutch gentleman find himself a wife?'

'Where?' Willem echoed.

'God has foreseen this problem, as He foresees everything.' With a flourish he swung the parchment pages back to the first text, indicating it with his left forefinger. 'Go back to your own country and be patient. Don't throw yourself away on local women, the way those idiots in Java do.' Pointing to the deck below, he added, 'Nor on slaves.'

'Am I to wait perpetually?'

'No, because when you debark with your slaves at the Cape, this fleet continues to Holland. And when we reach Amsterdam, I'll speak to your brother Karel and commission him to find you a wife from among the women of Holland, the way Isaac and Jacob found their wives in their native country. I'll bring her back to you.'

When Willem drew back in obvious distaste over having his life arranged by others, the captain closed the great book and rested his open hands upon it. 'It tells you what to do right here. Obey the word of the Lord.'

The visit to the captain changed nothing. Willem continued to keep his slave girl in his quarters, and it was she who obeyed the Bible, for like the original Deborah, she continued to sing, twisting herself ever more tightly about his heart.

Then abruptly everything changed. One afternoon as the east coast of Africa neared, Deborah sat on the lower deck whispering an old song to herself, but as Willem approached she stopped midway and told him, 'I shall have a baby.'

With great tenderness he drew her to her feet, embraced her, and asked in Javanese, 'Are you sure?'

'Not sure,' she said softly, 'but I think.'

She was correct. Early one morning, as she rose from Willem's bed, she felt faint and dropped to the deck, sitting there with her arms clasped about her ankles. She was about to inform Willem that she was certain of her pregnancy, when the mast-top lookout started shouting, 'Table Mountain!' and all hands turned out to see the marvelous sight.

Willem was overcome when he saw the great flat mountain standing clear in the sunlight, for it symbolized his longing. Years had elapsed since he left it, and he could imagine the vast changes that must have occurred at its base, and he was thinking of them when Deborah came to stand beside him.

Aware of the hold this mountain had on him, she said nothing, just hummed softly, whispering the words now and then, and when he took notice of her she placed her left hand, very small and brown, on his right arm and said, 'We will have a baby.' The mountain, the waiting cave and the indiscernible future blended into a kind of golden haze, and he could not even begin to guess what he must do.

When he was rowed ashore, leaving Deborah behind, for she must wait till an owner was assigned, he found a settlement much smaller than expected; only a hundred and twenty-two people inhabited the place. There was a small fort with sod walls threatening to dissolve on rainy days, and a huddle of rude buildings within. But the site! Back in 1647 when the shipwrecked sailors lived ashore, their beach headquarters had been nine miles to the north, and Willem had seen only from a distance the delectable valley at the foot of Table Mountain; now he stood at the edge of that good land, protected by mountains on three sides, and he believed that when sufficient settlers arrived this would be one of the finest towns in the world.

He was greeted by the commander, a small, energetic man in his late thirties of such swarthy complexion that blond Dutchmen suspected him of Italian parentage. He wore a rather full mustache and dressed as fastidiously as frontier conditions would allow. He spoke in a voice higher than usual in a mature man, but with such speed and force that he gained attention and respect.

He was Jan van Riebeeck, ship's chirurgeon, who had served in most of the spice ports, winding up in Japan after abandoning medicine to become a merchant-trader, a skill he mastered so thoroughly that he was making profits for both the Compagnie and himself. For each hour he spent in the former's interests, he spent an equal time on his own, until his profits grew to such dimension that the Compagnie had to take notice. Accused of private trading, he was recalled to Batavia, where he was dealt with leniently and shipped back to Holland for discipline. Forced into premature retirement, he might well have finished his life in obscurity had not a peculiar circumstance thrust him back into the mainstream and an honored place in history.

When the Lords XVII decided to establish a recuperation spot at the Cape, they selected as their manager one of the men who had guarded the trade goods following the wreck of the *Haerlem*. He had been chosen because of his familiarity with the area, but when he declined, a wise old director said, 'Wait! What we really need is a merchant of proved ability.'

'Who?'

'Van Riebeeck.'

'Can we trust him?' several of the Lords asked.

'I believe he's a case of what we might call "belated rectitude,"' the old man said, and it was Jan van Riebeeck who got the assignment.

In effect, his instructions were simple: 'Establish a refreshment station which will feed our ships, but do so at no cost to this Compagnie!' That charter, in force for the next hundred and fifty years, would determine how this land would develop: it would always be a mercantile operation, never a free colony. The charter already accounted for what Willem was seeing on his brief walk to the fort with Van Riebeeck, but he had the good sense not to share his observations: This is much finer than Batavia, but where are the people? The land beyond those hills! It could house a million settlers, and I'll wager it's not even been explored.

'I often saw your brother Karel in Amsterdam,' Van Riebeeck said.

'How is he?'

'Married to a wonderful girl. Very wealthy.'

Willem, observing that the commander evaluated even marriage in terms of commerce, changed the subject. 'Will there soon be more people?' he asked.

Van Riebeeck stopped abruptly, then turned as if to settle once and for all this matter of population, and from the sharp manner in which he spoke, Willem suspected that he had made this speech before: 'You must understand one thing, Van Doorn.' Although only six years older than Willem he spoke patronizingly: 'This is a commercial holding, not a free state. We're here to aid the Compagnie, and we'll enlarge the colony only when it tells us to. As long as we allow you to stay ashore, you work for the Compagnie. You do what the Compagnie says.'

Within the next few hours Willem learned his lesson. He was ordered where to put his bag, where to make his bed, where to eat, and where to work. He found that a farmer could till a plot of land but never own it, and that whatever he grew must produce profit for the Compagnie. Of course, as an old Java hand he was not alarmed by these rules, but he did recall that in Batavia there had been a lusty freedom, epitomized by his mother, whereas here at the Cape there was somber restriction. Worst of all, the tiny settlement suffered under two sets of masters: from Amsterdam the Lords XVII laid down the big principles, but from Java came the effective rules. The governor-general in Batavia was an emperor; the commander at the Cape, a distant functionary. In Java, grand designs effloresced; at the Cape, they worried about 'radishes, lettuce and cress.'

Three days later, when Willem stood before the commander in the fort, Van Riebeeck thought him a poor replica of his brother: Karel was tall and slim, Willem shortish and plump; Karel had a quick, ingratiating manner, Willem a stubborn suspiciousness; and Karel was obviously ambitious for promotion within the Compagnie, whereas Willem was content to work at anything, so long as he was free to explore the Cape. In no comparison was the difference more startling than in their choice of women: Willem, if the ship captain could be trusted, had formed an alliance with a Muslim slave girl, while Karel had married the daughter of one of the richest merchants in Amsterdam.

'Wonderful match,' Van Riebeeck said. 'Daughter of Claes Danckaerts.' And again he added, 'Very rich.'

'I'm happy for him,' Willem said. Actually, he could scarcely remember his brother and could not possibly have guessed how Karel had changed in the eight years since he had quit the wreck of the *Haerlem* to sail homeward. From what the commander said, he must be prospering.

'What we have in mind for you,' Van Riebeeck continued, 'is the vineyard. Have you ever grown grapes?'

'No.'

'You're like the others.' When Van Doorn looked bewildered, the energetic little commander took him by the arm, led him to a parapet from which the valleys lying at the foot of Table Mountain were visible, and said with great enthusiasm, 'This soil can grow anything. But sometimes we approach it the wrong way.' He winced, recalling one early disaster. 'From the start I wanted grapes. I brought with me the seeds, but our gardener planted them the way to plant wheat. Scattered them broadside, plowed them under, and six months later harvested weeds.'

'How do you grow them?'

'Rooted vines, each one separately. Then you make cuttings . . .'

'What are cuttings?'

Patiently Van Riebeeck explained the intricate proceedings whereby tiny plants imported from Europe turned eventually into casks of wine headed for Java. 'Why do we bother?' Willem asked, for he saw that fruit trees and vegetables would flourish.

'Java's demanding wine,' the commander said sharply. Hustling Willem back to his rude office, he pointed to a large map that showed the shipping route from Amsterdam to Batavia: 'Every vessel that plies these waters wants wine. But they can't fetch it from Holland, because that wine's so poor it sickens before the equator and reaches us as vinegar. Your task is to make wine here.'

So Willem van Doorn, now thirty years of age, was settled upon a plot of ground belonging to the Compagnie and given nine basketfuls of small rooted vines imported from the Rhineland. 'Make wine,' Van Riebeeck said peremptorily, 'because if you succeed, after twenty years you'll be free to head for Holland.'

'You also?' Willem asked.

'No, no! I'm here for only a brief time. Then I go back to Java.' His eyes brightened. 'That's where the real jobs are.'

Willem started to say that he preferred the Cape to either place, but since he had never seen Holland, he concluded that this might be presumptuous; still, the fact that Van Riebeeck thought well of Java made him more attractive.

For a man who had never done so, to make wine presented difficulties, but Van Riebeeck showed Willem how to plant the precious roots, then provide them with poles and strings to grow upon, and finally, prune them along the lines required. He learned how to use animal fertilizer and irrigation, but most of all, he learned to know the howling southeast winds that blew incessantly in some seasons, making the high ground near the mountain a grave for growing things.

'It didn't blow like this when we were here before,' he complained, but the Compagnie gardeners laughed at him, for they were weary of hearing his constant recollections.

'We were up there,' he said, pointing some nine miles to the north, where the winds had been gentler. The men ignored him, for in their opinion there could be no spot in this forlorn land where the winds did not howl. But they showed him how to plant trees to give protection, if they survived, and offered other encouragements, for they, too, needed wine.

Willem realized that he had been handed an unrewarding assignment in which failure was probable, but it gave him one advantage which he prized: everyone else at the Cape lived within the fortress walls in cramped, unpleasant quarters, while he enjoyed the freedom of living in his own hut beside his vines. True, he had to walk some distance for food and companionship, but that was a trivial price to pay for the joy he found in living relatively free.

But his freedom accentuated the slavery in which Deborah lived, and often at night, when he would have wanted to be with her, he was in his hut and she in the fort, locked in the guardhouse. The Malayan slaves had been thoughtfully placed by Van Riebeeck: 'One man and woman will work for my wife. The strongest man will work the ships. The other woman can do general work for the Compagnie.'

Deborah was the latter, and as she moved about the fort, Van Riebeeck saw that she was pregnant. This did not trouble him, for like any prudent owner, he hoped for natural increase, and since Deborah was proving the cleverest of his slaves, he assumed that she would produce valuable children. But he was distressed that the father of the unborn child was Van Doorn.

'How did this happen?' he asked Willem.

'On the ship . . . from Malacca.'

'We need women. Badly we need them. But proper Dutch women, not slaves.'

'Deborah's a fine person . . .'

'I've already seen that. But she's Malay. She's Muslim. And the Bible says—'

'I know. The captain read me the passages. "Thou shalt not take a wife from the Canaanites. Thou shalt go to thine own country and find a wife."'

'Excellent advice.' Van Riebeeck rose from his desk and paced for several moments. Then threw his hands upward and asked, 'But what shall we do here at the Cape? At last count we had one hundred and fourteen men, nine women. White men and women, that is. What's a man to do?'

He wanted to bar Van Doorn from visiting with his slave girl, but he refrained because he knew that to exact such a promise in these close quarters would not be sensible. Instead he warned: 'Keep marriage out of your mind, Van Doorn. What happens in Batavia will not be encouraged here. The child will be a bastard and a Compagnie slave.' Van Doorn, suspecting that what was law now would be altered later, bowed and said nothing.

But when he saw how far with child Deborah had come, he felt a pressing desire to stay with her and make her his wife, even though his experience in Java should have taught him that these marriages often turned out poorly. Such memories were obliterated by his recollection of those exceptional marriages in which Javanese women had created homes of quiet joy, half-Christian, half-Muslim, in which the husbands relinquished all dreams of ever returning to a colder Holland and a more severe society.

Deborah, to his surprise, seemed unconcerned about her future, as if the problems of pregnancy were enough. Her beautiful, placid face showed no anxiety, and when he raised questions about her status, she smiled: 'I'm to be a slave. I'll never see my village again.' And he supposed that this was her honest reaction, that she did not prize freedom the way he did.

'I want to care for you,' he said.

'Someone will,' she said, and when his emotion flared, tempting him to steal her from the fort, she laughed again and said that when the time came, Commander van Riebeeck would find her a man.

'Will he?'

'Of course. In Malacca the Portuguese owners always found men for their slave women. They wanted children.'

'I'll be that man.'

'Maybe you, maybe someone else.'

As the time neared for the birth of their child, Willem endeavored to visit with Deborah as much as possible, and it became known to everyone that he was the father. She walked with him sometimes to the vineyard, thinking with amusement of how a Portuguese grandee at Malacca would have scorned any fellow countryman who dipped his hands into the earth. But she was acquainted with growing things and said, 'Willem, those vines are dying.'

'Why? Why do they die?'

'The rows run the wrong way. The wind hits them too strong.' And she showed him how, if he planted his vines along the direction from which the winds blew, and not broadside to it, only the lead plants would be affected, while the sun would be free to strike all the vines evenly.

She was at the vineyard one day, singing with that extraordinary voice, when Van Riebeeck came to inspect the German vines, and he, too, saw that they were dying: 'It's the wind.' And he added grimly, 'No wine from these plants,' but he assured Willem that replacement plants were on their way from France. He was determined to produce wine for the Compagnie, even if he had to import new plants constantly.

When the women of the fort led Deborah to her confinement, Willem was overwhelmed by the realization that he was about to become a father, and this had an unexpected effect: he wanted to recover his Bible so that he could record in it the fact of birth, as if by this action he could confirm the Van Doorn presence in Africa. Since he had a hut apart from the others, it would be safe to produce the book without being required to offer explanations as to how he had acquired it. So in the evening after his son was born he slipped along the beach till he came to that ancient cave, and when he was satisfied that no one was spying, he entered it to claim his Bible.

A few days later Commander van Riebeeck appeared at the vineyard, said nothing about the birth of the boy, but did ask for Willem's assistance on a knotty problem: 'It's this Hottentot Jack. They tell me you know him.'

'Jack!' Willem cried with obvious affection. 'Where is he?'

'Where indeed?' And the commander unraveled his version of duplicity, stolen cows, promises made but never kept, and suspected connivance with the dreadful Bushmen who had edged south, enticed by Compagnie sheep and cattle.

'That doesn't sound like my Jack,' Willem protested.

'The same. Nefarious.'

'I'm sure I could talk with him . . .'

The complaints continued: 'When we arrived in the bay, there he was, uniform of an English sailor, shoes and all.'

'That's Jack,' Willem said.

The commander ignored him. 'So we made arrangements with him. He to serve as our interpreter. We to give him metal tools and objects.'

'He spoke English rather well, didn't he?'

'But he was like a ghost at twilight. Now here. Now gone. And absolutely no sense of property. Whatever he saw, he took.'

'Surely he gave you cattle in return.'

'That's what I'm here about. He owes us many cattle and we cannot find him.'

'I could find him.'

At this confident offer the commander placed the tips of his fingers together and brought them carefully to his lips. 'Caution. We've had killings, you know.'

'Our men shot the Hottentots?' Willem asked in amazement.

'There were provocations. It was this sort of thing Jack was supposed to—'

'I'll go to him,' Willem said abruptly. So Van Riebeeck arranged for three trusted gunners to accompany him in an exploration of those villages which Jack and his people had occupied when the *Haerlem* wrecked, but Willem refused the gunners: 'I said I'd go. Not with an army.'

That was the beginning of his difficulties with the Compagnie. Those in authority refused to believe that an unprotected Dutchman would dare to move inland, or survive if he did, but Willem was so confident that he could reach Jack and settle differences with him that he persisted. In the end he was ordered to accept the three gunners, and after strong protest which irritated everyone, he complied.

He had been right. When the Hottentots spied the armed men coming after them, they retreated into the farther hills, driving their sheep and cattle before them. In nine days of wandering, Van Doorn spoke with not a single Hottentot, so perforce he started homeward, but as the four men marched, one of the gunners said, 'I think we're being followed,' and after extra precautions had been taken, it was agreed that some brown man—or men—was keeping to the mounds and trees, marking their progress.

'It's got to be Jack,' Willem said, and when they came to those slight rises from which the Cape settlement could be seen—the point at which a prudent enemy would turn back—he told the three gunners, 'I know it's my friend. I'll go to meet him.'

This occasioned loud protest, but he was adamant: 'I'll go without a gun, so that he can see it's me, his friend.' And off he went, holding his hands wide from his body and walking directly toward the small mound behind which he knew the watcher waited. 'Jack!' he called in English. 'It's me. Van Doorn.'

Nothing moved. If the person or persons behind the rise were enemies, he would soon see the flight of deadly assegais, but he was certain that if anyone had the courage to track four well-armed men, it must be Jack, so he called again, loudly enough for his voice to be heard at a far distance.

From behind the hill there came the soft sound of movement. Slowly, slowly, a human form emerged, that of a Hottentot, unarmed and wearing the uniform of an English sailor. For several moments the two men faced each other, saying nothing. Then Van Doorn dropped his empty hands and moved forward, and as he did so, little Jack began to run toward him, so that the old friends met in a forceful embrace.

They sat on a rock, and Willem asked, 'How did these wrongs come to happen?'

It was too difficult to explain. On each side there had been promises unkept, threats that should never have been uttered, and petty misunderstandings that escalated into skirmishes. There had been killings; there would be more, and any possibility of reconciliation seemed lost.

'I don't believe this,' Willem said. His affection for the slave girl Deborah had intensified his attitudes, making it easier for him to look at this Hottentot as an ally.

'We talk too much,' Jack said.

'But we're going to stay here, Jack. Forever. A few now, many later. Must we live always as enemies?'

'Yes. You steal our cattle.'

'They tell me you steal our tools. Our European sheep.'

The Hottentot knew that this countercharge was true, but he did not know how to justify it. Enmity had been allowed to fester and could not be exorcised. But one charge was so grave that Willem had to explore it: 'Did you murder the white soldier?'

'Bushmen,' Jack said, and with his nimble fingers he indicated the three-part arrow.

'Won't you please come with me?' Willem begged.

'No.'

There was a painful farewell, the little brown man and the big white, and then the parting, but when the two men were well separated, with Van Doorn heading back to his gunners, one lifted his weapon and shot at Jack. He had anticipated such a probability, so as soon as he saw the gun raised, he jumped behind a mound and was not hit.

On a fine February morning in 1657 nine gunners and sailors assembled outside Van Riebeeck's office, and all in the fort stopped work and moved closer to hear an announcement that would alter the history of Africa:

> 'Their Honors in Amsterdam, the Lords XVII, wishing always to do what furthers the interests of the Compagnie, have graciously decided that you nine may take fields beyond Table Mountain and farm them under your own guidance, but you must not move farther than five miles from the fort.'

When the men cheered at this release from drudgery, Willem van Doorn heard the commotion and came in to listen with envy as Van Riebeeck spelled out the meticulous terms laid down by the Lords. The freedmen would work not individually but in two groups, one five, one four, and would receive in freehold as much land as they could plow, spade or otherwise prepare within three years. Their crops would be bought by the Compagnie at prices fixed by the Compagnie. They could fish the rivers, but only for their own tables. They were forbidden to buy cattle or sheep from the Hottentots; they must buy from the Compagnie, and one-tenth of their calves and lambs must be given back to the Compagnie. On and on the petty regulations went—and also the penalties: 'If you break one rule, everything you own will be confiscated.'

The men nodded, and Van Riebeeck concluded: 'Their Honors will allow you to sell any surplus vegetables to passing ships, but you may go aboard to do so only after said ships have been in harbor three days, because the Compagnie must have a chance to sell its produce first. You are forbidden to buy liquor from ships. And you must always remember that the Lords XVII are giving you this land not for your indulgence but in the hope that you will turn a profit for the Compagnie.' Van Doorn, listening to the restrictions, muttered to himself, 'He says they're free, but the rules say they're not free.'

Van Riebeeck, wishing to solemnize this significant moment, and totally unaware that he had imposed any unreasonable restrictions, asked the men to bow their heads: 'Under the watchful eye of God, you are now free burghers,' and to sanctify this status he read from the Bible that glowing statement of God's covenant which had excited Willem:

> 'And I will give unto thee, and unto thy seed after thee, the land wherein thou art a stranger, all the land of Canaan, for an everlasting possession . . .'

With this benediction these nine became the first free white men in South Africa, the progenitors of whatever nation might subsequently develop. Suddenly the quiet was broken with cheers for the commander, after which the two groups set forth to line out their future farms.

One of the Hottentots had listened intently to this ceremony, and late that afternoon he crept off, taking a route past the fields the free burghers were surveying. At a small stream he stopped to watch as two antelope dipped toward the sparkling water; then he moved to break the news to his people: 'They are taking our land.'

The joy with which the nine free burghers had greeted their release was short-lived, for during the first year of backbreaking effort they came to know the Compagnie's interpretation of freedom. Two of the more adventurous, alarmed by their growing indebtedness to the Compagnie stores began clandestine trading with the Hottentots for elephant tusks, rhino horns and ostrich feathers. For this they were severely disciplined, but Van Riebeeck did reluctantly agree that they might trade for cows, if they never paid more than the Compagnie did.

An argument arose over whether they might kill one of their own sheep for their personal use; the commander recognized this as a threat to the Compagnie's butchery, but he did compromise: 'You can slaughter one animal occasionally, but before you do so, you must pay a fee to the butchery.'

In the evenings, in their rude huts, the burghers grumbled, and sometimes Van Doorn would be present, for the things these men said he understood. No complaint was voiced more constantly than the one regarding labor.

'Is this what freedom means?' one farmer asked. 'We're peasants, working eight days a week.'

'The Hottentots are better off than us,' another said. 'They have their herds and all that free land out there. We're free . . . to be slaves.'

Relations with the Hottentots had deteriorated: few brought animals to be traded, almost none wanted to work for the burghers. Most kept their herds at the edge of the settlement, watching sullenly as the Dutchmen's cattle encroached.

'In Java no man would work like this,' one stout burgher complained. 'I think I'll hide in the next ship and sail back to Holland.'

And that's precisely what several of the free men did, so guards were posted about any vessel that put into Table Bay, and then one morning in 1658 the lookout atop the fort awakened everyone by hammering on a length of metal suspended from a post and shouting, 'Warship coming!'

Apprehension gripped the tiny group of settlers; as far as they knew, Holland was still at war with England, and since this intruder might be carrying a landing party, a quick muster was called, and Van Riebeeck said, 'We fight. We will never surrender Compagnie property.' But as the men prepared their muskets the lookout cried, 'Good news! It's a Dutch ship!' and all ran from the fort to greet the taut little craft.

Van Riebeeck was waiting when the ship's boat drew alongside the jetty his men were constructing, and as soon as the captain jumped smartly ashore the good news was announced: 'Off Angola we ran upon a Portuguese merchant ship headed for Brazil. Short fight. We captured her. A little gold, a little silver, but scores of fine slaves.'

Van Riebeeck could not believe the words; for years he had been imploring his superiors in Java for slaves to work at the Cape, and now the captain was saying, 'We found two hundred and fifty on the Portuguese ship, but seventy-six died in our holds.' Many of the others were seriously ill, and some were boys and girls, of whom Van Riebeeck complained, 'They'll be of little use for the next four or five years.'

'Fetch the big one,' the captain cried. 'You'll want him for yourself, Commander.' Then, lowering his voice: 'In exchange for extra beef?'

When the boat returned, there standing in the bow, shackled heavily, stood the first black from Africa that Willem and the other Dutchmen had ever seen; all previous slaves had been private acquisitions from Madagascar, India or Malaya.

This man must have come from a family of some importance in Angola, for he had what could only be called a noble bearing: tall, broad-shouldered, wide of face. He was the kind of young man a military leader promotes to lieutenant after three days in the field, and as soon as Van Riebeeck saw him he decided to give him an important assignment. He seemed destined to be the leader of the thousands of future slaves who would soon be joining the community.

'What's his name?' he asked, and a sailor replied, 'Jango.' It was an improbable name, corrupted no doubt from some Angolan word of specific meaning, and Van Riebeeck said, in the Portuguese dialect used by all who worked in the eastern oceans, 'Jango, come with me.' And as the tall black, hefting his chains, followed the commander to the fort, Willem thought: How majestic he is! More powerful than two Malays or three Indians.

For the next few days Commander van Riebeeck was occupied with assigning tasks to his new slaves, reserving eleven of the best for the personal use of his wife, and with the arrival of blacks in force he judged that he had better tidy up the status of the slaves already at the Cape. So he summoned Willem to his quarters and asked, 'Van Doorn, what are we going to do about this girl Deborah?'

'Van Valck wants to marry his Malaccan girl. I want to marry Deborah.'

'That would be most unwise.'

'Why?'

'Because you're the brother of an important official in the Compagnie.'

'She's to have another child.'

'Damn!' The preoccupied little man strode back and forth. 'Why can't you worthless men control yourselves?' He had brought his wife with him, and two nieces, so that he felt no lack of feminine companionship; he believed that men like Van Doorn and Van Valck should wait until suitable Dutch women arrived from Holland, and if this took nine or ten years, the men must be patient.

'I'm thirty-three,' Willem said. 'And I feel I must marry now.'

'And so you shall,' Van Riebeeck said, whipping around to face his vintner. Reaching out his hands, he grasped Willem's and said, 'You'll be married before the year's out.'

'Why not now?' Van Doorn asked, and he saw Van Riebeeck stiffen.

'You're most difficult. You spoil everything.' And from his desk he produced the copy of a letter he had sent some ten months before to the Lords XVII in Amsterdam, requesting them to find seven sturdy Dutch girls, no Catholics, and send them south on the next ship. Names of the intended husbands were given, and at the head of the list stood: 'Willem van Doorn, aged thirty-two, born in Java, brother of Karel van Doorn of this Compagnie, reliable, good health, vintner of the Cape.'

'So your wife is on her way,' the commander said, adding lamely, 'I would suppose.'

'I'd rather marry Deborah,' Willem said with that stolid frankness that characterized all he did. A more subtle man would have known that rejecting a woman the commander had taken pains to import, and for a slave, was bound to provoke him; it never occurred to Willem, and when Van Riebeeck pointed out that it would be highly offensive to any Dutch Christian woman to be sent so far and then discarded in favor of a Muslim slave, Willem said, 'But I'm practically married to Deborah.'

Van Riebeeck rose stiffly, went to his window, and pointed down into the fortress yard. Willem, following his finger, saw nothing. 'The horse,' Van Riebeeck said.

'I see no horse,' Willem said in a tone calculated to irritate.

'The wooden horse!' Van Riebeeck shouted.

There it was, a wooden horse of a kind that carpenters use for sawing, except that its legs were so long that it stood much too high to be useful for woodworking. Willem had often heard of this cruel instrument, but it had not seemed a reality until this moment.

Clapping his hands, the commander instructed a servant: 'Tell the captain to proceed.' And from below a prisoner who had transgressed some trivial edict of the Compagnie was led toward the horse, where a bag of lead shot was attached to each ankle. He was then hoisted into the air, poised spread-legged above the horse, and dropped upon it. The fall of the man's body, plus the weight of the lead shot dangling from his ankles, was so powerful that the body was almost broken in half, and he screamed terribly.

'Let him stay there two days,' Van Riebeeck told his orderly, and when the man was gone, he said to Willem, 'That's how we discipline workmen who disobey Compagnie orders. Willem, I'm ordering you to marry the girl I've sent for.'

Van Doorn was transfixed by the hideousness of the event, and that night when guards were asleep and he was supposed to be in his hut at the vineyard, he crept into the punishment area, gave the prisoner a drink of water, and lifted him slightly from the cruel wood, holding him in his arms through the hours. When the sun struck the man he fainted, and remained unconscious till nightfall. This night Van Doorn was kept from administering aid by a guard posted to watch the victim; as Willem stood in the shadows staring at the ugly horse, he understood why its legs were so high: they prevented the two bags of lead from resting on the ground.

Van Riebeeck spent some days pondering the problem of Willem and Deborah, and finally arrived at a solution that left Van Doorn aghast. The commander assigned Jango to the bed next to Deborah: 'Day after day they'll see each other, and I'll have no further problems with Van Doorn.'

But he did. When guards were not looking, Willem slipped into the slave quarters below the grain store to sit with Deborah and Jango, and in broken Portuguese the three discussed their situation. Jango listened briefly, then said, 'I understand. Your baby, when it comes. I care.'

Willem clasped his hand, then added, 'Jango, do nothing to enrage the officers.' He intended that such warning apply only to Jango, for he could not suppose that Deborah would in any way incur Compagnie displeasure. While Willem warned Jango of the horse and other punishments visited upon fractious men, she whispered a song, singing a lullaby as if her baby was already born.

Finally Willem said with a faith that impressed Jango, 'When the predikant arrives with the fleet, I'm sure Van Valck will be allowed to marry his Malaccan girl, and I know I'll get permission, too. Jango, protect her till I do.' The huge black man shifted his chains and nodded.

It was not only slaves that caused Van Riebeeck trouble. The Hottentots gave him no rest, this day smiling and gregarious, the next sullen and contentious, and when one enterprising brown fellow, hungry at the end of a long workday, slipped into the Compagnie kraal and stole a sheep, actual war broke out.

It was not a real war, of course, but when the white population was so small and the native so large, the loss of even one white man posed grave problems. The stolen sheep was soon forgotten, but tempers rose on both sides as cattle were taken, assegais thrown and muskets fired. And the situation was aggravated when many of the new slaves ran away, representing a huge cash loss to the Compagnie.

In the final clash, four men were slain, and then reason prevailed. To the fort came Hottentot messengers, calling, 'Van Doorn! Van Doorn!' He was finally found playing with his son and Van Riebeeck was irate when Willem, out of breath, finally reported.

'Isn't that thieving Jack's crowd?' the commander asked, pointing to where seven Hottentots stood under a large white flag.

'I don't see Jack,' Willem said.

'Let's talk,' Van Riebeeck said. 'Go bring them in.'

So Willem, unarmed, left the fort and walked slowly toward the Hottentots, and Jack was not among them. 'Where is he?'

'He stay,' replied a man who had helped at the fort.

'Tell him to come see me.'

'He want to know if it is safe?'

'Of course.'

'He want to know from him,' the man said, pointing to the fort.

So a further conflict between Van Doorn and the commander arose when Willem left the Hottentots, returned to the fort, and informed Van Riebeeck that Jack was demanding a guarantee given personally by the commander. Since this seemed an accusation of bad faith, Van Riebeeck refused. 'May I do so on your behalf?' Willem asked. There was a grudging nod.

The Hottentots were invited to approach the outer perimeter of the fort, where Van Doorn assured them that it would be safe for Jack to join them, but the little brown men still wanted recognition from the commander himself. So Willem again confronted Van Riebeeck, and after much angry discussion, he agreed to the meeting.

When Jack received the safe conduct, he remembered Java, and the way men of importance behaved. Donning his faded uniform and mounting his finest ox, he jammed his cockaded hat on his head and rode forth to meet the man whom some of his people were already calling the Exalted One.

The peace negotiations, as Van Riebeeck would grandiloquently call them in his report to the Lords XVII, were protracted.

'You've been taking too much of our land,' Jack said.

'There's room for everyone.'

'As long as we can remember, this was our place. Now you take all the best.'

'We take only what we need.'

'If I went to your house in Holland, would I be allowed to do the same?'

Van Riebeeck ignored this rhetorical question. 'Why don't you bring back our slaves when they run away?'

'We tend cattle, not people.'

'Then why do you steal our cattle?'

Jack said, 'We used to come to this valley for bitter almonds. We must have food.'

'You'll find other almonds.'

'They're far away.'

And so it went, until Van Riebeeck said wearily, 'We will draw a paper that says we shall always live in peace.' And that night, when Jack had ridden off on his ox, Van Riebeeck sat alone with his diary. As he had done every day since arriving at the Cape he penned a careful entry, which would be read with reassurance in both Amsterdam and Java:

> They had to be told that they had now lost the land, as the result of the war, and had no alternative but to admit that it was no longer theirs, the more so because they could not be induced to restore stolen cattle which they had unlawfully taken from us in our defensive war, won by the sword, as it were, and we intended to keep it.

And then the Cape forgot both slaves and Hottentots, for one clear December morning the settlement awakened to a breathtaking sight. In the night hours the ships of a great merchant fleet had moved into the bay and six medium-sized vessels rode tidily near the *Groote Hoorn,* a magnificent East Indiaman bound for Java. Tall and proud, she displayed her fine woodwork and railings of polished brass as if she were boasting of the distinguished passenger who occupied her stateroom, the Honorable Commissioner, personal emissary of the Lords XVII. He came with powers to investigate conditions at the Cape before sailing on to Java, where he would become governor-general: the merchant Karel van Doorn.

When he stepped carefully ashore, he looked disdainfully at the slaves who held his pinnace. He was dressed in black, with broad white collar, ribbed hose and brightly buffed shoes. He wore a broad-rimmed hat, carried a lace handkerchief, and guided himself gingerly with a silver-topped cane. He wore his hair in ringlets, which cascaded over his collar, and his beard in a trim point. He was tall and stiff and handsome, and when he was safely ashore, he turned to assist a lady even more carefully dressed than he. She reminded Willem of his mother, for she looked as if she had the same inborn sense of regal command, and he could visualize her occupying the big house in Batavia.

Karel, of course, did not see his brother; his attention was directed solely to Van Riebeeck as the senior Compagnie official, and even when these two had exchanged greetings, no attempt was made to summon Willem, so he stood lost in the small crowd as cheers were given while the entourage marched to the fort. Even there Karel did not ask to see his brother, for as commissioner, he deemed it necessary to impose his authority upon the settlement as promptly as possible.

'What are your major problems?' he asked Van Riebeeck as soon as the door was closed on the watching subordinates.

'Four, Mijnheer.'

Karel was forty-three years old that year, a man burdened with importance, and since Van Riebeeck was only thirty-seven, smaller and less imposing, Karel would normally have been able to lord it over the resident agent, but he had in addition full and sole jurisdiction to look into every aspect of the Cape occupancy and to draft whatever new instructions he deemed prudent.

Placing a sheet of valuable paper before Van Riebeeck, he asked, 'What are the four?'

'There has been no predikant here since the founding. We need marriages and baptisms.'

'Dr. Grotius is on his way to Batavia. He'll come ashore tomorrow.'

'The slaves run away constantly.'

'You must guard them more carefully. Remember, they're Compagnie property.'

'We guard them. We punish them if we recover them. We chain them. And still they seek their freedom.'

'This must be stopped, and harshly. The Compagnie does not purchase slaves to have them vanish.'

'But how do we stop them?'

'Every man, every woman must assume responsibility for keeping the slaves under control. Especially you. The third problem?'

'Desperately we need women. Mijnheer, the workmen cannot live here alone . . . forever.'

'They knew the terms when they signed with us. A place to sleep. Good food. And when they get back to Holland, enough money saved to take a wife.'

'I've begun to think that many of our men may never go back to Holland.'

'They must. There's no future for a Compagnie man here.'

'And this is the fourth problem. I detect an innate restlessness among the free burghers.'

'Rebellion? Against the Compagnie?' Karel rose and stomped about the room. 'That will not be tolerated. That you must knock down immediately.'

'Not rebellion!' Van Riebeeck said quickly, indicating that the commissioner should resume his seat and waiting until he had done so. 'What I speak of, Mijnheer. The men complain of the prices we pay for their corn . . . their expenses . . .' He stopped at the look Van Doorn gave him. 'They sometimes seem driven to probe eastward—on their own, not on Compagnie business at all. As if the dark heart of Africa were summoning them.'

Karel van Doorn leaned back. On three separate occasions the Lords XVII in Amsterdam had detected in Van Riebeeck's voluminous reports hints that the free burghers at the Cape were beginning to look beyond the perimeters set for them at the time of their original grants. This burgher baker had wanted an additional plot for himself. That farmer had suggested moving out to where the lands were more spacious. Even Van Riebeeck himself had petitioned for a hundred acres more so that he might extend his personal garden. On this heresy Commissioner van Doorn knew the Compagnie attitude and his own inclinations; leaning forward so that his words would have more weight, he said, 'Commander, you and your men must understand that you have been sent here not to settle a continent but to run a business establishment.'

'I understand!' Van Riebeeck assured him. 'You've seen how I protect the smallest stuiver. We waste not a guilder at this post.'

'And you make not a guilder.' Van Doorn did not relax his stern gaze. 'When the *Groote Hoorn* sails we would like to take aboard a large supply of vegetables, mutton, beef and casks of wine. And as of right now, I expect that we shall be disappointed in all four.'

'Wait till you see our cauliflower.'

'The wine?'

'The vines do poorly, Mijnheer. The winds, you know. But we've planted a protective hedge, and if the Lords could send us some stronger vines . . .'

'I bring them with me.'

Van Riebeeck, an ardent gardener, showed his joy at this unexpected bounty, but he was brought back to reality by Van Doorn's insolent questioning: 'The mutton and the beef I'm sure you won't have?'

'The Hottentots trade very few beasts with us. Indeed, I sometimes wonder at the ways of the Lord, that he should allow such unworthy people to own so many fine animals.'

Karel rocked back and forth in silence, then stabbed at the items in his dossier. 'You have cauliflower, but nothing else.'

Van Riebeeck laughed nervously. 'When I say cauliflower, I mean, of course, many other vegetables. Mijnheer will be astonished at what we've done.' Without allowing time for the commissioner to rebut this enthusiasm, the lively little man said, 'And of course, Mijnheer, there's a fifth problem, but this is personal.'

'In what way?' Karel asked.

'My letters. My three letters.'

'Concerning what?'

'My assignment to Java. When I accepted this task, and it's not been an easy one I assure you, it was with the understanding that if I did good work here for one year, I would be promoted to Java. At the end of that year I applied for transfer, but the Lords said I was needed at the Cape. So I stayed a second and petitioned again. Same answer. I stayed a third, and now it's in the seventh year.' He paused, stared directly at the commissioner, and said, 'You know, Mijnheer, this is no place to leave a man for six years.' When Van Doorn said nothing, the commander added, 'Not when a man has seen Java. Please, Mijnheer. Most desperately I long for Java.'

'On this the Lords gave me specific instructions.' From a leather box made in Italy he produced a sheaf of papers, riffled through them, and found what he wanted. Disdainfully he pushed it toward Van Riebeeck, then sat with his lips against his thumbs as the commander read it aloud: '"Your strong efforts at the Cape have been noted, as has your repeated request for transfer to Java. For the time being, your skill is needed where you are."' In a hollow voice Van Riebeeck asked, 'How many years?'

'Until you produce enough meat and wine for our ships.' Van Doorn was quite harsh: 'You must remember, Commander. You and your men are here not to build a village for your own pleasures, but to construct a farm that will feed our ships. Every sign I see about me testifies to the fact that you are wasting your energies on the former and scamping the latter.' With that he reached for a new paper and began reading off the vetoes and decisions of the Lords XVII, none of whom had ever seen South Africa, but all of whom had studied meticulously the detailed reports sent them by Van Riebeeck:

'Item: Hendrick Wouters is not allowed to keep a pig.

'Item: Leopold van Valck is not to plant his corn in the field beyond the river.

'Item: Henricus Faber is to pay nineteen florins for use of the plow.

'Item: Rice imported from Java must not be fed to any slaves acquired from Angola, but only to those who became accustomed to it while living in Malacca.'

On and on went the instructions: the blacksmith could shoe the gardener's horse only if the latter was to be used on Compagnie business; the
sick-comforter is encouraged to conduct worship on Sundays, but he must
never again preach from his own notes; he must restrict himself to reading
sermons already delivered by properly ordained predikants in Holland; the
wife, Sibilla van der Lex, must not wear sumptuary finery; there must be
no loud singing after eight in the evening and none at all on Sunday; and
the names of the four visiting sailors who were caught dancing with slaves
last New Year's, everyone naked, must be sent with Commissioner van
Doorn to the authorities in Java, where they are to be punished for immorality, if they can be found.

'You must stamp out the frivolous,' Van Doorn said, and only then did
he ask, 'Is my brother working well?'

'We have him at the vineyard.'

'You said the vines were poor.'

'They are, Mijnheer, but through no fault of his. They reached us in
poor condition. They were packed in Germany. Improperly.'

'The ones I bring are from France,' Van Doorn said sternly. 'I can assure you they've been properly packed.' Then, actually smiling at Van
Riebeeck, he said, 'I should like to see my brother. Don't say anything
about it, but I bring a surprise.'

Willem had been waiting patiently outside the door, a man of thirty-
three sitting with his hands folded like a refractory schoolboy. 'Commander wants you,' a servant said, and Willem jumped from his bench,
nodded as if the servant possessed great authority, and entered the office.
His brother looked resplendent.

'How are you, Willem?'

'I'm very glad to be here. Very glad to see you, Karel.'

'I'm commissioner now. In Java, I'm to be the assistant.'

'Mother?'

'She's fine, we understand. I want you to meet my wife,' he said, and
as he spoke a look of either compassion or amusement crept across his
countenance and he reached out to take his brother's arm.

They went to a part of the fort which had been specially cleaned and
provisioned for meetings during the visit. It was made of fine brick, recently kilned in the colony, with a floor pounded flat and polished with
liquid cow manure that had hardened to a high and pleasing gloss. It contained five pieces of handsome dark mahogany furniture carved in Mauritius by a Malayan slave: a table, three chairs and an imposing clothes cupboard that covered much of one wall. Seated on one of the chairs was the
noble lady Willem had seen coming ashore some hours before.

'This is your sister, Kornelia,' Karel said, and the woman nodded,
refraining from extending her hand.

She did, however, smile in the cryptic way that Karel had smiled only
a few moments earlier. 'And this,' Karel continued, 'is Dr. Grotius, who is

to conduct the marriages and baptisms.' He was a fearsome man, fifty years old, angular and with a heavy touch of righteousness. He wore black except for a white collar of enormous dimension and greeted everyone who approached him with a bleak nod softened by no change of expression.

'Dr. Grotius has been sent to vitalize religious observances in Batavia,' Karel explained, whereupon the predikant looked directly at Willem and bowed again, as if including him among the persons to be vitalized.

The marriage which Dr. Grotius performed occasioned no difficulty, once he was satisfied that the slave girl who was marrying Leopold van Valck understood the Christian catechism and was willing to abjure the heathenism of Islam, but when it came to baptizing the children, a real confrontation arose and Commissioner van Doorn was vouchsafed a new perspective on Van Riebeeck, who up to now had been so obsequious.

Baptism of the children who were clearly white presented no problem; their parents acknowledged Jesus Christ and the veracity of the Dutch Netherlands church, but when the slave girl Deborah, with no husband, offered her dark-skinned son Adam, Dr. Grotius sternly rebuked her, saying, 'Children born out of wedlock can in no way be baptized. It insults the holiness of the Sacrament.'

At this point Kornelia, a self-centered woman, lost interest in theological disputation and demanded to be taken back to the ship. As soon as she was gone Van Riebeeck resumed defending his position: 'Dominie, we live at the edge of a wilderness. A lonely few. After six years we have but one hundred and sixty-six. Nine women only. We need these slave children. Please, do baptize them.'

'The traditions of the Bible,' thundered Grotius, 'are not to be ignored simply because the place is a wilderness. Here more than in a civilized city must the rules be followed, lest we fall into contamination.' He refused to budge, and the ceremony broke up in confusion.

Five participants reacted in five sharply different ways. Dr. Grotius stormed back to the ship, unwilling to stay in the fort where such profanations took place. Deborah showed no concern whatever, her grave, placid face untroubled by the storm she had caused; it had not been her idea to baptize her son; Willem had insisted upon that, coming to her secretly when news of the ceremony became known. Willem was distraught and briefly considered disclosing the fact that the child was his, and that it was he who was insisting upon the baptism. Jan van Riebeeck was just as adamant as Dr. Grotius, except that he was determined that the slave children be baptized for the good of his little settlement. And Commissioner van Doorn, who sensed that sooner or later he would be called upon to break this deadlock, was morally agitated. Quite simply, he was eager to do the right thing. He wanted to be a good Christian patriarch, and when the others were gone, he prayed.

At supper that night Van Riebeeck and Willem discussed with him what ought to be done about the baptism, and Van Riebeeck made a strong plea that his request be honored: 'We are a Compagnie, Mijnheer van Doorn, not a church. You and I are to determine what happens at the Cape, not some predikant. In Java, as you know . . .' Whenever a Dutchman said this magical word he lingered over it: Yaaaa-wa, as if it possessed arcane powers. Whatever had been done in Yaaaa-wa was apt to be right. 'In Java, as you know, we baptized the children of slaves and raised them as good Christians. They helped us run the Compagnie.'

'I would not want to contradict a doctor of theology—'

'You must!' Van Riebeeck thundered. He suddenly seemed taller. 'If he wrote back to Amsterdam that we had profaned the Bible—'

Van Riebeeck pounded the table. 'The Bible says . . .'

And it was these words that sent the three men to Willem's hut to consult the Bible he had rescued from the *Haerlem*. Unclasping the brass fittings, he laid back the heavy cover and offered the book to his brother, who turned the pages reverently, probing those noble passages in which Abraham had laid down the laws for his people living in a new land, just as the Van Doorns and Van Riebeecks had to establish principles for their followers in this vast new territory. What was the right thing to do?

By candlelight they searched the passages, but found no guidance. Karel, accountable for healing this breach, was reluctant to surrender the Bible. Again and again he turned the pages, reading occasionally some passage that seemed to relate to their presence in the wilderness, then rejecting it. In the end he found nothing. They were adrift.

'Could we pray?' he asked, and the three knelt on the earthen floor, their somber faces illuminated by the candlelight as Karel pleaded for divine guidance. God had led the Israelites through such dark periods and He would lead the Dutchmen. But guidance did not come.

Then Willem, vaguely remembering passages in which Abraham faced difficult decisions, looked with real intensity through the chapters of Genesis, and after a while came upon those passages in which God Himself, not Abraham, instructed sojourners in the steps they must take to preserve their identity while in a strange land:

> This is my covenant, which ye shall keep, between me and you and thy seed after thee; Every man child among you shall be circumcised . . . He that is born in thy house, and he that is bought with thy money, must needs be circumcised . . .

> And Abraham took . . . all that were born in his house, and all that were bought with his money, every male among the men of Abraham's house; and circumcised the flesh of their foreskin in the selfsame day, as God had said unto him.

'It's what we sought!' Willem cried, and in the flickering light the two men responsible for this tiny settlement peered over his shoulder to find justification for whatever they might have to propose. Van Riebeeck was delighted: 'It's quite plain. Their covenant was circumcision, and God ordered the slaves to be circumcised. Our covenant is baptism, and He orders our slaves to be baptized.' He was so relieved that he cried, 'Commissioner, we must go to the ship at once, and have Dr. Grotius baptize the children,' and when Van Doorn protested at the lateness of the hour, Van Riebeeck jabbed his finger at the Bible and cried, 'Did not God command that it be done that selfsame day?'

Carefully Karel studied the Bible, and when he read the words *in the selfsame day* he knew he was obligated to have these children baptized before midnight. 'I think we should give thanks for God's guidance,' he said, and the three men knelt once more.

Bearing lanterns against the night, they carried their Bible to the waterfront, aroused the boatmen, and made their way to the *Groote Hoorn*, where they summoned Dr. Grotius. 'Dominie,' Karel cried when the predikant appeared in his nightgown, 'God has spoken!' And they spread the text before him.

For a long time Dr. Grotius studied the passages, reflecting upon them. Finally he turned to his visitors and said, 'Mijnheeren, I was wrong. Can we pray?' So for the third time they knelt, while Dr. Grotius, his hands firmly on the Bible, thanked God for His intervention and begged for continued guidance. But Willem noticed that the doctor was lingering over every item of his conversion, so that when Commander van Riebeeck suggested that he return to shore for the infants, so that they could be baptized within the day, Dr. Grotius said, almost triumphantly, 'That day is now passed. We shall perform the office before this day ends.'

With that he closed the Bible, but as he did so, a corner of the cloth upon which it had been resting caught in the leaves, and he fingered the pages to set the cloth loose, and this led him to reopen the book to the page on which Willem had inscribed the birth-facts of his first-born: 'Son Adam van Doorn born 1 November 1655.'

'Have you a son?' Dr. Grotius asked.

'Yes,' Willem said frankly.

'But . . .' There was a painful silence, after which the predikant asked, 'Wasn't the dark child to be baptized named Adam?'

'He is my son.'

The awfulness of this admission, that the brother of a distinguished merchant who was serving as commissioner for the Lords XVII should have been consorting with a pagan slave girl, struck Dr. Grotius and Karel dumb. Twice the former tried to form words of condemnation: 'You . . . you . . .' But he could think of no damnation proper for the crime. He had never served in the East and had little comprehension of the anxieties and hunger Dutchmen could feel. Karel, however, did know Java and the miseries that could ensue when men of promise married with native women . . .

'Oh, my God!' he cried suddenly. Looking at Dr. Grotius with shock, he indicated with his shoulder another cabin and cried, 'She's in there.'

'Oh, goodness!'

Whipping about, Karel jutted his face into his brother's and asked, 'Are you married?'

'I wanted to—'

'I wouldn't permit it,' Van Riebeeck said.

With fervor Karel clasped the commander's hands and cried, 'You were so prudent.'

'But Deborah—' Willem began. Karel brushed him aside and said petulantly, 'I wanted this to be a surprise.' With grandiloquent gestures he pointed to his right: 'Your future wife is in there, asleep . . . waiting to meet you in the morning.'

'My wife?'

'Yes. My wife's cousin. A girl of fine family, come all the way from Amsterdam.' And on the spur of that moment Karel rushed from the little cabin, ran down the hallway, and banged on a door: 'Katje! Come out!'

Katje, whoever she was, did not appear, but Kornelia did, tall and formidable in her night clothes. 'What's this noise?'

'Go back to bed!' Karel pushed her roughly away from the door. 'I want Katje.' And in a few moments came the girl—short, ill-favored when sleep was upon her, with frizzled hair and red face.

'What is it?' she asked peevishly.

'You're to meet Willem.'

'Not like this,' Kornelia said from the rear.

'Come!' Karel cried, agitated beyond control. And he jerked the protesting girl down the passageway and into the predikant's cabin, where with red eyes and sniffling nose she met her intended husband: 'Willem van Doorn, this is your bride, Katje Danckaerts.'

She was a country girl, a daughter of the poor Danckaerts, but a full cousin of Kornelia's and thus someone to be cared for. A year ago when Kornelia had asked, 'Whatever will we do with Katje?' her husband had said impulsively, 'We'll take her with us to the Cape. Willem needs a wife.'

So it had been arranged, and now the ungainly girl, twenty-five years old, stood in the cramped room where so many others were crowded and mistook Van Riebeeck as her betrothed, but when she moved toward him, Karel said sharply, 'Not him. This one!' and even the predikant had to laugh.

At this moment Kornelia appeared, wrapped in a coat and demanding to know what was happening. 'Go back to your room!' Karel thundered, hoping to prevent his wife from learning about the scandal, but she had been ordered about enough and elbowed her way to Katje's side.

'What are they doing to you, Katje?' she asked softly.

'I'm meeting Willem,' the girl whined.

Kornelia surveyed the men and realized immediately that they were making a botch of whatever it was they were trying to accomplish. Willem looked especially inept, so she said gently, 'Well, if you're meeting your husband, let's meet him properly,' and she pushed her cousin forward. Willem stepped up awkwardly to greet Katje, but she held back, and it was prophetic that the second utterance he heard her speak was also a complaint: 'I don't want to get married.'

She had barely finished this sentence when she felt Kornelia's firm hand in the middle of her back, giving her such a sharp push forward that she fairly leaped into Willem's arms. In that brief moment he looked at her and thought: How different from Deborah. But as he caught her he felt her womanliness and knew that he would be responsible for the years of her life. 'I'll be a good husband,' he said.

'I should think so,' Karel muttered, and then sensible Kornelia, who had acquired confidence from associating with the best families of Amsterdam, said forcefully, 'Now I demand to know what you men have been doing,' and Dr. Grotius, realizing that further dissembling was fruitless, directed her attention to the revealing entry in the Bible. She read it carefully, looked up at Willem, smiled, then read it again. Summoning Katje to her side, she showed her cousin the damaging news, then said quietly, 'It seems your husband has had another wife. But that hardly signifies.'

'She's pregnant again,' Willem blurted out.

'Oh, Jesus!' Karel moaned, whereupon Dr. Grotius reprimanded him.

'Neither does that signify,' Kornelia said.

'He's not really married to the slave girl,' Van Riebeeck said reassuringly, and Karel added, 'But they shall be married now.' When everyone turned to stare at him, he added lamely, 'I mean Willem and Katje.'

'They certainly shall,' Kornelia said, and it was she who proposed that the marriage ceremony take place right now, at one in the morning. But the predikant objected that it would be illegal to solemnize any marriage until banns had been read three times, at which Kornelia said, 'Read them.' So Karel rattled off the rubric, repeating it twice: 'Katje Danckaerts spinster Amsterdam and Willem van Doorn bachelor Batavia.'

'Cape,' Willem corrected.

'Marry them,' Karel snarled at the predikant, so the Bible was opened, with three witnesses to verify the sanctity of the rite about to be performed. In flickering light, while Katje and Willem kept their hands upon the open pages, the glowing phrases of the sacrament were intoned.

When the ceremony ended, Willem startled everyone by demanding a pen, and when it was provided, he turned to the page which had given such offense, and in the little spaces decorated with cupids and tulips where weddings were to be inscribed he wrote: 'Katje Danckaerts, Amsterdam. Willem van Doorn, Kaapstad, 21 December 1658.'

* * *

Through the mysterious system of communication that always existed in a frontier area like the Cape, the Hottentots learned that an Honorable Commissioner had arrived to adjudicate matters, and that he was older brother to the man who tended the vineyard. The news was of little significance to most of the brown men, but to Jack it was momentous, for it meant that he could pursue his major objective with someone capable of accepting it. Accordingly, he took his sailor's clothes from the bark-box in which he kept them, dusted off the heavy shoes he had made from cowhide, put on his wide-brimmed hat, and with a heavy stave cut from a stinkwood tree came westward to the fort.

On the parapet a lookout turned at intervals, scanning the land for signs of any trouble from the Hottentots, and the sea for the English or Portuguese ships that might some day attempt to capture the little Dutch settlement. Since the fort itself now contained only ninety-five men of fighting age, plus nine women and eleven children and the slaves, it was unlikely that any enemy from Europe could be repelled by them and the fifty-one free burghers, but a lookout was maintained nevertheless, and now he spotted Jack coming through the dust.

'Hottentot!'

Commander van Riebeeck ran to the wall and quickly saw that it was his old nemesis Jack, shuffling in with some new chicanery. 'Call the commissioner,' he instructed his orderly, and when Karel was rowed ashore and saw the newcomer, he cried, to Van Riebeeck's irritation, 'That's Jack!'

'How do you know him?'

'We were together in Java.' And he hurried out to meet the little fellow.

They did not embrace, Karel was too studious of his position for that, but they did greet each other with unmistakable warmth. 'I'm to be in charge at Java,' Karel said.

'Cinnamon, nutmeg, tin, cloves,' Jack recited, evoking the days when he had known the Van Doorn brothers at the Compagnie warehouses.

'All that and more,' Karel said proudly.

Blowing out his breath, Jack asked, 'You got any cloves?'

'No,' Karel said with a thin laugh. Together they walked to the fort, where Jack asked, 'Willem, he here too?' When the younger Van Doorn was sent for, with Van Riebeeck in attendance, Jack repeated the proposal he had made many years before.

'Time that you men, Hottentots work together.'

'Fine,' Karel said, sitting stiffly in his big chair. 'If you trade us cattle, we'll—'

'Not that,' Jack said. 'We need our cattle.' He was speaking English with a heavy Portuguese overlay and occasional Dutch words acquired lately—that grand mélange which was on its way to becoming a unique language—but everyone in the room understood him and was able to respond in the same vernacular.

'What, then?' Karel asked.

'I mean, we come here. Live with you. Have pasture here, huts, run your cattle, our cattle.'

Willem broke in: 'Nobody tends cattle better than a Hottentot.'

With considerable disdain Karel stared at his brother. 'Live here? You mean . . . Hottentots living in this fort?'

'They learn trades very rapidly, Karel. Those who become carpenters might live in the fort, or bakers, or shoemakers. Look, he made his own shoes.'

With disdain Karel looked at the shoes, big, misshapen affairs, and they epitomized his view of the Hottentot: capable of mimicking a few outward traces of civilization, but worthy of no serious consideration. He was dismayed at the way the meeting had turned, and without ever addressing himself seriously to Jack's proposal, he returned to the problem of the runaway slaves.

'What you can do for us is organize your people for tracking down our runaways. We'll give you weights of metal for every slave you bring back.'

Jack thought, but did not say: When we hunt, we hunt animals, not men. We're shepherds and cattlemen, and we could help you so much.

'As to the possibility of your moving into the vicinity of the fort,' Karel said with a deprecatory laugh, 'I fear that will never happen.'

'Commander . . .'

'He's the commander,' Karel said, indicating Van Riebeeck. 'I'm the commissioner.'

'Commissioner, sir. You white men need us. Not today maybe. Not tomorrow. But the time comes, you need us.'

'We need you now,' Karel said with a certain generosity. 'We need your help with the slaves. We need your cattle.'

'You need us, Commissioner. To live with you. To do many things.'

'Enough of this.' Van Doorn rose grandly, nodded gravely to his one-time friend, and left the room. He left the fort and returned to the ship, where he penned two recommendations for the Lords XVII that became law at the Cape:

> There must be no social contact with the Hottentots. The easy entrance that some have had to the fortress area must be stopped. In everything that is done, effort must be made to preserve the three distinctions: the Dutchman in command, the imported slave at his service, and the Hottentot in contact with neither. They are not to be used as slaves and are under no circumstances to be taken into any family. I would suggest that a fence be built around the entire Compagnie property. It might not be strong enough to repel in-

vaders, but it would serve the salutary purpose of reminding our people that they are different from the Hottentots, and it would forcefully remind the Hottentots that they can never be our equals. It would also impress upon our people that their job is the replenishing of Compagnie ships and not the exploration of unknown territories. If material for a fence is not available, a hedge of thorns might be considered, for this would keep our men in and the Hottentots out.

Already serious at this moment, and of the gravest potential danger in the future, is the fact that our Dutch are beginning to use the bastard Portuguese tongue adopted by slaves and idlers and petty traders throughout the Eastern Seas. During my stay I noticed the introduction of many words not used in Holland. Some were Madagascan, some Ceylonese, many were Malaccan but most were Portuguese, and if this were to continue, our Dutch language would be lost, submerged in an alien tide, to our detriment and the cheapening of expression. Compagnie servants at the Cape must address their slaves in Dutch. All business must be conducted in Dutch. And especially in family life, conversation must be in Dutch, with children forbidden to speak the language of their amahs.

When these new rules were explained at the fort, Commissioner van Doorn judged his responsibilities discharged, and he instructed his captain to prepare the ship for the long trip to Java.

On the evening before departure, a gala New Year's festival was prepared by Van Riebeeck and his gifted wife, Maria. It was attended by their two nieces, attired in the new dresses Kornelia had brought them, and music was provided by Malaccan slaves. Each item of food had come from the Cape: the stock fish, a leg of mutton, cauliflower, cabbage, corn, beets and pumpkin. The wine, of course, was provided by the ship, taken from casks being transported from France to Java, but as Karel said so gracefully when he proposed the toast: 'Before long, even the wine will come from here.' And he nodded toward his brother.

'Now for the dessert!' Van Riebeeck cried, flushed with the good wine. Clapping his hands, he ordered the slaves to bring in the special dish prepared for this night, and from the kitchen came Deborah, heavy with child, bearing in her two hands a large brown-gold earthen crock, straight-sided and with no handles. Looking instinctively at Willem, her grave face expressionless, she awaited a signal from him; with a slight nod of his head he indicated that she must place the pot before Kornelia, and when this was done, and a big spoon provided with nine little dishes, everyone saw with pleasure that it was a most handsome bread pudding, crusty on top and brown, with raisins and lemon peel and orange rind peeking through.

'Our Willem makes it,' Van Riebeeck said proudly as the diners applauded.

'Did you really make this?' Kornelia asked as she poised the spoon above the rounded crust.

'I had to learn,' Willem said.

'But what's in it?'

'We save bits of bread and cake and biscuit. Eggs and cream. Butter and all the kinds of fruit we can find. At the end, of course . . .' He hesitated. 'You wouldn't appreciate this, Kornelia, never having lived in Java . . .' He felt that he was not expressing himself well, and turning to his brother and Van Riebeeck, he concluded rather lamely: 'You Java men will understand. When the sugar's been added and the lemon juice, I dust in a little cinnamon and a lot of nutmeg. To remind us of Java.'

'You're a fine cook, Willem.'

'Someone had to learn,' he said. 'You can't eat fish and mutton four hundred days a year.'

At this curious statement the diners looked at one another, but no one thought to correct the speaker. At some spots in the world the year did have four hundred days, and even a small thing like bread pudding helped alleviate the tedium of those long, lonely days.

When the last wine decanter was emptied, two final conversations occurred. They were monologues, really, for the speakers lectured their listeners without interruption. Karel van Doorn told Commander van Riebeeck, 'You must strive very hard, Jan, to comply with all Compagnie rules. Waste not a single stuiver. Make your people speak Dutch. Fence in the Compagnie property. Discipline your slaves. Get more cattle and start the wine flowing. Because if you take care of our ships, I can assure you that the Lords will reward you with an assignment in Java.' Before Van Riebeeck could respond, Karel added reflectively, 'Didn't the spices in Willem's pudding . . . Well, didn't they remind you of the great days in Ternate and Amboyna? There's no place in the world like Java.'

At this moment Kornelia van Doorn was telling her red-complexioned cousin, 'Katje, help Willem grow his grapes. Because if he succeeds, he'll be in line for promotion. Then you can come to Java.' With a flood of gentleness and affection, she embraced her unlovely cousin and confessed: 'We haven't brought you to a paradise, Katje. But he is a husband and his hut is temporary. If you keep him at his work, you'll both soon be in Java, of that I'm sure.'

When Willem saw how meticulously the vines from France had been packed and learned how carefully they had been tended on the voyage, he felt that these new stocks would invigorate the Cape vineyard; the hedge of young trees was high enough to break the force of those relentless summer winds and he now knew something about setting his rows in the right direction. Before Karel sailed on to Java the vines were well planted, and one of the last entries the commissioner made in his report to the Lords XVII commended Willem for taking viticulture seriously and predicted: Soon they will be sending casks of wine to Java.

His last entry was a remarkable one, often to be quoted in both Amsterdam and Batavia but never to be comprehended there or in South Africa; it dealt with slaves and their propensity for running away. In his stay at the Cape he had listened to three days of detailed testimony on the frequency with which slaves of all kinds—Angolans, Malaccans, Madagascans—ran away. It was a madness, he concluded, which no measures open to the Dutch could eliminate, and he reported to the Lords XVII:

> Neither hunger nor thirst, neither the murderous arrow of the Bushman nor the spear of the Hottentot, neither the waterless desert nor the impassable mountain deters the slave from seeking his freedom. I have therefore directed the officers at the Cape to initiate a series of punishments which will impress the slaves with the fact that they are Compagnie property and must obey its laws. At the first attempt to run away, the loss of an ear. At the next attempt, branding on the forehead and the other ear to be cropped. At the third attempt, the nose to be cut off. And at the fourth, the gallows.

When the *Groote Hoorn* resumed its way to Java, it was decided that since the prompt production of wine loomed so important, Willem ought to have more assistance at the vineyard, so the slave Jango was excused from his duties at the fort. This was a happy decision, because he quickly displayed an aptitude for handling vines, and when the new plants took root, Van Riebeeck felt that the pressing of wine would soon be a reality.

But Jango had the weakness of every man of merit: he wanted to be free. And when Willem recommended that the chains be struck off his slave, 'so that he can move more freely about the vineyard,' Van Riebeeck reluctantly agreed.

'You may be courting trouble,' he warned Willem, but the latter said he felt sure Jango would appreciate this opportunity of working outside the fort and could be trusted.

He was partly right. Without chains, Jango worked diligently, but as soon as the new vines were pruned, he escaped into the wilderness. Two days passed before Willem reported his absence to the fort, where the news caused great agitation. Van Riebeeck was furious with Willem for having delayed the alarm, and in anger dispatched a field force to track down the escapee, but when a muster was taken he found that three other slaves had joined Jango, and their tracks indicated that they were heading directly into Bushmen country, where they would probably be slain. 'And that's the end of Compagnie property,' Van Riebeeck groaned.

But after a three-day search, Jango and the others were discovered huddled at the foot of a small cliff, cold and hungry. When they were roped together and on the march back to the fort, the soldiers began to speculate on how Commissioner van Doorn's draconian laws governing runaways would be enforced. 'You're going to lose your ears,' they told the slaves. 'You know that.' One Dutchman grabbed Jango's left ear and sliced at it with his hand: 'Off it comes!'

But when the lookout at the fort spotted the returning prisoners, and everyone gathered to see the mutilations, they were disappointed, for Van Riebeeck refused to lop off ears: 'I do not disfigure my slaves.' Two assistants argued with him, citing both the new law and the necessity for drastic punishment, but the stubborn little man rejected their counsel. The slaves were moderately whipped, thrown into a corner of the fortress that served as a jail, and kept without food for three days.

Five days after they were released, Jango ran away again, and Willem was summoned to the fort: 'We have reason to believe that the slaves have again made union with the Hottentots. Go find Jack and warn him that this must not continue.'

'And Jango?'

'We'll take care of Jango.'

So Willem went eastward to confer with Jack, while the usual troop of hunters went after Jango, who this time had taken only two others with him. Willem found Jack at a distant site, unwilling to admit that he was in league with the slaves, unwilling to cooperate in any way.

'What do you want?' Willem, exasperated, asked his old friend.

'What I said at the fort. Work together.'

'You heard my brother. That can never happen.'

'More ships will come,' Jack persisted. 'More cattle will be needed.'

Willem's frown ended the conversation. There was no hope that the kind of union Jack was proposing could ever be effected; white men and brown were destined to live their different lives, one the master, one the outcast, and any attempt to bridge the gap would forever be doomed by the characters of the persons involved. The white men would be stolid and stubborn like Willem, or vain and arrogant like Karel; the brown men would be proud and recalcitrant like Jack . . .

A visible shudder raced over Willem's face, for he had been accorded a glimpse of the future. Staring down the long corridor of Cape history—beyond the fortress and the branding of slaves—he saw with tragic clarity the total disappearance of Jack and his Hottentots. They were destined to be engulfed, overswarmed by ships and horses. Tears of compassion came to his eyes and he wanted to embrace this little man with whom he had shared so many strange adventures, but Jack had turned away, rebuffed for the last time. In his ragged English uniform and his big homemade shoes, he was walking alone toward the mountains, never again to approach the Van Doorns with his proposals.

When Willem returned to the fort he found that Jango had been retaken and that the heavy iron chains had been returned to his legs. Henceforth he would work at the vines slowly, dragging monstrous weights behind him. But in spite of this dreadful impediment, he ran away a third time, far to the north, where he survived three weeks prior to his recapture. This time, argued the junior officials, his ears really must be cropped, but once more Van Riebeeck refused to carry out the harsh measures which Commissioner van Doorn had authorized, and one of the commander's subordinates dispatched a secret message to Batavia, informing Karel of this nonfeasance.

The garden-hut in which Katje van Doorn started her married life echoed with an incessant chain of complaints; three were recurrent.

'Why do we have to live in this hut? Why can't we move to the fort?'

'Why can't I have four slaves, like the commander's wife?'

'How soon can we join Kornelia and your brother in Java?'

Patiently Willem tried to answer each complaint: 'You wouldn't like it at the fort. All those people. What would you do with so many personal slaves? And we'll have to prove that wine can be made here before they let us go to Java.' He deceived her on the last point: he had no desire whatever to return to Java; he had found his home in Africa and was determined to stay.

Katje was not convinced by his arguments, but she did appreciate it when he built a small addition to the hut so that she could have space of her own. Of course, when time came to finish the floor, and he brought in bucketfuls of cow dung mixed with water for her to smooth over the pounded earth not once but many times, she wailed in protest. So he knelt down and did the work for her, producing in time a hard, polished surface not unlike that of weathered pine. It had a cleansing odor too, the clean smell of barnyard and meadow.

He was startled upon learning that Katje had gone to Van Riebeeck, petitioning him for a servant. The commander pointed out that the only woman available was Deborah, adding delicately that it would hardly be proper for this girl to move into their hut, seeing that she was far pregnant, and with Willem's child. To his astonishment, Katje saw nothing wrong in this: 'He's my husband now, and I need help.'

'Quite impossible,' Van Riebeeck said, and Katje's complaints increased.

On the other hand, she was steadfast in tending the new vines, and so it was she who patiently watered the young plantings and wove the straw protections which shielded them from the winds. She watched their growth with more excitement than a mother follows that of a child, and when the older vines at last yielded a substantial crop of pale white grapes, she picked them with joy, placed them almost reverently in the hand press, and watched with satisfaction as the colorless must ran from the nozzle.

She and Willem had only the vaguest concept of how wine was made, but they started the fermentation, and in the end something like wine resulted. When it was carried proudly to the fort, Van Riebeeck took the first taste and wrote in his report to the Lords XVII:

> Today, God be praised, wine has been made from grapes grown at the Cape. From our virgin must, pressed from the young French muscadels you sent us, thirty quarts of rich wine have been made. The good years have begun.

But the next year, when a heavy harvest of grapes made the production of export wine a possibility, it received a harsh reception in Java: 'More vinegar than wine, more slops than vinegar, our Dutch refused it, our slaves could not drink it, and even the hogs turned away.' And because sailors aboard the big East Indiamen rejected it too, the Cape wine did not even help to diminish scurvy.

As a consequence, Willem fell into further disfavor at the fort; his deficiency was harming Van Riebeeck's chances—as well as his—of getting to Java; Katje, sensing this, constantly railed at him to master the tricks of wine-making, but there was no one from whom he could learn, and the pressings of 1661 were just as unpalatable as those at the start.

Willem had toiled faithfully at the vineyard and deemed himself eligible to become a free man, but he had to acknowledge that the Compagnie retained total control over all he did, so three times he prayerfully petitioned the commander for permission to proclaim himself a burgher, and three times Van Riebeeck refused, for his own release from this semiprison depended largely upon Willem's success.

'You're needed where you are,' Van Riebeeck said.

'Then give me another slave to help propagate the vines.'

'You have Jango.'

'Then strike off his chains . . . so he can really work.'

'Won't he run away again?'

'He has a woman now.'

Willem said these words with pain, for on those days when Katje upbraided him most sorely, he could not refrain from contemplating what his life might have been like had the Compagnie allowed him to marry Deborah. On trips to the fort he would see her with her two half-white sons, moving through her tasks with placid gentleness as she softly sang to herself, and he would return to his hut and by candlelight finger through the great Bible until he came to that passage in Judges which the ship captain had read to him during the long passage from Malacca: 'Awake,

awake, Deborah, awake, awake, utter a song.' And he would lower his head into his hands and dream of those golden days.

And then one day he learned at the fort that Deborah was pregnant again, not with his child this time but with Jango's, and as an act of compassion for her he insisted that Jango's chains be struck off, and the next day Jango, Deborah and their boys headed for freedom.

It was incomprehensible to the soldiers that these slaves would dare such a venture—pregnant woman and two children—but they were gone, headed north for the most dangerous roaming ground of the Bushmen and their poisons. Van Riebeeck, furious at having been talked into unshackling Jango, ordered a troop of soldiers to bring him back at any cost, and for seven days the fort spoke of little else.

No one was more apprehensive than Willem. He wanted Deborah to survive. He wanted his sons to live into manhood so that they could know this land. And curiously, he hoped that Jango would escape into the freedom he had so courageously sought through all the years of his captivity. Indeed, he felt a companionship with this slave who had tended the grapes so faithfully, dragging his chains behind him. Willem, too, sought freedom, escape from the bitter confines of the fort and its narrow perceptions. No longer did he merely want to be a free burgher; he now wanted absolute freedom, out beyond the flats toward those green hills he had first seen from the crest of Table Mountain fourteen long years ago. He was hungry for openness, and bigness, and at night he prayed that Jango and Deborah would not be taken.

'They caught them!' Katje exulted one morning as she returned from the fort, and against his will he allowed her to take him to the gate when the fugitives were dragged in. Jango was quietly defiant. Deborah, not yet visibly with child, held her head up, her face displaying neither anger nor defeat. It was Van Riebeeck who responded in unexpected ways; he absolutely forbade his soldiers to mutilate the slaves. In his regime there would be no cropping of ears, no branding, no nose lopped off. Back went the chains, on Deborah too, but that was all. Physically, Van Riebeeck was a smaller man than any to whom he gave these orders; morally, he was the finest servant the Compagnie would ever send to the Cape.

The more Willem had observed Van Riebeeck, the higher became his opinion of the man's ability. The Lords XVII had assigned him impossible tasks; like the ancient Israelites, he was supposed to build great edifices with faulty bricks. He was given a dozen things to do, but no funds with which to do them, and he was even begrudged his manpower. When he enticed sailors from passing ships to stay at the Cape, he built his garrison to one hundred and seventy men, but the Lords commanded him to reduce it to one hundred and twenty on the reasonable grounds that they were operating a commercial store and not a burgeoning civil community.

But one unexpected reaction startled Willem: 'I want you, and thirty slaves, and all the free burghers to plant a hedge around our entire establishment. I've been ordered to cut the colony off from that empty land out there.' With a broad gesture of his left hand he indicated all of Africa. 'We'll keep the slaves in and the Hottentots out. We'll protect our cattle and make this little land our Dutch paradise.'

He led Willem and the burghers in seeking the kind of shrub or tree that would make a proper hedge, and at last they found the ideal solution: 'This bitter almond throws a strong prickle. Nothing could penetrate these spikes when the tree grows.'

So a hedge of bitter almond was planted to separate the Cape from Africa.

In 1662 the glorious day arrived when a ship from Amsterdam brought the news that Commander van Riebeeck was at last being transferred to Java. Katje van Doorn immediately wanted to know why she and Willem could not go, too, and was distraught when she learned that Willem had never applied. Upon upbraiding him, she discovered that he had no intention of leaving the Cape: 'I like it here. There's no place for me in Java, with Karel in command.'

'But we must go, and force Karel and Kornelia to find us promotions!'

'I like it here,' Willem said stubbornly, and he refused to plead with Van Riebeeck for a transfer.

The new commander was an extraordinary man, not a Dutchman at all, but one of the many Germans who long ago had sought employment in the Compagnie. He had served in Curaçao, in Formosa, in Canton, in most of the Spice Islands and particularly in Japan, where he had been ambassador-extraordinary that year when more than one hundred thousand persons died during the vast fire that swept the capital city of Edo. When he reported to the Cape he was a weak, sickly, irritable man, much plagued with gout and a moody disposition. During the days of interregnum, when Van Riebeeck was making his farewells but before his replacement assumed command, the German behaved circumspectly. He had a German wife who had mastered the complexities of Compagnie rule, and together they studied conditions at the Cape. They were therefore well prepared to take charge as soon as their predecessor left. Especially they intended to halt—and punish—the evil and costly flight of slaves.

So on the day that Van Riebeeck sailed, his eyes aglow with visions of Java, the new commander faced the problem of a slave who had fled to join a Hottentot camp but had been recaptured by horsemen galloping across the flats. As soon as the escapee was brought within the fortress walls, the commander ordered that his left ear be chopped off and both cheeks branded.

A few days later another slave was caught eating a cabbage grown in the Compagnie gardens; he was promptly flogged and branded, after which both ears were chopped off and heavy chains attached to his legs, 'not to be removed for the duration of his life.' When similar punishments were meted out to other recalcitrant blacks, Willem slipped into the fort to talk surreptitiously with Jango and Deborah: 'I know you still seek freedom. For the love of God, don't risk it.'

Jango, sitting with Willem's two sons on his knees, laughed easily. 'When the time comes, we'll go.'

'The chains! Jango, they'll catch you before sunset.'

'Of course we'll go,' Deborah said quietly, and Willem looked at her in astonishment. He had lived with her, had sired two children with her, and had known almost nothing about her. He had assumed that because she had a quiet, placid face and spoke softly that her heart was placid too. It had never occurred to him that she hated slavery as much as Jango, and it appalled him to think that she would risk losing her ears and having her face branded, just to be free.

'Deborah! Think of what they might do to you,' he pleaded, but she merely looked at him, her eyes resolute, her face immobile. Finally she placed her hand on his and said, 'I will not remain a slave.'

On his way back to his hut he prayed: Oh, Jesus, help them come to their senses. But one night when the guards were inattentive, the four slaves set forth once more.

When they were dragged back, the new commander ordered everyone in the little settlement to assemble for the punishment: 'Jango, for the fifth time you have tried to escape your dutiful labors, depriving the Compagnie of its property.' Willem felt sick, wondering what awful thing was about to be done, but when he turned his ashen face to Katje, he saw that she was stretching forward to watch the proceedings.

'Jango, you are to have your ears lopped. You are to have your nose lopped. You are to be branded forehead and cheeks, and you are to carry chains for the rest of your life. Deborah, twice you have run away. You are to be branded forehead and cheeks, and shall wear chains for the rest of your life. Adam and Crisme, you are slaves—'

'No!' Willem shouted. The commander turned to take note of who had interrupted him. An aide whispered that this was the father of the two boys, which angered the commander even more: 'You are slaves, and you are to be branded on the forehead.'

'No!' Willem shouted again, determined that such dreadful punishment not be visited upon his children, but two soldiers pinioned him, and the sentences were executed.

A week later the slave Bastiaan stole a sheep belonging to the Compagnie and was hanged, and now the new commander had time to study the case of Willem van Doorn. He learned that he was the younger brother of the powerful Karel van Doorn, but he also learned that Karel had little regard for his brother and knew him to be troublesome. He knew that on four occasions Willem had petitioned to become a free burgher, stating that he had no desire to work endlessly for the Compagnie, and at the punishment he had, of course, behaved disgracefully. Here was a man begging for discipline, and the commander was determined that he receive it.

'Willem van Doorn,' he said at the public sentencing, 'you've been a disruptive influence. You've consorted with slaves. You were seen only last week slipping in to the slave quarters, and you require discipline. The horse, two days.'

'Oh, no!' Katje pleaded, but the words had been spoken, so Willem was grabbed and bound, while two heavy bags of lead pellets were attached to his ankles. The high wooden horse was dragged in and stationed where everyone could witness, and four men held him aloft while two others kept his legs pulled apart.

In the moment that he was held thus suspended, the mutilated slaves Jango and Deborah were brought forth to watch, and for the first time Willem saw the hideous face of the man, the deeply scarred face of the woman he had loved. 'No!' he screamed, and all who heard, except Jango and Deborah, supposed that he was protesting the cruel punishment he was about to receive.

'Now!' the commander called, and he was dropped. The pain was so terrible that he fainted.

When he recovered, it was night and he was alone, chained to the horse whose rough edges tore sullenly at his crotch, spreading it, cutting it, wounding it horribly. If he moved to alleviate the pain, new areas were affected. Against his will deep groans escaped, and when he tried to move to a new position, the awful weights on his legs pulled him back.

Twice that night he fainted, partly from the pain, partly from the vicious cold that swept in from the bay. When he awakened, he began to shiver, and by the time the dull sun rose, he was feverish.

Residents of the fort came to mock him, satisfied that he deserved what he was getting. They had envied him his home at the garden, the fact that he had a wife and they didn't, and his relationship to a powerful brother in Java. They noticed that he was shivering, and one woman said, 'He has the ague. They all do after the first day.'

That afternoon, when the wind rose, his fever intensified so that when dusk came, with rain whipping in from the bay, he was in grave danger. His wife, unwilling to visit him while others were mocking him, crept up to the horse and whispered, 'How goes it, Willem?' and he replied through chattering teeth, 'I'll live.'

The fact that he had said this made Katje suspect that he would not, so she forced her way into the commander's office and said, 'You're killing him, and Karel van Doorn will learn of this.'

'Are you threatening me?'

'I am indeed. I am the niece of Claes Danckaerts, and he's a man of some importance in Amsterdam. Take my husband down.'

The commander knew enough of Compagnie politics to appreciate the influences that might be brought against him if a determined Dutch family declared war upon a German hireling, and from the manner in which Katje spoke, he suspected that she would pursue her threat, so against his own best judgment he put on a cloak and went out into the storm.

He found Willem unconscious, his body trembling with fever, and when he twice failed to rouse him, he gave the brusque order: 'Cut him down.'

The stiff body was carried to the garden-hut and placed on the dung-polished floor, where Katje brought him slowly back to consciousness: 'You're home. It's over, Willem.' And their love, awkward and strained as it would always be, dated from that moment.

The ordeal of the wooden horse had a powerful impact on Willem van Doorn. For one thing, it crippled him; he would always walk with his body slightly twisted, his left leg not functioning like his right. And he would be susceptible to colds, a deep bronchial malaise affecting him each winter. An even more powerful result, however, was that he began to frequent the smithy in the fort, stealing pieces of equipment, which he kept sequestered behind the shed in which the vines were grafted.

One evening, when he had assembled a heavy hammer, a chisel and a bar for prying, he grasped Jango's arm as he dragged his chains homeward. Without speaking, he kicked aside a covering of grass, displaying the cache. Jango said nothing, but his eyes showed Willem his gratitude.

It was not easy to look at Jango. Instead of ears he had lumpy wounds. His face, lacking a nose, lost all definition. And the three bold scars on forehead and cheeks imprisoned the glance of anyone who saw that ugly, repulsive face. Willem looked only at the eyes, which glowed.

The two men never confided in each other. Jango refused to tell Willem what his precise plans were, or how he would carry out his final attempt. The instruments for his freedom lay there under the grape cuttings and would be called upon when time was proper, but how and where he would cut away his chains and Deborah's, neither man knew.

Then one afternoon, half an hour before sunset, Jango quietly quit his work and dragged his chains to the grafting shed, removed the covering grass and wrapped the chisel in a canvas bag. With strong blows, well muffled, he cut the chains that bound his legs, then tied them inconspicuously back together. Secreting the tools under his sweaty shirt, he walked unconcernedly past Willem, as he always did at close of day, and for a brief moment the two men looked at each other, one with face terribly scarred, the other with heart in turmoil. It was the last time they would ever be in contact, black and white, and tears came to Willem's eyes, but Jango refused to allow emotion to touch him. Clutching his tools, he moved toward the fort.

'You're very nervous,' Katje said when her husband limped in to supper, and when he stayed for a long time reading his Bible, she said, 'Willem, come to bed.' Desperately he wanted to go to the fort, to stand upon the wall, to witness how Jango and Deborah and the boys made their escape, and where her chains would be struck off, but he knew that he must betray nothing. He was not afraid of the punishment that would be meted out to him if the commander deduced his role in this escape; he was afraid only for Jango and Deborah and his sons. At nine, when Katje went to bed, she saw her husband still at his Bible, his head lowered as if in prayer.

They fled into the desert lands northeast of the fort, Jango the black from Angola, Deborah the brown from Malaya, Adam and Crisme, half-brown, half-white, and the baby girl Ateh, half-black, half-brown. When they were well away from the hedge of bitter almond, Jango struck off his wife's chains, then discarded his own, but she picked them up, thinking that they would be useful in trading with the Hottentots or Bushmen.

This time they escaped. As they entered into a wilderness unknown, uncharted, they exemplified that reverberating report of Karel van Doorn:

> Neither hunger nor thirst, neither the murderous arrow of the Bush-man nor the spear of the Hottentot, neither the waterless desert nor the impassable mountain deters the slave from seeking his freedom.

They survived, and in time the descendants of Adam and Crisme and thousands like them would not have to flee to freedom bound in chains. They would be able to live in places like Cape Town, where they would come to know a greater bondage, for they would be stigmatized as Coloured. They would be preached against by predikants, because they would be living testimony to the fact that in the beginning days whites had cohabited with brown and black and yellow: 'They are God's curse upon us for the evils we have done.' The land of their birth would be the home of their sorrow, and they would be entitled to no place in society, to no future that all agreed upon, but they would forever be a testimony.

The German commander was not really sorry about the disappearance of Jango and the Malayan girl. Had they been apprehended, he would have had to hang them, and there would be the ugly question of the three children, two with those heavy scars upon their foreheads.

Nor was he especially concerned when spies informed him that Willem van Doorn was showing signs that he might be preparing to quit the colony to head eastward for a farm of his own: 'He's building a wagon. He's putting aside any objects that fall his way. And he's collected more grape rootings than he needs for his fields.'

'When the time comes, we'll let him go. He's a troublemaker and he belongs out there with the Hottentots.'

In 1664, when one of the homeward fleets brought to the Cape an unexpected visitor, the German commander was pleased that he had not overreacted in Willem's case, because the visitor was Karel van Doorn, bringing the exciting news that he had been summoned home to become one of the Lords XVII. 'My father-in-law had something to do with it,' he said modestly. 'He's Claes Danckaerts, you know, the wealthy merchant.' He moved into the fort with considerable pomp, followed by Kornelia and her two children dressed in lace and satin. Celebrations were held for five nights, during which the commander confided that he was exhausted by this damned Cape, and that he hoped Karel would do everything possible to get him transferred to Java.

'I know how you feel,' Karel said. 'Van Riebeeck told me the same when I was last here. This is certainly no place for a man with ambitions.'

'What's Van Riebeeck doing?'

'Like everyone else, he wanted the supreme job.' Here Karel smiled weakly at the commander. 'But no one from the Cape would ever be given that.'

'What's he doing?'

'Governor of Malacca. And there he'll stay.'

'But at least he's near Java.'

'And you shall be, too. Not near it. In it.'

The commander sighed and started dreaming of that fortunate day when he would again be back in civilization. But he was interrupted when Karel asked, 'What's this I hear about my brother?'

The commander supposed that Karel was referring to the incident of the horse, and said, 'As you know, out of compassion I had him taken down—'

'I mean, his making himself a free burgher.'

'We'd never permit anyone to make such a decision on his own,' the commander said quickly.

'But might it not be a good idea to get him out of here?'

The commander, having served in foreign capitals, recognized a devious suggestion when he heard it: Good God, he's trying to get rid of his brother. Why?

He never discovered Karel's reason for proposing that Willem be allowed, even encouraged, to leave the fort. For some undisclosed family complication, it was to Karel's advantage to get rid of Willem, and sending him into the assegais of the Hottentots might be the most practical way. Maps were produced, sketchy affairs which represented almost nothing correctly, and the two men selected an area where a frontier post might profitably be established, supposing that Willem survived the bleak initial travel and the threats of Bushmen and Hottentots.

It lay to the east, where a lively river debouched from the first range of

mountains; exploring parties had commented upon it favorably, and here
Karel outlined an area of some sixty morgen: 'Let him try to raise his
grapes there. God knows we could use the wine.'

'How was the last batch he sent to Java?'

'Barely acceptable for the hospital. But each year it gets a little better.'

When arrangements were completed, the two officials summoned Willem, who limped sideways into the fort. 'Willem! We've great news!'

'How's Mother?'

'Oh, she died two years ago.'

'Her house? The garden?'

'The Compagnie took it back. It was theirs, you know.'

'Did she . . . was she in pain?'

'She died easily. Now, what we wanted to see you about . . . You tell
him, Commander.'

The German said, 'We are going to allow you to become a free
burgher. Far across the flats. Here.'

'That's about where I've decided to go,' Willem said softly.

The two officials ignored this rebuke to their authority. 'Look!' Karel
said. 'We're giving you sixty morgen.'

'You don't need sixty morgen to grow grapes. I could do it on twenty.'

'Willem!' Karel said with some harshness. 'Anytime the Compagnie
offers you something free, take it.'

'But I can't farm it.'

'Take it!' Karel shouted. A Lord XVII was offering a laborer sixty morgen of the choicest land, and the laborer was raising objections. This
Willem was beyond salvation; the only good thing about this visit was
learning that his brother's two bastard children had vanished somewhere
in the desert. It reminded him of Hagar—but did her bastards die?

The meeting between Katje and her cousin Kornelia was equally cold,
and shrewd Katje warned her husband, 'There's something wrong about
them, Willem. They've done something wrong and are ashamed to see us.'
She brooded about this for some time, then one evening at supper snapped
her fingers: 'Willem, they've sold your mother's house and are keeping the
money to themselves.'

'Let them have it,' Willem said, but Katje was the niece of a merchant,
and it galled her to think that she might have been defrauded of property
that was duly hers, or at least her husband's, so she went to the ship and
confronted the older Van Doorns: 'Did you sell your mother's property?'

'No,' Karel said carefully.

'What happened to it?'

'It was Compagnie property. You know that. Like the house you're living in—'

'It's a hut.'

'But it's Compagnie property.'

'I think you sold—'

'Katje!' Kornelia said sharply. 'You forget yourself. You forget that you were a poor farm girl—'

'Kornelia, you're a thief. You're stealing Willem's share.'

'We will hear no more!' The commissioner did not intend to sit by and listen to a member of his own family, an impoverished member at that, charging him with defalcations. 'Take her back to shore,' he directed the sailors, and during the remainder of the visit he refused to meet with his brother.

His farewell was a gala. There were fulsome speeches from the German commander and his staff, gracious responses from Karel and his wife. The new Lord XVII, the first to have had extended experience in the East, assured his listeners that the Compagnie would always have close to its heart the welfare of the Cape:

> 'We're going to find you additional settlers, not too many, never more than two hundred living here. It was I who proposed the hedge, and it seems a salient idea. Makes this a comfortable little establishment with enough room for your cattle and vegetables. I'm told that my brother Willem, whom you know favorably, is heading eastward to see if he can make some real wine instead of vinegar. [Laughter] But his going must not suggest a precedent. Your task is here, at this fort, which the Lords XVII have decided to rebuild in stone. As Abraham brought his people to their new home and made it prosper, so you have established your home here at the Cape. Make it prosper. Make it yield a profit for the Compagnie. So that when you return to Holland you will be able to say, "Job well done." '

Three days after Karel departed for Amsterdam and his duties as a Lord XVII, Willem started loading his wagon. After providing space for Katje and their son, Marthinus, he tucked in grape cuttings, the tools he had taken from the smithy, all household goods required by Katje, and two items which were of supreme importance to him: the brassbound Bible and the brown-gold crock in which he baked his bread puddings. Without them a home in the wilderness would be impossible.

As he did his packing, he heard from Katje a constant whine of complaints: 'You're taking too many grape vines. You'll never use that chisel.' And he would have shown his irritation at this cascade of words except for one thing: he had grown to love this petulant, difficult woman, for he had seen that when family interests were involved, she could be a lioness, and he sensed that on the frontier she would prove invaluable. Like a chunk of hard oak that grows to appreciate the rasp that grinds it down and makes it usable and polished, so he appreciated his wife.

Before the loaded wagon could reach the trail, it had to penetrate the hedge of bitter almond, and normally it would have gone down the farm road past the fort to the exit, but Willem had no intention of subjecting Katje and Marthinus to the crowd's derision. Instead, he chopped down four bushes, breaking his own path, and when spies reported this vandalism to the commander, they expected him to order Willem's arrest, but the commander knew something the spies did not: that the Honorable Commissioner, Karel van Doorn, wanted his abrasive brother lost in the wilderness.

'Let them go,' he said with disgust as they headed for more spacious lands.

IV. The Huguenots

IN the year 1560 in the little village of Caix in the northern wine region, when Mary, the future Queen of Scots, was Queen of France, society was well and traditionally organized. There was the Marquis de Caix, who owned the vineyards, as petty a nobleman as France provided, but petty only in land and money; in spirit he was a most gallant man, survivor of three wars and always prepared for a fourth or a seventh. He was tall, slim, handsomely mustached, and with a goatee of the kind that would in later days represent the France of this period. He could not afford dashing clothes, nor caparisons for his two horses, but he did take pride in his swords and pistols, the true accouterments of a gentleman. His great weakness, for a man in his position, was that he read books and pondered affairs that occurred in places like Paris, Madrid and Rome, for this distracted him from his local responsibilities, and his vineyards did not flourish.

Abbé Desmoulins, the priest of Caix, had infirmities almost as disabling. An older man who had seen the sweep of battle, he had been deeply affected by religious events in Germany and Geneva; the preachings of those two difficult Catholics Martin Luther and John Calvin disturbed him, for he saw in the fulminations of the former a justified challenge to the sloppiness of the church as he knew it, and in the transcendent logic of the latter, an answer to the confusions he was finding in religion as it operated in France. Had he stumbled into a curacy controlled by some unlettered nobleman secure in his faith, the Abbé Desmoulins would probably have remained in line, preached a standard religion, and died without ever having come to grips with either Luther or Calvin. He had the bad luck to find himself in a village dominated by a marquis whose faith was as mercurial as his military exploits, and in a subtle way these two leaders agitated each other, so that the village of Caix was in a rather tenuous position.

Head of the vineyards was a stalwart, conservative, taciturn semi-peasant named Giles de Pré, thirty years old and the father of three children who already worked with him in the fields, even though the youngest was only five. De Pré was a wonderfully solid man with an uncanny comprehension of agriculture. 'You're an oak tree yourself,' his wife often said. 'If the pigs rooted at your feet, they'd find truffles.' Like many farmers around Caix, the De Prés could read, and it was their pleasure to work their way through the French Bible the marquis had given them, noting with satisfaction that many of the noblest figures in that history had been associated with vineyards. But as they read, especially in the Old Testament, they acquired a suspicion that human lives had once been arranged somewhat better than they were now. In the days of Abraham or David or Jeremiah, society had known a sanctity which was now vanished; in those days men lived intimately with God, and rulers were acquainted with their subjects. Priests were devoted to great principles, and there was reverence in the air. Today things were much different, and even if the marquis did rule the area, it was with a most unsteady hand.

That was the village of Caix, in the year 1560: a marquis who could not be depended upon except in battle; a priest who had lost the assurances of his youth; and a farmer whose reading of the Bible confused him. It was to such men throughout France that John Calvin dispatched his emissaries from Geneva.

'Dr. Calvin is a Frenchman, you understand,' one of these austere visitors explained to the Marquis de Caix. 'He's a loyal Frenchman, and would be living here except that he made an unfortunate speech.'

'Why has he fled to Geneva?'

'Because that city has placed itself in his hands. It thirsts to be ruled by the institutes of God.' At this mention the emissary said, 'Of course, you've read Dr. Calvin's remarkable summary of his beliefs?' The marquis hadn't, and it was in this way that one of the greatest books in the history of man's search for religious truth, John Calvin's *Institutes of the Christian Religion*, reached Caix.

It was a profound book, written with strokes of lightning when Calvin was only twenty-six and published widely the next year. It was beautifully French, so clear in its logic that even the tamest mind could find excitement in its handsomely constructed thought. Martin Luther in Germany had made wild, explosive charges which repelled thoughtful men, while John Knox in Scotland had raged and roared in a way that often seemed ridiculous, but Calvin in Geneva, patiently and with sweet reason, spread out the principles of his thought and with irrefutable clarity invited his readers to follow him to new light springing from old revelation.

But it was also revolutionary, 'like nine claps of thunder on a clear night,' the Geneva man said when handing over the book, and he enumerated Calvin's shocking rejections: 'First, he rejects the Mass as an accretion in no way connected with our Lord. Second, he rejects compulsory confession as an ungodly intrusion. Third, he dismisses all saints. Fourth, their relics. Fifth, their images. Sixth, he denies out of hand that the Virgin Mary enjoys any special relationship to either God or man. Seventh, he has abolished all monasteries and nunneries as abominations. Eighth, he rejects priests as power-grasping functionaries. And ninth, it must be obvious by now that he rejects the Pope in Rome as unnecessary to the operation of God's church in France.'

The marquis was hesitant about accepting so radical a doctrine, but when he passed the *Institutes* along to the abbé, he confided, 'What I like about Calvin's system is the way it works with civil government to create a stable, just social order. I've become really irritated by the confusions in our land.' He was correct in assuming that Calvin sponsored civil order, for in Geneva he taught that the governance of his church must rest with four groups of serious men: first, a body of brilliant doctors to explicate theology and prescribe how men and women ought to behave; second, clergymen to interpret this theology to the general public; third, a body of all-powerful elders to assume responsibility for the church's survival and act as watchdogs of the community's behavior, and when they uncover a miscreant, turn him or her over to the city magistrates for civil punishment; fourth, a collection of deacons to perform God's great work of collecting alms, running orphanages, teaching children and consoling the sick.

'I like his sense of order,' the marquis said.

'Where would you fit in?' his priest asked.

'Certainly not a doctor. I'm a stupid man, really. I could never learn Greek, let alone Hebrew. And I'd not be pastor, that's certain.' When he shrugged his shoulders, the priest laughed, recalling the scrapes this handsome man had engineered.

'I don't think I'd like to be an elder,' the marquis continued. 'The women, you know. I'm not intended to be a watchdog of other people's morals. But I could be a deacon. I could work for the welfare of a system like Calvin's.' He paused to reflect upon the fact that for most of his life he had been just this, a man trying to help where needed. 'Yes,' he said loudly, 'I could be a deacon.' Then he burst into laughter. 'But I'd want to be very careful who the elders were. I don't want to enforce the rules of some damned snoop-snoot.'

When the Abbé Desmoulins returned the *Institutes* to the marquis he was deeply worried: 'The four orders we spoke about I understand. They're needed to ensure civil tranquillity and order in the church. But the doctrine that even prior to birth all men are divided between the few who are saved and the many who are perpetually damned . . . That's very unCatholic.'

'I knew you'd have trouble with that,' the marquis said eagerly. 'I did myself.'

He led the priest to a corner of the garden, where under branching trees beside a low stone wall erected some three hundred years earlier the two men analyzed this fundamental doctrine of the burgeoning religion, and the marquis offered the bald, simplified interpretation of Calvin's thought that was gaining currency among non-theological groups: 'It conforms to human experience, Abbé. In this village you and I can name men who were saved from birth and others who were doomed from the moment the womb opened. Such men are damned. God has put His thumb upon them and they are damned, and you know it and so do I.'

'Yes,' the priest said slowly, 'they are damned, and proof of their damnation is visible. But by faith they can be saved.'

'No!' the marquis said sharply. 'There is to be no more of this salvation by faith.'

'You speak as if you'd accepted the teachings of Calvin.'

'I think I have. It's a man's religion. It's a religion for all of us who want to move forward. There are the saved who do the work of the world. There are the damned who stumble through life headed only for a waiting grave.'

'And you're one of the saved?'

'I am.'

'How do you know?'

'Because God has given signs. This vineyard. My castle. My high position in this village. Would He have given me these if He did not intend to assign me to some great task?'

But when the abbé studied the *Institutes* with his background of religious speculation, he found that Calvin had preached no such fatalistic doctrine. Only God in the secrecy of His wisdom and compassion knew who was saved and who not, and high estate on earth was unrelated to one's ultimate estate in heaven. All children were to be baptized, because all had an equal hope for salvation: 'But I judge that most will not be saved, according to Dr. Calvin.'

An assignment which would encourage the marquis to believe that he was among the saved was at hand, for when the king in Paris heard of the growth of Calvinism in the towns along the Flemish border, he dispatched a Catholic general at the head of twelve hundred stout Catholic yeomen, and they lashed about the countryside, maiming and killing, and leading errant Protestants back into the customary fold. In late 1562, with the boy king dead and Mary on her way back to Scotland a widow, the Marquis de Caix rallied two hundred of his men who had never heard of John Calvin or Geneva, either, and marched forth to do battle. It should have been a rout, twelve hundred against two, but the marquis was so able in the saddle and so grand a leader to his men that they repelled the invaders, chasing them fifteen miles south and inflicting heavy damages.

Among the foot soldiers who routed the Catholics was the wine-maker, Giles de Pré, who, when he returned home weary and triumphant, announced to his wife that he was now a Huguenot. When she asked what this word meant, he could not explain, nor could he tell her what his new religion stood for, nor had he heard of the *Institutes*, or Geneva. But he knew with striking clarity what his decision entailed: 'It's an end of priests. No more bishops shouting at us what to do. That big monastery, we'll close it down. People will behave themselves, and there will be order.'

Slowly the village of Caix became a Huguenot center, but with almost none of the changes predicted by De Pré in effect. The good Abbé Desmoulins continued as before, arguing forcefully with the marquis against the theory of predestination. When the bishop arrived from Amiens he thundered in the same old way, except that now he fulminated against Calvin and the Huguenots. In 1564 John Calvin, the most significant Frenchman of his era, died in Geneva, but his influence continued to spread.

In 1572 the Marquis de Caix, veteran of nine battles in which Huguenots confronted royal armies, decided to visit Geneva to see for himself what changes Calvinism sponsored when it actually commanded a society, and with his chief farmer Giles de Pré, set out on horseback for the distant city. Any Huguenot had to be careful these days in traveling about France, for that old tigress Catherine de Medici waged ceaseless war against them, even though she had long since ceased being the legal queen; and if a Protestant like the Marquis de Caix, with his powerful military reputation, dared to move about, he was apt to be pursued by a real army and slain on the spot. So the two travelers moved cautiously, like two rambling farmers, eastward toward Strasbourg, then south to Besançon and across the low mountains into Geneva.

The visit was a disaster. The free-and-easy marquis found that Calvin's successors were terrified lest their Protestant Rome, as some called it, be overturned by Catholic princes storming up from the south. Extreme caution ruled the city, with synods condemning men to be burned for theological transgressions. When the marquis, wearied by his long journey, sought some inn where he could employ the services of a maid to ease his bones and comfort him, the innkeeper turned deathly pale: 'Please, monsieur, do not even whisper . . .'

'You must have some girls?'

The innkeeper placed his two hands upon the wrist of his guest and said, 'Sir, if you speak like that again, the magistrates . . .' He indicated that at some spot not far from there—where, he never knew—there would be spies: 'Catholics trying to destroy our city. Protestants ready to trap men like you.'

'I seek some merriment,' the marquis said.

'In Geneva there is no merriment. Now eat, and say your prayers, and go to bed. The way we do.'

Wherever they moved, the two Frenchmen encountered this sense of heavy censorship, and it was understandable. The city, inspired by fear of a Catholic attack on the one hand and Calvin's severe Protestantism on the other, had evolved what later historians would describe as 'that moral reign of terror.'

'This is not what I had in mind,' the marquis confided to his farmer. 'I think we had better quit this place while we have four legs between us. These maniacs would chop a man in half . . . and all because he smiled at a pretty girl.'

They slipped away from Geneva without ever having announced themselves to the authorities, and during the long ride back home they often halted at the edge of some upland farm, sitting beneath chestnut trees as they discussed what they had seen. 'The trouble must rest with Geneva,' the marquis said. 'We're not like that in France, spies and burnings.'

'The good far outweighs the bad,' De Pré argued. 'Perhaps they have to do this until the others are disposed of.'

'I caught the feeling they were doing it because they liked to do it.'

The travelers reached no conclusion, but the marquis's suspicions deepened, and he might have changed his mind about Protestantism as the solution to the world's evils had he not become aware that along the roads of France there was a considerable movement of messengers scurrying here and there, and he began to wonder if perchance they were looking for him. 'What are they after?' he asked De Pré, but the farmer could not even make a sensible guess.

Since it was mid-August, there was no necessity to frequent towns or cities in search of accommodation, so the men slept in fields, keeping away from traveled routes, and in this way moved across northern France toward the outskirts of Rheims. On the morning of August 25 they deemed it safe to enter a small village north of that city, and as they did so, they found the populace in a state of turmoil. Houses were aflame and no one was endeavoring to save them. Two corpses dangled from posts, their bowels cut loose. A mob chased a woman, caught up with her, and trampled her to death. Other fires were breaking out and general chaos dominated the village.

'What happens here?' the marquis called as one of the rioters rushed past with a flaming brand.

'We're killing all Protestants!' the man cried as he ran to a house whose inhabitants he did not like.

'Careful, careful!' the marquis whispered as he led his horse gingerly into the center of the rioting. 'Why are you hanging him?' he shouted to members of a mob about to throw a rope over the lower branches of a tree.

'Huguenot.'

'On whose orders?'

'Messengers from Paris. We're killing them everywhere. Cleansing the country.'

'Sir,' De Pré whispered, 'I think we should ride on.'

'I think not,' the marquis said, and with a sudden spur to his horse he swept down upon the rioters, knocked them aside, and grabbed the doomed man by his shoulders, striving vainly to swing him to safety. The man's feet were lashed so that he could not help himself, and he would have been stamped to death by the mob had not De Pré dashed in, grabbed him by the thighs, and galloped off beside the marquis.

When they were well out into the country they halted, and the nobleman asked the bound man what had taken place. 'Midnight, without warning, they leaped upon us. I hid in my barn.'

'Huguenot?'

'The same. My wife hanged. They had a list of every Protestant and tried to kill us all.'

'What will you do?'

'What can I do?'

'You can come with us. We're Huguenots too.'

The frightened man rode with De Pré until they reached an isolated farm, where the marquis asked, 'Is this a good Catholic farm?'

'It is indeed,' the owner said.

'Good. We'll take that horse. We're Huguenots.'

It would be remembered in history as St. Bartholomew's Day, that awful August massacre which the Italian queen mother, Catherine de Medici, instigated to destroy Protestantism once and for all. In cities and towns across France, the followers of Calvin were knifed and stabbed and hanged and burned. Tens of thousands were slain, and when the joyous news reached Rome, Pope Gregory XIII exulted, and a cardinal gave the exhausted messenger who had brought the news across the Alps a reward of one thousand thalers. A medal was struck, showing the Pope on one side, an avenging angel on the other castigating heretics with her sword. In Spain, King Philip II, who would soon be losing his Armada to Protestant sailors from England and Holland, dispatched felicitations to Catherine on her meritorious action: 'This is one of the greatest joys of my entire life.' Lesser people celebrated in lesser ways.

Even in a village as remote as Caix the slaughter raged, and if the marquis and his farmer had been at home that fateful night, they would have been slain. As it was, the marquis's barns were burned, his vineyards ravaged; and Giles de Pré's wife was hacked into four pieces. It was a fearful devastation, one of the worst in French history, and its hideous memory would remain engraved on the soul of every Huguenot who survived.

Some did. The Marquis de Caix resumed his residence in the village, always ready to sally forth on whatever new battle engaged his fellow Protestants. Giles de Pré married again, and took as his assistant in the refurbished vineyards the man he had helped rescue at Rheims. And in due course the Abbé Desmoulins found that he was more attuned to the sober precepts of John Calvin than to the rantings of his bishop at Amiens; like hundreds of priests in Huguenot areas, he changed his religion, becoming a stout defender of his new faith.

In this quiet way the village of Caix became again solidly Huguenot, and in 1598 held joyful celebrations when that fine and sensible king, Henry IV, issued the Edict of Nantes, assuring the Huguenots that they would henceforth enjoy liberty of conscience and even the right to hold public worship in certain specified locations outside towns. And as far as Paris was concerned, no closer than twenty miles.

The De Pré family continued as wine-makers, servants to the successive Marquis de Caix, until that fatal year of 1627 when the last marquis rode off to help defend the Huguenot city of La Rochelle against the Catholic armies that were besieging it. He fought gallantly, and died amidst a circle of enemy swords, but with him died his title; no longer did Caix have a marquis.

In later years members of the De Pré family stayed with their vineyards and the church started by Calvin, but never did these rural people descend to the harshness practiced at Geneva or to the burnings conducted there. French Calvinism was a quiet, stable, often beautiful religion in which a human being, from the moment he was conceived, was registered in God's great account book as either saved or damned. He would never know which, but if life smiled on him and his fields prospered, there had to be a supposition that he was among the saved. Therefore, it behooved a man to work diligently, for this indicated that he was eligible to be chosen.

This curious theology had a salutary effect in Caix: any person who presumed that he was among the elect had to behave himself for two reasons. If he was saved, it would be shameful for him to behave poorly, for this would reflect upon God's judgment; and if God saw him misbehaving, He might reverse His decision and place the offender among the damned. Prayer on Wednesday, church at ten on Sunday, prayer at seven Sunday evening was the weekly routine, broken only when some fanatical Catholic priest from a nearby city would storm into Caix and rant about the freedoms the heretical Huguenots were enjoying. Then there might be insurgency, with soldiers rioting and offering to slay all Protestants, but this would be quickly suppressed by the government, with the inflammatory priest being scuttled off to some less volatile area.

In 1660, when even these sporadic eruptions had become a distant memory and when all France glowed from the glories attendant upon King Louis XIV, the De Pré family celebrated the birth of a son named Paul. With the extinction of Marquis de Caix's title, distant female relatives had sold off the vineyards and the De Prés had acquired some of the choicest fields. At ten, young Paul knew how to graft plants in the field and supervise their grapes when they were brought in for pressing. The De Pré fields produced a crisp white wine, not of top quality but good enough to command local respect, and Paul learned each step that would ensure its reputation.

He was a sober lad who at fifteen seemed already a man. He wore a scarf about his neck the way old men did and was fastidiously careful of his clothes, brushing them several times a day and oftener on Wednesdays and Sundays. At sixteen, he astonished his parents by becoming in effect a deacon; he wasn't one, technically, but he helped regulate life in the community and served as visitor to families needing financial help.

'I should like to be an elder one day,' he told his parents that year, and he was so serious that they dared not laugh.

They were not surprised when, at the age of eighteen, he announced that he had decided to marry Marie Plon, daughter of a neighboring farmer, and he rejected their suggestion that they accompany him when he went to seek permission of the elders for the marriage. Gravely he stood before the leading men of the community and said, 'Marie and I have decided that we must get on with our lives. We're going to work the old Montelle farm.'

When the elders interrogated him, they found that he had everything planned: when the wedding was to be, how the Montelle farm was to be paid for, and even how many children they proposed to have: 'Three—two boys and a girl.'

'And if God should give you less?'

'I would accept the will of God,' Paul said, and some of the elders laughed. But they approved the marriage, and one man made Paul extremely happy when he said at the conclusion of the interrogation, 'One day you'll be sitting with us, Paul.' It was with difficulty that he refrained from retorting, 'I intend to.'

The marriage took place in 1678, launching the kind of strong, rural family that made France one of the most stable nations in Europe, and promptly, in accordance with the master plan, Marie de Pré gave birth to her first son, then her second. All that was now required was the daughter, and Paul was certain that since God obviously approved of him, a daughter would appear in due time.

But now, once again, there were ominous signs in French society. Devout Catholics were shuddering at the blasphemous liberties allowed Protestants under the Edict of Nantes and pressed for its repudiation. Always assisted by the mistresses who exercised the real power over the kings of France—Henry IV would have fifty-six named and recorded—the clerical faction succeeded in annulling one after another the liberties enjoyed by the Calvinists.

The minister at Caix explained to his congregation the restrictions under which they all now lived: 'You cannot be a teacher, or a doctor, or a town official, even though Caix is mostly of our faith. You have got to show the police that you attend one meeting a month to listen to government attacks on our church. When your parents die, Protestant burial services can be held only at sunset, lest they infuriate the Catholics. If you are heard speaking even one word in public against Rome, you go to jail for a year. And if either you as a citizen or I as a minister try to convert any person to our faith, we can be hanged.'

None of these new laws touched Paul de Pré, and he lived a contented life regardless of the pressures being applied to his community. But in 1683 two events occurred which terrified him. One morning two of the king's soldiers banged on the door and told Marie that they had been billeted to her home, whereupon, pushing her aside, they stamped into the farmhouse, selected a room they liked, and informed her that this would be their quarters.

Marie ran to the vineyard, calling for her husband, and when he reached the house he asked quietly, 'What happens here?'

'Dragooned,' the soldiers said.

'What does that mean?'

'We live here from now on. To keep an eye on your seditions.'

'But—'

'Room. We'll use this one. Bed. You can move the blue one in. Food. Three good meals a day with meat. Drink? We want those bottles kept filled.'

It was a dreadful imposition, which worsened when the lonely soldiers tried to drag local girls into their quarters. Forbidden by the Catholic priest from a neighboring village to behave so coarsely, they retaliated by inviting dragoons from other homes into the De Pré rooms, shouting through the night for more food and drink, and handling Marie roughly when she brought it.

But even so, the senior De Prés did not appreciate where the real danger lay until one Sunday morning when they found the soldiers behind the barn talking earnestly with the two boys. When Paul came upon them, the soldiers seemed embarrassed, and that afternoon he sought out the Calvinist minister for guidance.

'I might have killed them, for it seemed ominous,' he confessed.

'Indeed it was,' the clergyman said. 'You're in great peril, De Pré. The soldiers are interrogating your boys to trick them into saying something against our religion or in favor of theirs. One word, and the soldiers will take your boys away forever, claiming that they said they wanted to be Catholics but that you prevented their conversion.'

It happened in several homes. Children were tricked into saying things of which they could have had no understanding, and away they went, to another town, in another district—and they would never be heard of again. 'You warn your sons to be careful,' the minister said, and then came the anguished nights when mother and father secretly instructed their sons what to say.

'Do your parents lecture you at night?' one of the soldiers would ask the boys.

'No,' he must say.

'Did they ever take away pictures of the saints that you loved?'

'No.'

'Wouldn't you like to attend Mass with other boys and girls?'

'We go to our own church.'

Now nights became sacred, for when the family was alone in their part of the house, and the soldiers rioting in theirs, Paul took out his Geneva Bible and patiently read from the Book of Psalms those five or six special songs of joy and dedication which the Huguenots had taken to their hearts:

> 'As the hart panteth after the water brooks, so panteth my soul after thee, O God. My soul thirsteth for God, for the living God: when shall I come and appear before God?'

And the elder De Prés drilled their sons in how to avoid the peril which menaced them: 'Our lives would end if you were taken from us. Be careful, be careful what you say.'

In 1685 the axe which had been hanging over the Huguenots fell. King Louis XIV, judging himself to be impregnable, decided to rid himself of Protestants forever. With grandiloquent flourishes he revoked all concessions made to them by the Edict of Nantes and announced that henceforth France was a Catholic country with no place for Huguenots. Dragoons were dispatched to Languedoc, that ancient hiding place for heresy, and whole towns were depopulated. The massacre of St. Bartholomew's Day might have been reenacted across France, except that Louis did not want to inherit the moral stain of his forefathers.

Instead, a series of harsh decrees altered French life: 'All Protestant books, especially Bibles in the vernacular, to be burned. No artisan to work anywhere in France without a certificate proving him to be a good Catholic. Every Huguenot clergyman to quit France within fifteen days and forever, on pain of death if he return. All marriages conducted in the Protestant faith declared null and all children therefrom designated bastards. Protestant washerwomen not to work at the banks of the river, lest they sully the waters.'

And there was another regulation which the De Prés simply could not accept: 'All children of Protestant families must convert immediately to the true faith, and any father who attempts to spirit his children out of France shall spend the rest of his life on the oar-benches of our galleys.'

What did these extraordinary laws mean in a village like Caix, where the population was mainly Huguenot? Since it had long been an orderly place, it did not panic. The pastor summoned the elders, and when the deacons assembled, a large percentage of the adult males were present. 'First,' said the minister, 'we must ascertain if the rumor be true. Probably a lie, because four kings have assured us our freedom.'

But in due course official papers arrived, proving that the new laws were in effect, and a few families converted on the spot, parents and children noisily embracing the traditional faith. Other families met in conclave, and fathers swore that they would die with their infants rather than surrender them to Catholicism. 'We'll walk to the ends of the earth till we find refuge,' Paul de Pré cried flamboyantly, and when the pastor reminded him that the new edicts forbade taking either one's self or one's children out of France, De Pré astounded the assembly by shouting, 'Then the new laws can burn in hell.'

From that moment, others drew away from him. The pastor announced that he would go into exile at Geneva, and the Plons proclaimed loudly that they had never really approved of John Calvin. Paul observed such behavior without comment; they could abandon their religion and their duties at Caix, but not he. And then came the assaults that shattered his confidence.

One morning the soldiers billeted at his farm brought in a mob to ransack the place, searching for Huguenot books. With loud, triumphant voices the soldiers shouted, 'Calvin's *Institutes!* The Geneva Bible!' And he watched in sick dismay as these testaments were pitched into a bonfire, and as the flames consumed the books, with men roaring approval, one of the soldiers grabbed him by the arm and growled, 'Tomorrow, when the officials come from Amiens, we take your children too.'

That night Paul gathered the family in a room with no candles and told his sons, 'We must leave before morning. You can take nothing with you. Our vineyards will go to others. The house we abandon.'

'Even the horses?' Henri asked.

'We'll take two of them, but the others . . .'

Marie explained to the children in her own words: 'Tomorrow the soldiers will take you away. Unless we go. We could never give you up to others. You are the blood of our hearts.'

'Where are we going?' Henri asked.

'We don't know,' she said honestly, looking at her husband.

'We're heading north,' he said, 'and we've got to cross dangerous lands owned by Spain.'

'Won't they arrest us?' Marie asked.

'Yes, if we're careless.'

He had no clearer concept of where he was going than his infants; all he knew was he must flee oppression. Having once experienced the calm rationalism of John Calvin, he could not surrender that vision of an orderly world. He told his sons, 'I'm satisfied that God will lead us to the haven for which we are predestined,' and from that conviction he never deviated.

After midnight, when fowls were asleep and roosters had not yet crowed, he led his family north, abandoning all he had accumulated. How did he have the courage to take a wife and two small children into uncharted forests toward lands he did not know?

Calvinism placed strong emphasis on the fact that God often entered into covenants with his chosen people; the Old and New Testaments were replete with examples, and Paul could have cited numerous verses which fortified his belief that God had personally selected him for such a covenant. Lacking a Bible, he had to rely on memory, and his mind fixed upon a passage from Jeremiah which Huguenots often cited as proof of their predestination:

> They shall ask the way to Zion . . . saying, Come and let us join ourselves to the Lord in a perpetual covenant that shall not be forgotten.

Each sunset, when the travelers rose from their daytime sleep to risk the next stage northward, Paul assured his sons, 'The Lord is leading us to Zion, according to his covenant with us.'

When De Pré arrived in Amsterdam in the fall of 1685 he had with him only his wife, his two sons and a ragtag collection of bundles; the two horses had been sold at Antwerp, where Paul received for them a great deal more than the guilders involved. A crypto-Protestant had given him the address of a fellow religionist who had emigrated some years before to Holland, and it was to this man that the De Pré family reported.

His name was Vermaas and he held two jobs, each of which proved crucial to De Pré: during the week he worked in a dark, drafty weighhouse where shipments of timber, grain and herring from the Baltic were weighed and forwarded to specialized warehouses; on Sunday he served as custodian of the little church near the canals where only French was spoken. Here Protestants from the Spanish Netherlands and Huguenots from France gathered to worship God in the Calvinist manner, and few churches in Christendom could have had a more devout membership than this. Each person who came to pray on Sunday was an authentic religious hero who had sacrificed position, security and wealth—and often the lives of family members—to persevere in Calvinism. Some, like the De Prés, had crept at night across two enemy countries or three in order to sing on Sundays the Psalm that Huguenots had taken specially to their hearts:

> 'I called upon the Lord in distress: the Lord answered me, and set me in a large place.'

Amsterdam with its burgeoning riches and crowding fleets was indeed a large place, spacious in wealth and freedom, and Vermaas epitomized the spirit of the town, for he was a big man, burly in the shoulders and with a wide space between his eyes.

Intuitively he liked Paul de Pré, and when he learned how this resolute family had fled French tyranny, he embraced them. 'There's a good chance I can find you work at the weigh-house,' he assured Paul, and to Marie he said, 'I know a little house near the waterfront. Not much, but it's a foothold.'

Vermaas was master weigh-porter, and Paul sensed immediately the importance of this position. Never before had he seen such scales: huge timbered affairs with pans that weighed as much as a man, but so delicately balanced that they could weigh a handful of grain. To these scales, each taller than two men, came the riches of the Baltic. Stout little ships, manned by Dutch sailors, penetrated to all parts of that inland sea, selling and buying at a rate that would have dazzled a French businessman. At times the weigh-house would be occupied with timber from Norway; at other times copper, iron and steel from Sweden would predominate; but always there were tubs of North Sea herring waiting to be cured by a process known only by the Dutch, after which it would be transshipped to all the ports of Europe.

'Gold with fins,' the men at the weigh-house called their herring, and De Pré learned to tell when a ship with herring was about to unload; this was important, for when the workmen hauled in the tubs of gold, they were permitted to sequester a few choice fish for their families.

De Pré had deposited his wife and children in the miserable shack near the banks of the IJ River, trusting that he would in time be able to find them better quarters. It was a vain hope, for Amsterdam was crowded with refugees from all parts of Europe: Baruch Spinoza, the brilliant Portuguese Jew, had lived here while unraveling the mysteries of God; he had died only a few years ago. René Descartes had elected to come here to conduct his work in mathematics and philosophy, and a score of great theologians from all countries had considered Amsterdam the only safe place to conduct their speculations. The English Pilgrims had rested nearby before sailing on to Massachusetts, and it was still the major center for the rescue of Jews from a score of different lands.

Houses were not easy to find, but with the aid of timber Paul acquired at the waterfront and cloths with which to stuff the windy cracks, he and Marie converted their shack into a livable home, and although the dampness caused much coughing, the family survived. The boys—Henri, six, and Louis, five—reveled in the canals that cut across the city and the endlessly changing river up which the Baltic ships came.

'The Golden Swamp' Amsterdam had been called in the old days, for it was then four-fifths water, but engineers were ingenious in filling in the shallow lakes to build more land. Son Henri's first comment on his new home was apt, and the De Prés often quoted it: 'I could get in a boat, if I had a boat, and row and row and never come back.' And every year men dug new canals, so that the city became a network in which every house was connected by water with every other, or so it seemed.

The French church, seated on one of the most interesting small canals, had started in 1409 as a Catholic cloister, but during the Reformation it was converted into a refuge for generations of fleeing dissidents. Rebuilt many times, it became a monument not only to Protestantism but also to the essential generosity of the Dutch, for its ministers, a courageous lot of French-speaking Walloons, who had dared much in coming here, had always been given pensions by the Dutch government on the grounds that 'we are seekers after truth and are richer in having you among us.' No other nation in recorded history gave immediate pensions to its immigrants, or profited more from their arrival.

With pride Paul led his family to this church on Sundays, pointing out to the boys the various other Frenchmen who worked along the waterfront. It was an impoverished congregation, with many families subsisting only through the generosity of Dutch patrons, but invariably someone in the group provided flowers for the altar, and it was because De Pré commented on this that his good fortune commenced.

One Monday morning, as Paul and Vermaas were hefting bales of cloth onto their weigh-scales, the big man said, 'You like flowers, don't you, Paul?'

'Where does the church always find flowers?'

'The Widows Bosbeecq send them over. They're looking for someone to tend their garden.'

'Who are the widows?'

'Aloo! This one doesn't know the Widows Bosbeecq!' And the workmen came to joke with him.

'What ship have you been unloading?' When De Pré pointed, the men cried, 'That's their ship. And that one and that one.'

It seemed that seven of the best ships sailing the Baltic belonged to the widows, and Vermaas explained, 'Two country girls married the Bosbeecq brothers. The men were fine captains who worked the Baltic for many years. In time they had seven ships, like that one.'

'How did they die?'

'Fighting the English, how else?'

In 1667 the older Bosbeecq brother had accompanied the Dutch fighting fleet right into the river Thames, threatening to capture London itself; he had gone down with his ship the next year. The younger brother helped in three notable victories over the English, but he, too, had died at the hands of the English, and the family's profitable trade with Russia might have evaporated had not the two widows stepped forward to operate the fleet. Choosing with rural skill those captains who would best preserve their profits, they continued to send their doughty potbellied vessels to all parts of the Baltic.

Sometimes the widows would appear at the docks, always together and with parasols imported from Paris, and would primly inspect whichever of their ships happened to be in the harbor, nodding sagely to their captains and approving of the manner in which their cargoes were being handled. They were in their sixties, somewhat frail, dressed in black. They walked carefully, attended by a maid who shoved idlers aside for them. One was tall and very thin; the other was roundish, always with a broad smile. Never once did they complain about anything, but Vermaas assured De Pré that when they had their captains alone in the family office, they could be quite tart.

A few days after their conversation Vermaas ran up to De Pré with exciting news: 'It happened by accident. When the Bosbeecq factor was here the other day I told him you liked flowers. He became quite interested, because the Widows Bosbeecq are still looking for a gardener.' So it was arranged that Paul quit work early one afternoon and accompany the Bosbeecq factor to the tall, thin house on the Oudezijdsvoorburgwal (Old-sides-forward-city-dyke) where the widows waited.

'We have a large garden,' they explained, and from a narrow window Paul could see a garden so neatly trimmed that he could scarcely believe it was real. 'We like it neat.' There was also much work to be done inside the house, and the widows wondered if Paul had a wife. 'Is she able?' they asked. 'Is she encumbered with children?'

'We have only two boys.' Quickly he added, 'They're quite grown, of course.'

'How old?'

'Six and five.'

'Oh, dear. Oh, dear.' The sisters-in-law looked at each other in real dismay.

Paul sensed that his entire future depended upon what he did next, and he started to say, 'Those boys have walked all the way from . . .' Dramatically he stopped, for he knew that this was irrelevant. Instead he said quietly, 'Please! We live in a cold, damp shack, and my wife keeps it like a palace. She could do wonders here.'

The Widows Bosbeecq liked their servants to be at work at five in the morning; it discouraged sloth. But once on the job, the workers enjoyed surprising freedoms, the principal one being that they were exceptionally well fed. The widows liked to prepare the food themselves, leaving to Marie de Pré the cleaning of rooms, the sweeping of the stoep and the ironing of clothes sent upstairs by the slaveys. They were good cooks, and being country women, felt that one of man's major requirements was an adequate supply of food, and where growing boys were concerned, downright gorging was advisable.

'It must have been God who brought us here,' Paul said frequently, and on Sundays he led his brood across the canal to the French church for prayers. One Sunday the widows intercepted him as he was about to leave: 'You should attend our church now. It's just as close.'

The idea stunned De Pré. It seemed almost blasphemous that he should abandon the church of his fathers, the place in which French was spoken, and attend a different one which used Dutch. He had never considered this before, since he was convinced that God spoke to mankind in French and he knew that John Calvin did. It would have surprised him to know that Calvin's principal works had been written in Latin, for the solemn thunder of Calvin's thought had reached him in French translation, and he could not imagine it in Dutch.

He discussed this with his family, even though the boys were scarcely old enough to comprehend the difference between French, the correct language of theology, and Dutch, an accidental: 'Within the family we must always speak French. It's proper for us to speak with the widows in Dutch, and you boys must always thank them in that language when they give you clothes or toys. But in our prayers, and in the services at the church, we must speak French.'

He told the widows, 'I went to see your church and it must be the finest in Christendom, because ours is certainly a small affair. But we have always worshipped God in our own language . . .'

'Of course!' the widows said. 'We were thoughtless.'

The fact that De Pré now lived in the Bosbeecq house, with no further obligations at the weigh-station, did not mean that he lost touch with Vermaas. On Sundays, after church, they would often meet to discuss affairs pertaining to the Bosbeecq ships, and one fine April day they stood together at the bridge leading from the French church as the two widows came down the cobblestones, attended by their servant.

'Pity you're married,' Vermaas said.

'Why? Marie's wonderful . . .'

'I mean, if you weren't married, you could take one of the widows, and then the house . . .'

'The widows?'

'Never be deceived about widows, Paul. The older they are, the more they want to get married again. And the richer they are, the more fun it is to marry them.'

'They're older than my mother.'

'And richer—'

'Who are those men?' Paul interrupted, referring to the horde of strange-looking men who seemed always to be clustered about a building which abutted onto the French church.

'Them?' Vermaas said with some distaste. 'They're Germans.'

'What are they doing here?'

'They line up every day. You must have seen them before this.'

'I have. And I wondered who they were.'

'Their land has been torn by war. A hundred years of it. Catholics against Protestants, Protestants killing Catholic babies. Disgraceful.'

'I knew war like that,' Paul said.

'Oh, no! Not like the German wars. You French were civilized.' He made an ugly sound in his throat and drew his finger across it as if it were a knife. 'Slash across the throat, the Frenchman's dead. But in Germany you would . . .'

'Why do they stand there?'

'Don't you know what that building is? You've been working here for more than a year and you don't know?' In amazement he led De Pré across the bridge and into the Hoogstraat (High Street), where a sturdy building surrounding a courtyard bore on its escutcheon the proud letters V.O.C.

'What's that mean?' Paul asked.

'Vereenigde Oostindische Compagnie,' he recited proudly. 'Jan Compagnie. Behind those doors sit the Lords XVII.' And he explained how this powerful assembly of businessmen had started more than eighty years ago to rule the East.

'But the Germans?' Paul asked, pointing to the rabble that waited silently outside the courtyard.

'There's nothing in Germany,' Vermaas explained. 'These are men who fought for some count . . . some baron. They lost. For them there's nothing.'

'But why here?'

'Jan Compagnie always needs good men. The clerk will come out to-morrow morning, look them over, try to spot those likely to survive. And poof! They're off to Java.'

'Where's Java?'

'Haven't you seen the big Outer Warehouse of the East Indies Company?'

'No.'

'Well, after we weigh the goods here and assess the taxes, they're stored in the proper warehouses,' and on Sunday he took Paul on a leisurely stroll along various canals, past the house in which Rembrandt had lived and the place once occupied by Baruch Spinoza before he had to grind lenses to keep himself alive. They crossed a footbridge to an artificial island that contained a vast open space surrounded by row upon row of warehouses, a very long rope-walk and a majestic, five-storied building for holding valuable importations.

'The treasure chest of the Lords XVII,' Vermaas said, and he summoned a watchman, who granted admission. In the darkness the two men moved from one stack of goods to another, touching with their hands casks and bales worth a fortune.

'Cloves, pepper, nutmeg, cinnamon.' Vermaas repeated reverently the magic names, and as he spoke De Pré grew sick at heart for contact again with the soil, the real soil of trees and vines and shrubs.

'Now, these bales,' Vermaas was saying, 'they're not spices. Golded cloth from Japan. Silvered cloth from India. Beautiful robes from Persia. This is from China, and I don't know what's in it.'

'Where's it come from, all this richness?'

'From the gardens of the moon,' Vermaas said. All his life he had wanted to emigrate to Java, where a purposeful man could make his fortune. He had an insecure idea of where Java was, but he proposed one day to get there. Grasping De Pré by the arm, he said in a whisper, 'Paul, if you can't marry a rich widow, for God's sake, get to Java. You're still young.' And the sweet promise of this dark warehouse was overpowering.

In the morning De Pré asked permission from the widows to visit the offices of Jan Compagnie. 'Whatever for?' the women asked.

'I want to see what the Germans are up to. About Java.'

'Java!' The women laughed, and the older said, 'Go ahead. But don't you start dreaming of Java.'

So he walked only a few blocks to the Hoogstraat, where the crowd of Germans was vastly augmented, men extremely thin and pinched of face, but willing to undertake the severest adventure if only it would provide sustenance. He stood fascinated as clerks came out of the Compagnie offices to inspect the supplicants, selecting one in twenty, and he saw with what joy the chosen men leaped forward.

But when he returned to his work the widows said that they wished to talk with him: 'Don't get Java on your mind. For every guilder that reaches us from Java, six come from the Baltic. Yes, you'll see the big East Indiamen anchored off Texel, transshipping their spices and cloth-of-gold, and you'll hear that one cargo earned a million of this or that. But, Paul, believe us, the wealth of Holland lies in our herring trade. In any year our seven little ships serving the Baltic bring in more money than a dozen of their Indiamen. Keep your eye on the main target.'

They spoke alternately, with one making a point and her sister-in-law another, but when the roundish one repeated, 'Keep your eye on the main target,' the taller wished to enforce the idea: 'We've been watching you, Paul. You and Marie have been chosen by God for some great task.'

No one had ever spoken like this to him before; he had for some time suspected that he was among those elected by God for salvation, the basic goodness of his heart emitting signals that he was predestined. As of now, he lacked the financial wealth which would have proved his election, but he felt certain that in time it, too, would arrive, and in his self-congratulation he missed what the widows said next. It was apparently something very important, for one of them asked sharply, 'Don't you think so, Paul?'

'I'm sorry.'

'My sister said,' the taller woman repeated, 'that if you learn shipping, you could become one of our managers.'

With the bluntness that characterized most French farmers, and especially the Calvinists, De Pré blurted out, 'But I want to work the earth. You've seen what I can do with your garden.'

The widows liked his honesty, and the roundish one said, 'You're an excellent gardener, Paul, and we have a former neighbor who might use your services, too.'

'I'd not want to leave you,' he said frankly.

'We don't intend that you shall. But he's a friend, and one of the Lords XVII, and we could spare him three hours of your time a day. You can keep the wages.'

His hands dropped to his side, and he had to bite his lip to control his emotion. He had wandered into a strange land with no recommendation but his devotion to a form of religion, and in this land he had found a solid friend in Vermaas, who had gone out of his way to help him, a church whose members were encouraged to worship in French, and these two widows who were so kind to his wife, so loving with his sons and so generous with him. When the Huguenots fled France they found refuge in twenty foreign lands, where they encountered a score of different receptions, but none equaled the warmth extended to them in Holland.

On Tuesday morning at nine o'clock, after De Pré had put in his usual four hours of hard work, the Bosbeecq women suggested that he accompany them to the stately Herengracht (Gentlemen's Canal), along which his new employer lived, and there they knocked at the door of a house much grander than theirs. A maid dressed in blue admitted them to a parlor filled with furniture from China and bade them sit upon the heavy brocades. After a wait long enough to allow Paul time to admire the richness of the room, a gentleman appeared, clad in a most expensive Chinese robe decorated with gold and blue dragons.

He was tall and thin, with a white mustache and goatee. He had piercing eyes that showed no film of age, and although he was past seventy, he moved alertly, going directly to De Pré and bowing slightly. 'I am Karel van Doorn, and I understand from these good women that you wish to work for me.'

'They said you could have me three hours a day.'

'If you really work, that would be enough. Can you really work?'

De Pré sensed that he was in the hands of someone much harsher than the widows, but he was so captivated by the idea of Java that he did not want to antagonize anyone who might be associated with that wonderland. 'I can tend your garden,' he said.

With no apologies to the Bosbeecqs, Van Doorn took Paul by the arm, hurried him through a chain of corridors to a big room, and threw open a window overlooking a garden in sad repair. 'Can you marshal that into some kind of order?'

'I could fix that within a week.'

'Get to it!' And he shoved Paul out the back door and toward a shed where some tools waited.

'I must explain to the—'

'I'll tell them you're already at work.' Van Doorn started to leave, then stopped abruptly and cried, 'Remember! You said you could do it in a week.'

'And what do I do after that?' Paul asked.

'Do? You could work three hours a day for ten years and not finish all the things I have in mind.'

When De Pré returned to the Bosbeecq house, where the widows were preparing a gigantic meal because they knew he would be hungry, the two women suggested that he sit with them in the front room, and there, in forthright terms, they warned him about his new employer, speaking alternately, as usual, like two angels reporting to St. Peter regarding their earthly investigations.

'Karel van Doorn will pay you every stuiver you earn. He's fiercely honest.'

'Within limits.'

'And he can afford to pay you. He's very wealthy.'

'He is that. The Compagnie in Java had an iron-clad rule. No official to buy and sell for himself. Only for the Compagnie.'

'But his family bought and sold like madmen. And grew very rich.'

'And the Compagnie had another iron-clad rule. No one in Java to bring money earned there back to Holland.'

'She knows, because her uncle was one of the Lords XVII.'

'But when Karel's mother died in the big house along the canal in Batavia, he hurried out to Java, and by some trick which only he could explain, managed to smuggle all the Van Doorn money back to Amsterdam.'

'And he should have shared half with his brother at the Cape—'

'Where's that?' Paul interrupted. It was the first time in his life he had heard mention of this place.

'It's nothing. A few miserable wretches stuck away at the end of Africa, trying to grow vegetables.'

'Is Mijnheer van Doorn's brother there?' Paul asked quickly.

'Yes. Not too bright a lad. Born in Java, you know.'

'And Van Doorn should have shared the family money with his brother.'

'But he didn't.'

'He smuggled it into Amsterdam, and with it bought himself membership in the Lords XVII.'

'He took my uncle's place.'

'He's one of the leading citizens of Amsterdam. You're lucky to be working for him.'

'But watch him.'

'At the Compagnie, you'll see his portrait painted by Frans Hals.'

'And at the Great Hall of the Arquebusiers, you'll see him in Rembrandt's painting of the civic guard. He's there with my husband, standing beside him.'

'And you'll notice that her husband has his right hand closely guarding his pocket, which is a good thing to do when Karel van Doorn's about.'

'But for a young man like you, he's an influential person to know.'

'If you guard your pocket.'

The relationship was a profitable one, even though Karel van Doorn expected his gardener to work at such a speed that at the end of three hours he was on the verge of collapse. Anything less than signs of total exhaustion indicated laziness, and Van Doorn was apt toward the end of the third hour to slip away from his desk at the Compagnie and watch through the back wall, hoping to catch his workman resting. When he did, he would rush in and berate Paul as an idle, good-for-nothing Frenchman who was, if the facts were known, probably a Papist at heart.

But a hard-nosed French farmer was an adequate match for any avaricious Dutch merchant, and De Pré devised a score of ways to defeat his employer and end the daily three-hour stint in moderately rested condition. In fact, he rather liked the game, for he found Van Doorn meticulously honest in his payments, and when occasionally De Pré returned to the gardens on his own time to finish a job, his employer noticed this and paid extra.

'The one thing that perplexes me,' Paul told the widows one afternoon, 'is that during all the time I've worked for him, he's never once offered me anything to eat or drink.'

'He's a miserly man,' one of the women said. 'Anyone who steals from the Compagnie in Java and from the government in Amsterdam and from his own brother . . .'

'He never steals from me.'

'Ah! But don't you see? The Bible says that you must treat your servants justly. If word got out that he maltreated you, his entire position might crumble. He would no longer be among the elect, and all would know it.'

'I don't understand,' Paul said.

'It's very simple. A man can steal millions from the government, because the Bible says nothing about that. But he dare not steal a stuiver from a servant, because on that both the Bible and John Calvin are very strict.'

'But doesn't the Bible say anything about a little food and drink?'

'Not that I can recall.'

And then, on the very next day, Karel van Doorn offered his gardener Paul de Pré a drink, not at his house but in the Compagnie offices. He had come home at the beginning of the third hour and said abruptly, 'De Pré, let's go to my offices. I need your advice.'

So they walked across town to where a new batch of German mercenaries waited, imploring Karel as he passed, for they knew him to be one of the Lords XVII, but Van Doorn ignored them. When he was seated behind his desk he said without amenities, 'They tell me that in France you made wine.'

'I did.'

'What do you think of this?' From a drawer in his desk Karel produced a bottle of white wine and encouraged the Frenchman to taste it.

'How is it?' Van Doorn asked.

Pursing his lip and spitting onto the floor, De Pré said, 'The man who made that ought to be executed.'

Van Doorn smiled thinly, then broke into a laugh. 'My brother made it.'

'I'm sorry. But it's a very bad wine. It shouldn't be called wine.'

'My own opinion.'

'They told me your brother's in Africa?'

'This comes from his vineyard. He's been working it for thirty years.'

'He must have a very poor vineyard.'

'I wonder if he mixes in something beside grapes?'

'He wouldn't dare.'

'Then how can it be so bad?'

'In making wine, there are many tricks.'

'Could this wine be saved?'

Gingerly De Pré took another sip, not enough to strangle him with its badness but sufficient for him to judge the miserable stuff. 'It has a solid base, Mijnheer. Grapes are grapes, and I suppose that if a vintner started fresh . . .'

'I have a report here. It says the vines are still healthy.'

'But are they the right kind of vine?'

'What do you think should be done?'

De Pré sat with his hands in his lap, staring at the floor. Desperately he wanted to get back to the soil, in Java preferably, where gold proliferated, but his heart beat fast at the possibility of once more raising grapes and making good wine. Since he did not know what to say that might further his plans, he sat dumb.

'If the Compagnie were to send out some men who knew wine,' Van Doorn was saying as if from another room. 'And if those men took with them new strains of grape. Couldn't something be done?'

Ideas of wonderful challenge were coming at him so fast that De Pré could not absorb them, and after a while Van Doorn said, 'Let's look at the map,' and he led the way to a council chamber decorated with a

Rembrandt group portrait and a large map done by Willem Blaeu of Leiden. On it four spots showed conspicuously: Amsterdam, Batavia, the Cape of Good Hope, Surinam in South America.

'We're concerned with these three,' Karel said, jabbing at the Cape, which stood midway between Amsterdam and Java. 'If our ships sailing south could stop at the Cape and load casks of good red wine and strong vinegar, they could maintain the health of their men all the way to Java. And we'd save the freightage we now spend on bottles from France and Italy.' Suddenly the spot representing the Cape assumed considerable importance.

'But the soil—will good vines grow there?' De Pré asked.

'That's what we intend to find out,' Van Doorn said. 'That's why I've been watching you so closely.'

De Pré stepped back. So the watching had been spying—and since his experiences with the Catholics of France, this fact troubled him deeply.

'You didn't think that I hired you to clean up my garden?' Van Doorn laughed. 'I could have hired a hundred Germans to do that, good gardeners some of them.' He actually placed his arm about De Pré's shoulders, leading him back to the first office. 'What I sought, De Pré, was an estimate of you Huguenots. What kind of people you were. How you worked. How dependable you were religiously.'

'Did you find out?' De Pré was angered with this man, but his own canny approach to life made him respect the Dutchman's caution.

'I did. And your honest reaction to my brother's wine has made up my mind.' He rose and strode nervously about the room, galvanized by the prospects of new engagements, new opportunities to snaffle a florin here or there.

Resuming his seat, he said softly, 'De Pré, I must swear you to secrecy.'

'Sworn.'

'The Lords XVII are going to send three shiploads of Huguenots to the Cape. We like you people—your stubborn honesty, your devotion to Calvinism. Your family is going to be aboard one of those ships, and you' —he reached over and slapped De Pré on the knee—'you will take with you a bundle of first-class grape vines.'

'Where will I get them?'

'In France. From some area whose vines you can trust.'

'They won't send vines to Amsterdam. Forbidden.'

'No one sends the vines, De Pré. You go get them.'

'I'd be shot.'

'Not if you're careful.'

'The risk . . .'

'Will be well paid for.' Again he rose, storming about the room, tossing his white head this way and that. 'Well paid, De Pré. I hand you this first bag of coins now. I hand you this second bag when you return to Amsterdam with the grapevines. And if you get them to the Cape, you and I will sell them to the Compagnie and share the profits.'

De Pré studied the offer, and he was glad that the Bosbeecq women had alerted him to this canny gentleman: he was buying the vines with Compagnie money, then selling them back to the Compagnie for more of its money. He remembered something one of the women had told him: 'Van Doorn has a mind that never stops working. As a Compagnie official, he imports cloves from Java. And whom does he sell them to? To himself as a private trader. So he earns double, except that he trebles the price of cloves, since he's the only one who has any, and makes a princely profit.' Here was a man to be wary of, but he also remembered something else the women had said: 'But he dare not steal a stuiver from a servant.'

'Will you pay me the two other times?' he asked directly.

'Would I dare do otherwise? A member of the council?'

And then De Pré's stolid French honesty manifested itself: 'You didn't share with your brother.'

Van Doorn ignored the insult. 'In life,' he said, 'accidents occur. My brother was a dolt. He gave me no help in spiriting the family fortune out of Java. He was a man to be forgotten. You're a man to be remembered.'

When Paul informed his wife that he intended smuggling their eight-year-old son Henri into France with him, she was appalled, but after he explained that this might prove to be the one disguise that would disarm the border guards—'A father traveling back to the farm with his son'—she consented, for she had long suspected that French families ought not to stay too long in congenial Holland. The boys were beginning to speak only Dutch, and the strict Calvinism of the French was being softened by the easier attitudes of the Dutch. She knew also that her husband longed to get back to the making of wine, and this seemed an opportunity engineered by God Himself. So she packed her son's clothing, kissed him fondly, and sent him off on the great adventure.

There was no problem as long as the pair remained in Holland: Amsterdam to Leiden to Schiedam and by boat to Zeeland, where another boat skirted Antwerp and set them down in Ghent. But on the approaches to Amiens, spies could be expected, so the pair shifted eastward and slipped by back roads into the country north of Caix, and when Paul saw the fine fields his eyes filled with tears. This was the good land of France, and it was only an error of magnitude that had driven him from it.

When he passed several small villages where Protestants had once worshipped freely and saw the ruined churches, he was desolated, and late one night he tapped lightly at the window of a farm he knew to be occupied by his wife's family, the Plons.

'Are you still of the true religion?' he whispered when an old woman came to the door.

'It's Marie's man!' the woman cried.

'Sssssssh! Are you still of the true religion?'

When no one dared answer, he knew that they had reverted to Catholicism, but it was too late to retreat. He must rely upon these farmers, for they controlled his destiny. 'This is Marie's boy,' he said, thrusting Henri forward to be admired by his kinfolk.

'If you're caught,' an old man said, 'they'll burn you.'

'I must not be caught,' Paul said. 'Can we sleep here tonight?'

In the morning he told the cautious Plons that he must have four hundred rootings from grapes which made the finest white wine. 'You'd not be allowed to take them across the border, even if you were Catholic,' they warned.

'I'm taking them to a far country,' he assured them. 'Not Holland or Germany, where they would compete.'

He spent four days with the nervous Plons, carefully compacting the vines they brought him, and when he had three hundred and twenty he realized that they formed about as big a bundle as he could reasonably handle on the long journey back to Amsterdam, and the work ended. On the last night he talked openly with the Plons, who by now were satisfied that officials were not going to break down their doors for harboring a Huguenot, and the old people told him, 'It's better now that the village is all one faith.'

'There are no Protestants?'

'None. Some ran away, like you and Marie. Most converted back to the true religion. And a few were hanged.'

'Did the priest escape to Geneva?'

'He was hanged.' Plon's wife interrupted: 'He offered to convert, but we couldn't trust him.'

Then Plon summed up the matter: 'Frenchmen were supposed to be Catholics. It's the only right way for us. A village shouldn't be cut down the middle. Neither should a country.'

'You'd like it much better here,' his wife agreed. 'Now that we're all one.'

But when Paul went to bed on that last night he realized that he could never turn his back on Calvinism; the cost of his emigration was modest in comparison with what he had gained by remaining steadfast. The quiet rationalism of Amsterdam was something the Plons would not be able to comprehend; he wished he were able to explain how content their daughter Marie was in her new home, but he judged he had better not try. He had come back to Caix for its good grape rootings, and he had them.

When he delivered the vines to Mijnheer van Doorn at the Compagnie offices, Karel paid him promptly, but Paul noticed that the sum was slightly less than promised, and when he started to complain, Van Doorn said crisply, 'We contracted for four hundred, you remember,' and Paul said, 'But it would have been impossible to carry so many,' and Van Doorn said, 'Contract's a contract. The solidity of Holland depends upon that.' And Paul dropped the subject, pointing to the large black bow resting on Van Doorn's left arm.

'A death?'

'My wife.' The chairman of the Lords XVII lowered his voice as if to say, 'That subject's closed,' but then he realized that Paul would be interested in what was about to happen as a consequence of his wife's death. 'She was a wonderful woman. Sailed to Java with me. Helped arrange matters there.' Paul wondered why the great man was telling him this, and then came the thunderbolt: 'I'm marrying Vrouw Bosbeecq next Saturday.' Lamely he added, 'At the Old Church. You'll be invited.'

'Which widow?' Paul asked.

'Abigael, the tall one,' and when he saw the incredulity on Paul's face, he explained, 'This way we can combine our two houses and save a good deal of money.'

'What of the other widow?'

'She moves to the Herengracht . . . with us. The other good part is that the seven ships will come . . .' He hesitated, then said, 'Well, under my management.'

Paul wanted more than anything else at that moment to run out and find Vermaas who might be able to explain this absurdity, a wealthy man over seventy conniving to get hold of a few ships, but Van Doorn wished to discuss news that was even more exciting: 'We're assembling a Compagnie fleet right now. They sail for Java within the week, and two hundred and ninety Huguenots will be aboard. It works out well, Paul, because when we close down the Bosbeecq house you and your wife won't be needed any further . . .'

Paul was disgusted. He had risked his life to find three hundred and twenty vines for an experiment, and while he was gone this tall Dutchman had sat in this office scheming, burying his wife and proposing to another before the earth on the grave had settled.

'Mijnheer van Doorn, my trip to Caix was possible only because my little boy Henri accompanied me. He's eight, and I wonder if you would like to make him a special present? For his bravery?'

Van Doorn reflected on this, then said judiciously, 'I don't think so. The contract was with you.' He showed Paul to the door, where he said warmly, 'I hope the boys will enjoy life aboard ship. It's an exciting trip.'

As soon as Paul was free of the Compagnie quarters he ran to the weigh-house to consult with Vermaas: 'I heard the Widow Bosbeecq with my own ears warn me that Van Doorn was a thief, that he could not be trusted . . .'

'And you come home to find she's about to marry him?'

'Yes! It passes understanding.'

'Except for what I told you, Paul. Every widow who ever lived wants to get married again. I said even you could marry one of them, if you were single.'

'But I know she despises Van Doorn.'

'If a widow can't find a real man, she'll take Van Doorn.' Then, with a cry of animal delight, he shouted, 'Good God, Paul! Don't you see how it happened?'

When De Pré looked blank, the big warehouseman cried, 'They took you over to Van Doorn's to work his garden because they wanted to be close to him in case his wife did die. They were using you as bait.'

Paul reflected on this for some time, then asked, 'Do you not think, Vermaas, that Dutchmen make use of everybody?'

'They're in business, Paul.'

The wedding was a solemn affair, with most of the business leaders of Amsterdam in attendance at the Old Church beside the canal. Some came in barges, poled along by their servants, but many walked, forming long processions in black, as if this were a funeral. The church was filled, and when the choir chanted the metrical Psalms so beloved of Calvinists, the place reverberated. The Widows Bosbeecq did not weep; they marched steadfastly to the front of the church, where they waited for the arrival of Karel van Doorn, tall, stately, handsome and whiskered. The marriage couple made a fine impression, two old people joining their lives and their fortunes for the remaining years of life.

'Oh, no,' the roundish widow said that night in the old house as she talked with De Pré about his adventures in France. 'They're not uniting their fortunes. You think a woman as clever as my sister would allow a scoundrel like Van Doorn to lay his hands on our ships?'

'But Mijnheer van Doorn told me himself—'

'When did he tell you?'

'Last week.'

'Aha!' the woman chortled. 'That was last week. Well, this week we presented him with a contract, specifying everything. This house? We sell it and keep the money. The farmland? We join it to his. The seven ships? They're all put in my name, not his.'

'I should think he'd back out.'

'He wanted to. Said we were robbing him. So we revised the contract to keep him happy.'

'Did you give him the ships?'

'Heavens, no! But we did agree that when my ships took their salted herring to Sweden, he should be the agent for selling them, and he keeps the commission.'

Paul was amazed at the cold-blooded quality of this transaction, and started to comment upon it, when the old woman placed her hand on his arm and said softly, 'You know, Paul, it was partly your fault that Abigael decided—that we decided, really—to get married.'

'How me?'

'Because Mijnheer van Doorn came to us the night of his wife's burial and said, "Good women, your man De Pré is sailing shortly for the Cape. You'll be alone again, so why don't we arrange something?" And he was right. We would be alone again, and you reminded us how pleasant it was to have a man in the house.' She laughed. 'Any man.'

When the Bosbeecq house was emptied and the shutters closed, the widows suggested that the De Pré family move with them to the Van Doorn house for the few days before the ships loaded for the Cape, but Mijnheer would have none of this. 'Let them sleep in the old place,' he said, and a few blankets were taken there. But the widows did carry hot food to them, which they ate sitting on the floor.

'You must be sure that Van Doorn pays you all he owes,' they warned Paul, and on the last day in Amsterdam, Paul went to the Compagnie offices and reminded Van Doorn that the third part of the payment was still due him.

'I have it in mind,' Mijnheer assured the émigré. 'I'm handing this packet to the captain of our ship, and the moment you land the vines at the Cape, you get your final payment. See, it says so here. Ninety florins.' But Paul noticed that he did not hand over the promissory note; he kept it, saying, 'This goes to the captain of your ship.'

At dusk that night the Huguenots gathered in the old French church, two hundred and ninety children and women and men who had dared the terrors of this age to retain their faith. They had braved dogs that hunted them, and men who rode after them on swift horses, and frontier guards who shot at them. They had crossed strange lands and come to towns where their language was unknown, but they had persevered, these wood-workers, and vintners and schoolteachers. They had sought freedom as few in their generation had sought it, volunteering their fortunes and their lives that they might live according to the rules they believed in. And now they were embarking upon the final adventure, this long passage in rolling ships to a land about which they knew nothing—except that when they reached it they would be free.

'Cling to your God,' the minister cried in French. 'Cling to the inspired teachings of John Calvin. And above all, cling to your language, which is the badge of your courage. Bring up your children to respect that language, as we in exile here in Holland have respected it against all adversity. It is the soul of France, the song of freedom. Let us pray.'

In the morning Paul led his family from the Bosbeecq home and lined them up on the bridge over the canal. 'Oudezijdsvoorburgwal,' he said for the last time. 'Always remember that when we were naked, the good people on this canal clothed us, as it says in the Bible. Keep that name in your heart.'

He then led them to the house of Mijnheer van Doorn, where he knocked on the door, asking that the Widows Bosbeecq appear, and when they did, he told his sons, 'Remember these good women. They saved our lives with their generosity.'

Next he took them to the French church, where the doors were opened for families to say their last prayers, and inside its warm hospitality he and his family prayed in French, committing themselves again to the promises made the night before.

When they left the church and started toward the waterfront where the ships waited, Paul saw as if for the first time the quiet grandeur of this city, the solid walls behind which sat the solid merchants, the stout churches with their stout Dutch ministers, and above all, the charity of the place—the simple goodness of these burghers who had accepted refugees from all the world because they knew that if a nation could feed and manage itself, it could accommodate strangers.

He was sorry to leave. Had he reached Holland sooner in his life, he might have become a Dutchman, but he was French, indelibly marked with the mercurial greatness of that land, and Holland was not for him.

Seven different Compagnie ships would carry the Huguenots to their new home. They left at various times and encountered various conditions. Some made the long run in ninety days; the poor *China*, buffeted all the way by adverse winds, required a hundred and thirty-seven, by which time many of its Frenchmen were dead. The De Prés and sixty others were loaded upon the *Java*, but not by plan. There were two ships at the wharf that day, *Java* and *Texel*, and Paul was inclined to choose the latter, but his friend Vermaas would not allow it: 'Look at the planking, Paul.' He looked and saw nothing amiss, but Vermaas said, 'It's uneven, not laid on carefully. Bad in one, bad in all.' And he led the family to the gangway of the *Java*.

This occasioned some difficulty because friends of the De Prés were already aboard the *Texel*, and the boys wanted to stay with them. But Vermaas had convinced Paul that the *Java* was safer, so there were tearful farewells, and kisses blown and promises to farm together in the new land —and it was appropriate that the parting should have been sorrowful, for after the *Texel* passed Cape St. Vincent at the tip of Portugal, where Prince Henry the Navigator had dreamed of voyages like this, it ran into heavy seas and perished.

The *Java* was a medium ship, not small and swift like a flute, nor large and wallowing like an East Indiaman. It was a slow ship, requiring a hundred and thirty days for the tedious passage, and it carried no lemons or pickled cabbage. For four long months the passengers ate only salted meat, and scurvy rampaged through the lower decks.

They were dreadful, these low-ceilinged hovels below the waterline. Fresh air was unknown, cleanliness impossible. Men emptied their bowels in corners and children lay white and gasping on filthy bunks. During the transit of the equator the temperatures were intolerable and dying people pleaded for a breath of air, but when the lower latitudes were reached, the next to die cried for blankets.

At the hundredth day Paul became aware that his wife, Marie, was not handling the long passage at all well. Her life in the cold, damp shack close to the river IJ in Amsterdam had started a lung congestion which had never really mended, and now, with worsening conditions below-decks, she began to cough blood. Frantically Paul sought assistance among the passengers, but to no avail. There were scholars aboard the *Java,* and a failed clergyman, and some excellent farmers, but no doctors or nurses, and Paul had to watch in despair as his wife declined.

'Marie,' he pleaded, 'we must walk on deck. To catch the breezes.'

'I cannot move,' she whispered, and when he forced her to her feet, he saw that her knees crumpled, so he returned her to the filthy bed.

He sought counsel among the women passengers, and all they could do was look gloomily at the stricken Frenchwoman and shake their heads lugubriously. It was no use appealing to the crew, for they were a miserable lot. Dutch sailors of merit preferred to work the Baltic ships, from which they could return to their homes periodically; also, the pay was better. For the long passages to Batavia, the Lords XVII had to rely principally on those untrained Germans whom De Pré had seen outside the Compagnie offices. They were not sailors, nor were they disciplined. For twenty years they had been conducting religious warfare back and forth across Germany, and it was unreasonable to think that they would now settle down and obey orders. Uncertain of what their Dutch officers were saying, totally unable to comprehend the French emigrants, they barely kept the ship afloat, and it was probably they who had been responsible for the sinking of the *Texel:* the Dutch captain had surely shouted the right order at the moment of peril, but his sailors had not responded.

So the *Java* rolled and pitched through the South Atlantic, with all hands praying that the wind would steady so they might make land before everyone was dead. Under these circumstances it was not strange that Marie de Pré should sink closer and closer to unconsciousness; her husband watched in horror as her vital signs diminished.

'Marie!' he pleaded. 'We must go aloft. You must walk and regain your strength.' As he argued with her three sailors moved through the filthy quarters collecting bodies, and Paul ran to them begging for fresh water for his wife. The Germans looked at him and grunted. The Cape would soon be reached and then these troublesome passengers would be gone, such of them as had survived.

Long before any sailor could win his silver schilling for crying, 'Table Mountain!' Marie de Pré fell into a coma, and since there was no proper clergyman aboard the rolling ship, the Dutch sick-comforter was summoned. He was a small, round fellow with rheumy eyes and the self-effacing manner of one who had tried to pass the courses at Leiden University and failed. Forbidden to preach like a real minister, he discharged his deep convictions by serving as general handyman to the Dutch church; especially he comforted those who were about to die.

As soon as he saw Marie he said, 'We'd better fetch her children,' and when Henri and Louis appeared he took their hands, drew them to him, and said softly in Dutch, 'Now's the time for courage, eh?'

'Could we pray in French?' Paul asked, hoping that his wife would be heartened by the language she had used as a child in Caix.

'Of course,' the sick-comforter said, but since he spoke not a word of French, he nodded to Paul, indicating that he must do the praying. 'It will ease her,' he said, even though he knew that she would never again hear human speech.

'Great God in heaven,' Paul prayed, 'we have come so far in obedience to Thy commands. Save Thy daughter Marie that she may see the new home to which Thou hast brought us.' When he finished, the sick-comforter clasped the two boys and prayed with them in his language, after which he said in a low voice, 'We can call the sailors now. She's dead.'

'No!' Paul shouted, and the fury with which he embraced his wife, who had accompanied him so far and with so gentle a compliance, made those about him weep.

'Call the sailors,' the sick-comforter said forcefully. 'Boys, you must kiss your mother goodbye,' and he edged them toward the pitiful bier.

In due time two German sailors shoved their way through the passengers, took the corpse away, and holding it aloft, pitched it into the sea, after which the sick-comforter indicated that he would lead public prayers for those who were still ambulatory. A stout Dutch merchant who had once served as deacon at Old Church pushed him contemptuously aside as unworthy; he would do the praying, and all on deck bowed their heads.

When the *Java* finally anchored in the lee of Table Mountain, Paul de Pré, thirty pounds lighter than when he sailed, reported to the captain, asking for his final payment for acquiring the grapevines, but instead of handing over any money, the captain informed Paul that Mijnheer van Doorn had arranged for the delivery of some one hundred and twenty acres of land toward the eastern mountains, and he produced a document affirming this: 'The Compagnie Commander at De Kaap is directed to give the French emigrant Paul de Pré sixty morgen of the best land, contiguous to the farm of Willem van Doorn in the settlement of Stellenbosch, there to raise grapes and make wine.'

By paying De Pré in Compagnie land rather than his own money, Van Doorn had saved himself ninety florins.

Paul—brooding over the loss of his wife—was halfway across the desolate flats before the immensity of Africa struck him, and he was suddenly overcome with dread lest this enormous continent reject him, tossing him back

into the sea. The land was so bleak, the vast emptiness so foreboding that
he began to shiver, feeling himself rebuked for his insolence. Clasping his
sons to protect them from the loneliness he felt, he muttered in French,
'Our grapes will never grow in this godforsaken soil.'

That night the Dutchman in whose wagon he was riding pitched
camp on the loneliest stretch of the flatlands, and Paul stayed awake, listening to the howling wind and testing the harsh, sterile earth with his
fingers. Driven with fear, he rose to inspect his grape cuttings, to see if
they were still moist, and as he replaced their wrappings he thought:
They are doomed.

But toward the end of the second day, when the laden wagon completed its traverse of the badlands, he was allowed a gentler view of
Africa, for they now traveled along the bank of a lovely river edged by
broad meadows and protected by encompassing hills. He thought: This is
finer than anything I knew in France or Holland! A man could make his
home here!

Begging the driver to halt, he lifted his sons down so that they could
feel the good earth that was to be their home, and when he had filtered it
through his fingers he looked up at the Dutchman and shouted in French,
'We shall build a vineyard so great . . .' When the driver looked at him
in stolid unconcern, for he understood not a word De Pré was saying,
Paul cried in Dutch, 'Good, eh?' and the driver pointed ahead with his
whip: 'Ahead, even better.'

They camped that night beside the river, and by noon next morning
they saw something that sealed Paul's love of his new home. It was a
farmhouse, low and wide, built of mud bricks and wattles, and so set
down against the hills rising behind it that it seemed always to have been
there. He noticed that it stood north to south, so that the west face looked
toward Table Mountain, still visible on the far horizon. From this secure
house a lawn of grass reached out, with four small huts along each side for
tools and chickens and the storage of hay; they were so placed, and at
such an angle, that they seemed like arms stretching to invite strangers,
and when Paul had seen the entire he whispered to himself, '*Mon Dieu!* I
should like to own this farm!'

'Has the master a daughter?' he asked the driver.
'He does.'
'How old?' he asked casually.
'Nine, I think.'
'Oh.' He said this in such a flat, disappointed voice that he added
quickly, lest he betray himself, 'That's good. Someone for my boys to play
with.'
'He has sons, too. Nine and eight.'
'Interesting.'
'But you understand, the farm really belongs to the old man.'
'Who?'

'Willem van Doorn. And his old wife Katje.'

'Three generations?'

'Working the fields, you live a long time.'

When they reached the farmhouse, walking down the lane between the eight huts, a tall Dutchman, broad of face and open in manner, came out to greet them: 'I'm Marthinus van Doorn. Are you the Frenchman?'

'Paul de Pré, and these are my sons Henri and Louis.'

'Annatjie!' the farmer cried. 'Come meet our neighbors!' And from the house came a tall, gaunt woman with broad shoulders and big hands. She was obviously quite a few years older than her husband, in her late thirties perhaps, and she bore the look of one who had worked extremely hard. She did not smile easily, as her husband had done when greeting the strangers, but she did extend a practical welcome: 'We've been waiting for your knowledge of grapes.'

'Is it true, you've made wine?' her husband asked.

'A great deal,' Paul said, and for the first time the woman smiled.

'The old man is out with the slaves,' Van Doorn said. 'Shall we go see him?'

But before they could depart, a high, complaining whine came from the back of the house: 'Who's out there, Annatjie?'

'The Frenchman.'

'What Frenchman?' It was a woman's voice, conveying irritation that things had not been explained.

'The one from Amsterdam. With new vines.'

'Nobody tells me anything,' and after a bit of shuffling, the door creaked open and a white-haired woman, partially stooped, came protestingly into the sunlight. 'Is this the Frenchman?' she asked.

'Yes,' her daughter-in-law said patiently. 'We're taking him into the fields to meet the old man.'

'You won't find him,' the old woman muttered, retreating to the shadows of the house.

They did find him, a crippled old man in his mid-sixties, walking sideways as he supervised the slaves in pruning vines. 'Father, this is the Frenchman who knows how to make good wine.'

'After thirty years they send someone,' he joked. Since that first joyous pressing decades ago, hundreds of thousands of vines had been planted at the Cape, assuring a local supply of wine, but even the best vintage remained far inferior to those of Europe.

The old man jammed his pruning knife into his belt, walked awkwardly to greet the newcomer, and said, 'Now let's figure out where your land's to be.'

'I have a map . . .'

'Well, let's fetch it, because it's important that you get started right.'

When the map was spread, the old man was delighted: 'Son, they've given you the very best land available. Sixty morgen! With water right from the river! Where will you build your house?'

'I haven't seen the land yet,' Paul said hesitantly.

'Let's see it!' the old man cried, almost as if the land were his and he was planning his first house. 'Annatjie, Katje! Get the boys and we'll go see the land.'

So the entire Van Doorn establishment—Willem and Katje; Marthinus and Annatjie; and the children Petronella, Hendrik and little Sarel—set off to see the Frenchman's land, and after they had surveyed it and assessed its strengths, all agreed that he must build his house at the foot of a small mound that would protect it from eastern winds. De Pré, however, said with a certain stubbornness, 'I'll build it down here,' but his reasons for doing so he would not divulge. They were simple: when the Van Doorns indicated the spot they were recommending, he immediately noticed that it did not balance the house they had built, and he wanted his home to be in harmony with theirs, for he was convinced that one day these two farms must be merged, and when that time came he wanted the various buildings to be in balance.

'We'll put it here,' he said, and when several of the Van Doorns started to protest the obvious unwisdom of such a location, old Willem quieted them: 'Look! If the house is put here, it balances ours over there. The valley looks better.'

'Why, so it does,' Paul said, and soon the building commenced. The Van Doorns sent their slaves to work on the walls, as if the house were to be their own, while the three De Prés toiled alongside the swarthy Madagascans.

'De Pré's a Frenchman,' Willem said approvingly. 'He knows how to work for what he wants.' And as the house grew, its mud bricks neatly aligned, the Van Doorns had to concede that it was not only spacious, but also solid and attractive.

'It's a house that needs a woman,' old Katje said, and on the next evening when the Frenchman ate at her house, she asked him bluntly, 'What are your plans for finding a wife?'

'I have none.'

'You better get some. Now, you take Marthinus'—she pointed to her sturdy son—'he was born at the Cape when there were no women, none at all available for young men. So we moved out here to Stellenbosch, except it wasn't named that in those years, and here I was—the only woman for miles around. So what to do?'

Paul looked at Marthinus and then at Annatjie, and asked, 'How did he find her?'

'Simple,' Katje continued. 'She was a King's Niece.'

This news was so startling that Paul stared in a most ungentlemanly manner at the tall, ungainly woman. 'Yes,' Katje said, 'this one was a King's Niece, and you'd better be sending for one of them, too.'

'What do you mean?'

'Orphans. Amsterdam's full of girl orphans. No one to give them in marriage, no dowry, so we call them the King's Nieces, and he gives them a small dowry and ships them out to Java and the Cape.'

'How did . . .'

'How did Marthinus know that Annatjie was his? When news of the ship reached out here, we supposed all the girls would be gone. But I told Marthinus, "Son, there's always a chance." So he rode at a gallop, and when he got to the wharf all the girls were gone.'

She placed her work-worn hands on the table, then smiled at her husband. 'I was what you might call a King's Niece also. My rich uncle shipped me out here to marry this one. Never saw him before I landed. Thirty years ago.'

'But if the girls were all gone, how did your son . . .'

Old Katje looked at Marthinus and laughed. 'Spirit, that's what he had. Like his father. You've heard that Willem chopped down four bitter almond so we could escape from the Cape. I predicted he would be hanged. I said, "Willem, you'll be hanged."'

'What did Marthinus do?'

'Got to the ship, all the girls gone. But before he rode back empty-handed he heard that one of the men at the fort didn't like the girl he got, so he shouted, "I'll take her!" And one of the other men said, "You haven't seen her!" But Marthinus shouted again, "I'll take her," and the girl was sent for, and there she is.'

Paul could not determine in what spirit the woman pointed to her daughter-in-law, whether in derision for being so much older than her son, or in disgust at her being so ungainly, or in pride for having had the strength to surmount such a poor beginning. 'Look at her fine children,' the old woman said, and Paul noticed that the three youngsters were looking at their mother with love. He would never have told his children such a story, but when he got his sons back into their house, he was startled to hear Henri say, 'Father, I hope that when you go to the ship, you get someone like Annatjie.'

The Huguenot boys were finding their new home even more exciting than the canals of Amsterdam. The spaciousness enchanted them; they loved the flashing sight of animals moving through the swards of long grass; and playing with the Van Doorn children was a joy. But the Dutchman they loved was old Willem. He moved slowly among his vines, his left leg out of harmony with his right, and he coughed a lot, but he was a reservoir of stories about Java and the Spice Islands and the siege of Malacca.

He took delight in arranging surprises for them: cloves to chew on so their breath would be sweet, and games with string. He let them watch the Van Doorn slaves, great blacks from Angola and Madagascar, and then one afternoon he told them, 'Boys, tomorrow night I have the real surprise. You can try to guess what it's to be, but I shan't tell you.'

At home they discussed with their father what it might be: perhaps a horse of their own, or a slave boy whom they could keep, or a hunting trip. They could not imagine what the old man had for them, and it was with trembling excitement that they crossed the fields at dusk to join the seven Van Doorns.

The old lady was complaining that too much fuss was being made, but even so, no one told the French boys what the surprise was to be, and with some anxiety they sat down for the evening meal, where the old ones talked endlessly as a slave woman and two Hottentots served them.

'Tell me in simple words,' Marthinus said, 'what a Huguenot is.'

'I'm a Huguenot,' Paul said. 'These two boys are Huguenots.'

'But what are you?'

'Frenchmen to begin with. Protestants next. Followers of John Calvin.'

'You believe as we do?'

'Of course. You in Dutch, we in French.'

'I hear you Huguenots were badly treated in France.'

'Tormented and thrown in jail and sometimes killed.'

'How did you escape?'

'Through the forests, at night.' No one spoke. 'And when we were safely in Holland, your brother, Karel . . . He's an important man, you know, in the Lords XVII. He sent me back to fetch the vines I've brought you. I took my son Henri with me to confuse the Catholic authorities. This boy crept through the forest with me to steal the grapevines, and if we'd been caught by the soldiers . . .'

'What would have happened?' young Hendrik asked.

'I'd have been chained to a ship for life. He'd have been put where they turn Huguenot boys into Catholic boys in a jail, and his brother here would never have seen him again.'

'Was it really so cruel?' Marthinus asked.

'It was death to be a Calvinist.'

'It was in our family, too,' Willem suddenly said. 'My great-grandfather was hanged.'

'He was?' Louis asked in awe, all thoughts of the surprise buried in this revelation of family courage.

'And my grandfather died in war, fighting for our religion. And as a little girl my mother used to gather with her family like this and do something that would have caused her execution . . .'

'What do you mean?' Louis de Pré asked.

'She would have been hanged if they had caught her.'

'What did she do?'

'Blow out the candles,' Willem said, and when only one flickered he produced from the next room the old Bible, which he opened at random, and when the children were quiet he read a few verses in Dutch. Then, with his hand spread out upon the pages, he told them, 'In those days your grandfathers died if they were caught reading like this.' Closing the heavy cover, he told the children, 'But because we persisted, God came to comfort us. He gave us this land. These good houses. These vines.'

Young Hendrik van Doorn had heard these tales before, but they had made no impression on him. Now, with the Frenchman telling comparable stories, he understood that tremendous things had happened in France and Holland, and that he was the recipient of a powerful tradition. From that night on, whenever the Dutch Reformed Church was mentioned, he would visualize a young boy creeping through the forest, a man chained to a galley bench, one of his ancestors hanged, and especially a group of people huddled over a Bible at night.

'Light the candles!' old Willem cried. 'And we'll have the surprise!'

'Hooray!' the Huguenot boys shouted as Annatjie left the room, to reappear bearing a brown-gold crock with no handles. As she came to the table she looked momentarily at her father-in-law, who nodded slightly toward Louis. Going to him, she placed the crock before him, and he looked in to see the golden brown crust with the raisins and lemon peel and cherries peeking through.

'Oh!' he cried. 'Can I have some?'

'You can have it all,' Willem said. 'I made it for you.'

The three Huguenots stared at him, unable to conceive that this wrinkled old farmer could also cook, but when the crock was passed to Paul, so that he could serve, he jabbed his spoon into the crust and they applauded.

While the others ate, Paul studied the old Dutchman and was confused. Willem had proved the most generous of neighbors, lending slaves whenever needed; he laughed with the children and now proved himself an able cook. He was in no way the dour and heavy Dutchman Paul had expected, but he did have one mortal failing: he could not make good wine. In a way, this was not surprising, for none of his countrymen could, either. For a thousand years Frenchmen to the south of Holland and Germans to the east had made fine wine, but the Dutch had never mastered it.

'Van Doorn,' Paul said one day in exasperation, 'to make good wine requires fifteen proper steps. And you've done all of them wrong except one.'

Willem chuckled. 'What one?'

'The direction of your vines. They don't fight the wind and the sun.' De Pré studied the lines and asked, 'How did you get that right?'

And then an inexplicable thing happened. The old man stood among his vines, and dropped his hands, and tears came to his eyes. His shoulders shook, and after a long time he said, 'A girl instructed me a long time ago. And they branded her on the face, here and here. And she fled into the

wilderness with my sons. And by the grace of God she may still be alive
. . . somewhere out there.' He placed his hands over his face and bowed
his head. 'I pray to God she's still alive.'

So many things were implied in what the old man said that Paul concluded it was wisest to ask nothing, so he returned to the making of wine:
'Really, Mijnheer, you've done everything wrong, but because your vines
know you love them, they have stayed alive, and when my good grapes
join them, I do believe we can blend the musts into something good.'

'You mean, we can make wine they won't laugh at in Java?'

'That's why I came,' De Pré said, and his jaw jutted out. 'In two years
they'll be begging for our wine in Java.'

Inadvertently he brought dilemmas into the Van Doorn household. One
day, while listening to his sons at play, he realized to his dismay that they
had shouted at one another for upwards of half an hour without once having used a French word. They had begun to conduct their lives wholly in
Dutch, and no matter how carefully he spoke to them in French at meal-
time or at prayers, they preferred to respond in Dutch. He recalled the
farewell sermon of the clergyman at the Huguenot church in Amsterdam:
'Above all, cling to your language . . . It is the soul of France, the song of
freedom.'

When it became apparent that no discipline from him was going to
make his sons retain their language, he appealed to the Van Doorns for
help, but they were aghast at his effrontery. 'You're in a Dutch colony,'
Katje said bluntly. 'Speak Dutch.'

'When you want to register your land,' Willem said, 'you'll have to do
it in Dutch. This isn't some French settlement.'

'It's quite proper that church services should be in Dutch,' Marthinus
continued. 'Ours is a Dutch church,' and when De Pré pointed out that in
Amsterdam the Dutch had not only permitted a French church to operate
but had also paid the salary of the foreign minister, Marthinus growled,
'They must have been idiots.'

Despite their arguments, Paul still felt that the Compagnie should duplicate the Dutch government's generosity and provide the Huguenots
with a church of their own, and he started looking about for fellow
Frenchmen, but found none, and for good reason. The Lords XVII, afraid
that the immigrants might coalesce, just as De Pré was now proposing,
and form an indigestible mass within the settlement, speaking an alien
language and demanding extraterritorial rights, had issued an edict to prevent this error:

> The Huguenots shall be scattered across the countryside rather than
> settled in one spot, and every effort shall be made to stamp out their
> language. Legal proceedings, daily intercourse, and above all, educa-

tion of the young must be conducted in Dutch, and no concession whatever shall be made to their preferred tongue.

The threat of a divided colony was not trivial, for although the number of Huguenots was small—only one hundred and seventy-six in the main wave of immigration—so was the number of Dutch, for in 1688 when De Pré and his first group landed, the entire Compagnie roster listed only six hundred and ten white people, counting infants, and a frightening portion of these were of German descent. At times it seemed that the Germans must ultimately submerge the Dutch, except for two interesting factors: on the rare occasion that a German found a marriageable woman, she was invariably Dutch; and the Germans tended to be ill-educated peasants who readily accepted the Dutch language.

Not so the Huguenots. They were both well educated and devoted to their language, and if left to cluster in xenophobic groups, might form an intractable minority. Since the Dutch did not propose to let this happen, the French were scattered, some to Stellenbosch, some higher up in a place called Fransch Hoek, and others in a choice valley well to the north. But no matter where they found refuge, they encountered this driving effort to eradicate their language, which De Pré was determined to resist. In the letters he dispatched to the other settlements he wrote:

> The most sacred possession a man can have, after his Bible, is his native tongue. To steal this is to steal his soul. A Huguenot thinks differently from a Dutchman and expresses this thinking best in his native language. If we do not protect our glorious French in church, in law and in school, we surrender our soul. I say we must fight for our language as we would for our lives.

This was such open subversion that Cape officials felt obligated to send investigators to Stellenbosch, and after brief questioning, these men proposed throwing De Pré in jail, but the Van Doorns protested that he was a good neighbor, needed for the making of wine. The latter point impressed the officials, who lectured De Pré at a public hearing: 'Only because your friends have defended you do you escape imprisonment. You must remember that your sole duty is to be loyal to the Compagnie. Forget your French. Speak Dutch. And if you circulate another inflammatory petition, you will be ejected from the colony.'

Despite this censure, De Pré did gain one of his objectives: the refugees were given permission to build a small church for the minister who had sailed in one of the ships from Amsterdam, and behind its whitewashed walls only French was heard. But the children, and especially Henri and Louis de Pré, continued to speak mainly in Dutch, and it became apparent that the Compagnie's efforts to stamp out French would in the end succeed.

It was agreed between the Van Doorns and the De Prés that the question of language would be discussed no further; each side had made its position clear and only animosity could ensue if the arguing continued. Of course, no one supposed that any peace treaty would be honored by old Katje, and whenever she gave the De Pré boys a goodie she would tell them, 'Say thank you, like a good Dutch boy,' and the boys would say, 'Hartelijck bedanckt, Ouma!'

One night she asked Paul, 'Why did you come to a Dutch land if you don't like it?'

'I do like it,' Paul said. 'Look at my fields.'

'But how did you get here?'

'Your husband's brother sent me to steal the grapevines, as I told you.'

'How is the old thief?'

'Katje!' Willem protested.

'Well, he is an old thief, isn't he?' she demanded of De Pré.

'If he is, he's a smart one,' Paul said. 'He married one of the richest widows in Amsterdam.'

'I'm sure of that,' Katje snapped, and when De Pré revealed the clever manner in which the Widows Bosbeecq had outmaneuvered Karel in the matter of their seven ships, she chortled.

'Nine cheers for the widows!' she cried, then grabbing her granddaughter Petronella, she said solemnly, 'If you ever become a widow, outsmart them, Petra. Keep your wits about you and outsmart them.'

'Grandmother!' Annatjie said sharply. 'Don't talk like that to a child.'

'And you too!' the old lady said. 'If you become a widow, which God forbid, watch yourself. Women are smarter than men, much smarter, but in times of emotion—'

'But you see,' Paul broke in, 'the Widows Bosbeecq were forewarned about Karel. They knew he was a tricky man.'

Suddenly Katje leaned forward, and reaching out to grasp the Huguenot by his arm, she asked, 'How did they know that?'

'They warned me about him when I went to work at his big house. They were ready to marry him, you understand, either of them, but they knew he was a thief . . . because of what he had done to you.' At this point he addressed Willem.

Katje tugged at his arm: 'What do you mean?'

'The way he stole from your husband.'

Sharp tug: 'Stole what?'

'When he sold your mother's house in Batavia. Everyone knew that half the money was for Willem, but he kept it for himself . . . all of it.'

'I knew it! I knew it!' the old woman shouted, jumping from her chair and rampaging back and forth from table to door. 'I told you he was a thief.' Halfway back to the table she stopped, remembered old days, and cried, 'I told him to his face. "You're stealing from us."' On and on she recalled scenes of that last confrontation when she had divined what the couple was up to. At the end she fell into her chair, dropped her head on the table and wept.

'There, there,' Willem whispered.

'But we could have had that money. We could have gone back to Holland in style. We didn't have to work like slaves . . .'

'I would never have gone,' Willem said, and his wife looked up at him in astonishment, then with slow understanding as he asked, 'Would you have missed this valley for a smelly house on a smelly canal?'

But as the De Prés started to walk home they could still hear the old woman haranguing her family: 'Always remember, your uncle was a thief. He stole what was rightfully yours.' On and on, until they could hear no more, she lectured on how she had been right, back in 1664.

It annoyed Paul that his sons used Dutch to refer to Katje. It was 'Ouma gave us a cookie.' 'Ouma said we could sleep over there.' It meant *old mother*, hence *grandmother*, and was a term of endearment, for if Ouma gave her husband a bad time over the various mistakes he made in his life, she compensated by her love for children. She knew they needed discipline and she was the one to dispense it, but she also knew they needed love, and she was as indulgent with the De Pré children as with the Van Doorn.

One morning, when Henri and Louis had gone to the big house to beg sweets from the old lady, they ran home in tears. 'Ouma's dead! Ouma died last night!' Three days later she was buried at the foot of a hill, and on the way back from the grave Marthinus said, 'She's had time to get to heaven, and right now she's advising St. Peter, sternly.'

Her death had a curious aftermath. Old Willem, recalling how often she had badgered him to enlarge the farmhouse—seeking by this means to finally compensate for the cramped hut at the Cape—decided that he would at last accede to her wishes. When he announced that he was riding to the Cape to buy a Malay carpenter, his son asked why, and he replied to Annatjie, as if she were old Katje's surrogate, 'It's about time I made this house the way she wanted it.'

By starting early and riding hard through the heat of day, the old man reached the Cape before dusk, and what he saw always delighted him. The bay now had a quay at which ships could tie, a handsome new fort of gray stone, streets with solid houses and spacious orchards growing pears and lemons and oranges and plums and apples. More than half the white people in the colony lived in the town, which had every aspect of a thriving community—except one: the entire place contained not a single formal store; the Compagnie felt that the duty of the Cape was to refresh its fleets and collect goods for use in Java. What local buying and selling might be necessary would be done by the Compagnie, from its offices, and no merchant class would be allowed at the Cape.

But Amsterdam was a world away from the raw settlement in Table Valley, and its restrictions had the opposite effect from those intended: practically everyone at the Cape became a secret huckster, dealing directly with passing ships, hoarding clandestine stores in their homes, selling, bartering, smuggling until they became so skilled that they earned their entire living at the business. Corruption was also rife among Compagnie officials, as poorly paid as they were resentful of service at this insignificant and forsaken outpost; venality reached to the top, as proved by the vast private estates operated by some Compagnie men.

The Lords XVII had never sought a proper settlement here and constantly proclaimed that free burghers were to keep within the bounds established by the authorities in Amsterdam. Physical and spiritual lives alike were minutely prescribed, for the truth was that the Lords were both perplexed and frightened by the vastness of Africa. Holland was a small, hemmed-in country and provided the scale by which their Cape entrepôt would always be judged. The Lords believed that if, through their Council of Policy at the Cape, they were able to dictate what could be read, or spoken in church, or discussed publicly, they would retain control; so they instructed the farmers how to conduct their leisure hours, their wives how to dress, and all citizens when to go to bed at night.

But Willem had the Lords XVII to thank for providing him with an opportunity to purchase a carpenter; the Lords had ordered: 'No homeward-bound official may bring his slaves with him to Holland.' So Willem picked up a bargain and hurried to the Castle, as the new five-bastioned fort was now called, to register his property, but he found the officials more interested in Paul de Pré than in the deed of sale.

'Tell us, does De Pré still converse in French?'

'Not with us. We don't speak it.'

'But with his children?'

'When his boys are with us, they speak Dutch.'

'Is he circulating any more petitions?'

'He's too busy with the grapes.' Had De Pré been manufacturing grenades, Willem would not have betrayed him.

With visible reluctance the Compagnie granted permission to buy the young Malay carpenter, Bezel Muhammad, whose name betrayed his mixed origin—the first deriving from his black Madagascan mother, the second from his brown Malaccan father. He spoke five pidgin languages, none well, and was a master of saw and hammer. He was reluctant to leave a town which contained other Coloureds, with whom he liked to associate, but he saw advantages in moving closer to where trees grew. He preferred the timber of Africa to the mahogany of Mauritius or the heavier imported woods from Java. He also liked the forthright manner of Van Doorn, and promised, 'I build good.'

As they were leaving the Castle an official called out after them, 'Remember, you're responsible for that slave! See that he doesn't run

away!' Willem agreed, thinking: How men change. When Jango wanted
to run, I helped him. But for this slave I paid my own money, so I must
guard him.

Willem could not have foreseen the effect that Bezel Muhammad
would have upon the valley. The children loved helping him with his
tasks, accompanying him into the forest in search of stinkwood, that heavy
dark wood which smelled so foul if a tree rotted, but looked so grand
when planed down and polished. Annatjie, now in sole charge of the
house, appreciated his helpfulness, but it was Paul de Pré who was
affected most deeply.

He quickly discovered that Bezel was an artist, not only in wood but
in all building, and it was he who argued Willem into allowing the slave
to refinish the west façade of the house, the side facing Table Mountain:
'What we should do, Willem, is make the long house not only a little
bigger, but a little more pleasant.'

'That's what Katje always wanted.'

'We'll do it for her,' Paul said, but often as Willem watched the en-
ergy with which the Huguenot worked he gained the impression that
Paul was building not for Katje, but for himself. On important points the
Huguenot was adamant.

'The front must be kept long and low, but over the door we want a
beautiful gable, like the ones I knew in Holland.' He sketched the graceful curves that would define the gable and determine its height, and although he consulted the two Van Doorn men on what materials Bezel
Muhammad should use, it was he who directed each stage of the construction.

It was De Pré's idea also to build a wing projecting backward from the
front door, so that the house took the form of a T, with the kitchen and
serving areas in the stem at the rear. When the house was completed, he
found a way to finish off its long clean walls with cow manure, which
hardened like stone, and then to whitewash them so that they gleamed
pure-white. But because the mud-and-manure produced an uneven surface,
when the whitewash was applied, it assumed magnificent planes and dips
and protuberances which reflected light in a thousand different ways. Like
a crystal jewel set among trees, the gabled whiteness symbolized the scin-
tillating Dutch-Huguenot alliance which, with its strong German component, was forming a new society.

'And now the surprise!' De Pré announced as all looked with pleasure
at their new dwelling. 'What I have in mind is something else Katje
would have liked.' And he sketched in the dust his plan for a stoep, a
front porch on which to rest when the sun went down behind Table
Mountain. It was agreed by all that Katje would indeed have liked this,
would have sat there at the end of day; so the gallant old woman, who
had rarely been given a moment to rest while alive, was memorialized by a
stoep on which her descendants would sit doing nothing.

'It mustn't be a high stoep,' De Pré cautioned, 'for that would mar the face. Just two courses of stone and only wide enough for two rocking chairs.' When it was finished, the Van Doorns applauded, and on the first evening when Annatjie tested the rockers, looking out to Table Mountain, she told her son Hendrik, 'It will be your job to care for these fields when your grandfather and your father are no longer here.' Later she would remember that when she said this, her son had turned away from the Cape and said, 'Grandfather always wanted to go that way. Didn't you?' And old Willem had agreed with his grandson: 'Go beyond the mountains. If I were younger, I'd build my farm out there, and to hell with the Compagnie.'

Bezel Muhammad had his own surprise for his new family. Having found several large stinkwood and yellow-wood trees, he had built a standing clothes cabinet, nine feet high, with finely polished swinging doors in front, a set of four drawers below, and feet carved in the form of an eagle's talon grasping an orb. In simple design the closet would have been handsome, but when the two woods, near-black and glowing gold, were alternated, the result was quite dazzling. It was a gift for Annatjie, but everyone agreed that Katje would have loved that armoire.

When De Pré used this word the Dutchmen looked at him askance, and even when he explained its meaning they resented it. 'That thing's a wall cupboard,' Marthinus said, and he was aghast at what De Pré suggested next. Leading the entire family to a spot well west of the remodeled house, he asked them to look at its quiet perfection as it nestled among its hills: 'See how all things fit together. The gable not too high, the stoep not too big, the walls reflecting the light. It's our palace in Africa.'

The Dutchmen did not like the analogy. Palaces were occupied by Spaniards and Frenchmen, and they had meant death to Calvinists. 'I want no palace on my land,' Marthinus said.

De Pré ignored him: 'There's a new palace building near Paris. Trianon it's called. Our African palace should be called that, too.'

'Ridiculous!' Marthinus cried, but De Pré said quietly, 'Because when we start to sell our wine, we'll need a good name for it. And if we call it Trianon, we'll catch everybody. A few will know it to be a good Cape wine. The main will think it's French.'

This made sense, and when De Pré saw that the Van Doorns were wavering, he dispatched Henri to fetch a bundle by the door, and when the lad rolled in the wrapped parcel, Paul carefully folded back the covering to display a beautifully made oaken cask, capable of holding a leaguer of wine, which Bezel Muhammad had decorated with a most handsome replica of the gabled house and the single word TRIANON.

Old Willem accepted the cask, and after he had studied it in various lights, said: 'We'll call it Trianon. Because my wine wasn't worth a stuiver till this fellow came along.'

* * *

In the years that followed, when the wine of Stellenbosch was gaining favorable attention both in Java and Europe, Bezel Muhammad continued to build, but only occasionally, his wall cupboards of the two contrasting woods, and whereas he took great pains to design each one in lovely balance—making his art the only one of high degree that flourished in the colony in these decades—he never exceeded that first handsome design. It stood in the bedroom to the left as one entered Trianon and was admired by all.

His cupboards were sold as soon as he could finish them, and at various farms in the Stellenbosch area they were prized. The slave who made them was in great demand when it came time to build a gable or enlarge a house, and this caused Annatjie some uneasiness, for although she was quite willing that her family profit from the work of their slave—Marthinus sold the cupboards and kept all but a few rix-dollars on each—she was not content that this skilled man should be without a wife, and it perplexed her as to how she might find him one.

When she raised the question at supper one night, Marthinus said, 'Most men who come out here live without women for years. Look at De Pré.'

'Yes,' she said, 'and I wonder about him, too.'

'Let him get one of the King's Nieces. The way I did.'

When next De Pré ate with them she raised the question: 'Paul, it's time you should ask the Compagnie to bring you a wife. You could write to Karel. He'd find you someone.'

'He'll not deal with that one,' Willem said sternly.

'But he can't always live alone,' Annatjie said, and she was so persuasive that De Pré drafted a careful letter to his old employer, asking for a wife. A year later Trianon received word that Karel van Doorn had died, his estate going to the Widows Bosbeecq.

So Annatjie turned her attention to Bezel, dispatching letters to the Cape to ascertain if there were any Muslim slave girls, or black ones, for that matter, seeing that he was half-black, who might be purchased, but there were none, and Bezel continued to live alone, building the houses and the furniture that became a feature in the elegant town of Stellenbosch.

It had a fine church now, broad streets lined with young oak trees, and a score of tidy small houses whose floors were smoothed brown with cow manure. It looked nothing like Holland, not too much like Java; it was a unique little gem of a town born of the South African experience, and no house excelled that one called Trianon.

And then a farm family moved nearby with a marriageable daughter, Andries Boeksma and his pretty child Sibilla. 'She's God's answer to our prayers,' Annatjie told Paul as soon as she heard the good news. Using the excuse of taking spiced apples to the newcomers, she studied Sibilla and drove back to Trianon, exultant—'Paul, Marthinus! She's just what we've prayed for'—and she insisted that the two men dress properly, kill a lamb and take it to the Boeksmas. She very much wanted to go along, but felt that to do so might betray her interest in having Sibilla meet the Huguenot widower.

'What happened?' she asked breathlessly when she and her husband were alone.

'I don't really understand,' Marthinus said. 'They took an instant dislike. They were barely civil.'

'What could have happened?'

'Well, Boeksma walked to the cart with me, and while Paul was saying goodbye to Mevrouw he confided that Sibilla would never marry a Frenchman, and on the way home Paul confided that he had no interest in her. He was most emphatic. Told me, "None whatever."'

With the most obvious stratagems Annatjie endeavored to ignite a romance between the two, inviting the Boeksmas twice to her table and lending Bezel for the building of their house, but Paul wanted nothing to do with Sibilla, and she in turn showed herself to be most uneasy in his presence. Before long she was betrothed to a widower from a farm at the north edge of town, and Paul was still without a wife.

When he left his sons with Annatjie for two weeks so that he could journey to Fransch Hoek, she was convinced that he had gone in search of a wife among the other Huguenots, but when he returned alone she found that he had only been agitating—as he had so often before—for the establishment of a French school. When Marthinus upbraided him for this, he repeated stubbornly, 'If a man loses his language, he loses his soul.'

Two interests kept the families united: their desire to produce a good wine, and their deepening faith in Calvinism. Like all Huguenots, Paul was fanatically devoted to his religion, and because his experience of repression was recent, he was apt to be more fiercely protective than his Dutch neighbors, none of whom had known the Spanish persecution personally. Had the Dutch of Stellenbosch wanted to relax the austerity of their Calvinism, the Huguenot immigrants would have protested. Back in Holland the Dutch were making gestures of conciliation with Catholics, especially their German neighbors, and occasionally a strain of this liberalism would surface at the Cape; when French ships put into the bay, officers and men were treated with respect, even though they were Catholic; but for the Huguenots that religion remained unspeakable, and whatever steps their church took had to be diametrically opposed to Rome.

This preoccupation with religion was illustrated when a band of raiders struck at the cattle of the Stellenbosch farmers. The attackers were a wild bunch of outcasts, slaves and renegade Hottentots who crept into Dutch kraals and in repeated sorties carried off many of the best animals.

Neighboring farmers assembled to retaliate, but their efforts made little impression along a hundred-mile frontier, so the burgher militia had to be summoned to launch a serious offensive. Every adult male in the district reported to Stellenbosch, and it was to this meeting that Farmer Boeksma rode up with three of his Hottentot servants equipped and armed for war.

'Madness!' several of the old-timers argued. 'You heard what the governor told us. "To allow them to bear arms is nothing less than putting a knife in their hands to slash our throats." '

'He was talking about slaves,' Boeksma reminded the men.

Over the years the Dutch had had so much trouble with their slaves, who persisted in trying to escape to freedom, that the most bizarre punishments were instituted: when one black woman enraged the community, the commander ordered that she be stripped, broken on the wheel, and tied to the ground while her breasts were ripped off by red-hot pincers, after which she was to be hanged, beheaded and quartered. When certain settlers protested this barbarity, the commander granted clemency: the woman was sewn into a canvas bag and thrown into the bay, where she struggled for half an hour before drowning.

'We must never arm slaves,' a cautious man warned.

'But these aren't slaves,' Boeksma pleaded. 'They're loyal. They believe in me like my own children.'

As he spoke, the armed servants stood silent. One could still be classified as a Hottentot, but the other two were Coloureds, and when Boeksma called them part of his family he spoke the truth, for there was no tribe or captaincy surviving in this area to which they could give their allegiance, no homeland, no human being except 'Groot Baas Boeksma.' They had accepted his God, his church, his way of life, and this was demonstrated daily in the language they spoke, an exciting mixture of Dutch-Malay-Portuguese-Hottentot. It was a good patois and it served them well in field and kitchen. A farmer might not be able to afford many slaves, but every settler was able to attract his complement of Hottentot-Coloured families; they tended the vineyards; they served his meals; they nursed his infants and minded his children, scolding when needed and whispering instructions in the language they were building from their disparate backgrounds.

Still, the idea of arming even such placid dark men was repugnant, and an impasse was reached between Boeksma, who wanted to do so, and the sager heads, who warned against it. It was the Huguenot De Pré who resolved the argument: 'I seem to remember a passage in our Bible. In the years when Abraham was still called Abram, his nephew Lot fell into trouble, and there was discussion as to how the commando might rescue him. And did not Abraham arm his servants and sally forth to save his nephew?'

None of the Dutchmen remembered this incident, but all agreed that if Abram really had armed his servants, that would constitute permission for them to do the same, so they consulted Willem, who offered his Bible to the worried men, and in the fourteenth chapter of Genesis, De Pré found specific instructions telling them what to do, but when he encountered trouble reading the Dutch he almost spoiled things by saying, 'In French it's clearer.' It had never occurred to his neighbors that God's word had ever appeared in any language but Dutch:

> 'And when Abram heard that his brother was taken captive, he armed his trained servants, born in his own house, three hundred and eighteen, and pursued them . . . And he brought back all the goods, and also brought again his brother Lot, and his goods, and the women also, and the people.'

What astounded these devout men was that when they added up those servants in the Stellenbosch region capable of fighting, they totaled three hundred and eighteen, and Andries Boeksma shouted, 'It's a revelation—a revelation from God Himself! A thousand years ago, nay, ten thousand, He foresaw our plight and instructed us to arm our servants.' And he asked the men to pray, expressing their thanks for this guidance, and when they rose they organized a punitive expedition, and for every animal the Hottentots had taken away, the Dutchmen brought back three.

From then on, no commando sallied forth without its complement of Hottentot-Coloured fighters, and few farmers would venture into the wilderness without their dark families trailing along with them. For generations this alliance would maintain, fortified sometimes by bloodlines when lonely men needed companionship, but more often based on a kind of acknowledged and gentle servitude, for they were, as Boeksma had said, 'Loyal.' As the Dutchmen traveled, the little dark men and women might not be visible, and they never ate at table, but they were there, one step behind the Groot Baas.

Willem did not accompany the raiders, and he refused for a good reason: he still hoped that some kind of peace might be brought about between white settlers and brown. 'You're no longer a good Dutchman,' Andries Boeksma chided when the victorious commando returned. 'You don't think like a man from Holland, and you don't act like a man from Java.'

'I've thought of that myself,' Willem said. 'I suppose I'm an Afrikaner.'

'A what?' Boeksma cried.

'An Afrikaner. A man of Africa.' It was the first time in history this designation had been used, and never would it apply more accurately. And when the day came that Willem's persistent lung disease, incurred by his hours on the horse, attacked and he lay dying, he counseled his grandchildren never to war with the Hottentots: 'Share Africa with them in peace.'

His sickbed stood in the left-hand room facing Bezel Muhammad's first cupboard, and he passed the pain-choked hours by studying afresh the lovely relationship between the two woods, dark and light. They seemed an augury of what the country he had discovered and settled might become.

No amount of Biblical glossing helped when the Van Doorns faced their real catastrophe, nor were the teachings of the Dutch Reformed Church of much assistance, either. One spring morning when Marthinus was working at the vines and the three De Prés were far away, he was summoned by the frantic ringing of a bell, and suspecting that this meant fire, he ran toward the big house, shouting, 'De Pré! De Pré! Where in hell are you?' But when he reached the house, and found only Annatjie, tall and red-faced, standing in the kitchen with Petronella, he was glad he had come alone.

'Send the boys away,' his wife said brusquely, and the two lads were dismissed, even though Hendrik, now thirteen, could guess that the emergency had something to do with babies.

When the boys were gone, Annatjie gasped, 'This one wants to marry Bezel Muhammad!' And when Marthinus looked at his fifteen-year-old daughter, she nodded so vigorously that her pigtails bobbed, giving her the look of a child.

Marthinus sat down. 'You want to marry a slave?' When his daughter nodded again, he asked, 'Does he know about this?' And before she could reply, he demanded, 'Do you have to get married?'

She shook her head and held out her hands to her father. 'I love him, and he's a good man.'

Marthinus ignored this for the moment and said, 'I could find you a dozen husbands at the Cape.'

'I know,' Petronella said, 'but I would not be happy with them, Father.'

The way she said *Father* melted Van Doorn. Extending his arms, he said, 'Before he died, old Willem told me he had wanted to marry a slave. Said he regretted not doing so every day of his life. Oh, he loved old Katje, you could see that . . .'

'Then, I can marry him?'

Marthinus looked at his wife, a woman who had contracted a marriage almost as bizarre: in her case she accepted a white husband she had never seen; Petronella was taking a black-brown man she had known for three years. When Annatjie shrugged, the girl took it as a sign that her marriage was approved, but her father said quietly, 'Leave us now, Petronella,' and when she was gone he raised questions too delicate for her ears: 'You know how the Compagnie feels about white and black . . .'

'The Compagnie's worried only about their sailors and soldiers who creep to the slave quarters.' Annatjie sniffed.

'And about men like Boeksma.'

'We all know about Boeksma and his servant girls.'

'With Petronella it is different. She's in love with her slave.' In his confusion Marthinus turned to his Bible, but found no guidance. Abraham had married his slave girl Hagar, and her offspring had populated half the earth, but they could find no account of an Israelite woman's taking a slave husband. There was, of course, constant fulmination against Israelite men marrying Canaanite women, but nothing about the reverse, and it began to look as if God was much more concerned about young men than about their sisters. They even found the obscure text in Ezra in which God, speaking through His prophet, commanded all men to put away their strange wives. They read aloud that extraordinary list of nearly a hundred men who had taken wives from among the Canaanites:

> 'And of the singers also; Eliashib: and of the porters; Shalum, and Telem, and Uri . . . And they gave their hands that they would put away their wives; and being guilty, they offered a ram of the flock for their trespass.'

In the end Marthinus realized that the decision must be made by the Van Doorns alone, and when reached, must be defended by them against whatever opposition the community might organize, so one afternoon he asked his wife to sit with him at the kitchen table, to which they summoned the young lovers.

'Are you determined to marry?' Marthinus asked.

'We are.'

The Van Doorns sat with folded hands, looking at the couple, and the more they studied Bezel the more acceptable he became. 'You are clean and hard-working,' Marthinus said. 'You're a good carpenter. You never praise your own work, but I can see you prize it.' Annatjie said, 'It's as if you combined the best of your two races, durable like the blacks, poetic like the Malays.' But then Marthinus observed ominously, 'And you also represent two very difficult problems.'

When Petronella asked what these were, he said, 'First, he can't marry a white woman while he remains a slave.'

'That's simple,' she said. 'Set him free.'

'Not so simple,' Marthinus said. 'Bezel, you must buy your freedom.'

The slave, having anticipated this impediment, nodded to Petronella, who from the folds of her dress produced a canvas bag containing coins, which she emptied onto the table.

'How did you collect them?' Marthinus asked.

'From the wall closets he makes,' Petronella explained. 'I save the money for him.'

Head bowed, Marthinus fumbled with the coins but did not count them. After a while he cleared his throat and pushed the money back toward his daughter. 'He is free. Keep the coins.' Then, sternly, he added, 'But the marriage will still be impossible unless he's a Christian.'

'He's willing to become one,' Petronella said.

'I was speaking to Bezel.'

'I think I'm already a Christian,' Bezel said, and when this was explored, the people at the table were satisfied that he told the truth, but when they approached the predikant to have him verify the fact, Paul de Pré heard of the negotiation and fell into a rage.

He was so eager to gain possession of Trianon, a house he had practically built, with vineyards he alone had saved from decay, that he had been quietly devising his own plans for Petronella. True, she was only fifteen and he thirty-four, but on a frontier where wives often died in childbirth, it was not uncommon for a patriarch to take himself four wives in sequence. The bride was always about seventeen, the man growing older and older. He had been giving serious thought to Petronella and now he heard with dismay that she was about to be married to a slave.

Frantic, he ran across to Trianon, bursting through the doors he had rebuilt. 'I've come to seek your daughter's hand in marriage.'

'She's already taken,' Annatjie said.

'Muhammad? The slave?'

'Yes.'

'But there hasn't been a wedding!'

'Perhaps there was, perhaps there wasn't,' Annatjie said calmly.

'You would never allow a slave . . .'

'Perhaps we will, perhaps we won't,' she said, and when he started to rave, she said without any show of anger, 'Neighbor De Pré, you're making a fool of yourself.'

Paul appealed to Marthinus, but he remembered too vividly his father's dying comment on what marriage meant at the edge of a wilderness: 'Tell Hendrik and Sarel to find the best women they can and cling to them. I could not have lived my life without Deborah's singing in my ears. I could never have built this refuge without Katje's help.'

'I think we'll let things work themselves out,' Marthinus said, and for five months he did not see De Pré at the vineyard, but when the time came to blend the wine, with Trianon's harsher grapes giving character to De Pré's gentler ones, Paul could not stay away, and it was he who made the final selections: 'This wine in barrels, for the slaves in Java. But this good one we put in casks for Europe.' And it was with this vintage that Trianon became an established name, even in Paris and London.

It was Annatjie who first detected Paul de Pré's grand design. She was a hard-minded woman who even as a child had learned to calculate what others might be wanting to do to her. Other unmarried girls at the orphanage had been afraid of emigrating to Brazil or South Africa, but she had perceived this as her only avenue of escape and had never moaned over the consequences of her act. When the man who chose her first at the Cape rejected her, she did not fly to tears, satisfied that someone else would want her in this lonely outpost, and when Marthinus stepped forward to claim her, she was not surprised.

She remembered that first long ride across the flats; how bleak they seemed, how destructive of hopes! But at the worst part of the transit she had known that something much better must lie ahead, and she had gritted her teeth, held fast to the reins, and thought: He wouldn't have settled here if the land were all like this—so that when the river appeared, with ibis and cranes gracing its banks, and ducks of wild variety diving to its bottom, she did not feel triumphant relief, but only that this was what she had expected.

Her life with Katje had been difficult at times, for that quarrelsome woman loved to complain, accusing her daughter-in-law of being too lazy or too careless, but after two or three harsh battles in which Annatjie stood her ground, Katje realized that she had a strong woman in her house, and the two mistresses worked out compromises. Occasionally it had been necessary for Annatjie to shove Katje aside, when something had to be done quickly and in what she thought was the proper way. When this first happened, her mother-in-law exploded, but Annatjie said, over her shoulder as she did the work, 'Yell your heart out, old lady, but don't get in my way.' In later years, when the younger Van Doorns had three children, Annatjie appreciated Katje's presence, for she proved a loving grandmother, instilling decent behavior into the children while stuffing them with goodies.

Annatjie's relationship with Willem had been more placid. She felt sorry for the crippled old farmer and admired the stalwart way he tended his vineyard, never complaining of the pain that kept him walking sideways, always ready to help any newcomer get started in the Stellenbosch area. She had worked with him in building the huts that had accumulated about the farmhouse: one shed for pigeons, one for farming tools, one for the storage of grain. She enjoyed that heavy work, for with every building that went up, she felt that the Van Doorns were securing their hold upon the land; she, more than his son Marthinus, was a projection of Willem's dream for South Africa.

With her three children she was a firm-minded mother, insisting that they work on the land with the slaves and Hottentots during the day and learn their letters at night after the table was cleared. She was desperately afraid they would be illiterate, and made them read with her from the only book the family owned, the big Bible whose Dutch words were printed in heavy Gothic script—and for a child of seven to try to decipher them was much like unraveling a secret code, but the ability to do so was the mark of a good human being, and patiently she drilled her offspring. In this she succeeded, but in her determination to make them hard-working farmers, like the ones she had known as a girl in Holland, she failed, for as the years passed, the white men of Africa grew accustomed to seeing black bodies bent down over the fields. It seemed God's ordination that labor be divided so that men like the Van Doorns could supervise while slaves and servants toiled. The expression 'Oh, that's slave's work' became current.

Annatjie was distressed when Hendrik showed no real interest in reading, and learned only under duress. For some reason that she did not understand, he inclined toward the wilderness, the tracking of animals and the exploration of valleys yet unsettled. She often wondered what would happen to him, for he was not tractable like the De Pré boys; he had a quick temper, a stubbornness much like his grandfather's; indeed, the only hopeful aspect of his character had been his affection for Willem. It was he who had listened most intently to what the old man had said about the siege of Malacca and his voyages to Japan. The De Pré boys were hungry for news of the France their father had known, but her children were content with Africa.

Petronella she always loved with special affection; the girl was much as she had been, stubborn, helpful, considerate of others and with a vast capacity for love, and it was with this in mind that Annatjie had approached her daughter's marriage to Bezel Muhammad, a free man and a Christian. She had learned to look not at a man's skin but at his soul, and she was quietly amused when Farmer Boeksma revealed his. A hypocritical man, he ranted in church, but at home had three little servant girls who bore a remarkable resemblance to him; their black grandfathers had ridden at his side on commando; their black mothers had served at his table. But now he denounced the proposed Van Doorn marriage: 'It's all right, when the pressure's on a man, to sleep with a slave, but, by God, you never marry them.'

Quickly another farmer corrected him: 'What you mean, Andries, it's all right for white men to sleep with black women. Never white women with black men.' When this was enthusiastically approved, Boeksma endeavored to prohibit the marriage, and might have succeeded except for two reasons: local people needed the wine Marthinus made and the wall closets Bezel built. So the slave became free, the dark man married the white woman, and in a score of unexpected ways the community profited.

Not long after the wedding, Boeksma approached Annatjie with an interesting proposition: 'Mevrouw, would you allow your slave to build me a stinkwood closet?'

'He's a free man. Ask him direct.'

Bezel accepted the commission, and Annatjie was pleased to see the beauty of the gigantic piece. It was, she believed, the best work her son-in-law had ever done, and she watched with wry amusement as he loaded it on his cart for delivery to the man who had been his adversary.

With her daughter married, Annatjie's concern turned to little Sarel, whose reticence had worried her from cradle days. As long as he had to be compared only to Hendrik, who was himself quiet, she could rationalize: 'Sarel's a good boy. He just doesn't attract much attention.' But when he had to be judged against the De Pré lads, his deficiencies became apparent. He spoke more slowly, reacted tardily to externals, and never showed anger the way boys should. She was not yet prepared to admit that Sarel was slow-witted and would have fought anyone who said so, but she did worry: 'He's a slow developer. Not to be compared with the others.'

Annatjie herself was without vanity, or envy, or senseless anger. She was a woman born without prospects who had stumbled into a life infinitely better than she could have anticipated, with a young husband who appreciated her, an older son who gave promise of becoming outstanding, and parents-in-law who had been exceptional. Furthermore, she lived in a valley that had no equal in South Africa and in a house that would one day be hailed around the world as a masterpiece of Cape Dutch invention.

She was therefore quite capable of handling Paul de Pré's obvious determination to gather all the land in this valley into one vast holding, of which the principal part would be the vineyards of Trianon. The Van Doorns now owned their original sixty morgen, plus an additional hundred and twenty acquired since coming to the valley. Paul de Pré owned only the sixty granted him by Karel van Doorn in lieu of cash, but already he had plans to pick up another farm, and had sharp eyes for several bits of unclaimed land beyond that.

He had tried to marry Petronella in order to establish some kind of claim on Trianon, and had been rebuffed. Indeed, he had been ridiculed by Annatjie, who had told him he was making a fool of himself, but this had not deterred him from proceeding with his ambition, and one evening some months after the funeral of old Willem he came to the Van Doorns with an astonishing proposal: 'Why don't we merge the two farms? I'll contribute mine so that we can operate the vineyards as a single unit.'

'But what would you do?' Marthinus asked.

'Work with you. We can make this the best wine farm outside of France.'

'You'd give up your morgen?'

'We'd be partners. What difference does it make who owns this piece of land or that?'

Marthinus said, 'But we own one eighty morgen. You have only sixty. What kind of partnership is that?'

'If I stop tending the grapes, how much are yours worth, eh?'

'We'd farm it, some other way. But we'd never give up our land.'

'Think about it,' De Pré said, and after three weeks, when the subject was not returned to, he announced one night, 'I now have a hundred and six morgen and will soon have two hundred.'

When he was gone, Annatjie sent the boys to bed and talked seriously with her husband. 'I'm sure Paul has plans to take over Trianon. He rebuilt our house to his taste. He named it. He designed the motif for our casks. And his slaves work the fields better than ours do. I often wondered why he never planted a hedge between our properties. Now I know.'

'I think he just wants a good relationship. As he said—working the fields as a single unit.'

'Marthinus, he's a peasant. A French peasant. And French peasants do not surrender their land easily. Never.' When her husband started to uphold the Huguenot, she interrupted: 'Remember how you defended your land when he proposed a partnership? "We'd never give up our land." What made you say that? Old Willem's sacrifices to get the land? Old Katje's long years of hardship here? Well, if you love your land, Paul de Pré worships his. And if he's willing to give us his, it's only because he thinks he sees a way to gain control over the whole estate later on.'

Marthinus pondered this. He and Annatjie were older than De Pré and would probably die sooner. But there were the three Van Doorn children to inherit Trianon.

'Don't count on that,' Annatjie warned. 'If Petronella has a dark husband, they won't try to hold the land. And I've had grave suspicions that Hendrik won't want to stay here. He's like his grandfather. Eyes to the east. One day he'll wander off and we'll see him no more.'

'There's still Sarel. He loves the soil.'

'De Pré is sure he can outwit Sarel. De Pré knows that Petronella and Hendrik don't count. It's him against Sarel, and he intends to win.'

'But he could well be an old man before this happens. You and I aren't going to die tomorrow.'

'De Pré himself—yes, he will be old, but his boys will be young. And able. And older than Sarel. Three determined Huguenots against one young Dutchman who's not . . .'

'Not what?' Marthinus asked aggressively, and the words she had sworn never to utter came forth: 'He's not too quick.'

'What do you mean?' He spoke in anger, for his wife had opened a subject he had for some time been trying to avoid, and he reacted defensively: 'There's nothing wrong with Sarel!'

The forbidden subject having been broached, she plowed ahead: 'He's a wonderful child and we both love him, but he's not too quick. No match for the De Prés.' And when she began slowly to recite the deficiencies which could no longer be masked, Marthinus had to admit that his young son was limited: 'Not a dull boy. I'd never confess that to anyone. But I do sometimes see that he's not . . . well, as you say . . . quick.' Then he voiced the hope that kept him working so hard at the vineyard: 'One of these days Hendrik will see the light. When the time comes for him to take command.'

'Hendrik has seen other horizons,' Annatjie said. 'He talked too long with old Willem. One of these days he'll be gone.'

'So how do we protect ourselves against De Pré?'

'I think we look first at the land,' she said. 'What's good for the land?'

Marthinus sat for a long time, staring at the flickering candle, and finally said, 'The sensible thing would be to join the two farms, operate them as one, and make some really fine wine.'

'I think we should do so,' Annatjie said.

'But you said you were afraid of De Pré?'

'I am, but I think that together you and I will prove a match for him.'

So to De Pré's astonishment, the Van Doorns came to him and said that papers should be drawn combining the two holdings and that De Pré should go to the Cape to formalize the documents, for such joining of land would never be permitted without Compagnie sanction. And it was this trip which altered everything at Trianon, for when Henri and Louis had a sustained opportunity to see the bustling town, now with about a thousand inhabitants of myriad coloring, they were enchanted by it.

Malays in turbans, Javanese in conical hats, swarthy Madagascans in loincloths, handsome dark women from St. Helena, and high Compagnie officials in fine suitings with lace at the collar—these were the people who formed the Cape parade. While the elder De Pré arranged for the uniting of the farms, a French East Indiaman put into the bay, and stately parties were held at the fort, and one night the Huguenots, as fellow Frenchmen, were invited to attend, and the boys heard their native language spoken with elegance, and saw for themselves what a superior group the French were.

The captain of the French vessel, impressed by the manliness of the boys, invited them to visit his ship, where they ate with the officers and spoke of France. When the ship departed, the boys stood on the quay, saluting, and after that they had no interest whatever in working the fields at Trianon or inheriting the grand design their father was putting together.

In 1698 Henri announced that he was sailing back to Europe. This was not unusual; every return fleet which stopped at the Cape enticed a few free burghers to abandon the settlement, disgusted with the difficulties of farming or terrified by the prospect of being forever lost in the African wilderness. Soldiers, too, who served at the Cape without acquiring land usually wanted to return home at the earliest possibility, and over ninety percent of Compagnie officials quit the Cape when their tour of duty ended. It was the unusual man who followed the steps of Willem van Doorn, choosing the Cape once and for all as his future home and committing himself totally to its development. Young Henri de Pré was not such a pioneer; he was haunted by the gracious canals of Amsterdam, the good fields of France, and he longed to see them once more.

As for young Louis, eighteen years old, the sights and adventures of the Cape had corrupted him. He wanted no more of the wilderness farm or the placid offerings of Stellenbosch: 'I want to work at the Cape.'

'But what can you do, with no land?'

'The Compagnie's wine contractor needs an assistant. I'll join him. I'll work with the men at Groot Constantia, and learn the wine trade. The Huguenots at Paarl will need help.' With that quickness of mind that Annatjie had detected, the boy had visualized a complete way of life: 'I'll marry some Dutch girl.' He could have said, had he wished to confide his entire dream, 'And we'll have many sons and our name will live here forever.'

It was in this way that the Huguenots, that small group of refugees, would make their mark on South Africa. Their names, modified in passing generations, would reverberate in local history and would at times seem to monopolize elite positions: the athletic DuPlessis; the legalist DeVilliers; Viljoen, adapted from the name of the poet's family Villon; Malherbe; the poet Du Toit, who would help build the Afrikaans language; the military Joubert; the Naudés of religious fervor; the extensive, rugged Du Preez family. All of them were devout Calvinists, dedicated to learning and to conservatism. It was no accident that the man who would lead the Afrikaners to their final nationalist victory and become prime minister came from this stock—Malan, whose ancestors had fled persecution from a small town in southern France.

In 1700 Louis de Pré left the aggrandized vineyards of Trianon and settled in at the Cape, where, according to plan, he married a Dutch girl and prospered in all he attempted. He would have seven sons, who would in time be called Du Preez.

His father's plans fared less well. He was forty years old, the best wine-maker in the district, full partner in the profitable Trianon winery, but a man now without children or a wife. He lived alone in his small house, took some of his meals at Trianon, and fended off the Van Doorns when they persisted in trying to find him a wife. 'Why is he so obstinate?' Marthinus asked one night after Paul had left to walk the short distance to his lonely house.

'You know what I think?' Annatjie said to her husband. 'I think he is interested in only one thing—he still hopes that Hendrik will leave us and that he can bring Louis and his sons back here to take over. He intends that this shall be a De Pré farm before he dies.'

'He is dreaming.'

'I saw him the other day drawing designs in the dust—uniting all the little huts into fine buildings stretching out like arms from this one. It could be quite fine, as he plans it.'

'Let him do it. Bezel likes nothing better than to start carpentering a new building.' The wings that De Pré had sketched could easily be erected between seasons, but Annatjie guessed correctly that he would not start until the farm was more securely in his grasp.

Trianon now comprised about three hundred and eighty acres, all with access to water. It owned more than thirty slaves from various parts of Africa, the eastern ocean and Brazil. Fifty Hottentots and Coloureds worked also from five-thirty at dawn till seven at night, receiving no wages; they were given food, tobacco, an occasional blanket, and the right to graze the few animals that remained from their once-vast herds. Once each day they would queue up with the slaves for a spendid reward: a pint of raw wine.

One evening Farmer Boeksma arrived to buy a cask of Trianon at the very time the slaves and servants were lined up for their tot, and he observed, 'Maybe they have bartered away their freedom, but what a marvelous way to forget the past.' Marthinus, thinking of what old Willem had told about Jango's lust for freedom, and the prices he had been willing to pay, said nothing.

And then the Bushmen struck. The little brown people had watched with dismay as white farmers kept extending their holdings farther into traditional hunting grounds. At first they had merely observed the invasion, retreating ten miles ahead of the plow, but now they were beginning to fight back, and on many mornings a farmer on the outskirts of Stellenbosch would awaken to find his kraal broken, a prize ox slaughtered in a gully, and the spoor of Bushmen leading north toward the open country.

Every tactic had been used to combat the voracious raiders: armed Hottentots had been sent against them, commandos had been mounted, guards had been posted on twenty-four-hour duty, but the little men loved animal meat so much, and the placid cows of the Dutchmen were so inviting, that they circumvented every device the farmers tried. Losses were beginning to be intolerable, and in August of 1702 most of the farmers of Stellenbosch decided they must eliminate the pests.

They were led by Andries Boeksma, who argued that since the Bushmen were not human, they could be wiped out ruthlessly. Others, guided by Marthinus van Doorn, contended that Bushmen did have souls and must not be shot down like wild dogs; he was willing to have the worst offenders disciplined and even hanged if they persisted, but their basic humanity he defended. At first the community divided evenly, the tougher old men insisting that the Bushmen were not much different from dogs or gemsbok, the younger granting that they just might be human.

After a week of debate it was agreed that the argument be settled by recourse to the Bible, but no guidance could be found there, because little people with enormous bottoms and poisoned arrows had never molested the Israelites. When a vote was taken, it stood eleven-to-six in favor of exterminating the Bushmen, since it was decided that they were animals and not human. But before the commando could be started north, young

Hendrik van Doorn, twenty-one years old, startled the assembly by volunteering a special piece of evidence:

> 'When I was tracking with the Hottentots we followed a rhinoceros
> for some days, and when we had it well located in a valley, we went
> to bed expecting to shoot it in the morning, but when we reached its
> resting spot, we found that the Bushmen had slain it in a pit. This
> angered us, and we started tracking the Bushmen, and at last we
> came upon where the clan was camped, and we saw that they had
> tame dogs with them, and we concluded that if they could tame
> dogs, they must be human beings like us and not animals as many
> had proposed.'

His evidence stunned the eleven men who had voted to kill off all the little people in the way hyenas were destroyed if they came too near a farm,
and Andries Boeksma said gravely, 'If they can tame dogs, they're human,
and we cannot shoot them all.' To hear the leader of the commando
reason thus impressed the others, and the final vote was sixteen-to-one that
the Bushmen were human, the lone dissident arguing, 'Human or not, if
they steal my cattle, they have to be dealt with.' He would say no more in
public meeting, but he planned to kill every Bushman he saw.

The seventeen horsemen found a substantial spoor to follow, the trail
of five or six Bushmen dragging cattle parts back to camp, and for several
days they narrowed the gap between the two parties. On the fourth day
Andries Boeksma saw signs which satisfied him that the Bushmen must be
close at hand, hiding perhaps behind low rocks: 'They know we're after
them, so they won't lead us to their camp. That proves this bunch are
scavengers, and we can kill them all.' This was agreed upon, even by
those who had defended them: the little things might in principle be
human, but this particular group were cattle thieves who must be slain.

So the commando, practicing extreme caution, since everyone feared
that terrible flight of thin arrows which brought agonizing death, moved
toward the rocks that could be hiding the thieves, and when Boeksma saw
twigs move, he shouted, 'There they are!' and his followers cheered as
they swept down on their target.

There was so much gunfire that none of the Bushmen had any chance
of escape, but as they fell, one man maintained control and calmly aimed
his arrow at a specific rider, launching it just before he collapsed with
four bullets through him. The arrow struck Marthinus van Doorn in the
neck, lodged deep within, and broke apart.

By nightfall he felt painfully dizzy and asked Andries Boeksma to cut
the arrowhead out, but the big Dutchman said, 'I can't do it, Marthinus.
I'd cut your throat.' So the agony increased, and at dawn Marthinus was
again pleading that the arrow be cut out, but the men agreed with
Boeksma that this was impossible. They built a litter and slung it between

two horses, hoping to get Van Doorn back to the apotheek at Stellenbosch, but by midday the poison had spread furiously, and in the late afternoon he died.

'Shall we bury him here?' Boeksma asked Hendrik. 'Or would your mother want him at Trianon?'

'Bury him here,' Hendrik said. The Van Doorns had never feared the veld. So the men of the commando broke into two groups, one to dig a grave, one to gather stones that would mark it, and when the hole was deep enough to keep away hyenas, Marthinus van Doorn, forty-three years old, was buried. Andries Boeksma, as leader of the commando, said a brief prayer, then tied the bridle of Van Doorn's horse to his and started homeward.

Hendrik would never forget what happened at Trianon when the mournful procession rode in to inform Annatjie of her loss. It was not what his mother did that shocked him; she was resolute, as he had expected—a tall, gaunt woman of fifty-one, with rough hands and deep-lined face. She nodded, started to cry, then pushed her knuckles into her eyes and asked, 'Where did you leave the body, Andries?'

'Decently buried . . . out there.'

'Thank you,' she said, and that was all.

Nor was it her impersonal reaction that appalled young Hendrik—he knew that she was not the wailing kind—it was what happened after the commando had ridden off. No sooner had the horsemen left Trianon than Paul de Pré hastened over from his house, crying in a loud voice, '*Mon Dieu*, is Marthinus dead?'

'Why do you ask?' Hendrik said.

'I saw the empty horse. The way the bridle was tied to Boeksma's.'

'And what did you think?'

'I thought, "Marthinus must be dead. I must go comfort Annatjie." '

'He's dead,' Hendrik said. 'Mother's inside.' And he saw the avidity with which the Huguenot hurried through the door. Hendrik should not have listened, but he did, hearing De Pré say with great excitement, 'Annatjie, I've heard the dreadful news. My heart is pained for you.'

'Thank you, Paul.'

'How did it happen?'

'Bushmen. Poisoned arrow.'

'*O mon Dieu!* You sorrowful woman.'

'Thank you, Paul.'

There was a silence which Hendrik could not interpret, and then De Pré's voice, urgent and nervous: 'Annatjie, you'll be alone, trying to work the vineyard. I'll be alone, trying to do the same. Should we not join forces? I mean . . . well, I mean . . . What I mean is, should we not marry, and hold the place together?'

Hendrik quivered at the brazenness of such a question, at the awful impropriety of its coming on this day, but he was restrained from bursting into the room and thrashing the Frenchman by what his mother replied: 'I knew you would come quickly to ask that question, Paul. I know you've been plotting and scheming and wondering how you could gain control of the Trianon. I know you're nine years younger than I am and that not long ago you wanted to marry my daughter, not me. And I know how shameful it is of you to ask that question this night. But you're a poor, hungry man, Paul, with only one desire, and I have pity on you. Come back in seven days.'

De Pré spent those days in drawing plans, in adding up acreages and in supervising the slaves and the Hottentots as they prepared the grapes for harvest. He neither went to the big house nor attended the memorial service in Stellenbosch at which the predikant and the members of the commando told the community of Marthinus van Doorn's heroism. He stayed completely apart, working as he had never worked to get Trianon in top condition, and at eight o'clock in the morning of the eighth day he walked over to Trianon in his pressed and dusted clothes.

He did not find Hendrik there. The young man had loaded his wagon —first putting in it, carefully wrapped, his grandfather's Bible and brown-gold crock—with the equipment necessary for a life on the veld, and with a slave and two Hottentot families, had departed for the lands beyond the mountains, taking with him a small herd of cattle and sheep. Before leaving he had said farewell to Petronella and Bezel Muhammad; he judged they were as happy as human beings were allowed to be on this earth, but he could not know that their two dark children would soon be lost in that human wilderness called Coloured; for a brief while they and their descendants would be remembered as Van Doorns, but after that, their history, but not their bloodline, would vanish as surely as would the antecedents of the three little girls fathered by Andries Boeksma. Later, it would become fashionable to claim that all such half-castes were the spawn of those lusty sailors who could not control their urges at the halfway house between Europe and Asia. That a Van Doorn or a Boeksma had contributed to the Coloureds would be unthinkable.

Hendrik had no feeling about his brother Sarel; the boy showed no courage, no deep interest in anything, and he guessed that with the De Pré boys gone, Sarel would inherit the vineyards; but in this development he had no interest whatever. He did have enormous feeling for Annatjie and supposed that in her place he would do as she was doing; she had been a most excellent mother, loving and understanding; he had seen how tenderly she cared for old Katje when the grandmother was troublesome, and she had been just as attentive to Paul de Pré's two motherless boys. Tears came to his eyes as he admitted to himself that after this day he might never see his mother again, that this break was final; Trianon and the lovely river and the white walls and the gables were lost forever.

With his wagon he headed eastward, as old Willem had done years before; the difference was that he traveled without a wife.

* * *

The wedding took place in the church at Stellenbosch at eleven in the morning, and by three that afternoon Paul de Pré, now master of Trianon, had his slaves tearing down the huts that stood in front of the house, and when the space was cleared, he and Bezel Muhammad paced off the dimensions of the proposed wings.

'It's important,' Paul explained, 'that they come away from the main building at an angle, and that the two angles are the same.' When the stakes were driven and the two men had gone far down the entrance road to satisfy themselves that they had found the proper relationships, Paul said, 'I think that's it,' and he could visualize the finished buildings, stark-white but with shadows playing across the surfaces like breezes in a glade, the arms extended in welcome, with the two flanks helping to form with the house a spacious enclosure such as farms in France sometimes had.

'It will be glorious!' he cried with deep pleasure as the sun began to sink, throwing bold colors on the hills behind the house, and he could visualize travelers from the Cape approaching this haven of white buildings and generous spaces.

Construction started immediately. Ten slaves dug foundations, piled rocks, and mixed mud for the walls. Cadres were sent into the fields to cut the heavy thatch that would form the roofs, and Bezel Muhammad led still others into the forests to find yellow-wood for the rafters. Under the constant urging of De Pré, the two rows of buildings seemed to spring from the soil, and when they were nearing completion, and Muhammad's supervision was no longer needed, Paul took him aside to explain what would later prove to be the most engaging aspect of the buildings.

'What I want,' he told Bezel, 'is for each of the eight compartments to have over the door, in the darkest stinkwood you can find, an oval plaque, carved in high relief, indicating what goes on in that segment of the building.' And he stepped along the two flanks, suggesting by big movements of his hands what he had in mind.

'As we ride in, first door on the left, a pigeon, dark against the white wall. Next a pig, because we'll use this as part of the sty. Next a stack of hay, and over this door near the house, a dog. Now let's go back and look at the right-hand side. First a rooster, then a measure for grain, then a pot of flowers, and on the one nearest the house, a rake and a hoe.' Bezel nodded, already planning in his mind how he would carve certain of the signs, but as he started for the two-room home he had built for Petronella some distance from the main house, Paul called him back: 'On the right-hand side, have the tools over the next-to-last door. Save the flowers for the door nearest the house, so that Mevrouw de Pré can get to them easily.'

In all he did, he consulted the wishes of Mevrouw. He might have been tempted to be unpleasant with Annatjie, for she was both older and plainer than he; fifty-one years of ceaseless work had roughened her face, while he remained a handsome youngish man of only forty-two. Girls from surrounding farms, and sometimes their mothers, too, had looked at him with affection, but he had so desperately yearned for control of Trianon that he was willing to pay the price, and that was faithful attention to Annatjie, through whose hands he had acquired it. He would never belittle her, or mention her advanced age, or in any way fail to pay the debt he owed her.

He gave evidence of this attitude on the day the two outreaching buildings were completed, each door with its splendid identifying oval, for after Annatjie had inspected everything and approved this handsome addition, Paul said, 'And now we attend to your needs.'

'I have none,' she said.

'Oh, yes. Your house is too small for you.' She noticed with approval that whereas he often said 'my farm, my vineyard,' and even 'my fields at Trianon,' he invariably referred to the house as hers. There she was mistress, and he proposed making it worthy of her.

Leading her inside, he showed how the T could be improved by the simple device of adding two large rooms to the stem. 'What we'll do,' he explained, 'is change it from a T to an H.' And he pointed out that if this were done, she would also gain two small gardens in the empty parts of the H. 'In hot summers, the cool wind will come at us from all sides.'

When the H was completed, it worked exactly as he had foreseen, and the De Prés now had the finest house in Stellenbosch, a low gracious set of buildings beautifully associated with meadow and mountain. But still his insatiable urge to build drove him on: 'Bezel, I want you to carve me a monstrous oval, six times bigger than the little ones.'

'Showing what?'

'Wine casks decorated with vines.' And while the Malay carpenter carved the symbols, Paul directed his slaves in building a huge wine cellar at the rear of the house but closely attached to it, so that a Spanish-style patio resulted. Trianon now had four lovely gardens: the big one in front, the two little ones tucked into the angles of the house, and this quiet, restricted one at the rear, closed in by white walls and dotted with small trees. When Bezel Muhammad bolted his carving into position, Paul said, 'Here's a building in which wine of distinction might be housed.'

His building mania was almost ended. When the great wine casks from France were placed in position, and the pigeons and chickens and pigs were in their cubicles, he informed Annatjie that he would build one final thing for her, and when she tried to guess what it might be, he told her to visit with the Boeksmas in Stellenbosch for five days. When he came to the Boeksma farm to fetch her, she asked what he had done, and he told her, 'You must see for yourself,' and as they drove up the lane, and into the areaway between the two embracing arms, she could detect nothing new, but as they approached the house she gasped, for at each end of the low stoep on which they sat in the evening Paul had directed his workmen to build two ceramic benches perpendicular to the front wall and faced with the softest white-and-blue tiles from Delft. They showed men skating on frozen canals, women working at the river, views of old buildings and sometimes simply the implements of Dutch farm life. They converted ordinary benches into little jewels, glistening in sunlight, and the great house of Trianon was complete.

It was great in neither size nor height, nor was it Dutch. Its chief characteristics had been borrowed from Java, its secondary ones from rural France, but the spirit that animated it and the manner in which it hugged the earth came only from South Africa. Dutch workmen had helped build it, and a French megalomaniac, and a Malay carpenter, and slaves from Angola, Madagascar and Ceylon, with Hottentots doing much of the light work. It was an amalgam, glorious yet simple, and its chief wonder was that when one sat on the Delft benches at close of day, one could see the sun setting behind Table Mountain.

Paul's attitude toward his five children would always be ambivalent. Concerning Annatjie's boy Hendrik, who had vanished into the wilderness, he was glad to see him go, for he recognized him as a threat. He did not worry about his own son Henri, now in Amsterdam, for he judged this one would never have wanted to farm; indeed, he felt some relief at the boy's disappearance, for he sensed that sooner or later he would have had trouble with him. Annatjie's boy Sarel he considered a dolt and was pleased to see that girls thought so, too, for the boy was not married, would produce no heirs to claim the vineyards, and could be dismissed. His son Louis was a different matter; Paul was still convinced that after a few years at the Cape, the boy would want to come back to the farm, and it would be to him that Trianon would ultimately revert; often he consoled himself by thinking: The experience with the Compagnie will make him a better manager. He'll know about ships and agents and markets. That the boy would ultimately return he never doubted, and that Louis could wrest the vineyard from silly Sarel was evident. 'Trianon of the De Prés' he saw as the ultimate title, and if the French name should be submerged in the Dutch Du Preez, that would be all right with him.

It was his attitude toward Petronella that surprised Annatjie, for he had bitterly opposed her liaison with Bezel Muhammad, but now his opinion changed radically. One day he said, 'Annatjie, I'm not using my house, and the boys seem to have fled. Why not give it to Petronella and Bezel?'

'I think they'd like that,' Annatjie said, and she was astonished when he not only gave the young couple the house, but also helped Bezel erect a workshop in which his tools would have an orderly place. He even assigned three slaves to the task of cutting stinkwood trees for Bezel and shaping them into timbers.

Later, of course, Annatjie discovered that Paul had talked Bezel into building only wall cupboards, which were carted to Louis de Pré, who sold them at top prices at the Cape. Bezel was given less than a third of the profits, but he and Petronella did occupy their new home rent-free, and he appreciated the fact that Paul's patronage was of great value to a carpenter who had been a slave.

Then came the years of conflict. Paul was determined that Louis come back to inherit the vineyard; Annatjie was equally insistent that her son Sarel pull himself together, take a wife, and produce the Van Doorn children who would supervise Trianon far into the future. In this struggle De Pré used vicious weapons, denigrating Sarel at each opportunity, spreading in the community rumors that he was an imbecile. He spoke casually of the day when Louis would return to take command: 'He's studying the wine business, you know. The Compagnie has sent him to Europe to ascertain who the trustworthy merchants are.'

The struggle took an ugly turn whenever Annatjie maneuvered her self-conscious son into contact with any marriageable girl, for then Paul would arrange to meet, by happenstance, her parents, to whom he would drop bits of intelligence: 'I don't really suppose he's an idiot. He can buckle his shoes.' And since Sarel, who blushed beet-red at the sight of a girl, did nothing to advance any courtship, the meetings arranged by his mother came to naught.

She wondered what to do. She was fifty-seven now and did not expect to live far into her sixties; Sarel was not deficient, of that she was certain, but he was shy and awkward and he needed a wife most urgently. But where could she find one for him?

She arranged an excuse for taking him to the Cape, but accomplished nothing, so in desperation she looked toward Holland and the orphanage from which she had come. She very much wanted to commission Henri de Pré to make contact with the women who supervised the girls, but her peasant instincts warned her that Henri could be trusted no more than his father, so in desperation she sat in her corner of the big house and penned a secret letter to a woman she had never seen, the mistress of the orphanage where the King's Nieces resided:

Dearest Mevrouw,

I am a child of your house, living far away where there are no women. Please find me a healthy, strong, reliable, Christian girl of seventeen or eighteen, well-bred and loyal, who can be trusted to come here to marry my son. She will have to work hard but will be mistress of nearly four hundred morgen and a beautiful house. My son is a good man.

Annatjie van Doorn de Pré
Trianon, Stellenbosch, The Cape

She forwarded the letter without letting her husband know, and nearly a year of anxiety passed before a courier arrived with news that a Compagnie ship from Amsterdam would soon be putting in with a wife for Sarel van Doorn.

'What's this?' De Pré demanded.

'Someone's sending out an orphan, I suppose. The way I came.'

'But who asked for an orphan?'

'Many people know that Sarel needs a wife.'

'What would he do with a wife?' This was a difficult moment for De Pré. Never had he transgressed his resolve to treat Annatjie with respect and even love, and he did not propose to treat her poorly now; but he was determined that Trianon stay in his family, and if Sarel married and had children, such inheritance might be in question. If he forbade himself to abuse Annatjie, he felt no such restraint where Sarel was concerned, and now he made gross fun of the hesitant young man.

'What would that one do with a wife?' he repeated, and Annatjie, wanting most earnestly to slap his insinuating face, left the house.

She ordered slaves to inspan her horses, then asked Bezel Muhammad to accompany her to the Cape, where she would greet the arriving bride. 'Why not take Sarel?' he asked, and without thinking, she replied, 'He might not know what to do.'

She would. When they reached the Cape, the promised ship had not yet arrived, but others of its convoy assured the officials that it was on the way, so she waited. And then one morning guns fired, and a pitifully small ship limped into harbor with almost half its passengers dead. For a dreadful moment she feared that she might have lost her orphan, but when the survivors came ashore Geertruyd Steen was among them, twenty-two years old, blond, squared-off in every aspect, and smiling. She had a large square face, a stout torso, big hips, sturdy legs. Even her hair was braided and tied so that it accentuated the squareness of her head, and Annatjie thought: Dearest God, if there was ever a woman destined to breed, she is it.

The girl, not knowing what to expect, looked tentatively about her for some young man who might be awaiting a wife, but saw only sailors and Hottentots, so she took hesitant steps forward, saw Annatjie, and knew instinctively that this woman must be her protector. There was a slight pause, after which the two women ran at each other and embraced almost passionately.

'You've come to a paradise,' Annatjie told the girl. 'But it's a paradise you must build for yourself.'

'Are you to be my mother-in-law?'

'I am.'

'Is your son here?'

'It's an important story,' Annatjie said, and on the spur of the moment she directed Bezel Muhammad to take one of the horses and ride on ahead. It was important that she talk with this girl, and a long ride across the flats would give her just enough time.

She whisked Geertruyd out of the Cape that morning, afraid lest she be infected the way Louis de Pré had been, and as they entered the flats, she began talking: 'I shall have to tell you so much, Geertruyd, but every sentence is important, and the order in which it's told is important, too. My husband, your father-in-law, is a remarkable man.'

She explained how he had fled persecution in France, the courage with which he had made his way to Holland, and his great bravery in risking a return trip to fetch the vines which now accounted for the prosperity of Trianon. She told how tough old Willem van Doorn and his nagging wife had ventured out into the wilderness to build their farm, and how Paul de Pré had transformed it into a rural palace.

The first hours were spent in these details, but when they stopped to have their midday meal, Annatjie changed the tone of conversation completely: 'You'll see a dozen kinds of antelope, and hear leopards at night, and maybe one day you'll find a hippo in the river. We have a flower called protea, eight times as grand as any tulip, and birds of all description. You'll live in a land of constant surprises, and when you're an old woman like me you still won't have seen everything.'

She asked Geertruyd to look about her at the endless flatness. 'What do you see?' she asked.

'Nothing.'

'Always remember this moment,' Annatjie said, 'for soon you'll see such a place of beauty that your eyes will not believe it.' Geertruyd leaned forward as her mother-in-law-to-be added, 'If you do your work well, you'll build a little empire here, but only you can do it.'

All elderly people claim that the future lies in the hands of the young people, but few believe it; Annatjie de Pré knew that alternatives of the most staggering dimension depended upon how this particular young girl behaved herself and with what courage she attacked her problems.

'What problems do you mean?' Geertruyd asked.

'Inheritance,' Annatjie said. 'Yesterday you were an orphan girl owning a few dresses. Tomorrow you'll be a significant factor in the ownership of the finest vineyard in the land.'

Geertruyd listened and did not like what she heard. 'I am not penniless,' she said. 'I have guilders in my package.'

Annatjie liked her response, but goaded her still further: 'You come bringing nothing. Except your character. You're being offered everything, if you demonstrate that character.'

'I am not a pauper!' Geertruyd repeated, her square face flushing red.

'I was when I came across these flats,' Annatjie said, and without emotion she told the girl of how she, too, had left that orphanage, and of how her first man had rejected her, and of how she had slaved to improve the farm. 'You say you have a few hidden guilders. I had nothing.'

Abruptly she turned to the problem of her son, the proposed husband: 'Sarel is a fine, honest young man. He's always been overshadowed by the four children he grew up with. My husband, who despises him because he's afraid of what he might become, will tell you within the first ten minutes that Sarel's an imbecile. Sarel will be especially afraid of you, and if you believe my husband, you may shy away.' She paused and took Geertruyd's hands. 'But we never know, do we, what a man can become until we treat him with love?' They talked no more.

When they came off the flats, and the river hove into view, and the horses entered the long lane leading to Trianon, Geertruyd Steen saw for the first time the stunning sight of those enveloping arms, the clean white façade of the house and the two Delft benches defining the ends of the stoep. 'It's beautiful,' she whispered.

'And remember,' Annatjie whispered back, 'it was Paul de Pré who made it this way.'

'Halloo there!' Paul cried as he bounded out of the door to greet his wife and the stranger from Amsterdam. As soon as Geertruyd stepped forward, shining like a red Edam cheese, he thought: *Mon Dieu!* That one was bred for having children. 'Sarel!' he called. 'Come out and meet your bride!'

These were words well calculated to embarrass the young man, and Annatjie sought to soften them by calling, 'Sarel, here's the most pleasant girl I've ever met.'

From the doorway came the young man, twenty-six years old, weighing not much more than his intended and many times as shy, but when he saw Geertruyd and the frank joy that wreathed her face, he was drawn to her immediately and came forward, stumbling in his eagerness.

'Mind your step,' Paul said, extending a hand to help.

Sarel brushed aside his stepfather's hand as he moved to greet Geertruyd. 'I'm Sarel,' he said.

'My name's Geertruyd.'

'Mother says you come . . . from the same place she did.'

'I do,' the girl said, and the meeting was so agreeable that Sarel was put at ease. He wondered if he should volunteer to kiss the girl, but the question was resolved for him; she stepped forward and kissed him on the cheek. 'We're to be married soon, I think,' she said.

'Let's not rush things,' Paul said cautiously, but Annatjie said, 'It will be arranged. The banns will be read.'

Paul objected seriously to having Petronella and her husband attend the wedding, but when Annatjie insisted, a compromise was worked out. Petronella and Bezel would sit in the rear of the church but not participate; Annatjie said that this was a strange way for Paul to act, seeing that he had given the young couple his house, but Paul said, 'What we do at home's one thing. What we do in public is quite another,' and he simply would not listen to Annatjie's further plea that the couple be allowed to sit in the family pew.

When the wedding party returned to Trianon, Paul said graciously, 'Isn't it lucky we built the extra two rooms? The young people can have one of them.' So they were installed, and he began to watch Geertruyd meticulously, to see if she showed any signs of pregnancy, for with the birth of her first child, the Van Doorns would have a potential inheritor of the vineyard, and his own design would fall into confusion.

He knew it was inevitable, yet the possibility made him irritable, and one night at supper he threw down his spoon and cried, 'Damnit all, it's been four months since I've spoken a word of French. Everybody in this house speaks Dutch, even though I own the place.'

'You don't own the place,' Annatjie reminded him, 'you own part of it.'

'Then we should speak part French.'

'I know not a word,' Geertruyd said, and this simple statement angered him further.

'They're even threatening to halt the sermons in French,' he wailed. 'Every time I attend a funeral, it means one less French voice in the colony. And none to come to replace it.'

'Paul,' his wife said with a certain harshness. 'Stop this. It's long past the time to acknowledge what you already are, a good Dutchman.' The tone of her voice, her easy assumption infuriated him, and he stomped from the room and slept that night among the wine casks.

There in the darkness the ugly thought leaped forward in his mind: Annatjie can't live forever. She's almost sixty. One of these days she's got to die. He had respected her for all she and her family had done for him, and had honored his obligation to treat her with civil affection, but now the world that he had built was being threatened, and he wished that she were dead—and he began to watch her health as closely as he did Geertruyd's.

Annatjie did show signs of rapid aging. Her hands were withered and heavy lines marked her face. She moved more slowly than when he had married her, and her voice cracked now and then. Her deficiencies were the more notable in that he continued as young as ever—a vital, hard-working man with a smooth face that displayed his enthusiasm: After all, I am nine years younger. If I had this place by myself . . . He was thrilled by the prospect of what he could accomplish; and this was not fatuous, for one had only to look at the buildings of Trianon, those handsome, well-proportioned masterpieces, to realize what this man could achieve.

* * *

And now the battle for Trianon began. Sometimes at meals De Pré would seem to strive for breath; he felt surrounded by enemies who were trying to wrest his vineyard from him, and all he could see in the kitchen were hostile faces. Annatjie he could dismiss; she was almost sixty and must soon die. Sarel showed no signs of improving because of marriage, and could be ignored. With peasant cunning Paul saw that his real foe was Geertruyd, this deceptively quiet orphan from Amsterdam. Watching her closely, he found to his dismay that she was watching him. No matter what he did to make his good wine, he could feel Geertruyd spying on him, noting how he acted and why.

She never confronted him, for in the orphanage it had been drilled into her that the sovereign quality in any woman was meekness. So when De Pré railed at her, she kept her eyes lowered and made no response. She also refrained from trying to defend Annatjie when Paul shouted at her, for she was determined to avoid diversionary squabbles. But when De Pré, in his strategic assault, humiliated Sarel, trying to convince the young man that he was incompetent, she felt her anger rise. But still she fought to maintain self-control.

Four times, five times at supper Paul scorned his stepson, without rebuttal from Geertruyd or Annatjie, and this convinced him that he could beat down these women. One evening he launched a series of destructive attacks: 'Sarel, wouldn't it be better if you kept away from the slaves? They ignore your orders.'

Sarel said nothing, only fumbled with his spoon, so De Pré stormed on: 'And don't meddle with the wine casks. Certain things around here have to be done right.'

The young man reddened and, still silent, looked down at his plate, but when De Pré dredged up a third humiliating point—'Stay clear of the new vines'—Geertruyd had had enough. Very quietly, but with frightening determination, she interrupted: 'Monsieur de Pré . . .'

'Haven't I told you to call me Father?'

'Monsieur de Pré,' she repeated menacingly, 'since Sarel will take over the vineyards when you are dead . . .' She delivered the word with such brutal finality that De Pré gasped. He had often contemplated his wife's death, never his own.

'So Sarel and I have decided,' she continued, her face flushed with anger, 'that he must become familiar with all stages of making wine.'

'Sarel decided?' De Pré burst into derisive laughter. 'He couldn't decide anything.'

Everyone turned to look at Sarel, and he realized he ought to respond, both to combat his stepfather and to support his wife, but the pressure was so ugly that he could not form words.

So in her first attempt at defiance, Geertruyd lost, and she noticed that this made De Pré even more arrogant. For the first time he put aside his pledge to treat Annatjie with the respect due a wife and became publicly contemptuous. This grieved Geertruyd, for quite properly she placed the blame on herself; she went to Annatjie and assured her: 'I shall do whatever I must. Let his wrath fall on me, but you and I together are going to make Sarel strong. You'll see the day, Annatjie, when he runs this vineyard.'

'Have we the time?' Annatjie whispered.

'I hoped last month I was pregnant,' Geertruyd confided. 'I was wrong, but one of these days you'll have a Van Doorn grandson. This vineyard must be protected for him.'

So in the second year of Sarel's marriage the two women intensified their efforts in educating him to be a responsible man and themselves to be masters of viticulture. They studied everything about the process and compared notes at night, but what gave them greatest hope was that Sarel appeared to be learning, too. 'He's not dull,' Geertruyd whispered one night when De Pré had left the table, 'it's just his inability to express his thoughts.' They found that he was developing sound ideas on how to tend vines, make casks, protect the must, and manage slaves effectively, and one afternoon, out in the bright sun, Geertruyd cried joyously, 'Sarel, you'll run this vineyard better than De Pré ever did.' He looked at her as if she had voiced some great truth, and he tried to convey his appreciation, but words did not come easily. Instead he embraced her, and when he felt her peasant body, warm in the sun, he was overcome with love and said haltingly, 'I can . . . make wine.'

That night Paul was unusually obnoxious, for he sensed that Geertruyd, this orphan from nowhere, was on the threshold of transforming Sarel, and it embittered him to think that all the good things he had done at Trianon—and he had done many—would ultimately be for the benefit of strangers. 'Sarel!' he lashed out. 'I told you to stay clear of those casks—'

'Monsieur de Pré,' Geertruyd interrupted instantly. 'I told Sarel to mind the casks. How else can he run these vineyards when you are dead?'

There was that horrid word again, thrown at him by this twenty-three-year-old peasant girl. He beat on the table till the spoons rattled, and cried, 'I want no imbecile meddling with my casks.'

'Monsieur de Pré,' Geertruyd said with an infuriating smile, 'I think Sarel is ready to take complete charge of the casks. You won't have to bother any longer.'

'Sarel couldn't . . .'

Annatjie had heard enough. Sternly she said, 'Paul, must you be reminded that I still have authority in this place? It was I who decided that Sarel must learn how to run it.'

Geertruyd, strengthened by her mother-in-law's support, said firmly, 'Sarel will start tomorrow.'

'That one couldn't line up three staves,' De Pré snarled, and he was about to hurl additional insults, but under the table Geertruyd quietly pressed her hand against her husband's knee, and with courage thus imparted, Sarel spoke slowly: 'I am sure that I . . . can build good casks.'

The battle for the control of Trianon was interrupted by an event so arbitrary that men and women argued about it for decades: it seemed that God had struck the Cape with a fearful and reasonless scourge. One day in 1713 the old trading ship *Groote Hoorn* docked with an accidental cargo that altered history: a hamper of dirty linen. It belonged to a Compagnie official who had been working in Bombay; upon receiving abrupt orders to sail home, he had been required to depart before he could get his shirts and ruffs washed, so he tossed them into the hamper, proposing to have them laundered while he stopped over at the Cape. Unfortunately, the hamper was stowed in a corner where men urinated and where a constant heat maintained a humidity ideal for breeding germs. This condition was pointed out to the owner, who shrugged and said, 'A good washing ashore and more careful stowage on the rest of the trip will correct things.'

At the Cape the hamper was carried to the Heerengracht, the canal where slaves did the laundry. Six days later these slaves began to show signs of fever and itching skin; three days after that, their faces erupted in tiny papules, which soon enlarged to vesicles and then to pustules. The lucky slaves watched these festering sores change to scabs and then lifetime scars; the unlucky ones died of shattering fevers. Smallpox, that incurable disease, was on the rampage, and whether an afflicted person lived or died was not related to the care he was given.

Forty out of every hundred slaves died that year. Sixty out of every hundred Hottentots at the Cape perished, making their survivors totally dependent on the Dutch. The turbulent disease traveled inland at the rate of eight miles a day, ravaging everyone who fell within its path. One strain leapfrogged the flats to strike at Stellenbosch, and on some farms half the slaves died. The Hottentots of this region were especially susceptible, and many white farmers perished also.

It struck with peculiar fury at Trianon, killing Petronella in the first days and annihilating more than half the slaves. No one in the area tried more diligently to stem the awful advance than Paul de Pré; he went to every afflicted house, ordering the people to burn all clothes related to the dead, and in certain instances, when an entire family had died, he burned the house itself. He quarantined the sick and dug a clean well, and in time the tide abated.

But on the sixteenth day he fell ill, and began to tremble so furiously that Annatjie and Geertruyd put him to bed in the little white outbuilding marked with rake and hoe. There these good women cared for him, assuring him that they would send for Louis at the Cape—if that young man had survived the plague. Wrapping their faces in protective linen, they moved like ghosts about the improvised hospital, comforting him and promising to protect his vineyards.

They were heartsick when the pustules on his face proliferated until they covered all parts of his skin; and when his fever rose so that he shook the bed, and his eyes grew glassy, they knew he could not survive. Still wrapped in cloth to protect themselves from infection, they stayed with him through the night, their candle throwing shadows on the white interior, their forms moving like phantasms come to haunt him for the ill will he had borne them.

He did not become delirious. Like the fighter he was, he followed each step of his decline, and asked, when morning broke, 'Am I dying?'

'You still have a chance,' Annatjie assured him.

When he began to laugh wildly, she tried to ease him, but he would not cease cackling. Then, looking at the ghosts, he pointed at Annatjie and said in a hollow voice, 'You should be dying, not me. It was intended that you should die, you're so much older.'

'Paul, lie still.'

'And you!' he shouted at Geertruyd. 'I hope your womb is dry.'

'Paul, stop—please stop!'

But the agony of death was upon him. The vast dreams were vanishing. His sons were alienated; the slaves were dead; the vineyards would be withering. 'It's you who were supposed to die!' he screamed, and the sores on his face showed fiery red as he dragged his fingernails across them. 'It wasn't planned for me to die. You infected me, you witches.'

He tried to leap from the bed to chastise his tormentors, but fell back exhausted. He began to weep, and soon pitiful sobs racked his body as mortal grief attacked him. 'I was not meant to die,' he mumbled. 'I am of the elect.' He stared accusingly at the shrouded figures waiting to collect his fever-wasted body—and then he died.

Geertruyd, shattered by his hideousness, tried to throw a sheet over him, then broke into convulsive sobs, whereupon Annatjie took hold of her, shook her vigorously, and whispered, 'These are things that are not to be remembered.' And they prepared his body for quick burial.

As soon as Paul was buried, and trenches were dug for the accumulated corpses of the slaves, Annatjie and Geertruyd made a sober calculation of their position, and it was the younger woman who perceived most clearly the danger threatening Trianon and the strategy by which it might be averted.

'At the Cape, in Java, and in the offices of the Lords XVII men will argue, "No women should be allowed to operate a treasure like Trianon," and steps will be taken to deprive us of it.'

'They will not remove me from these fields,' Annatjie said.

'They will try. But we have two very strong points in our favor. The

wines that De Pré blended three years ago are still in our casks. They'll
protect us at the beginning.'

'But when they've been shipped?' Annatjie asked.

'By that time we'll have our second protection.'

'What?'

'Sarel. Yes, Annatjie, by the time Amsterdam orders you and me off
the place, because a man must run a vineyard, we will put Sarel forth,
and convince the authorities that he can run this place better than any
other man they might propose.'

'Could he do that?'

'We shall help him do it,' Geertruyd said. And then, looking away, she
added, almost in a whisper, 'Each night of my life I shall seek God's help
to become pregnant. When Sarel realizes that he is to be a father . . .'
Suddenly she whipped about and caught Annatjie's hands. 'He is a good
man, Annatjie. We shall prove to him that he can run this vineyard.'

Geertruyd was right in expecting that the men of the system would
resent leaving two women in charge of a property upon which the Compagnie depended for revenue, but she was quite wrong as to where that
animosity would originate. Their good neighbor, Andries Boeksma, who
could not resist sticking his nose into everything, including his maids'
sleeping quarters, began raising doubts both at Stellenbosch and at the
Cape.

'The young wife knows nothing, an Amsterdam castaway, and as you
know, the boy's an imbecile. The old lady was capable, but she's dying,
and I ask you, what's to happen with this valuable property?'

Carrying his concern to the officials at the Castle, he encouraged them
to ask the very questions that Geertruyd had anticipated, and one night
after drinks when the governor asked Boeksma, 'Who could we get to run
the vineyards,' Andries said boldly, 'Me. I know the wine business better
than De Pré ever did. We don't need Huguenots to teach us how to make
wine.'

'That's a sensible idea,' the governor said, and next morning he dispatched letters of inquiry to both Java and Amsterdam.

No one warned Geertruyd that her good neighbor Andries Boeksma
was plotting to steal Trianon, but one day as she came from the fields
where she had been inspecting grapes, she saw him with his wagon
stopped beside their fields, inspecting them, and when she walked over to
speak with him, she saw that he was smiling and nodding his head as if
engaged in pleasing calculations.

Hurrying home, she sought Annatjie, and found her in bed, too weak
from illness to rise, and for a moment the perilous position in which Geertruyd found herself overwhelmed her, and she fell into a chair beside the
bed and wept. When Annatjie asked what had happened, she whimpered,
'Now I lose your help, my dear, lovely mother, when I need it most. I just
saw Andries Boeksma spying out our land. Annatjie, he intends stealing it

from us, just as I warned.' She wept for some moments, then broke into sardonic laughter: 'Stupid me! I thought the enemy would be in Java or Amsterdam. And he was waiting in the next village.'

'My fever will subside,' Annatjie assured her. 'If we can hold off the Lords XVII, we can hold off Andries Boeksma.' And from her bed, which held her prisoner far longer than she had expected, she took charge of everything, dispatching slaves to perform specific tasks and explaining to Sarel her reasons for each act.

She was especially eager to have the Compagnie import large numbers of new slaves to replenish the work force, but in this she was disappointed; a young official from Amsterdam had landed at the Cape during the last stages of the epidemic and had seen it not as a vast destruction but as a heaven-sent opportunity for reform. In his report to the Lords XVII he wrote:

> The pox, which did have grievous consequences, offers an opportunity to set Africa on the right path. Our Dutch farmers living there have accustomed themselves to a life of ease. Their daily routine carries them away from their lands to partake of wine, smoke sundry pipes of tobacco, gossip like women, complain about the weather, and pray constantly that their afflictions might pass. It is ironical that they call themselves Boers, for farmers they are not. They regard all such work as our farmers perform at home as labor fit only for slaves.

> I recommend that you use this plague as a God-sent opportunity to halt further importation of slaves, and to curtail the use of Hottentot and half-caste labor. Let us comb from Holland honest men and women who know how to work, Boers who will create in Africa a peasant class of true Dutch character, unspoiled by sloth and privilege.

For a brief moment in history there was a chance that this advice might be followed, converting South Africa into a settlement much like the northern American colonies and Canada, where in good climates free men built strong democracies, but before the proposed Dutch farmers could be imported, the problem was resolved in an unusual way.

Hottentots from independent captaincies east of Stellenbosch had been cruelly ravaged by the pox. Their cattle dead, their traditional hunting lands depleted, they wandered in pathetic groups to farmhouse doors, begging for any kind of work so long as it provided food. This was their only chance of survival, and before long, Geertruyd had accepted so many that Trianon was back to its full complement of workers, proof that if the white man succeeded in his economic enterprises, the brown and the black man would find a way to participate in his prosperity. The only requirement was that the black do his sharing not for free wages but in some form of servitude.

When the fortunes of the plantation were at their lowest ebb, and rumors circulated that it might be taken from the women, Annatjie in her sickbed conceived a strategy which had to be acted upon quickly. Summoning Sarel and his wife, she told them, 'Now's the time to buy back any claims the De Pré boys might have on their father's share of Trianon. They'll think it's worthless. We know it's going to be invaluable.' To her delight, it was not Geertruyd who responded, but Sarel, who said very slowly, 'They will know our troubles . . . and they will sell . . . at a lower price.'

'Oh, Sarel!' his mother cried. 'You do understand, don't you?'

'And this year . . . the three of us . . . we will make even better wine.'

That night Annatjie composed a letter to Henri de Pré in Amsterdam, offering him a shockingly few rix-dollars for his share, and she wanted to carry the letter herself to the Cape, where she would bargain with Louis, but her health would not permit, so she coached her daughter-in-law: 'Sarel's not quite able yet to conduct such a negotiation. And when you've paid Louis his money, you must go to the Castle and meet with the governor and sound him out.'

'I would feel ill-at-ease,' Geertruyd said, looking at her work-stained hands.

'We do what we must,' Annatjie said, and when the cart was ready, she left her bed to bid the girl farewell.

The meeting with Louis went much better than she had anticipated, but it contained one very painful moment. After the deal was concluded, and the papers signed, Geertruyd was led into another part of the house, where coffee and rusks had been prepared, and there she saw De Pré's four sons, and gasped, 'You have four and I have none,' and her barrenness lay heavy upon her.

At the Castle the governor said it was most fortunate that she had come to the Cape, for an Honorable Commissioner had arrived from Java and was awaiting a ship from Amsterdam which would bring him instructions from the Lords XVII. 'We're particularly interested in Trianon,' the governor said as he led her in to dinner.

When she entered the Compagnie mess she was startled by two things: the richness of the huge teakwood table set with gold-and-blue plates kilned in Japan, each bearing the august monogram V.O.C. and accompanied by five pieces of massy silver from China; and the presence of her neighbor Andries Boeksma, who had obviously been instructing the Honorable Commissioner from Java about what he considered the troubles at Trianon.

It was a chilly dinner. The three men, each so much older, wiser and more capable than she, stared down their noses at this girl who presumed to manage a great vineyard. 'What are your plans for restoring Trianon?' the man from Java asked.

Taking a deep breath, she said, 'My husband Sarel already has the fields in good order.'

'Sarel?' Boeksma echoed.

'Yes,' she replied, looking straight at him. She hesitated, wondering if she dared say what was in her mind, but then she found her courage. Turning to the governor, she said with the tenderness of a young wife, 'I'm sure you've been told that Sarel's not capable. I assure you that he is. It's just that he expresses himself slowly.'

'Why isn't he on this mission?'

'Because he is very shy. And I am doing all I can to cure him of that affliction.'

'Many call him slow-witted—' Boeksma said.

'Sir!' the man from Java interrupted. 'This lady . . .'

'It was a most rude remark,' the governor said, 'but I would like to know . . .'

'Three years from now, your Excellency, you will bring important visitors to Trianon . . . to show them with pride what my husband has accomplished.'

During the journey back to Trianon, Geertruyd van Doorn sat very erect, staring straight ahead as if she were a wooden doll, and when she reached the welcoming arms of her little buildings she did not even glance at them. At the big house she ignored the waiting servants and ran directly to Annatjie's room, where she threw herself on the bed beside the sick woman and broke into convulsive sobs.

After her mother-in-law had comforted her, she controlled herself enough to report on her disastrous visit to the Castle: 'They humiliated me. Three great men staring at me, making fun of you and me. Forcing me to say whether or not Sarel was an imbecile. Oh, Annatjie, it was so shameful. And they mean to take Trianon from us.'

Leaping away from the bed, she stormed about the room, uttering curses she had learned in whispered sessions as a child. 'I will not let them do it. Sarel van Doorn will stand before them and face them down. He will run this vineyard to perfection, and within one month I will be pregnant with the son who will inherit Trianon.'

'That's up to God,' Annatjie said.

'I am telling God. "Make me pregnant. Give me the son I need." '

'You are blaspheming, Geertruyd.'

'I am taking God into my partnership. Annatjie, we have two months at most. They're waiting for instructions from the Lords.'

Annatjie, against her children's advice, rose to supervise fields while Geertruyd worked with Sarel: 'It all depends upon you, my dearest friend.

When the men come here to inspect us, you must meet with them, and assure them that all is well.'

'Men?'

'Yes, three tall men, old, powerful.' She acted out their roles: 'The Honorable Commissioner is a gentleman, but he can be very stern. He'll ask the difficult questions. The governor . . . well, he knows everything. Andries Boeksma . . .' She studied how to characterize this evil, unpleasant man: 'He's a worm. But if you try to step on him, Sarel, the others will rise to protect him. Let him insult you.'

Since the ship bringing instructions from Amsterdam was tardy in arriving, the committee of inspection had to postpone its visit for more than half a year, which gave the Van Doorns added time to organize their efforts; but Andries Boeksma also had time to establish his attack, and when the long-awaited letters arrived, with instructions that their commissioner from Java must settle everything, Boeksma convened a planning session at the Castle.

'I've been keeping an eye on the vineyard,' he reported. 'Dreadful shape.'

'The wine seems to be standing up,' the governor said.

'But don't you see, your Excellency? These women are clever. That's wine that De Pré blended.'

'What will the three people do if I dispossess them?' the commissioner asked, turning to the governor.

'They own the land. We'd compensate, one way or another. Maybe a little farm that they could handle. Perhaps a gin shop here at the Cape . . . for sailors.'

'When we get there,' Boeksma coached his superiors, 'you must insist that we meet with Van Doorn alone. The women will protest, but you must order them away. So that you can see for yourselves how defective he is.'

And when the three men finally reached Trianon, Geertruyd awaited them on the stoep, gloriously pregnant, and smiling broadly as she brought Annatjie forward to greet them.

'I was right,' Boeksma whispered. 'They aren't going to let us see Sarel. I told you they kept him locked up.'

At that moment, from the lovely half-door that marked the entrance to the house, Sarel appeared, a tallish, good-looking, thin young man whose smile showed two rows of very white teeth. 'Distinguished gentlemen,' he said, emphasizing each syllable, 'we welcome you . . . to Trianon.' With that he offered the two women his arms and held them back as the visitors entered the hallway.

There they received another surprise when Geertruyd detached herself, smiled at the men, and led them into the room designated for their meeting. It had been decorated with flowers and a small cage of goldfinches, and after arranging the four chairs she graciously excused herself: 'My husband feels it would be better if he met with you alone.' She bowed and left.

Once removed from the room, she ran into the one adjoining it, pressed her ear against a small hole in the wall, which had been covered at the other end by the flowers, and listened nervously as Sarel started the discussion. 'Please, God,' she whispered, 'forgive me for when I was insolent. Help Sarel to do what we planned.'

In the opening minutes Sarel's interrogators were quite insulting, treating him as if he were indeed defective, but when Boeksma completed his charges of mismanagement at Trianon, Sarel surprised them by answering slowly and intelligently, 'Gentlemen, aren't you referring to the days when we all suffered . . . from the loss of servants to the plague? We have none of those problems now.'

Boeksma started to refute this claim, and Geertruyd listened anxiously to hear how her husband would handle him, and she was relieved when Sarel said firmly, 'So I have asked our servants to bring before you a selection of our wines.'

He waited until Boeksma started to protest that these had to be wines that Paul de Pré had been responsible for, then added quietly, 'I know that you must suspect . . . that I am offering you wine laid down by De Pré.' He laughed. 'That would be a naughty trick. These are my wines, as you shall see . . . when we visit the cellars.'

Geertruyd, hearing this complicated statement, left her listening post and ran to where Annatjie waited. Taking her mother-in-law by both hands, she exulted: 'He's even better than we had hoped!'

The visitor from Java tasted the new wines and was impressed: 'This is very good, really.'

'And next year it will be great,' Sarel said. 'We intend to make great wines . . . at Trianon.'

Geertruyd, back at her post, clasped her hands and held her breath. What Sarel was to say next represented an enormous gamble, but also a vindication, and as a fighting woman, she had deemed it a proper risk. 'Honorable Commissioner, we at Trianon have no desire to force our product on Java. That's unfair . . . to Java. So what we did two years ago was make quiet inquiries of European . . .' He hesitated, trembling at the bold thing he must say next. Then he smiled and continued: 'What we did was seek buyers in Europe. And I am pleased to inform you that both France and England will buy our wine . . . at an excellent price.'

'Wait!' the commissioner protested. 'If you can make wine this good, we would . . .'

'But where did you get the authority,' the governor asked, 'to make inquiries in Europe?'

'Not in Europe, your Excellency. My wife carried samples to captains when their ships docked at the Cape. I wanted to save you trouble, your Excellency.'

And there the discussion ended as Geertruyd appeared in the doorway. 'Oh,' the man from Java cried. 'Here's your wife now, coming with tea and rusks. You must be very proud, Mevrouw van Doorn, of the excellent wine your husband is making.'

'I am,' she said, and when the interrogators were gone, and Sarel had laughed at how Andries Boeksma had tried to insert irrelevant probes, Geertruyd took her husband's hand and led him to where Annatjie, exhausted, slumped in a chair.

'Your son was magnificent,' Geertruyd said. 'He saved our vineyard.'

'Did I?' Sarel asked, and from the way he straightened up when he spoke, his women were satisfied that he was at last ready to be the master of Trianon.

V. The Trekboers

I N 1702 Hendrik van Doorn became a trekboer, one of those wandering graziers who moved eastward across virgin land at the slow pace of an ox.

Turning his back on any further claim to Trianon, because his mother had married the Huguenot only eight days after his father had been slain by Bushmen, he had penetrated the mountains, taking his wagon apart and carrying it piece by piece up precipices, then reassembling it for tortuous descents into the valleys.

He kept on till he reached a stream where kingfishers flashed blue as they dived toward crystal water, and when he saw the good pastures nearby, he knew he had reached his temporary home. For the first years he grazed his cattle and sheep, lived himself in the meanest reed-and-mud hovel, and shared his austere food with the one slave and the two Hottentot families who had come into exile with him.

Each spring he swore, 'This summer I shall build me a real house,' but as the season lengthened, his resolve weakened, and he watched idly as his Hottentots ranged deep into surrounding valleys, seeking their own people who still dwelt in the region, raising their own cattle, which they would readily barter. His herd increased, and every other year he was able to drive some of his stock back to a Compagnie buying-station; there he would acquire the supplies needed for the approaching two years, then vanish, for he was growing to treasure the freedom he had attained and feared contact with the merchants of the Cape.

Each year, two or three wandering white men might pass his way, or some other young trekboer 'finished with the Cape,' or one of the hunters who ventured far into the interior for months at a time, seeking his fortune in ivory or hides. Once Hendrik joined with a hunter who probed far to the south, where a mighty forest of stinkwood and yellow-wood concealed a herd of elephant.

In the fourth year, drought struck, spreading its ashen terror, choking the river where the kingfishers danced and destroying the pasture. The Hottentots, always aware of water, led them sixty miles to the edge of a great pan containing a little water, and here Hendrik remained with two other trekboers. When the rains finally came, he returned to his stream, but it was never quite the same again, for in the evenings when he sat near the fire with the Hottentots and his slave he felt a sense of restlessness, of loneliness. It never occurred to him that this feeling might terminate if he married, for there were no Dutch girls in that vast region.

In 1707, on a journey home from the cattle station, the Hottentot who guided the oxen realized that Hendrik was not pleased. There had been talk among the Compagnie buyers of a proposed rent for farms such as Van Doorn occupied—nothing definite . . . no legal placaats . . . just rumors of rix-dollars to be paid. 'Verdomde Compagnie!' the Hottentot heard the baas mutter over and over, and it was in this mood that Hendrik stomped alongside his wagon as it approached his hut. It helped his temper none to see another trekboer outspanned there.

The man shuffled toward him and held out his hand. He, too, had braved the mountains and carried his wagon piece by piece down the precipices. The difference was that he had women with him, a haggard wife and a pigtailed daughter named Johanna. Hendrik was twenty-six that year, the girl sixteen, and during the three months the itinerant family stayed at the hut he became enraptured of her. She was willow-thin, a most energetic worker, and the one who held her small family together, for her father was irresolute, her mother a complainer. It was Johanna who mended the clothes and did the cooking. Hendrik, who had lived off the simplest fare, learned to enjoy the curries this girl made; she had acquired the trick of making even the poorest meat taste acceptable by adding the fragrant spices concocted by the Malays at the Cape. She carried with her a plentiful supply, and Hendrik asked, after a particularly fine supper based on steenbok flanks, 'On eastward, how will you find curry?'

'We have enough for three or four years. You don't use very much, you know. By that time traders will be coming through, won't they, Pappie?'

Pappie was an optimist: 'Smous . . . two, three years, there'll be a flow of such peddlers.'

One evening at supper, when they were rested and well prepared for the journey ahead, the father said, 'Tomorrow we move on,' and it was then that Johanna became aware that she did not wish to leave Hendrik. At the edge of the mysterious wilderness she had found a man, sturdy, gentle, and reasonably capable, and although he had said or done nothing to reveal his interest in her, for he would always be hesitant about his own capacities, she felt assured that if she could stay with him a little longer, she would find some way to encourage him.

She was not yet distraught about the passing years—sixteen years old and no husband—but she did foresee that if her family moved far east, it might be some time before a marriageable man came along, so after everyone had gone to bed she crept close to her parents and whispered, 'I would like to remain here with Hendrik.'

The old people fell into a frenzy: 'Would you leave us alone? Who will help us?' They had a dozen reasons why their daughter must not desert them, and each was compelling, for they were an inadequate pair and knew it. Without Johanna they saw little chance of survival in the bleak years ahead, so they pleaded with her to come with them. Tearfully she said she would, for she knew that without her they could perish.

But when she was alone, staring at the empty years ahead, she could not bear the thought of the solitude that was being forced upon her, so she moved silently to Hendrik's litter and wakened him: 'Our last night. Let's walk in the moonlight.'

Trembling with excitement, he slipped into his trousers, and barefooted they left the hut. When they had gone where none could hear them but the ruminating cattle, she said, 'I don't want to leave.'

'You'd stay here? With me?'

'I would.' She could feel him shivering, and added, 'But they need me. They'll not be able to survive without me.'

'I need you!' he blurted out, and with that she dropped any maidenly reticence and embraced him. They fell on the ground, grappled hungrily with each other, and assuaged the loneliness and uncertainty that assailed them. Twice they made fumbling and inconclusive love, aware that they were not handling this matter well, but also aware that gentleness and love and passion were involved.

Finally she whispered, 'I want you to remember me.'

'I'll not let you go. I need you with me.'

She wanted to hear these reassuring words, to know on the eve of her departure for strange fields that she had been able to inspire such thoughts in a man. But now when Hendrik said in a loud voice, 'I'm going to speak with your father,' she grew afraid, lest a confrontation occur that could have no resolution.

'Don't, Hendrik! Perhaps later, when the farm . . .'

Too late. The stocky trekboer marched to the hut, roused the sleeping pair and told them bluntly, 'I'm going to keep your daughter.'

Perhaps they had anticipated such a denouement to their extended stay; at any rate, they knew how to deal with it. With tears, accusations of filial infidelity and pleadings they besought her to stay with them, and when morning came she had to comply.

After they left, Hendrik experienced the most difficult days of his life, because now, for the first time, he could imagine what it would be like to live with a woman; he would lie in his hut and stare at the rolling land she had traversed, picturing himself on horseback galloping after her. He went so far as to worry about how they could marry, with no predikant in the region.

Four times he resolved to leave his hut and herds in care of his servants and ride east to overtake her, but always he fell back on the dirty paillasse he used for a bed, convincing himself that even if he did find her, she might not want to come back with him. But then the awful reality of how impoverished his life would be if he had no wife overcame him, and he would lie for days immobile.

After a year he conquered this sickness, and had almost forgotten Johanna, when his slave came running with news that people were approaching. Leaping from his bed, he instinctively looked to the west to see who had come across the mountains, and when he saw nothing, the slave tugged at his arm and cried, 'This way, Baas.' And from the east, shattered and nearly destroyed by their experiences on a bleak and distant tract, came Johanna and her family.

For two weeks Hendrik and his servants treated the sick, defeated travelers: 'Our Hottentots ran away with most of our cattle. We planted a few mealies, but in the wrong soil. The winds. The drought and then the flooding rains. We had to eat our last sheep.'

The father assailed himself. His wife complained bitterly of their wrong choices. And Johanna, pitifully thin, lay exhausted on Hendrik's paillasse, blaming no one, but obviously near death from having had to do all the work. For ten days Hendrik tended her gently, washing her wasted body and feeding her with broth made by the Hottentots at their open fires; on the eleventh day she got out of bed and insisted upon doing the cooking.

This time the family stayed for six months, and when it came time for them to resume their westward journey to the Cape, Hendrik gave them four oxen, a small cart and a servant, but as they were preparing to depart, Johanna moved to his side, took him by the hand, and without speaking to her parents, indicated that this time she would stay with him. Her thin face showed such anguish at the thought that they might force her to go with them that they could make no more protest; they knew that she loved this man and had lost him once through filial obedience, but she would not surrender him a second time. It was a solemn moment, with no minister to confer society's approbation, no ritual of any kind to mark one of the great rites of human experience. There was no talk, no prayer, no chanting of old hymns. The girl's father and mother faced a perilous mountain traverse on their retreat to the Cape, and there seemed little chance that they would ever return to see their daughter.

The Hottentot flicked his hippopotamus-hide whip. The oxen moved forward, and the broken couple retreated from their sad adventure.

* * *

In the fifteen years since that informal marriage, Johanna had borne nine children, each delivered in the corner of the harsh hut with the assistance of little Hottentot women, whose wails of apprehension and joy equaled the howls of the newborn. Two children had died, one struck down by a yellow Cape cobra in the dust outside the dwelling, another taken by pneumonia; but the seven survivors swarmed about the huts and hillsides. Johanna kept track of her brood, fed and swept and sewed clothes for them all, and kept her ramshackle home in reasonable order.

But she herself deteriorated, and one traveler described her as a slattern, a word she merited, since she had no time for her appearance. At thirty-three she was used up and practically dead, except that she refused to die. She had entered that seemingly endless period in which a scrawny woman, inured to work, moved almost mechanically from one bitter task to the next, perfecting herself in a ritual of survival.

'The only attention she allows herself,' the traveler wrote, 'comes at dusk when, with her brood about her, she holds court as her two Hottentot women servants bathe her feet. Whence this custom came, I know not, nor would Mevrouw van Doorn explain.'

No matter how bleak her life, no matter how unattractive she became, she retained one assurance: Hendrik loved her. She was the only woman he had known, and that first night in the fields she had shown him that she needed him; without books to read or the ability to read them, without other Dutch people to consort with, she had been content to hold Hendrik as the core and source of her life, while he, able to read the great brassbound Bible, could envision no life other than the one he led with her. Sometimes, after reading a chapter of Genesis or Exodus to his family and relating the wanderings of the Israelites to the tribulations of a trekboer, he would speculate on the future of the children: 'Where will the girls find husbands?'

And then in 1724 came the worst drought Hendrik had known, and even when the Hottentots galloped to the edge of the northern pan, thinking to herd the cattle there, they found that it, too, had retreated to a mere pond. Hendrik now had four hundred cattle, three times as many sheep, and he realized that his depleted lands could no longer support them. Even the modest garden that Johanna tended had withered, and one evening Hendrik directed all his clan to go down on their knees and pray. With thirty-five supplicants around him—his own eight, the twenty-two Hottentots, plus the slaves—he begged for rain. Night after night they repeated their prayers, and no rain came. He watched his cattle, his only wealth, grow scrawny, and one dark night as he crept into bed Johanna said, 'I'm ready,' and he replied, 'I do believe God wants us to move east.'

'Should've moved five years ago,' she said without rancor.

'I figure to move east. Maybe sixty, seventy miles.'

'I been east, you know.'

'Was it as bad as you said?'

'It was worse. We was seventy miles east of here, just where you're heading, and it was even worse than Pappie said.'

'But you're willing to try again?'

'This place is used up. We better go somewheres before the drought ruins us.'

'You'd be willing to try again?'

'You're a lot smarter than Pappie. And I know a lot more now than I did then. I'm ready.'

The older children were not. Conservative, like all young people, they complained that they wanted to stay where they were, especially since families were beginning to move into the area, but there were two boys at the farm who looked forward to the proposed move with considerable excitement. Adriaan was a mercurial stripling, lean and quick like his mother. He was twelve that year, illiterate where books were concerned but well versed in what happened on the veld. He understood cattle, the growing of mealies, the tracking of lost sheep and the languages of his family's slaves and Hottentots. He was not a strong boy, nor was he tall; his principal characteristic was an impish delight in the world about him. To Adriaan a mountain had a personality as distinct as that of a master bull or his sisters. He certainly did not talk to trees, but he understood them, and sometimes when he ran across the veld and came upon a cluster of protea, their flowers as big as his head, he would jump with joy to see them whispering among themselves. But his chief delight lay in walking alone, east or north, to the vast empty lands that beckoned.

The other boy who was cheered by news of an eastward trek was the half-Hottentot Dikkop, fathered nineteen years earlier by a Coloured hunter who had lain with one of Hendrik's servants. It was unfair to call him a boy, for he was seven years older than Adriaan, but he was so unusually small, even for a Hottentot, that he looked more like a lad than Adriaan did. He had a large bottom, a handsome light-brown skin and a shy nature that expressed itself principally in his love for the Van Doorn children, especially Adriaan, with whom he had long planned to set forth on a grand exploration. If the family now moved a far distance eastward, after the new hut was built and the cattle acclimated, he and Adriaan would be free to go, and they would be heading into land that few had seen before. Nothing could have pleased Dikkop more than this possibility, and when the wagons were loaded he went to Hendrik: 'Baas, come new farm, Adriaan, me, we head out?'

'It's time,' the baas agreed, and that was all the promise Dikkop required. On the journey he would work as never before, proving to his master that the proposed exploration was justified.

Two wagons heavily loaded, a tent to be pitched at dusk, a white family of nine, two slaves, two large families of Hottentots, two thousand sheep, four hundred cattle and two span of oxen—sixteen in each—formed the complement of the Van Doorns as they headed into totally unfamiliar land. Johanna had a meager collection of kitchen utensils, five spoons, two knives but no forks. Hendrik had a Bible published in Amsterdam in 1630, a few tools and a brown-gold crock in which on festive occasions he made bread pudding for his family. He also had a small assortment of seeds, which he was confident he could expand into a garden, and sixteen rooted cuttings of various fruit trees, which, with luck, would form the basis of an orchard. In the entourage he was the only one who could read, and he took delight in assembling all people connected with him for evening prayer, when he would spread the Bible on his knees and read from it in rich Dutch accents.

The trekboers traveled only modest distances on any day. The oxen were not eager to move and the herds had to be allowed time to graze. Hottentots had to scout ahead to locate watercourses, so that five miles became a satisfactory journey. Also, when a congenial spot was found, the caravan lingered three or four days, enjoying the fresh water and the good pasturage.

At the end of three weeks, when some sixty-five miles had been covered, Hendrik and Johanna stood together on a small rise to survey a broad expanse of pasture, where the grass was not excessive or the water plentiful, but where the configuration of land and protective hills and veld looked promising.

'Was your father's farm like this?'

'Almost the same,' Johanna said.

'And he failed?'

'We almost died.'

'This time it's different,' Hendrik said, but he was reluctant to make the crucial determination without his wife's approval. At a score of intervals in their life together she had been so prescient in warning him of pitfalls that he relied on her to spot weaknesses that he missed.

'Would you worry, Johanna, if we chose this spot?'

'Of course not! You have sons to help you. Trusted servants. I see no trouble.'

'God be praised!' he shouted with an exuberance which startled her. 'This is it!' And he started running toward the center of the plain he had selected, but Johanna cried, 'You won't have time before sunset! Wait till tomorrow!'

'No!' he shouted with an excitement that activated his children and the servants. 'This is ours! We mark it out tonight.' And he kept running to a central position, where he directed his Hottentots to collect rocks for a conspicuous pile. As soon as it was started, he cried to everyone, 'Where's north?' He knew, of course, but wished their confirmation for the sacred rite he was about to perform.

'That's north,' Dikkop said.

'Right.' And he handed Johanna a pistol. 'At half an hour, fire it. I want everyone here to witness that I walked only half an hour.' And with that he strode off to the north, not taking exaggerated steps, and not running, but walking with grave intent. When he had covered about a mile and three-quarters, Johanna fired the pistol, whereupon he stopped, gathered many rocks and built a pile somewhat smaller than the one at the center. Then, shouting with joy, he sped back to the center, leaping and kicking like a boy.

'Where's south?' he yelled.

'Down there!' several voices cried, whereupon he said again to his wife, 'Give me half an hour,' and off he went, never running or cheating, for the testimony must be unanimous that he had defined his land honestly. When the pistol fired, he built a cairn and hastened back to the central pile.

'Where's west?' he shouted with wild animal spirits, and off he went again, taking normal strides but with abnormal vigor. Another shot, another cairn, another dash.

'Where's east?' he cried, and the men bellowed, 'There's east!' But this time, as he headed for the vast unknown that had so lured his crippled grandfather, and had seduced him away from the pleasing security of Trianon, it seemed to him that he was participating in a kind of holy mission, and his eyes misted. His steps slowed and diminished much in scope, so that his farm was going to be lopsided, but he could not help himself. He had walked and run nearly eleven miles at the close of a demanding day, and he was tired, but more than that, he was captivated by the mountains that ran parallel to his course, there to the north, hemming in the beautiful plains on which the great farms of the future would stand. And to the south he could feel the unseen ocean, reaching away to the ice-bound pole, and he had a sense of identification with this untrammeled land that none before him had ever felt.

'He's not walking,' Adriaan said at the center.

'He's slowing down,' Johanna said.

'Give him more time,' the boy pleaded.

'No. We must do it right.' But Adriaan grabbed his mother's hand, preventing her from firing, and of a sudden his father leaped in the air, throwing his arms wide and dashing ahead to recover the lost time.

'Now!' Adriaan said, dropping his hand. The pistol fired, the eastern cairn was established, and Hendrik van Doorn tramped slowly back to his family. The new loan-farm, six thousand acres of promising pasture, had been defined.

The next three months, April through June, were a time of extraordinary effort, since the farm had to be in stable operating condition before the onset of winter. A spacious kraal was built of mud-bricks and stone to contain the precious animals, trees were planted, a small garden was dug and a larger field for mealies was plowed and allowed to lie fallow till spring planting. Only when this was done were the servants put to the task of building the family hut.

Hendrik paced out a rectangle, forty feet by twenty, then leveled it with a mixture of clay and manure. At the four corners long supple poles were driven into the ground, those at the ends bent toward each other and lashed together. A sturdy forty-foot beam joined them, forming the ridge pole of the roof. The sides of the hut, curving from base-line upward, were fashioned of wattles and heavy reeds interwoven with thatch. A crude door entered from the middle of one side, but the two ends were closed off and the whole affair was windowless.

The house contained no furniture except a long table, built by the slaves, with low benchlike seats formed of latticework and leather thongs. Wagon chests held clothing and the few other possessions, and atop them were stacked the plates, pots and the brown-gold crock. The fireplace was a mud-bricked enclosure to one side, with no chimney. Children slept on piles of softened hides, their parents on a bed in the far corner: four two-foot posts jutting above ground, laced with a lattice of reed and thong.

The name for the rude domicile in which the nine Van Doorns would live for the next decade, and the other trekboers for the next century, would occasion endless controversy. It was a hartbees-huisie, and the contradictory origins proposed for the word demonstrated the earthy processes at work shaping a new language for the colony. The hartebeest, of course, was the narrow-faced, ringed-horn antelope so common to the veld, but there was no logical reason why this lovely animal who roamed the open spaces should lend his name to this cramped residence. A better explanation is that the word was a corruption of the Hottentot /harub, a mat of rushes, plus the Dutch *huisje*, little house. Others claimed that it must be *harde* plus *bies* plus *huisie*, hard-reed house. Whatever, the hartbees-huisie stood as the symbol of the great distance these Dutchmen were traveling physically and spiritually from both the settlement at the Cape and their progenitors in Holland.

The first winter was a difficult time, with little food in store and none growing, but the men scoured the hills and brought in great quantities of springbok and gemsbok and handsome blesbok. Occasionally the Van Doorns, in their smoky hartebeest hut would dine on hartebeest itself; then Johanna would cut the meat into small strips, using a few onions, a little flour and a pinch of curry. Hendrik would roam the lower hills, looking for wild fruits which he could mangle into a chutney mixed with nuts, and the family would eat well.

The children begged their father to make one of his bread puddings, but without lemon rind or cherries or apples to grace it, he felt it would be a disappointment, and he refrained, but toward September, when the long winter was ending, an old smous driving a rickety wagon came through from the Cape with a miraculous supply of flour, coffee, condiments, dried fruits, and things like sewing needles and pins.

'You'll be the farthest east,' he said in a high, wheezing voice.

'How'd you get over the mountains alone?' Hendrik asked.

'Partner and I, we broke the wagon down, carried the parts over.'

'Where's your partner?'

'Took himself a farm. Down by the ocean.'

'How you getting back to the Cape?'

'I'll sell the things. I'll sell the wagon. Then I'll walk back and buy another.'

'You plan to come back this way?' Johanna asked.

'Maybe next year.'

'This'll be a nice place then,' Hendrik said. 'Maybe I'll build us a real house.'

No one believed this. Four years on this farm, a drought or two, a more fertile valley espied on a cattle drive, and the Van Doorns would all be impatient for a move to better land. But now there was food at hand, and a few rix-dollars to pay for it, so the entire family joined in fingering through the old man's stock.

'I'm not eager to sell,' he said. 'Lots of people on the way back want my things.'

'How many people?' Hendrik asked.

'Between here and the mountains . . . ten . . . twenty farms. It's becoming a new Stellenbosch.'

Johanna saw to it that they bought prudently, but at the end of the bargaining she said, 'Bet you haven't had a good meal in weeks.'

'I eat.'

'If you let us have some of that dried fruit, some of those spices, my husband will make you the best bread pudding you ever tasted.'

'That one?' The old man looked almost contemptuously at Hendrik, but when Johanna pressed him on the exchange, he began to waver.

'You got any mutton? Just good mutton?'

'We do.'

'Mutton and pudding. I'd like that.' So the barter was arranged, and while Johanna and Hendrik worked inside the hut, the old man sat on a rickety stool by the entrance, savoring the good smell of meat. Trekboers liked their meat swimming in grease.

It was a gala meal, there at the farthest edge of settlement, and when the meat had been apportioned and there was much surplus, Adriaan said, 'I'd like to give Dikkop some.' No one spoke, so he added, 'Dikkop and me, we're going on the walk, you remember.' So it was approved that the Hottentot could come to the doorway of the hut while Adriaan passed him a tin plate of mutton. 'Stay here,' he whispered.

Now Hendrik brought forth the crock with no handles, placing it before the old man: 'You first.'

This was a mistake. The old fellow took nearly half the pot; he hadn't had a sweet in ages, and certainly not one with bits of lemon rind and dried apples. The Van Doorns divided the remainder evenly, but Adriaan split his portion in two. 'Whatever are you doing?' Johanna asked, and her son said, 'I promised Dikkop a share,' and he passed it quickly out.

Their journey was planned for November, when protea blossoms were opening like great golden moons. Dikkop, brown and barefooted, nineteen years old and well versed in frontier living, would be in charge. Adriaan, well clothed in rugged leather vest and moleskin trousers, and exceptionally informed regarding animals and trees, would be the spiritual leader. They would head for a wild terrain with lions and hippos and elephants and antelope unnumbered. And in the end, if they survived, they would wander back with nothing whatever to show for their journey except rare tales of cliffs negotiated and rivers swum.

In the late spring of 1724 they started east, carrying two guns, two knives, a parcel of dried meat and not a fear in the world.

It was a journey that could rarely be repeated, two young fellows heading into unexplored land without the least concept of what they might be finding, except that it would be an adventure which they felt confident of handling. Dikkop was an unusual Hottentot, skilled as a carpenter, like a Malay, but also beautifully adapted to the wild, like many Hottentots. He had a sense of where danger might lie and how to avoid it. He dreaded physical confrontations and would travel considerable distances to escape them; he was, indeed, something of a coward, but this had helped him stay alive in difficult surroundings and he did not propose altering his philosophy now.

Adriaan, in the wilderness, was a remarkable boy, afraid of nothing, confident that he could confront any animal no matter how big or powerful, and alive to all the sensations about him. If his grandfather Willem had been the first Afrikaner, he was the second, for he loved this continent more devoutly than any other child alive at that time. He was part of it; he throbbed to its excitement; he lived with its trees and bushes and birds; and if he could not read books, he could certainly read the documents of nature about him.

They had no tent, no blankets. At night Dikkop, drawing upon knowledge ten thousand years old, showed Adriaan how to form a declivity in the earth for his hip and then to place bushes against his back to break the breeze. They drank whatever water they came upon, for none could be polluted. They ate well, of ripening berries, nuts, roots, an occasional river fish, grubs and abundant meat whenever they wanted it.

They climbed trees to survey distant areas, guided themselves by the stars, keeping a middle path between the mountains to the north, the ocean to the south. Occasionally they spied Hottentot clans, but they preferred to avoid them, for this was an adventure they did not want to share with others. In this way they covered more than a hundred and fifty miles due eastward. On the banks of one river, where all things seemed to be in harmony—grass for cattle had they had any, flat fields for seed, good water to swim in, fine trees for timber—they remained two weeks, exploring the river north and south, testing the herds of game. In later years Adriaan would often remember that river, and would ask Dikkop, 'What do you suppose the name of that river was? Where we stayed those weeks doing nothing?' But they could never deduce what river it must have been: Groot Gourits, Olifants, Kammanassie, Kouga, Gamtoos. It was a river of memory, and sometimes Adriaan said, 'I wonder if it was real. I wonder if we dreamed that river.' It was statements like this, heard by practical men, that gave him his name Mal Adriaan: Mad Adriaan. Daft Adriaan. Crazy Adriaan who sleeps in trees.

Thus the great journeys of boyhood mark a man, showing him possibilities others never see, uncovering potentials that stagger the youthful mind and monopolize an entire life in their attaining. A boy of twelve, sleeping in a tree, looks down upon an alien landscape and sees a lioness, lying in wait to trap an antelope at dawn, and as he watches in silence, a zebra moves unconcernedly into the arena, and the antelope skips free when the lioness leaps upon the zebra's back, breaking its neck with one terrible swipe of claw and snap of teeth. Mal Adriaan, the boy who knows how a lion thinks.

At the midpoint of their journey, when it was about time to turn back with enough stories to fill a lifetime of evening recollections, an accident occurred—nothing of great importance and no harm done—which in its quiet way symbolized the history of the next two hundred and sixty years in this region. Adriaan and Dikkop, white and brown, were traveling idly along a swale that showed no sign of animals, when suddenly Dikkop halted, lifted his head, pointed eastward and said, with some concern and perhaps a little fright, 'People!'

Instinctively the two boys took cover, fairly certain that their movements had been so silent that whoever was approaching could not have detected them. They were right. From the far end of the swale came two young men, shimmering black, hunting in an aimless, noisy way. They were taller than either Adriaan or Dikkop, older than the former, younger than the latter. They were handsome fellows, armed with clubs and assegais; they wore breechclouts and nothing more, except that around the right ankle they displayed a band of delicate blue feathers. They had apparently failed in this day's hunting, for they carried no dead game, and what they intended eating this night, Adriaan could not guess. However, on they came at a moderate pace which would soon put them abreast of the hiding watchers.

It was a tense situation. The newcomers might pass on without discovering the two boys hiding, but then the problem would be how to skirt either north or south to avoid them. More likely, the newcomers would soon spot the strangers, and then what might happen no one could foretell. Dikkop was trembling with apprehension, but Adriaan merely breathed deeply. Then, without preparation, he spoke loudly but in a gentle voice, and when the two blacks turned in consternation, he stepped forward, holding his empty hands forth and saying in Dutch, 'Good day.'

The two blacks automatically reached for their clubs, but now Dikkop moved out, his hands before his face, palms out with fingers extended: 'No! No!' The two blacks continued their movements, held up their clubs, brandished them, and faced the strangers, whose hands were still extended. After a very long time, while Dikkop almost dissolved in fear, they slowly dropped their clubs, stood looking at the unbelievable strangers, then moved carefully forward.

In this way Adriaan van Doorn became the first of his family to meet blacks inhabiting the land to the east. Willem van Doorn had landed at the Cape in 1647, but it was not until 1725 that his great-grandson stood face-to-face with a South African black. Of course, from the early days at the Cape, men like Commander van Riebeeck had owned black slaves, but these were from Madagascar and Angola and Moçambique, never from the great lands to the east. Thus the Van Doorns had occupied the Cape for seventy-eight years before this first contact, and in those fatal generations the Dutch had become committed to the policy of Europeans in whatever new lands they encountered: that whatever they desired of this continent was theirs. During all those years they had paid scant attention to reports from shipwrecked mariners and Hottentot nomads that a major society existed to the east. Because of arrogance and ignorance, the impending confrontation would have to be violent.

'Sotopo,' the younger said when the matter of names was discussed. He came, he said, from far to the east, many days travel, many days. The older boy indicated that they, like Adriaan and Dikkop, had gone wandering at the end of winter and that they, too, had been living off the land, killing an antelope now and then for food. But this day they had been unlucky and would go to bed hungry.

How did they say this? Not a word of the black language was intelligible to the farm boys, and nothing that Adriaan or Dikkop said was intelligible to the other pair, but they conversed as human beings do in frontier societies, with gestures, pantomime, grunts, laughs, and incessant movement of hand and face. The problem of talking with these strangers was not much different from the problem of talking to strange slaves that the Van Doorns would buy from time to time. The master talked, and that was it. The slave understood partially, and that was enough. What really counted was when Dikkop tried to tell them that with the stick he carried he could catch them an antelope for supper. They were too smart to believe this. A witch doctor could do many things with his magic, but not to an antelope. So the four boys crept quietly to the edge of the swale, waited a long time for animals, and finally spotted a herd of springbok drifting along the veld. Very patiently Dikkop moved into position, took aim at a healthy buck, and fired. When the noise of the gun exploded, the two black youths exclaimed in fear, but when the springbok fell and was collected by Dikkop, they marveled.

The canny Hottentot, aware that this night would probably be spent in the company of these two, used many gestures to warn them that if his stick could kill a springbok far away, it could certainly kill them close at hand. And he further showed them that even if they stole the stick, they would not be able to kill the white man, because they would not have the mystery, which he was not going to explain. They understood.

Onto the embers of the blazing fire went the springbok meat, and as it roasted, the four young men made careful calculations of their situation, each pair speaking freely in its own language, assured that the other could not understand whatever strategies were proposed. Dikkop, who was terrified of the situation, suggested that as soon as they finished the evening meal, he and Adriaan should start back toward the distant farm, relying on their guns to keep the blacks at bay should they attempt to follow. Adriaan laughed at such an idea: 'They can run. You can see that from their legs. We'd never escape.'

'So what we do, Baas?' Dikkop asked, almost impertinently.

'We stay here, keep watch and find out as much as we can.'

To Dikkop such a strategy seemed irresponsible, and he said so, sternly; the compromise that evolved was ingenious. As Dikkop explained it, 'We sleep in that tree, Baas. With our guns. You sleep first and I keep guard. Then I waken you, you keep your gun trained on them. Shoot them down if they try to kill us.'

But after they had eaten, the strangers licking the antelope fat from their fingers, Adriaan and Dikkop were astonished to see that the blacks headed immediately for a tree, disposing themselves so that they were protected should the two young men try to kill them in the night. Adriaan, as he hollowed out a place on the ground from which he could aim his gun at the tree, noticed that they had taken their warclubs aloft with them.

And so they spent the night, two above, two below; two awake, two asleep. Only when daylight came did the blacks climb down out of their tree.

They were together four days, with Dikkop in a state of near-exhaustion because of the fear that gripped him. The blacks were so much bigger than he, so powerfully muscled, that he could not avoid imagining them swinging their clubs at his head, so that even at the moment when he fired his gun to bring down another antelope, he expected to be brained. He was not unhappy when the accidental partnership showed signs of breaking up, the blacks explaining that they must return eastward eighteen days walking, Dikkop saying with relief that he and Adriaan must go westward their thirty days. He told Adriaan, 'About same distance, Baas. They move much faster.'

The parting involved no great emotion, but all felt it to be a pregnant moment. There was no shaking of hands, no *abrazos* in the Portuguese style, only a moment of intense quiet as the two pairs looked at each other for the last time. Then, as if to epitomize the unfolding history of these racial groups, Sotopo thrust out his hand to grasp Adriaan by the arm, but the Dutch boy was frightened by the unexpected movement and drew away. By the time he recovered his senses and wanted to accept the farewell touching, Sotopo had stepped back, mortified that his gesture had been rejected. Dikkop, the Coloured man, merely stood aside and watched, participant in nothing.

The two blacks moved off first, but after they reached the eastern end of the glade they stopped and turned back to watch the strangers walking to the west, and there they stood as the two figures grew smaller and smaller, their miraculous fire-sticks over their shoulders.

'Who were they?' Sotopo asked his older brother.

'Like the ones who came across the sea, before Old Grandmother's time.' The lads had been told about these mysterious creatures; they had arrived by sea in a floating house that had broken to pieces on the rocks, and they had come ashore. There had been a few killings, on each side, after which the strangers had split into two parties, one walking overland and perishing in the empty spaces, the other waiting by the shore for many moons—many, many moons—until another floating house came to take them away.

They had left no visible impact on the tribes, only memories to be talked about at night by warriors in the kraals. But clearly, the little fellow with the white hair had been of that breed. As for the other? 'Who was he, Mandiso?'

'He looked like one of the brown people from the valleys,' the older boy replied, 'but there's something different.'

And when the strange pair vanished in the western distance, the two black travelers turned toward their own homes.

They were Xhosa, members of the great and powerful tribe that lived beyond the big river, and when they returned to their family they were going to have much explaining to do. They could hear Old Grandmother screaming at them: 'Where have you been? Where did you take your little brother? What do you mean, a white boy with a stick that threw flame?' Each night as they moved closer to home, they devised a different strategy.

'You explain it, Mandiso. You're older.' And that night it was arranged that Mandiso would tell how they had wanted to know what lay west of the big river, beyond the hills where the red-paint earth lay.

But on the next evening it would seem desirable that Sotopo do the speaking, since he was younger and would be accorded a more sympathetic hearing: 'We followed the spoor of a large beast, but could not find him, and before we knew it we were beyond the hills.'

On some nights they would mutually acknowledge the fact that neither of these explanations sounded convincing, but how to explain their hegira they did not know. The truth would surely be rejected. 'The reason we were away so long,' Mandiso said as they gnawed on roots from a succulent shrub, 'was that day after day we felt that when we reached the top of the next hill we would see something of magnitude.' He hesitated, and Sotopo continued the narrative: 'But whenever we reached the crest of the hill, all we saw was nothing. More forests, little rivers and a great many more hills.'

'Shall we tell them of the two boys?' Mandiso asked.

'That's difficult,' Sotopo said, 'because the little one with the yellow skin—I don't think he was a boy. I do believe he was a Khoi-khoi, maybe twenty summers.'

'I liked the big one,' Mandiso said. 'He wasn't afraid, you know. The little one, you could smell him sweating in fear. But the white-haired boy, he seemed to like us.'

'But at the end he, too, jumped back in fear.'

'He did,' Mandiso agreed. 'You moved toward him and he leaped back, afraid like the little one.'

When they reached the banks of the big river and knew that they must soon encounter other Xhosa, they stopped speculating and faced up to the fact that before nightfall they would have to explain their absence. 'What we'll do,' Mandiso said with a touch of resignation, 'is simply tell them that we wanted to see what lay far to the west.'

'But shall we tell them of the two strangers?'

'I think we better had,' the older boy said. 'If we could smell fear in the little one, Old Grandmother will see excitement in our eyes, whether we speak of it or not.' So it was agreed that they would tell the entire story, embellishing nothing, hiding nothing, and this resolve pacified their fears, and they went forward boldly to meet the scouts that guarded the perimeters, and with them they were quite brave and forthright, but when Old Grandmother started shouting at them, they crumpled and told a very disjointed story.

The Xhosa people took their name from a historic chieftain who ruled around the year 1500. Among his many accomplishments was securing for them the lovely chain of valleys they now occupied between the mountains and the shores of the Indian Ocean. For half a thousand years they had been drifting easily south and west, enticed from in front by a succession of empty pasture lands, edged from behind by the movement of other tribes. They had been traveling at the rate of only a hundred and twenty miles a century, and although this had accelerated recently, as their population and especially their herds increased, they could have been expected to reach the Cape, and the end of their expansion, about the year 2025 had not the Dutch occupied the Cape and started their own expansion eastward. After the meeting of the four young men, it became obvious that trekboer and Xhosa would have to come face-to-face, and that this would take place rather soon, probably along the Great Fish River.

Well to the east, in a valley unusually well protected, lived the Great Chief, who had never even visited the western frontier where the family of Sotopo and Mandiso lived. All tribes owed allegiance to the Great Chief, though his effective powers over them were limited to precedence at festivals and rituals, and determination of the rights of the royal family, to which all chiefs of the tribal group belonged. The constituent tribes were organized geographically, Sotopo's being the westernmost. Tribal chiefs appointed headmen of various clans or 'neighborhoods,' which were large enough to permit their members to intermarry. The 'neighborhoods' were broken down into kraals, where intermarriage was forbidden, and Sotopo's father, Makubele, was kraal headman; he carried orders from above, served at ceremonies and postured a good deal, but everyone knew, especially Makubele himself, that the kraal was really ruled by the tongue of Tutula, Old Grandmother. The family consisted of forty-one members.

To say 'They owned a wooded hillside well inland from the sea' would confuse the entire point of this story, because nobody *owned* any part of the land. Sotopo's father owned many cattle, and if the cows continued to produce calves, he might well become the next chief. Old Grandmother owned the beautifully tanned animal skins she used as coverlets in winter. And Sotopo owned his polished hard-wood assegais. But the land belonged to the spirits who governed life; it existed forever, for everyone, and was apportioned temporarily according to the dictates of the tribal chief and senior headman. Sotopo's father occupied the hillside for the time being, and when he died the older son could inherit the loan-place, but no man or family ever acquired ownership.

The beauty of the system was that since all the land in the world was free, when a dispute over succession occurred or a kraal became crowded, the aggrieved could simply move on; if an entire kraal decided to move west, as happened continually, they left behind unencumbered land open for others to occupy. In some other distant valley as acceptable as the one they had left, they would settle down, and life would continue much as it had done for the last eight hundred years. All that was needed to ensure happiness was unlimited land.

'What we should get on with now,' Makubele said, puffing his pipe after the excitement over the boys' trip quieted, 'is Mandiso's circumcision.' Everyone agreed, especially Mandiso, who was seventeen years old now and eager to become a man. The running away to the west had been a last childish adventure; now girls in the valley were beginning to look at him with extra interest, and unless he went through the painful ordeal of officially becoming a man, there was no chance that he could ever attain one of them, no matter how much lobola he assembled for a purchase. Their valley already contained one man, now in his forties, who had evaded circumcision, and no one would have much to do with him, women or men, because he had not certified his manhood.

Young Sotopo, only fourteen that year, had become aware during their expedition that his brother was changing, growing more serious; sometimes Mandiso had remained silent for most of a day, as if he were anticipating the rites that lay ahead, and now no one was more attentive to the impending rituals than Sotopo. He kept wondering how he would perform, were he Mandiso.

He watched as the family elders visited other families to ascertain which of their boys wished to participate, and he stayed with his father when the men visited the witch doctor to determine when the moon would be in proper position to build the secluded straw lodge in which the manhood-boys would live for three months after the ritual. He saw the designated boys set out to collect red-earth clay for ceremonial adornment, watched as they wove the curious rush-hats they would wear for a hundred days: three feet long, tied at one end, open at the other, but worn parallel to the ground, with the tied end trailing behind. He could imagine Mandiso in such a hat; he would look much like the crowned crane, sacred bird of the Xhosa.

The day came when the man who had been appointed their guardian assembled the nine manhood-boys and led them to the river, where in the presence of men only, with a few lads like Sotopo watching from hiding places among the trees, they stripped, went into the waters, and painted themselves totally with white clay; when they emerged, they were like ghosts. In this uniform they marched to the secluded lodge, where the guardian entered with them, initiating them into the verbal secrets of the tribe. After a long time he led the boys outside, where all checked to be sure there were at least nine ant hills; Mandiso identified his with two sticks, and the guardian left.

All that night the boys chanted old songs inherited from the days when the Xhosa people lived far to the north, long before the time when Great Xhosa gave them their name, and Sotopo, still watching, envied them their fellowship, and the singing, and the fact that they would soon be men.

Next morning, when the sun was well up, the guardian returned with his knife-sharp assegai, strode purposefully into the lodge and cried in a loud voice, 'Who wishes to become a man?' and with pride Sotopo heard his brother answer, 'I wish to be a man.' There was a silence during which Sotopo could imagine the flash of the assegai, the burning pain, and then the triumphant shout: 'Now I am a man!' Against his will, Sotopo burst into tears of pride; his brother had not cried out in pain.

When the nine were initiated, they left the lodge one by one, each carrying in his right hand the foreskin that had been cut away. This was hidden in the ant hill, each to his own, so that evil spirits could not find them and create spells. For three days a guard was posted at the ant hills to keep sorcerers away; by then the ants would have devoured all traces of the ritual.

It was important, in this valley, to watch out for spirits, and when the nine boys had been in their shack for six days, the dreaded fire-bird struck to remind everyone of his power. Only a few people had ever seen this bird, which was fortunate, because it was so terrifying. It lived behind the mountains and ate prodigious quantities of stolen mealies, growing so fat that it became larger than a hippopotamus. Then, because it was a hellish bird, it set itself on fire, its body fat throwing long flames as it flew through the sky, screaming with a mixture of joy at destroying kraals and pain at the consuming of its own body: thus came thunder and lightning.

When the fat was nearly burned away, the fire-bird dove to earth in a tremendous clap of thunder, buried itself deep and laid one egg, large and very white, which burrowed underground till it reached the bottom of some river. There it ripened until another full-grown fire-bird leaped out of the river to gorge mealies, set itself afire, and bring more thunder and lightning.

On this day, when Mandiso and his eight companions huddled in their lodge, the fire-bird was especially vengeful, sweeping back and forth across the valley until the earth seemed to tremble, so loud were the claps of thunder. As at any kraal, it was imperative that the headman go out into the storm with his assegais, stand by the kraal where the beasts lowed in confusion, and with such magic as he had, defend his cattle and his family from the lightning. If the fire-bird did succeed in blasting a kraal, it was proof that the occupants had done something wrong, and then they would have to pay excessive fees to the witch doctor to get themselves made clean again.

Indeed, one had to pay the witch doctor for almost every act of life, but when the fire-bird wept, that was powerful proof that someone had transgressed. In certain storms, when the bird's fat burned too swiftly, the pain became unendurable, and the wild-flying bird began to cry, just like a baby, and as its tears fell they turned to hail, each grain bigger than a bird's egg, and this peppered the valley unmercifully.

In this storm the fire-bird wept so pitifully that vast sheets of hail came thundering down, breaking thatch and hurting cows until their cries penetrated the hut where Sotopo and his family huddled. One flurry of especially heavy stones struck Makubele as he stood outside endeavoring to protect his family, and he fell to the ground. Sotopo, seeing this, realized that if the witch doctor heard of it, he would take it as proof that it was Mandiso who had sinned in some way, causing the fire-bird to torment the valley. So although it was forbidden, Sotopo jumped from the safety of the hut, ran to his father, raised him to his feet, and then assisted him in fighting off the bird.

When the fire-bird left the valley to dive into the earth behind the hills, and the lightning ceased, Sotopo quietly gathered the three assegais he had laboriously made and his one calf, harbinger of the herds he would one day own, and walked purposefully to the witch doctor's hut.

'I come seeking aid,' he said twice at the low entrance. From the dark interior a heavy voice said, 'Enter.'

Since the boy had never before visited a diviner, he had little concept of the mysterious world he was entering: the owl on the dead branch; the stuffed hornbill in the corner, red-wattled and forlorn; the sacs of dead animals; lizards and herbs; and above all, the brooding presence of the old man who wrestled with evil spirits, preventing them from overwhelming the community.

'I hear your father was knocked down by the fire-bird,' the witch doctor said.

'No,' Sotopo lied. 'He slipped when rain made the slope muddy.'

'I hear you left your hut.'

'I went to help fight off the fire-bird.'

'Why do you come to me? What other great wrong have you done?'

'I come to plead for my brother.'

'Mandiso? In the circumcision lodge? What great wrong has he done?'

'Nothing. Oh, nothing. But I want you to intercede for him, that he conduct himself bravely during these weeks.'

The diviner coughed. This was a bright boy, this Sotopo son of Makubele, grandson of Old Grandmother. He knew that it was all-important how a young manhood-boy behaved himself during the initiation; two years ago one applicant fainted with pain, and although it was discovered that his wound had festered, that was no excuse for fainting, and he was consequently given second status, which would mar him for the rest of his life. That Sotopo should be enough concerned about his brother to offer three assegais and a cow . . .

'You bring me the assegais?' the witch doctor asked.

'Yes, and my cow.'

'You're a strong boy. You'll be a wise man one day. Leave them with me.'

'And you will protect my brother?'

'He will do well.'

'And you'll forget that my father slipped in the mud?'

'I will forget.'

'Diviner, we thank you. All of us thank you.' Sotopo told no one of his clandestine visit to the witch doctor, and he was much relieved when he heard rumors from the ritual lodge that Mandiso was conducting himself especially well.

In the days that followed, Sotopo became aware that another resident of the valley was taking an unusual interest in his brother's progress; it was Xuma, the attractive girl who lived in the kraal at the far end of the valley. She was fifteen, a year older than Sotopo, with a smiling face, supple lips, and an accumulation of ear bangles, beads and ankle charms that made her approach a musical interlude. Sotopo had known Xuma all his life and liked her better than any other girl, even though she was older than he and in some ways stronger, and it pleased him that this lively girl, above all others, had focused her attention on Mandiso.

'How do they say, about the lodge?' she asked as she came easily down the path to Sotopo's kraal.

'They say well. He's strong, Xuma.'

'I know.'

It was permissible, in Xhosa custom, for boys who were not yet men to play at night with girls past puberty, always mindful that there must not be any babies, and Sotopo was aware that Xuma had begun to go into the veld with his brother, even spending nights with him, so he was not surprised that she should now be inquiring after him, and he was pleased. Because he loved his brother, and cherished the long exploring trip they had taken together, he looked forward to the day when Mandiso would be chief of the clan and he the assistant.

His family lived in a collection of huts, seven of them, scattered about the kraal in which the cattle were kept. They were dome-shaped, formed by rows of saplings implanted in a circular pattern, bent inward and bound together, then thickly thatched. The huts were handsome of themselves, and when seen against the rolling hills, formed pleasing patterns.

Xuma, honored to become part of this family, volunteered to help collect thatch for replenishing the huts, and often she went down to the river with her shell knife to cut rushes. Sotopo went with her, to help carry the large, but light, bundles homeward, and on one trip Xuma confided that her father had fallen into trouble with the witch doctor and had been forced to pay him excessive gifts.

'That's troublesome,' Sotopo said, not revealing that he, too, had had a minor confrontation with the powerful diviner.

'I don't know what Father did that was wrong,' Xuma said. 'He isn't a man who angers anyone easily, but the witch doctor was most angry.'

It was like that among the Xhosa. As a nation, the tribes were a gentle people, eschewing vast armies for war against their neighbors, but there were clashes with the Hottentots. Some of the conquered little people allied themselves with the Xhosa, intermarrying and occasionally even attaining power within the hierarchy. This interaction with the Hottentots continued through many centuries, and one of the lasting legacies was a unique language: from the Hottentots, the Xhosa borrowed the click sounds, and these distinguished their speech from that of the other southern black tribes.

Although they did not war on the grand scale, no Xhosa warrior ever hesitated to snatch up his assegais if his cattle had to be defended, or if he saw a good chance to capture his neighbor's. Cattle raiding was the national pastime; success conferred distinction, for cattle were in many ways more important than babies. Everything depended upon them: a man's reputation derived from the number of cattle he held; the kind of bride a young man could aspire to was determined by how many cattle he could bring as lobola to the girl's parents; and the good name of a kraal like Sotopo's sprang almost entirely from the number of cows and oxen and bulls it possessed. The cattle did not have to be good beasts, nor produce copious milk, nor excellent eating meat; there was no merit in having a prepotent bull which threw fine animals. Only numbers counted, which meant that year by year the quality of the great herds deteriorated, with five thousand beasts needed to perform the functions that nine hundred really good animals could have fulfilled.

So although the Xhosa lived without fear of warfare, they lived in dreadful fear of what might happen to their scrawny cattle, and it was the diviner who established and policed the intricate rules for the preservation of the herd. For example, during her entire lifetime no Xhosa woman could ever approach or lay her hand upon the rocks which enclosed the kraal, and if any dared to enter the sacred area, she would be punished. A boy set to tending his family's cattle as they roamed the hills had better come home with every calf, or his punishment would be savage. There was a time to perform every function connected with cattle, a proper way to handle them. No boy dared milk a cow, and for a girl to do so was a grave offense; of course, in special circumstances, when no adult males were available, a daughter was permitted to milk a cow, but she was forbidden to touch the milk sac itself. Every act of life, it seemed, was circumscribed by rules, and Xuma's father had broken one of them. He was, as Xuma intimated to Sotopo, in deep trouble.

But this was forgotten as the time approached when the nine manhood-boys in the lodge reached the end of their confinement, and now a sad thing happened: Sotopo, who had been so close to his brother, became aware that henceforth a gulf would exist between them. Sotopo was still a boy; Mandiso was a man, and his allegiance to the eight others who had undergone the ordeal with him would always be much stronger than his friendship for his own brother, who had not, and it was with sorrow that the boy watched the emergence of the man.

The lectures on manhood delivered by the headman and the guardian were now ended. The intricate rituals, the secrets of the tribe had been shared, and the time for burning down the lodge and all its pains was at hand. But first the nine new men must go to the river in sight of the entire community and cleanse themselves of the white clay that had marked them for the past hundred days. In stately procession, naked, with the mark of their circumcision plain for all to see, the new-men marched to the river, immersed themselves, and spent several hours trying to clean away the adhesive mud. When they emerged, their bodies, long protected from the sun, were lean and pale. Anointed with butter and red-earth, they glimmered in the unaccustomed light; never again in their lives would they appear so manly, so promising of noble conduct.

Then came the celebration! Dried gourds, their seeds intact, were rattled in fine rhythms. Musical instruments, consisting of a single cord of cured gut tied tight between the ends of a bowed piece of wood, were plucked, the musician keeping one end of the wood between his teeth, and altering the sound by altering the movements of his mouth. Old women held two sticks, beating them together, and young men who had completed their ritual three or four years before dressed themselves in wild costumes of feather, rush and reed, ready to dance till they collapsed in exhaustion.

Before the manhood-boys were free to join the celebration, their guardian lighted a brand, carried it solemnly to the ceremonial lodge and set it ablaze. Now the nine inductees rushed from their place of seclusion for the last time, dressed in gaudy costumes topped by their elongated hats, which they still wore horizontally. Turning their backs to the blazing lodge, they kept their eyes rigidly forward as they walked away, for if they dared look back, evil spirits would doom them.

Free of the lodge, they became like wild men as they joined their exultant families and friends, cavorting without rule and leaping into the air as if to challenge the fire-bird himself. Then slowly order began to take over, the clapping of hands assumed a stately rhythm, and all associated with the ceremony leaned forward to see which new-man among the nine would step forward as spokesman for the group.

It was Mandiso, and at this moment of honor Sotopo gave a cry of joy and nodded to the diviner, who did not nod back.

'Today we are men,' Mandiso said, and with these words he began the great dance of the Xhosa, keeping his feet planted on the ground but gyrating all parts of his body as if each were a separate entity. He was especially adroit at sending his belly in one direction, his buttocks in another, and at the moment when he did this to perfection, the other eight new-men leaped in the air, tore about the dancing ground and settled into their version of this dance, so that the entire area was filled with wildly twisting bodies, cries, and the rumble of approval.

The feasting lasted two days. At times both the young men and the spectators collapsed in exhaustion, slept in a kind of daze, awakened, drank large draughts of mealie-beer, and with fresh shouting and renewed vigor, resumed the dance. Dust rose from the kraals; soot from the burned shack was scattered joyously; Sotopo, numb with pride because of his brother's outstanding performance, watched the proceedings from the edge of the crowd and observed how carefully Xuma followed the dancers, never participating herself but applauding quietly whenever Mandiso performed his solos.

When Mandiso returned to the family kraal, the first thing he did was to ask Sotopo's help in laying out the floor for a new hut; it was not as big as his father's, nor would it be as tall; it was a hut for two people, not ten.

'You can attend the ant hills,' the new-man told his brother, and Sotopo was delighted to be given this honor. Taking a large basket, he circulated among some fifteen large ant hills, scooping up excess earth in which the ants had deposited their larvae, dead bodies and bits of their saliva. This fine, granular earth, when spread in a thick layer and watered down and allowed to bake in the sun, formed a substance harder than most stone, and when polished with cow manure, made the best possible base for a hut. Sotopo, guessing that he was building for Xuma, made a floor that would last a generation.

The young women of the family had to gather the saplings for the walls, but when it came to the thatching, that all-important part, Old Grandmother herself wanted to go down to the fields and cut the grass, and although she was too weak to gather all that would be required, she did deliver the first bundles and then stood noisily directing the design of the lovely, rounded finish.

It was a jewel of a hut, and now Mandiso was eligible to visit Xuma's parents, but on the eve of doing so, the most disturbing word reached Sotopo via one of his playmates: 'A sorcerer has placed a curse on Xuma's father.' This could be such a fatal impediment to any union of the two families that Sotopo borrowed two of his brother's best assegais and a goat and went directly to the witch doctor, hailing him from a distance: 'All-powerful One! May I approach?'

'Come' echoed the mournful voice.

'I seek counsel.'

'I see that this time you bring only two assegais.'

'But they are better, All-powerful.'

'And a cow?'

'The boy is holding a goat outside.'

'What is the question?'

'Will my brother marry Xuma?'

There was a long silence, perhaps five minutes, during which the old man carefully weighed the complex problems raised by this inquiry. Sotopo's family was one of the most powerful in the valley and could be expected, in the years to come, to provide both leadership and wealth; it would not be wise to affront them. But on the other hand, Xuma's family had long been troublesome and there was good cause to believe that the last flight of the fire-bird had been evoked by malperformances on the father's part. Twice the witch doctor had warned the man, and twice the injunctions had been ignored. Now he was under a curse, and it seemed highly improbable that he would ever be allowed to escape from it, for it was the duty of a diviner to police the health of his clan, to remove all forces that might work against central authority, and Xuma's father was an irritation.

But what to say about this proposed marriage? And the more the old man pondered this difficult question, the angrier he became at this boy Sotopo who had raised it. Why had he dared to come with such an impertinent question? Why had he stepped forth as champion of the girl Xuma, which was clearly his intention in this affair? Damn him. Sotopo, son of Makubele, a boy to be marked for remembrance.

The old man temporized: 'I suppose that Xuma herself has had no part in her father's misbehavior. I suppose a marriage could go forward.'

'Oh, thank you!' Sotopo cried, but after he had surrendered the two assegais and the goat and had gone running down the footpath, the diviner stared after him, mumbling, 'Two assegais, not three. A goat, and not one of the best. Damn that boy!'

The wedding ceremonies covered eleven days, and in certain respects they were a triumph for Mandiso, since he got himself a strong, beautiful and darling wife; but in another way they were a disaster, for through her he acquired the enmity of the diviner. As to the wedding itself, there was a good deal of marching back and forth between Mandiso's kraal and Xuma's: he had to take a heifer there as proof of his good intentions; she had to bring rushes here as an indication of her willingness to work; he had to go there in his finest ornaments to dance before her family and break two saplings across his knee, thus pledging that he would never beat his wife; she had to come and dance before his cattle kraal to show that she revered the cows and would show them the respect they merited. And through it all, the old witch doctor watched sardonically, aware that no matter what rituals they observed, nothing good could come of this marriage. It was doomed.

But he did not interfere, and even officiated in certain of the hallowed rites, going so far as to protect the new hut against evil. He did this for good reason: he suspected that within a year Mandiso and Xuma would flee the place, after which he could see that one of his nephews gained possession.

To that end, as soon as the young couple moved into the handsome hut, he began asking questions through the community, never directing them at Mandiso, but always at Xuma's father: 'Who do you think it was that caused the fire-bird to fly?' and 'Have you noticed how the mealies at his kraal have grown bigger than any others? Could he be casting spells?'

Week after week these poisonous suspicions were broadcast, never a substantiated charge, only the nagging questions: 'Have you seen how Xuma's cattle become pregnant so quickly? Could her father be weaving a spell there, too?' The assumption in this question was most effective; that her father was casting a spell over the new hut was problematic, but that he had done so at his own was accepted: 'He's bringing this valley into sore trouble.'

During this time Sotopo was preoccupied with the last days of boyhood. Having seen his older brother through the twin ordeals of circumcision and marriage, he returned to those things that gave his own life significance. Beyond the family kraal, at the edge of the river, there was a level place where in the morning the wagtails danced, those delicate little gray-brown birds that bobbed their tail feathers up and down as they paraded. They loved insects, and darted their long bills this way and that, plucking them off dead leaves.

They were the good-omen birds, the ones that made a kraal a place of joy, and Sotopo had always found delight in being with them, he on a log, they on some rock at the edge of the river; he sprawled out on the ground, they dancing back and forth oblivious of him, for they seemed to know that they were protected: 'No one but a man near death from frenzy would disturb a wagtail, for they bring us love.'

He also felt increasingly attached to Old Grandmother, as if, like Mandiso, he must soon move away from her influence. He stayed with her about the house, watching as she prepared the dish he liked the most: mealies well pounded in the stump of a tree, then mixed with pumpkin, baked with shreds of antelope meat, and flavored with the herbs which only she knew how to gather.

'Tell me again,' she said as she worked. 'When you ran away from us, you say you met two boys, one brown, one white?' When her grandson nodded, she asked, 'You say one spoke like us? The other didn't? How could that be?'

She had a dozen questions about this meeting; the men in the family had listened to the story, nodded sagely and forgotten the matter, but not Old Grandmother: 'Tell me again, the brown one was small and old, the white one was young and big. That goes against the rule of nature.'

But when he explained, with increasing detail, for he enjoyed talking with the old woman, she told him what he had heard many times before: 'I didn't see it myself, because it happened before I was born. But men like that boy came to our shore once in a house that floated on the waves, but they died like ordinary men.' It was her opinion that what the white-skinned boy had said was probably true: 'I think there are other people hiding across the river. I don't think I'll ever see them, but you will, Sotopo. When you marry and have your own hut and move to the west . . .'

At this point she would always stop what she was doing and ask her grandson, 'Sotopo, who are you going to marry?' And he would blush beneath his dark skin because he had not yet addressed this problem.

But one day he did ask the question whose answer could reveal the dangers that lay ahead: 'Old Grandmother, why do you always say that when I take a wife, we'll move across the river?'

'Ah-hah!' she cackled. 'Now we're ready to talk.' And she sat with him and said, 'Can't you see that the witch doctor is determined to drive Xuma's father out of the valley? And that when he goes, Mandiso will surely go with him? And that when Mandiso and Xuma flee, you'll join them?'

She had uncovered thoughts which had been germinating deep in the boy's mind; he had chosen to stay by himself, away from the others, to communicate with the wagtails and his other friends of river and forest, because he was afraid to face up to the tragedy that he saw developing in the valley, with families quietly turning against Xuma's father, and by extension, against Xuma and Mandiso. He knew instinctively what he had been afraid to voice: that before this year was out he would have to choose whether to stay with his parents, whom he loved, and with Old Grandmother, whom he loved most dearly, or go into exile with Mandiso and Xuma.

His solution for the moment was to draw even closer to his grandmother, for she was the only person who would talk with him; even Mandiso was so occupied with starting a new family that he had little time for his brother.

'Why does the diviner torment us?' he asked the old woman one day.

'He doesn't. No, he doesn't. It's the spirits. It's his job to keep the spirits happy or they'd devastate this valley.'

'But Xuma's father . . .'

'How do we know what he's done? Tell me that, Sotopo! How do we know what evil things a man can do without the rest of us being aware?'

'You think he's guilty?'

'Of what? How should I know. All I know is that if the witch doctor says he's guilty, he's guilty.'

'And Mandiso must go into exile with him, if he leaves?'

'Oh, now!' She thought about this for some time, sucking at her corncob pipe, then said to her grandson, 'I think the time comes for all of us when we should move on. The field is no longer fertile. The neighbors are no longer kindly. For an old woman like me, death comes to solve the problem. For a young person like you, move on.'

Neither of them said another word that day; they had stepped too close to the ultimate realities of life, and it would require weeks of reflection before complete meaning could be known, but in those days of silence Sotopo became aware that all things had deteriorated sadly in the community. Xuma's father had been found one morning in a ditch with a gash on his head. Xuma's cooking pot was shattered when she left it dry-ing in the sun.

So young Sotopo, now approaching sixteen, gathered the two assegais he had made of dark wood and went for the last time to see the diviner. 'Come in,' the old man said.

'Why is Mandiso being punished?'

'You bring me only two assegais? And a calf, perhaps?'

'I have no more cattle, All-powerful One.'

'But you still ask my help.'

'Not for me. For my brother.'

'He is in trouble, Sotopo, deep trouble.'

'But why? He's done nothing.'

'He's associated with Xuma, and her father has done much evil.'

'What evil, All-powerful?'

'Evil that the spirits see.' Beyond this fragile explanation the old man would not go, but he allowed his visitor to sense the implacable opposition all good men ought to show against a member of the tribe guilty of evil practices, even though those practices were never identified.

'Can you do nothing to help him?' Sotopo pleaded.

'It isn't him you're worried about, is it?'

'No, it's Mandiso.'

'He shares the guilt.'

'Can he do nothing?' the boy asked.

'No. The evil is upon him.' And no amount of pleading, no amount of future gifts would alleviate this dreadful curse. The community, through the agency of their diviner, had named Xuma's father as a source of con-tamination, and he must go.

Shortly after this visit he was found beaten to death at the gateway to his kraal, an especially ominous way to die, implying that even the sleek and growing cattle had been powerless to protect him.

That night Mandiso and Xuma came to the big hut, the wife sitting circumspectly to the left among the women as the fateful discussion began. 'You must leave us,' Old Grandmother said without any show of sorrow.

'But why must I surrender . . .'

'The time has come to go,' she said forcefully. 'Tell him, Makubele.' And the boys' father referred only to his own selfish interests: 'The old one's right. You must go. Otherwise the curse will apply to us all, won't it, Old Grandmother?'

But she refused to allow her own predicament or that of her family to intrude in this matter: 'What is important, Mandiso, is not what will hap-pen to your father, but what will happen to you and Xuma. What do you think your future is now, with her father killed in that manner, at the gateway to his kraal?'

'If there is one sacred place—' Mandiso began, but Xuma broke in: 'We must go. And we must go before nightfall tomorrow.'

'Can it really be so!' her husband said, appalled at the implications of what Xuma had said.

'Isn't that true, Old Grandmother?' the girl asked.

'I'd go tonight,' the old woman said. And it was agreed that before the next sun set Mandiso and Xuma would start for the west, to a new settlement, to a new home. They would take cattle, and skin bags of mealies for seed, and other oddments—but they must go, for the consensus of their community, arrived at in complex ways, had decreed that they were no longer wanted.

But where did this leave Sotopo, not yet a man but deeply devoted to his brother and his brother's wife? When the family conclave broke up, he remained with his grandmother a long time, discussing his difficult alternatives: remain, with the diviner probably opposed to him; or flee, when he had not yet been ordained a man? He had absolutely no hard evidence that the witch doctor had declared war upon him, but he knew it had happened and that sooner or later the rumors would begin to circulate against him. But he also knew that to face the future without the sanctions of circumcision entailed dangers too fearful to contemplate. Having watched his brother's joyous entrance into married life, with a girl as admirable as Xuma, he had begun to sense how awful it would be to have the girls of his community categorize him as less-than-man and to be deprived of their companionship.

This was something he could not discuss with his grandmother, so in the dead of night he crept to his brother's kraal and whispered, 'Mandiso! Are you awake?'

'What is it, brother?'

'I shall go with you.'

'Good. We'll need you.'

'But how will I ever become a man?'

Mandiso sat in the dark with his left hand over his mouth, considering this perplexing question, and then, because he felt he must be truthful, he listed the impediments: 'There'd be no guardian to bless the hut. There'd be no other boys to share the experience. We probably couldn't find clay to cover your body. And at the end there'd be no grand celebration.'

'I've thought of that, Mandiso. I've thought of it all, but still I want to stay with you.' And he added, 'With you and Xuma,' for he was not ashamed of his love for his sister-in-law.

'It seems to me,' Mandiso said, 'looking back on everything that happened, that a boy becomes a man with the pain, with the courage. He becomes a man not with the dancing and the food and the cheers of others. He becomes a man within himself, through his own bravery.'

They pondered this for a long time, during which Mandiso hoped that his brother would speak up, would volunteer proof of his courage, but Sotopo was too confused by this necessity to make at age sixteen a decision more difficult than most men make in their entire lives. So finally Mandiso tipped the scales: 'In the woods that time, when we met the two strange men'—in his thinking, they were men, now—'it was you, Sotopo, who devised the plan for sleeping in the tree. I believe I might have slipped away.'

'Really?' the boy asked, and the possibility that he had been brave, there in the woods, so captivated his mind that he said no more that night. Nor did he sleep. At dawn he was at the river saying farewell to the wagtails. At full-sun he was watching a pair of monstrous hornbills waddling across the fields, and at midmorning he had collected his remaining goats, falling in line behind five of the young men who had shared the ritual circumcision with Mandiso and who now elected to go with him because of the profound brotherhood they felt. Three girls who hoped to marry with the young exiles trailed along for a short distance, then turned back tearfully, knowing that they must wait till their suitors brought lobola to their fathers.

In this way units of dissidents had always broken off from the main body of the Xhosa. Perhaps the diviners performed a vital function in identifying those potentially fractious individuals who might ultimately cause trouble in the community; at any rate, the diviners served as the agencies of expulsion. For eight hundred years groups like Mandiso's had broken away to form new clans on the cutting edge of expansion. They never moved far; they retained contact with the rest of the tribe; and they still acknowledged a hazy kind of allegiance to the Great Chief, who existed far to the rear but whom they never saw.

This time the wandering unit proceeded to the east bank of the Great Fish River, which they settled upon because of the vast empty grazing fields on the west bank. 'We'll use those fields,' Mandiso told his followers, 'for the cattle that like to roam.'

In this time-honored tradition the Xhosa innocently launched a westward move which would bring them into direct conflict with the Dutch trekboers, who with equal innocence were drifting eastward. These two great tribes were so similar: each loved its cattle; each measured a man's importance by his herds; each sought untrammeled grazing; each knew that any pasturage it saw belonged to it by divine right; and each honored its predikant or diviner. A titanic confrontation, worse than any storm the fire-bird had ever generated, had become inevitable.

When, in February 1725, Adriaan and Dikkop approached their farm at the conclusion of their wanderings, they faced none of the uncertainties that had perplexed the two Xhosa lads. True, they had been gone almost four months when only three had been intended; but their people knew what they were doing, and the extended absence was no cause for alarm.

As Hendrik assured his wife several times: 'If the lions don't eat them, they'll be back.'

So when they straggled in, with the dust of distant horizons on their eyebrows, no one made much fuss, for Hendrik, too, had been wandering, six weeks to the north to trade for cattle with the Hottentots. He had returned with two hundred fine animals, the largest-ever addition to his herd. He asked Adriaan to ride with him to the easternmost part of the grazing lands, and from a low hill the two Van Doorns looked down approvingly. 'God has been good to us,' Hendrik said. ' "All the land that is Canaan He has given to us and the generations which will follow you." ' For a long time they sat astride their horses, watching the cattle, and there was joy in their hearts.

The hartebeest hut had been lived in so thoroughly that it could scarcely be distinguished from the one on the previous farm, and on the perimeter of the holding, Hendrik had placed four more cairns, midway between the compass points. In less than a year the Van Doorns had themselves a stable farm, six thousand acres well marked and so far removed from any neighbor that intrusion of any kind was unlikely for years to come.

The family was deeply interested in Adriaan's report of the two black youths and this proof that a tribe of some magnitude occupied the lands farther east. Again and again the older Van Doorns asked their son to repeat exactly what he had learned during his four-day meeting with the blacks.

'They speak with clicks,' Adriaan said, 'so they must be of the same family as the Hottentots, but Dikkop understood none of their words. They were a strong, really handsome people, but their only weapons were clubs and assegais.'

Hendrik was so interested that he summoned Dikkop, who conveyed the important information that so far as he could discern, they called themselves the Xhosa: *Hkausa,* he pronounced the word, giving it a pronounced click in the back of his throat. 'They said they were the Xhosa, who lived beyond a big river.'

'What river?' Hendrik asked.

'There were so many,' Adriaan and Dikkop said together, and for the first time they spelled out the geography of the vast lands to the east, and it was this report, laboriously written down in archaic language by Hendrik van Doorn, that ultimately reached the Cape, adding to the Compagnie's comprehension of the lands they were about to govern, whether they wanted to or not:

> The land east of our farm is not to be traversed easily, because heavy mountains enclose it on the north, a chain unbroken for many miles that cannot be penetrated, for there seem to be no passes across it. Travel to the south along the seacoast is no easier, because

deep ravines cut in from the shore, running many miles at times, not passable with wagons. But in between these impediments are lands of great productivity and greater beauty. Our farm lies at the western edge of what must be the finest lands on earth, a garden of flowers and birds and animals. Copious rivers produce water for every purpose, and if fruit trees can be made to grow there as easily as they do here, you will have a garden paradise. But we have reason to believe that black tribes are pressing down upon it from the east.

When Hendrik finished this writing he was proud to have remembered so much of his education, and ashamed that he had neglected it. At Trianon his parents had taught him his letters and to speak correct Dutch, but long years in the company of Hottentot and slave, and then with an illiterate wife, had caused him to speak in rough, unlettered sentences. Worse, he had taught none of his children to read.

But he engaged in no recriminations, for life was bountiful. With June came harvest time, and the family was busy gathering not only enough vegetables for the long winter, but also more than enough to dry for seeds: big yellow pumpkins, gnarled green squash, mealies, radishes, onions, cauliflower and cabbage for pickling. The fruit trees, of course, were too young to bear, but in his explorations of the surrounding terrain Hendrik had found wild lemons whose thick and oily skin proved so useful, and bitter almonds like the ones from the hedge his grandfather had cut down during his escape from Compagnie domination.

One heard little of the Compagnie out here. The farm was so distant from headquarters—one hundred and sixty-two miles in a straight line, half again more according to the wandering path over the mountains—that no official could easily reach it. No predikant ever arrived for marriages and baptisms, and certainly no assessor or tax collector. Still, a kind of supervision prevailed, distant and unenforced, but ready for implementation when roads should penetrate the area. A petulant Compagnie official who crossed the mountains in vast discomfort had come as far east as four farms short of Van Doorn's, and he had written upon his return to the Cape:

> Wherever I went I heard of divers Dutchmen who occupied stupendous farms, Rooi van Valck to the north, Hendrik van Doorn to the east. They graze their cattle on our land without the Compagnie deriving any benefit. They plant their seeds on Compagnie land without any profit to us, and I think the Compagnie deserves better treatment from these rascals. I recommend that every man who occupies a farm pay to the Compagnie a tax of twelve rix-dollars a year plus one-tenth of whatever harvest of grain or fruit or vegetables or

animals he produces. But how this tax is to be collected from farms as distant as Rooi van Valck's and Hendrik van Doorn's, I have not decided.

The loan-farm law was passed, but as the perceptive emissary had predicted, it could rarely be enforced. Distant farmers were instructed to carry their taxes to either the Cape or Stellenbosch, and they simply ignored the law. On farms close in, the officials did make a brave show of riding out in midwinter to demand overdue tithes, but with obstinate and dangerous renegades like Rooi van Valck, no collector dared approach his outlaw domain lest he be shot through the neck.

In these years Adriaan had little concern with tax collectors; he was so occupied with extending his knowledge of the wilderness that weeks would pass without his being seen at the farm. It was then that the soubriquet Mal Adriaan was fastened most securely to him; he would come home from an exploration and say, 'While I was sleeping in the tree . . .' or 'As I climbed out of the hippo's wallow . . .' or 'In the days when I lived with the gemsbok . . .' He caused outrage among his family and the slaves by insisting that lions could climb trees, for it was commonly accepted that they could not and that a man was secure if only he could find refuge in a tree.

'No,' said Adriaan, 'I've seen a tree with seven lions sleeping on the higher branches.' This was so crazy that even the slaves called him Mal Adriaan, and once when he was twenty he experienced for the first time the loneliness that comes upon a young man when he is ridiculed by his peers. The family was eating in the hut, scraping away at bones of mutton and cabbage, when his father asked, 'Have the animals moved closer to our valley?' and he replied automatically, 'When I was staying with the rhinoceros . . .' and his brothers and sisters said simultaneously, 'Oh, Adriaan!' and he had blushed furiously and started to leave the table where they huddled, except that his mother placed her hand upon his arm to restrain him.

That night, as they sat outside the hut, she told him, 'It's not good for a man to wait too long. You must find yourself a wife.'

'Where?'

'That's always the question. Look at our Florrie. Where's she to catch a husband? I'll tell you where. One of these days a young man will come by here on his horse, looking for a bride. And he'll see Florrie, and off she'll go.'

And sure enough, within four weeks of that conversation Dikkop, always frightened of new movement, came rushing to the hut, shouting, 'Man coming on horse!' And in came a dusty, lusty young farmer who had ridden a hundred and twenty miles on hearing the rumor that Hendrik van Doorn out beyond the river had several daughters. He made no secret of his mission, stayed five weeks, during which he ate enormous quantities of food, and on the night Hendrik offered him a bread pudding crammed with lemon rind and cherries and dried apples, he belched, pushed back the soup plate from which he had gorged himself, and said, 'Florrie and me, we're heading home tomorrow.'

The Van Doorns were delighted. It might be years or never before they saw this daughter again, but at her age it was proper that she ride away. Illiterate, barely able to sew a straight line, a horrible cook, a worse housekeeper, off she went with her illiterate husband to found a new farm, to raise a new brood of tough-minded trekboers to occupy the land.

Two nights after they departed, Johanna sat with Adriaan again and said, 'Take the brown horse and be going.'

'Where?'

'Three people now have told us that Rooi van Valck has a mess of daughters. Ride up and get one.'

'They also say Rooi's a bad one. Defames the Bible.'

'Well.' She hardly knew how to say what was required, but she had thought about this matter for some time, keeping her mouth shut lest she irritate her husband. But now she said in a low voice, 'Adriaan, it's possible to take the Bible too seriously. I can't read it myself—never had my letters—but sometimes I think your father makes a fool of himself, scouring that book for instructions. If Rooi van Valck has a daughter, and she looks as if she'd be good in bed, grab her.' When Adriaan said nothing, for these ideas were shocking to him, raised as he was with absolute faith in the Bible, even though he could not read it for himself, his mother added, 'Living in a hut is no pleasure. It's not much better than what the Hottentots have. But to love your father and go to bed with him when you children are asleep. That can be enough to keep a life going.' With a sudden jerk of her hand she pulled him around to face her in the darkness. With her eyes close to his she whispered, 'And never forget it. You leave for Van Valck's at sunup.'

Adriaan took the brown horse and rode far to the north, across the empty plains, across the muddy Touws River, and well to the west of the Witteberge Mountains, until he saw ahead the columns of dust that signified a settlement. It was the farm, the little empire, of Rooi van Valck, and to get to the hartebeest huts in which Rooi and his wild collection of attendants lived, he had to pass through valleys containing twenty thousand sheep, seven thousand head of cattle.

'I'm looking for Rooi,' Adriaan said, overwhelmed by the magnitude of his wealth.

'Not here,' a Madagascan slave growled.

'Where is he?'

'Who knows?'

'Can I speak to his wife?'

'Which one?'

'His wife. I want to speak with his wife.'

'He's got four. The white one, the yellow one, the brown one, the black one.'

'Which one has the daughters?'

'They all got daughters, sons too.'

'I'll see the white one.'

'Over there.' And the slave pointed to a hut not one bit better than the one the Van Doorns occupied.

All these cattle, Adriaan said to himself as he crossed the clearing to the hut. And he lives in a hut like us. He was pleased rather than disturbed, and when the white Mevrouw van Valck invited him to sit with her, he was relieved to see that she was much like his mother: old beyond her years, well adapted to the dirt, independent in nature.

'What do you want?' she asked, squatting on a log that served as a bench.

'To see your husband.'

'He's around somewheres.'

'When will he be back?'

Like the slave, she answered, 'Who knows?'

'Today? Three days?'

'Who knows?' Looking at him carefully, she asked, 'What farm?'

'Hendrik van Doorn's.'

'Never heard of him.'

'Trianon. Those Van Doorns.'

The name had a startling effect on her. 'Trianon!' she roared, following the name with a string of Dutch and Hottentot curses. Then, going to the open end of the hut, she bellowed, 'Guess who's here? A Van Doorn of Trianon!'

'I'm not from Trianon,' Adriaan tried to explain, but before he could establish this fact, numerous people had erupted from the many huts, women of varied colors bringing with them children of the most mixed appearance.

'This one is from Trianon!' Mevrouw van Valck shouted, hitting him in the shoulder playfully and ringing out a new string of obscenities. 'And I'll wager he's come to find him a wife. Isn't that right, Van Doorn? Isn't that right?'

And before he could control his blushing and explain in an orderly manner the purpose of his mission, the tough woman had yelled for different people, and a procession of bewildering types came to her hut. 'You can have this one,' she shrilled, pointing to a nubile girl of seventeen with dark skin and black hair. 'But you can't have that one because he's a boy.' This occasioned great laughter among the women, and the parade continued.

'This one you can have,' she said more seriously, 'and I'd advise you to take her.' With these words she brought forth one of her own daughters, a girl with bright red hair that fell almost to her waist. She seemed to be about fifteen or sixteen, not shy, not embarrassed by her rowdy mother. Going directly to Adriaan, she extended her hands and said, 'Hello, I'm Seena.' When her mother started to say something obscene, the girl turned in a flash and shouted, 'You, damn fool, shut up.'

'She's the good one,' Mevrouw van Valck shouted, cackling with the other wives, who formed a circle of approbation.

'She has lovely hair,' a Malay woman said, reaching out to fluff the girl's red tresses.

Adriaan, overcome with embarrassment, asked Seena, 'Is there somewhere . . .'

'Get away, you . . .' The girl uttered an oath equal to her mother's and chased the women back. 'We can sit here,' and she indicated an old wagon chest at the entrance to the hut in which she lived with a ramshackle collection of other children.

'Where's your father?' Adriaan asked.

'Out killing Bushmen,' she said.

'When will he be back?'

'Who knows? Last time it took him four weeks to clean out the valleys.'

'Can I stay here?'

'Was my mother right? Are you looking for a wife?'

'I'm . . . I'm . . . looking for your father.'

'You don't have to wait for him. He doesn't care what happens. Have you a farm?'

'I live a long way off.'

'Good.' That was all she said, but the single word conveyed her longing to get away from this tempestuous place.

It was worse when Rooi himself roared in from the manhunt. He was a huge man with a flaming head of red hair that gave him his name. He was really Rupertus van Valck, from a family which had settled early at the Cape. Rooi van Valck, Rooi the Falcon, the red-haired terror who submitted to no control, whether from the Cape governor, the Lords XVII, or God Himself.

The Van Valcks first had trouble with authority in the time of Van Riebeeck, when Leopold, the stubborn soldier who had founded the family, sought permission to marry a Malaccan girl. The Compagnie dillydallied so long that when permission was finally granted, Rooi's grandfather was a sire twice over. The next serious clash came when Mevrouw van Valck, a lively, independent-minded woman, wanted to dress in a way becoming her prettiness. From Amsterdam the Lords XVII specifically ordered that 'Mevrouw van Valck must not wear bombazine, and certainly not a bright yellow bombazine, and especially since she is not the wife of a senior Compagnie official.' When she persisted, with her husband's encouragement, soldiers were sent to rip the dress apart, whereupon Van Valck thumped the soldiers—and spent a long day on the wooden horse.

Since he had not been dropped onto the killing horse from any height, he escaped the permanent injury that had marred Willem van Doorn's later life, but he never escaped the corroding resentment, and when some months later one of the soldiers who dropped him was found with his throat cut, it was assumed that Van Valck had done it. Nothing was proved, but subsequently, when Willem and Katje made their escape through the bitter almond, this Van Valck followed the same route. But he went north.

There, in a wild and spacious valley, he built his huts, assembled slaves and runaways, and launched the infamous Van Valcks. He had four sons, and they proliferated, but all kept to the initial valley, where they farmed vast herds of animals and planted whole orchards of a single fruit. They sheared their own sheep, wove their own cloth, and tanned their hides to make leather shoes. They timbered, built rude roads, and had a community which needed to move out for nothing except periodic journeys to graze, and into which officials were afraid to enter.

It was the other side of the African coin. At the Cape, citizens came to attention when the Lords XVII handed down a directive; they lived for the Compagnie's profit, from the Compagnie's largesse, and in obedience to the Compagnie's strict laws. But at Van Valck's frontier, the red-haired adventurers said, 'To hell with the Compagnie!' and enforced it.

No predikant had ever preached at Rooi van Valck's, or ever dared to castigate the master for having four wives. For two generations no Van Valck had been legally married, and in this generation none wished to be. The mélange of children could not be distinguished, and their bounding health and good spirits belied the Compagnie's belief that children must be reared in strict accordance with the Bible. At Rooi's, there were no Bibles.

'So you come looking for a bride?' the huge man said as he studied Adriaan. 'You the one they call Mal Adriaan?'

'How did you hear of me?'

'The smous. In what way are you crazy?'

'I like to wander. I study the animals.'

'Eh, Seena! Kom hier, verdomde vrouw.' When she came to him, he rumpled her hair and said, 'No question she's my daughter. Look at that hair! I don't have to worry the smous got to her mother.'

When Adriaan blushed a deeper red than Rooi's shock of hair, the renegade tossed his daughter in the air, catching her under the arms. 'If you get her, you're getting a good one,' he cried. And again he snatched her up, throwing her far into the air, but this time she fell not back to his arms, but across the open space into Adriaan's. The first time he touched Seena, really, was as she came flying at him.

'She's yours, son, and don't go wandering too much, Crazy Adriaan, or the smous will catch her when you're not looking.'

'Shut up, damn you!' the girl cried, making a face at her father. 'If Adriaan was bigger, he'd thrash you.'

With a huge hand, Rooi reached out, grabbed Adriaan, and almost broke his collarbone. Shaking him like a dog, he said, 'He better not try. And, son, you treat this girl right, or I'll kill you.' It was obvious that he meant it, but to Rooi's surprise, Adriaan broke loose, swung his fist in uncontrollable fury, and smashed the huge man on the side of his face. It was like a monkey swatting an elephant, and Rooi roared with delight.

'He's a spunky one, Seena. But if he tries to hit you, kick him in the stomach.' And with a sudden swipe of his right boot, he aimed a shot at Adriaan's crotch. Perhaps the fear of the awful pain that impended activated the young man, for deftly he sidestepped, caught the up-swinging foot, and toppled the big redhead.

While still flat on the ground, Rooi lashed out with a swinging leg, caught Adriaan at the ankles and brought him down. With a leap, the big man fell upon him, wrestling him into a position where he could gouge his eyes with big knuckles. As Adriaan felt the man's superhuman strength and saw the dreadful knuckles coming at him, he thought: I am wrestling with the devil. For the devil's daughter. And he jerked his knees up to smite the evil one in the gut, but Rooi fended off this last attack.

'I'll teach you,' he grunted, and he would have done so had not Seena grabbed a log and struck him on the head, knocking him quite silly. When he recovered, blinking his eyes and spitting, he roared, 'Who hit me?' and Seena said, 'He did.' And there stood Adriaan, fists clenched, waiting for what might come next.

'By God!' the huge redhead shouted as he raised himself to his knees. 'I do believe Seena's got herself a good one.' And when he hoisted himself back onto his feet, still groggy, he embraced Adriaan in one huge arm, Seena in the other, and dragged them into his hut, where he broke out a jug of brandy.

They drank through the night, and toward four in the morning, when Adriaan was almost insensible, Rooi insisted that the bridal couple be given a hut to themselves, so children were swept out of the hovel occupied by the Malayan wife, and onto her filthy pile of straw the young pair were thrown. At first Adriaan wanted only to sleep, a fact which was circulated through the camp by youngsters who watched from a peephole, but Seena certainly did not propose to spend her wedding night in that manner. So, as the children shouted to the elders, she roused him from his stupor and indoctrinated him into the duties of a husband.

'That's good, that's good!' Rooi van Valck said when the children reported to him. 'I think Seena's got herself a man to be proud of. He's a little crazy, that's obvious, but he's quick with his fists, and I like that. What's his name again?'

'Adriaan,' the children said. They knew everything.

* * *

Sotopo's achievement of manhood did not come easily. As his brother Mandiso had predicted when the matter of the boy's joining the exodus to the Fish River was discussed, the new settlement had no guardian to supervise the circumcision rites, no other boys to share it, and certainly no large community to arrange a celebration. But Sotopo knew that the ceremony had to be performed, and it was, in a lonely and gruesome way.

A small hut was built, big enough for one boy. Since white clay could not be located, red had to suffice. There being no older man familiar with a sharp cutting edge, a young amateur volunteered, and with a dull assegai performed a hideous operation. Without the proper herbs to medicate it, the wound festered so badly that Sotopo almost lost his life. For a hundred days he remained in isolation, only his brother slipping in occasionally to share the experience he had had when he was inducted into manhood.

When the seclusion ended, the small hut was set aflame, as custom required, and time was at hand for him to dance. He did so alone, with no gourd, no stringed instrument; tail feathers projected from the rear as he waved his buttocks, and the shells about his ankle reverberated when he stomped. At the conclusion he delivered a speech of profound import. Looking at the adventurous little band, he said in a loud, clear voice, 'I am a man.' It was toward men like him that the trekboers were advancing.

Seena and Adriaan met Nels Linnart of Sweden in a most improbable way. In 1748 a horseman came rushing up from the south with the exciting news that a great ship had foundered off Cape Seal, with so much cargo to be salvaged that all farms in the area could replenish their stocks for a dozen years. At Van Doorn's, every able man saddled his horse to participate in the looting, and when Adriaan galloped south, Seena rode with him, her long red hair flashing in the wind.

They arrived at the wreck about two hours before sunset the next day, to find an even richer store than the messenger had indicated. Some thirty trekboers had formed a rescue line with ropes and were bringing the ship's passengers ashore, but as soon as the lives were saved, these same men rushed back through the waves to plunder the ship, and the eager Van Doorns arrived in time to reach the foodstuffs before the water damaged them. Whole barrels of flour and herring were rafted ashore. One family concentrated on every item of furniture in the captain's cabin, and when he protested, a huge trekboer glowered at him and said, 'If you'd kept your ship off the rocks, we wouldn't be plundering it.'

All that night, with the aid of a shadowy moon and rush lanterns, the avaricious trekboers ransacked the ship of its movable treasures, but at dawn a young man not over thirty came to Adriaan and said, in highly accented Dutch, 'Please, sir, you and your wife look decent. Will you help me get my books?'

'Who are you?' Adriaan asked suspiciously.

'Dr. Nels Linnart, Stockholm and Uppsala.' When Adriaan's blank face showed that he understood nothing, the young man said, 'Sweden.' Adriaan had never heard of this, either, so the man said, 'Please, I have fine books there. I must save them.'

Still Adriaan registered nothing, but Seena said impatiently, 'He needs help,' and in the doctor's wake the two Van Doorns swam out to the ship, clambered up the side and boarded the vessel that could not stay afloat much longer. To them it was a weird universe of dark passageways, pounding waves and the dank smell of steerage. The treasured books were in a cabin, forty or fifty large volumes published in diverse countries, and these Dr. Linnart proposed to move ashore, but to get them through the waves without destroying them posed a problem.

Seena devised a way. She would jump down into the waves, grasp the rope, then accept an armful of books, which she would hold aloft as Adriaan struggled beneath her, holding her above the waves as they moved slowly ashore. 'Bravo!' cried the doctor from the deck as he saw the couple deposit his books well inland and come back for another cargo.

In this manner the little library was rescued; it would form the foundation of a notable collection of books in southern Africa: Latin, Greek, German, Dutch, English, Swedish, and fourteen in French. They covered various branches of science, especially mathematics and botany, and among them was Systema Naturae by Karl von Linné, also of Stockholm and Uppsala. 'He's my uncle,' the young doctor said, stamping the water out of his boots.

'What kind of book is this?' Adriaan asked, for it was the first one other than his father's Bible that he had ever held in his hands.

'It deals with plants and flowers.'

And there on the beach by the wrecked ship Adriaan said the words that would determine the remainder of his life: 'I like plants and flowers.'

'Have you seen many here?' the young scientist asked, concerned always with his basic subject even though his ship had sunk.

'I have walked many miles,' Adriaan said with immediate recognition of the young man's intense interest, 'and wherever I went, there was something new.'

'That's what my uncle said. My job is to collect the new plants. The ones we haven't heard of yet in Europe.'

'What do you mean, collect?' Adriaan asked, but before the young doctor could explain, Hendrik shouted, 'Come on! There's lots more to take before she sinks.' And the two young Van Doorns continued with the plunder, but when there was nothing left and the ship started to break apart, Adriaan was drawn back to the scientist, and while the other trekboers helped the shipwrecked passengers build temporary huts to protect

themselves till rescue ships arrived, he and Seena stowed the precious
books upon their two horses and started walking back to the farm, accompanied by the young Swede.

> I had intended [he wrote in his report published by the London
> Association] doing my collecting in India, but Providence sent my
> ship upon the rocks at the southern tip of Africa, where I was
> rescued by a remarkable couple with whom I spent the four hap-
> piest months of my life, living in a wattled hut. The husband, who
> could not read a word of any language, had made himself a well-
> trained scientist, while his wife with flaming red hair could do posi-
> tively anything. She could ride a horse, handle a gun, drink copious
> quantities of gin, swear like a Norwegian, prune fruit trees, sew,
> cook, laugh and tell fabulous lies about her father, who, she
> claimed, had four wives. I remember the morning that I cried in my
> bad Dutch, 'God did not intend me to go to India. He brought me
> here to work with you.' They opened a new world for me, showing
> me wonders I had not anticipated. The husband knew every tree,
> the wife every device required for a good life, and when the four
> months ended in their hut, I was better prepared to start my collect-
> ing than if I had matriculated in a university. To my great joy and
> profit, this wonderful pair wanted to join me, even though I warned
> them that I might be gone for seven months. 'What's that to us?'
> Mevrouw van Doorn asked, and they rode off with me as uncon-
> cerned as if headed for a *fête champêtre* in some French park.

They traveled farther east than Adriaan had gone on his first exploration,
then due north into a type of land which not even he had ever seen. It lay
well north of the mountain range and was desert, yet not desert, for whenever rain fell, a multitude of flowers burst across the entire landscape, sub-
merging it in a carpet of such beauty that Dr. Linnart was amazed: 'I
could spend a lifetime here and identify a new flower every day, I do believe.' When Adriaan inquired further as to why the Swede was collecting
so avidly, Linnart spent several nights endeavoring to explain what the expedition signified, and in his report he referred to this experience:

> Van Doorn wishing to know what I was about, I decided to unravel
> for him the full extent of my interest, holding back nothing. I laid
> forth Karl von Linné's organizing principle of *genus* and *species*,
> and within the first hour this natural-born scientist understood what
> I was saying better than most of my students at the university. He
> then asked me why Linné bothered with such a system, and I in-
> formed him that my uncle intended to catalogue every plant grow-
> ing in the world, which was why I had come to South Africa, and
> he asked me, 'Even these flowers on the veld?' and I said, 'Especially

these flowers, which we do not see in Europe.' So with that bare instruction, he proceeded to collect some four hundred flowers, not less, arranging them in grand divisions according to Von Linné's principles. It was a remarkable feat which few scholars in Europe could have duplicated.

The caravan consisted of Dr. Linnart, the two Van Doorns, Dikkop in charge of everything, and ten Hottentots paid by the Swede. Two wagons accompanied the expedition, loaded with small wooden boxes into which the specimens collected by Adriaan went. On four separate occasions Linnart said that he could not credit the wealth of flowers on the veld, and each time Adriaan assured him that if he went farther, he would find more.

But interested as Dr. Linnart was in botany, he was even more captivated by Seena's remarkable capacity for keeping the camp lively, and he was enchanted one morning when she said briskly, 'Biltong's gone. You, Linnart, shoot us an eland.' So he and Dikkop had gone hunting, and although they failed to get one of the huge antelopes, they did knock down two gemsboks, which they butchered on the spot, bringing back to camp large stores of thinly cut strips of the best lean meat.

'Looks good,' Seena said approvingly as she tended a pot in whose liquor the meat would be marinated.

Linnart, hungry to know the procedures of every operation, asked, 'What's in the pot?' and she showed him: 'A pound of salt. Two ounces of sugar. A heavy pinch of saltpeter. A cup of strong vinegar, a little pepper and those crushed herbs.'

'What herbs?'

'Any I can find,' she said. And into this cold mixture she dropped the strips of meat, stirring them occasionally so that each would be well penetrated. When she was satisfied that the gemsbok was properly marinated, she directed Linnart to remove the strips, take them to the sunny side of the camp where the wind could strike them, and leave them there to dry.

When they were hard as rock, with flavor permeating every cell, they were packed in cloth, to be gnawed upon when other food was lacking. 'The best meal for the veld,' Linnart exclaimed as he nearly broke his teeth chewing. 'Better than the pemmican our Reindeer People make. More flavor.'

The best part of each day came in the late afternoon when Seena and the Hottentots were preparing supper, for then Dr. Linnart sat with Adriaan, discussing Africa and comparing it with other lands he had seen. He liked to take down his atlas and press flat the maps of areas he spoke of, and then little Dikkop would crowd in, look at the incomprehensible pages and nod sagely in agreement with whatever the Swede said. Adriaan, who could not read the words, grasped the geographical forms and he, too, approved.

'Look at this map of Africa,' Linnart told the men one evening. 'Your little colony is truncated. It ought to run all the way north to the Zambezi, its natural boundary. And east to the Indian Ocean.'

'Here in the east,' said Adriaan, tapping the map, 'are many Xhosa.'

'Who are they?'

'Tell him, Dikkop.' And the Hottentot expressed his apprehension over the large tribes of blacks that Sotopo had described during their meeting in the glade.

'Mmmm!' Linnart said. 'If that's the case, sooner or later . . .' And with his forefinger he indicated the blacks moving westward and the trekboers eastward. 'There's got to be a clash.'

'I think so too,' Dikkop said.

'But up here? Toward the Zambezi? Have any of you gone up there?'

'The Compagnie wouldn't allow us,' Adriaan said.

'But the Compagnie lets you live where you are, hundreds of miles from the Cape. What stops you from exploring the north?' When neither of the men responded, he said, 'Men should always move out till they reach the final barriers. East to the ocean. North to the Zambezi.'

If he implied that the trekboers were delinquent in comparison with other peoples who had explored other lands, he had some justification, but if he thought that they held back through lack of adventurousness, he was wrong, as he discovered when at the end of seven months they came back south through the mountains, looking for signs of the Van Doorn farm:

> Then I learned what *trekboer* means, for when we approached the farm where I had spent those four happy months, I saw to my horror that the place had been wiped out. The roof of the hut was flapping in the wind. The kraal was deserted. The gardens had gone to weeds and there was no sign of sheep or cattle or human beings. It was total desolation, and I looked with anguish at the young Van Doorns, trying to anticipate how they would accept this tragedy. They were unconcerned. 'Father moved, I suppose' was all my extraordinary guide said, and with no more concern than if the journey involved perhaps a mile, we set off eastward toward a destination we could not guess. At the forty-mile mark I asked, 'Will they be here?' and Van Doorn merely shrugged his shoulders, saying, 'If not here, somewhere else.' I was especially impressed by the indifference of red-haired Seena. When I asked her one night after an especially difficult day fording rivers, 'Where do you think they are?' she spoke like a sailor: 'Who cares a goddamn? They've got to be out here somewhere.' And at the end of the seventy-fifth mile, by my calculation, we came upon a handsome valley in which the old man had staked out a circular farm comprising, I calculated, not less than six thousand acres of the best. For this he paid only a handful of rix-dollars annually, was not obligated to fence it, and when he

judged the pastures to be exhausted, he was free to abandon it and move some seventy miles to some other spot of equal beauty, to treat it as roughly. 'Tiptoeing through paradise,' they call it.

It became a tearful moment when this brilliant young man left the Van Doorn farm and headed toward the Cape with his two wagons filled with specimens. Adriaan and Seena did not cry, of course, for they had known for some time that he must leave them. The tears came from Dr. Linnart, who tried three times to make a flowery farewell speech to the effect that he had lived for nearly a year with nature and with two people who understood it better than he did, but every time he looked at Seena he was so overcome with love and fellowship that tears choked him and he had to start over. It was an expedition, he affirmed, that he would never forget; he ended his comments rather awkwardly: 'My uncle, who publishes his books under his Latin name, Carolus Linnaeus, would send you a copy of the volume in which this material will appear, except, of course, neither of you can read.'

Several of his comments regarding his trip to the Cape were widely circulated in Europe and America; after recounting his horrendous experience in crossing the final mountains, when his specimens ran the risk of being lost in a sudden fog, he told of coming to Trianon:

> It was impossible to believe that the same family which occupied the huts in the wilderness also owned this delectable country mansion, laid out as meticulously as any French palace. It boasted four separate gardens, each with its special quality, and a façade which, while not ornate in any way, displayed an elegance that could not be improved upon. These Van Doorns make two kinds of wine, a rich sweet Trianon for sale in Europe, where it is highly regarded, and a pale, very dry white wine of almost no body or fragrance until the last bottle has been drunk. Then it remembers beautifully . . .

> At last we reached the Cape, which had been described by several Dutchmen as something comparable to Paris or Rome. It was a miserable town of less than three thousand souls, unkempt streets and flat-roofed houses, with some recollection of Amsterdam in the canals that brought water down from mountain streams. The Castle and the Groote Kerk, a fine gabled octagonal building, dominate life here, the former telling the people what their hands must do, the latter instructing their souls.

> The avaricious Compagnie utilizes the Cape not as a serious settlement but as a provisioning station on the way to Java. Compagnie law dominates all: the church, the farmer, the clerk and the future. There are no schools of any distinction, the scholarchs barely able to

keep ahead of their students. Yet the Compagnie officials and the few persons of wealth live indulgently, as I witnessed during a splendid dinner at the Castle, where no fewer than thirty-six fine dishes were offered, and even the ladies, who ate separately, partook most liberally of the governor's largesse.

My visit to the Cape occurred two years prior to my collecting tour in the English colonies of America. These colonies were launched more or less at the same time as the Dutch venture in Africa, and I was constantly oppressed by comparison of the two. The colonies had scores of printing presses, the most lively newspapers and journals, and books in every town. I was able to consult with scholars at several fine colleges, Harvard, Yale and Pennsylvania among them. But my most doleful concern grew out of my extended meeting with Dr. Franklin in Philadelphia, that self-educated genius. He reminded me precisely of Adriaan van Doorn, for the two had identical casts of mind. But because of the cultural opportunities in the English colonies, Dr. Franklin is acknowledged to be a great scholar, while Van Doorn, who can neither read nor write, is called at home Mal Adriaan, Crazy Adriaan . . .

It was my own ignorance that caused a major disappointment. Although I knew some Dutch, I had expected to speak mostly French, because of the large number of immigrants who reached the Cape from that country. I had taken mainly French books with me, but when I tried to use the language, which I speak moderately well, I found no one to talk with. Custom and the stern measures of Compagnie rule have eradicated the language, and throughout the colony no sound of French is heard.

Adriaan and Seena had four children, who were reared in the same slapdash manner that prevailed at Rooi van Valck's, and to a degree, at the hartebeest huts of the Van Doorns. They were raised with love and boundless physical affection, much as if they were young puppies, and they showed signs of becoming close copies of their wandering father or their rowdy and profane mother. The first and third had red hair inherited from the Van Valcks; the second and fourth, light blond hair like the Van Doorns; and in 1750 it seemed probable that they would be frontier nomads like their parents, illiterate, contemptuous of Compagnie authority, and delightfully tied to the soil of which they were a part. In a few years strange young men would wander in to court the girls and then start eastward to launch loan-farms of their own, stepping off the six thousand acres to which they felt they would always be entitled. 'The land out there is limitless,' the trekboers proclaimed. 'We can keep moving till we meet the Indian Ocean.' And if a man kept his farm for about ten years before leapfrogging to virgin soil, the process could continue for another hundred years.

'Of course,' Adriaan said when such predictions were being made, 'sooner or later you're going to run into the Xhosa.'

'The what?' the newer trekboers would ask.

'The Xhosa.'

'And what in hell are they?'

'The blacks. They're out there, beyond the big river.'

But since he was one of the very few who had seen them, and since the farms were prospering in the new lands, the Xhosa barrier was ignored.

In many ways the Van Doorn farm now resembled that of Rooi van Valck: grandfather, grandmother, Adriaan's family and his brothers', the numerous grandchildren, and many servants, and the large herds of cattle. Life was good, and when one of the women cried at midmorning, 'I want someone to chop this meat,' any man in hearing distance was eager to help, because this meant that the cooks were going to make bobotie, and there was no dish better than this on the veld.

Seena, who had often made it for her father, usually took command. In a large, deep-sided clay baking dish she placed the chopped beef and mutton, mixing in curry and onions, all of which she allowed to brown while she pounded a large handful of almonds mixed with additional spices. When all was blended and seemingly done, she whipped a dozen eggs in such milk as was available, and threw this on top, baking the entire for about an hour. While the smell permeated the area, she boiled up some rice and took the lid off her crock of chutney. No matter how big the baking dish, no matter how few the diners, there were never any scraps when Seena made bobotie. 'All credit to the curry,' she always said.

To sit at a table after a hard day's work and to have a mug of brandy and a huge plateful of bobotie was the kind of treat that kept a farm contented.

Occasionally Grandfather Hendrik brought out his big Bible, hoping to instruct the children in their alphabet, but they felt that if their parents and their uncles and aunts survived without reading, so could they. But once or twice the youngest boy, Lodevicus, who was now eleven, showed signs that he might be the one who would return to the earlier scholarship of the Van Doorns who had lived in Holland. He would ask his grandfather, 'How many letters must I learn if I want to read?' and Hendrik, referring to the Dutch alphabet, would reply, 'Twenty-two.' And he would show the boy that each letter had two forms, small and capital, taking unusual care in explaining that in Dutch, unlike other languages, capital IJ was not two letters but one. It was all too confusing for Lodevicus, and soon the boy was out rampaging with the others.

However, old Hendrik noticed that it was this same Lodevicus who was beginning to show impatience whenever Adriaan disappeared on one of his explorations: 'Why isn't Father here to help with the work?' And he became quite agitated if Seena accompanied her husband, as she liked to do: 'Mother ought to be home, making us bobotie.' The three other children accepted their father's strange behavior and showed no concern when he was absent for months at a time. Moreover, they enjoyed it when their parents began to say, 'People are crowding in. Too many Compagnie rules. That valley where the cattle grazed last year looks better.' But Lodevicus said, 'Why can't we stay in one place? Build us a house of stone?'

Hendrik and Johanna, always willing to move when they were younger, now sided with their grandson: 'Lodevicus is right. Let's build a house of stone.' And they argued that this piece of land was good for another twenty years, if properly managed. But Adriaan became increasingly restless, and red-headed Seena backed him up: 'Let's all get out of here!' So the wagons were loaded, the huts were abandoned, and with little Dikkop in the lead, everyone moved eastward, but along the way, Hendrik whispered to his grandson, 'Lodevicus, when you're older, you must stop wandering and build your house of stone.'

It was during one such journey that old Hendrik, now sixty-nine, collapsed and died. This was no great tragedy; his years had been full and he had lived them at the heart of a lively family whose future seemed secure. But there was the matter of burial, and this posed a difficult problem, for whereas Hendrik had been a religious man who would have wanted God's words to be read over his grave, the family no longer contained anyone who could read. Johanna brought out the old Bible and there was serious talk of burying it with the old man who had loved it, but at this moment Lodevicus happened to look away and saw a rider coming down the hills to the west.

'A man comes!' he called to the mourners, and Dikkop hurried off to ascertain who it might be. Within a short time a stranger rode up, tall and thin, wearing dark clothes and broad-brimmed hat, but no gun of any kind. When he reined his horse he looked with piercing eye at each of the Van Doorns, and said in a voice that seemed to come from deep within the earth, 'I have been searching for you, Van Doorns, and I see that my arrival is timely.' Alighting, he strode to the grave, looked down and asked, 'What sinner has been called to face the judgment of his Lord?'

'Hendrik van Doorn.'

'The same,' the tall man said. 'He alone among you was saved, is that not true?'

'He knew the book,' Johanna said, pointing to the Bible.

'Let us bury him with prayer,' the stranger said, and while the commingled family bowed, he launched into a long supplication, beseeching God to forgive the grievous sins of his wayward child Hendrik, whereupon red-headed Seena began to snicker, for if there had been any Van Doorn who was not wayward, it was Hendrik.

The stranger paid no attention to this irreverence, but continued his endless prayer. The Hottentots who had worked for Baas Hendrik, some from the earliest days, stood respectfully to one side. They had loved the old trekboer as a father, and the old patriarch had often seen them as children, using the whip when he felt it was needed, rewarding the industrious when he returned with cloth and implements from the cattle trading. He never understood why they so readily drank themselves into a stupor, or why their children ran away to become vagrants rather than work for him. He had acknowledged them to be master herdsmen, far better than the pesky Bushmen still out there sniping at colonists with their poisoned arrows. When the prayer finally ended, the stranger said peremptorily, 'Now you can bury him. He's on his way to meet his Maker.'

'He's dead,' Seena said brusquely. 'He had a damned good life and he's dead.'

'I take that you're the daughter of Rooi van Valck. By your red hair, I mean.'

'I am.'

'I have been sent by the Compagnie to bring the word of God to the wilderness. I am Dominee Specx, of Huguenot lineage, and I have been living at the new town of Swellendam. I am commissioned to marry and baptize, and to bring families like yours back to the ways of the Lord.'

'You're welcomed,' Johanna said, as matriarch of the sprawling family.

'You're on your way to a new farm?'

'We are.'

'They're going to collect the rents on farms now.'

'They'll get none from us,' Adriaan said sharply. 'We've farmed where we willed and paid taxes to no one.'

'That's ending,' the stranger said. 'Beginning this year, all will be collected.'

'All but us,' Adriaan said. 'We explored this land. We occupied it alone. And it belongs to us, not the Compagnie.'

Predikant Specx asked if he could ride with them to the new site, and Johanna said, 'Yes, if you will read to us from the Bible.'

And it was in this way that Lodevicus van Doorn memorized the great, stirring passages of the Old Testament, the experiences of Abraham and Joshua in their wildernesses, the love stories of David and Ruth. Night after night, as the tall dominee sat by the candle, intoning timeless stories of men who wandered into strange lands, Lodevicus reflected on how much he had missed in the years when he could not read the Bible, and he asked Specx how long it would take him to learn, and the dominee said, 'One week, if God commissioned you.'

To the surprise of the Van Doorns, he proved to be a congenial traveling companion, eager to share the work, willing to share the hardships. At the riverbanks he was often up front with the Hottentots to guide the oxen across, and he was a strong man with an axe when they settled on their new land and it came time to cut wood. Nor was he reticent, as some predikants were apt to be. He entered any argument, made his statement, and listened to those who tried to rebut him. He was fun at meals, for he had a most voracious appetite and startled the children with the amounts of food he consumed: 'I do believe I could eat that entire bobotie.'

'I'm sure you could,' Seena said. She alone displayed animosity toward the predikant, an inheritance from her father, who had fought the church incessantly, and one afternoon he took her aside and said, 'Seena, I know your father. I've fought with him. Last year he threw me off his farm when I went there to talk with him about God. He roared, "I need no God meddling in my affairs." And now you're roaring at me.'

'We don't need you here, Dominee. We're doing very well.'

'I'm sure you are, Seena. You and Adriaan are falling into the footsteps of your father—'

'Not a bad way to fall,' she said sharply.

'I'm sure it isn't. I've shared great love and happiness living with you.'

'And great pans full of bobotie, too.'

'I would gladly pay, Seena, had I the money. But I travel alone, I travel with nothing, like the original men who did the work of Jesus.' When Seena started to comment scathingly on his acceptance of charity, he took her by the hands and said, 'For myself, I am ashamed to come to you with nothing. But I bring you a gift greater than any you will ever know. I bring you the love of God.'

'We have His love,' Seena said harshly. 'He prospers our farm. He increases our flocks. We worship Him in our way.'

'But you cannot always accept everything and give nothing.'

'You seem to.'

'I give you the greatest gift, salvation.'

'You just said the greatest gift was love, or something. Now it's salvation. Dominee, in some ways you're a fool.'

He was not insulted by her rejection. Without ever trying to divert her criticism, he plodded on with his message: 'Seena, I've come to marry and baptize. I want the first marriage to be yours.'

'I need no prayers said over me. I have four children . . .'

'Legally, if you are not properly married, and Adriaan died . . .'

'Adriaan dies, I keep this farm,' she said defiantly.

Specx ignored this bravado and said, 'But your children should be baptized, Seena.' And when she started to protest that they were getting along all right as it was, he interrupted sharply: 'Seena, the world's changing. Swellendam has legal offices now. Soon there'll be an effective arm of government out here. Taxes will be collected. Laws will be enforced.'

'You mean this noble land will be hammered down till it looks like the Cape?'

'Exactly. God and law and decency follow each the other. Seena, allow your children to be baptized.'

But Seena was adamant, and for the time being, Specx dropped the subject. Working alongside them, he helped the Van Doorns establish themselves on what might be called a double farm: six thousand acres to Adriaan van Doorn, six thousand to his brothers, side by side. But when the hartebeest huts were started, the dominee returned to the matter of baptisms: 'I most urgently plead with you to have your children brought into the holy family of the church. You owe it to them. They're not going to live out their lives in this wilderness. There will be churches here before they marry, and they must belong or their lives will be cut off.'

'I've lived without churches for thirty-four years,' Seena said. 'Now get back to work and leave me to my cooking—so that you can gorge yourself before you leave.' He replied that he did not intend to depart before the children were baptized.

The argument changed dramatically when Seena's two daughters rode up from the south, accompanied by their husbands and two baby girls: 'We want to be married. We want our children to be baptized.'

'God be praised,' the dominee said, and Johanna said, 'We'll make one of Willem's bread puddings to celebrate,' and Adriaan was surprised at how vigorously his mother participated in the preparations, for Johanna was visibly delighted that her granddaughters were to be properly married, that her great-grandchildren were to be baptized.

None of the huts was finished when the various ceremonies were performed, but this did not stop the women from preparing a grand feast of mutton, dried fruits, baked cauliflower, carrots, pickled cabbage and pudding, with a whole ox roasted for the servants. And the conclusion of the day was marked by a strange occurrence: the boy Lodevicus came before the dominee and said, 'I, too, wish to be baptized.' And when this was done, he added, 'I want it written in the Bible.'

So the old book was brought out, and Predikant Specx shuddered when he saw how it had been neglected, lacking a whole generation on the page of marriages and births; he called for some implement for writing, but of course there was none.

So he sat with the Bible on his lap and pointed at the various squares where Johanna should have been entered as the wife of Hendrik, and Seena as the wife of Adriaan. He showed them where the daughters and their husbands should be printed, and then where Adriaan's two sons should be placed: 'Lodevicus, this is your square, right here, and when you learn to write, you're to put your name here, and your wife's here, and your children down here. Do you understand?'

Lodevicus said he did.

* * *

Adriaan made a fearful mistake when he confided to his four children the
thoughts he'd had while wrestling with Rooi van Valck for the hand of
his daughter: 'You have no idea how big your grandfather was. Tell them,
Seena.' And with profane descriptions she told the awe-struck children of
her life at the Van Valcks', and of the numerous wives and the score of
children. Three of the young Van Doorns relished these tales, for they explained the red hair in their family and the lustiness of their mother.

But when Lodevicus, the youngest child, robust, white-haired, very
Dutch in appearance, heard his father actually say, 'I knew I was wrestling with the devil, and he would have gouged out my eyes, except your
mother bashed him in the head with a log,' he was overcome by a feeling
of loathing, for he was convinced that Rooi van Valck was the devil. Judging his mother and her harsh ways, he was convinced that she was the
devil's daughter, and that if he did not exorcise himself, he would forever
be contaminated with hellish sin.

In 1759, when he was twenty years old, he experienced a theophany
so palpable it would dominate the remainder of his life. Whenever a crisis
approached he would be able to evoke this sacred moment when God
spoke to him beside the stream, commanding him to go to the Cape to find
for himself a Christian wife who would counteract the satanic influence of
his mother: 'You cannot read. Go to the Cape and learn. You live in sin.
Go to the Cape and purify yourself. Your father and mother are of the
devil. Cross over the mountains, go to the Cape and find a Christian wife
to save them.' The Voice stopped. The night fell silent. But a light glowed
to the north toward the mountains, and he fell on his knees, begging God
for strength to obey His commands, whereupon the light intensified and
the Voice returned: 'You are the hammer who shall slay the infidel.'
There was no more.

For the next few weeks Lodevicus walked by himself, pondering how
he might get to the Cape to fulfill God's commandments, and he spent
much of this time watching his parents for signs of their satanism. He
found none in Adriaan, whom he dismissed as an ineffectual, but he did
see in Seena's robust paganism much evidence of her damnation. She
swore. She drank gin whenever any was available. And she was most
offensive in teasing him about when he was going to find himself a wife.

'Get on a horse, ride in any direction, and grab the first young thing
you see,' she said. 'One's about as good as another, when it comes to running a farm.'

He shuddered at such blasphemy, remembering that the Voice had
told him that he was destined for a special bride who would bring light
and Christianity to the trekboers. And one night, when he could bear his
mother's abuse no more, he went to the kraal, saddled a horse, and rode
westward in the darkness.

He moved from farm to farm, always aware that when he and his
bride returned they would bring decency into this wilderness. On two oc-

casions he stayed with families that had marriageable daughters, and there was a flurry of excitement when he rode up, for he was a big and handsome man, with broad shoulders and blond, almost white, hair, but he had no eye for these girls, dedicated as he was to his commission. At this stage in his life he knew the Bible imperfectly, but he imagined himself to be a son of Abraham heading back to the homeland to find a bride of decent heritage.

In this frame of mind, his entire being focused on the Cape, he approached the small settlement of Swellendam, nestled among hills and distinguished by some of the loveliest white houses in the colony. As he entered the village he wondered where he might stay, for already people in towns had become less hospitable than those in the country, where a traveler could expect an enthusiastic welcome wherever he stopped, and he was walking aimlessly when he heard the resonant voice of Dominee Specx: 'Isn't this Lodevicus of the Van Doorns?' When Vicus said, 'Yes, Dominee,' the predikant asked, 'And what brings you to this fair village?' and the young man made the startling explanation: 'Because God has ordered me to the Cape to take a wife.'

By no gesture did Predikant Specx betray any reaction to this extraordinary statement; instead he invited Lodevicus to the parsonage, informing him that a widow nearby would provide him housing for a small fee; then, sitting him upon a chair, he asked, 'Now what was it that happened to you?' When the epiphany was described, Specx said, 'I believe God has visited you.' And he suggested that they pray, but before they could do so, a young woman of twenty-two, her hair drawn tightly back against her head, revealing a face of calm austerity, came into the study with a forthright question: 'Who came here with you, Father?'

'Lodevicus, of those Van Doorns I told you about.'

'Oh, yes. How are your parents?'

'Poorly,' Lodevicus said, and before she could say she was sorry, he added, 'They know not God.'

'Yes, Father told me.'

'He has been called of God,' the dominee said, 'and we were about to give thanks.'

'May I join?' the girl asked.

'Of course. This is my daughter, Rebecca,' and the first thing young Van Doorn did in the presence of this quiet, stately girl was kneel beside her and pray.

When they rose, Specx explained to his daughter: 'The Lord commanded him to learn how to read and write. I think we could teach him.'

So for the next four weeks father and daughter instructed Lodevicus in his letters, and by the end of the period he was reading in the Bible. He also attended every service conducted by Specx, and later asked for extensions of the sermon's main theses. It was a time of great awakening, with ideas ricocheting about the white walls as the young man formulated the large concepts that would animate him the rest of his life. So powerful was the influence of his epiphany that not once in these days did he contemplate terminating his journey at Swellendam and asking for Rebecca's hand in marriage; the Lord had said that his bride awaited him at the Cape, and he intended setting forth for that town as soon as he was satisfied that he could read.

But when he reached the Cape he felt like one of the angels who looked down upon Sodom and Gomorrah. Sailors roaring off the ships to riot with the slaves and Coloureds. Indecencies at night. A world so alien that the idea of taking a wife from these quarters was repellent, and he prayed for guidance. He had been instructed to come here and take a wife, but to do so was repugnant. And now he did not know where to turn.

For three weeks he remained in this state of indecision, obedient to God's major dictate but unable to accept the detail. Again and again he walked along the shore, expecting another revelation, but none came. He saw only the vast and frightening sea and he wanted to run from it to recover the sweet assurance of the valleys across the mountains, and he was reminded of that lovely phrase in the Bible, 'the other side Jordan,' where he felt sure goodness would be found.

In profound conflict of spirit, he decided to quit the Cape, recross the mountains, and seek counsel from Predikant Specx; it never occurred to him that he was seeking not the dominee, but his daughter. All he remembered in later years was that when he came down off the hills and approached the beautiful town, he broke into a run, galloped like a runaway animal down the main street, and burst into the parsonage with the cry: 'Dominee Specx, I've come back.' But all members of the predikant's family knew why he had come back.

Three prayerful sessions were held, with Lodevicus laying bare his inability to obey the final detail of his conversion and Dominee Specx explaining that God often moves in mysterious ways, His wonders to perform: 'When you departed, I prayed that you would return because I knew that you and Rebecca were destined for majestic things.'

'Rebecca?' Lodevicus asked.

'Yes, she planned to marry you from the day you arrived.'

'But the Lord told me to find my wife at the Cape.'

'Exactly what did the Voice say?' Dominee Specx asked, and when Lodevicus replied that he could not remember exactly, the clergyman said, 'You told me that it said, "Go to the Cape . . ." and then "Find a Christian wife." That doesn't mean that you must take your wife from the Cape. It merely means that God wanted you to have the experience of the Cape. And you were quite right to come back here for your bride. God directed you, don't you see?'

The explanation was so logical that Lodevicus had to accept it, and neither then nor afterward would he admit to himself that he had returned to Swellendam to marry Rebecca, for she had seemed too mature and superior to be attainable.

They were married by her father in the newly built church, and after a honeymoon that revealed the quality of the two young people—he fanatically determined to exhibit God's handiwork, she unflinching in her resolve to take Christianity to the frontier—they saddled two horses, and with a minimum of possessions, set forth to tame the wilderness.

Their reception at the Van Doorn farm was not a pleasant one. On the trip east Lodevicus had warned his bride that Seena might prove troublesome: 'Adriaan's an infidel, but he's quiet. My mother's the daughter of Rooi van Valck, and she'll be difficult, even hostile.'

When they rode into the farmyard the first voice they heard was Seena's, loud and raucous, shouting to her husband, 'Adriaan! He's back. With a bride.'

When the family assembled, Lodevicus, with new-found assurance, attempted to share with his parents the miracle of his epiphany: 'God called to me to go to the Cape to take a wife.'

'Adriaan heard a call like that once,' Seena said, 'but I doubt God had much to do with it.'

'So I stopped at Swellendam to pray with Dominee Specx, and Rebecca taught me the letters and how to put them together . . .'

'I'll warrant that wasn't all she taught.'

The young couple ignored these interruptions, and Lodevicus continued: 'And when I learned to write, I got down on my knees and thanked God and told Him that as soon as I returned home I would write our names in the Bible. Fetch it.'

He issued this request as a command, and Seena was somewhat irritated when her husband complied. Going to a wagon chest in which he kept the odd valuables that accumulate even in a hartebeest hut, he brought forth the old Bible, opening it to the page of records between the two testaments. 'This time,' Lodevicus said gravely, 'we have a pen,' and with everyone watching, he carefully inscribed the missing names: 'Adriaan van Doorn, born 1712. Seena van Valck born . . .'

'Maybe 1717,' she said.

'Father, Rooi van Valck. Mother . . .'

'I never knew for sure.' Lodevicus and Rebecca stared at her, and he said, 'We've got to put something.'

'Put Fedda the Malayan. I liked her best.'

'Put Magdalena van Delft,' Adriaan said. 'You know she was your real mother.'

Seena spat: 'That for Magdalena.'

Hurriedly Lodevicus wrote in the names of his brother and his two sisters, then, with a flourish and a smile for his wife, he wrote: 'Rebecca Specx, Swellendam, daughter of the Predikant.'

When he put the pen aside, satisfied with his work, Seena asked, 'When you reached Swellendam, were you married?'

'Oh, no!' her son said. 'When I had learned to write I marched on to the Cape, as God had directed.'

'Over the mountains?' Adriaan asked, showing respect for such a trip.

'Over the tall mountains, but when I reached the Cape, I found Sodom and Gomorrah. Indecencies everywhere.'

'What indecencies?' Seena asked.

Again he ignored her, telling of his revulsion, his rejection of the town and his return over the mountains. 'We were married and spent the next weeks in a revelation. The four of us, Dominee Specx and his wife, I and my wife, we sat together and read the entire Bible.'

For the first time Rebecca intruded. In a low voice, but with great firmness, she said, 'The Old Testament, that is.'

'And we discovered,' Lodevicus continued, 'how we trekboers are the new Israelites. That we have reached the point where Abram was when he changed his name to Abraham and settled in Canaan while Lot chose the cities of the plain, to be destroyed. And I learned that the time of our traveling is ended. That we must settle and build our houses of stone.'

'Did you and the dominee,' Adriaan asked, 'ever discuss the fact that you new Abrahams would be building your houses of stone on land that can be worn out? That we have to move on from time to time to find ourselves better land?'

'They're not moving at Swellendam,' Lodevicus replied, whereupon his mother said, 'We are. This verdomde farm is worn out.'

And while the old couple planned their next leap eastward, the young couple journeyed to the southern farms, there to advise the people how they ought to live.

It was on their return journey that Lodevicus first shared with another human being the mysterious fact that at the stream God had told him that he was to be the hammer, the trekboer who brought order into shapeless lives, and as soon as he said the words, Rebecca understood. With great excitement she said, 'It was why Father and I prayed that you would return from the Cape. And take me with you. That we could perform the tasks that lie ahead.'

'God spoke to you, also?'

'I think He did. I think I always knew.'

It was with this common understanding of their salvation and their mutual reinforcement that the younger Van Doorns came back to the farm, secure in their knowledge of what was required, and the first person their wrath fell upon was Dikkop, now fifty-seven years old and as inoffensive as always. Because of the many years they had shared, and the adventures, Adriaan gave the little fellow unusual prerogatives, and Lodevicus decided that this must stop: 'He is of the tribe of Ham, and he must no longer live with us or feed with us, or in any way associate with us, except as our Hottentot servant.'

When Adriaan protested such a harsh decree, Lodevicus and Rebecca explained things carefully, step by step, so that even Seena would understand: 'When the world started the second time, after the flood, Noah had three sons, and two of them were clean and white like us. But the third son, Ham, was dark and evil.'

'Now, Ham,' Rebecca continued, 'was the father of Canaan and all black people. And God, acting through Noah, placed a terrible curse on Canaan: "Cursed be Canaan! A servant of servants shall he be to his brethren." And it was ordained that the sons of Ham shall be hewers of wood and drawers of water, for as long as the world exists. Dikkop is a Canaanite. He is a son of Ham, and is condemned to be a slave and nothing more.'

It really didn't matter to Adriaan and Seena what the Hottentot was called; he was necessary to their lives, and as such, he was well treated. Seena especially liked to have him in the hut when food was being prepared or eaten, and it was this that caused the first open rupture with her daughter-in-law, for one day Rebecca said in some exasperation, 'Seena, you must not allow Dikkop in the hut ever again.' Then she added, in a voice of honest conciliation, 'Except, of course, when he cleans up.'

'But he's always been with me when I cook.'

'That must stop.'

'Who says so?' Seena asked belligerently.

'God.'

With the snap of a cloth and a sharpness of tongue that invited trouble, Seena said, 'I doubt that God troubles Himself over a woman's kitchen.'

'Lodevicus!' Rebecca called. 'Your mother refuses to believe.' And when Vicus came into the hut to hear the complaints, he, of course, sided totally with his wife, taking down the Bible and turning to those short, inconsequential books that end the Old Testament, and there in Zechariah he found the concluding passage which had loomed so large in the teaching of Predikant Specx at Swellendam: '"And in that day there shall be no more the Canaanite in the house of the Lord of Hosts."' He added that from this time on, the hut was the house of the Lord, and since Dikkop was clearly a Canaanite, he must be banished.

Curiously, Adriaan did not support his wife in this argument, for he was coming to believe that Rebecca spoke for the future; it was time that order be brought to the frontier, although he himself wanted none of it. The truth was, he rather liked his daughter-in-law, for she was capable, intelligent and forthright, and he suspected that Lodevicus had been lucky to catch her. Seena, however, saw her as a moralizing menace to be consistently opposed: 'You think your Bible has an answer for everything?'

'It has.'

'Well, when you and Vicus make the Xhosa mad, and they come clicking over that hill armed with assegais, what does your Bible say about that?'

With absolute assurance Rebecca said, 'Vicus, fetch me the Bible, please,' and in later years he would often remember this moment, when his wife and his mother argued over what might happen if the Xhosa struck.

Turning the pages expertly, Rebecca came to that passage in Leviticus which formed a keystone of her father's belief, and read triumphantly: '"And ye shall chase your enemies, and they shall fall before you by the sword. And five of you shall chase an hundred . . ."' And then, as if this solved all problems of the frontier, she glared at her mother-in-law and said, 'We will have five to defend this farm.'

Of course, the little brown men knew nothing of this prophecy and had no difficulty whatever in breaking through. One night a clan of Bushmen living beyond the mountains crept down, found large numbers of cattle roaming freely, and made off with some sixty fine beasts.

'That's enough,' Lodevicus said, his voice betraying iron but no fire. 'That's just enough. And now we settle the problem of the Bushmen.'

He organized a commando, all the men from thirty miles around, and he set forth, inviting Adriaan to come along but ignoring him when decisions were required. They went north about seventy miles, so far that Adriaan was certain they had left the Bushmen far behind, but when he started to alert his son to this fact, Vicus, grim-lipped, sat astride his horse, saying nothing.

The old man was right. The commando had far outrun the little brown raiders, but Vicus had devised a super strategy, and when the riders reached a spot where whole families of Bushmen might be expected to congregate, he ordered his men to dismount and hide themselves near a spring that broke out from between the rocks. Adriaan, unable to discern his son's plan, expected the hunting party to arrive with the stolen cattle and walk into an ambush, but instead, just at sunset, a huge rhinoceros lumbered in to catch his evening swill of water, and as he drank noisily, switching his wiry tail, Lodevicus dropped him with one powerful shot behind the ear.

There the great beast lay, beside the spring, and before nightfall vultures gathered, perching in trees and waiting for the dawn. They were seen, of course, both by the Bushmen families awaiting the return of their men and by the cattle stealers coming north, so that by midafternoon some sixty Bushmen, counting the women and children, had gathered at the spring to gorge upon the unexpected feast of the dead rhino.

During the first excitement as the little people butchered the huge beast, Lodevicus kept his men silent, and this was prudent, for the wait allowed another thirty brown people to assemble, and when they were all there, about ninety of them, cutting the rhino steaks and laughing as the blood ran down their wizened faces, Vicus leaped up and cried, 'Fire!'

Caught in the crossfire of a score of guns, the banqueters fell one by one. Cattle stealers, grandmothers, the makers of arrows, the young women who collected the beetles from which the poisons were made, and the little children, even the babies—all were exterminated.

Lodevicus the Hammer he was called after that exhibition, God's strong right arm, and whenever trouble threatened he was summoned. He organized the first church in this remote region and served as its sick-comforter during the years when it had no predikant. He read sermons from a book printed in Holland and sent him by Rebecca's father in Swellendam; he was punctilious about never posing as a real clergyman, for that was a holy vocation requiring years of formal study and the laying on of hands, but he did enforce religious law on both his own family and the scattered farms. Whenever a young man and woman started living together, he and Rebecca would visit them, take their names down in a book, and make them promise that as soon as a predikant came their way, they would marry. He also kept a register of births, threatening parents with damnation if they failed to have their infants baptized when the dominee came.

One night as he rode back after lecturing two young couples living carelessly down by the sea, he took Rebecca by the hand and led her a safe distance from the hut: 'I'm sorely worried. I've been reflecting on Adriaan and Seena. It's an affront to God for me to travel far distances to enforce His ordinances when in my own home . . .'

'What are we going to do about them?'

'It would be a dreadful act, Rebecca, to evict one's own parents. But if they persist in evil ways . . .'

When he paused to weigh the gravity of the problem, Rebecca enumerated the nagging difficulties she faced with Seena, the worst being her mother-in-law's paganism: 'She sneers at our teaching, Vicus. When you were gone she brought Dikkop back into the hut, even though she knows the Bible forbids it. When I pointed this out, she snapped, "Either he stays or you starve."'

'Rebecca, we should pray,' and they did, two earnest and contrite hearts seeking the right thing to do. They considered themselves neither arrogant nor unforgiving; all they sought was justice and sanctification, and in the end they resolved that Adriaan and Seena would have to leave: 'They're still young enough to build their own hut, they and that Canaanite Dikkop.'

They rose early so as to be strengthened for the unpleasant scene that must ensue, but when they looked out to the meadow they found Adriaan and Dikkop already up, two horses laden with enough gear to last them for an extensive journey.

'What are you doing?' Lodevicus demanded.

'Seena!' Adriaan shouted. 'Come out here!' And when the redhead appeared, her husband said, 'Tell them.'

She did: 'He's tired of your preaching. He's ashamed to keep a hut in which his friend is not welcome. And he doesn't like the new type of life you're trying to force on us.'

'What is he going to do?' Rebecca asked.

'He and Dikkop are going up to the Zambezi River.' The blank look on her son's face betrayed the fact that he had no idea of where such a river might be. 'The Swede told us about it. It's up there.' And with a careless wave of her arm she indicated a wild river of the imagination some fifteen hundred miles to the north.

'And you?' Rebecca asked.

'I'll stay here. This is my farm, you know.'

And in those few words Seena underlined the impossible situation that faced the young Van Doorns. They could not force his mother off this farm, nor could they in decency abandon her here. They would have to share the hut with her until her husband returned. 'How long will you be gone?' Lodevicus asked in chastened voice.

'Three years,' Adriaan said, and with a flick of his whip he started his oxen north.

It was in October 1766, when Adriaan was at the advanced age of fifty-four, that he and Dikkop left. They took with them sixteen reserve oxen, four horses, a tent, extra guns, more ammunition than they would probably need, sacks of flour and four bags of biltong. They wore the rough homemade clothes of the veld and carried a precious tin box containing Boer farm remedies, medicinal herbs and leaves, their value learned through generations of experience.

They moved slowly at first, seven or eight miles a day, then ten, then fifteen. They let themselves be diverted by almost anything: an unusual tree, a likelihood of animals. Often they camped for weeks at a time at some congenial spot, replenished their biltong and moved on.

As the two went slowly north, they saw wonders that no settler had ever seen before: rivers of magnitude, and vast deserts waiting to explode into flowers, and most interesting of all, a continual series of small hills, each off to itself, perfectly rounded at the base as if some architect had placed them in precisely the right position. Often the top had been planed away, forming mesas as flat as a table. Occasionally Adriaan and Dikkop would climb such a hill for no purpose at all except to scout the landscape ahead, and they would see only an expanse so vast that the eye could not encompass it, marked with these repetitious little hills, some rounded, some with their tops scraped flat.

In the second month of their wandering, after they had rafted their luggage wagon across a stream the Hottentots called Great River, later to be named the Orange, they entered upon those endless plains leading into the heartland, and late one afternoon at a fountain they came upon the first band of human beings, a group of little Bushmen who fled as they approached. Throughout that long night Adriaan and Dikkop stayed close to the wagon, guns loaded, peering into the darkness apprehensively. Just after dawn one of the little men showed himself, and Adriaan made a major decision. With Dikkop covering him, he left his own gun against the wheel of the wagon, stepped forward unarmed, and indicated with friendly gestures that he came in peace.

At the invitation of the Bushmen, Adriaan and Dikkop stayed at that fountain for a week, during which Adriaan learned many good things about the ones his fellow Dutchmen called 'daardie diere' (those animals), and nothing so impressed him as when he was allowed to accompany them on a hunt, for he witnessed remarkable skill and sensitivity in tracking. The Bushmen had collected a large bundle of hides, which Dikkop learned would be taken 'three moons to the north' for trade with people who lived there.

Since the travelers were also headed in that general direction, they joined the Bushmen, and twice during the journey saw clusters of huts in the distance, but the Bushmen shook their heads and kept the caravan moving deeper into the plains till they reached the outlying kraals of an important chief's domain.

The Bushmen ran ahead to break the news of the white stranger, so that at the first village Adriaan was greeted with intense curiosity and some tittering, rather than the fear which might have been expected. The blacks were pleased that he showed special interest in their huts, impressed by the sturdy, rounded workmanship in stone and clay and the walls four to five feet high that surrounded their cattle kraals. As he told Dikkop, 'These are better than the huts you and I live in.'

News of their arrival spread to the chief's kraal and he sent an escort of headmen and warriors to bring these strangers before him. The meeting was grave, for Adriaan was the first white man these blacks had seen; they came to know him well, for he stayed with them two months. They were excited when he demonstrated gunpowder by tossing a small handful on an open fire, where it flamed violently. The chief was terrified at first, but after he mastered the trick, he delighted in using it to frighten his people.

'How many are you?' Adriaan asked one night.

The chief pointed to the compass directions, then to the stars. There were so many people in this land.

When Adriaan studied the communities he was permitted to see, it became obvious to him that these people were not recent arrivals in the area. Their present settlements, the ruins of past locations, their ironwork traded from the north, their copious use of tobacco—all signaled long occupancy. He was especially charmed by the glorious cloaks the men made from animal skins softened like chamois. He liked their fields of sorghum, pumpkins, gourds and beans. Their pottery was well formed, and their beads, copied from those brought to Zimbabwe three hundred years earlier, were beautiful. He accepted their presence on the highveld as naturally as he accepted the herds of antelope that browsed near the fountains.

In succeeding months he would never be far from such settlements, scattered over the lands they crossed, but he rarely contacted the people, since he was preoccupied with reaching the Zambezi. Besides, he worried that other chiefs might not be as friendly as the man who danced with joy at the flash of gunpowder.

As they moved north they shot only such food as they required, except one morning when Dikkop became irritated with a hyena that insisted upon trying to grab her share of an antelope he had shot. Three times he tried in vain to drive the beast away, and when she persisted he shot her. This might have occasioned no comment from Adriaan but for the fact that when she died she left behind a baby male hyena with fiery black eyes; she had wanted the meat to feed him, and now he was abandoned, snapping his huge teeth at Dikkop whenever he approached.

'What's out there?' Adriaan called.

'Baby hyena, Baas,' Dikkop replied.

'Bring him here!'

So Dikkop made a feint, leaped back, and planted his foot on the little beast's neck, subduing him so that he could be grabbed. Struggling and kicking but making no audible protest, the baby hyena was brought before Adriaan, who said immediately, 'We've got to feed him.' So Dikkop chewed up bits of tender meat, placing it on his finger for the animal to lick off, and by the end of the third day the two men were competing with each other to see who would have the right to feed the little beast.

'Swartejie, we'll call him,' Adriaan said, something like Blackie or the Little Black One, but the hyena assumed such a menacing stance that Adriaan had to laugh. 'So you think you're a big Swarts already?' And that's what he was called.

He showed the endearing characteristics of a domesticated dog without losing the impressive qualities of an animal in the wild. Because his forequarters were strong and high, his rear small and low, he lurched rather than walked, and since his mouth was enormous, with powerful head muscles to operate the great, crunching jaws, he could present a frightening appearance, except that his innate good nature and his love of Adriaan, who fed and roughhoused with him, made his face appear always to be smiling. Short tail, big ears, wide-set eyes, he made himself into a cherished pet whose unpredictable behavior supplied a surprise a day.

He was a scavenger, but he certainly lacked a scavenger's heart, for he did not slink and was willing to challenge the largest lion if a good carcass was available. But once when the two men came upon a covey of guinea fowl and wounded one, Swarts was thrown into a frenzy of fear by the bird's flapping wings and flying feathers. As winter approached and the highveld proved cold, whenever Adriaan went to his sleeping quarters— eland skin formed like a bag, with soft ostrich feathers sewn into a blanket —he would find Swarts sleeping on his springbok pillow, eyes closed in blissful repose, his muscles twitching now and then as he dreamed of the hunt.

'Move over, damnit!'

The sleeping hyena would groan, lying perfectly limp as Adriaan shoved him to one side, but as soon as the master was in the bed, Swarts would snuggle close and often he would snore. 'You! Damnit! Stop snoring!' and Adriaan would shove him aside as if he were an old wife.

They saw animals in such abundance that no man could have counted them, or even estimated their numbers. Once when they were crossing an upland where the grass was sweet, they saw to the east a vast movement, ten miles, twenty miles, fifty miles across, coming slowly toward them, raising a dust that obliterated the sun.

'What to do?' Dikkop asked.

'I think we stand where we are,' Adriaan replied, not at all pleased with his answer but unable to think of any other.

Even Swarts was afraid, whimpering and drawing close to Adriaan's leg.

And then the tremendous herd approached, not running, not moving in fear. It was migration time, and in obedience to some deep impulse the animals were leaving one feeding ground and heading to another.

The herd was composed of only three species: vast numbers of wildebeest, their beards swaying in the quiet breeze; uncounted zebras, decorating the veld with their flashy colors; and a multitude of springbok leaping joyously among the statelier animals. How many beasts could there have been? Certainly five hundred thousand, more probably eight or nine, an exuberance of nature that was difficult to comprehend.

And now they were descending upon the three travelers. When they were close at hand, Swarts begged Adriaan to take him up, so the two men stood fast as the herd came down upon them. A strange thing happened. As the wildebeest and zebras came within twenty feet of the men, they quietly opened their ranks, forming the shape of an almond, a teardrop of open space in which the men stood unmolested. And as soon as that group of animals passed, they closed the almond, going forward as before, while newcomers looked at the men, slowly moved aside to form their own teardrop and then pass on.

For seven hours Adriaan and Dikkop stood in that one spot as the animals moved past. Never were they close enough to have touched one of the zebras or the bounding springbok; always the animals stayed clear, and after a while Swarts asked to be put down so that he could watch more closely.

At sunset the western sky was red with dust.

In the next months the landscape changed dramatically. Mountains began to appear on the horizon ahead, and rivers flowed north instead of east, where the ocean presumably lay. It was good land, and soon they found themselves in that remarkable gorge where the walls seemed to come together high in the heavens. Dikkop was frightened and wanted to turn back, but Adriaan insisted upon forging ahead, breaking out at last into that wonderland of baobab trees, whose existence defied his imagination. 'Look at them!' he cried. 'Upside down! How wonderful!'

For several weeks he and Dikkop and Swarts lived in one huge tree, not up in the branches, which would have been possible, but actually inside the tree in a huge vacancy caused by the wearing away of soft wood. Swarts, responding to some ancient heritage in a time when hyenas had lived in caves, reveled in the dark interior spaces, running from one to the other and making strange sounds.

He had become an exceptional pet, perhaps the finest animal Adriaan had ever known, placid like the best ox, brave like the strongest lion, playful like a kitten, and of tremendous strength like a rhinoceros. He enjoyed playing a fearsome game with Adriaan, taking the trekboer's forearm in his powerful jaws and pretending to bite it in half, which he could have done. He would bring his teeth slowly together and impishly watch Adriaan's face to see when pain would show. Tighter and tighter the great teeth would close until it seemed that the skin must break, and then, with Adriaan looking directly into the animal's eyes, Swarts would stop, and laugh admiringly at the man who was not afraid, and he would release the arm and leap upon Adriaan's lap and cover him with kisses.

At times Adriaan would think: These years can never end. There will be enough land for everyone, and the animals will multiply forever. When he and Dikkop left a carcass it was good to hear the lions approaching, to see the sky filled with great birds waiting to descend and clean the feast.

They came at last to the river, not the Zambezi, as Adriaan had promised, but the Limpopo, that sluggish stream that marked the natural northern borders of the subcontinent. Dr. Linnart had said the natural border was the Zambezi; Portuguese explorers had said the same; and anyone who had a map, rude and rough, saw that the Zambezi was the natural boundary, but reality dictated that this boundary be the Limpopo. South of here, the land was of a piece; north of here, it altered radically and could never be digested as an inherent part of a manageable unit.

Perhaps Adriaan realized this in December 1767 when he stood at the

Limpopo beside his irreparably broken wagon and his oxen and horses dying from disease. 'Dikkop,' he said, 'we can't go any farther.' The Hottentot agreed, for he was tired, and even Swarts seemed relieved when the trio started south on foot. It was as if the hyena had a built-in compass which reminded him of where home had stood; he seemed to have known that he was heading away from where he ought to have been, and now that he was homeward bound he manifested his joy like a sailor whose ship has turned into a proper heading.

They formed a curious trio as they came happily down the spine of Africa. Swarts, with his big head and small bottom, took the lead. Then came Dikkop, with small head and enormous bottom. Finally there was Adriaan, a lean, white-haired trekboer, fifty-six years old and striding along as if he were thirty. Once Swarts insisted upon leaving the trail made by antelope and heading to the west, and when the men followed they found a small cave which they were about to ignore, until Dikkop looked at the roof and discovered a marvelous canopy showing three giraffes being stalked by little brown men; it had been painted there millennia ago by the ancestors of the Bushmen they had met. This way and that, men and animals moved, colors unfaded, forms still deftly outlined. For a long time Adriaan studied the paintings, then asked, 'Where have they gone?'

'Who knows, Baas?' Dikkop replied, and Adriaan said, 'Good boy, Swarts. We liked your cave.'

Summer that year was very hot, and even though the trio was moving south, away from concentrated heat, Adriaan noticed that Dikkop was exhausted, so he looked for routes that would keep them away from the hot and dusty center and lead them out toward the eastern edge of the plateau, where they were likely to encounter cooling rains; and on one such excursion they came upon that quiet and pleasant lake where the flamingos had flown and Nxumalo had hunted his rhinoceros.

It was at its apex now, a broad and lovely body of water to which a thousand animals came each evening, in such steady profusion that Swarts was benumbed by the possibilities he saw before him. Lurching here and there, chasing birds and elephants alike, he watched for any weakling, placing himself well back of the lions that were also stalking it, and ran in for bits of meat whenever an opportunity arose. When the bigger predators were gone, he would waddle into the lake to drink and wash himself, and he obviously enjoyed this part of the trip above any other.

Dikkop was faring less well. It was 1768 now and he was sixty-three years old, a tired man who had worked incessantly at a hundred different tasks, always assigned him by someone else. He had lived his life in the shadow of white men, and in their shadow he was content to end his final days. He was not indifferent about his fate; eagerly he wanted to get back to the farm to see how Seena was doing, for he loved her rowdy ways and usually thought of himself as 'her boy.' He would be very unhappy if anything happened to him before he saw her again.

He was to be disappointed. As the summer waned, so did he, and it became apparent that he would not be able to endure the long return journey: 'My chest, he hurts, he hurts.' Adriaan berated himself for having brought so old a man on so perilous an expedition, but when Dikkop saw this he said reassuringly, 'Impossible to come without me. But you get back safe, I think.'

He died before the chill of winter and was buried beside the lake he had grown to love; it was when Adriaan collected the stones for Dikkop's cairn from the ruins of an ancient village dating back to the 1450s that he began talking seriously to his hyena: 'Swarts, we're piling these stones so your filthy brothers don't dig him up and eat him, you damned cannibal.' Swarts showed his enormous teeth in what could only be a grin, and after that whenever Adriaan consulted with him about which eland path to follow or where to spend the night, Swarts bared his teeth and nuzzled his master's leg.

Adriaan now had every reason to pursue vigorously his way homeward, but for reasons he could not have explained he lingered at the quiet lake, not exploring its hinterland but simply resting, as if he realized that this was a place to which men fled for refuge. From his sleeping place he studied the low mountains to the east, the twin peaks that looked like breasts, and the flatlands hungry for the plow. But most of all he kept his eyes upon the rim of the lake, where animals came to drink and across whose placid surface the flamingos flew.

'Vrijmeer!' he cried one day. 'Swarts, this is the lake where everything that moves has freedom.' That night he could not sleep. Restlessly he stepped across the inert body of his hyena to stand in moonlight as undisciplined thoughts assailed him: I wish I were young again . . . to bring a family here . . . to live beside this lake . . .

It was not easy for Adriaan to admit that he was growing lonely. He had never talked much with Dikkop, nor looked to him for intellectual companionship. He was not afraid of traveling alone, because by now he knew every trick for avoiding dangers; he sensed where the kraals of the black people lay, and he swung away from them; he slept where no lion could reach him, relying upon Swarts to alert him if unusual developments occurred. The hyena was not really a good watchdog, he slept too soundly on a full belly, and with his master's constant hunting he had a good supply of guts and bones to gorge upon; but he had a marked capacity for self-defense, and many animals that might have attacked Adriaan sleeping alone would think twice before risking a hyena's great jaws and flashing teeth.

The loneliness came from the fact that he had seen Africa, had touched it intimately along the mountains and the veld, and had reached the point where there were no more secrets. Even the fact that a majestic waterfall lay only a short distance to his northwest would not have surprised him, for he had found the continent to be greater than he had imagined or Dr. Linnart had suggested.

Again the vagrant thought struck, this time with pain, and he said in a loud voice, 'God, Swarts, I wish I were young again. I'd cross the Limpopo. Go on and on, past the Zambezi all the way to Holland.' He had not the slightest doubt that given a good pair of shoes, he could walk to Europe. 'And I'd take you with me, little hunter, to protect me from the dik-diks.' He laughed at this, and Swarts laughed back at the idea of anyone's needing protection from the tiniest of antelopes who leaped in fear at the fall of a leaf.

Perhaps this recurrent loneliness was a premonition, for as they came down off the spacious central plateau to cross the Great River, he saw that Swarts was becoming restless. The hyena was two and a half years old now, a full-grown male, and as they came into territory where other hyenas hunted in packs, Swarts became aware of them in new ways, and sometimes at dusk gave indications that he wanted to run with them. At the same time he knew deep love for his human companion and felt a kind of obligation to protect him, to share with him the glories of the hunt.

So he vacillated, sometimes running toward the open veld, at other times scampering back in his lurching way to be with his master; but one night, when the moon was full and animals were afoot, he suddenly broke away from Adriaan, ran a short distance into the veld, stopped, looked back as if weighing alternatives, and disappeared. Through his sleepless night Adriaan could hear the sounds of hunting, and when day broke, there was no Swarts.

For three days Adriaan stayed in that area, hoping that the hyena would return, but he did not. And so, with regret almost to the point of tears, Adriaan set out for the mountains that protected his farm, and now he was truly alone, and for the first time in his life, even afraid. From the latitude of the stars he calculated that he might be as far as three hundred miles north of his destination, afoot, with a diminishing store of ammunition and the necessity of covering that expanse of open country when he was not quite sure where he was.

'Swarts,' he shouted one night, 'I need you!' And later, as he lay fitfully sleeping, he heard the sound of animals, many of them, trampling near to where he was hiding, and he began to shiver, for he had not heard this noise so close before. Then slowly he came awake, and was aware of something pressing upon him, and it was Swarts, snoring in the old manner.

Now he talked with the animal more than ever, as if the hyena's return laid bare his need for companionship; Swarts, for his part, kept closer to his master, as if after tasting the freedom of the wild, he realized that partnership with a human being could have its rewards, too.

Down the long plains they came. 'It must be over this way, Swarts,' Adriaan said, looking at the last line of hills that rose from the veld. 'The farm is probably down there, and when you meet Seena you two are going to have fun. She's red-headed and she'll throw things at you if you don't look out, but you'll like her and I know she'll like you.' He was not at all sure how Seena would take to sharing her hut with a hyena, but he kept assuring Swarts that it would be all right.

But the hyena's recent experience in the wild had revived animal habits, and one evening after Adriaan shot a gemsbok, a beautiful creature with white-masked face and imperial horns, a lioness thought it safe to move in and command the kill, whereupon Swarts leaped at her, receiving a horrible slash of claw across his neck and face.

When Adriaan, screaming at the lioness, reached his companion, Swarts was dying. Nothing that the man might do could save the beast; his prayers were meaningless, his attempts to stanch the blood fruitless. The great jaws moved in spasms and the eyes looked for the last time at the person who had been such a trusted friend.

'Swarts!' Adriaan shouted, but to no avail. The hyena shuddered, gasped for air, got only blood, and died.

'Oh, Swarts!' Adriaan moaned repeatedly through the night, keeping the misshapen body near him. In the morning he placed it out in the open where the vultures could attend it, and after an anguished farewell to a constant friend he resumed his journey south.

Now he was truly alone. Almost everything he had had with him at the start of his exploration was gone: ammunition, horses and oxen lost to the tsetse fly, the wagon, the trusted Hottentot, his shoes, most of his clothing. He was coming home bereft of everything, even his hyena, and his memories of the grandeurs he had seen were scarred by the losses he had sustained. Most of all he mourned for Swarts; Dikkop, after all, had lived his life, but the hyena was only beginning his, a creature torn between the open veld and the settled farm that was to have been his home.

As he slogged his way south Adriaan began to feel his age, the weight of time, and idly he calculated the farms he had used up, the endless chain of animals he had bred and passed along, the huts he had lived in and never a house: 'Swarts, I'm fifty-seven years old and never lived in a house with real walls.' Then he braced his shoulders, crying even louder, 'And by God, Swarts, I don't want to live in one.'

He came down off the great central highland of Africa—not defeated, but certainly not victorious. He could still walk many miles a day, but he did so more slowly, the dust of far places in his nostrils. From time to time he shouted into space, addressing only Swarts, for now he was truly Mal Adriaan, the crazy man of the veld who conversed with dead hyenas, but on he went, a few miles a day, always looking for the trail he had lost.

* * *

When he broke through the mountains into unfamiliar terrain he calculated correctly that he must be a fair distance east of his farm, and he was
about to turn westward to find it when he said, 'Swarts! If they had any
sense, they'd have moved to better land over there.' And like earlier
members of his family, he headed east.

But when he reached the territory that ought to have contained the
new farm, he found nothing, so he was faced with the problem of plung-
ing blindly ahead into unknown territory or turning back, and after long
consultation with Swarts he decided on the former: 'Stands to reason,
Swarts, they'd be wanting better pastures.'

At the farthest edge of where he could imagine his family might have
reached, he came upon the shabbiest hut he had yet seen, and in it lived a
man and wife who had taken up their six thousand acres with only the
meagerest chance of succeeding. They were the first white people Adriaan
had seen since setting out, and he talked with them avidly: 'You hear of
any Van Doorns passing this way?'

'They went.'

'Which direction?'

'East.'

'How long ago?'

'Before I got here.'

'But you're sure they went?'

'We stayed in their old huts. Four months. Trekboer came through,
told us they had gone.'

Since Adriaan needed rest, he stayed with the couple for a short time,
and one morning the woman asked, 'Who's this Swarts you keep talking
to?' and he replied, 'Friend of mine.'

After two weeks, during which the trekboer gave him a supply of ammunition, which he used to bring meat to the hut, Adriaan announced
casually that he was about to try to locate his family. 'How long you been
gone?' the woman asked.

'Three years.'

'Where'd you say you were?'

'M'popo,' he said, using a name the blacks had taught him.

'Never heard of it.' For a moment Adriaan felt that he owed it to his
hosts to explain, but upon reflection, realized that to do so adequately
would require another two weeks, so he departed with no further comment.

On and on he went, well past the place where he had met Sotopo, the
Xhosa, and one morning as he reached the crest of a substantial line of
hills he looked down to see something which disturbed him greatly; it was
a valley comprising some nine thousand acres and completely boxed in by

hills. 'It's a prison!' he cried, alarmed that people would willingly submit themselves to such confinement.

What dismayed him especially was that at the center, beside a lively stream that ran from the southwest to the northeast, escaping through a cleft in the hills, stood not the usual Van Doorn huts but solid buildings constructed of clay and stone. Whoever had planned this tight enclave intended to occupy it not for the ordinary ten years, but for a lifetime. It represented a change of pattern so drastic that in one swift glance Adriaan realized that his old trekboer days were ended, and he groaned at the error these people were making: Stone houses! Prisons within a prison! To reach this at the end of three years on the most glorious land in Africa was regrettable.

But he still was not certain that this was his new farm until an older woman with fading red hair came out of the stone house and walked toward the barn. It was Seena. This stronghold was her home, and now it would be his.

He did not call out to his wife, but he did say to Swarts, 'We've come to the end, old fellow. Things we don't understand . . .' Slowly and without the jubilation he should have felt at reaching the end of so long a journey, he came down the hill, went to the door of the barn, and called, 'Seena!' She knew immediately who it was and left the gathering of eggs, running to him and hugging him as if he were a child. 'Verdomde ou man,' she cried. 'You're home!'

After the children had screamed their greetings and Lodevicus, now a solid thirty, had come forth with Rebecca, Adriaan asked the adults, 'How did our farm get to this place?'

'We wanted security,' Lodevicus explained. 'The hills, you know.'

'But why the stone houses?'

'Because this is the last jump that can be made. Because on the other side of the Great Fish River the Xhosa wait.'

'This is our permanent home,' Rebecca said. 'Like Swellendam, a foothold on the frontier.'

'I saw a place up north. It had hills like this, but they were open. There was a lake, and it was open too. Animals from everywhere came to drink.'

The younger Van Doorns were not interested in what their father had seen at the north, but that night when Adriaan and Seena went to their bed after the long absence she whispered, 'What was it like?' and all he could say was 'It's a beautiful country.'

That had to stand for the thundering sunsets, the upside-down trees, the veld bursting in flowers, the great mountains to the east, the mysterious rivers to the north, but as he was about to close his eyes in sleep, he suddenly sat upright and cried, 'God, Seena! I wish we were twenty . . . we could go to a place I saw . . . that lake . . . the antelope darkening the fields.'

'Let's go!' she said without hesitation or fear.
He laughed and kissed her. 'Go to sleep. They'll find it in time.'
'Who?'
'The ones who come after.'

Lodevicus and Rebecca never once asked about the northern lands; their preoccupation was in building a paradise at hand; but in the afternoons their children gathered with Adriaan to hear of Swarts, the cave with leaping giraffes on the ceiling, the boisterous blacks who danced at the flash of gunpowder, and of the place he called Vrijmeer.

When the excitement of his return died down, the battle between Seena and Rebecca resumed, with each woman confiding to her husband at night that the other was intolerable, and Adriaan would lie awake listening to his wife's litany of complaint: 'She's a nasty tyrant. She has a withered lemon for a heart. It's her intention to run this entire area, and Lodevicus supports her.'

He shared with her his impression upon first seeing their new home: 'This room with its tight walls is a prison cell—within the stone house, which is the small prison, within these hateful hills, which form the biggest prison of all.'

'No,' she corrected. 'The big prison is the ideas he wants to enforce. Every person on every farm must behave the way he says. You know, he's started fighting with the Xhosa when they come over the river to feed their cattle.'

When Adriaan asked his son about this, Lodevicus said, 'Three times I've heard you speak poorly about having our farm within these hills. Well, war with the Xhosa is inevitable. They're pressing westward more strongly each month, and soon we'll have real warfare.'

'Let them graze their cattle,' Adriaan said.

'They'll never be content with that. Mark my words, Father, they'll want everything. They'll overrun this farm. That is, if it wasn't protected by hills.'

In 1776 Lodevicus was proved right, for a large group of Xhosa, led by Guzaka, son of that Sotopo with whom Adriaan had spent four days of friendship, became increasingly angered by the constant pressure from the white farmers.

As in the beginning days of Dutch-Hottentot contact, when an attempt was made to confine the settlement so as to avoid irritations, once again the Compagnie, trying vainly to rule an area already ten times greater than Holland, forbade any further barter with blacks. But on the frontier their proclamations were like sand thrown in the wind. Daring white men crossed into the lands occupied by those they called Kaffirs, Arabic for infidels, reasoning that it was simpler to fire their guns and take what land they needed rather than sit out a protracted bargaining session with the Xhosa. No bitter-almond hedge could possibly demark hundreds of miles of borderland; also, Sotopo's people provoked rage, for, when the white men's herds moved placidly within range, they reverted to old ways, sang old songs, sharpened their assegais, and shouted with glee as they stole the trekboers' cattle.

And so the battles began, the blacks claiming land which was theirs by hereditary right, the trekboers grabbing for the same land because it had been promised to the children of God.

Guzaka's men struck south, smiting an isolated farm not far from the sea, killing everyone and driving some five hundred cattle back across the Great Fish. They then rushed northward to the Van Doorn farm set among hills, recognizing it as the major impediment to their westward expansion.

'It will not be easy,' Guzaka warned his men.

'You said that about the other farm,' one said.

'It was not defended. At this place there are the hills.'

'Which means they're trapped inside.'

'It could mean something else,' Guzaka cautioned.

'What?'

'That we will not be able to break in.'

'We have so many. They have so few.'

'But they have the guns.'

'The others had guns.'

'But only two to use them. Here there will be many.'

'Are you afraid, Guzaka?'

'I am,' and before the others could ask if they should turn back, he added, 'But we must wipe out this farm, or it will oppose us always.'

It was he who led the charge down the eastern hill, coming first to the cattle byres and the other small buildings, and it was here that the Xhosa met their punishing taste of what real trekboers could do in defense of a farm. From crannies that the blacks could not have anticipated, gunfire snapped at them, cutting and killing until they had to retreat. No invader even came near the house.

On the hillside, surveying what amounted to the first trekboer fort, Guzaka and his men consulted on what to do, and their leader reminded them: 'I told you this would be different.' He did not yet know that his father's friend, Adriaan of the Van Doorns, occupied the stone house, nor would he have recognized the name had it been spoken, but he carried in the back of his mind stories his father had told of that compelling meeting with the white man and of the man's capacities. Guzaka understood that there were degrees in manhood and that the futile defenders of that first farm stood rather low on the rod of measurement. The men in this house resembled more the one that Sotopo had encountered.

'Shall we turn back?' his men asked.

'No. Then they would think it was too easy to defeat us. We will attack from two quarters.' And he devised a plan whereby one group would come down the eastern hill, while a larger body would swing in from the south.

In the stone house Adriaan said, 'They're not stupid. This time they'll come at us from two directions.' Looking at the hills and the position of the stream, which though small would prove difficult to ford under gunfire, he concluded that they would have to come in from the south, so along that wall he stationed three of his guns.

'But they'll try the east again,' he warned. 'Just to test us.' So he alone went to the byre, satisfied that the number of eastern invaders would be smaller than before.

When Guzaka saw that his own groups were in position, he gave the signal and dashed for the outlying buildings; to his delight, there was no gunfire, so with a wild yell he urged his men on to the house, but when they were abreast of the cattle byre, a deadly fusillade struck from the flank, and two of his men fell.

Then from the south wall of the house, gunfire erupted, and that invading contingent was also thrown back.

When the Xhosa regrouped on the eastern hill it was obvious that this farm could not be taken. Turning away from that stronghold, the blacks forded the stream well east of the house, rounded up such cattle as grazed in the far fields, and retreated through the northeast opening.

'They'll be back,' Lodevicus warned. 'Not today, but they'll know that ours is the kraal that must be reduced.'

'Kraal?' Adriaan asked.

'This refuge enclosed by hills,' and from that time on the farm was called De Kraal, the protected place.

The trekboers, having lost none and slain seven, should have celebrated, but they didn't, for old animosities between Seena and Rebecca continued to smolder, always ready to burst into flame. Usually the brawls involved religion, with Seena ridiculing her daughter-in-law's stern devotion and Rebecca complaining of her mother-in-law's agnosticism. No compromise seemed possible, and when the old folk were alone, Seena resumed her pestering: 'Let's leave and build a little hut where we can live the way we used to. I'm tired of having the Bible thrown at me.'

'It's being thrown at your father, too,' he said, referring to the rumor that a military expedition had been sent to eliminate Rooi van Valck's outlaw empire. Some even claimed that Rooi had been hanged.

Seena doubted this: 'They'd have to catch him first. And then they'd have to get a rope around his neck. Not many at the Cape would like to try.'

'If you'd be more patient with Rebecca,' Adriaan began, whereupon his wife gave him a lesson on the future of South Africa: 'She'll never let up. With her quiet manners she'll press on and on. The way her father did.'

'What do you mean?'

'He came here singing Psalms. Accomplished nothing with you and me. But he worked on Lodevicus, sowing seeds. And later on he trapped him.'

'What do you truly think of our son?'

'He's going to grow stronger every day. As a boy he was like a piece of soft limestone lying in water. You can cut it with your fingernail. But when it stands clear of the water, and dries in the sun, it becomes harder than granite, and no one can cut it. Rebecca and Vicus, they'll form a terrible partnership.'

As she uttered this prediction, Rebecca was arguing with her husband: 'Vicus, I know I've said it many times before, but I can no longer tolerate that woman. I can't have her godlessness continue to contaminate my house.'

'In point of fact,' Lodevicus said, 'the house is hers and my father's, not yours.'

'Very well, we'll leave it to them and go build our own.'

'But I worked three years building these walls. Be patient. They can't live forever.' Lodevicus was hardening, but he had not yet reached the point at which he could throw his parents out of their own house.

Rebecca was sterner: 'God has directed you and me to bring a new order into a pagan land. We're to form a new life here among the trekboers. We're to raise children according to the Holy Book and not the way that godless old woman raised you and the others.' When Vicus started to protest, she silenced him: 'Don't you realize that God performed a miracle so that you could be saved? Suppose Father had not stopped at your farm to plant the holy seed? Suppose you had not visited Swellendam to have it nurtured? You've been set aside for a noble mission, and we cannot allow it to be diverted.'

Of the four adults engaged in this continuing battle, Mal Adriaan was the only one who saw its dimensions clearly, for he possessed a childlike simplicity which he was willing to turn even upon himself: 'I'm a man of the past, Seena. There's no place in this family for wanderers. Frightened people want to retreat into stone forts.' When his wife asked what he thought of her, he laughed. 'You're a pagan. Daughter of a pagan. There'll be no place for pagans in the world Vicus and Rebecca are building.'

As for Lodevicus, Adriaan supposed that Seena had been correct when she described him as limestone-about-to-become-granite: 'I don't think I'll like the finished result. Too stiff, too unforgiving. And I pity those who cross him.'

Rebecca he saw with unflinching clarity: he sensed that she had declared war upon Seena and him and was probably agitating for their expulsion; but he also saw that she was an exceptional woman whom he might have wanted to marry had he been younger. She was passionate and clean and shining, like a white stone at the bottom of a moving river. Her courage merited enormous respect, for in her zeal to discipline the trekboer world, which he had to admit was lawless, she was like some great mother elephant crashing through the underbush, headed for a destination which she alone perceived, and nothing would stop her. That she felt herself to be driven by God only made her more formidable. She was not cruel, nor did she try to overwhelm her opposition; like a cascade running to the sea, she simply kept moving in her predestined direction.

She would be the inner strength of the new religion developing in South Africa, the silent woman who sat serene in church while the men roared and ranted and announced the Psalms to be sung; but in the privacy of the home it would be she who determined what the day-to-day applications of that public religion were to be, and if ever the men carelessly fumbled their way toward some wrongdoing, she would summon them back to the stern path of duty. She would be against change, against relaxation, against new ideas from abroad, against any bizarre interpretation at home. She would form the granite core of the church, and her quiet teaching would prevail.

In short, Adriaan had grown to respect his daughter-in-law not only as the inexorable force of the future but also as the hard-grained, just human being who was needed at this moment in history. She was a stalwart wife, a compassionate mother; he liked her caustic wit and her capacity to hew to a single line. She was, all told, a good woman, and if she opposed him, the fault must be his.

It was always this way when generations clashed: the best of the old found it easy to appreciate the merits of those among the new who displayed integrity. It was the second echelons, deficient in understanding and empathy, who caused the trouble, and now Lodevicus was prepared to do just that.

It was the second expedition against the Bushmen which demonstrated how stonelike he had become and how justly he merited the title Hammer. This time there had been no massive theft of cattle, only the constant spiriting away of a cow here, an ox there, but all farmers in the region were enraged with the little brown men, and when Lodevicus said, 'They're like vermin. Periodically they have to be exterminated,' they agreed, and once more a commando was sent north to cleanse the area.

On this expedition no rhinoceros was used as bait, and for good reason: there were now no herds of large animals in the region; most had been killed off or driven away. Rhinoceros, hippopotamus, lion, zebra, those glorious beasts who had roamed these hills had vanished before the horse and gun, and now these dreadful weapons were to be turned against the Bushmen.

What Lodevicus did was separate his commando into three groups operating like a vast pinwheel, riding in circles that tightened toward the center, and as the men rode they watched for little brown men who might be trapped within their circle. As the bewildered Bushmen ran this way and that in sad confusion, the horsemen picked them off, one by one. There was no mass slaughter of ninety, as before, but only the deadly attrition of knocking down running targets—until two hundred were slain.

Adriaan, remembering his friendship with the Bushmen, had spoken against the hunt, but he had been ignored. He was appalled at its inhumanity, and when one old man, hampered by a kind of belt he wore, stumbled about in confusion, Adriaan rode to rescue him, but Lodevicus swept in, lowered his rifle, and killed the man.

'What have you done?' Adriaan cried.

'We're clearing the land,' Vicus shouted from his horse.

'Damn you! Look at him!' And Adriaan dismounted to inspect the dead man's belt, and found it to be of rhinoceros hide imbedded with eight tips of eland horn. Holding the belt aloft, he cried, 'What is it, Vicus? Tell me, what is it?'

His son reined in his horse, rode back, and looked contemptuously at the leather. 'Seems like a belt.'

'Dip your finger into one of the horns,' and when he did, the finger came out a deep-stained blue.

'What is it, Vicus?' And when his son said he didn't know, Adriaan cried in pain, 'They're the pots of an artist. Who paints the living veld on the roof of the cave. And you murdered him.' Looking up at his mounted son, he said with bitter scorn, 'Lodevicus the Hammer. I won't share my house with you one day longer.'

'It's my house,' Lodevicus said. 'I built it.'

Whereupon the old man cried in terrible rage, 'Read the Bible you prate about! It was Abraham's house as long as he lived. But you've tainted it . . . with red blood . . . and blue paint. And I'll have no more of it.'

Turning his back on his son, he mounted his horse, hurried over the hills, and shouted as he rode into De Kraal, 'Seena! Come on, old Redhead. Get yourself ready to leave this pitiful place.'

'Good!' she shouted back. 'Where do we go?'

'I'll find a place,' he assured her, and at sixty-five the old wanderers began scouting far lands to determine where they would build their own hut.

In 1778 the Hollanders who came to Cape Town to govern the colony, spending temporary terms in a land that confused them, gave honest proof of their desire to administer the area justly, for they devised a solution to frontier problems that was more humane and considerate than any being offered at this time by either the British or the French in their colonies. The governor himself trekked all the way from Cape Town, on horseback and by slow oxcart, to talk with trekboers like the Van Doorns and native chieftains like Guzaka, and after painful consideration of what was best for all, sent an emissary back to De Kraal with a written order that was concise and unmistakable:

> We have decided that the only practical solution to the problem of having settled white farmers mingling with roaming black herdsmen is to separate the two groups severely and permanently. This will provide justice and security for each segment, leaving each free to develop as it deems best. Since the Compagnie plans to import no new settlers, and since the blacks certainly have sufficient land for their purposes, we order that each shall stay in their present places and move no farther. There shall be no contact of any kind between white and black.

> The Great Fish River shall be the permanent dividing line between the races, and a strict policy of apartness shall be maintained, now and forever. No white man shall move east of the Great Fish. No black man shall move west. In this manner, peace can be maintained perpetually.

When the emissary rejoined the governor's party he was able to state with assurance: 'The frontier problem is settled. There can never again be conflict, because each side will keep to its own bank of the river.'

The day after he said this, Adriaan van Doorn loaded his wagon, handed his wife a walking stick, and bade farewell to his son's family. To Rebecca he said with sorrow, 'You and Lodevicus have set a course so harsh I cannot follow. May your God give you strength to finish it.'

'He's your God, too.'

'Mine is a gentler God,' he said, but when this rebuke caused blood to leave her face, he kissed her and said, 'The world throws up mountains, and sometimes we must live in separated valleys.'

And he forded the river and built his hut right in the center of the area which the governer had promised would never again be touched by white men.

When Xhosa spies informed Guzaka that a trekboer had violated the order before it was seven days old, he concluded that the only reasonable response was warfare, so he assembled a party and led his men in a swift charge that engulfed the trespass hut.

Before Adriaan could reach for his gun, assegais flashed and Seena was dead. Swinging the butt of his rifle, he tried to beat off the attackers, but they overwhelmed him, and when his arms were pinioned, Guzaka lunged at him with a spear.

Now Lodevicus became indeed the Hammer, exacting a terrible revenge. Inflamed by the knowledge that it had been he who forced his parents' exodus, he confessed his guilt to no one, but led his commandos far across the Great Fish, rampaging deep into Xhosa lands, destroying forever the hopeful truce the governor had arranged. He burned and slaughtered, and for every cow the Xhosa had stolen, he took back a hundred. With flashing guns he rode against unmounted men armed only with spears, shouting, 'Kill! Kill!'

When he returned to De Kraal he claimed, in his apologetic report to the governor, that he had been lured across the Great Fish by Xhosa infamy, but that the border was now secured for all time. Although he convinced the governor, he was not persuasive with Guzaka, who heard of this report, and now it was he who planned revenge.

'Every kraal must be destroyed,' he thundered at night meetings, and if Vicus van Doorn had sought retribution after the death of his parents, Guzaka wanted nothing less than extermination.

It was, in most respects, as uneven a war as would ever be pursued in Africa, with each side having outrageous advantages. Blacks outnumbered whites by a ratio of one hundred to one and could extirpate any single white farm; but the whites possessed guns and horses, and when the latter galloped through a kraal, they spread such terror that one white gunman could methodically reload and shoot a dozen fleeing natives.

It was a confusion, a clash of interests that could not even be defined. Guzaka was committed to moving his cattle slowly onward, as his people had been doing for eight hundred years, while Lodevicus felt that God Himself had ordered him to establish on the far bank of the Fish River a Christian community obedient to the rules of John Calvin. Land ownership was a constant problem, Guzaka's tribe having always held their land in generality and believing that they were entitled to every lush pasturage reaching to the Cape, while the trekboers cherished a tradition which their Dutch forebears had defended with their lives: that a man's farm merited the same respect as a man's soul.

It was impossible to detect at any moment in this vast struggle who was winning. At the beginning of 1778 Guzaka gained a signal victory by razing the hut of Adriaan van Doorn, but in the spring of that year Vicus retaliated with his famous 'tobacco commando.' Recalling his tactics with the Bushmen, when he used a rhinoceros to wipe them out, he scattered tobacco on the ground a Xhosa war party would traverse; when they bent to grab at this prize, they perished in a hail of lead. In 1779 recognized warfare erupted, black regiments pitted against white field forces, and this was repeated in 1789 and 1799, bloody preludes to the more terrible wars that would continue through the next century.

During the battles Lodevicus never equated the Xhosa with the Bushmen, those troublesome little animals that had to be exterminated. Since the Xhosa were large men like himself, they commanded respect. As he told Rebecca, after one arduous expedition, 'When we pacify them, they'll be good Kaffirs.'

Guzaka had no intention of becoming a good Kaffir. Six separate times he threw his warriors against De Kraal, still convinced that if he could humble it, he could break the spirit of the trekboers, and six times the protecting hills enabled the embattled farmers to repel the invaders, and in the chase that always followed, to massacre them. But on the seventh try, in 1788, Guzaka and his warriors broke into the valley unexpectedly and came upon Rebecca van Doorn as she was going from the cattle byre to her house. With flashing assegias they cut her down, and she died before Lodevicus could reach her.

In contrast to the rage he felt at the similar death of his mother and father, this time he fell silent, brooding upon the harsh fact that God was not giving him the easy victories Dominee Specx had spoken of in those exciting days of revelation at Swellendam. He was also plagued by memories of that morning when his wife and his mother resorted to the Bible to answer the question of what would happen when the Xhosa struck, and the mocking words reverberated: 'An hundred of you shall put ten thousand to flight.' One of that ten thousand, the damned Guzaka, had killed his father, his mother and his wife. The New Jerusalem had not been established on the far side of the Great Fish; the Canaanites had not been expelled from the house of the Lord; indeed, they seemed to be chopping that house to bits.

And then, in the depth of his despair, when it seemed that his mission and that of the trekboers had been completely frustrated, God visited him again, in the person of a girl of nineteen who came riding alone into De Kraal on the back of a white horse. She was Wilhelmina Heimstra, from one of the irreverent families down by the sea, and her mission was forthright: 'I cannot live in idolatry. I cannot exist without the presence of God.'

'You can't stay here,' Lodevicus said. 'I have no wife.'

'That's why I came,' the girl said. 'When the messenger told us that the Xhosa had killed Rebecca, whom I knew . . .'

Lodevicus, then forty-nine, the Hammer of the frontier, stood silent. In all the territory he commanded there was no predikant to give direction, not even a sick-comforter other than himself, and he did not know what to do. But then he recalled the patristic figures of the Old Testament and how often they had been faced by such problems on their lonely frontiers: older men without wives, heads of families with no one to assist them, and his mind fell especially on Abraham, the first great trekboer:

And Sarah was an hundred and seven and twenty years old . . .
and Sarah died . . . and Abraham came to mourn for Sarah, and to
weep for her . . . Then again Abraham took a wife, and her name
was Keturah.

It became apparent that God had sent this girl to comfort him in his old
age, but the problem of how a Christian marriage could be performed
without a cleric was perplexing. 'You cannot stay here, when I have been
so demanding of others that they follow in righteous paths.'

'You demanded, Lodevicus, that's true, but no one obeyed. Everyone to
the south lives as they always lived. I'm the one who listened and obeyed.'

This was so similar to his own experience, when Predikant Specx, now
dead three years, had preached to scores who did not listen, and to one
who did, that Lodevicus had to be impressed, and when he looked at the
flaxen-haired girl, so smiling and so different from rigorous Rebecca, he
was tempted.

It was really quite simple. Wilhelmina pointed out that since she
could not very well return to the south, having run away, there was no alternative but for her to stay at De Kraal, and this she did, moving into the
room that Adriaan and Seena had once occupied; and on the third night,
as she slept, her door opened and Lodevicus said, 'Are you willing to be
married of God? Without a dominee to enter it in the books?' and she
replied, 'Yes,' and nine months and eight days later the boy Tjaart was
born.

In 1795 news reached De Kraal which stunned the Van Doorns, news so
revolutionary that they had no base for comprehending it. A courier from
Cape Town had dashed across the flats to Trianon, then over the mountains to Swellendam, then along the chain of farms to De Kraal, and
wherever he stopped to give his report, men gasped: 'But how could this
have happened?'

'All I know, it's happened. Every Compagnie holding in South Africa
has been surrendered to the English. We're no longer attached to Holland. We're citizens of England and must be obedient to her.'

It was incomprehensible. These frontier farmers had only the vaguest
notions of a revolution in France or of the new radical republic that now
controlled Holland. They knew that France and England were at war, but
they did not know that the new government sided with France while the
old Royalists supported England. They were bewildered when they heard
that their Prince of Orange, William V, had fled to London, and from
that refuge had ceded the Cape to his English hosts.

And what they heard next was even more confusing: 'The English
warships stood in the bay. But Colonel Gordon behaved valiantly.'

'Was he English?'

'No, Scot.'

'What was he doing in the fort, fighting the English?'

'He was a Dutchman, fighting for us.'

'But you just said he was a Scot.'

'His grandfather was, but he came to live in Holland. Our Gordon is a born Dutchman . . . joined something called the Scots Brigade.'

'So the Scots made him a colonel, in Scotland?'

'No, the Scots Brigade is Dutch. We made him a colonel, and he was in command at the Castle.'

'Did he drive away the English?'

'No, he surrendered like a craven. Never fired one of our guns and invited the English to take everything.'

'But you said he was brave.'

'He was. Brave as a tiger defending her young. Because after the disgrace of surrender, he blew his brains out, as a brave man should.'

Lodevicus and Wilhelmina asked the courier to go over the details again, and at the conclusion the courier returned to the astonishing truth: 'This colony is now English. You are all to be confirmed in the ownership of your farms. And English soldiers will be here soon to establish peace on the border.'

When the young messenger rode on, to spread his confusion among the other trekboers, Lodevicus assembled his family, and with little Tjaart upon his knee, tried to pick out the truths that would govern their new life: 'What do we know about the English? Nothing.'

'We know a great deal,' his wife contradicted, bowing quickly to ask forgiveness for her impertinence. 'We know they don't follow the teachings of John Calvin. They're little better than Catholics.'

That was bad enough, but soon a man rode in from Swellendam announcing himself as a patriot, and he lectured the Van Doorns about America, where England had once had colonies and where the citizens had risen in revolt against English rule. 'What I learned when I was in New York,' he said, 'is that when English magistrates come ashore, English troops are always ready to follow. Mark my words, you'll see Redcoats on your frontier before the year is out. They'll not have Lodevicus van Doorn telling them how to handle Kaffirs.'

From a corner of the room, where he had been sitting with Tjaart, Lodevicus spoke of the real problems facing the Dutch in Africa: 'New rulers who have not our traditions will attempt to alter our church, recast it in their mold, destroy our ancient convictions. To preserve our integrity, we shall have to fight ten times as hard as we fight against the Xhosa. Because the English will be after our souls.

'Since they do not speak our language, they'll force us to speak theirs. They'll issue their laws in English, import books printed in English, demand that we pray from their English Bible.' Pointing like an Old Testament prophet at the various children in the room, he said with an ominous voice, 'You will be told that you must not speak Dutch. That you must conduct your affairs in English.'

In later years Tjaart would say, 'First thing I remember in life, sitting in a dark room while my father thundered, "If my conqueror makes me speak his language, he makes me his slave. Resist him! Resist him!"'

And when the Redcoats came, followed by the magistrates, the Van Doorns did resist, and looked very foolish for having done so, because within a few years everything was thrown again into wild confusion, for the same messenger came galloping eastward over the same route with news more startling than the first: 'We're all Dutch again! England and Holland are allies, fighting a man called Napoleon Bonaparte. You can ignore English laws.'

So the Redcoats were withdrawn; Van Doorn's fears proved groundless; and life resumed its orderly way, which on the frontier meant without any order at all. Guzaka continued his raids across the Great Fish, and Vicus hammered him for his insolence. Killing became so commonplace that often it was not even reported to Swellendam.

Restoration of Dutch rule had one curious side effect: a minor but condescending official came out from Holland to inspect the frontier, and upon finishing his tour he commented on the sad deterioration of speech in the colony: 'At times I would scarcely know I was listening to Dutch, the way your people mishandle the language.' From his pocket he produced a slip of paper on which he had noted certain unfamiliar words. 'You borrow words with a most careless abandon, adopting the worst of the native languages and forgetting your good Dutch words.' And he read off neologisms like *kraal, bobotie, assegai* and *lobola*. 'You should purify yourself of such abominations,' he said, proceeding to criticize also the local word orders and mispronunciations. When he was finished, Lodevicus said with some asperity, 'You make us sound like barbarians,' and the visitor said, 'That's what you'll become if you lose your Dutch,' and that was the beginning of the Van Doorn family's distrust of the homeland Dutch. They were a snobbish, metropolitan, unpleasant lot, with no appreciation of what frontier life involved.

When the stranger left, Lodevicus called his group together and said, 'We'll speak Dutch the way we want it to sound.' And the result was that they drove an even deeper wedge between their inherited Dutch language and the new tongue they were building.

Despite these years of uncertainty and war, Lodevicus prospered as a stock farmer, extending his acres far beyond mountain-girt De Kraal. When he required more help and found it impossible to lure Xhosa warriors to work his farm, he grumbled about their arrogance, then drove his wagon to Swellendam, where he purchased slaves: two Madagascans, three Angolans. Because of his visible wealth, he was appointed veldkornet for his district, and he presented a dominating appearance; tall, heavy, white-haired, with whiskers down the sides of his face, he wore substantial clothes, holding up his heavy trousers with both belt and suspenders. When he walked among strangers he strode ahead, with Wilhelmina a respectful four paces behind. In public she always referred to him as the Mijnheer, and he was gratified to see how easily she assumed Rebecca's role as a driving religious force, but of a different quality. She was amiable, forgiving of minor defections and most eager to be of help to everyone who came past the farm. She sang as she worked and was overjoyed to learn that a real church had been built at Graaff-Reinet, ninety-odd miles to the northwest: 'We must report to the predikant for our marriage.'

'I can't leave the farm.'

Wilhelmina laughed. 'You call yourself a trekboer?'

'No more. The Van Doorns are through wandering. This is our home.'

'But Tjaart's got to be baptized,' she said with such simplicity that he could not refuse her. So the older Van Doorn children were left in charge while their stepmother led Lodevicus and young Tjaart to their religious duties.

It was a glorious ride, with Tjaart old enough to recall in later years the vast empty spaces, the lovely hills with their tops flattened. He would never forget the moment when his parents halted their horses some miles south of the new village to observe that extraordinary peak which guarded the site: from flat land it rose very high in gentle sweeps until it neared an apex, when suddenly it became a round turret, many feet high, with sheer walls of solid gray granite. And at the top, forming a beautiful green pyramid, rose wooded slopes coming to a delicate point.

'God must have placed it there to guide us to things important,' Lodevicus said, impressing upon his son the stunning significance of the place, and Tjaart remembered this peak long after he had forgotten his parents' marriage and his own baptism.

The boy now had three memories upon which to build his life: that the Dutch way of life must be defended against the English enemy; that Graaff-Reinet was a center of excitement; and that far to the north, as Grandfather Adriaan had told the other children before he died, lay an open valley of compelling beauty which he called Vrijmeer.

And then, in 1806, when the Van Doorns were congratulating themselves upon having resisted the English threat and preserving the countryside for Calvinism, the final shocking news arrived. Because the ordinary citizens of Holland had joined forces with Napoleon, England felt it must reoccupy the Cape to keep it from falling into French hands, which would cut the life line to India. It was now an English possession, and neither the local Dutch government nor the mother country Holland would exercise further control. All of Lodevicus' apprehensions about suppression at English hands revived.

The Cape, having been a stopping place between Holland and Java during the years 1647 to 1806, now became one between England and India, and the indifference with which Holland had always treated this potentially grand possession would now be matched by English imperiousness.

In these days of change it was inevitable that assessments be made of Holland's long rule, and it was remarked by certain observers—Dutchmen who had known their country's holdings in other parts of the world, Englishmen who had fought in the American war, and Frenchmen who knew many parts of the world—that her rule had been almost without parallel in world history. The home country had allowed neither its royalty, its parliament nor its citizens any voice in the rule of this distant possession; control had rested in the hands of a clique of businessmen who made all decisions with an eye to profit. True, these profits had sometimes been widely distributed, with the government grabbing a healthy share, but in essence the colony had been a narrow business venture.

This had imposed limitations. The surging colonization that marked the French, Spanish and English settlement of North America, with excited citizens pushing exuberantly into the interior, was discouraged in South Africa. Always the Lords XVII preached caution, a holding back lest rambunctious elements like the Van Doorns stray so far afield that they could not easily be disciplined. If one major charge could be leveled against the Compagnie, it was that it restricted normal growth. The borders which should have extended to logical boundaries, perhaps the Zambezi, as Dr. Linnart suggested, never did, which meant that the generic entity never came into being. Absentee businessmen, seeking only profit, do not generate a sense of manifest destiny; indeed, they fear it lest it create movements that get out of hand, and without this spiritual urge, no nation can achieve the limits to which geography, history, philosophy and hope entitle it. Because of Compagnie policy, rigorously enforced through sixteen decades, South Africa remained a truncated state, with only a few single-minded pioneers like the Van Doorns eager to dare the unknown.

Comparison with North American development was inescapable. In 1806, when the English assumed final control, South Africa had 26,000 white settlers. Canada, which had been started at about the same time as Cape Town and on less favorable soil, had 250,000, and the young United States more than 6,000,000. Mexico, a century older than South Africa, had 885,000. The main reason was simple: the Lords XVII were so reluctant to allow any immigration from which they could not immediately profit that during the entire eighteenth century they permitted only 1,600 new settlers to land! Sixteen newcomers a year cannot keep any new society healthy, or an old one, either.

But the Lords XVII were not entirely to blame, for on the rare occasions when they did advocate immigration, the response from those already living at the Cape was uniformly negative. 'It is absolutely impossible,' those holding land reported, 'to introduce any more whites into the country because they could find no livelihood.' What this really meant was that positions of advantage already filled by those in place would not be shared. There were no vacancies for the tough, impoverished migrant seeking a new country and a new chance, because the work that such people would normally start with was already being done by slaves.

In the time it took the cautious Lords XVII to approve inward movement of a hundred miles, settlers in North America had penetrated a thousand. While the Compagnie grudgingly allowed the establishment of a few small towns like Stellenbosch and Swellendam relatively close to the Cape, the free French and English settlers were already building communities like Montreal and Detroit far inland, thus laying the foundation for further movement westward.

It was not that the Dutch were commercially minded and the English not; had the English merchants been allowed to dominate North America they might have duplicated the folly of the Dutch, but English commercialism was never free to dictate to their colonies the way the Compagnie did.

Wherein lay the difference? The Dutch system of government not only permitted but encouraged its businessmen to rule without supervision, whereas the English government, which started in the same direction, quickly turned matters over to Parliament, a free press, and the innate longing for freedom of its citizens overseas. English businessmen might have wanted to ape the Dutch precedent, but the institutions of freedom forestalled them.

In no respect did the Dutch deficiency show itself more clearly than in the field of education and the dissemination of culture. Because the population was meager and dispersed over thousands of square miles, the development of large schools was impractical, and those that were attempted in the towns were atrocious. On the veld, where countless children like the Van Doorns grew up, education was left to a group of vagabond itinerants with only a meager knowledge of reading and writing. Usually discharged servants of the Compagnie, these inept clerks roamed from farm to farm dispensing their rudimentary wisdom while they supplemented their income with anything from composing love letters to making coffins. The trekboer Van Doorns were not alone in producing children who were illiterate; one traveler estimated that seventy-five percent of the colony's children were unable to read.

This was not surprising, because the Compagnie ran the colony for nearly a century and a half before it allowed the colonists to import a printing press, or publish any kind of book, or print a newspaper. In Canada these things happened almost automatically, and America could not have been the same without its itinerant printers, inflammatory broadsides and contentious newspapers; but it was precisely such potential troublemakers that the Compagnie sought to inhibit, and did.

In such a climate there could, of course, be no institutions of higher learning, and here the comparison with other colonial settlements was shocking. The Spaniards, who conquered Mexico in 1521, had by 1553 opened a major university. They took Peru in 1533 and sponsored a university in 1551. The English, who landed at Plymouth Rock in 1619, had a functioning college at Harvard in 1636, and before the revolution started in 1776 they had sixteen great colleges in operation. During the entire Dutch rule the Compagnie never even came close to starting a college.

Of course, bright boys at the Cape sometimes found their way back to Leiden or Amsterdam, where splended universities were available, but an emerging nation needs speculative intelligence bred in local institutions; they provide the fine yeastiness that produces strong new ideas applicable to local situations. The entire history of South Africa might have been modified if there had been a strong school system topped by a university staffed with local luminaries dedicated to the creation of a new society. Instead, fresh ideas either did not germinate or were stamped out.

Much of the blame must be shared by the church; its leaders were convinced that they could trust only predikants trained in the conservative centers of Holland, and they were terrified of the possibility that a Cape seminary might arise to sponsor alien ideas. Missing in South Africa were those gaunt Pilgrim ministers of New England who cut themselves off from European dictation and initiated a local approach to religious problems.

'The Night of Darkness in which the South African nation had its birth,' some historians would describe this period of the trekboers, when the merchant mind stifled the scientific, creative and political urges of the citizens.

But there was another side to this coin, and it shone brightly. A few Dutch children, through assiduous teaching within the family, did gain an education almost comparable to that available in the average European country, and although the Boers lacked an Oxford or a Harvard, they did have their own unique university, and its curriculum was one of the most effective in the history of education. They had a massive Bible, which accompanied them wherever they went; their curriculum was the Old Testament, whose narratives predicted each event that might arise. There were, of course, many trekboer families like the Rooi van Valcks and the Adriaan van Doorns who ignored the Bible, through either illiteracy or indifference, but the majority studied and obeyed.

Few nations were ever as solidly indoctrinated in one group of principles as the Dutch in South Africa, and this begat a Volk—a people—with tremendous driving force, self-assurance and will to persist. With constant support from this theological university, which each man could carry with him as he moved, the Dutch colony became a conservative, God-fearing state, and so it would remain despite English occupation, English persecution, English wars and the constant threat of imposed English values. In

South Africa the Old Testament triumphed over the university because it was the university.

On one major point Lodevicus was wrong. When he thundered 'South Africa is Dutch and will always remain so' he misrepresented the composition of his white community: Dutch ancestry, forty percent; German ancestry, thirty-five percent; Huguenot component, twenty percent; and although this would later be denied by Van Doorn's descendants, a Malay-Hottentot-black component of at least five percent. This creative mix had produced a handsome, tough, resilient Volk infused with the trekboer spirit, and no English governor would have an easy time trying to discipline them into the ways he wanted them to go.

VI. The Missionary

THE Englishmen who came so late to South Africa, and with such pervasive power, were men of courage, as the Saltwoods of Salisbury, that cathedral town southwest of London, proved. On Midsummer Day 1640, after three years of daring enterprise among the Spice Islands, Captain Nicholas Saltwood of the little ship *Acorn* came sailing into Plymouth harbor with a bulging cargo of nutmeg, clove and cinnamon. It was so valuable that it made all his partners—who had counted him dead, and their investments lost—men of substantial wealth.

His own fortune was increased when he sold the *Acorn* within two hours of anchoring. When his partners, eager to send him forth again, asked why he had acted so precipitately and against his own best interests, he snapped, 'You invested money. I invested my life against pirates, storms and Portuguese forts. No more.'

When he was alone with his wife, Henrietta, who had spent these three years in near-poverty, he kissed her vigorously and led her in a small dance about their meager rooms: 'Years ago, sweets, I saw the cathedral at Salisbury, and I swore that if I ever reached the Spice Islands and made my fortune, you'd have a home in the meadow, beside the River Avon. And you shall!'

With his bags of silver and his drafts upon the spice merchants of London, he packed Henrietta in a diligence and his household goods in two drays. Taking his position at the head of his armed guards, he led the way through the lovely lanes of southern England until he reached that broad and noble plain in the middle of which stood Salisbury Cathedral. There, on the right bank of the Avon, he purchased nine good acres and the seven swans that guarded those gentle waters.

Like many a prudent Englishman, Captain Saltwood planted a garden before starting on a house, but since he was a man of vigor he preferred trees, and he located his so that they framed the handsome cathedral on the far side of the river. To the left he placed nine cedars, well rooted, whose dark limbs swept the ground. In the center, but not exactly so, he planted eleven strong chestnuts; in spring they would be white with flowers; in autumn, heavy with fruit for children to play with. Well to the right and safely back from the river, he started a group of slender oaks; in time they would be massive of trunk and stout of limb, and under them swans would nestle when they came ashore.

Sentinels he called his trees, and that name was given the house that later rose among them. It was notable as reflecting an older style of construction known as hang-tile. It was two-storied, with the lower walls built of conventional brick; nothing unusual about that. But the top story was faced in a most peculiar manner: instead of using brick, ordinary roof tiles had been hung vertically! The effect was resoundingly fourteenth century, as if the roof had slipped, abandoning its accustomed place to come down and cover the walls. The true roof was of thatch, sixteen inches thick and carefully trimmed like the hair of a boy about to leave for choir.

Generations of Saltwoods had gathered under the sentinel trees to discuss family problems while contemplating the spire of the cathedral; under strictures laid down by Captain Nicholas, they continued to be cautious in protecting their investments but daring in investing their profits. About 1710 a Timothy Saltwood had had the good fortune of making the acquaintance of the Proprietor, that gentleman of august lineage who owned much of the region, and before long Timothy was serving as the Proprietor's agent, an occupation of dignity which passed from one Saltwood to the next.

One afternoon during the first years of the 1800s, Josiah Saltwood, the present master of Sentinels, sat with his wife on a bench beneath the oaks and said, 'I deem it time we meet with the boys.' He paused, as if matters of gravity impended, then added promptly, 'Nothing serious, of course. Merely their entire future.'

His wife laughed. 'They're all about somewhere. I could summon them.'

'Not just yet. I must ride to Old Sarum with the Proprietor. The election, you know.' And with his wife at his side, and the swans following, he walked across the lawn to where his horse was being saddled.

The beautiful cathedral had not always stood in its present location. In the early days of Christianity in England a much different cathedral-castle-fort, keystone to security in this part of the country, had rested on a low hill some two miles to the north, and here devout bishops exercised as much leadership as the masters of the castle would permit. It was called by a bewildering variety of Roman and Saxon names, but in time it came to be known as Sarum, and from it came that set of orders and regulations for worship known as the Use of Sarum, which would be adopted by much of the English church.

The first cathedral, begun in 1075, was a large, rugged building in the French manner, set down within the walls of the castle-fort; between the two groups of occupants, clergy and soldiers, so much friction arose that rupture was inescapable. Rarely has a formal complaint been more comprehensive than that issued by Pope Honorius III in 1219 when he summarized the difficulties of his priests at Sarum:

> The clergy cannot stay there without danger to their persons. The wind howls so furiously that priests can hardly hear each other speak. The building is ruinous. The congregation is so small it cannot provide repairs. Water is scarce. People wishing to visit the cathedral are prevented by the garrison. Housing is insufficient for the clergy, who must buy their own houses. The whiteness of the chalk causes blindness.

The bishop solved these difficulties by offering to move his cathedral from Sarum to a vacant field well to the south, where the town of Salisbury would belatedly arise. The exchange worked and the cathedral at Sarum was abandoned, to the pleasure of the bishop; he owned the vacant field and sold it to the church for a nice profit.

With the loss of its cathedral, Sarum declined. Once it boasted more than two thousand residents, then one thousand, then five hundred, then only a handful, and the day came in the early 1700s when it had almost none. Cathedral and castle alike were in ruins.

But tradition dies hard in England, and in rural England, hardest of all. When Parliament convened in the late 1200s, Sarum as a major settlement and support of the king, was awarded two seats; in its heyday it sent some mighty men to London. With the disappearance of its cathedral and its population, those seats, in any other country, would have been lost. But not in England, where precedent was prized. If Sarum had once been entitled to two seats, Old Sarum, as it was now called, was still entitled to them, and these empty fields with barely a single human being residing on or near them retained the right to send two members to Parliament and arrogantly exercised that right.

It became famous as 'the rottenest of the English rotten boroughs,' referring to those former towns, now abandoned or much reduced in population, which clung to ancient privileges on the principle that 'Parliament represents land, not people.' So that even in these early years of the nineteenth century one-fourth of the members of Parliament came from boroughs which in common sense should have returned nobody, and a shocking percentage of these were from boroughs like Old Sarum, which contained almost no one.

When a sitting Parliament was dissolved and a new one authorized, who selected the men to represent a rotten borough, especially when it had no voters? Custom said that whoever owned the land reserved the right to nominate whom he wished to represent it. What made this system repugnant to people of sensible intelligence was that an empty spot like Old Sarum could have two members of Parliament while great towns like Birmingham and Manchester had none.

At Old Sarum, in the first decade of the 1800s, an election was held for members of the new Parliament that would soon be convening, and the Proprietor rode out to the site in his carriage from Salisbury Town, while his factor, Josiah Saltwood, forty-nine years old, accompanied him on horseback. They started from the south side of River Avon, crossed the stone bridge five centuries old, passed the marvelous cathedral with its tall, clean tower, and made their way through the cluster of inns from which the stagecoaches departed for London. As they left the North Gate they entered the lovely rolling hills that led to Old Sarum, and after a pleasant rural passage, came to the south side of the rise on which the ancient ruins stood.

They did not climb that hill, but stopped at an elm tree whose spreading branches created a kind of shady amphitheater. Stepping carefully from his carriage, the Proprietor, an old man with white hair and kindly blue eyes, looked about him and said, 'Rarely have we known a finer voting day, eh, Josiah?'

'It was thoughtful of the old Parliament to end when it did,' the factor agreed.

'I can remember storms,' the old man said, recalling voting days when rain dripped from the elm. 'But our work never takes long, be praised.'

The coachman led his horses some distance from the tree, and after another servant placed a collapsible table on cleared ground, steadying the legs with twigs, the Proprietor unfolded a set of legal papers.

'I trust you find everything in readiness,' Saltwood said.

'Seems to be,' the old man said. He wore white side whiskers and showed a military bearing, for he had served his nation in many capacities abroad. It was curious that he had never elected to take one of his Parliament seats for himself; always he had picked other men who showed promise of good judgment, as had his father before him, so that whereas Old Sarum was indeed a rotten borough and an offense to reason, it had sent to London a succession of notable politicians, most of whom had never set foot in Old Sarum or even Salisbury. Indeed, none had ever lived within fifty miles of the dead town, but they had accepted the nomination as their right and had performed well. William Pitt the Elder, one of the outstanding English statesmen of the previous century, had been able to function as independently as he did only because he was sent to Parliament from Old Sarum, whose invisible electors he did not have to appease.

'Who's it to be this time?' Saltwood asked.

'A surprise, and not a surprise,' the Proprietor said, taking from his pocket a private memorandum. 'Dear old Sir Charles is to keep his seat, of course. He never speaks in the House, proposes no bills and might as well stay at home, but he's never done any harm, either, and many of us deem him the best member in recent history.'

The name was properly entered in the report of the election that Saltwood would forward to London. 'It's with the second name we get our surprise,' the Proprietor said, thrusting the paper at his factor. 'See for yourself.'

And there it was, in second position in the memorandum: 'Josiah Saltwood.'

'Me, sir?'

'You've a better head than most, Josiah, and I wish to reward it.'

The factor gasped. A seat like this, from one of the rotten boroughs, could cost an aspiring politician as much as a thousand pounds, and it might have to be paid anew periodically, but considering the money a clever man could come by if he held a seat, the cost was minimal. To have such a boon handed to one was only to be dreamed of, and here came a gift he had not even solicited.

'You're the man for the job,' the Proprietor said. 'But I want you to take it seriously. During the first four years it'll be better if you say nothing. Just listen and vote as I instruct, and after four or five years, you might begin to do things. Nothing flashy. You're not to be noticed. Men from the provinces are apt to make asses of themselves and don't last. Show me one from Old Sarum who ever spoke much and I'll show you one who lasted only a session.'

Saltwood very much wanted to ask, 'How about William Pitt?' but had the good sense to keep his mouth shut. Indeed, as he stood silent in the manner the Proprietor liked, the old man said, 'Even Pitt, he talked too much. Much better if he'd sat silent more often.'

With the necessary papers signed, and endorsed by Saltwood, the old gentleman signaled for the horses, and when he was safely inside his carriage for the ride back to the cathedral for evensong, he flicked his hat to his factor, riding behind, and said, 'We've done a good day's work.'

Behind them stood the great elm, its branches covering an immense spread. For three hundred years this venerable tree had witnessed elections like this, but never one conducted so speedily. A significant percentage of Parliament had been elected by one man in the course of seven minutes.

* * *

When Josiah Saltwood assembled his family under the oak trees to inform them of the surprising event at Election Elm, his wife Emily did not try to anticipate what her husband was about to announce; her task had been the rearing of four sons, and it had occupied her exclusively. Her principal recreation had been walking the mile or so to the cathedral to listen to the choristers; she did not care much for the sermons.

The four boys came to the meeting with eagerness; for some time they had been speculating on what they must do to find a settled place in life, and any sudden change in their father's position excited them for the possibilities it might uncover for them. Peter, the eldest, had come down from Oxford some years back and was serving as a kind of junior clerk for the family estate while vaguely learning the tasks involved in his father's role as factor to the Proprietor. He was not accomplishing much.

Hilary Saltwood, twenty-four years old that day, presented a serious problem. As a younger son he could not look forward to inheriting either the Saltwood house or his father's occupation. He must look to the army or to the church for his life's sustenance, and up to now he had decided on neither. He had done well at Oxford and could possibly have aspired to work in India, but he had dallied, and now all positions for which he might have been eligible were filled by young men with greater concentration. In some respects he was brilliant; in others, quite confused, so that the family often speculated on what might become of him.

Richard Saltwood, however, though he had done poorly at Oxford and left with the most meager degree awarded, had bought his way into what was always called 'the Gallant Fifty-ninth,' a regiment stationed in India. His father had told the Proprietor, 'That boy was destined for the army from birth, and I'm damned relieved he's found a place!' Then, with proper deference, he added, 'Thanks principally to you.' It had been the Proprietor who had put up the money to purchase the commission and who had recommended young Saltwood to the commanding colonel. Richard would soon be on his way to India and was delighted with the prospect.

It was young David who was most worrisome. He had managed to stay at Oriel in Oxford—the college to which Saltwoods had gone time out of mind—only one term, after which he was sent down 'with prejudice,' meaning that he need not reapply when and if he ever learned Latin. To be dismissed from Oriel was rather shameful, for even the most backward scholar should have been able to get a degree from that feckless college. If a lad had real promise, he went to Balliol; if he sought preferment, he went to Christ Church; and if he wanted to cut a figure, he went to Trinity. If he came from some rural cathedral town like Salisbury, with little Greek and less social footing, he went to Oriel. Indeed, the archetypal Oriel student was a Saltwood from Sentinels, and had been for over a hundred and fifty years. What with four Saltwood boys of child-producing age, it looked as if the college was assured of an endless future supply of its preferred students.

What to do about David, no one knew. As his father once said, 'If a boy can't handle it at Oriel, what on earth can be expected of him?'

Saltwood coughed as his family sat in the picnic chairs, awaiting his revelations. 'It's rather surprising news,' he said modestly. 'I'm to be the new member of Parliament from Old Sarum.'

'Father!' It was difficult to separate what the various boys were saying, but that they were honestly pleased with this turn of fortune was apparent, and they were gratified not only because of what it might mean to them, but especially because their father had been such a hard-working, responsible citizen.

'No better choice!' Richard said. Striking the pose of a politician arguing a point, he cried, 'Sirs, sirs! I beg of you! Attention, please.'

'When do you leave for London?' Peter asked, but before his father could reply, young David leaped to his feet, ran to his father, and embraced him.

'Good on you!'

Quietly Mrs. Saltwood said, 'Let's hear your father's plans.'

'They're simple,' Josiah said. 'You and I leave for London immediately, find a flat, and stay there for the season.'

'I shouldn't like to leave the trees,' Emily said, pointing to the cedars and chestnuts.

'We've new fields to consider,' he said abruptly, and his wife spoke no more.

'Who's to mind our interest?' Peter asked hesitantly, afraid lest his question seem like begging.

'You, Peter. And you're to become the Proprietor's manager. He asked for you.'

'And I'm off to India,' Richard said brightly. 'How about you, Hilary?'

The second son blushed, for he was being importuned to disclose his plans before he was entirely ready, but in such a conclave, when issues of gravity were being decided, he could not refrain. Very softly he said, 'I've been wrestling . . . for many days . . . I've been away, you know, in the fields mostly . . .'

'And what did you decide?' his father asked.

Hilary rose and slowly moved among the oaks, coming back to stand before his mother. 'I'm to be a missionary,' he said. 'God has called me out of my confusion.'

'A missionary!' Emily repeated. 'But where?'

'Wherever God sends me,' he replied, and again he reddened as his brothers gathered to congratulate him.

'I'm going overseas, too,' David broke in.

'You're what?' his father cried.

'I'm emigrating. Four chaps I know in London . . . we're off to America.'

'Good God, those rebels!'

'It's a settlement scheme. Ohio, some place like that. I'm sailing next month.'

'Good God!' his father repeated, aghast at the prospect of a son of his in such a wilderness. 'David,' he said seriously. 'We'll be at war with those rebels within a year. As soon as I get to Parliament, I'm to vote for war. The Proprietor said so.'

'I'll be fighting your troops somewhere in Ohio, wherever that is.'

'When will you be back home?' Emily asked.

'It'll take some years to get the plantation going,' the young man said. 'Slaves hoeing the cotton, and all that. But I'll be back.'

'You must never take arms against England,' Josiah said gravely. 'You'd be shot for a traitor. And there will be war.'

'Father, America's a sovereign nation. Don't send a lot of silly troops like Richard—'

'Brother against brother!' Richard cried. 'Wouldn't that be jolly?'

So under the oak trees at Sentinels in the County of Wiltshire the Salt-woods reached decisions on the destinies of their sons. Peter, who had brains, would take charge of the family business. Hilary, who had character, would go into the ministry. Richard, who had courage, would enter the army. And young David, who had neither brains, nor character, nor courage, would emigrate to America.

The shock caused by Hilary's announcement that he intended becoming a missionary instead of a proper clergyman grew into a firestorm when his family learned that he proposed joining the Missionary Society operated not by the Church of England but by the dissidents, and more especially, the radical Congregationalists. 'You'll ruin your prospects,' his mother warned, but he was adamant, assuring his family that when he reported to the training headquarters at Gosport, not far from Salisbury, he would not be required to convert to the rebellious faith. 'I'll serve my time with Jesus overseas and come back to Salisbury,' but even as he promised this he announced that he was not going to be a part-time missionary but one wholly dedicated to the cause: 'I've elected to go for a complete theological education, terminating with ordination as a full-fledged minister.' His father, now in Parliament and a resident of London, encouraged him in this decision: 'In for a penny, in for a pound. Choose the highest possible, because one day, when this missionary foolishness is over, your mother and I expect to see you dean of Salisbury Cathedral.' At tea one afternoon, during the later stages of his training, his mother said, 'Hilary, you must discharge your duties quickly, because the Proprietor has promised most faithfully that when you're through and safely back in the Church of

England, he plans to exert every influence for your assignment as dean of the cathedral.'

Hilary's brothers approved heartily: 'We could sit here under the oaks and look across the meadows and tell each other, "That cathedral's in good hands." Do hurry and finish with the savages, wherever you go.'

He would have made a flawless dean, tall, slightly stoop-shouldered, his head bent a little forward as he walked along the cloisters, as if he were looking for something a few yards ahead, diffident, rather brilliant in his studies and of deep conviction religiously. He should have stayed at home, progressing from one small living to another until his reputation as a sound young man was established, then moving into the larger positions from which he would write two incomprehensible books. Such books were a prudent step in English advancement; no one bothered to read them, but one's superiors were gratified that the effort had been made. And in due course, fortified with credentials from the noble houses of the county, including the Proprietor's, he would move on to professor at Oriel and then the deanship.

What had interrupted this pleasant, routine progression? Hilary Salt-wood had religious insights far deeper than those of the ordinary Oxford graduate, and he had paid attention to those ringing commandments of Paul in the New Testament in which young men were charged with the duty of spreading the gospel. Indeed, his favorite book in the Bible was Acts, in which the birth of a new religion, and especially of a new church, was portrayed so vividly. With Paul he had traveled the Holy Lands and penetrated to those surrounding nations which knew not Jesus and where Christianity began as an organized religion.

He felt a deep affinity with Paul, and a thorough knowledge of Acts prepared him for the Pauline letters that outlined the next steps in the spread of Christianity. His own discovery of Christ was less dramatic than Saul's conversion into Paul on the road to Damascus, but it had been real. He was not, like others he knew, turning to religion because as a second son he had nowhere else to turn; the church was by no means his secondary choice. Long before his father had been nominated for Parliament he had been on the verge of announcing his commitment to Jesus, and would have done so regardless of his family's fortunes.

His conversion was deep if not spectacular, and he enjoyed the opening months of his ministerial education; the London Missionary Society, as it was being called in some quarters, was becoming famous in various parts of the world, even though it had been in existence for barely a decade. Its stern, intense young devotees, coupled with the older, practical artisans, had penetrated to remote areas, often serving as the cutting edge of civilization as it reached unsettled lands. The LMS was a revolutionary force of the most persistent power, but in his early months at Gosport, Hilary did not discover this.

Instruction was principally in the propagational theories of the New

Testament, an extension, as it were, of Acts and the missionary letters of St. Paul. He enjoyed the abstract philosophizing and profited especially from the droning lectures of an older scholar who expounded the basic theories of the New Testament, instructing him in facts that sometimes surprised him:

> 'The Book of Acts is significant for two reasons. It was written by the same hand that gave us the Gospel According to St. Luke, and that unknown author is extremely important because he is probably the only non-Jew to have composed any part of our Bible. All the other authors were rabbis like Jesus and St. Paul, or ordinary lay-men like St. Matthew, the tax collector. In Acts we receive the first message about our church from a person like ourselves.'

But apart from knowledge, there was also deep conviction. These mature ministers truly believed that it was the duty of young men to 'go forth unto all the world' to spread the word of God; they were convinced that unless this word was taken to the remotest river, souls worthy of salvation might be lost.

For these simple English clergymen there was no predestination whereby all men were sorted out as either saved or damned; such belief would make missionary work a futility. The Society taught that every human soul was eligible for salvation, but this could be attained only if some missionary could instruct it. The task was to deliver Christ's precious message to savages who were in darkness, and few young Englishmen of this period who absorbed that teaching ever doubted that they personally could bring this salvation.

There was much prayer, and many learned discussions as to how salvation might be conveyed, and crude geography lessons outlining the problems to be encountered in Africa or the South Seas, where the young men were to go. It was studious and pious and soporific. But when Reverend Simon Keer, after having served four years on the frontier, burst into headquarters, every aspect of Hilary Saltwood's life was altered.

Keer was a Lancashire activist, son of a baker and lacking a university education. He was a short, round man, not over five feet two, with an unruly mop of red hair and a pair of wire spectacles that he kept shoving back onto the bridge of his nose. His station had been South Africa, a land that Hilary had scarcely heard of; vaguely he knew that through some accident or other a vast area had fallen under English rule. The students were spellbound when Keer, bounding up and down like the bobbin on an active line, launched his impassioned speeches:

> 'There is a land down there in our care which cries for the word of God, a land of black souls thirsting for redemption. Lions and hyenas ravage these people by night, slavery and corruption by day.

We need schools, and hospitals, and printing presses, and trusted men to teach farming. We need roads and proper houses for these children of God, and dedicated men to protect them from cruel abuse.'

After he had listed another dozen things the natives required, one young man whose father was a butcher asked, 'Don't we need churches, too?' and Reverend Keer replied, without halting the flow of his impassioned oratory, 'Of course we need churches.' But in the days that followed he never again mentioned any need for them. Instead, he captivated his eager listeners by his explicit accounts of what it was like to be a missionary:

'I landed at Cape Town with my Bible and my dreams, but before I preached my first sermon I traveled three hundred miles over almost impassable mountains, across arid lands and up and down ravines where there was no road. I lived for weeks with white men who spoke not a word of English and black men who knew nothing of Jesus Christ. I slept on the barren veld with only my coat to cover me and ate food that I had never seen before. The first task I was called to perform was aiding the birth of a baby girl, whom I baptized. The first service I conducted was under a thorn tree. When I finally reached my post I was alone, with no house, no food, no books and no congregation. All I had was another thorn tree under whose spreading branches I conducted my second service. Young men, in South Africa a thousand thorn trees wait to serve as your cathedrals.'

He had an overpowering effect upon the young dreamers of the LMS, for with his exhortations to face the practical problems of the world he combined a devout conviction that what he had done, and what they must do, was missionary work over which God exercised a personal supervision. Again and again he cited those stirring commands issued by St. Paul when he struggled with his frontiers, and as he lectured, the reality of the New Testament materialized before the eyes of his listeners.

It was not till the third week of his fiery declamation that he began to confide the real problem that had brought him back to London. In his preliminary lectures he had disposed of the physical world of the missionary and in subsequent ones he had treated knowingly the theological basis of conversion. Now he sought to instruct his future replacements in the realities:

'I care not whether you have planned to work under the palm of the South Seas or the frozen wastelands of Canada. I care not what commitments you have made to your parents or your ministers here. We need you in Africa, and I implore you to dedicate yourselves to the salvation of this continent. Especially do we need you in our new colony, for nowhere else on earth are the challenges to Christ's teaching more clearly dictated. A dozen men like you, dedicating your lives to the task, can set patterns for a new nation.'

Whenever he spoke on this theme, and he returned to it constantly, he became like a man possessed of special insights: his voice soared; he seemed to become taller; his eyes flashed. He was engaged in a kind of spiritual Armageddon and conveyed his thundering sincerity to any listener. In the fourth week, after a series of such flights, he told the young missionaries what the great problem was:

'Slavery! The Dutch who have occupied the Cape for a hundred and fifty years are among the finest people on earth. They're all good Protestants, much like the Presbyterians of Scotland. They tithe; they listen to their predikants; they support their churches; but they have fallen into the great evil of slavery. For generations they have been owners of imported slaves, and now the wonderful brown and black people with whom they share the land they also hold in cruel bondage, and it is our solemn, God-given mission to rescue all these souls from that bondage. If you join me in this task, and I pray that you will, you must expect that men will revile you, and misrepresent your motives, and even threaten you with bodily harm. But you will persist. And God will strengthen you, and in the end we shall build an English nation of which God will be proud.'

In the fifth week, realizing that he had been painting too somber a picture of the missionary's life in South Africa, he stopped ranting, and began to amuse his listeners with affectionate stories of his life there, using an exaggerated North Country dialect:

'Half an hour before dawn comes a rrrroar! It's a lie-yon, but he's retreating from the sunrise. You learn to know that by the manner in which his voice rrrrecedes. Comes a knock on your tent, and it's the little girl informing you that her baby sister is about to be born and Mother says can you hurry. There are days on the veld with hunters and nights under the starrrrs with more lie-yons and protea flowers, bigger than your mother's washbasin.'

What the young men never forgot, however, were the two brief sermons Keer delivered in the Kaffir language—in them they heard for the first time the click sounds which the Xhosa had borrowed centuries before from the Hottentots. He explained to them that he had mastered the language in order to compile a dictionary, from which a translation of the Gospels for the Xhosa would soon be made.

His first sermon dealt with the Good Samaritan, and since he played all the roles, dancing about the stage, his red hair flying, and since he altered his voice and manner for each of the participants in the parable, the missioners could easily follow the story without understanding the words. But his second sermon dealt with Christ's love for all people, and now there were no clues to its meaning except the overwhelming conviction that filled the room when he stood on his toes, eyes closed, deep voice throbbing with the repeated words *Jesus Christ.*

As he reached the climax of his preachment a hush fell over the room, and when the last click sounds had echoed, Hilary Saltwood knew that his destiny lay in South Africa. Waiting till the other students had left the room, he stepped forward to the podium, but before he could speak, Reverend Keer jumped down and held out his hands: 'Laddie, you've decided to join the Lord's work in Africa?'

'I have.'

'God be praised.'

That night, after he had written explanatory letters to his parents, he felt an enormous sense of having been set free. He had been impelled toward this decision both spiritually and intellectually, and would never question it. It had been God's miracle that sent Simon Keer at this particular time, and Hilary thanked Him for that with a full heart.

But before he fell asleep a most curious reflection flashed across his mind: In all the time I've been here, I've rarely heard the Old Testament mentioned. We're men of the New Testament, the personal followers of Jesus and St. Paul . . .

When Hilary completed his studies, Parliament was not in session, so before sailing for South Africa he returned to Sentinels on Salisbury Plain, and there he sat under the oak trees with his parents and his two brothers. Peter was now in full charge of family affairs and spent half his time on them, the other half devoted to the interests of the Proprietor. Richard had his commission in the Wiltshire regiment and was on leave prior to embarking for India; he joked that when he was a general he would stop off at Cape Town to meet with his brother, the bishop. Their father did not appreciate such remarks, for he still insisted that what Hilary ought to do was serve routine time as a missionary, then hurry back to enter competition for the deanship of the cathedral: 'When a young fellow has backing as strong as the Proprietor's, and as vigorous . . .'

One day the entire family went for a picnic at Old Sarum, where Josiah showed them the ancient elm under whose noble branches he had been elected to Parliament, and the older Saltwoods remained there while the three brothers climbed the low hill to view the ruins. It was both remarkable and moving that they could pick out the lines of those very old buildings which represented a heroic age of England, but after the first moments they paid scant attention to the ruins, for this was a cloudy day, and while they were standing among the fallen rocks a portion of the sky cleared, allowing great shafts of light to fall upon Salisbury to the south, and there the cathedral stood, bathed in radiance, a most noble monument, perhaps the finest in all England, situated on its almost empty meadow with no smaller buildings encroaching, and beyond it, outlined in the same accidental light, the three clumps of trees at Sentinels.

'Oh, look!' Peter cried. 'It's a signal!'

'For what?' Richard asked.

'For us. For us Saltwoods.' Grasping the hands of his brothers, he cried in excited syllables, 'Wherever you go, you're to come back here. This is always to be your home.'

Richard said, somewhat gruffly, 'It looks a far distance from India.'

Peter ignored his brother's dampening comment and asked, in a flush of emotion, 'Hilary, will you say a prayer for us?'

It seemed a most natural thing to do when three brothers, who had shared an old house beside a river of heavenly beauty and in the shadow of a great cathedral, were parting: 'Dearest God, Thy home is everywhere. Ours is here. Let us cherish both.'

'Damned fine prayer, Hilary,' Richard said, and the outing ended, but four days later their father proposed a more serious expedition, one that would require horses and considerable preparation.

'You'll be gone for some time,' he said to Hilary and Richard. 'I've spoken to the Proprietor and he wants to come along. Says it may be his final visit.'

'To where?' Peter asked.

Their father had a welcome surprise. Through the centuries when Saltwoods sent their sons to Oxford, the boys invariably went by carriage north through Wiltshire and then easterly through Berks, a route that carried them past one of the noble monuments of the world, and generations of the family had come to look upon this place as symbolic of their fortunes, so that occasionally, when no lad had gone north to university for some decades, the Saltwoods would convene and go that way without excuse, simply to renew their acquaintance with Stonehenge.

The monument lay only eight miles north of Salisbury, and a visit could be completed within a day, but the Saltwoods liked to pitch a tent there overnight so as to catch the dawn rising over the ancient stones. This expedition consisted of the Proprietor, still traveling by carriage, with the four Saltwood men on horseback and five servants following with tents, the food and the flagons of wine. The road was a rough one, not much traveled, since most people leaving Salisbury headed either east to London or west to Plymouth. Only the occasional scholar on his way to Oxford went north to Stonehenge, or someone headed to the port at Bristol or the towns in Wales.

Toward the close of day Josiah said, 'I rather think that at the rise of the next hill we shall see it,' and he told the boys to rein in their horses and allow the Proprietor to be in the lead when Stonehenge was first sighted.

'There they are!' the old man cried, and to the east on a small mound which caught the first rays of the rising sun and the last light of day stood the hallowed stones, some fallen, some leaning, some erect in the location they had occupied for more than four thousand years. It was an awesome place and no Englishman conversant with his nation's history could fail to be humbled upon approaching it.

'D'you think it was the Druids?' the Proprietor asked as the group surveyed the somber monument.

'It was here centuries before anyone heard of Druids,' Josiah suggested.

'My own thoughts,' the Proprietor said. 'Sturdy bastards, whoever they were.'

Hilary had always been enchanted by Stonehenge. He had seen it first as a boy of ten on a family excursion much like this. He had seen it again when he accompanied Peter to Oriel, and of course on his own travels to Oxford. It was timeless, old beyond counting when Jesus was born, and it reminded men of the long sweep of history and the periods of darkness. The stones turned red as the sun dipped to its horizon, shimmering in the fading light.

'We'll pitch the tents over there,' the Proprietor suggested, and that night they slept within the shadowed circle.

Long before dawn the Proprietor was up, cursing the night and abusing his servants for not having lighted candles. 'I want to see the sun striking it,' he grumbled, and as the Saltwoods joined him he said, 'I'm sure they used to conduct human sacrifice here. At the solstices, anyway. Probably killed off two old men like me and three young virgins. Let's go to the sacrifice.'

And they stood among the ancient stones, hauled here from sources far removed, as the sun broke upon them.

'D'you think you could offer us a prayer, Hilary?' the old man asked.

'Let us bow our heads,' the new minister said, and as day came in earnest he prayed: 'God, Who marks our passage back to Salisbury and to India and to South Africa, and also to America where our brother hides, watch over us. Watch over us.'

The Proprietor said that while these were fine words, he would have appreciated some mention of the fact that this might be his last journey to the stones, whereupon Hilary uttered another short prayer, instructing God on this additional matter, and the old man was appeased.

They spent that day inspecting the fallen rocks and making cautious guesses as to how old they might be, but as dusk approached, Hilary experienced a surge of religious emotion and moved apart from the others. Standing among the untoppled pillars, a gaunt, angular, stoop-shouldered figure who might well have been an ancient priest of this temple, he whispered, 'O God, I swear to Thee that I shall be as faithful to Thy religion as the men who erected these stones were to theirs.'

He landed at Table Bay one morning in the spring of 1810, expecting to be greeted by representatives of the LMS who would probably spend some weeks indoctrinating him in his duties and perhaps even accompanying him to his place of assignment. Instead, as soon as he stepped ashore he was grabbed by a sturdy Dutch farmer with very broad shoulders and full beard who asked in heavily accented English, 'Is it true, you're a disciple of Simon Keer?'

Modestly Saltwood conceded that he was, whereupon the farmer pushed him away, muttering, 'You ought to be ashamed, spreading lies.'

He was not allowed even one night's rest in Cape Town, for at noon he found himself in a caravan of sorts heading eastward to a river on the far side of the mountains, where he had been directed to launch a mission. During the arduous journey he learned much about South Africa but even more about Reverend Keer, for wherever he stopped, people asked about the red-headed Lancashire man. The few Englishmen spoke of him with obvious regard, the many Dutchmen with unmasked contempt, and one night he asked an English missionary's wife to explain this contradiction.

'Simple,' she said. 'Simon Keer always stood up for the Hottentots and the Xhosa.'

'Isn't that our duty? To bring them to Jesus Christ?'

'Reverend Keer treated the Hottentots more like workmen in England. Always fighting for their rights. Decent pay. Decent homes for them to live in. Things like that.'

'Did the Dutch object?'

She put down her cooking pans and turned to face Hilary. 'You must keep one thing in mind, if you're to be an effective missionary. We English have been here four years. The Dutch have been here a hundred and fifty-eight. They know what they're doing and they do it well.'

'Keer says that what they do so well is slavery.'

She placed her two hands on Hilary's and pleaded, 'Don't use that word. Reverend Keer was given to exaggeration. He lacked education, you know.'

'He's translating the Gospels.'

'Oh, he was excellent at identifying himself with the Xhosa. He could stay up all night transcribing their words.'

'I thought it was my duty to do the same.'

'To bring them Christ, yes. To become their advocate against the Dutch, no.'

'You speak harshly.'

'The Xhosa killed my son. They'd have killed me, too, except that a Dutch commando arrived in time.'

'And you stay?'

'It was an incident. We were at war and our troops had killed their people. Simple retaliation.'

'Aren't you afraid?'

'I am, and you will be, too. And pray God that you don't get caught up in it.'

As he penetrated farther into the country he became increasingly aware of how different the long-established Dutch were from the lately arrived English, and in his first letter home he shared his observations with his mother:

> The Dutch speak of themselves in three distinct ways. Those in the environs of the Cape call themselves Dutch, although many of them have never seen Holland or ever will. In truth, they speak harshly of the old country, holding in contempt those real Dutchmen who came out from Holland to lord it over the locals with sneers and assumptions of superior education. Some of these long-time Dutch have taken themselves a new name, for they are more of Africa than of Europe. 'We are *Afrikaners*,' they say, but where I am traveling now these Afrikaners are named *Boers* (farmers). But farther east toward the lonely perimeter of the country, where the roughest of the Dutch dwell, they call themselves *trekboers* (migrating graziers), which is appropriate, for they are constantly moving on with their herds, until I am reminded of Abraham and Isaac. My mission is to be established in the lands of those trekboers who have stopped their wanderings.

At his next halt, where only Boers lived, Hilary received his harshest view of Reverend Keer: 'Arrogant, stupid man. Kept saying he loved the Xhosa and the Hottentots, but every action he took damaged them.'

'In what way?'

'Made them dissatisfied with their lot.'

'What is their lot?'

'At school in England, did they teach you the Book of Joshua?'

'I've read it.'

'But have you taken it to heart? God's story of how the Israelites came into a strange land? And how they were to conduct themselves there?' It was obvious to the Boer listeners that the new missionary knew little of Joshua, so the oldest farmer took down his huge Bible and slowly leafed the pages until he came to the familiar instructions, which he translated roughly for the newcomer:

> 'You shall not marry with the daughters of Canaan . . . You shall keep yourself apart . . . You shall destroy their cities . . . You shall

hang their kings from trees . . . You shall block up their graves with stones, even to this day ... You shall take the land, and occupy it and make it fruitful ... One man of you shall chase one thousand of them ... You shall keep yourselves apart ... And they shall be your hewers of wood and your drawers of water ... And all this you shall do in the name of the Lord, for He has commanded it.'

Closing the big book reverently and placing his hands upon it, he stared directly into Hilary's eyes and said, 'That is the word of the Lord. It is His Bible which instructs us.'

'There is another part of the Bible,' Hilary said quietly, leaning his thin shoulders forward to engage the debate.

'Yes, your Reverend Keer preached quite a different message, but he was an idiot. Young friend, believe me, it is the ancient word of God Himself that we follow, and you will break your teeth in this country if you contradict it.'

Across the southern plains of Africa, wherever he stopped, Hilary found himself engaged in argument over the merits of Simon Keer, and the Boers were so forceful in their rejection of the little redhead that in his quiet moments Hilary began to read Numbers and Joshua, finding in them not only the passages which his first Boer mentors had cited, but scores of others which applied directly to the position of the Dutch who had come into this land like the Israelites of old, who had entered their land of Canaan. The parallels were so overwhelming that he began to see local history through Dutch eyes, and this was a salvation when he opened his own mission.

The spot selected for him lay on the left bank of the Sundays River, four hundred miles from Cape Town. When he reached it, not a building stood, not a roadway existed. The river, suffering from drought, carried little water, and there were no trees. But the spot itself was congenial, perched on a broad bend of the river and graced with level fields acceptable to plowing. In the distance was a forest with an abundance of usable wood; and at hand, enough stones to build a city. Hilary, visualizing what this bleak spot might become, named it from a passage in the twentieth chapter of Joshua, where God instructs His people to erect cities of refuge to which any accused could flee and be assured of temporary safety:

And on the other side Jordan . . . eastward they assigned . . . Golan . . . that whosoever killeth any person at unawares might flee thither, and not die . . . until he stood before the congregation.

This will be Golan, my city of refuge, Hilary thought, and when the last members of his caravan disappeared, leaving him majestically alone in the heart of a strange land, he prayed that he might be allowed to build well.

* * *

The first night, as he lay on the ground close to his belongings, he listened to strange sounds, and the darkness of Africa assailed him with a wild discordance, a sense of awe and anticipation rather than fear. When he awakened at dawn, he found a group of brown people watching him, squatting on their haunches a hundred feet away. For months there had been rumors that a missionary was coming.

Hilary beamed at the sight. Surely the Lord Himself had brought this little gathering into the arms of His servant Saltwood. Dusting himself off, he rose to greet them, overjoyed when one man spoke to him in broken English.

'We stay with you. We your people now.' His name was Pieter, son of that Dikkop who had traveled with Mal Adriaan. It was ten years since he had lived with the Van Doorns; he had run away after a beating for eating a melon from the family garden. He had drifted from farm to farm, working just enough to avoid being classified as 'Vagrant Hottentot,' which would allow his being assigned arbitrarily to any farmer who wanted him.

In truth, Pieter was a man who saw virtue in idleness; he could happily pass an entire day with his back against a tree, eyes firmly shut.

But before sunset that first day the Hottentots had shown Hilary how to dig a foundation to keep out rain, and by the second nightfall they had cut enough saplings to frame out a dwelling. Hilary saw in his imagination how Golan should look: rows of huts facing each other, a meeting hall and a church to close off one end of the rectangle.

He was pleased with the rapid growth of his little community—six Hottentots to forty within three weeks—and within a short time Hilary and his followers had the mud-and-clay walls of a mission church in place. Before the thatching of the roof was complete he preached a message of dedication inside the little structure. Having mastered several words of the Dutch-like language these people spoke, and some Hottentot with its click sounds, he delighted his congregation by offering the benediction in their language. In the days that followed he heard members of the mission saying gravely to one another as they worked, 'Peace be unto you.'

Peace was a commodity almost unknown. Young Xhosa warriors persisted in raiding cattle from white men's farms, and not long after Hilary's first sermon English troops, fortified by a Boer commando, had launched a massive attack against the black men, driving twenty thousand of them back across the Great Fish River and liberating, as they phrased it, vast herds of cattle. The gallant leader of this rout would be honored by having a newborn town named after him: Grahamstown.

Hilary was untouched by these events; but it grieved him that after six months he had not met one Xhosa, and he began to fear that he had made a mistake in locating Golan here. During his studies at Gosport he had imagined himself bringing Christianity to black savages, wrestling with their pagan beliefs and finally welcoming them to Jesus. Instead he was surrounded by brown Hottentots, more than ninety in the huts that faced the rectangle, while all the Xhosa lurked far across the river, a gang of cattle thieves.

In his reports to the LMS he called his flock 'my Hottentots,' knowing that few were of the pure strain; they ranged from light, yellow-skinned half-Malays to very dark half-Angolans. They were not inclined to hard work, and a distressing number loitered about the mission doing nothing. But Hilary always remembered the name he had given this place, Golan the refuge, and he believed that these 'mild and peaceable folk,' as he wrote of them, merited all the sanctuary they could find. Many had come to him with terrible tales of beatings, chains, and years of labor without pay from Boers who made their lives a misery. Simon Keer's impassioned indictment of the colonists echoed in his ears, and he saw it his duty to succor the weak.

Even his hopes for the Xhosa soared when a black man finally came to Golan, an elderly fellow from a kraal to the east. He proclaimed himself to be a Christian, stating in halting English that he had been baptized by a missionary with red hair called 'Master Keer,' and he indicated that his village contained several other blacks who had been converted by 'our dear little man who could speak Xhosa.'

His Christian name was Saul, and Hilary promptly sent him back to Xhosa lands to spread joyful news about Golan, and because of Saul, at the end of six months the mission was home to one hundred and forty Hottentots and twenty Xhosa. The latter taught Hilary the traditions of their people, and he developed respect for the ease with which they adjusted to life at Golan. As he worked with them he found himself constantly referring to the practical instructions he had acquired from young Simon Keer, rarely to the theological indoctrination of the older LMS clergymen. 'Missionary work,' Keer had predicted, 'is one-tenth disputation, nine-tenths sanitation.'

The first white man Hilary met was a Boer living at a remote spot twenty-eight miles to the northeast, across hills that separated the Sundays River from the Fish. He rode into Golan one afternoon, a tall, rough-clad, white-haired old man who looked like someone from the early books of the Bible, his beard trembling in the wind. 'Name is Lodevicus,' he said in halting English. 'Lodevicus van Doorn.' He had come to warn Hilary not to allow any Hottentots from the north to take refuge at Golan.

'Why not?' Hilary asked.

'They . . . my laborers . . . they signed papers,' he growled, obviously disliking the necessity of speaking in a foreign tongue. 'They to work . . . not pray.'

'But if they come seeking Jesus Christ . . .'

Lodevicus showed his irritation that Saltwood made no effort to address him in Dutch: 'If you here . . . missionary . . . damnit . . . learn Dutch.'

'I should! I should!' Hilary agreed enthusiastically, but to continue the conversation it was necessary to find someone who had both languages, which put Lodevicus in the awkward position of lodging a complaint against Hottentots through the agency of a Hottentot. It was fortunate that Lodevicus did not recognize the melon thief, and insensitive to the impropriety, went on talking, with Pieter listening respectfully and saying 'Ja, Baas' at least once a minute.

'Baas say, "His Hottentots not come seek Jesus. They run away from work his place." '

'Tell him that even so, if any of his workmen were to come seeking refuge with me . . .'

No sooner had the interpreter started this sentence than Lodevicus interrupted.

'Baas, he say, "My goddamn workers come here, no trouble for you. I come gettim." '

'Tell him that if any Hottentot or Xhosa seeks Jesus Christ . . .'

Once more Lodevicus issued a string of threats, only some of which the Hottentot bothered to repeat. So this first meeting between the Boer and the Englishman ended in disarray, with Lodevicus shouting as he remounted his horse that Saltwood was no better than that damned idiot Simon Keer. He sputtered what sounded like curses, and Hilary was told: 'Baas say damn-fool Master Keer come back, he meet him with sjambok.'

'Assure him that Reverend Keer is safely in London and will not be seen again in these parts.' When this was delivered, Lodevicus directed the Hottentot to say, 'Damn good thing.'

As a Christian, Hilary could not allow his first acquaintance with a neighbor to end so poorly, and with a complete change of attitude he said to the Hottentot, 'Ask Mijnheer van Doorn if he will join us in evening prayer?'

This sudden switch to the Dutch *mijnheer* softened the old man somewhat, but only for a moment, for he soon realized that the prayers would be conducted in English, whereupon he spat: 'I pray Dutch church.' And with that he galloped off, even though night was almost upon him.

And that was the way things stood between the mission station of Golan and the nearest white man to the north until the end of the first year—when the Reverend Simon Keer burst upon the South African scene with a reverberation that would last for two centuries, making his name accursed. He did not appear in person, which was prudent, since he would have been whipped, but a booklet that he published in England did arrive by ship. It bore the pejorative title *The Truth About South Africa*, and was a compilation of accusations against the Dutch so horrendous that the civilized world, meaning London and Paris, simply had to take notice.

It charged the Boers with having already killed off the Bushmen, annihilating the Hottentots, and beginning to abuse the Xhosa—expropriating their land, stealing their cattle, and killing their women and children. It was especially harsh in allegations that the Hottentots and Coloured brethren were being tricked into slavery and denied ordinary decencies. It was a blanket indictment, its charges so melodramatic that they might have been ignored had he not added one accusation which more than any other inflamed the Christians of England and Scotland:

> The Boers refuse to allow their Hottentots to attend mission schools or to convert to that one true religion which could save their immortal souls. Indeed, one gains the impression that the Boers refuse to believe that their laborers have souls, and each day that dawns sees Jesus crucified anew in order for the Boer to gain a few more shillings through the toil of these mild and peaceable people forced into a servitude worse than that of the true slave.

Such charges ignited action throughout England, especially since that nation now had responsibility for the governance of South Africa, and protests of the most vigorous force were launched. What made government intervention inevitable was Reverend Keer's closing statement that he personally could indict a hundred Boers for forced enslavement, criminal abuse and even murder.

When the four dozen copies of *The Truth About South Africa* reached the Cape and were distributed, with Dutch translations being rushed to the frontier, a sullen resistance developed. Even prospering townsmen in Cape Town and Stellenbosch who had clearly benefited from the English takeover protested that Keer had unjustly maligned the entire colony. And the frontier Boers! Each man felt that he was being specifically accused, and wrongfully. Pamphlets were prepared, rebutting the absent missionary, and practically the entire population combined to defend South Africa's reputation.

But the power of an inspired missionary to inflame English public opinion would always be great, and while at the Cape a few people were defending South Africa, in London a multitude called for action, and before long, commissions were on their way to the Cape to look into Keer's charges, and the mournful day came when formal accusations had to be lodged against some fifty Boers, who were commanded to stand trial before judges who would circulate throughout the colony. The Black Circuit, this exhibition would be called, and in due course it would reach Graaff-Reinet, several days' ride to the northwest, and there Lodevicus van Doorn would be tried for physically abusing his Hottentots, starving them and denying them the right to attend religious services. He was also accused of murder.

Before the Black Circuit reached Graaff-Reinet, Lodevicus, convinced that no judge appointed by the English would accord a Boer justice, swallowed his pride and rode back to Golan, where he found that Hilary could now speak moderately good Dutch. The two men conducted an impassioned conversation.

'All I ask, Saltwood, is that you come with me, now. Look at my farm. Talk with my Hottentots and slaves.'

'I'll not be party to this lawsuit.'

'It's not a lawsuit. It's a charge of murder.'

'And other things, if I hear correctly.'

'And other things. Trivial things. And it's those you must inspect.'

'I'm not a witness, Mijnheer van Doorn.'

'All men are witnesses, Dominee.'

The sudden use of this Dutch appellation caught Hilary's imagination, and he had to admit that in a situation so grave, all men were witnesses, so that even though Van Doorn had been an unpleasant man, if he now appealed for help, it had to be given. On the spur of the moment he said, 'I'll ride with you, but I'll not testify in court.'

'No one asks you to,' Lodevicus said gruffly.

Leaving Golan in care of Saul, Hilary left for the north, finding a ride with Van Doorn a moving experience: 'These vast lands with no markings —how do you find your way?'

'The look of things,' Lodevicus said, and Hilary thought: That's what I'm being asked to judge—the look of things.

As in the days when Mal Adriaan wandered these lands with Dikkop, this Van Doorn and his English clergyman formed a bizarre pair, the first an old man with heavy frame and white whiskers, the second a tall and gawky young man with the open face of a child. They were unlikely associates, Boer and Englishman, with different heritages, different attitudes toward life and vastly different religions, one Old Testament, the other New. Yet they were joined in a forced association that would prove, for better or worse, inescapable.

When they entered the low hills that separated the mission station from the farm, a wholly new vista opened, the vision of a land immense in its dimensions, softly varied in the rise and fall of its low ridges, but ominously grand in the substantial mountains that rose to the north. They seemed to warn Saltwood: This is a greater land than you have envisaged. The challenges are vaster than Simon Keer defined.

At the crest of the last rise Lodevicus reined in his horse and pointed down to a small valley hemmed on all sides by hills of varying height. It was as tight a little world as Saltwood had ever seen, a secure haven cut by a river which brought fruitfulness to the rolling fields. The river entered the area at an opening to the southwest, ran diagonally across the meadows and exited at a pass in the northeast. If ever a frontier settler had a farm that was secure, this was it.

'De Kraal,' Van Doorn said gruffly but with evident pride. 'Safe place for keeping cattle.'

'Have you cattle?'

'The Hottentots have taken our herds north to graze. But this kraal is for human beings. A nest within the hills.'

Hilary turned in his saddle to inspect the land, and from his experience with meadows on the Salisbury Plain estimated that De Kraal ran five miles west to east and something less than three north to south. Making such calculations as he could, he said in astonishment, 'You have nine thousand acres down there.'

'Yes,' said Lodevicus. 'This is the land of the Van Doorns.' And he rode down into his little empire as if he were Abraham riding a camel to Canaan.

The three days Hilary spent at De Kraal were a revelation, for he was in an enclave removed from any outside influence and ruled by one man. It was into this fortress that English justice presumed to force its way. Lodevicus had a wife, of course, and Hilary was surprised when he met her, for she seemed not at all awed by her austere husband, even though he was at least thirty years older. Wilhelmina van Doorn was a big, amiable woman who obviously set the laws to be observed in her house. She had one son, Tjaart, a square-bodied young farmer with a lad of his own.

De Kraal had nine Madagascan and Angolan slaves, few by comparison with the intensively farmed vineyards near Cape Town, but it also had thirty-two Hottentot and Coloured workers and their families, some whose ancestors had become affiliated with the Van Doorn family generations ago. By law they were contract laborers duly registered at Graaff-Reinet; whether they were de facto slaves was moot. No outside observer like Saltwood would be allowed to ascertain the facts.

'Thirty-two Hottentots?' Saltwood asked. 'Isn't that a lot?'

'They have to herd our cattle sixty miles north of here.'

'Sixty miles! Doesn't that put them on other people's land?'

'There are no other people.'

Lodevicus invited Saltwood to inspect every aspect of De Kraal, where the slaves and Hottentots ate and where they slept and worked. Since Hilary now understood much of the Dutch-Portuguese-Malayan-Madagascan dialect spoken between master and servant, he was able to conduct his investigations without the interference of Van Doorn. He was especially eager to interrogate the Hottentots, for Golan's people had said that the Boers were constantly abusing them, but when the herders were brought in he found them a jovial lot who loved their horses and the open range.

'How much do you get paid?' he asked the lead man.

'Paid? What is paid?'

'Wages. Money.'

'We got no money.'

'Not now, but how much does Mr. Van Doorn pay you?'

'He not pay nothing.'

Saltwood started again: 'You work? Seven days a week? How much do you get paid?'

'Baas, I no understand.'

So with great patience the missionary explained that everywhere in the world, when a man performed a certain task, like herding cattle . . .

'We like cattle . . . sheep . . . big land.'

'But what do you get paid?'

After many false starts Hilary discovered that they got paid nothing in cash. They did receive their clothes, and their horses, and their food, and when they fell ill, Mrs. Van Doorn medicated them.

'Are you free to leave De Kraal?' Hilary asked.

'Where would we go?'

Three times Saltwood questioned the Hottentots, trying to ascertain whether they were in fact slaves, but he never reached a satisfactory answer, so he broached the subject with Van Doorn himself: 'Would you call your Hottentots slaves, like the Madagascans?'

'No! No! They can leave any time they wish.'

'Have any ever left?'

'Why should they?'

Hilary dropped this line of investigation, turning his attention to the slaves, whom he found to be in good condition but surly in manner, unlike the Hottentots who worked the free range. One of the Madagascan men showed scars, and when Saltwood inquired about them, he found that the man had run away, been recaptured and punished.

'Why did you leave?' he asked.

'To be free.'

'Will you run away again?'

'Yes, to be free.'

'Will you be punished again?'

'If he catch me.'

When Hilary asked Van Doorn about this, the Boer could not mask his disgust: 'He's my slave. I paid good money for him. We can't let our slaves get the idea they can run away at will. Of course they have to be punished.'

'You seem to have whipped him rather harshly.'

'I disciplined him.' When he saw how Saltwood flinched, he said sharply, 'Dominee, in the old days he'd have had his nose cut off, his ears, one hand if he persisted. These are slaves, and they must be disciplined, as the Bible says.'

Apart from the Madagascan, the Van Doorn slaves and Hottentots showed evidences of good treatment, and Saltwood said so, whereupon Van Doorn confessed: 'We live at the edge of the world, Dominee. We spend years without seeing a predikant. We must have slaves to operate the farm. We must have Hottentots to run the cattle and sheep. We rely upon instructions from God and the direction we receive from this.' He indicated a huge old Bible, and when Saltwood took it in his hands, and pried open the brass clasps, and saw the heavy pages within, and the one on which Van Doorns had for a hundred and fifty years kept their family records, he was awed by the simple righteousness of this frontier Boer, and knew that if Van Doorn asked him to be a witness at his trial in Graaff-Reinet, he would out of simple decency have to at least testify as to his character.

He was little prepared for what Lodevicus asked him to do now: 'Dominee, we live alone, terribly alone. Would you baptize our grandson?'

Saltwood stiffened. 'At the mission you refused to pray with me.'

'I was a fool,' the old man said. 'Wilhelmina, come in here!'

The smiling Wilhelmina came into the room, bowed to the missionary, and stood with arms akimbo. 'Tell the dominee,' her husband said. 'Tell him what I told you when I reached home.'

'From where?'

'From the mission,' he snapped. 'When I got home from that visit to the mission.' When she stood bewildered, he said more gently, 'When I told you I had refused to pray with him.'

'You said you were a damned fool, and you were.' Smiling at the visitor, she started to retire, but her husband said, 'I've asked him to baptize the boy, and he's agreed.'

'I do indeed,' Hilary said, and the little boy, struggling with a puppy, was brought into the room, and water was provided by one of the slaves, and the solemn rite was performed. But as it ended, Reverend Saltwood noticed that the little girl who had fetched the water lingered, twisting her fingers in her gray dress, and it was in this sanctified moment that he met the child Emma, daughter of the Madagascan.

She was ten that year, a bright child often perplexed by what she witnessed. Her face had that sooty-blackness which seemed almost blue, and was so attractive, as if God had said, 'Emma, since you're to be black, why not be really black?' Her face was composed of handsome interlocking planes, so that when she smiled, showing her white teeth, it broke into lovely patches of light and shadow. When she was six and living on the farm from which Lodevicus had purchased her parents, she had been instructed sketchily in Christianity by Simon Keer and had from him acquired a vision of a world somewhat different from the one the slaves knew. Now, as the Van Doorns took their baptized grandson out in the yard to resume play with his puppy, she lingered to ask Reverend Saltwood, 'Can I come to your mission?'

'You are a slave, my child,' he said softly. 'You belong to Baas.'

'Baas, he follow me, cut off my nose?'

'You know he wouldn't do that. But you also know what happened to your father when he ran away. If you run away, you'll be punished.' As he spoke he recalled the words of Jesus: 'Suffer the little children to come unto me'—and he knew that he was being less than heroic in failing to support this child. But his reflections were broken by a shout from one of Van Doorn's Hottentots: 'Riders! Riders! From north!'

A bailiff from the Black Circuit sitting at Graaff-Reinet had come to inform Lodevicus that he must appear before that court. 'For what?' the old man blustered, whereupon the nervous little Dutchman who had joined the English service puffed out his chest and in faltering voice recited the charges: 'Enforced slavery of Hottentots. Abuse of slaves. Murder of a slave.'

'By God, I will destroy that judge,' the old Boer cried, but the bailiff whispered in rapid Dutch, 'Lodevicus Hammer, you have friends at Graaff-Reinet. Many Boers owe their farms to you. You'll never hang.'

'But I'm to be dragged into a Kaffir court . . .'

'Please, Lodevicus, I'm just starting in my job. Don't make trouble.'

It was humiliating, but the old fighter realized he must comply, so after giving orders to his son and bidding Wilhelmina farewell, he came to Saltwood and said humbly, 'Dominee, you must ride with me.'

Despite his earlier resolution, Saltwood now faltered, and asked weakly, 'Why?'

'To testify. You've seen me. You've seen my slaves.'

'But the charge of murder—'

'Ask the slaves.' And Lodevicus was so obviously shaken by his arrest that Hilary wanted to help in some way. Certainly he could testify that by Boer standards, the De Kraal slaves and Hottentots were reasonably treated, and he was willing to say so to the court, but he was not willing to be called on to aid any man charged with murder. Van Doorn, seeing his hesitation and guessing as to its cause, said again, 'Ask them.'

So Hilary took the girl Emma aside. 'Do you know who God is?'

'I do,' she said in a childish voice.

'And do you know what hell is?'

'Master Keer, he tell me.'

'And do you know that if you don't tell the truth, you will go to hell?'

'Master Keer tell me.'

'The old baas, has he ever killed a slave?'

The little girl's dark face froze into a scowl, her soot-black features betraying her agitation. Finally she said, moving nervously from foot to foot, 'He beat my father. Sometimes he thrash my mother. But he never kill nobody.'

'Do the slaves ever talk at night, Emma?'

'All the time.'

'Do they ever speak of a killing? Long time ago? When the old baas angry?'

'No killing.'

Saltwood was impressed by the girl's willingness to speak but also by her obvious fear, so he asked abruptly if she would fetch her parents, and when they appeared, as nervous as their daughter, he asked them in their dialect, 'Has Baas ever killed a slave?'

They looked at each other, then at their daughter, after which the husband said, 'He beat me too much. He beat my wife sometimes.' He showed Saltwood the scars that he had shown before. They were gruesome and deep.

'But has he ever killed a slave?'

'No.' When he said this, his wife tugged at his shirt sleeve and they whispered for a while.

'What's she saying?' Hilary asked Emma.

'About the other time.'

'What other time?'

And the father told in broken, agitated words that on another farm, where they had lived prior to being purchased by Van Doorn, the master had killed a slave, and had been arrested at the insistence of Simon Keer, and had been fined two pounds. Also, his right to own other slaves was taken away, which was why these Madagascans had been sold to De Kraal. There had been murder, but never by Van Doorn.

'Does your father know who God is?' Hilary asked the little girl.

'No.'

'Then he does not know what hell is, either?'

'No,' the girl said. 'But he knows what true is. There was no murder.'

Saltwood went to the door and called to Van Doorn: 'I'll ride with you.'

The Black Circuit at Graaff-Reinet was an explosive affair. Inspired by Simon Keer's incendiary reports, a score of indictments had been issued based on the accusations of missionaries, Hottentots and Coloureds, all charging the Boers with gross abuses. Granted, there had been serious evils: Hottentots had been forced to work on after their legal contracts had expired; their women and children had been threatened with violence if they left; slaves had been excessively flogged; there had been murder.

But many of the charges were wild, without foundation, so that what should have been a serious judicial inquiry became a shambles. The countryside rallied so strongly in support of the Boers, and perjured itself so willingly, that no demonstrable lawbreakers could be found guilty, while dozens of reasonably honest frontiersmen like Lodevicus van Doorn were publicly humiliated by being forced to stand in the dock and answer to preposterous accusations.

Three Hottentots were brave enough to testify against Van Doorn, but what they said was so chaotic that the court had to be suspicious, and when Reverend Saltwood stepped forward to defend him, the court had to be attentive. The verdict was 'Not guilty,' but this absolved nothing, for the Boers who had been so abused by the English courts would never forget their humiliation. Thus the Black Circuit joined that growing list of grievances, some real, some fancied, which would be recited in every Boer family for the next century and a half.

The English were mortified that one of their own ministers had given testimony enabling a Dutchman to escape punishment: 'He was guilty as sin, you know. Indictment said so.' A rumor was floated that Saltwood had defended the Boer in anticipation of favors to come: 'Perjured himself, of course. They're taking up a collection for him right now, among the Boers.' It was agreed that Hilary Saltwood must be ostracized insofar as the English community at the Cape was concerned: 'From now on he's the darling of the Boers.'

How wrong they were! The Van Doorn–Saltwood armistice lasted only two days, for when they rode back to De Kraal, Wilhelmina van Doorn met them at the gate, crying, 'Lodevicus! Emma's run off.'

'Get her back.'

'We don't know where she's gone.'

'Set the Hottentots tracking. They'll find anything.'

Saltwood found it difficult to visualize that little child in her gray dress running anywhere, but if she was indeed gone, he was fairly sure why: 'Probably went to the mission.'

As soon as he uttered these words he knew they were ill-advised, for Van Doorn's look of petty irritation turned to one of hatred: 'She cannot do that.'

'But if she wants to know about Jesus.'

'I teach my slaves and Hottentots all they need to know about Jesus.'

'But, Mijnheer Van Doorn—'

'Don't Mijnheer me!'

'Obviously, this child hungers for Jesus. It's been four years since she heard about him and still she—'

'Where did she hear about Jesus?'

'At the other farm. From Simon Keer.'

What a sad mistake to have spoken that name! Van Doorn began shouting Dutch phrases so fast that Hilary could not follow, then jutting his white-whiskered face forward and growling, 'Any slave of mine has dealings with Simon Keer, I'll beat her till she's—'

He stopped, aware of the dreadful thing he had been about to say, and aware also that his new friend, Saltwood, knew how the sentence would have been completed. It was then, at the moment of their triumphant return from the Black Circuit, that the veil dropped between these two men.

Saltwood was first to speak: 'If Emma has run to Golan, she will have my protection.'

'If my slave is at your mission, you can be sure I'll come and take her.'

'Van Doorn, don't fight the law.'

'No law gives you my slave. I paid good money for her. She belongs here.'

'She belongs in the care of Jesus Christ.'

'Get out!' Throwing open the door, he ordered Saltwood to be gone, but when the latter headed for the hill, he summoned two Hottentots and directed them to speed west, keep out of sight, and fetch the slave girl Emma from the mission.

Saltwood, anticipating such a maneuver, traveled at forced speed, but when he reached Golan he found the place in an uproar, for the Hottentots had preceded him and were in the process of carrying off the little girl, who was weeping and struggling in their arms.

Without hesitating, Saltwood dashed to his quarters, grabbed his gun, and confronted the kidnappers: 'Drop your hands. Back on your horses and ride home.'

'Baas say bring Emma.'

'I say take your hands off her.'

'No! She belong us.'

At this moment Emma broke loose and ran to Saltwood, throwing herself at him, and when he felt this child seeking his protection, he determined to rescue her at any cost; and as the Hottentots reached out to seize her, he fired his gun over their heads, frightening them and terrifying himself. Fortunately, the two brown men scuttled to their horses and galloped away, for had they lunged at Saltwood again, he would have been quite incapable of firing at them, even had his gun contained a second chamber.

Hilary now placed the child with Saul's family, where she began learning the alphabet, the catechism and the refulgent promises of the New Testament. She proved an able student, as gifted in singing as in sewing, and before long it was her glowing black face and gleaming teeth that showed in the front rank of the mission choir.

She was practicing under the trees one evening when Lodevicus van Doorn rode in like a white-haired avenging angel, two guns resting carelessly on his saddle. 'I've come to fetch you, Emma,' he said quietly.

'She will not go,' Saul said, trembling at the sight of the menacing guns.

'If you try to stop me, Kaffir, I'll blow your head off.' Lodevicus did not touch either of the guns, but he did move his horse closer to Emma.

With a dignity many of the blacks acquired at the mission, old Saul moved to protect the child, whereupon Lodevicus raised one of his guns.

'For God's sake!' a voice cried from one side. 'Are you mad?'

It was Saltwood, coming to lead the choir. Unarmed, he walked directly to the muzzle of the gun, looked up at Lodevicus, and ordered: 'Ride back to De Kraal.'

'Not without my Madagascan.'

'Emma lives here now.'

'I have an order from the court at Graaff-Reinet which says—'

'Such orders apply to runaway slaves, not to little girls seeking Jesus.'

Van Doorn's neck muscles stood out like the vines of a squash. 'You goddamned meddler . . .'

'Old friend,' Saltwood said quietly, 'get off that horse and let's talk.'

'I'm going to take my slave.'

'Come here, Emma,' and the little girl in her blue mission dress ran to clasp her protector.

Van Doorn was infuriated. Emma was his property, worth a great deal of money, and he had a proper order directing her return. If he shot this Englishman now, the frontier Boers would support him and to hell with the English, but as he raised his gun, Saul stepped quietly in front of the missionary and the child, extending his arms to protect them, and there was something in this gesture which caused the Boer to hesitate. If he fired now, he would have to kill three people, and one of them a little girl. He could not do such a thing.

But as always, Saltwood said the wrong words: 'If you kill me, Lodevicus, the entire force of the British Empire will hunt you down to the ends of the earth.'

From his saddle the Boer burst into a contemptuous laugh. 'You English. You goddamned English!' Without further comment, he wheeled his horse and headed back to the veld. He would ride through the night rather than spend it with fools like this English missionary.

When word circulated through the farms of the Boer community that the English missionary Saltwood had stolen the slave girl Emma and provided her refuge at Golan, consternation spread among them, and meetings were convened to which participants might have to ride for fifty miles. At each the principal orator was the patriarch Lodevicus the Hammer, who saw more clearly than most the dangers men like him faced.

'I can see the inevitable,' he ranted. 'The English want our Hottentots to live like Boers. Our lands are to be whittled down till we crowd together like Kaffirs. And mark my word, one day our slaves will be taken from us. And then our language will be outlawed and we'll hear predikants delivering their sermons in English.'

A farmer from near Graaff-Reinet, who had seen the fairly amicable relations that existed there between Boers and English officials, said, 'False fears. We can abide the English till they leave again.'

Quiet happenings proved that he was wrong. This time the English invaders showed no sign of quitting the country, and indignation ran through the isolated community when three new clergymen were assigned to remote districts; all were Scotsmen.

'You'd think we had no predikants of our own,' the farmers cried, truly distressed at this radical change.

'It's England pressing us under the heel,' Lodevicus announced, and he refused to send any further tithing to the church.

The fault was not England's. The government knew that frontier congregations longed for predikants who could speak Dutch, and those in charge wanted to send out such men, but there simply were none. Considering all the colonization under way throughout the world at this period, South Africa was the only major settlement in which organized religion failed to provide enough ministers to accompany the outward thrusters. When this deficiency became apparent, the government did the next best thing: it imported large numbers of young Scots Presbyterians who made the easy jump from John Knox to John Calvin; they were fine public servants, men of great devotion and a tribute to their religion.

Lodevicus, of course, was unaware of England's good intentions in this matter, and even if they had been explained to him, he would have damned them; all he was concerned with was that the new predikants were from an alien country, and would be bringing alien ideas. It was clear to him that they had been inserted to destroy Boer influence; one element of his gloomy prediction was being proved true.

Since there were no schools anywhere near De Kraal, Lodevicus was not personally involved in the next scandal, but he was outraged when he heard from farmers in settled areas like Swellendam that English was invading the schools.

'Shocking!' one man told a group of Boers. 'My son Nicodemus goes to school on Monday—what does he find? A new teacher. An Englishman who tells him, "From now on we speak English," or something like that. Nicodemus, he don't speak English, so how does he know?'

Bitter resentment developed among the Boers, and many a family, after the Bible reading at night, reflected on the warnings Lodevicus had uttered: 'It's coming around the way he said. First our church, then our school. Next we'll be forbidden to speak Dutch in court.'

This prediction had scarcely been voiced when a farmer near Graaff-Reinet who wanted to lodge a complaint about a boundary was informed that he must submit his brief in English. This provoked further argument, with Lodevicus resuming his role as prophet: 'Most sacred possession a man can have, even surpassing the Bible, I sometimes think, is his native tongue. A Boer thinks different from an Englishman and expresses that thinking in his own language. If we don't protect our language everywhere, church and court, we surrender our soul. I say we must fight for our language as we would for our lives, because otherwise we can never be free.'

Lodevicus, like all the Van Doorns, was obsessed with freedom, but only for himself. When one Englishman argued: 'Historical parallelism, old man. When the Huguenots came here, you Dutch were in command and forbade them to speak French. Now we're in charge, and we want you to speak English. Only fair.'

At such reasoning the old man exploded: 'Goddamn! This place was never French! Only Dutch! It will never be English either. You learn the

Dutch of the Afrikaner, damn you.' He would have chastised the visitor had not others intervened. The Englishman sought to apologize, but Lodevicus was caught in a mighty rage and, his neck muscles bulging, he shouted, 'Never, never will our soil be English.' Storming about the room like a Biblical patriarch, he thundered, 'You will have to kill me first . . . and then my sons . . . and then their grandsons . . . forever.'

It was against this background of rebellious thought that Lodevicus the Hammer rose against the English in 1815. Tjaart was absent with the herds when a horseman came riding up to De Kraal late one evening. 'Van Doorn! Lodevicus van Doorn!' he shouted, leaping from the saddle.

The white-bearded old man stepped outside. 'Ja, broeder, wat is dit?'

Breathlessly: 'Hottentots are killing Boers!' And when Lodevicus grabbed him by the neck, he stuttered: 'Frederick Bezuidenhout . . . lives thirty miles north of here . . . the court at Graaff-Reinet . . .'

'I know that court,' Lodevicus snapped. 'What's it done now?'

'Summoned Bezuidenhout . . . charges of abusing a servant.' It seemed that when the accused, a rough, unlettered renegade, refused to appear, a lieutenant and twenty soldiers were sent to fetch him. Unwisely, all the soldiers were Hottentots, and when Bezuidenhout retreated to a cave, gunfire was exchanged, and the highly trained Hottentots shot him dead. The Bezuidenhout family vowed vengeance.

Lodevicus reacted spontaneously: 'Good riddance. Those thieves.' He knew the Bezuidenhouts as border ruffians who respected neither English rule nor Dutch, and as veldkornet he had often been required to discipline them. 'Afrika voor de Afrikaner!' was their battle cry, and they hated the English with a passion equaled only by their abhorrence of those Dutch who served what they called 'The Lords of London.'

They were an unregenerate lot and Lodevicus could not feel sorry over the death of Frederick. 'Van Doorn!' the messenger shouted. 'Are you listening? Hottentots sent by the English Kaffir-lovers murder a Boer.' He shook the master of De Kraal and cried almost plaintively, 'We need you, Lodevicus Hammer.'

'For what?'

'To lead the Boers.'

'Against who?'

'The English. Who plan to kill off all us Boers.'

Van Doorn, much as he hated the English, could not accept this ridiculous statement. He started to tell the messenger that he was forgetting the early days when trekboers armed their Hottentots to fight the Xhosa, but the man was persistent.

'Lodevicus Hammer, if we let the English do this thing to one of us, they will do it to all,' and his arguments were finally so persuasive that the old man asked, 'What do you want of me?' and the messenger said, 'Lead us against the English.'

'And where would we get the troops?'

Softly the messenger said, 'The Bezuidenhouts say we must go to Kaffirs.'

Neither man spoke, for this was the moment of treason, the moment when loyalties and moral judgments hung in the balance. Lodevicus van Doorn knew well that the ultimate battle his people would have to fight would be against the blacks, and he had seen how fearful that struggle could be. His father Adriaan, his mother Seena, his wife Rebecca had all been slain by the Xhosa, and he in turn had decimated their ranks. To ally with them now was unthinkable.

'The only Kaffir this Boer wants to speak with is a dead one,' he growled.

'No, no! Van Doorn, listen to me. With the Kaffirs we can drive out the English. When that's done we can settle with the Kaffirs.'

'They butchered my family,' Lodevicus said grimly.

'And now we use them for our purposes.' He explained how this could be done, and concluded: 'I've heard you say yourself, Vicus, that the English will destroy us. They will stamp on the backs of the Boers. They will make us say "Mister" to the Hottentots eating at our own table.' On and on he went, driving home the message that the Englishman was the real enemy: 'Look what he did to you in the Black Circuit.'

This was the telling blow. Lodevicus, who had hammered the Kaffirs, took a great step down the road to treason: 'The enemy that matters is the enemy of today. He is white and English.'

'I know where we can meet with the Xhosa generals,' the messenger whispered, and without conceding that he would actually unleash these fearsome warriors against the English, Lodevicus did agree to talk with them.

Through the dark night the two conspirators rode east to the Great Fish, forded it upstream from a rude fort, and sought the dwelling of Guzaka, son of Sotopo. When at last Lodevicus faced the warrior, the two adversaries glared at each other in silence. Guzaka had slain three members of the Van Doorn family; the Hammer had captained the destruction of more than three thousand Xhosa. Finally Guzaka rose, extended his two hands, and said, 'It is time.'

They sat outside Guzaka's hut, two grizzled warriors licking their wounds like old tomcats, their claws blunted by the years. 'Ja, Kaffir,' Van Doorn said slowly, 'here stands a Van Doorn asking your help. God knows it's not right, but what else is there?'

'The Redcoats will destroy both of us,' the white-haired Xhosa said.

'We must kick them out.'

'Killings, too many killings,' Guzaka said.

'Settle with them, then we'll settle peace between us.'

'But you Boers steal our lands, too.'

'Did we ever drive twenty thousand across the Big Fish? It was the English who did that.'

'It's still our land,' Guzaka said, confused by the drift of the conversation.

'Old man, you and I don't have too many years. Let us solve the land question now. We drive out the English, then you and I make peace. We each herd cattle. We share the land.'

'Can we defeat the Redcoats?' the old warrior asked.

'Together we can do anything,' Lodevicus said with fervor, and impulsively he clasped his enemy's hand, for at that moment he truly believed those words.

Inspired by this show of friendship, Guzaka said, 'Tonight I shall discuss this with my headmen. Tomorrow we make the treaty.' It was a word he knew well, for along this contested border there had been more than fifteen treaties, none with prospects more hopeful than this: Boer and Xhosa against the enemy.

But during this parley, which might have meant so much to the frontier, a young Xhosa warrior with wild and shifting eyes who claimed to see visions and exercise prophecy—a thin man with a ridged scar across his forehead—had sat off to one side, carefully watching, his heart smoldering with hatred for Van Doorn. He remembered that years ago this huge Boer had scattered tobacco on the ground as a trap; his father had stooped to retrieve it—and fifty warriors had perished.

So after Lodevicus and the messenger withdrew, the trembling prophet harangued his tribesmen: 'Jackals! Cowards! Men without skins! Who is this Van Doorn who comes begging? Is he not the sorcerer who uses tobacco to slay his enemies? The blood of my people is on his hands.'

'The blood of his people is on our hands,' Guzaka replied. 'This is the time to halt the bloodshed.'

'What can this monster do for us?' the prophet demanded.

'He will help us fight the English,' Guzaka argued. 'With the Boers we can live in peace. With the English, never.'

'If we help these Boers today,' the scarred prophet warned, 'they will steal our land when the battle is over. I say kill them tonight.'

But Guzaka saw a chance to gain that lasting peace without which his people would suffer unbroken travail, and he tried vainly to support the concept of a combined attack on the English; he achieved nothing, for the prophet, inflamed by an apocalyptic vision of long-dead Xhosa generals rising mysteriously to launch an attack on both the English and the Boers, expelling them from the land, cried, 'He is old and frightened!' And three young warriors struck Guzaka, leader of many battles, to the ground and killed him.

They then raged out into the night, seeking the trail by which Lodevicus had left the camp. In the mists, sixty warriors, spurred on by the prophet, fell upon the tent where Lodevicus slept. The old man reached for his gun, but before he could fire even one shot, assegais pierced his chest and he fell back.

As he lay dying in treachery he moaned, 'Merciful God, forgive me. Forgive me.' As he fell back, blood gushing from his lips, he mumbled, 'Adriaan, Seena. Rebecca, me. The circle . . .'

News of the death of Lodevicus had not yet reached De Kraal when Hilary Saltwood entered the valley with Saul. Tjaart, returning from the cattle drive, eyed the missionary suspiciously, seeing him only as the Englishman who had stolen the slave girl Emma. Clasping the sjambok at his side, he flicked the long hide over the grass and growled, 'Off these lands, Saltwood.'

Hilary, perched on the riding seat of a small cart, felt Saul trembling next to him. 'Put that down, Tjaart. This is no time for argument.'

'Back to your Hottentots, Englishman, and take that damned Kaffir with you.'

Saltwood's eyes followed the line of the menacing whip, then crept up to Tjaart's face. The Boer recognized a look of anguished appeal, and his next words were less intemperate: 'What is it you want?'

'It's your father, Tjaart.'

Wilhelmina and Tjaart's wife, who had been listening inside the house, stepped outside and stood glaring at the intruder; at the sight of the women Saltwood held back his words.

'What about my father?'

'He rode with the rebels.'

'Damnit, man, I know that. And I join them tomorrow.'

Lord, why me? Hilary asked himself as if in prayer. Why does it always have to be me who faces this family.

'Tjaart, your father is dead.'

The younger Van Doorn ground out his words: 'What you say, Englishman?' Till now they had been conversing in the language of the Boers, but in his agitation Tjaart used the missionary's language.

The color drained from Wilhelmina's face. Putting her arm about her daughter-in-law's shoulders, she drew her close to her bosom, and in that instant she thought of the long years since the day she rode north from a godless past to offer herself to Lodevicus the Hammer. They had been good years and violent. Twice her lips formed his name, and when she looked up at the stricken, bean-thin missionary she knew that he was telling the truth. Her wild old man was dead.

'The Kaffirs killed him,' Saltwood repeated. Quietly he explained that his Xhosa, Saul, had been visiting across the Great Fish and had learned of the mission to Guzaka and of the dual tragedy that ensued. When he assured them that Saul would be able to lead them to the body, Wilhelmina said softly, 'Dominee, you must be tired. Come in.'

That afternoon they started the grim journey; Wilhelmina was insistent that the Hammer should be buried where he fell. 'He was a man of God but not of churches,' she said, and she refused Saltwood's offer of burial at the mission. At noon next day, while the Xhosa were lamenting the death of the general, Guzaka, the white men and women piled rocks above the grave of Lodevicus, whereupon the missionary offered a prayer in Dutch, after which he recited the somber passages of the Ninetieth Psalm:

> 'The days of our years are threescore years and ten; and if by reason of strength they be fourscore years, yet is their strength labour and sorrow; for it is soon cut off, and we fly away . . . So teach us to number our days, that we may apply our hearts unto wisdom.'

On their return, the mourners reached the point at which Saltwood and Saul must head east for Golan, and it seemed to the missionary that his life and Tjaart's were as divergent as the directions they would now follow; he had been as close to a Van Doorn during these past days as he would ever be, and this moved him to say fervently, 'Tjaart, don't ride with the rebels. Don't seek tragedy.'

'You?' Tjaart asked. 'You worry about my soul?'

'Concerning the slave girl, Emma, who has caused so much bitterness. I want to buy her.'

'A dominee? Buying a De Kraal slave?'

'Her and her parents.'

'Where would you get the money?'

'I'd write home . . . to my mother.'

The fatuousness of this statement amused all the Van Doorns, and for the first time since the death of the Hammer they broke into laughter. 'He'll write home to his mother!' Tjaart mimicked. But he did agree to sell the slaves.

Even as the laughter echoed, the final scenes of the futile uprising were being enacted to the north, where well-trained English soldiers pinned down a ragtag commando of seventy dissident Boers, most of whom surrendered without a shot. A few of the ringleaders escaped to fight a bitter-end clash, but when it ended, Johannes Bezuidenhout, brother of Frederick, who had started the troubles, lay dead. The first abortive rebellion was ended.

It was a sound that never before had been heard in this part of the world: two slow-footed drummers marching alongside a cart in which stood six manacled men and beating out the pace of death. The two horses, groomed for the occasion, hauled the last of the Bezuidenhout rebels into a beautiful valley surrounded by comforting hills. The six men had been sentenced to death, but one had been reprieved: before his life in jail began he must stand tied by the neck to the gallows while his five companions were hanged.

The place chosen for the hanging was so appallingly named, and the events it would witness so hideous, that it would reverberate in South African history: Slagter's Nek—The Neck of the Slaughterer.

The crowd of witnesses was great. All revolutionaries not condemned were required to stand in the shadow of the gallows, as were members of the men's families, and the two widows of the Bezuidenhouts already dead. Near three hundred militia were present to control passions: English troops in red, Hottentot militia in marching gear, and loyal Boers in the rough dress of the commando. And in command of all rode a most extraordinary man: the son of the mayor of Albany, New York, in the new United States of America.

Colonel Jacob Glen Cuyler, forty years old and a fine figure of a man, had been born on the eve of the American Revolution into a loyalist family. When his parents refused to support the revolution, they fled to Canada, where young Jacob joined the British army. Because of his Dutch heritage, it seemed sensible to send him to South Africa, where he landed with the second English invading force of 1806. A man of courage and intelligence, he prospered in the new colony, rising to rank of colonel and magistrate of a large district south of Graaff-Reinet.

He was a foe of revolutionaries. They had driven him from his home in America and left him with indelible memories: when he came to South Africa he brought with him two handsome portraits of his parents, completed shortly before his death by Major John André, who lived with the Cuylers before his execution as an English spy.

Colonel Cuyler, acting under strict orders from Cape Town, was determined that these hangings be conducted with propriety. It was he who had suggested the two drummers; it was he who had stopped at Golan Mission on the way north to tell Missionary Saltwood: 'It's always proper to have a clergyman present at a hanging. Gives religious sanction and helps control the doomed men.'

No one who attended the hangings at Slagter's Nek would ever forget them; women and men would sometimes cry in the night, not because of the hangings, which occurred often in those days, but because of the soul-wrenching thing that happened.

When the five condemned men were led to the gallows, they were forced to climb upon movable platforms and stand at attention, hands and feet tied, as the ropes were attached to their necks and knotted. Some of the men accepted blindfolds, others ignored them, and when all was in readiness Cuyler ordered the drums to roll, and the platforms were kicked away. For a long, terrible moment the doomed men struggled in the air—

and then the miracle happened! Four of the five ropes broke, allowing those men to fall free.

When this occurred a great shout of joy rose from everyone, even the rows of Hottentot corpsmen. Reverend Saltwood actually jumped up and down, throwing his arms in the air and crying, 'God be praised!' In a frenzy of relief he clasped the men who had been so miraculously saved and knelt in the dust to untie their ankle fetters. Then he led them in prayers, which seemed to gush forth as if God Himself were rejoicing. In his exultation at this happy escape from tragedy, even though the unlucky fifth rebel dangled dead, he found himself next to Tjaart van Doorn, and in mutual joy the two enemies embraced. 'Thank God, thank God!' Hilary mumbled repeatedly as he and Tjaart danced in the shadow of the gallows.

'Tjaart!' Saltwood cried ecstatically. 'You must come and worship with me. We can be friends, truly we can.'

'Maybe we can,' Tjaart said, and it was in that moment of reconciliation that the awful thing happened.

'Re-form!' Cuyler shouted. 'Bring new ropes.'

'What?' Saltwood cried, unable to comprehend what he was hearing. 'New ropes!'

'But, Colonel! In English law . . . if the rope breaks, the man goes free!'

As soon as Hilary voiced this ancient edict, and a good one it was, for it acknowledged that God Himself sometimes intervened to save the condemned, the crowd took up the cry, and those relatives who had been rejoicing with their reprieved men ran to the officer, reminding him of this honored tradition.

'They are saved!' the people cried. 'You cannot hang them a second time.'

'True,' Saltwood pleaded, tugging at Cuyler's sleeve. 'It's a custom all men honor. The hanging was completed when God intervened.'

Suddenly Cuyler's eyes hardened. He had a job to do, a revolution to quell. Having been driven away from Albany, he understood the terror that could engulf a land when revolutionary ideas were allowed to gallop across a countryside, and he intended having none of that in Africa. These men must die. So it was frustrating when this damn-fool English priest started making trouble. With a vigorous shove he knocked Saltwood back and cried to his orderly, 'Bind that silly ass and take him away.'

'No, sir, no!' Hilary protested. 'You will defile this land if you—'

'Take him away,' Cuyler said coldly, and soldiers seized the missionary, clapping a hand over his mouth so that he could protest no further, and dragged him off.

Then the four survivors whom God had touched were placed once more upon the platforms, their faces ashen as fresh ropes were tied about their necks.

It was not a roar that came from the crowd. It was not a military challenge to the new government. It was only a vast sigh of anguish that so foul a thing should be done on so fair a day. Then, from the area in which he was being held, came Saltwood's high begging scream: 'No! No!'

Once more the platforms were kicked aside. This time the ropes held.

When Tjaart van Doorn returned to De Kraal he was silent for a long while, then grimly he summoned his mother, his wife, his children, and in solemn conclave lined out the mystical litany that would be recited in diehard Boer families from that day forward: 'Never forget the Black Circuit when Hottentots and liars bore testimony in English courts against honest Boers. Never forget how the English have tried to banish our language. Never forget Slagter's Nek, where an English officer hanged the same men twice, in disobedience to God's law.'

Tjaart was twenty-six now, a quiet, stubborn man emerging slowly from the shadows of his father's flaming exuberance to assume responsibility for De Kraal. His character was not yet fully formed; he supported all his fiery father had done, even his near-treason, convincing himself that 'Father was driven to it in desperation over the illegal acts of the English.' But he knew he could never take the Hammer's place as champion of the Boers; his was a calmer approach, that of the self-confident bull who rules the pasture without bellowing. It became obvious to him that English rule would have to be challenged, but when and how, he could not guess. He supposed that the invaders would make one small mistake after another, digging their own graves, until that day when the Boers would be able to resume control of their native land.

When Colonel Cuyler returned from the hangings at Slagter's Nek, he was so disgusted with Reverend Saltwood's pusillanimous behavior—for so he considered it—that he submitted an angry report to Cape Town, confirming what many government officials had begun to suspect: that Hilary was an irresponsible character whose loyalties were questionable. From then on, the English segment of South Africa had little to do with the gawky missionary at the eastern edge of settlement.

During these years Captain Richard Saltwood was conducting himself rather well in India; at Hindu hangings, of which he saw not a few, he gave way to no hysterics: 'Blighter was caught, he gets hanged, that's that.'

In 1819, as a newly commissioned major with six campaigns to his credit, two with Ochterlony against the Gurkhas, losing 1814, winning 1816, he shipped home to England from his regiment, and when his transport lay to at Cape Town he fully expected to unite with his brother, who was serving somewhere as a missionary, but when he found that Hilary was four or five hundred miles distant, he was amazed: 'This place is as big as India.' And he surrendered any idea of trying to find him.

He was not pleased with what he heard in Cape Town regarding Hilary's curious behavior; one army wife said, 'It's the frontier, Richard. The Kaffirs, the Hottentots, the Boer farmers who can't read or write. Our army men are stationed there only seven months. That's about all they can take. How long's your brother been there? Nine long years? No wonder he's acting up.'

An army captain who had been stationed at Graaff-Reinet was more specific: 'It's the moral loneliness . . . the intellectual loneliness. The church in London sends them books and all that, but there they are, stuck away and gone. I wouldn't dare leave one of my men out there for even two years. They'd go to rot.'

'In what way?'

'They begin to see everything from the point of view of the natives. They learn the language, you know. Eat Kaffir food. Some of them, God forbid, take Kaffir wives.'

'Not missionaries, certainly.'

'Yes, even marry them. And there have been cases . . .' He dropped his voice significantly to allow Major Saltwood to guess what those cases had consisted of.

'Is there anything I can do?' Richard asked.

'There certainly is. Find him a wife.'

'Can't he find—'

The captain interrupted, wishing to elaborate on a point which he had often considered: 'Fact is, men everywhere are sounder stuff if they have wives. Keeps them responsible. Go to bed earlier. Eat better-prepared food. Missionaries are no different. Your brother needs a wife.'

'Why doesn't he take one?'

'None to be had.'

'I saw lots of women at the dance last night.'

'None single.' He ran off a list of the pretty women Richard had met, and every one was married.

'They didn't seem so last night,' Richard said.

'What you must do,' the captain said, 'is when you get home, find your brother a good wife. One who accepts missionaries.'

'And ship her out?'

'That's the way we all do. Every ship comes into Table Bay has its quota, but never enough.' He looked reflectively into his cup. 'When you're in England, and women are everywhere, they seem rather ordinary. But when you're overseas and there are none—no white ones, that is—

damn, they seem important.' It was under this urging that Richard Saltwood drafted a letter to his brother:

> I was most fearfully disappointed not to have met you during my
> visit. The regiment's home to Wiltshire with me a major, thanks to
> some lucky work against the Gurkhas. I find myself quite homesick
> for Sentinels, and wish to God you were going to be at home when
> I get there.
>
> Several people in Cape Town, religious and military alike, urged me
> to find you a wife when I get back to Salisbury, a task I face for my-
> self. Send Mother a letter, quickly, telling us whether we should
> proceed and how. Your woman could be aboard one of the next
> ships to Cape Town, and I could be, too, because I've taken a great
> liking to your land. I think an English soldier could do well here,
> and I'm afraid I've gone about as far as I can in the Glorious Fifty-
> ninth.

When Hilary received the letter he was at low ebb, for Golan Mission
was not doing well. The rows of huts were filled with Hottentots and
Xhosa seeking to avoid work under the Boers, but few were sincere Christians. Not even Emma's parents had converted, and there was a problem
with Emma herself. She was nineteen now, and a true Christian, but
plans of some kind had to be made for her future; the most she could hope
for was marriage to some half-Christian Xhosa; more probably she would
slip back into servitude at some Boer kraal.

Funds to support the mission were slow in coming from England, and
one young man who had been seconded to relieve Hilary had taken one
look at South Africa and scrambled back aboard his ship, preferring to
trust his luck in India. Hilary kept himself insulated from such disap-
pointments by cherishing his trivial accomplishments and sharing them
with Emma: 'Phambo appeared at prayers again, and I do believe he is on
the way to salvation.' Three days later, when Phambo ran off to the Xhosa
camp on the other side of the Great Fish, taking with him three Golan
cows, Hilary did not condemn him: 'Poor Phambo heard temptation and
could not resist, but when he returns, Emma, as I am convinced he will,
we must greet him as our brother, with or without the cows.'

Hilary refused to acknowledge the ostracism directed against him by
both the Boers and the English: the former because he was an agent of
the English repression; the latter because he had 'behaved poorly' at
Slagter's Nek. And both sides viewed him with scorn for supporting the
Kaffirs against white men. One good reason why he was able to ignore the
ostracism was that he rarely participated in any public gathering. His
world was his church.

But his brother's letter suggesting that he take a wife made great sense;

he was thirty-four now, worn and wasted by his exertions on a difficult frontier, and he felt the need for someone to share his spiritual burdens; if his mother, in consultation with her other sons, could comb the Salisbury scene and locate a suitable wife, the years ahead might prove more profitable both to Jesus and to His servant Saltwood. So he wrote a careful letter, advising his mother as to the requirements for a missioner's wife in South Africa.

He was distracted from such personal matters when Tjaart, accompanied by four Boers, galloped into the mission one morning, shouting in anxiety, 'We need every man! The Kaffirs are marching on Grahamstown.'

The commando waited some fifteen minutes for Saltwood to arm himself, and Hilary spent ten of these in agonizing inner debate as to whether it was Christian for him to participate in armed combat against the Xhosa, a people he loved; but he realized that until the frontier was pacified, not even missionary work could proceed, so reluctantly he took his rifle.

'Bring your Hottentots, too!' Tjaart cried, and six of them eagerly mounted up. For the English to have used armed Hottentots against the Boers had been criminal; for the Boers to use them against the Kaffirs was prudent.

It was seventy miles from Golan Mission to the little military post at Grahamstown, and as the Boers urged their horses onward, Saltwood reflected that only Englishmen lived in the village, yet here were the Boers galloping full speed to aid them. He was aware that Tjaart despised the English, inveighing against them at every chance, but when an English outpost was threatened by Kaffirs, the Boer commandos were always ready to saddle up. It was confusing.

The twelve newcomers were given a cheering welcome at Grahamstown, where fewer than three hundred English and Hottentot soldiers, plus two cannon, awaited the Xhosa attack. Tjaart's contingent meant that thirty civilians would aid the soldiers; he was distressed when the English commander divided his troops: 'Half to the barracks southeast of town, half here with me to defend the empty town.' He sent the women and children to the safety of the barracks, except for five, who said, 'We'll fight with our husbands in the town.'

Throughout the night Hottentot scouts crept in to report the steady advance of the Xhosa horde, but Tjaart and Saltwood could not credit the numbers they recited. 'Hottentots always exaggerate,' Tjaart explained. 'Whites and blacks are so much bigger, they think there's more of us.' But at dawn the defenders gaped in sickening awe as the slopes northeast of Grahamstown showed more than ten thousand warriors descending in three massed divisions. The noise of this multitude as they began dashing toward the settlement caused fear in every heart.

The brow-scarred Xhosa prophet had predicted certain victory: 'When Grahamstown falls, we have a clear run through every frontier farm from the ocean to the mountains at the north!' Behind the exulting regiments came hundreds of women with their cooking pots and gourds, for the prophet had promised them: 'At sunset we shall feast as never before. Redcoats and Boers alike, destroyed.'

Tjaart, imbued with the spirit of the Hammer, perceived the impending attack as one more clash in a never-ending battle. There stood the enemy, here stood the men of God—and the only obligation of the latter was to chastise the former. Turning to the men near him, he said, 'Anyone afraid to fight, ride off now.' And he looked directly at Saltwood, half expecting him to flee, but throughout history no Saltwood had ever deserted, and Hilary would not break that tradition. Turning to his six Hottentots, he asked, 'Are you ready?' and the brown men nodded.

'Then let us pray,' and when he had done so in English, Tjaart asked if he might add words of his own, and in Dutch he prayed: 'Like Abraham we face the Canaanites. Like him we place our lives in Thy hands. Great God, guide us good Christians as once again we smite these Kaffirs.'

The attack came in early afternoon, wave after wave of shrieking Xhosa roaring down the hill to hurl themselves against the soldiers in the town. Those in the barracks had to watch, helpless, as the regiments rushed at the little houses.

'We must go to help them,' Saltwood said.

'Stay!' a lieutenant ordered. 'Our time will come.'

The most daring of the Xhosa got to within one hundred feet of the soldiers, but then massed gunfire raked their ranks and the two cannon wreaked devastation. Hundreds of blacks fell in the front ranks, until their commanders, seeing that the English line could not be broken, gave the order to swing onto the barracks. Here they were more successful, penetrating the small collection of buildings. This landed them in the center of the barracks square, where they were safe, since the cannon could not be brought directly against them for fear of killing fellow Englishmen and Boers. The fighting would have to be hand-to-hand.

Tjaart and Saltwood were in the midst of it, shoulders pressed. They saw two Hottentots go down, a Redcoat fall. A huge Xhosa leaped at Saltwood, swinging his war club, but Tjaart twisted about to drop him with a pistol shot. For almost an hour the battle raged in the square, then finally the gallant Xhosa, facing gunfire they had not anticipated, had to retreat. A jubilant cry arose from the white and Hottentot fighters as the warriors fled in uncontrolled panic. Grahamstown had been saved!

In the aftermath of battle Saltwood was missing, and for a while Tjaart wondered if this missionary, who had fought so bravely, had been dragged away by the fleeing Xhosa, but as Tjaart searched a field he saw Hilary, bloody and disheveled, kneeling beside a dying Xhosa. Tears streamed down his face, and when he saw his neighbor Van Doorn approaching he looked up in bewilderment.

'Seven hundred of them dead,' he mumbled softly. 'I've counted more than seven hundred lying here. Three of our men dead. May God forgive us for this slaughter.'

'Dominee,' Tjaart reasoned, 'God wanted us to win this battle.' When the missionary muttered something incoherent, Van Doorn added, 'In warfare like this, so few of us against so many of them, it's no time to love thy enemy. Destroy him. Because where would you be now if they'd broken through? Can you see Golan burning?'

Saltwood looked up at the man who had saved his life. He tried to justify his feelings of repugnance, but he could form no words. 'It's all right, Dominee,' Tjaart said. 'We taught the Kaffir bastards a lesson they'll remember. Till next time.'

'Next time?'

Tjaart tugged at his beard. 'It will never stop, Dominee. Not till one side is victor in this land.'

Saltwood had to admit, though reluctantly, that what Van Doorn was saying was true, but he did not voice this thought, for next to him the young Xhosa warrior, no more than a boy, shuddered and lay still.

When Hilary Saltwood's letter reached Sentinels in the shadow of Salisbury Cathedral, his mother was fifty-four years old, a widow and eager to help her distant son find the proper wife. The commission was not an unusual one in rural England. Sons of distinguished families would venture to all parts of the world, serving for years as outriders of civilization in places like India, South America and Ceylon, without ever thinking of marrying local women the way Portuguese and French colonizers did. An Englishman remembered the girl left behind, and when he was in his mid-thirties he would come home, and some gaunt woman in her early thirties, who in another society would never find a husband, would be waiting, and they would repair to the village church, two people who had been terrified of missing life, and they would be married, and flowers would be scattered, and the local curate would dry his eyes at this little miracle, and soon the pair would be off to some other remote spot.

Or, as in this case, the son would write home to his parents and ask them to pursue his courtship for him, and they would visit only the daughters of families they had known for a generation, and again some older woman who might never have married would find that she was needed in some far country by a man she could only vaguely remember. This was the English pattern, and men who deviated from it by marrying local women were apt to find their lives truncated, if not ruined.

Emily Saltwood, upon reading her son's appeal, retired to her room for two days and reflected upon the marriageable daughters of her friends, and after trying her best to judge the girls from a man's point of view, and a missionary's, she decided that the family she must visit was the Lambtons, who lived across the bridge within the purlieus of the cathedral.

Wishing not to share her secret mission with any servant, she elected not to use her carriage but to walk to the village, where she sought out the bricked path leading to the Lambton residence, at whose door she knocked quietly. After an interval that troubled her, because it seemed that no one was at home, she heard shuffling feet approach, and an elderly maid creaked open the door. 'Mrs. Lambton is not at home,' she said. Nor was Miss Lambton there, but there was a possibility that they could be found near the cathedral grounds, for they had planned on having tea in that vicinity.

Emily said, 'You know, it's frightfully important that I see Mrs. Lambton immediately, and I think you'd better go fetch them.'

'I couldn't leave the house, ma'am.' The maid was insistent.

'On this day you'd better.' Emily Saltwood could be just as insistent. 'Couldn't you go and meet them at the cathedral?'

'No, I couldn't. Because what I have to discuss is not for an open park. Now you scurry off and find your mistress, or I'll take this umbrella to you.'

This the maid understood, and after a while she returned, leading both Mrs. Lambton and her daughter Vera. This was rather more than Emily had expected, so she said quite brusquely, 'It was your mother I wished to see,' and the tall girl, twenty-nine years old and somewhat timid, dutifully vanished.

'I've had a curious letter from my son Hilary, in South Africa,' Emily began, and without another word being spoken, Mrs. Lambton grasped the significance of this abrupt meeting. Keeping her hands under discipline, lest they tremble, she said, 'Vera and I remember Hilary well. The soldier, wasn't he?'

'The missionary,' Emily said.

'Yes, yes.' Her hands were now trembling furiously, but she kept them hidden. She knew she'd made an unforgivable mistake, confusing the Saltwood boys, but she recovered admirably by throwing Emily on the defensive: 'Didn't you have a son who went to America?'

'Alas, we did. Never hear of him.'

'They tell me that your boy Richard's thinking of returning to India . . . without the regiment.'

'He's headstrong. He'll be off to some remote spot.'

'Tell me, Emily, how does a mother feel when her chicks are so scattered?'

'You may soon know, because Hilary has asked me to ascertain whether Vera . . .' It was most difficult to say such a thing bluntly, without preparation of any kind, but it was inescapable. 'He wonders if Vera would like to join him in South Africa—in the mission field, that is.'

'She's a devout girl,' Mrs. Lambton parried. 'All us Lambtons are devoted to the church.'

'I know, I know. That's why it's been so easy for me to approach you on so delicate a matter.'

'I don't know how Vera . . .' Mrs. Lambton spoke defensively, as if her daughter were accustomed to weighing such proposals, but Emily Salt-wood was not going to have any of that. Abruptly she said, 'Vera's at the age when she must make up her mind . . . and quickly. Hilary's a fine lad and he needs a wife.'

'How old is he?' Mrs. Lambton asked sweetly.

'Thirty-four. The proper age for such a marriage.'

'And has he prospects?'

'His older brother—Peter, that is—he'll inherit the house, of course. But we expect Hilary to be dean of the cathedral one of these days. When his tour ends, of course.'

'Most interesting.' Mrs. Lambton knew of three young clergymen who were being considered for that promotion. Besides, Hilary suffered an im-pediment which completely disqualified him, and it was important to knock down Mrs. Saltwood's bargaining position early in the game: 'Didn't I hear that your son took orders with the Methodists, or something quite awful like that?' She beamed her benign Sunday-in-church smile.

'Merely for his ordination to do Christ's work. He'll scamper back into the proper fold, once he returns.' She, too, smiled. 'You've heard, I'm sure, that before he died, the old Proprietor, who was extremely fond of Hilary, made special overtures for him at the cathedral.'

'Pity he died,' Mrs. Lambton said. She had other solid objections to sending her daughter to a land so remote as South Africa, but she was realist enough to know that Vera was aging and had better catch a suitor promptly. Even a ghost like the absent Hilary had to be considered, so she extended Mrs. Saltwood a courtesy she did not fully feel: 'I think we should discuss this, Emily.'

'Shall we involve Vera?' Mrs. Saltwood asked.

'Not at this point, I think. And certainly not the two of us. It would make everything seem too important.'

'It's just that,' Emily said with that charming frankness that charac-terized so many elderly English women who no longer felt restraints. 'It's very important for my son, and frankly, it ought to be for Vera too. She's not getting any younger.'

She walked home across the old bridge, turned right, and went down the quiet lane leading to Sentinels, where she felt vaguely uneasy, al-though unaware that national events were about to do her work for her.

In London her eldest son, Peter, now a member of Parliament for Old Sarum, had become a leader in the movement to alleviate English unem-ployment by the device of granting large funds for shipping unwanted families out to South Africa:

> This interesting action will serve two noble purposes. In England it
> will remove large numbers of unfortunate people from our charity

rolls, and in South Africa it will correct the imbalance that now exists between the many Dutch and the few English. If our new colony below the equator is to become properly English, as it must, we shall have to throw many Englishmen into the balance pans, and this act will do just that.

A gigantic effort was mounted to convince impoverished Englishmen that they must quit their hopelessness at home and venture into the new paradise. Articles were published extolling the agricultural possibilities, the beauty of the landscape, and the salubriousness of the climate on the right bank of the Great Fish River, in the vicinity of that splendid rural capital Grahamstown. No mention was made of the recent attack by ten thousand assegaied Xhosa on said capital or the deaths among those who had defended it.

Most helpful were the speeches and writings of Reverend Simon Keer, who assured Englishmen that those lucky enough to be included in the roster of immigrants—whose boat fare would be paid by the government and whose land would be given free, a hundred rolling acres to each family—would be entering a paradise to which America and Australia were niggardly in comparison. To residents of crowded England, where a family could live well on twenty acres, the vision of a hundred, rent-free, tax-free, was compelling.

Ninety thousand citizens, well mixed as to occupation, education and ability, volunteered to emigrate, a superior lot, really, to those who had emigrated earlier to Canada and America, and had they all been moved to Cape Town, the history of Africa would have been sharply modified, for at this time there were only some twenty-five thousand Boers in the entire colony, and the infusion of so many Englishmen would have made South Africa much like any other British colony. But enthusiastic members of Parliament, such as Peter Saltwood, promised much more than they could deliver, and when the time came to fill the ships, only enough money to transport four thousand settlers was provided, so that the eighty-six thousand who might have restructured a nation had to be left behind.

Among those lucky enough to be included was a young man of twenty-five named Thomas Carleton, a carriage builder by trade, whose enthusiasm matched the rhetoric of speakers like Peter Saltwood and Simon Keer. From the first moment he heard of the emigration plan, he wanted to go, and with letters of approval from his minister and sheriff, he was among the first interviewed: 'My business is solid, but it's not really thriving. I want to go where distances are great and men must have wagons.'

'Have you any money saved?'

'Not a penny, but I have strong arms, a willing back and a complete set of tools fully paid.'

The examiners doubted if they would find many men so qualified and unanimously recommended that he be accepted, so he was given a slip of paper guaranteeing his passage and the allocation of one hundred acres. He was to report three months hence to Southampton, where the ship *Alice Grace* would be loading. 'That'll give you time to find yourself a wife,' the examiners explained.

'Not me!' Thomas said. 'I haven't a penny to feed a wife.'

When the news of this grand scheme reached Salisbury, the Lambtons listened with more than casual attention, and the more they heard, the more convinced they became that this was the kind of adventure to which an unmarried girl of good breeding might subscribe. Of course, Vera would not be sailing as an ordinary charity case, her way paid by the government; as the intended bride of a clergyman who might one day be dean of the finest cathedral in England, and the sister-in-law-to-be of an important member of Parliament, she would have preferment.

But the grand decision hung in the balance until Salisbury was visited by the one man in England who spoke as if he knew most about the new colony, Dr. Simon Keer, as he now called himself, a power in the LMS. He announced a public meeting in the cathedral cloisters, where chairs lined the hallowed square and where against a background of gray stone he explained everything. He was now middle-aged, a short, plump little man with red hair, a Lancashire accent and a powerful voice that boomed as it echoed from the noble walls; his oratory rolled like thunder as he spoke of challenges and flashed like lightning when he outlined the potentialities:

> 'If we grapple courageously with the problem of slavery in this colony, we shall show the way for Canada and Jamaica and Barbados and, yes, the United States itself. Any Englishman or woman who accepts this invitation to perform God's duty will be serving all of mankind. I wish I could sail in those ships, for all who do will be rebuilding the world.'

When the Lambtons lingered to ask him if he knew anything of Grahamstown, where the new settlers would be given their land, he showed his frank astonishment that a family as distinguished as theirs might be interested in emigrating: 'It's for the poorer type, you know. The solid workers of the world.'

'Of course,' Mrs. Lambton said. 'But we're told that the Golan Mission, run by your Society . . .' She had to say no more. With a wild clap of his hands and a leap in the air he cried, 'I know! I know!' And he took Vera's hands and danced a jig with her, even though she was a head taller than he. 'You're going out to marry Hilary Saltwood.'

He spent an hour assuring the Lambtons of how fine a man this missionary was. He reviewed the steps by which Hilary had reached conversion, and said that whereas he himself had not yet visited Golan Mission, for it had not been in existence when he served in that area, he had excellent reports of it. But then Vera took him aside for a confidential assessment.

When he finished she was convinced that she could profitably sail to South Africa, but her mother raised one serious objection: 'With whom can Vera travel? I don't fancy her alone on a ship for four months, surrounded by God knows whom.'

'That's a real problem,' Dr. Keer conceded, 'but I've been working closely with the shipping companies. Real gentlemen, you know.' To hear the former missionary speak, he consorted only with the best families, stayed only at the great houses, and one gained the impression that he enjoyed missionary work far more when lecturing in England than he had when serving on the Xhosa frontier. 'I'm sure we'll find persons of quality among the ship's officers. I'll make inquiries.'

This wasn't necessary, for within a week of Dr. Keer's lecture in the cloisters, Richard Saltwood came down from London, where he had been consulting with his brother in Parliament, and his news was exciting: 'Mother! I've resigned my commission. Wasn't going anywhere down that lane. And Peter's arranged with the colonial secretary for me . . . Point is, I'm to have a government job at Grahamstown! David lost in America. Me lost in South Africa.'

'Are you contemplating staying there?' his mother asked.

'There's nothing for me here. I've neither the money nor the talent to be a colonel of the regiment. So I'm off to the new land. I saw it and liked it. Much better than India.'

'This could be providential,' his mother said. 'We've found a bride for Hilary. The Lambton girl. You knew her years ago. She's a tall, thin thing now and is desperately hungry for a husband, although she won't admit it.'

'She's sailing to Cape Town? Splendid for Hilary.'

'She's ready to sail,' Emily said hesitantly, 'but she's afraid of going out with the emigrant mob—unattended, as it were.'

'I'll take her!' Richard said with the spontaneity that had gained him the affection of any troops with whom he served in close quarters.

'That's what I had in mind, the moment you spoke. But there are grave dangers . . .'

'Our laddies have the savages whipped into shape. A skirmish now and then, nothing to fear.'

'It wasn't that I was thinking of. Richard, will you go fetch Vera? Right now?'

They sat under the oak trees in the picnic chairs John Constable had used for his paints two years earlier when doing the large canvas showing Salisbury Cathedral in sunlight; as an appreciation for his constant use of this lawn, he had dashed off a wonderful watercolor sketch of the towers, which he had given Emily on his departure; it hung in the main room in a fine oak frame which she had cut and nailed herself.

The Saltwoods of Salisbury had not survived for nearly two centuries, during which people of influence had tried to wrest Captain Nicholas Saltwood's fortune from them, without acquiring certain shrewd skills, one of which was to marry young women of the vicinity who showed ability. Emily Saltwood had been one of the most resilient, mother of four good boys and counselor to all. She had never been afraid to pinpoint inherent dangers, nor was she now.

'How old are you, Richard? Thirty-one?' He nodded. 'And you, Vera? Twenty-nine?' She nodded.

'Then you're old enough to realize that a four-month sail to Cape Town, aboard a small ship, in close confinement . . .'

The couple found it embarrassing to look at her, so she spoke with extra vigor, demanding their attention: 'Inherently dangerous, wouldn't it be?'

'I suppose so,' Richard said.

'Old romances are full of this sort of thing. Tristan and Iseult over in Cornwall. One of the Spanish kings, if I recall, and his brother escorting the bride. Are you listening to what I'm saying?'

Richard placed his hand on his mother's and said, 'I'm taking a little girl I knew at playtime . . . out to marry my brother. When I seek a wife, I'll find one for myself.'

'Those are insulting words,' Vera snapped, and for the first time the two Saltwoods looked at her as an individual and not as a prospective answer to a Saltwood family problem. She was, as Emily said, twenty-nine, tallish, thinnish, not especially beautiful of face, but lovely of voice and smile. Like many young women her age she knew how to play the piano and had taken watercolor instruction from Mr. Constable when he stayed in the village. For the moment she was reticent, but as she grew older she would become much like the woman now counseling her: a strong English wife with a mind of her own.

She had never yet been kissed by any man other than her father, and by him only rarely, but she had no fear of men and had always supposed that when the time came, her parents would find her a husband. She was a girl of spirit and rather looked forward to an interval on the frontier, always supposing that her husband would return to a position of some importance at the cathedral, in whose shadow she had been raised and intended to die.

'I'm fully aware of the dangers,' she told her putative mother-in-law, using a low, calm voice even though she realized that Mrs. Saltwood's questioning reflected on her as much as on her son.

'That's good,' Emily said with an inflection that signified: 'This meeting's over. We understand one another.' But Richard had one thing more to say: 'You must tell Vera where the idea came from that sent you to her house . . . seeking a wife . . . for Hilary, that is.'

Emily laughed vigorously and took the young people's hands in hers. 'Vera, when Richard passed through Cape Town various army friends advised him that Hilary needed a wife. It was Richard who set this all in motion. And now he proposes to complete the transaction.'

'I don't think of myself as a transaction,' Vera said.

'We're all transactions. My husband married me years ago because the Saltwood holdings needed close attention, much more than he needed a wife.'

They rose from their chairs under the oak trees and looked across at the stunning beauty of the cathedral—which some of them might never see again.

The *Alice Grace* was a small commercial barque accustomed to freighting cargo to India but now commissioned to carry some three hundred emigrants to Cape Town, in conditions which would have terrified owners of cattle being shipped across the Channel to France. Her burthen was two hundred and eighty tons, which was significant in that by law she was entitled to carry three passengers for every four tons; this meant that she should have sold passage to no more than two hundred and ten emigrants. Thus, when she left port she was ninety over complement, but since most of the passengers were charity cases, government inspectors smiled and wished her 'Good voyage!'

She departed Southampton on 9 February 1820 on a gray, wintry day when the Channel looked more immense than the ocean, its waves far more menacing. For seven painful days the little craft tossed and pitched in waves that seemed determined to pull her to shreds, and all aboard who had not sailed before were convinced that they must perish. Major Richard Saltwood, retired, who had sailed to and from India, reassured the cabin passengers that once the Bay of Biscay was reached, the passage would settle into a pleasant monotony in which the limited movement of the ship 'would be like a gentle lullaby, no worse.'

Especially pleased to hear this was the woman whose welfare lay in his hands. She did not accept the violent motion of the ship easily, and this irritated her, for she was grimly determined to 'make a brave show of it,' as she had promised her mother she would, and when her stomach was wrenched into convulsions by her sickness, she was ashamed of herself. She was the sole occupant of the cabin next to her brother's, as she called him, but he shared his with a captain going out to join the Gallant Fifty-ninth on the Afghan frontier, so that during the bad days she had two gentlemen to assist her.

Sure enough, when the *Alice Grace* entered the great Bay of Biscay the storms subsided and the gentle, reassuring motion which Saltwood had predicted replaced the tossing. Vera came to like the motion of the ship, as he was certain she would, and for the third and fourth week the three travelers had a congenial time together, with Richard discovering what a sterling person this Vera Lambton was. Her determination was obvious, her sense of humor reassuring. When children were ill, she acted as general nurse, and whenever any of the women passengers in steerage needed attention, she was eager to help. My brother's getting a strong woman, Richard told himself, but because of a reticence which he could not have explained, he did not inform his cabin mate of Vera's destination. 'She's a family friend' was all he'd say. 'Heading out to South Africa.'

'She'd make some chap quite a decent wife,' the captain observed several times, but since he was much younger than Vera, and since his regiment would not allow him to marry till he was thirty, his interest in her could only be that of an observer.

Once Cape Finisterre was passed, that bleak and ominous last outpost of European civilization, the long reach to the bulge of Africa began, and now the three travelers began to be aware of a remarkable young man, a wagon builder by trade, who had more or less assumed command belowdecks. He was an attractive fellow, careful of his appearance even though the ship provided him no water for washing. His curly head and broad grin appeared wherever there was trouble. It was he who organized the teams that handled the slops; he supervised the distribution of food; and he sat as judge's clerk when the rump court belowdecks handed out penalties for such infractions as theft or pummeling another passenger.

'Name's Thomas Carleton,' he told Saltwood and the captain when they asked if he could fix their door, which had come off its hinges during a blow. 'I can fix it, sirs. With wood I can fix anything, it seems.' And as he worked, devising ingenious tools for getting around corners, he told them of his apprenticeship in a small Essex village and his removal to the more important town of Saffron Walden, not far from Cambridge University, which he had once visited.

He was a chatterbox, intensely excited about his prospects for starting a new life in the colonies: 'I can work eighteen hours a day and sleep four. Saffron Walden had prospects for everyone except me, so I kicked up me heels and was off to sea. The town's a fascinating place, you understand. Named by the father of Henry VIII, him with the wives. One of the two places in England entitled to trade in saffron, precious stuff. It makes meat taste better, but in all me days I never took a pinch of it into me mouth. Reserved for rich people.'

Vera, returning to her cabin after a stroll on the minute deck—fifteen steps forward, fifteen back—heard this last observation and interrupted: 'Saffron's a yellow powder, I think, and it's not used for meat. It's used for rice.' She blushed and added, 'Here I am explaining India, and both you men have been associated with it.'

'Not I, not yet,' the captain said gallantly.

'But she's right,' Richard said. 'Saffron is yellow—orange, really—and they do use it a great deal in India. You'll grow to like it.'

'While you're here,' Vera said to the wagon builder, 'could you fix the lock on my box? The workmen threw it aboard, I'm afraid.'

Thomas Carleton left the men's cabin and moved a few paces to Vera's, where, after one quick glance at the portmanteau in which she kept her dresses, he told her that a small piece of wood must be replaced so that the screws holding the hasp could catch. 'It's no problem,' he assured her, 'always providing we can find the wood.' Together they made a quick tour of the deck, finding nothing, but when they went to the 'tween deck, where the ship's carpenter kept his cupboard, they found the piece they needed, and it was so small that the carpenter refused any payment from Vera: 'Take it and be blessed.' He was giving it not to this amiable girl but to the wagon builder, whose good work among the passengers he had noted.

When the box was fixed, Vera thanked the young man, four years her junior, and then talked with him about conditions belowdecks. She was by no means a philanthropist, as those seeking always to do good for others were called in England—those busybodies who were agitating against slavery in Jamaica and child labor in Birmingham—because families like hers in Salisbury were too sensible for that. But she was interested in whatever was occurring on this tedious voyage, and on subsequent days she visited various parts of the ship with Carleton, and one night about half after ten the captain who occupied the bunk closest to the dividing wall in Richard's cabin whispered, 'I say, Saltwood! I think something interesting's going on next door.'

'Mind your business,' Richard said, but any chance of sleep was destroyed, so toward three in the morning, after assuring himself that the captain was asleep, he peered into the night and saw young Thomas Carleton, he of the glib tongue, slipping out of the next-door cabin and down the ladder to his proper place below.

The next weeks, half of March and half of April, were a dismal time for Richard Saltwood; it was apparent that Vera Lambton was entertaining the young man from belowdecks three and four times a week. During the day their behavior was circumspect. They spoke casually if they chanced to meet each other as he pursued his duties, but they betrayed no sign of intimacy. On one very hot day after the Cape Verdes had been passed and the ship was heading sharply southeastward, the ship's captain summoned both Saltwood and the young officer to assist him in a court-martial; the accusing official was young Carleton, who, as an officer in charge of maintaining discipline belowdecks, had brought charges against a pitiful specimen who on four different occasions had been caught stealing.

When the court learned that he had been shipped aboard after a chain of similar offenses in London, there could be only one logical verdict:

'Twelve lashes.' And Thomas Carleton was charged with bringing on deck all the passengers so that they could see for themselves how crime was punished. When all were in place, ship's officers led the convicted on deck, where he was stripped to the waist, tied with his arms about the mast, and lashed with a club from whose end dangled nine cattails of knotted leather. He made no sound till the fifth stroke, then cried pitifully and fainted. The last seven lashes were delivered to an inert body, after which he was sloshed with salt water. There was no more stealing.

The flogging had a sobering effect upon theft belowdecks; some of the passengers were a sorry lot, but most were from the sturdy and moral lower classes, women and men who would engage in no misconduct, and they rebuked those who did. One man, nearing fifty and with two sons, grabbed Carleton's arm as the young man hurried past one afternoon and pulled him into a corner.

'Laddie,' he said bluntly, 'you're treadin' on very dangerous ground.'

'What do you mean, old man?'

'Meddlin' with a lady of quality, that's what I mean.'

'I'm a man of quality,' Thomas said quickly. 'I am as strong—'

'Those men in the cabin next hers, they're officers. They'll shoot you in a minute, laddie.'

'Those men are not involved with the lady, and take your hand down.'

This the older man refused to do. Instead he tightened it, saying, 'Laddie, this is a small ship. If I know, don't you suppose they know?'

For six days the warning deterred young Carleton from visiting Vera, and Richard sighed with relief at having avoided the necessity of intervening where his brother's honor was involved. At night he listened for sounds that would betray an assignation, and was pleased when none came echoing through the thin wall. But on the seventh day he spotted Vera talking intently with the young wagon builder, and that night, about eleven, her door creaked open and someone slipped in.

It was, in many ways, the worst night of Richard Saltwood's life, for the lovers, having been separated for a week, clutched at each other with such passion and noisy delight that the young captain was awakened.

'I say, Saltwood, listen to this! I say, like a pair of goats!'

The noise of love-making could not be masked. There were rumblings of the bulkhead, the squeals of a woman who had waited till her twenty-ninth year for love, and harsh pantings. Without even moving to the captain's bed, Richard could hear the lascivious echoes, and after a long, wild ecstasy in the other room, when the captain said, 'I say, that's prolonged!' confused Richard blurted out, 'And she's going out to marry my brother!'

In Saltwood's room there was silence, broken by the sounds bouncing off the bulkhead, and after a long time the captain asked in barrack-room accents, 'Well, whad'ja goin' to do?'

'What do you mean?' Saltwood asked in the darkness.

'Damnit all, man. Aren't you goin' to shoot him?' And Richard heard the hard clang of a revolver being slammed onto their table.

It was there when daylight came into the cabin, accusing him. He did not shave that morning, nor take any food. The young captain left him severely alone, but at midafternoon he returned, picked up the revolver, and banged it down again: 'Good God, man! It's your duty. Shoot the filthy blighter.' When Richard was unable to respond, the young man said, 'I'll testify. I've heard everything, God knows. If you want to shoot 'em both, I'll testify for that, too.'

But the Saltwoods of Salisbury were not a family that solved problems by shooting. In Parliament, Peter had been challenged to a duel by a foolish city member and had ridiculed the man into retreating. In the wilds of Illinois, young David had refused to gun down an Indian caught trespassing, although his neighbors shot them for much less. And in the South Atlantic, with storms rising as the coast of Africa hove into sight, Richard could not bring himself to shoot a young wagon builder and perhaps the man's mistress as well. Instead he waited till dusk, then told his cabin mate to put away the revolver while he went next door to talk with his sister-in-law, as she had sometimes phrased herself.

'Vera, your behavior's been shameless.'

'What do you mean?' she said, bristling.

'The bulkhead. It's very thin.' She looked at the wall in amazement, tapped upon it and heard nothing. 'We don't make noises, the captain and I,' Richard said. 'We're gentlemen.'

She tapped again, whereupon the captain, lounging in bed, tapped back. It sounded like the explosion of a gun. 'My God!' she said, covering her face.

'Yes. The captain offered me his gun, wanted me to shoot you both.'

This had quite the opposite effect from what he had intended. Vera stiffened, lost any sense of contrition, and faced him boldly. 'I'm in love, Richard. For the first time in my life I know something that you've never known, will probably never know. What it's like to be in love.'

'You're a foolish woman on a lonely ship . . .'

Instead of attempting to defend herself, she laughed. 'Don't you think I know that your poor little Hilary is sadly damaged? That you're desperate to find him a wife . . . to get him back on course? I know that. Everyone knows it.'

'Who told you?'

'Simon Keer. The Reverend Simon Keer. Oh, at the public meetings he extolled your brother. So did your mother. But when I spoke with Keer alone, what do you think he said? That Hilary's a bit of an ass. Those were his words. He said I might be able to do something with him, the LMS certainly wasn't able to.'

'He told you that?'

'What else could he tell me, if I asked him in all honesty?'

'But Keer's the reason . . . He sent Hilary to Africa.'

'What he said was "Some young men, especially from Oxford . . ."'

'Natural envy from a man without an education.'

'". . . some young men from Oxford take religion too seriously. It addles them."'

'But Keer marches up and down England, lecturing about the missions.'

'He does so for a purpose, Richard. He wants to end slavery. Doesn't give a damn about religion . . . in the old sense.'

'What do you mean?'

'And neither do I.'

The blasphemy staggered Saltwood, and he sat down abruptly, whereupon Vera confided in a rush of words that it had been she, not her mother, who was desperate to find a husband. She loathed being a spinster, the afternoon teas, the sober dresses. Hilary, off in Africa, had been a last chance and she had grabbed at him. 'Your mother was so afraid I'd be put off by the long sea voyage.' She laughed nervously. 'I'd have fought my way aboard this ship. It was my last chance.'

Richard had never heard a woman talk this way, had never imagined that a Lambton of Salisbury could. And now the girl was saying, 'The journey's changed everything. You're no longer responsible for me. I'm going to marry Thomas.'

'No minister would—'

'Then we'll marry ourselves. When we reach South Africa he'll go to his land, and I'll go with him.'

'But Hilary will be there. Waiting.'

She did not even reply to that. She laughed in a way that caused her shoulders to shake, after which she took Richard by the arm, pulled him to his feet, and helped him out the door. She would discuss the matter no further, and that night both Richard and the captain could again hear rumbles from the adjoining cabin.

'You goin' to shoot 'em?' the captain asked.

'No! No! Stop such questions.'

'Then I will.' And there had to be a scuffle before Richard could wrest the captain's revolver from him. But this did not deter the violent young man, who felt that somehow his honor, and that of his regiment, had been impugned, for he burst out of his cabin, knocked loudly on the adjoining door, and demanded that Carleton go below 'to your proper quarters, damn you.' When the young wagon builder tried to slip past, the captain swung a mighty blow at his head, knocking him down the ladder.

'I hope he broke his neck,' the officer growled as he returned to bed, and after some painful moments of silence he felt compelled to say, 'Saltwood, I can understand why you had to leave the regiment. You were a disgrace to the uniform.' For two days he refused to speak to his cabin mate, but on the third day, with tears in his eyes, he clasped Saltwood's hand as if they were brothers and said, 'Richard, dear boy, is there any-thing I can do to help?'

'There is,' Saltwood replied in deep gratitude. 'When we stop at Cape Town, have that miserable blighter thrown ashore. I promised Mother I'd deliver this girl to Hilary, and by God, I shall, damaged or not.'

So when the *Alice Grace* put in for replenishing, none of the passengers belowdecks were allowed ashore, for they were docketed to Algoa Bay, three weeks more sailing along the coast. But the young wagon builder who had dared to make love to a lady of quality was thrown onto the wharf, with his axes and angles, while the lady of quality wept for him from the railing.

She was rudely dragged away by Richard, who said with fierce determination, 'You must go on to Hilary. As you promised Mother.' And all the time the *Alice Grace* stayed in Cape Town, she was kept prisoner in her cabin, guarded by the brother-in-law who stood guard outside, relinquishing his position to the captain when sleep was necessary. Even when the governor invited all the captain's guests to a gala, she was not allowed to attend lest she meet with Thomas Carleton and run away.

She remained in her cabin even when the ship resumed its journey, as did everyone else who had one, for a wintry gale blew up, driving the vessel far south, reminding the sailors of Adamastor, the tempestuous giant who guarded the Cape in the time of Vasco da Gama, and of whom Luis de Camoens had written with such brilliance.

Day after day the winds raged, forcing waves so high across the bow of the ship that they flooded cabins. At times the vessel plunged downward in such steep and sickening falls that everyone belowdecks was sent flying in one direction and then another as shrieks and wails competed with the howling winds. Sleep was impossible and food unthinkable; at numerous times, when her wet and lonely cabin shivered as if its bulkhead might splinter, Vera huddled in a corner, fearful of the moment when the voyage would end, terrified of its continuance, but never did she give way to superstition and castigate herself or her actions with Thomas as being in any way the cause of this violent storm. She was glad she had known him, even for just their brief passage through the tropics, and she prayed that in some mysterious way she might meet him again.

Alone, at the heart of a shattering tempest, she changed from being a meek English spinster and became a mature woman with a surprisingly independent mind. She had enjoyed being loved by a strong man and realized that she could never return to the dreamy afternoons of a cathedral town. As for marrying a missionary, that was quite impossible, but what she would do she did not know. Once, as the ship fell sideways in a plunge that could have torn it apart, she clung to her bed to prevent being swept away and cried, 'If we make land, I'm an African.' And she shook her fist in some wild direction, supposing the storm-girt continent to lie in that quarter.

On the seventh day of the storm, when the little barque was well down toward polar waters, passengers began reciting old tales of ships, rudderless and sails gone, being driven relentlessly southward till ice entrapped them, holding them forever in its embrace: 'A graveyard of ships down there, masts erect. Everyone aboard frozen stiff and standing erect till judgment day.' They told also of the Flying Dutchman: 'Captain van der Decken, out of Rotterdam. One of his great-grandsons settled at the Cape years ago. Swore he could round the Cape in a storm like this, swore an oath to do so. He's out there somewhere, still trying to breast the Cape, and will be till the people frozen down there are called to judgment.'

The poor ship was so knocked about that when the storm finally abated and the sun allowed the captain to calculate his position, all were shocked to learn how far south they had been driven; they were indeed on their way to the ice, and now, as they turned north toward Algoa Bay, they were humbled and chastened in spirit, so that even the young captain felt remorse at the way he had wanted to treat the awakened young woman in the cabin next to him, and he knocked on her door to apologize.

'I'm sorry,' he said.

'I'm not,' she replied.

'In the storm,' the captain confided, 'I thought once or twice we must surely sink. And do you know what I thought next?' He smiled at her engagingly, a man much younger than herself, endeavoring to reach understanding. 'I thought how utterly insane I'd been to interfere in your affairs. I wanted to shoot you, you know.'

'I was told.'

'Madam, would you allow me to make amends? I was such an ass. Whom you love makes no difference to others.' And to her astonishment, he fell to one knee, took her hand—and kissed it.

The scene at Algoa Bay in the winter of 1820 was one of historic confusion, confusion because five ships like the *Alice Grace* were trying to unload passengers in the open roadstead without a wharf to aid them, historic because a whole new type of person was coming ashore to add a new dimension to South African life.

The confusion was monumental, both in the bay and ashore. Captains endeavored to anchor their ships as securely as possible, but wind and tide tossed them vigorously, so that anyone trying to debark was in peril. Long ropes were led ashore through the water; they would be used to haul the boats to the beach. Women and children, of which there were aplenty, were crowded into the rude boats and taken ashore through the surf. Occasionally a boat broke loose to wander off, passengers screaming, until some stout-hearted swimmer came to rescue it.

Some women, having come seven thousand miles to their destination, flatly refused to debark, trusting neither the frail boats nor the men guiding them, but bellowed orders from the ship's officers usually forced them loose from the railings to which they clung; a few had to be dropped bodily into the tossing boats, and these ran the risk of broken limbs. Some daring children, unable to wait any longer to reach the paradise about which they had been constantly told, leaped gaily into the water as the lighters neared the beach, gasped and spat and spluttered toward shore, screaming their delight. Their mothers watched anxiously till they were lifted out of the water and onto the shoulders of men who would carry them through the surf. Among those who helped the immigrants to safety were some Xhosa who only a year before had flung themselves against Grahamstown.

Ashore the confusion worsened: 'The party from Manchester, over here! Liverpool, over there! Glaswegians, stay by that dune. Please, please! The Cardiff people must come over here to the big man with the top hat!' Dashing from one end of the beach to the other, instructing everyone what to do, was Colonel Cuyler of Albany, New York, now in charge of a much more pleasant task. But even here the energetic man encountered troubles, for the government had appointed him to instruct the immigrants in harsh facts overlooked in England when the glories of South Africa were being extolled: 'This is not yet a land of milk and honey. It's a land of guns. Never, never go into your fields without your muskets.'

In addition to the scrambling immigrants, the shore was cluttered with Boer farmers who had driven in, from sixty and seventy miles away, in heavy wagons pulled by fourteen or sixteen or twenty oxen, and these men forced hard bargains with the newcomers, offering to cart them and their possessions to their new homes for outrageous prices. But what alternative did the immigrants have? So day after day wagons were loaded, whips were cracked, and teams of stolid oxen began the long journey to the new paradise.

In the waiting crowd ashore was Reverend Hilary Saltwood, come to greet his bride. He was still extraordinarily thin and visibly entering middle age, for he was thirty-five and showed the effects of his hard life. He was certainly not an attractive bridegroom, and few women would have sailed so far to claim him, but when his present duties ended and he could be got back to England for some fattening up, and settled in some quaint rural parish, he might prove acceptable. The outstanding thing in his favor was the gleam that suffused his face: it was the countenance of a man who believed in what he was doing and found constant reassurance in the honesty of his calling. He loved people; his expedition to Grahamstown with the commando had taught him even to love the Boers who opposed him so vigorously, and the fact that he had fought well against the Xhosa warriors had earned him respect, so that the ox wagon that waited to take his bride to Golan Mission had been volunteered by Tjaart van Doorn himself.

There the two men waited amidst the wild confusion: the tall dark-suited missionary so ill-at-ease; the short, squared-off Boer with the heavy beard; the sixteen lumbering oxen indifferent to the whole affair. 'Dear God!' Hilary cried. 'It's Richard!' And he ran to the beach to embrace his brother coming wet and dripping out of the waves.

'Where's the lady?' Hilary asked in some apprehension, forgetting to introduce Van Doorn, who stood nearby, testing his hippopotamus-hide whip.

'She'll be coming,' Richard said. 'Who's this?'

'Oh, this is my neighbor, Tjaart van Doorn.'

'You live at the mission?'

'Thirty miles north.'

Richard blinked. Neighbors at thirty miles? But then he heard a shout from the *Alice Grace*'s lighter. It was the captain, with Vera Lambton beside him: 'Richard! Ho, Saltwood! Here comes the bride!'

His cry was so hearty, and the message so warm in this scene of new lives beginning, that everyone in the vicinity stopped work to watch the arrival of Miss Lambton, who looked quite pretty in her rough traveling clothes. Three cheers went up as the lighter was slowly pulled ashore, strong hands grasping the rope and guiding it to the beach.

Ashore, men quickly learned that she was the intended of Reverend Saltwood, and cheers were raised in his behalf. Even Tjaart van Doorn, moved by the spectacle of a wife arriving in such manner, relaxed and clapped the minister on the back: 'Exciting, eh?' And he moved forward to help bring his neighbor's betrothed ashore.

In the boat Vera sat rigid, her eyes down; she did not want to scan the shore lest she see the missionary she had been sent to marry. She did not want him, her heart lay elsewhere, and she doubted she could ever mask that fact; but the fierce rejection she had voiced during the storm had subsided, and now, faced with the prospect of making her way alone in a strange continent, she supposed that she must accept him: God forgive me for what I am about to do.

At the last moment she looked up, and what she saw banished all her fears—and although she endangered herself, she stood up in the boat, waved both hands, and screamed, 'Thomas!'

Thomas Carleton, wagon builder of Saffron Walden, had galloped at breakneck speed across the flats, across the mountains and the long reaches, to intercept the boat, and there he stood, arms outstretched, to greet his love. Disdaining the hands that waited to lead her onto dry land, Vera leaped into the shallow water, lifted her skirts, and ran through the waves, throwing her arms wide to embrace the one man she could ever love. She was twenty-nine, he twenty-five; she was educated in Bible, painting and music, he in wood-handling; but they were joyously committed to living in South Africa the rest of their lives. They were the English settlers of 1820.

Vera's arrival in this dramatic manner dominated the attention of everyone, even Richard Saltwood, who stood aghast as he watched her. Reverend Hilary was left standing alone, off with the oxen and the waiting wagon that would never carry his bride to the mission. Gradually people on the shore became aware of him, and turned to look at the forlorn figure, and as they did so, they broke into laughter. Harsh words were thrown, and ribald ones, and he stood apart, allowing them to fall over him like a cascade of icy water. He sought condolence from no one, nor did he try in any way to dissuade Miss Lambton from her extraordinary behavior. He could not guess what had precipitated it, but he was sure it must have been an emotion of powerful force, and certainly it was God's will that she should go with the other and not with him.

He did not demur when Tjaart came back and asked apologetically, 'Since I'm here, I'll cart the couple to their new home . . . if it's all right with you?'

'That's what you should do,' and when Richard, having assembled his own gear, said that he, too, must find a carter and be on his way, Hilary nodded. In the end, all the immigrants found transportation of some kind or other and were off to try raising wheat and mealies on land that could scarcely grow weeds; the government had not been entirely honest with these settlers, neither in Cape Town nor in London. They were not supposed to be farmers and merchants in the old sense; they were to form forward hedgehogs of self-defense along the border, keeping the Xhosa away from the established farms farther inland. Vera and Thomas, in their frontier home, were supposed to take the brunt of any Xhosa attack, so that established settlements like Grahamstown could exist in safety.

Hilary, who understood this conniving strategy, was saddened to see his intended bride and his brother heading eastward into such a situation, and as he stood alone he prayed for them, that God would give them strength for the trials that lay ahead. That done, he watched their wagons disappear, then mounted his horse and rode slowly back to Golan Mission.

He would never forget 1820. For him it was a year of tragedy, with both the Boer and the English communities sneering at him, not even conceding that he was a well-intentioned dominee. His mission was characterized as a farce where blacks could escape honest work; his attempts at agriculture were pitiful; and his constant insistence that Hottentot and Xhosa be given fair treatment was seen as weakness of character. The Boers de-

spised him for his antagonism to coerced labor, the backbone of their existence, while the English dismissed him as socially unacceptable.

His position worsened whenever Dr. Keer, in London, issued a new
publication or caused an inquiry to be made in Parliament. The little agitator was finding that his diatribes against the Boers were popular with the
English press and his passkey to the highest ranks of English society. He
wrote and preached and lectured, uttering the most inflammatory accusations against the Boers, but whenever he thundered from the safety of
London, the lightning struck Hilary Saltwood in his exposed mission, and
there was serious talk among the farmers of burning the place.

He seemed sublimely indifferent to the ostracism and to the threats.
He maintained a kind of Christian charity at his mission, accepting all
who stumbled in, finding them clothes and food in unlikely quarters. He
kept the converts working, more or less, and spent much time with the
choir, believing that a soul that sang was closer to God than one that
brooded in silence, and many travelers of that period wrote amusingly of
coming to Golan and hearing at evening prayers a glorious choir singing
old English hymns, all faces dark except that of the missionary, which
stood a good foot higher than the others. The writers always implied that
Saltwood was out of place, but that was not accurate. He belonged with
these people.

It may have been that God devised this loneliness, when all white men
scorned him, so that his attention could be focused on the future of South
Africa; at any rate, one night as he lay sleepless he was vouchsafed a vision of such crystal purity that in the morning he had to share it with his
parishioners. He spoke in a mélange of English, Dutch, Portuguese and
Xhosa:

'With the coming of our English cousins, and in such numbers, we
can see that this land can henceforth never be of one unit. It must
always be broken into fragments, many different people, many
different languages. We stand this morning, in 1821, like a river
moving along the crest of a ridge. Sooner or later it must come down
one side or other, and how it comes will make all the difference in
this land. Let us pray that it will come tumbling joyously down as a
cascade of love and brotherhood, in which Hottentot and Xhosa and
Englishman and Boer share the work and the rewards. Golan Mission must no longer be for blacks alone. We must open our hearts to
all people, our school to all children. [Here he frowned.] I cannot
believe that our great river of humanity will go rushing down the
wrong side of the mountain, creating a hateful society in which men
of different colors, languages and religions will go their separate
ways in bitter little streams, each off to itself. For we are all brothers
in God and He intended that we work and live together.'

Among his listeners that morning, when he shared his vision of a new South Africa, were many who could not comprehend what he was talking about; common sense told them that white men who had wagons and guns and many horses were intended to rule and to have lesser people work for them. But there were a few who understood that what the missionary was saying was true, not at this moment perhaps, but in the long reach of a man's whole life, or perhaps within the lives of his grandchildren.

Among this latter group was the gifted soprano Emma, whose family had escaped slavery through Hilary's charity, or rather his mother's, for she had sent the funds which purchased their release. Emma was now twenty-one, smallish in size, and her face was as jet-black as ever, her teeth even and white. She had a wonderfully placid disposition, worked well with children, and guided the mission whenever Saltwood had to be absent.

For some time she had been thinking of Golan's future, and because she was a Madagascan and not a Xhosa, she was able to see more clearly than some. She found the Xhosa in general a superior people, and could name a dozen ways in which they excelled: 'Baas, they could be as good farmers or hunters as any Boer.'

'Never, never call me Baas again,' Hilary admonished, 'I am your friend, not your baas.'

She was aware, of course, that Hilary had gone to Algoa Bay to fetch a wife, and speedy rumors had reached even Golan, describing the hilarious scene in which he had stood on the shore, arms open to receive his woman, while she ran right past him to embrace another. Emma, better than most, appreciated the agony this sensitive man must have known then, and upon his return she had discharged most of the managerial duties until he had time to absorb his disgrace, and bury it.

Emma, with no last name, understood the subtle process by which Saltwood had sublimated his personal grief and found, in doing so, his vision of South Africa as a whole, and she supposed that no one would ever understand this country, in which she, like Hilary, was a stranger, until he had experienced some sense of tragedy. She supposed also that once he expressed his vision, he would see its impossibility and would shortly thereafter leave the area and return to England, which must lie very far away.

So she was surprised one day, and perhaps pleased, when he said, 'I shall stay here the rest of my life. I'm needed for the building.'

She believed him, and knowing this, moved closer to him, for it was apparent that no man as fragile as he could survive without strong assistance, and she further observed that he was held in such scorn by the two white communities that there was little possibility that he could ever find a wife in those quarters.

She was, in some respects, even more solidly informed than Saltwood himself and exercised a sounder judgment, and this had been true when she was ten and realized that her life depended upon escaping from slavery at De Kraal. Her parents had been afraid; the other slaves, all of them, had been terrified of consequences; but she had fled into the night without horse or guide and had made her way to freedom. Now it was she who saw that Hilary must have a partner, and she perceived this on the simplest base: that he could not survive without one.

Reverend Saltwood, after his vision and his willingness to commit his life to it, was thinking along much different lines. He felt that God had brought him to Golan for some specific and perhaps noble purpose, and he was sure that it was God who had vouchsafed him the vision; in this respect he was much like Lodevicus the Hammer, except that Lodevicus had known that God had visited him personally.

Therefore, if he had been chosen for some exalted design, it was obligatory that he conform to the inherent patterns of that design—and what were they? That all men in South Africa were brothers, that all were equal in the sight of God and that all had just rights, none standing higher than another. He recognized that there were managerial degrees, and he was certainly no revolutionary; in the Missionary Society, for example, he stood on the very lowest rung of the hierarchy, and in his humility he suspected that he deserved little more. In Cape Town lived officials who gave him orders, and in London lived other officials who sent orders to South Africa, and above all, stood the little group of powerful thinkers like Simon Keer who directed everything. He was quite satisfied with the abstract structure, but he was somewhat troubled by the fact that everyone in the chain of command was white, as if this were a prerequisite for power. At Golan he had delegated command and it had worked rather well.

He had turned the mission choir over to Emma, and it was she who had trained the voices into a beautiful instrument, not he. He had found that in his absences Emma had run the establishment at least as well as he, and perhaps better. She certainly was as good a Christian, having braved true hardships in forging her allegiance to Jesus, and she was kind and humble in dealing with Boers when they came to complain about their runaways. 'Humble, but firm,' he wrote in one report, 'she displays the true sense of Christ's teaching. If she is required to face down some arrogant Boer screaming for the return of his Hottentots, she stands there, a little figure in a gingham dress, hands on hips, defying them to desecrate the house of the Lord. One man thrashed her with his whip, but she would not move, and in some confusion he rode away.'

Another line of thought was pushing its way into Saltwood's reflections, and he would have been astonished if its historic parallel had been pointed out to him, but like many men from superior cultures who are placed in association with large numbers of persons of inferior mechanical culture, he was beginning to think that salvation lay in rejecting the inherited superior culture and marrying some simple woman from the less advantaged, and in so doing, establishing connection with the soil, with the elementary. Thus, at this very time in Russia young men of the ruling class were coming to believe that they must marry serfs to attain contact with the real Russia, and in France writers and philosophers contemplated marriage to fallen women, so that together they might start from a solid base, as it were, and climb to new understandings. In Brazil gruff Portuguese planters defiantly married blacks: 'To hell with Lisbon. This is my life henceforth.' And in India certain mystic-driven young Englishmen were thinking that to understand the land to which they were now committed, they must take Indian wives.

There was a sense of self-flagellation in all this, and many observers were amused by it, but there was also a sense of primordial experience, of identification with a new land, and of deep-rooted psychological suspicions that in a flowering culture marked by too many books and far too many parties, something fundamental was being lost. When religion, with its example of Jesus Christ's abnegation, was thrown into the scales, there built up a solid impulse toward actions that would never otherwise have been contemplated, and one bright morning when life at Golan Mission was as placid as it would ever be, Reverend Hilary Saltwood entered upon three days of prayer and fasting.

He was thirty-six now, and as far in promotions as he would ever go. He was aware that his mother still fondly imagined him coming home to the deanship at Salisbury, but he knew that lustrous prize was lost forever; indeed, he sometimes doubted that he could even secure some inconspicuous English living. He suspected also that his term at Golan had better be ended; he had built so well that any new man from London could take charge. But his productive life was by no means finished; he felt an urgent call to the north, where many lived in ignorance of Jesus, and he envisioned his life as spent in one lonely outpost after another. But to live like that he needed a companion.

He remembered how excited he had been when his mother wrote that she was sending him a wife. How often he had read that letter, how carefully he had studied his mother's description of Miss Lambton, visualizing her working with him in outpost stations. In his loneliness he would sometimes recall every item of her dress as she came through the surf that day in Algoa Bay. 'I need a wife to share the veld,' he cried aloud.

But what wife? Dare he ever again enlist his mother in a search? He thought not. Could he ride over to Grahamstown to see if it contained any eligible women, new widows, perhaps, among the immigrants? Not likely. There they would laugh at him and jeer, and no woman would want to share that humiliation. Should he return to Cape Town? Never. Never. His life was on the frontier with the black people he loved.

Loved! Did he love Emma, his marvelous little assistant with the laughing eyes? He believed he did, but he wondered whether God would approve of such a union.

His thinking thus far had required one full day; he spent the next two in trying to ascertain whether a man totally devoted to Jesus Christ dared risk such a marriage, and just as the Boers searched the Old Testament for guidance in their time of tribulation, so he took down the New Testament and tried to decipher the teachings of Jesus and St. Paul, and the old familiar phrases leaped and tumbled in contradiction through his mind: 'It is better to marry than to burn . . . He that is unmarried careth for the things of the Lord . . . Husbands, love your wives . . . It is good for a man not to touch a woman . . . So ought men to love their wives as their own bodies,' and St. Paul's specific command to celibacy: 'I say therefore to the unmarried, "It is good for them if they abide even as I."'

It was a confusing doctrine, generated in a time when people were living in agitated communities much like the South Africa of 1821, and a searcher could find Biblical justification for either marrying or not marrying, but in the end one incident in the New Testament superseded all others: when a poor couple in Cana were being married without enough money to provide wine for their guests, Jesus stepped forward and converted water into wine so that the celebration could proceed. Laughter possessed Hilary when he thought of it: I've always liked that miracle best of all. A celebration. A blessing. And at the end the governor himself saying, 'At most parties they serve good wine at the beginning, rubbish as soon as the guests are drunk. But you've brought us the best wine at the end. Stout fellow!' I believe that Jesus and his disciples must have danced at this wedding.

He spent the third night praying, and in the morning he went to Emma and said, 'Jesus Himself would dance at our wedding. Will you have me?'

They were married quietly by Saul, who now served as deacon at the mission—this tall white man, this short black woman. They shared a wattled hut beside the church, and since no announcements were broadcast, news of the extraordinary marriage did not circulate.

It certainly did not reach Grahamstown, seventy-five miles to the east, where Richard Saltwood had found himself a saucy bride, Julie, the Dorset girl who had ridden her own horse to Plymouth to take passage on one of the last emigrant ships. Alone and unprotected, she lacked the funds to hire a sixteen-oxen wagon to freight her to Grahamstown, so she had walked, bringing with her barely more than the clothes on her back. Within a week six men had wanted to marry her, and in her flirtatious way she had chosen Richard. She could not read, but when he explained that one day he would take her back to the cathedral town of Salisbury, she said brightly, 'Then, by God, I better learn,' and she had sought out Mrs. Carleton to teach her, and the two women, so unlike in breeding, so similar in courage, had a fine time wrestling with the alphabet.

When Richard proposed that he send for his brother to conduct the wedding, Julie cried, 'Capital! It'll give us a chance to introduce him to the town.'

So a servant was sent west on horseback to invite Hilary to perform the ceremony, and the invitation seemed so sincere and the opportunity to establish connections with the new settlement so favorable that the missionary accepted. He would take Emma with him so that the Grahamstown people could witness the depth of his conviction that a new era was beginning in the colony.

Hilary, Emma, Saul and the servant made the eastward journey, with Bible reading each evening, prayers each dawn, and much conversation about Richard and his experiences in India. Hilary, having found great happiness in his own marriage, speculated on what kind of bride his brother was taking, and in his prayers repeatedly asked God to bless Richard.

As the quartet rode into Grahamstown, Hilary pointed out the little houses that had seemed like secure fortresses that day when he faced the screaming Xhosa, and he showed Emma the site on which Tjaart van Doorn had saved his life.

As they rode down the principal street they came to the spacious parade ground where a small church stood on land which would be occupied later by a fine cathedral, and another of Richard's Hottentot servants hailed the procession to say that Baas was at the shop of Carleton, the wagon builder, so the horses were turned in that direction while the slave hurried on ahead, shouting, 'De Reverend kom! Look, he kom!' And to the door of the rude shed in which Carleton worked came his wife, his friend Richard Saltwood and lively Julie, the intended bride. All four looked up at the horsemen and saw Hilary sitting high among them.

'Hullo, Hilary,' Richard said with the casualness that had always marked his behavior toward his brother. 'Glad you could come.'

'Hello, Richard. I hear God has blessed you with a bride. He has blessed me, too. This is my wife, Emma.'

From her horse the petite Madagascan smiled warmly at the two women, then nodded to their men. She remembered them later as four gaping mouths: 'They were astounded, Hilary. Didn't you see them, four mouths wide open?'

No one spoke. Emma, with a deep sense of propriety, felt that it was not her duty to do so first, since she was being presented to them, but they were too dumbstruck even to speak to Hilary, let alone his extraordinary wife. Finally the missionary said, 'We'd better dismount,' and he extended his hand to his wife.

The story sped through Grahamstown: 'That damned fool Saltwood's married a Xhosa bitch.'

It was an agonizing three days. No one knew where to put Emma, or how to feed her, or what to say to her. They were surprised to learn that she could speak good English and write much better than Julie. She was modest, of good deportment, but very black. There was no way to alleviate the awfulness of her reality, no explanation that could soften the dreadful fact that a decent Englishman, although a missionary, had married one of his Xhosa Kaffirs. When it was pointed out that she was really a Madagascan, one man said, 'Know the place well. The bastards ate my uncle.' And now a rumor circulated that Emma had been a cannibal.

Richard quietly insisted that the marriage proceed as planned, with his brother officiating, and the temporary church was crowded, most of the spectators having come to see the cannibal. It was a moving ceremony, filled with the soaring phrases of the Church of England wedding ritual, perhaps the most loving in the civilized world.

> 'Dearly beloved, we are gathered together here in the sight of God, and in the face of this company, to join together this Man and this Woman in holy Matrimony; which is an honourable state, instituted of God in the time of man's innocency . . . which holy estate Christ adorned and beautified with his presence, and first miracle that he wrought in Cana of Galilee . . . Wilt thou love her, comfort her, honour, and keep her in sickness and in health . . . so long as ye both shall live . . . forsaking all others . . . for better for worse, for richer for poorer, in sickness and in health, to love and to cherish, till death us do part . . .'

When Hilary intoned these mighty words, standing tall and gaunt, like someone St. Paul might have ordained in Ephesus, he gave them special meaning, for it seemed to him that he was solemnizing not only his brother's marriage but his own, and when he came to the cry, ' "O Lord save thy servant and thy handmaid!" ' he felt that he was asking blessing upon himself, and some of the congregation suspected this and looked with horrid fascination at Emma, wondering if she could qualify as a handmaiden whose fate concerned God.

The highlight of the ceremony came with the singing of Psalm Sixty-seven, required by The Book of Common Prayer, for then little Emma, who stood facing the crowded church, let her voice soar as she did at the mission, and other singers stopped to listen:

> 'O let the nations rejoice and be glad: for thou shalt judge the folk righteously, and govern the nations upon earth.'

The congregants heard the song but not the words.

On the return trip Hilary said, 'It was a dreadful mistake to have come. They saw nothing. They understood nothing.'

'What did you think when you met Vera?'

'It was strange. I'd never seen her, you know. Not really. I moved forward. She moved back. And I thought, "How lucky I was not to have married her."'

'You never had the chance,' Emma said.

'I'm convinced God took care of that. He had you in mind.'

'I liked Thomas very much,' she said. 'He'll do well in this country. We need wagons.'

'You and I need one, particularly.'

'Why?'

'Because we've got to move north. We're not wanted here any longer.'

So when they reached Golan and satisfied themselves that Saul could maintain the mission with Hottentot and Xhosa deacons until some young clergyman arrived from England, they started packing in earnest. They acquired a small wagon and sixteen oxen, a tent of sorts and some wooden boxes for their goods. With this meager equipment they set forth.

They headed northwest for a destination unknown, one man, one woman traversing barren lands that held no water, moving into canyons where desperadoes might be lurking, and crossing lands often ravaged by wandering bands of Hottentot and Bushmen outlaws. They had no fear, because they carried almost nothing of value that could be taken from them, and if they were to be slain, it would be in God's service. They were traveling to take His word into a new land, and they would maintain their steady progress for fifty days. Alone, walking slowly beside their oxen, they went into lands that no white man had ever penetrated before.

In later decades much would be made of treks conducted by large groups of Boers armed with guns, and these would indeed be remarkable adventures, but equally so were the unspectacular movements of solitary English missionaries as they probed the wilderness, these lonely harbingers of civilization.

By accident, and surely not by design, the Saltwoods came at last into that bleak northern country which had provided refuge to the slaves Jango and Deborah, who had fled here with their children. The land was now occupied by a few Bushmen, a few Hottentots who led a vagrant life after their last herds had been bartered away, quite a few runaway slaves from various parts of the world, and a scattering of ill-defined ne'er-do-wells and outcasts. In the veins of these fugitives there was Dutch blood aplenty, German, too, from settlers and sailors off ships, and not a little contributed by English officers on their way home from India and freed during their Cape Town leaves from the confines of British respectability. There was every color, from the purest black to the fairest white, the last being provided by the new missionary, Hilary Saltwood of Oxford.

He had settled on land in the northern part of the Great Karroo, that rolling semi-desert which occupied so much of the country. It was a thirstland whose treeless expanse frightened most people but enchanted those who found refuge here. The Saltwoods built their meager hartebeest hut close to a meandering stream, which went dry much of the year. When it was finished, they surrounded it with a thicket of protective thorn, exactly as Australopithecus had done five million years earlier.

The site would have seemed quite miserable, except for the cluster of five hills, each separated from all the others, perfectly round at the base, handsomely leveled off at the top. Their beauty lay in their symmetry, their classic purity of form; from a distance they resembled five judges huddling for an opinion, but from within their circles—say at the entrance to the missionaries' hut—they became protective sentinels guarding the Karroo from the vast herds of animals that wandered by and from the titanic storms that swept across it. When a man elected to serve God at this forsaken spot, he had the presence of God with him at all times.

One traveler, standing at the door to Saltwood's hut, avowed that he could 'see north to portals of heaven and west to the gates of hell without spotting a human being.' He was, of course, wrong. In various nooks and secret places families had their huts. Behind the flat-topped hills there were whole villages whose residents hunted small animals for their hides, great ones for their ivory tusks. Others traded to the north, crossing the Karroo to where substantial numbers of people congregated. And others, with remarkable diligence, actually farmed the area—one hundred and fifty acres to feed one sheep—and found it profitable. One man mended wagons for customers as far distant as a hundred miles.

But everyone in the Karroo shared in one miracle, and joyously. When spring rains came to this arid land, usually in early November, the rolling plains exploded with flowers, millions of them in a sweeping carpet of many hues. It seemed as if nature had hidden here her leftover colors, waiting for the proper moment to splash them upon the world. In one of his sermons Hilary Saltwood said, 'The stars in heaven, the flowers on the Karroo, they're God's reminder that He stays with us.'

His duties were many. It was he who marked with ritual the passages of life: to christen, to marry, to bury. He served as arbitrator in family brawling. He taught school. His wife was general nurse to the scattered community. Messages were left at his rectory, the hut by the water pan, and he counseled with all who sought advice on anything. He helped at brandings, attended slaughterings in the hope that he might come home with a leg of something. And he participated in extended hunts when food was needed. He was a vicar of the veld.

But most of all he conducted services, in the open, beside the stream, with the five hills looking down. He read from the New Testament, lingering on its revolutionary messages of social justice, equality and brotherhood. In simple terms, devoid of cant, he talked with his people about new fashions of living in which all men would share responsibility, and he bore constant testimony to the fact that black and white could live together in harmony:

> 'That the white man is temporarily in a position of command because of his gun, his horse and his wagon is as nothing in the eyes of the Lord, or in the passage of history. How brief is the life of man. A hundred years from now it may be the black man who will be in a position of authority, and how little that too will matter in the eyes of the Lord. White man up, black man up, the perpetual problems remain. Where do I get my food to eat? How do I pay my taxes? Am I safe at night when I go to sleep? Can my children learn the lessons they need? It is answers to those questions that we seek, and it matters not who is powerful and who weak, because in the great rolling away of history, all things change but the fundamentals.'

Whenever he spoke like this on Sunday morning, he spent Sunday afternoon wondering about the education of his own children. He and Emma now had three dark-skinned rascals, with their father's height and their mother's flashing white teeth. They were bright children, masters of the alphabet at five and their numbers at six. With others in the area, they studied with Emma and took their catechism from Hilary; some of these children were instrumental in bringing their parents to the mission, encouraging them to go through the motions of worship, and all participated when Reverend Saltwood organized a picnic with games and songs and food.

Then the young ones, twenty or thirty of them, of every shade, would venture outside the five hills and play on land that reached forever. A dozen kinds of antelope would watch from a distance, and sometimes lions would move close to listen and then to roar with chilling thunder.

Adults always sought permission to join these safaris, and sometimes it seemed as if they enjoyed the outings more than their children, especially when great flocks of ostrich loped past or when boys found a settlement of meerkats. Then there was joy indeed as everyone gathered to watch the furry little animals scamper to their burrows, stand upright to see who was watching, and duck swiftly below ground. 'Meerkats are like people,' Emma told the children, 'they must run around, but they're happiest when they go back into their homes.'

Hilary could find in the Bible no precedent for a picnic, and he sometimes wondered if he was sponsoring a pagan ritual. There was no instance in which Jesus had participated in such a gathering, but the missionary felt sure that the Master would have approved this glowing combination of fellowship in watching the meerkats and reverence in singing the hymns that followed. And one night he asked Emma, 'Isn't it possible that the miracle of the loaves and fishes should be considered a picnic? Or when He asked that the children be allowed to come to Him. Maybe the Cana wedding guests assembled on the side of some hill in Galilee.'

Such days imparted a happiness that Hilary had never known before. His wife was a woman of infinite richness; her children were a joy; the tattered people who comprised his congregation loved his curious manners and forgave his intrusions into their spiritual lives; and the great, barren land, once one became accustomed to it, provided a congenial home. Best of all, there were no Boers and Englishmen contesting for power, no social stigma because this man was white, that woman black.

And then the relative peace was broken by Dr. Simon Keer, thundering back to South Africa to collect incidents to be used in another book. He was in his fifties now, at the apex of his political power and a furious fighter for causes worthy of his support. He had recently assumed leadership of the philanthropic movement, as it was now called, and had learned how to excite huge crowds in London and Paris with his fiery oratory and dramatic examples of Boer misconduct. His first book, *The Truth About South Africa*, had run its course, and he felt he could best inflame opinion by producing a sequel showing that the horrors of Dutch occupancy at the Cape still persisted, even though Englishmen of higher moral standards held the reins of government. A supporter had given him a generous loan to fund this trip, counting upon Dr. Keer's sensationalism to cover the investment.

In short, the volcanic little man had found in the philanthropic movement his golden Ophir, and he was coming back to South Africa to increase his treasure.

Wherever he went he caused turmoil, lecturing the locals about morality, threatening them with the laws his friends in Parliament were about to pass, and accusing the Boer farmers of crimes that would have been rejected even by the Black Circuit of 1812. Always he made the confrontation one between the honest Englishmen of the empire and the dishonest Boers of the backveld, and when one man who had seen the real horrors of slavery in the English islands of the Caribbean said in public meeting, 'Don't come preaching to us. Clean up your own islands,' he silenced the man with the thundering response: 'Your observation is irrelevant.'

When rumors circulated that two Boers had tried to assassinate him at Swellendam, his audiences increased in size, as did his fury; he was certainly not without courage, for he took his message to all parts of the colony, and in due course he convoked at Grahamstown a meeting of all LMS personnel, and when messengers had ridden to the outposts, a strange, ungainly group of men and women began to straggle in. They were the forward agents of God, an impassioned, dedicated, unlikely lot made old before their time by the bleak conditions under which they lived, but intensified in their beliefs by the problems they had succeeded in solving.

Strangest of all the couples were the Saltwoods of Great Karroo, he walking in long strides, staff in hand, his black wife riding a small horse. They had come three hundred miles, their eyes ablaze at the prospect of meeting the leaders of their calling. When they entered the thriving mercantile center the first sign they saw was THOMAS CARLETON, WAGON BUILDER. It was a real building now, with stone walls, tiled roof; in fact, it was two buildings, one the foundry and carpenter's shop, the other a sturdy house.

'We must halt here,' Hilary said, anxious to try to heal any wounds that might still exist between him and the man who had stolen his bride. 'Hello, Thomas!' he called, and when the builder appeared at the door of his forge, Hilary was astonished to see how the years that had handled him so roughly had scarcely touched this bright-faced young man.

'I'm Saltwood,' Hilary said hesitantly.

'Why, so it is! Vera, come here!' And from the house beside the shop came the former Miss Lambton of Salisbury, now a matron with two blond children. No longer the timid spinster studying watercolors, she was now in her mid-thirties, mistress of a house and keeper of accounts for her husband's thriving business.

'Good morning, Hilary,' she said graciously. Then, with a mischievousness she could never have disclosed back in Wiltshire, she teased: 'You're the reason I sailed so far.'

'Are these your children?'

'They are.'

'I have three now,' he said quietly.

'We haven't stopped, you know,' Carleton said, putting his arm about his wife.

'Has my brother any little ones?'

'Like all of us. He has one.'

During this colloquy Emma had remained on her horse, quietly to the rear, and now Vera cried warmly, 'Here is your wife!'

'It is. Emma, as you know.'

The wagon builder helped her alight, took her by both hands, and asked, 'Didn't you tell us you're a Madagascan?'

'I did.'

'How in the world did you get down here?'

'I was born here,' she said in the slow, beautiful English she had acquired from her Oxford-educated husband. 'But my parents were . . . How do you say it, Hilary?'

'Kidnapped.'

'They were kidnapped by Portuguese slavers. It was quite common. Still is, I think.'

'Little woman like you, three children!' Carleton shook his head and returned to his work.

In the days prior to Dr. Keer's arrival, the Karroo couple participated in many friendly meetings like this, for the indignation caused by their marriage had abated. Grahamstown was now a typical rural English settlement with a thriving marketplace to which many Boer wagons came. They were heartily welcomed, not only for their trade but also because of the commandos they provided whenever untamed Kaffirs from across the Fish River attacked.

Hilary overheard one tough English farmer joking with a Boer: 'After we were here eighteen months, and the Kaffirs had attacked us once and you Boers five times, our minister said on Sunday, "See how the heathen restrain themselves in the face of God! They always prefer to raid the Boers." And a man in the back of the church cried, "It isn't God, Dominee. It's cattle. We don't have any and the Boers do!"'

Hilary was particularly pleased to renew acquaintance with his brother Richard, whose exuberant wife Julie had undergone a transformation somewhat similar to Vera Lambton's, except that whereas the latter had descended from the role of Salisbury elite, Julie had climbed the ladder from Dorset illiterate to solid gentlewoman, wife of a former major in the Fifty-ninth. She found no difficulty in accepting Emma Saltwood as her sister-in-law, partly because everyone knew that Emma would be returning to the Karroo as soon as the convening ended, and could thus pose no problem with her miscegenation, but partly also because of Christian charity. Julie saw that Emma was a remarkable woman and no doubt a fine mother, and as such she merited acceptance.

The trouble came with Dr. Keer, for when he dismounted, tired and hungry after the long ride from Golan, he gasped when he saw Hilary, and thought: Dear God, this man's ten years younger than me, and look at him! To reach Keer's hand, Hilary had to stoop, which made him appear even older and more haggard than he was; in missionary work a man on the frontier aged much more rapidly than an official back in London. And when Keer realized that the little black woman trailing behind must be the Kaffir his informants had spoken of, he almost gagged: It's another case of a man's taking his missionary work too personally.

In private discussions with the people of Grahamstown he spoke with some force against the awful error of a missionary's marrying a woman of any tribe with which he worked: 'It's a fatal mistake, really. Look at poor Saltwood. How can he ever return to England? I need an assistant. Work does pile up. Parliament and all that, you know. But could I ask him to help me? With a wife like that, how could he solicit funds from important families?'

One night, at a small gathering, he asked Richard Saltwood directly, 'My dear boy, how did you ever allow this to happen to your brother?' and

Richard replied with amusement, 'I think you'd better ask Mrs. Carleton
over there. You and she were responsible, you know.'

'Me? Carleton? Never met the man. What's he do?'

'He builds wagons. It's his wife you know.'

'Can't believe it,' Keer said, but when he was led across the room to
where Vera stood, she reminded him that they had met in Salisbury when
she was still Miss Lambton. 'Of course, of course! When I was giving my
lecture on slavery.' He coughed modestly. 'I visit the entire country, you
know. Becomes very tiring.' He was rambling on so that he might have
time to collect his thoughts, and suddenly he remembered: 'But you were
to marry Hilary Saltwood!' He stopped, then added in a pejorative way,
'But I hear you've married the carpenter.'

It fell to Vera Carleton to puncture this little man's balloon, and with
the quiet assurance she had gained from doing hard manual work to aid
her husband, she said, 'Yes, I did marry the carpenter. Because after your
lecture that night I took you aside and asked for your personal opinion,
and you confided that Hilary Saltwood was rather a silly ass. Which I
confirmed later, so I thank you for your good advice.'

Dr. Keer was nonplused at the direction this conversation was going,
but Vera forged ahead, her voice rising: 'So on the ship coming out I decided not to marry Hilary. I sought out Thomas Carleton, the wagon
builder, I asked him to sleep with me, and then to marry me. So I am dou-
bly indebted to you, Doctor.'

When Keer retreated several steps, she followed him. 'And I am indebted in a third way. For when I see what a great fool you are, and what
a man of nobility Hilary Saltwood is by comparison, I realize that you
aren't fit to tie his boots, or my husband's, or, for that matter, mine. Now
you scamper back to London before the Boers hang you.'

She was still fuming when she reached home: 'It was awful, Thomas,
that little prig. I suppose you'll have to apologize tomorrow, but Hilary really is Christ-like, and Keer's so stupid he wouldn't recognize Jesus if that
carpenter walked in here tonight.' Then she laughed. 'Didn't you see the
way Keer patronized you? And me? He seems to forget that a carpenter
was once important in this world, and may be so again.'

Angered by Keer's open abuse of one of his missionaries, Vera was inspired to move closer to Emma Saltwood, and when the two had tea together, or when they walked with Julie Saltwood, there developed a kind
of frontier solidarity which was possible among these pioneer women who
had come long distances to a strange land and who had conquered it in
limited ways. No one of the three had escaped battles—ten-year-old Emma
running away from De Kraal, Vera battling the physical and emotional
storms south of the Cape, wild Julie riding a horse to Plymouth to escape
stupid parents and more stupid brothers—and each had won through to
the reassuring plateau of strong husband and lively children.

Common experience allowed them to be friends, but this could happen only in their generation. Already forces were at work which would drive them forever apart, and in the second generation companionship like this would be unthinkable. Then a woman of good heritage from a cathedral town would not care to associate with a runaway illiterate from Dorset, and neither would dare invite into her home a Kaffir, whether married to a white missionary or not.

The cruel wedge that would separate people was driven deeper by everything that Dr. Keer did or said during his convention. In public meetings he excoriated the Boers, making any future relationship between Boer and missionary impossible. In private he continued to ridicule Saltwood for having taken a Kaffir wife; on this subject he did make one important observation: 'What Hilary's done, the silly fool, is place a weapon in the hands of our adversaries. Critics accuse us of being nigger-lovers—kaffir-boeties, the Boers call us—and when one of our own people makes such a disastrous marriage, it proves that everything they said against us is true. It sets missionary work back fifty years.' In general, he spoke and acted as if the welfare of the world depended upon his conciliating the better families of England so that they would bring pressure on Parliament to pass the laws he wanted.

His damage to the Hilary Saltwoods was mortal. As head of the LMS, he dictated that Hilary was to be kept in seclusion on the farthest veld, and at the final reception, when it seemed that he had done as much damage as an intruder could, he delivered his ultimate insult.

He was standing in a reception line, bestowing grace upon the locals, when the wagon builder Carleton and his sharp-tongued wife approached. Since apologies had been made, he was able to nod austerely, as he would to anyone in trade, but then he saw Hilary Saltwood, who had lacked the common sense to leave his Kaffir wife at home. She trailed along behind him, and when she reached Dr. Keer she held out her hand, intending to bid him safe journey home, but he found an excuse to turn away so that he would not have to acknowledge her. She kept her hand extended for just a moment, then—without showing any disappointment—dropped it, smiled, and passed on.

The wagons that arrived to carry Dr. Keer back to the Cape brought a parcel of mail from London, including a letter from Sir Peter Saltwood, M.P., Old Sarum, advising Richard that their mother was failing. Sir Peter was providing passage which would enable Richard to sail immediately, and it was hoped that he would bring his wife, whom the Salisbury Saltwoods were eager to meet.

This was quite impossible, for after a shaky start, the Richard Saltwoods had now developed a good business in trading ivory, and it was imperative that he journey to the eastern frontiers to buy such tusks as he could from the Kaffirs, but it occurred to him and Julie that since the

Hilary Saltwoods were in town, they should go. Much argument was advanced, with Emma pleading that she must return to her children, but as Hilary said, 'Those children love to stay in the veld.' So a messenger was posted north with news that the Saltwoods were extending their absence for a year or two.

In their innocence, they supposed it to be what essentially it was, the visit of a son to his aging mother, the presentation of a wife at the ancestral home. Just as Emma had been untouched by Reverend Keer's refusal to take her hand, so she and Hilary would be unmoved by either acceptance or non-acceptance. And it never occurred to them that in places like Cape Town, London and Salisbury they would encounter open hostility. Raised eyebrows, yes. Amused chatter, yes. Even the repugnance which the Boer farmer felt toward an Englishman who had taken a Kaffir wife, they expected some of that, too. But they had lived so amiably together that they felt certain there could be no cruel surprises.

They were wrong. Even while their wagon traveled slowly westward toward the Cape, curious people clustered to see the long-legged missionary who had taken the short Kaffir wife, and there were many giggles. At some houses where transients customarily slept, they were not welcomed, and occasionally they encountered real difficulty in finding quarters. At Swellendam they were a surprise; at Stellenbosch, a scandal.

When they were safely across the flats and entering Cape Town, they assumed that there they would escape the unkind curiosity, but again they were mistaken. Dr. Keer had spoken rather harshly of his stupid outcasts in the Karroo, and many people went out of their way to see them, not as missionaries, but as freaks. They spent a trying time before their ship arrived, but once aboard it, their real troubles began. Four families of some distinction, returning home from India, refused to be seated in the same salon as the blackamoor, so Hilary and his wife had to take their meals apart. They were not welcomed on deck, nor were they included in any of the ship's activities. On Sundays church services were held without the participation of a clergyman, since none but Hilary was aboard, and he was not invited to preach, for his presence would be offensive to the better families.

The ostracism worried him not at all. As he told his wife, 'We're in an age of change, and it's going to take time.' That it would require two hundred years or more would have stunned him, for he moved about the ship unconcerned with the present, assured that the future would see a better balance between the races. With anyone who would speak with him, he talked quietly of mission life, explained the various regions of South Africa, and shared his vision of the future:

'In India you'll have every problem we have. How can a few white Englishmen continue to govern huge numbers of people who aren't? In a hundred years situations will be quite different from what they are now. I see the same happening in Java with the Dutch, or in Brazil with the Portuguese. In New Zealand and Australia, I'm told, the problem is somewhat different, because there the white man forms the majority, but he's still got to rule decently or he'll lose out. Like it or not, we must devise systems of government to meet unforeseen conditions, and I for one am convinced it must be done on a basis of Christ's brotherhood.'

He was so persuasive in his quiet way that toward the end of the voyage certain passengers approached the captain and said that they would like to recommend Reverend Saltwood as minister for one of the last Sundays, but this was dismissed abruptly: 'Passengers wouldn't hear of it.' To which the men replied, 'We're passengers, and we think the others would accept.' The appeal was denied.

However, little Emma had been active among the children, telling them outrageous accounts of lions and leopards, of hippos in the river and rhinos crashing through the forest. Strangely, what interested the children most was her depiction of the Karroo:

'Think of a land as flat as this deck. Here, here and here, what do we have? Little hills, round at the bottom, flat on top, never touching. Scores of them. And from these hills one morning comes a blesbok. You want to see what a blesbok looks like? [Here she took some blacking and transformed a boy's face into the white-and-black glory of the blesbok.] So here comes our blesbok. And then another. And another. You're all blesboks, so get in line. And then another and another, until the world is full of blesboks. Marching in line. As far as you can see, faces like this. That's where I live.'

When Blesbok number one returned to his parents, they wanted to know what in the world had happened to him, and he said, 'I'm a blesbok, on the Great Karroo.' This started inquiries, and several parents discovered that Mrs. Saltwood had been entertaining their children for some time, and when they discussed this with their boys and girls, they found further that she had become something of an idol: 'She can sing, and make games with string, and she tells us about ostriches and meerkats.'

So now certain women joined their husbands in an appeal to the captain, but he was adamant against allowing Saltwood to conduct services, on the very good grounds that whereas a few families may have come to accept the missionary, those that really counted were still set against it; he knew from past experience that to irritate the rabble signified nothing, but to infringe in the slightest upon the prejudices of the ruling families meant that letters would be written to management and black marks cast. He'd have none of that on his ship.

On the second to last Sunday those families who still wanted to hear

Reverend Saltwood preach arranged an alfresco worship on the afterdeck, and to it came most of the children, hoping to hear the missionary's wife tell one of her stories about ostriches, or perhaps even to sing. She did the latter. When her husband called for one of the Church of England hymns, and there was no organ to set the tune, her voice rose in unwavering volume, a beautiful voice that seemed to fill that part of the ship. Then her husband spoke briefly of Christ's mission in Africa. He raised no difficult points, ruffled no sensibilities, and when the service ended with another hymn, many of the families congratulated him on an excellent performance. 'We're so glad you sailed with us,' one man said at the exact moment when the captain, in something of a rage, demanded to know who had authorized the service on the afterdeck.

'It just happened,' a junior officer said.

'Don't let it happen again,' the captain said. Several passengers had already protested that such a service was a mockery, since the real service was being held in the salon.

At Salisbury there was confusion. Emily had expected her son Richard to appear; she was not prepared for Hilary, and certainly not for his black wife. Had she wanted them to come, she would have sent for them, but when they arrived she simply could not behave poorly. She was glad to see Hilary again, even though he did look older than she, and she was respectful of his choice of a wife.

In the second week she confided to her friend Mrs. Lambton: 'Thank God, I behaved myself. That Emma's a treasure.'

'Can you stomach the blackness?'

'I'm happy if my son's happy. You must feel the same way about Vera, married to the wagon builder. Emma tells me your daughter is quite content, with two—or was it three?—lovely children.'

'To tell you frankly, Emily, long ago, before you talked with me, I dreamed that about this time Vera would be coming back to Salisbury with Hilary—that he'd be taking up his duties at the cathedral . . .' Suddenly she burst into uncontrollable tears, and after they were stanched she said bitterly, 'Damn! Damn! How dreadfully wrong things happen. How can you stand having that blackamoor in your house?'

Emily wanted to weep, too, not for the black woman in her house, but for her son David, lost God knows where in Indiana, for Richard with his illiterate stable girl, and most of all for Hilary, that sad, mixed-up man about whose head such ugly rumors flew.

'You know what they're saying in London?' Mrs. Lambton said after her sniffles were brought under control. 'Dr. Keer himself said to a small gathering . . . Our Cousin Alice was there and heard him. He says that poor Hilary is an outcast, that he's made a perfect ass of himself, with English and Dutch alike.'

'I suppose it's true,' Emily said. 'But I wonder if it matters. In God's eyes, I mean. The other day I received a letter from London. Someone who'd been on the ship with Hilary. They said his sermon on the voyage was like Christ Himself walking among men and restating His principles. He said he thought I'd like to know.'

At this Mrs. Lambton dissolved completely, and after a series of racking sobs, mumbled, 'I had so wanted them to marry. Vera could have saved your son, Emily. She'd have made him strong and proper. He'd have been dean over there, mark my words. He'd have been dean.'

'The rest of the letter,' Emily continued, 'said that Hilary had been denied use of the proper chapel aboard ship. The salon, I think they call it. He had to preach in the open. I think Jesus often preached in the open. I don't think even Vera could have gained permission for my son to preach inside. I think he was ordained to—' Against her will she broke into fearful sobs: He was so gaunt. He looked so sickly. The house they lived in on the desert, it sounded like a peat-gatherer's hut. He looked so very tired. And his poor wife had to make all the decisions.

With an unexpected thrust of her hand, she took hold of Mrs. Lambton's arm and cried, 'Laura, why do these things happen? I'll never see Richard or David again in this life. You'll never see Vera or the children. We sit here like two old spiders in a web, with the flies far, far away. Karroo! Karroo! Who gives a damn about Karroo? Or Indiana, either? Life is here, and we've let it slip away. We have a cathedral, the loveliest in England, but the choristers have fled. I feel such grief for that poor black woman in my garden. Laura, I could die of grief.'

Things improved not at all when Sir Peter came down from Parliament, well aware of what an embarrassment Hilary's visit was causing. Several London newspapers had run cartoons showing an elongated missionary accompanied by his fat dwarfish wife with bare breast and grass tutu, entitled 'The Bishop and His Hottentot Venus' or other amusing jests, and the ridicule was beginning to have wide effect. Lady Janice was both mortified and apprehensive, fearing that it would be hurtful to the good work her husband was trying to accomplish, and she came to Salisbury intending to take stern measures and insist that her brother-in-law and his wife leave immediately.

But when Sir Peter saw his younger brother and was reminded of that emotional moment at Old Sarum when he had invited his brothers always to come back to Sentinels, he relaxed, and pleaded with his wife to do the same, so although he could not express any warmth over this reunion, he did extend courtesies. Even Lady Janice was reasonably decent to her black sister-in-law.

In long discussions on the benches under the oak trees, Sir Peter sought guidance from his brother as to how England ought to conduct itself in this new colony: 'You know, Hilary, that I'm rather the leader in the House on these matters. Yes, government's given me free rein to work something out. Close touch with the Colonial Office, and all that. And you create such a different impression from what Simon Keer's been telling me that I wonder if we shouldn't call him down here for some serious consultation.'

'That would be capital,' Hilary said, not the least vengeful over Keer's treatment of him at Grahamstown. So the fiery leader of the Africa philanthropists was sent for, and in the meantime Emma Saltwood was exploring Salisbury. Each morning she helped serve breakfast, then donned a little white cap, took an umbrella, more as a stick for walking than for rain, and crossed over the Roman bridge into the village, where she spoke softly with anyone who wished to ask her about Africa and nodded deferentially to those who did not. She frequented all the shops, marveling at their intricacies, purchasing one small gift after another for her children.

Her reception was uneven. Women of good family who enthusiastically supported Dr. Keer's philanthropic movement loved the blacks in Africa, which they proved by their generous contributions, but were uneasy when a specific black took residence in their village and looked askance when Emma passed their way. It was the clerks in the shops and the housewives marketing who came to regard the missionary's wife as one of themselves, greeting her warmly when they met. They began to talk with her about lions and mealies and meerkats and the tanning of hides. But mostly they marveled at her clear voice when she sang at services, and one man who knew music said, 'I cannot believe so much voice can emit from such a small frame.' He asked if she would sing for him in his study, and there, with the assistance of two pupils, he tested the range and power of her voice. She liked the experiment, took deep breaths, and sang a chain of wonderful notes.

Now cartoons appeared entitled 'The Hottentot Nightingale,' and she was asked to sing at various affairs and even to travel to Winchester to sing in the cathedral there. Always she maintained her smile, her willingness to work and talk with others. England at this period had an insatiable interest in her colonies and the strange peoples they contained, and many persons like Emma had been imported to serve as nine-day wonders, but only a few reached the provinces. In Wiltshire, Emma Saltwood was a sensation.

Therefore, when Dr. Keer arrived in town he could no longer ignore the little Hottentot, as everyone called her. Remembering that she was Sir Peter's sister-in-law, he had to treat her decently, and insofar as he could unbend to an inferior, he did.

Hilary, who could bear no animosity toward anyone, was actually pleased to see the dynamic little agitator, although, as he told Emma, 'He doesn't seem so little now. Success and moving with important people have made him taller.'

'It's a game with him,' Emma said shrewdly. 'The pieces on the board are no longer plain checkers. Now they're knights and parliaments.'

'But don't forget. It was this man who taught me to love Jesus,' Hilary said.

'Don't you forget!' Emma laughed. 'He taught me, too. He was like thunder and lightning.'

They speculated on what could have caused the profound change, and reached no conclusion, but when the three men sat beside the River Avon, admiring the swans that moved through the rippled reflections of the cathedral, Hilary was willing to concede that Keer was motivated by one ambition: to end slavery. Everything else was secondary; he had moved from the veld onto a world stage: 'The pressing task no longer concerns the Cape Colony. It focuses solely on Parliament. We must pass the anti-slavery measure. We must force the colonial secretary to issue the ordinances I've drafted. We must press forward, always forward.' It was obvious that he had little concern with Boers, Kaffirs or Englishmen as human beings, but only with a rationalized system, and confessed this: 'In the government of nations the time often comes when the establishment of a principle ensures freedom for centuries to come. We're at such a marking point.'

'You don't agree?' Sir Peter asked his brother.

'Oh, but I do. Dr. Keer's right. We are at a turning point. But I believe it involves specific human beings and not abstract principles. Peter, in whatever you do, you must ask how this will affect the Boer farmer, for he is white South Africa. And how it will affect the Xhosa—'

'You mean the Kaffirs?'

'I never use that word. They're individual tribesmen. The Xhosa, the Pondo, the Tembu, the Fingo, the Zizi. And one day they'll be Africa. So be careful what you do to them. And finally you ought to ask yourself, "How will this affect the Englishman?" Because I assume we'll govern the place for generations to come, and we must do so with justice.'

'Can't we protect both Dr. Keer's general interest and your specific ones?'

'I'm afraid not. I think that when governments regulate in general, they stifle the individual, and then he festers and grows revolutionary and upsets everything. Start with individual justice and you'll guide the general.'

'Quite wrong,' Keer said with some force. 'Unless the principles are laid down, nothing good can follow.'

Sir Peter addressed his brother: 'How about the abolition of slavery? Surely Dr. Keer is right on that.'

'Indeed, indeed,' Hilary said, twisting his long, thin legs in knots as he tried unsuccessfully to make his point. 'What I mean is, the abolition must be done without infuriating the white. Otherwise we've accomplished nothing.'

'With a stroke of the pen we accomplish everything,' Keer said, his voice assuming the messianic glory he adopted when addressing church groups.

Hilary, twisting his legs into even tighter knots, began to laugh. 'Peter, you've never known a Boer, and, Simon, you've forgotten. Let me tell you about my neighbor Tjaart van Doorn. Built square like a corncrib. No neck. Big whiskers down the side of his face. Wears a belt and suspenders, and shoes he makes himself. Controls maybe sixteen thousand acres and lives in a fort. How many slaves? Half a dozen?'

'What's your point?'

'South Africa is filled with Tjaart van Doorns, and one day his white ox runs away. He goes after it, brings it back, and puts it to work. No punishment. No swearing. Two days later the ox runs off again. Again Tjaart goes after him. Same thing. I was there, baptizing a baby, and I saw him. Not a harsh word. So next day the white ox runs away a third time, and this time I go with Tjaart to help surround the beast, and when I get a rope around its neck, Tjaart comes up, blue in the face, and with a mighty roar he hits the ox between the eyes with a huge club. The ox drops dead, and Tjaart says to the fallen body, "By damn! That'll teach you."'

The two listeners said nothing, and before either could respond, Emma appeared with glasses of a drink she and Emily Saltwood had made: cold cider with honey and a dusting of cinnamon.

'Point I'm making, Peter, is that if the laws you pass goad the Boers, they'll listen once and accept what they don't like, and they'll listen twice. But I assure you, if you come at them a third time, they'll grab that club and bash you between the eyes.'

Very carefully Simon Keer delivered his next observation: 'What it comes down to—it appears to me—are we ruling South Africa, or are the Boers, from whom we took the colony some years ago and whom we have cosseted outrageously?'

With equal calm Hilary said, 'We did not take it from them. We took it from their supine government in Europe. They're still there, every one of them, and increasing by the year.' Then he became urgent: 'But more important are the Xhosa, the Pondo, the Tembu and the Fingo. They've always been there, and they always will. They're also increasing, and we must act to keep everyone on balance.'

'Can this be done?' Sir Peter asked, and before there could be a reply to a question that permitted no reply, Emma came rushing across the lawn, and when she reached the oak trees she gasped, 'Hilary! It's Mrs. Saltwood. I think she's dead.'

In the aftermath of the funeral Mrs. Lambton said, in the presence of the two Saltwood boys and their wives, 'Hilary, get back to Africa. You should be forever ashamed of yourself. You killed your mother.'

'Now wait!' Sir Peter said.

'She sat with me day after day, weeping. Once she broke into wild laughter and said, "The fault's all mine. I bought that black girl for him. Yes, I sent him the money and he bought himself a wife."'

'Now, Mrs. Lambton,' Sir Peter interrupted, but she had scorn for him, too: 'If you'd had any love for your mother, you'd have thrown this pair out—'

'Mrs. Lambton, just last week my mother told me that it was God's providence that sent Hilary home, and not Richard. We didn't want Hilary to come. We were embarrassed when he did. But as we lived with him—and these were my mother's words . . .'

He broke down. All he could do was grasp his wife's hand and nod to her, indicating that she must continue.

Lady Janice said, 'There was a reconciliation. Among all of us.' She reached for Emma's hand, welcoming her at last to Sentinels. But at the door Mrs. Lambton cried, 'You killed your mother. Go back. Go back.'

It could never be determined who murdered the two missionaries. Before dawn one morning in 1828, when Hilary was only forty-three but looked sixty, distant herders saw fire at the hut, and when they reached it they found the two Saltwoods with their throats cut and all their possessions gone.

Fire consumed the place, so that gathering clues proved impossible. Speculation centered on six groups of suspects: Bushmen who liked to creep into such settlements and steal cattle, but none of the mission cattle were gone; Hottentots who rebelled against authority, but the local Hottentots loved the Saltwoods, who had no servants; Kaffirs who were quick with their assegais, but the Kaffirs in the area were mission hands who knew only peace; Boers who despised most missionaries, but the only Boers in the area lived sixty miles away and they rather liked Saltwood; Englishmen who hated the Saltwoods for besmirching the good reputation of the LMS through their miscegenation, but there were none in the area; and wandering Singhalese thieves off some ship, but the nearest harbor was seven hundred miles away. Perhaps society in the abstract had finished with them.

They had fallen victims to that terrible affliction which brings certain crucifixion: they took religion too seriously; they trusted Jesus Christ; they believed that the bright, soaring promises of the New Testament could be used as a basis for government; and they followed these precepts unfalteringly in the one part of the world where they would cause offense to three powerful groups of people: the old Boers, the new English, the timeless blacks.

In one of his most perceptive sermons Hilary had told his mission: 'The perpetual problem of government remains, "Am I safe at night when

I go to sleep?" ' Like many others asleep in South Africa, he had not been safe.

It was an act of God, many alleged, that the three Saltwood children were absent when assassins struck. They were trekking in the Great Karroo with a Hottentot family, gathering ostrich plumes for sale in Paris. When they returned, their parents were already buried, and there was heated discussion as to what should happen to them. Some said they should be freighted down to Grahamstown on the next wagon heading south, but word was received that they were not wanted there. So there was some talk of sending them along to LMS headquarters in Cape Town, but they already had a flood of Coloured orphans and abandoned children. It would be quite improper to ship them off to England, where their ancestry would damn them.

Put simply, there was no place for them. No one felt any responsibility for the offspring of what from the start had been a disastrous marriage. So the children were left with the Hottentots with whom they had hunted ostrich plumes.

For a few years they would be special, for the older ones could read and write, but as time passed and the necessity for marriage arrived, they would slide imperceptibly into that amorphous, undigestible mass of people called Coloured.

VII. Mfecane

THE boy Nxumalo, like his distant ancestor, the Nxumalo who left the lake for Great Zimbabwe, had been reared to believe that what his chief said was law, no matter how contradictory or arbitrary. 'If the chief speaks, you leap!' his father told him, and the boy extended this sensible rule to all who gave orders. He was born to obey and trained to do so instantly.

One bright, sunny day in 1799, when he was eleven, he learned the real meaning of obedience. It would be an especially bitter lesson, since it came about because his father, an energetic man who loved the bursting flowers of spring, felt such a surge of joy that he could not keep from whistling whenever he walked through the fields near the kraal.

The sound of Ndela's happiness reached the ears of a suspicious woman who had concealed herself next to the footpath. A gnarled hunchback, she was the most powerful diviner in the region, a woman who held in her hands the balance of good and evil, of life and death. Now satisfaction spread across her face, for the spirits who lived in darkness had finally given her a sign. 'Ndela whistled!' she cackled to herself. 'Ndela whistled!' At last she knew why sickness lay like a cloak of winter mist over the herds of the Sixolobo. She was ready to act.

That afternoon the entire Sixolobo clan was summoned to the chief's place and the exciting word was passed: 'The diviner is going to smell out the wizard who has infected our cattle.'

Ndela arrived with no reason to suspect that he might be connected with the sick animals, but even so, when the divination began he behaved with his usual circumspection, because there was always the possibility that it was in his body that the evil forces hid without his knowing it.

A divination was a fearful experience. The old woman's body was smeared with a loathsome mixture of animal fats; her arms and parts of her face were streaked with a whitish clay; her hair was rubbed with red powder; and about her neck hung strings of roots and bones. Animal bladders dangled from her waist and in her hand she carried a weapon of dreadful power: a switch of wildebeest tail. About her shoulders, obscuring her hump, was draped a cloak of black material, while strips of animal skin were fastened to various parts of her body.

'I bring words, my people,' she intoned in solemn accents. 'I have dreamed these many nights and I have seen the evil that attacks our cattle. I have walked in darkness and Lord-of-the-Sky has made all things known.'

She began to dance, her bare feet slapping the earth, and when her pace had increased to leaps and bounds, the onlookers sang to give her encouragement, for they knew that she was reaching out for the spirits of the clan's ancestors. There was not one in the audience who doubted a life after death; they were also convinced that spirits who had gained more than the normal wisdom of the earth guided the destinies of the clan through the being of the diviner. Words that fell from her mouth were not hers, but the wishes and judgments of their forebears; they must be obeyed.

Suddenly she stopped dancing to take from a gourd at her side a pinch of snuff. When this caused a paroxysm of sneezing, the onlookers applauded, for they knew that spirits of the dead dwelt deep within the body of the living, and any tempestuous sneeze released their powers. Now came a hysterical screech of laughter, following which the diviner slowly and dramatically sank to the earth. Squatting, she took the cloak from her shoulders and placed it over her knees so that it cast a shadow before her. Opening a skin bag, she exhaled into it a pungent odor of the herbs she had been chewing and then removed from it the charms which would encourage the spirits to identify the contaminating wizard. For each item she laid before her she chanted words of praise:

> 'Oh, Claw of Great Leopard
>   slayer of the weak . . .
> In my hand, Little Rock,
>   trembler of the stream of sorrow . . .
> Fly to me, Talon of Hawk,
>   watcher of all from above . . .
> Hear my voice, Flower of Night,
>   keeper of eternal darkness . . .'

With a flourish she threw the items on the ground in front of her, swaying above them. Keeping her head downcast for a long time, she muttered and moaned, then pointed with her left forefinger at one grisly treasure and another. All were silent, for the terrible moment was at hand. Finally she rose and walked boldly toward the chief, and many gasped, for it seemed that she was about to accuse him.

'They have given me the answer, my Chief!'

'What did they show?'

'A great black beast with a hundred legs and a hundred eyes and the mightiest of horns. And it was revered by my chief, for it was the fattest animal in the land, because in it dwelt all those that had gone before. But this great beast was grieved. At a time when your cattle are ailing, one of those men out there'—and here she pointed generally at the silent crowd—'one of them, at this time of sorrow, did not lament. One of them was happy that the animals are sick.'

'Who was that one, Mother-with-Eyes-That-See-Everything?'

'The one who sings like a bird has brought this evil.'

When the diviner had said these fatal words, Nxumalo remembered immediately that his father sometimes 'sang like a bird' with his whistling, and he had a terrifying premonition that Ndela might be the man carrying the evil spirit that caused the cattle sickness. He watched with horror as the diviner began to stalk among the people, her wildebeest switch dangling loosely at her side. Whenever her eyes met those of another, the one under scrutiny would shake with fear, then breathe again as she passed on.

But when she reached Ndela, the whistler, she leaped high in the air, screaming and gesticulating, and when she came down, the switch was pointing directly at him. 'Him!' she shrieked. 'The happy one! The ravager of cattle!'

A cry rose from the crowd, and those nearest Ndela moved away. The great hump beneath the animal skins on the diviner's back was accented as she twisted about to address the chief: 'Here is the wizard, the one who has brought the evil.'

Briefly the chief consulted with his councillors, and when they nodded, four warriors seized Ndela and dragged him forward. 'Did you whistle?' the chief asked.

'I did.'

'While my cattle were dying?'

'Yes.'

'Did you have this dark evil in your heart?'

'I must have had it.' It was impossible for Ndela to doubt that he was guilty, for if the spirits of the clan had advised the diviner that he was the guilty one, it must be so.

'Why did you do it, knowing it was wrong?'

'So many flowers. The birds were singing.'

'So you sang too, while my cattle were dying?' Ndela had no explanation, so the chief growled, 'Isn't that true?'

'Yes, my Chief.'

'Then let there be judgment.' As he turned to consult his councillors, the men of the kraals moved closer while the women and children drew back.

'Ndela,' intoned the chief, 'the ones who came before have pointed to you as the wizard.'

'Praise them!' cried the crowd, paying deference to the spirits that guarded this clan.

'What shall be done with him?'

'Death to the wizard!' cried the men, the women ululating their assent. So the chief delivered the sentence: 'Let the lips that whistled, whistle no more. Let the tongue that pushed air, push no more. Let the ears that heard birds, hear no more. Let the eyes that were made drunk by the flowers, see no more. Let the wizard die.'

As soon as the words were out, the four warriors grabbed Ndela and rushed him toward the stout poles encircling the kraal, where the cattle languished. The screaming victim was hoisted up, his legs pulled apart, and with one downward thrust, impaled so that the sharp pole entered deep into his body.

Nxumalo, watching this without uttering a sound, wanted to run to the hideous scarecrow figure to mumble a farewell to his singing, loving father who had been so good to him, but any show of sympathy for a wizard was forbidden. Later, the corpse, the pole and even the ground at its base would be burned, and the ashes thrown into the swiftest river so that nothing might remain.

Nxumalo could bear no resentment against the chief or the diviner, for they had merely carried out the customs of the clan. No one in the audience that day could have questioned the fairness of the judgment: the spirits had advised the diviner; she had exposed the guilty man; and he had been executed in the traditional manner.

Hundreds of intricate rules governed a Sixolobo from birth till death, and beyond. Unquestionably the spirits of past members of the clan existed; unquestionably there was a Lord-of-the-Sky who had placed all men on earth. No phase of life could be without regulation: a man's hut must bear a certain relation to the chief's; women must move only in certain areas; a child must watch carefully his attitude toward elders; a man must observe formalities when approaching a stranger's kraal; and the treatment of cattle was minutely supervised. For any infringement of any of the rules, there was instant punishment, and death was obligatory for some fifty or sixty offenses, about the same number as applied in Europe at this time.

Deeply ingrained in a boy like Nxumalo were the beliefs that differentiated good and evil; these were notions which had come down from his earliest ancestors in Africa, observed by the Nxumalo of Great Zimbabwe, and brought by his descendants southward. These rules could be as petty as where cooking utensils were to be placed at night, or as grave as an accusation of wizardry, for which death by impaling was prescribed.

Nxumalo conceded that his father had been possessed by an evil spirit; he understood how Ndela could confess to a crime of which he had no knowledge; and he fully agreed that his father must die.

He had observed that the chief never killed for sport, or whimsically, nor did he exact cruel punishment or torture; he did only what tradition dictated must be done. He was a good man, burdened with duties and responsible for the lives of his thousand followers.

There existed, in this paradise tucked in between the mountains and the sea, some two hundred clans, many smaller than the Sixolobo, some larger, and the chief had to behave according to his status: imperious to the smaller clans, obsequious to those with more cattle, and most careful with any group that might raid the Sixolobo. Whatever decisions he made must be for the security of the clan, and chiefs before him had learned that even the slightest infringement of law had best be dealt with immediately.

The diviner was subsidiary to the chief, but as the earthly communicant with spirits, she wielded immense power and at moments of crisis might even overrule the chief. But the majority of her days were spent treating cuts and bruises, or relieving headaches, or brewing concoctions to ensure the birth of a son. But if a wizard crept into the tribe, spreading evil, she must seek him out, and then medicines were of no avail: that wizard must be impaled and burned.

Nxumalo understood all this and felt no bitterness, but since he was a bright lad he understood one thing more: that when a boy's father had been executed, the boy lived under a shadow. It was quite probable that one day the diviner would come for him. He had not the slightest idea as to what it would be that he would do wrong, but experience warned him that the son of a man who had been impaled ran a strong chance of repeating that prolonged death.

Caught in a conflict between obedience and self-preservation, he solved it in this manner: If I stay with the Sixolobo, I must do what the chief says, and I shall, but here the dark spirits are against me. So I shall run to a new tribe where I can start afresh, and give my allegiance to its king. He told no one of his decision, not even his mother, and before the moon showed midnight he was moving swiftly through the glorious valleys which led to the tribes of the south. To the west rose the forbidding peaks reaching eleven thousand feet into the sky, to the east swept the waters of the ocean.

He did not know where he was running to, but he was certain that there would be a welcome for a sturdy lad who showed promise of becoming a good warrior. But he wanted his new home to be at a safe distance from the Sixolobo, because he knew that if they ever found him fighting against them, he would receive a much harsher punishment than his father had suffered. Traitors were punished with four bamboo skewers.

He was headed for a river whose fame he had always known, the Umfolozi, which drained some of the most handsome land in Africa, tumbling out of the great mountains and running almost eastward to the sea. It marked a division between the tribes of the north and those to the south. It was not a massive river; few of the rivers of southern Africa compared to the great waterways of Europe or America, but it brought richness to all who lived along it, for its fields yielded good crops and its banks were crowded with animals of all description.

When moist and heavy winds blowing in from the south warned Nxumalo that he was approaching water, he concluded that he had come to the legendary Umfolozi, and he began to look for kraals to which he might report his presence, but there were none, and for two nights he patrolled the land well back from the river; on the third morning he came upon a group of nine boys his own age, naked like him and herding cattle.

With trepidation, but also a determination to protect himself regardless of what the boys attempted, he warily picked his way among the rocks guarding the pasture where the cattle grazed, and from a fair distance, prepared to announce himself. But at this moment the herders launched into a cruel game of throwing one of their younger companions into the center of a circle, while they kept a tough round tuber the size of a ball away from him, tripping him as he lunged for them and kicking him when he fell.

'Little penis!' they screamed at him. 'Little penis! Can't do anything!'

The boy in the center was himself not little; he was quite handsomely proportioned in all but his genitals, and probably able to handle any one of his eight tormentors taken alone; but when the entire group conspired against him, shouting words that wounded, he could only stand them off in a kind of blind rage.

His fury gave him added strength, and the incessant jibes about his penis drove him to extraordinary efforts; at one point he leaped high in the air, almost intercepted the ball, and did succeed in driving it off course and over the fingertips of his enemies. He, seeing its flight, was able to break through the circle of bullies and leap for it before any of them could change direction.

The ball rolled directly to Nxumalo's feet, and when the abused lad reached it he found a stranger handing it to him. In this way Nxumalo, a voluntary outcast from the Sixolobo, met Shaka, an involuntary exile among the Langeni.

With Nxumalo as his ally and ready to defend him, Shaka, a twelve-year-old, moody, difficult boy, received less tormenting. True, the entire Langeni clan continued to make fun of his undersized penis, and there was no way this particular abuse could be halted, but whenever rough play was involved, the newcomer and the moody one formed a resilient companionship. Yet, strangely, they were not friends, for Shaka would admit no one to that privileged position.

Yet he must have someone to talk with, and one night, his voice bursting with pride, he told Nxumalo, 'I'm a Zulu.'

'What's that?'

The tormented one could not mask his disgust at such ignorance: 'Zulu will be the most powerful tribe along the Umfolozi.'

'In the north we haven't heard of them.'

'Everyone will hear when I'm chief.'

'Chief! What are you doing herding cattle in this small tribe?'

'I was cast out of the Zulu. I'm son of their chief, and he banished me.' Then, with a bitterness Nxumalo had never witnessed before, Shaka unfolded his account of the intrigue which had driven him from the tiny, inconsequential tribe of the Zulu:

> 'My mother Nandi—you'll meet her one day. Look at her well. Remember her face, because before I die she's going to be proclaimed Female Elephant. People will bow down to her. [His voice trembled.] She was the legal wife of the chief, and he rejected her . . . cast us both out of his kraal, but I'll go back, and take my mother with me. [He clenched his fists.] I'm an outcast. You hear them make fun of me. Remember their names. Nzobo, he's the worst. Mpepha, he's afraid to hit me. He uses a club. Mqalane, remember him. I will always remember Mqalane. [He named the other five, repeating some.] They laugh at me. They refuse me permissions. But most of all, Nxumalo, they ridicule my mother. [Here he began trembling furiously.] I tell you, Nxumalo, one day she will be the Female Elephant. [Silence, and then the real burden.] No, the worst isn't that. It's the way they make fun of me. [It was impossible for this boy, tenser than the string of a bow, to weep, but he did tremble, grinding his heel in the dust.] They make fun of me.'

The simple sentence that Nxumalo uttered next would save his life on the day of retribution, but now it seemed only a gesture of decent friendship. He reached out, touched Shaka on the arm, and said, 'Later it will grow bigger.'

'Will it?' the older boy cried impetuously.

'I've often seen it happen.' He had no authority for what he was saying, but he knew it must be said.

Shaka said nothing more, just sat there in the grass, pounding his fists against his knees.

Like any confused boy his age, Shaka had shaded the truth, so far as he was able to understand it. Senzangakhona, chief of the Zulu clan, had impregnated Nandi, a virgin of the Langeni. When the elders of the latter tribe heard of this shocking breach of tribal custom, they insisted that Senzangakhona do the proper thing and accept her as his third wife, which he did, but she proved more disagreeable than sand in the mouth. Her son was worse, and at the age of six allowed one of his father's favorite animals to be slain, a mistake which precipitated banishment. Shaka was no longer a Zulu; he and his mother must take refuge in the kraals of the despised Langeni.

On the day they left, Senzangakhona was most pleased; they had given him nothing but trouble, and he recalled what his councillors had said that first day when Nandi claimed she was pregnant: 'She had no baby in her. It's only the intestinal insect they call iShaka.' The king agreed, and now watched with undisguised pleasure as his unwanted wife disappeared, taking her 'insect' with her.

In 1802 famine swept the valley of the Umfolozi, the only time that men could remember when the richest of rivers betrayed her children, but now the lack of food was so critical that the chief of the Langeni began to drive unwanted persons out of his kraals, and among those who had to leave were Nandi, mother of Shaka, and her son, who was liked by no one in the clan. As they were departing southward, using a ford that crossed the river, the outcast boy Nxumalo overtook them, saying that it could not be long before he, too, would be forced out and asking permission to join them in their exile. Nandi, a powerful woman who wasted little effort in sentiment, said, 'Stay behind.' But her son, remembering various behaviors of the younger boy, said, 'Let him come.' And the exiles moved south.

In time they straggled into the lands of Dingiswayo, most important of the southern chiefs, and when he saw the two stalwart fellows he wanted them for his regiment: 'You look like warriors. But can you fight?'

Long-shafted assegais were produced, but when Shaka hefted his he disliked its balance and demanded a replacement. 'Why?' asked the chief, and brusquely Shaka said, 'A warrior must have confidence.' And not until he had a spear he liked did he say, 'I'm ready.'

Dingiswayo laughed at his impudence, saying to his attendants, 'He looks like a warrior. He boasts like one. Now we'll see if he can fight.'

Hearing this implied insult, Shaka pointed to a distant tree: 'There is your enemy, Great Chief.' And with a short run he launched his assegai far and true, so that Dingiswayo laughed no more. 'He fights like a warrior, too.' To the young man he said, 'Welcome to my regiment.'

For the next years Shaka and Nxumalo shared a wild experience. As members of the region's greatest regiment, the iziCwe, they helped fortify their tribe's position, participating in the vast raids that kept the territory pacified and augmented. Nxumalo was content with his good fortune in gaining a position, however menial, in the land's finest fighting unit, but Shaka was as disconsolate and irritable as ever: 'There's a better way to fight. There's a much better way to organize a regiment than this. If they made me commander for one month . . .'

For example, in the great battle against the Mabuwane he was outraged, even though it was judged that he had been the foremost warrior. What happened was a standard battle, which, in Nxumalo's opinion, the iziCwe regiment had dominated.

Four hundred of Dingiswayo's troops marched north in noisy stages, announcing at every stop that they were about to engage the Mabuwane. Two hundred women, children and old men trailed behind, throwing a cloud of dust that could be seen for seven miles. In the meantime, the Mabuwane, who had known for two weeks that a battle was to be fought, had been scouting not the enemy, whose dispositions they always knew, but for a suitable spot on which to fight. One of the major considerations was that on the Mabuwane side at least, and on both sides if at all possible, there be commodious hills from which the audience could watch, and a comfortable and level place on which to place the chief's chair as he followed the ebb and flow of the battle.

The Mabuwane did their job well, and an ideal battleground was selected, a kind of pleasant amphitheater with exactly the kind of sloping sides the spectators preferred. When the two armies lined up, there were dances, formations, shouted insults and a good deal of foot-stamping. Then from each side four men moved forward, brandishing their shields and shouting fresh insults. The mothers of the opposing warriors were excoriated, the condition of their cattle, the poor quality of their food, and their known history for cowardice.

Each warrior carried three assegais, and at maximum distance each threw one that came so far in such good light that the big shields had ample time to deflect them. Unfortunately, one of the Mabuwane warriors shunted a spear aimed at him right onto the foot of one of his own men. It didn't pierce the foot, but it did bring blood, whereupon the multitude on Shaka's side cheered wildly. Nxumalo was especially excited, dancing up and down until Shaka, standing beside him, grasped his arm in a terrible grip. 'Stop that! This isn't warfare.'

Then, from a distance almost as great as the first, a second flight of assegais was released, again with no consequences. At this point it was obligatory for the four warriors on each side to run forward and to throw their last spears from a distance of about twenty-five feet. Again they could be fended off easily.

Now the main bodies of the two armies were required to mingle; however, they did so under carefully understood rules: vast flights of assegais, thrown from far distances so they could be easily deflected, and when both armies were thus disarmed, a fragmentary melee without weapons in which one side pushed a little harder than the other and took a few cap-tives. The observers could readily see which side had won, and when this was determined the other side fled, leaving its cattle to be captured and a few women to be taken home by the victors. Of course, in the scuffling some warriors were injured, and now and then some inept fighter would be killed, but in general the casualties were minimal.

A convenient feature of such a battle was that when it ended, each side could pick up about as many assegais as it had carried at the beginning, but of course they were not the same ones.

Disgraceful! Shaka brooded. This is no way to fight. Imagine! And he kicked his right foot in the air, sending his cowhide sandal in a wide arc: Men fighting in sandals. It slows them down. They can't maneuver. And it was after this fight that he began running up and down hills barefooted, until his feet were tougher than sandals and his breath inexhaustible. He also required Nxumalo to stand in the sun hour after hour, holding a big shield in his left hand, an assegai in his right.

Forty times, fifty Shaka told Nxumalo, 'I am your enemy. You must kill me.' And with a wild leap Shaka sprang forward, bringing the left edge of his shield far to his right. When Nxumalo tried to throw his assegai, as warriors were supposed to do, Shaka suddenly swept his own shield-edge brutally to the left, hooked Nxumalo's shield and half-spun him around so that the entire left side of his body stood exposed. With one swift lunge, Shaka thrust his spear at Nxumalo's heart, halting it inches from the skin.

'That's the way to kill,' he cried. 'In close.'

One afternoon, when he had slain Nxumalo many times, he took his own assegai and in a rage broke the shaft, kicking the halves in the dust. 'Spears are not the weapons for a fight. We need stabbers.' And in fury he grabbed Nxumalo's spear and shattered it, too.

'What's the matter?' Nxumalo asked.

'So stupid!' Shaka cried, kicking at the spears. 'Two armies approach, like this. You throw your first spear. I throw mine. Second spear. Third spear. Then when we have no weapons we rush at each other. It's madness.'

Retrieving only the metal points of the two spears, he went with Nxumalo to the best iron forger along the river and asked him whether he could combine these two points into one—a massive, heavy, blunt stabbing sword. The artisan said that might be possible, but where would Shaka find a haft heavy enough for such a spear.

'It's no longer a spear,' Shaka said. 'It's something quite different.' And he worked with all the blacksmiths, trying to find the man who could make the terrible weapon he visualized.

In these days, when the two were still living in mutual exile, Nxumalo noticed several unusual aspects of his friend's behavior, and once when they talked idly of their possible futures in this alien chiefdom, where warriors were respected but where real warfare was unknown, Nxumalo was goaded into telling Shaka of those obvious curiosities.

'For one thing, you cleanse yourself more than anyone I've ever known. Always under the bowl of thrown water.'

'I like to be clean.'

'I think you like to stand naked before the others. To show them that your penis is now big, like theirs.' Shaka frowned, but said nothing. 'And with girls, you're not like the rest of us. You often avoid the pleasures of the road.'

This was a lovely euphemism for one of the most gracious of the local customs. Since among these clans premarital intercourse was severely forbidden, the habit had evolved of 'taking the pleasures of the road,' meaning that youngsters were permitted to reach out for a likely love and take her into the bushes for any imaginable kind of frolic so long as pregnancy did not result. The men in the iziCwe were notorious for their gentle debauches, and none enjoyed them more than Nxumalo, but he had noticed that Shaka was indifferent to this love-play.

'No,' Shaka said reflectively on this particular day, 'I am destined to be a king. And it's perilous for a king to have children. They fight for his throne. When he grows old they kill him.' He was in his mid-twenties when he said this, and so far as Nxumalo could remember—and he knew this moody warrior better than anyone else—Shaka had never once boasted of his sexual exploits as other young men did. Nxumalo suspected that his friend had never lain with a woman, even though he was six foot three, with no fat about his middle, and the target of many eyes.

'When it's time to marry,' Nxumalo predicted, 'watch out! You'll be the first.'

'No,' Shaka said quietly. 'For me no children.'

'We'll see,' Nxumalo said, whereupon Shaka gripped him by the shoulder: 'You say I lie?'

'Oh, no,' Nxumalo replied, brushing his hand away. 'But you love women more than any man I've ever known. Your mother.'

In a rage so violent that the grass trembled, Shaka leaped up, sought madly for a stone, and would have crushed Nxumalo's head had not the latter slithered away like a frightened snake.

'Shaka!' he cried from behind a tree. 'Put that down!'

For several moments the warrior stood there, gripping the stone till his dark hands showed pale at the knuckles.

As the routine of army life absorbed them, disclosing no alternatives for the years that loomed, Nxumalo saw with some anxiety that his friend was becoming almost suicidal, dreaming hopelessly of goals he could never attain, and he felt that he must help him assuage this corrosive bitterness:

'When you said, "One day I'll be chief"—of what? There's no chance here. There's no chance of returning to the Langeni.'

'Oh! Wait!' Shaka said with fiery determination. 'One day I will return to the Langeni. There are men there I want to see again.' And he began to recite the names of the boys who had tormented him in the pastures: 'Nzobo, Mpepha, Mqalane.'

'You want to become chief of the Langeni?'

'Chief of them?' He laughed, and began to stride back and forth. 'I want to be king of a real tribe. And with my men to march upon the Langeni. And ask them about their laughter.' Suddenly he changed completely and asked Nxumalo, 'Wouldn't you like to go back and be chief of the Sixolobo?'

'I don't even remember them.'

'Don't you want to meet the men who killed your father?'

'I wouldn't know them. My father broke a rule. He was executed.'

'But if we could take the iziCwe and march into Langeni land one year, then Sixolobo the next . . .' His big hands had their fingers extended and slowly he brought them together. 'There's only one clan I want to lead,' Shaka said. 'The Zulu.'

Nxumalo grew grave: 'You must forget the Zulu. They banished you. Your father hasn't seen you in years, and he has many other sons. What are the Zulu but a tiny flea compared to this clan?'

'But if I were King of the Zulu . . .' He hesitated, reluctant to share his aspirations. Lamely he concluded: 'The Zulu are real men. By the end of the first day they'd understand my dreams.'

In 1815 he revealed his vision of what warfare in his territory was to become. It was an engagement with the Butelezi, and everyone else supposed it was to be an ordinary confrontation, with the two chiefs seated in their chairs as thousands applauded the desultory skirmishing, but when the ground was selected and everyone was in place, a single Butelezi warrior stepped forward with mocking, insolent gestures. From Dingiswayo's ranks a tall man, lean as lion sinew, dashed barefooted at the enemy, hooked his shield deftly into his opponent's, twirled him about like a top, and plunged his short, terrible assegai into the heart.

Then, with a wild yell, he bounded toward the front ranks of the Butelezi, a signal for the rest of the iziCwe to swarm upon the amazed enemy and slay them.

Fifty enemy dead. Kraals burned. Nearly a thousand cattle led home in triumph. More than a dozen women captured. There had never before been a battle like this, and there would never again be a battle in the old style.

As a consequence of this stunning victory, Shaka gained Dingiswayo's favorable attention and was promoted rapidly to regimental commander, a post of honor which he should have held in quiet distinction for the remainder of his life. But such limited achievement was not what Shaka had in mind, not at all. At night he whispered to Nxumalo, 'This Dingis-wayo goes to battle as if it were a game. He returns cattle to the van-quished. Leaves them their women.' In the darkness Nxumalo could hear him gritting his teeth. 'This isn't war. This is the quarreling of children.'

'What would you do?'

'I will bring war to the world. Real war.'

In 1816, when Reverend Hilary Saltwood, many miles to the southwest, was teaching the little Madagascan girl Emma the geography of Europe, Shaka's father, chief of the Zulu, died, and after an obliging assassin had removed the son intended for the succession, Shaka at last seized com-mand of the clan, one of the smallest, with a total population of only thir-teen hundred and an army, if all the able-bodied were mustered, of three hundred, plus two hundred novices.

It was a clan of little distinction, smaller than either the Sixolobo or the Langeni; it had no special history, had expanded its lands not at all during the preceding hundred years, and had provided no regional leader-ship except Shaka's promotion to command of the iziCwe. Normally the Zulu would have remained of these dimensions, crouched along one of the better reaches of the Umfolozi River.

But when Shaka assumed command, he moved in with an iziCwe regi-ment to support his takeover, and one of the first things he did was to require that every Zulu soldier throw away his three long-shafted assegais and replace them with one short stabbing weapon. He then increased the height and width of their shields, until a standing man, with knees only slightly bent, could hide his whole body behind two layers of rock-hard cowhide. But in some ways the most important thing he taught was how to dance.

First he appointed a knobkerrie team of six, choosing the tallest, strongest and most brutal men from his new recruits. Brandishing their clubs, they would stand behind him at all future public functions, await-ing his instructions. Then he assembled his Zulu regiment at the edge of a flat piece of ground well covered with three-pronged thorns. When they stood at attention in the moonlight he stepped before them, barefooted as always.

'My warriors,' he said quietly. 'Four times I have told you that if you want to be the greatest regiment along the Umfolozi, you have got to fight barefooted. And four times you have returned to your sandals. Now take them off. Throw them in a pile. And never let me see them again.'

When the recruits stood barefooted before him, he said, in the same low voice, 'Now, my warriors, we're going to dance.' And he led them onto the thorn-studded land and began a slow dance, accompanied by a chant they knew well. 'Sing, my warriors!' he cried, and as the rhythms began to throb, he danced upon the projections, which caused him no trouble, for he had made his feet tougher than leather. But for his soldiers those first tentative steps were agony, and some began to falter from a pain greater than they could bear.

Now came Shaka's first lesson to his Zulu. Watching hawklike, he spotted a man whose legs simply could not force his feet down onto the piercing thorns. 'That one!' Shaka cried, pointing at the soldier.

What happened next became invariable. Two of the knobkerrie team grabbed the offender from behind, pinioning him with great force. Another dropped down and grasped his ankles, spreading his legs apart. Reaching around from in back, the burliest of the gang seized the man's chin, and with a terrible swing of his arms, twisted it halfway around till the face was looking backward. Then an equally powerful man from in front grasped the chin and continued the awful wrenching until the man's face was again looking forward, having made a complete circle. The face looked the same, but the man was forever altered.

'Now dance!' he cried, and twice more he detected soldiers who were less than enthusiastic, and when he designated them, the slayers descended upon them, twisting their heads about in full circles.

Faster and faster Shaka set the beat until even he was tired. Then, with a gentleness that Nxumalo would never forget, he looked up at the moon and said, 'My dear warriors. It's three nights till the moon is full. Now go and harden your feet, for at the full moon after this, we shall all dance again. You have thirty-one days.'

When they resumed, at the next full moon, only one soldier's neck had to be twisted; the rest kept pace with Shaka until at the end all were jumping up and down on the thorns, driving them into the ground, and singing their regimental songs, and shouting with joy as they danced with their chief.

The next day Shaka explained to his troops why the foot-hardening had been necessary: 'We shall have an army unlike any that has ever swept along the Umfolozi. And its power will be speed. You and I will fly over the rocks, body-arms-head.'

That would be the secret of Shaka's irresistible army of Zulu: 'The body is the big concentration at the center. This is all that the enemy is allowed to see. The arms are swift outreaching movements on the flanks. These are concealed from the enemy.'

'And the head?' Nxumalo asked.

'You are the head, trusted friend. You're now in charge of my best regiment, and during the first stages of a battle your men hide behind a hill, at the center. With your backs to the fighting. You sit with your faces away from battle.'

'But why?'

'Because you must not know how the battle progresses. You must be neither excited nor dismayed. At the crucial moment I'll tell you what to do, and without thinking or trying to adjust, you roar forth and do it.'

It was the kind of commission at which Nxumalo excelled, for it required only allegiance and blind obedience, the two virtues that characterized him. Some men require a leader in whom they can place absolute trust; in his shadow they grow strong. And Nxumalo was such a man. Convinced that Shaka was a genius, he found it rewarding to obey him, and in doing so, became the young chief's only trusted advisor. One morning when the two stood before the regiments the difference between them was obvious. Both were dark of skin, both were battle-hardened. Shaka, only a year older, stood much taller than his aide, broader of shoulder and quicker of movement. In all ways he seemed superior, until the observer looked at Nxumalo's stocky middle, and then he saw a powerful heaviness: a massive chest that would never tire, a belly that could stand punishment, very stout legs prepared to climb hills, and a general endurance that was unmatched. They formed a good pair: Shaka the mercurial planner, Nxumalo the stolid executor.

Early in their strategy discussions they realized that if Shaka's battles were to depend upon fluidity, swift communication among the various segments was vital; equally important was accuracy. So one morning they assembled the four regiments that had been formed, and Shaka initiated this training exercise: 'Speed and accuracy. They're to be the heart of our success. Now the vice-commanders of our regiments are to go one mile from here, each in a different direction, then stand and wait. Each regiment, nominate four signal-runners, place one here with me, the other three at intervals along the way. When you're all in position, I'll give the signal-runners here a message. And off you go. Run to the first waiting man, give him the message, and he carries it to the second, and so on till it reaches the end of the line. Then you vice-commanders dash back here and tell me what the message was. Speed and accuracy.'

When the sixteen outlying men were in position, Shaka studied the field as if this were a real battle, and with Nxumalo and three other regimental commanders at his side, he said in a loud, clear voice, 'Run forty paces forward. Turn and go to the three trees. Leave half your men there. Move forward eighty paces.'

As soon as he had said this he clapped his hands, and the first signal-runners were off. With amazing speed these barefooted men, their feet inured to rocks and thorns, sped over the difficult terrain, ran up to the first waiting men, and delivered their messages. With some satisfaction, Nxumalo saw that his runners were doing rather better than the others, but this was to be expected, and when the final runners carried their messages to their waiting officers and those men began their dash back to Shaka, again Nxumalo saw that his vice-commander was in the lead.

Running at breakneck speed, this man approached the chief, knelt and delivered the message exactly as it had been stated earlier, and so did the next two officers, but the fourth not only lagged in speed but also in the accuracy of his message; indeed, it was badly garbled.

Shaka showed no displeasure. Instead he waited for the sixteen signal-runners to come gasping back to the center, whereupon he praised Nxumalo's men, nodding graciously to him as he did so. The second and third teams he also praised, but when he came to the five delinquent men, he merely pointed at them, whereupon the knobkerrie team grabbed them one by one and burst open their skulls.

'Speed and accuracy,' he said grimly, leaving the field.

Shaka placed major reliance upon Nxumalo because of his unflinching obedience. Some commanders questioned orders, but never his old companion: 'If I told the iziCwe to swim a river, climb a mountain and fight five thousand enemy along the way, Nxumalo would do it.' And he confessed to the other regiments that he depended upon the iziCwe as his one certain arm in battle, for its performance was terrifying.

Shaka's vision of the campaigns that would make him king required total war, total obedience to his personal rule, total destruction of anyone who raised even a whisper against him. He saw Dingiswayo's limited forays as a perpetuation of the petty rivalries which allowed every minor chief a separate development that made him weak and without direction. He was determined to sweep all clans into one great Zulu nation, and to do this his warriors must move like vast herds of antelope, leaving no blade of grass untouched.

While Shaka drilled his regiments, his mother, Nandi, asserted herself in the Zulu kraals. She became indeed the Female Elephant, trampling on those who had rejoiced at her departure years before. The long years of exile which mother and son had shared had forged an extraordinary bond of love and understanding, and now Nandi pushed her son ever forward toward the mighty destiny she saw for the outcast they had called 'that insect.'

Thus, when Shaka judged that his amaZulu were ready for the massive tasks ahead, he told his commanders one evening in 1816, 'We move against the Langeni,' and he was so determined to humble the clan which had treated his mother badly that he rehearsed his battle plan for three tiring days: 'Nxumalo, you were a dog of the Langeni. This time your regiment will form the body. I'm giving you that position because I want total discipline. No Langeni man is to be killed unless absolutely necessary. The two flanks. You must move with greater speed than ever before and capture the enemy alive.' Ominously, on the final evening he commissioned four additional bullies to serve in his knobkerrie team and gave one of them a club suitable for driving stakes. With all steps planned, he went to sleep.

Shortly after dawn Nxumalo assembled the four regiments in a hollow-square formation, each in its distinctive uniform, with headdress of identifying color and large shields of different-colored cowhide.

When all was ready, with a bright sun creeping over the hilltops, Shaka himself stepped into the center of the square, a giant of a man, completely naked, conspicuously muscled, and at a signal from Nxumalo the waiting soldiers cried 'Bayete' and gave foot-stomping applause.

His three personal attendants now dressed him for battle. First they put on a loincloth apron of tanned leather, then a girdle of bright leopard skin about two inches wide fastened tightly to support an ashy gray kilt made of twisted genet fur which ended well above his knees. About his shoulders they placed a loose garland of animal tails kept so short they would not flop when he ran, and on his head a kind of crown formed by tufts of small red feathers and topped by a backward-curving blue-crane feather at least two feet long.

He was barefooted, of course, and carried in his hands only two things: his massive shield almost as tall as himself and pure white, except for a small black dot in the middle; and his stabbing assegai with haft two feet long and iron point one foot. But what imparted a sense of awful majesty were the four adornments the attendants now attached. About each arm, just below the shoulder, an armband of white cowtails was tied, the tips reaching down to his elbows and very full, so that they fluttered when he moved. And below each knee, reaching to his ankles, a similar band was fastened, and it was these white ornamentations, combined with the stark whiteness of the shield, that caused his brown-black body to glow with imperial grandeur.

'We march!' he cried as he faced his regiments, and his five hundred warriors replied, 'Bayete!'

Like a serpent the Zulu army snaked through the hills, and at dawn next morning the Langeni were surprised to find, upon waking, that enemy regiments surrounded their kraals. Shaka's orders were obeyed, and the amazed Langeni, expecting their huts to be fired, their people slaughtered, found no assegai raised against them except in silent warning. Could this be Shaka, whose heralds referred to him as The-One-Who-Will-Swallow-the-Land? The answer would come with shocking clarity.

Nxumalo was sent quietly among the huddled Langeni, nodding at one, then another, until he had identified more than thirty. These men were taken to the main kraal, where they looked up at a face that seemed strangely familiar. 'I am Shaka, son of the Female Elephant Nandi, whom you reviled.' He sang out the names of the tribal leaders, and as each was shoved forward, the knobkerrie team began the slaughter.

The execution squad worked in different ways. If a victim had ever displayed one redeeming virtue, his head was swiftly and almost painlessly twisted in a complete circle. Death was instantaneous. But if there were remembered grudges, without extenuating circumstances, clubs were used, a heavy rain of blows to all parts of the body except the head, and this death was painful. The older Langeni died in this manner.

But when Shaka pointed out those who as herd boys had tormented him, he ordered the guards to stand them aside, and in the end he had eleven, and when he looked at them, his face grew dark as a thundercloud and reason seemed to leave him, for he was a boy again, back in the fields, and when he saw his chief aide and most trusted friend, Nxumalo, he shouted, 'You, too, were one of them!' and the knobkerrie team seized him and threw him with the others.

'Nzobo,' he now screamed at one of the former herd boys. 'Did you not scorn me?'

The Langeni, now a man of substance, stood silent. 'Take him!' Shaka bellowed, and in that instant Nzobo was taken hold of and stripped. Then two men held him by the knees while another two bent him forward in a final, terrible bow, as if he were a suitor seeking Shaka's approval. Another produced four bamboo skewers, each about fourteen inches long, fire-hardened and needle-sharp. One of these was inserted into Nzobo's rectum, and with a wooden pounder the last member of the knobkerrie team hammered it home deeply, slowly.

Another, and then another, and then a fourth was hammered in, whereupon a rope was slung under the armpits of the screaming victim and he was pulled aloft to hang from the limb of a tree. After sixteen hours of mortal agony he would be dead.

Nxumalo, seeing this horrible punishment and aware that he was destined for it, tried to make some appeal to Shaka, but the awful judgment was proceeding: 'Mpepha, did you not throw rocks at me?' A list of grievances, kept alive for twenty years, was hurled at the terror-stricken man, who was then stripped and skewered.

Mqalane was next, and when he, too, dangled from the tree, Shaka was finished with the three whose long-ago behavior rankled deepest. The next eight were impaled on the poles of the cattle kraal, where he could not see them. 'It's repugnant to watch traitors die,' he told his men, but now two were dragged forward whose death he would cherish. 'Did you abuse me?' The men nodded. For that he would forgive them, and they sighed, but then he asked, 'Did you abuse my mother?' and when they stood, heads down, he screamed, 'Let them die as women!' whereupon the death squad fell upon them and tore away their privates.

Now only Nxumalo remained, and at him Shaka looked with loathing, but also confusion. He had been one of the herd boys; clearly Shaka remembered that, but he could not recall what exactly the Sixolobo refugee had done that merited skewering. The guards were already stripping him when the king's mind cleared slightly and he realized that his regimental commander ought not to be included, and with humility he brushed the guards aside and stood facing Nxumalo.

'What did you do against me when we were herd boys?'

And Nxumalo replied, 'Nothing, my Chief.'

'What did you ever do for me?'

And this time Nxumalo said, 'I cannot speak it, Mighty One. But I will whisper it.'

So Shaka moved everyone back, ordering the guards to let Nxumalo have his uniform, and as the naked commander stood with his leather skirt in his hand, he whispered to the chief, reminding him of that afternoon when they sat upon the grass and Nxumalo had assured him that one day he would have a penis of normal size.

Shaka put the fingertips of his left hand over his eyes and bowed his head. 'Are you Nxumalo of the iziCwe?'

'I am.'

'Dark spirits are on this field,' Shaka mumbled, and with a great strangling cry he demanded that the diviners conduct a smelling-out to identify the men in this gathering who housed these spirits, and the wild ones with snake skeletons dangling about their necks, dried gall bladders in their hair and black wildebeest tails in their hands ran helter-skelter among the Zulu, sniffing and listening and finally touching with their switching tails those who had brought evil upon the chief. As soon as a victim was designated, the knobkerrie men killed him.

Toward midnight, as Shaka sat drinking beer with Nxumalo, he began to feel pity for the impaled men. 'It would be too cruel to leave them hanging through the night,' he said, and he directed his people to gather huge mounds of grass and sticks to pile under the dangling men. 'See,' he cried to his victims, 'I no longer hold bitterness against you.' And he lit the grass so that the men might die quickly and escape the terrible agonies that would otherwise have come with the morning, when the hot sun began to shine upon them.

As a gesture of conciliation Shaka absorbed the Langeni regiments into his growing army, launching a policy that would result in a powerful force. When Dingiswayo, to whom he still owed nominal allegiance, died in battle with a northern tribe, the entire iziCwe contingent marched over to the Zulu, and Shaka said, 'Nxumalo, my truest friend, from this day you eat with the iziCwe.' This thrilling announcement had nothing to do with the manner in which the new general of the regiments would take his meals; it referred to the terrifying battle cry that would soon echo through the land whenever a Zulu warrior killed an enemy: 'I have eaten!'

In every direction Shaka lashed out with devastating speed, devouring small clans, and one morning he cried brusquely, 'Today we destroy the Ngwane,' and within a few hours the regiments had crossed the Umfolozi River and were dashing north to the kraals of a tribe which had given repeated trouble. Without signals or warning, other than the cries of astonished herd boys who saw the amazing army approaching, the Zulu took battle position, body-arms-head, and fell upon the community.

The Ngwane, like all subsidiary tribes in this region, were stalwart men and they did not propose to lose their cattle easily, for they supposed this to be another cattle raid in which two or three men might get hurt. So they quickly formed into their rude battle formations, with their throwing assegais at the ready. They saw the body of Shaka's army, and it looked much like any traditional raiding party, but as they moved forward to engage it, they suddenly discovered that the wings were widespread, like the horns of some enraged buffalo, so that wherever they turned they confronted swift-running Zulu.

'They'll take all our cattle!' the Ngwane commander shouted, but it was not cows that the Zulu sought this time. With terrifying force they fell upon the Ngwane, stabbing and killing, and when the latter bravely tried to regroup and fight in earnest, from out of nowhere sprang the iziCwe, their brutal assegais slashing like the knives that slaughtered oxen for the sacrifice.

Under this tremendous onslaught the Ngwane defenses crumbled, and those warriors who were spared the Zulu cry 'I have eaten!' scattered and kept on running. In their flight from terror they would become outlaws, seeking in the blood of others vengeance for their own crushing defeat. The kraals from which they fled were now in ashes, their herds driven off, their boys dragooned into Zulu regiments and their women distributed among the Zulu kraals.

The old people were 'helped along to the other place,' their slayers killing them with joy, for the Zulu saw nothing cruel in shortening the days of any who were aged or infirm. But when this savage battle was over, the Ngwane had ceased to exist as a clan.

Their extinction had been made possible by the disciplined performance of the iziCwe, and when the regiments returned to the Zulu kraals, Shaka praised the men and told them, to the envy of the other warriors, 'You may now enjoy the pleasures of the road.'

Shaka had introduced his own variation of that sexual custom: no warrior could marry until his chief gave him permission, and this was usually delayed until the soldiers were in their mid-thirties and growing too old for the crack regiments. Then, in a grand ceremony, they were permitted to search the woods for a combination of vine, gut and gum, from which they made a wide headband, woven into the hair when moist and worn for the rest of life as proof of marriage.

But since it was illogical to expect grown men, and the bravest warriors at that, to remain continent till they donned their headbands, the soldiers were granted the 'pleasures' after any battle.

So Nxumalo's warriors fanned out through the community, looking for young women, and the girls, long wondering about husbands and lovers, eagerly allowed themselves to be found. For three long days the men reveled in the glades, loving the women with passion born on the battlefield, yet practicing an almost savage restraint because they knew the fearful penalty they must pay if they got the women pregnant.

Nxumalo, no less excited about the fraternizing reward than his men, had gone seeking his pleasure of the road at a kraal whose daughter he had been noticing for some time. He was now a powerfully organized man who had been in the forefront of seven battles; he had a right to assume, therefore, that one of these years he would win permission to take a wife, but he knew that in Shaka's regime, sex was utilized as the ultimate weapon of control.

So he was determined to excel in battle so that he could go to Thetiwe to ask her to be his wife. Thetiwe, sixteen years old and the daughter of a neighboring chieftain, a girl of lovely demeanor and flashing eyes, had expected the iziCwe to perform well, which meant of course that its commander would come calling. So she waited alone, and when night fell she heard his steps.

'How was the battle?' she asked as he led her into a scattered wood beside the river.

'They are no more, the Ngwane.'

'They were a troublesome people.'

'No more.'

They spent three exciting days together, and often they talked of how soon Shaka might allow them to marry. Nxumalo, better aware than most of Shaka's intentions, was not overly hopeful: 'Consider the situation. More than anything else, Shaka wants to build the Zulu into the commanding nation, of which he will be king. To achieve this, constant warfare is necessary. And in battle he must have one regiment he can rely on. It'll always be the iziCwe. And I shall be fighting at its head until I'm fifty.'

'Oh, no!' Pressing her small hands against her face, she pondered the empty years till Nxumalo could claim her, and with great sadness, asked, 'Doesn't he know that his men should marry?'

'Thetiwe,' he replied gravely, 'you must never let anyone hear you ask such a question.'

'But why not?'

'Because Shaka is different. He doesn't think of families. He thinks only of armies and the glory to come.' He paused, wondering if he dare discuss this matter honestly with an untested girl of sixteen, but his passion for her was so intense that he felt he must. 'How many wives does the chief have now?'

'In the various kraals, sixty . . . I think.'

'Are any of them pregnant?'

'Oh, no!'

'But the last chief, Shaka's father. Were his wives usually pregnant?'

'He had scores of children.'

'The difference is that Shaka never sleeps with his wives. You know what he calls them? "My beloved sisters." Always he calls them his sisters.

You see, he fears women for two reasons. He wants no children, especially no sons.'

'Why not? You want sons, don't you?'

'I do. I would quit the army now . . .' He dropped that dangerous topic and continued speaking of his chief: 'And the other reason he fears women . . . it goes back to when he was a boy. The others teased him. Told him he could never have babies. They laughed at him constantly and said no wife would ever want him.'

'Now he has sixty wives,' Thetiwe said, 'and they'll probably put twenty of the captured Ngwane girls aside for him.'

'But you mustn't speak of this to anyone,' Nxumalo warned, aware of what might happen to her and to him if Shaka suspected them of irreverence.

She laughed. 'I've known everything you've said. What do you think the women in the kraals joke about when no one can spy on them? That Shaka keeps his beloved sisters aside till a real man comes along to claim them.'

'Thetiwe! Never speak of that.' And having observed the wrath of Shaka, the lovers were afraid even to think such thoughts, let alone voice them.

Shaka had now absorbed four troublesome tribes, 'embracing them in my arms,' as he said. In his utilization of the body-arms-head tactic he had become incredibly deft. Sometimes he sent one of his flanks far out and thinly spaced, their broad shields with the edges forward and thus nearly invisible. Hidden in the grasses behind lurked a second group. As his army advanced, the opposing general spotted the undermanned flank and wheeled his principal force against it, but when the enemy was committed, Shaka flashed a signal, whereupon the front line of Zulu whipped their shields front forward, while the hidden men leaped into position, showing the full width of their shields also. In an instant, what had been a line of stragglers became a solid phalanx looming two or three times larger than it actually was. Often this struck such terror that the enemy soldiers who had been marching confidently to engage an outnumbered foe fled in panic, disrupting the lines behind and inviting the massive body of the Zulu army to overwhelm them.

Zulu messengers, in reporting victories, gave details in rigorous order: so many cattle taken for the chief's pastures, so many boys for his regiments, so many girls for his kraals. The watchmen of the women selected twenty or thirty of the choicest maidens and turned the others over to the clan, and although Shaka appeared to pay little attention to his wives, any male caught lurking about the women's compound was instantly strangled, and if the girl to whom he had been making advances could be identified, she, too, was slain.

Nxumalo, obedient to each rule Shaka promulgated, spent whatever time was legally allowed with Thetiwe, and told her many things: 'Shaka is the greatest man who ever lived. A genius like no other. I've known four chiefs, and beside him, they were boys. It's in his plans for our nation that he excels. All tribes combined into one. From the rivers on the north to the rivers on the south. One family, one king.' He paused as he said this, then added, 'Shaka, King of the Zulu.'

'But you said he almost impaled you.'

'It was the evil spirits, not Shaka himself. They came and blinded him, but as soon as I told him who I was and his eyes opened, he spared me.'

'But didn't you often tell me that when the tribes were united, there'd be no more war?'

It was the kind of probing question that Thetiwe often asked him. But he knew there must be an answer: 'It's like this. We're still faced by many tribes that we must defeat. This will go on for some years, but one day there will be peace. Shaka has said so.'

The king's next actions belied this, for he authorized the formation of two new regiments. The first was composed only of girls Thetiwe's age, and because of her impeccable lineage and her bright intelligence, she was made vice-commander of this new regiment. The girls were not intended for battle; they were kept to the rear, performing services such as cooking, the mending of weapons and the nursing of the wounded, and quickly they learned the basic rule of Shaka's battle plan: 'If a Zulu is wounded, speak to him. If he can understand what you're saying, mend him. If he can't, call the guards.' When the girls did summon the knobkerrie men, the latter studied the case briefly, then usually took the wounded man's assegai and plunged it into his heart, for as Shaka said, 'If he can't walk, he can't fight.' And this the nurses understood.

The second new regiment was of quite a different character. It was almost laughable to look at, a collection of older men halt of leg and bad of eye. It was inconceivable that they could move with the alacrity demanded of Shaka's regiments, but gradually the king's strategy became evident: 'These men are to receive half-rations. They're to be worked constantly, and the sooner they die off, the better the Zulu nation will be.'

Now everyone, except the child-bearing women, was in a regiment and the nation was at last efficiently organized. Nxumalo liked the certainty this provided, the orderly progression through life with no chance for accidental deviation: a boy was born; he tended cattle; at eleven he was assigned a place in the cadets, a kind of pre-regiment that performed tasks for the king; at fourteen he joined the youth's regiment, carrying water and food to men in battle; at nineteen he could, if he were fortunate, become a member of some renowned regiment like the iziCwe. For the next quarter of a century he would live in barracks in an orderly way, traveling to far parts of the nation where enemies existed; and if he proved obedient, the time would eventually come when he could marry;

he would have a brief, happy life with his wife and children, and then pass on to the old men's battalion, where he would die decently without prolonged imbecility. It was the way life should be managed, Nxumalo thought, for it helped men avoid erratic behavior and produced a disciplined, happy nation.

Nxumalo also appreciated the advantage that came from having the young girls collected into their own regiment: at the conclusion of some harsh battle, when the warriors were exhausted, these girls would be sent to the proper area, and for three or four days the victors could sport with them and thus avoid the burden of returning long distances to the kraals, where girls would have to be searched for. In later days Nxumalo was astounded by an additional simplicity the king's strategy permitted: once when the amaWombe regiment had performed especially well, Shaka rewarded it brilliantly. He marched the entire force to the parade ground, then summoned one of the girls' regiments and announced: 'The men may marry the women.' And by nightfall the pairings had been made and six hundred new families were launched without interrupting army procedures.

By 1823 Shaka had consolidated the major portion of his nation, bringing into carefully defined order what had previously been a mass of contending chiefdoms. He was an excellent administrator, offering positions of considerable importance to any gifted members of defeated tribes, and recalling his own unhappy days as an alien among the Langeni, he made the newcomers totally welcome, so that within a few months they began to forget that they had ever been anything but Zulu.

Nxumalo saw that iron rule was necessary if such a patchwork of clans was ever to become a unified kingdom; brutal punishments were accepted, for in the black tribes the chief served as father of the people, and what displeased him displeased his children, who became almost eager for retribution. Shaka started his reign in accordance with tradition; his rule was no more bloody than that of his predecessors, but as his authority widened he was tempted, like all burgeoning tyrants, to make his whim the law of the land.

In this he was encouraged by a curious personal motivation: he looked with scorn at all diviners and witch doctors, for although he knew they were necessary, he also knew they were a sorry lot. But the more he denigrated them, the more he was tempted to usurp their power; he became his own diviner, and those about him lived in terror. A nod when he was speaking, a belch, an injudicious fart, and Shaka would point to the offender, signaling his knobkerrie team to strangle that one.

But never in the early days was he a senseless tyrant; he gave the Zulu an able, generous government. He was especially careful to ensure that his people had reliable water supplies, stable sources of food, and his care of cattle would never be excelled. His personal herds numbered above twenty thousand, and he expressed his love for them in various ways. As a Zulu, he cherished cattle above any other possession, for he knew that a man's stature depended on the number of cattle he had been able to accumulate and that a nation's welfare was determined by the care with which it protected its animals.

His herds were so large that he was able to segregate them by color, which had not only an esthetic result but also a very practical one, because the cowhide shields of various regiments could be differentiated. The iziCwe, for example, carried only white shields with black fittings. Others had black, a choice color, or brown or red, the red finding little favor, for it was thought to be unlucky.

He was most careful with the animals intended for sacrifice, for upon them depended the spiritual safety of his kingdom, as well as his own. He never felt more secure than when he attended a ritual slaughter, stripped naked and washed himself in the still-warm chyme of a freshly slain bull. This thick liquid, the contents of the animal's stomach at the completion of the digestive process, was life-giving, and to feel one's self cleansed by it was an assurance of immortality.

Even more important, however, was the precious little sac, about as big as a child's fist, which fastened to the dead animal's liver. This was the gall bladder, in which rested the bitter fluid that symbolized life: it was acrid, like the taste of death, yet the bladder in which it lived was shaped exactly like the womb from which life sprang. Also, mysteriously, it resembled the beehive hut in which man lived, and the grave in which he ultimately rested, so that the whole of life was encompassed in this magical appendage. Once its bitter contents had been sprinkled to consecrate, it was dried into a thin leather, inflated and worn in the matted hair of witch-seekers.

He was extremely loving with his mother, turning over to her the supervision of the kraals in which he kept his wives, and it was because of her attentiveness that he became aware of Thetiwe, vice-commander of one of his women's regiments.

The Female Elephant was beginning to show her age, and Shaka was terrified by the possibility that one day she might die, so he tended her lovingly, and once when she caught something in her eye and could not dislodge it, she began to wail so loudly that messengers were sent for the king, and when he found her in despair, he summoned all his herbalists, but before they arrived, Thetiwe, whose regiment barracked nearby, was called to the queen's hut, and with the deftness she exhibited on so many occasions, extracted the thorn-tip which had tormented the queen. Nandi was ecstatic, and told her son, 'There's a splendid woman. I've waited all these years for you to give me a grandson. There's the one.'

When Shaka studied his young military leader he saw quickly that his mother was right, and this frightened him, for he did not want a Paramount Wife nor did he want any children by one. On both accounts his thinking was clear and accurate. A king, when he was making his way, could have as many wives as he wished; Shaka had twelve hundred now. And with them he could have as many children as he was capable of siring; some chiefs had sixty or more. But none of this counted; the early mothers had no special standing, for among the Zulu there was no primogeniture.

What a prudent king did was wait till his reign had been securely established; then he carefully chose from some family that could assist him in time of trouble a young woman of proved stability. She became his Paramount Wife, acknowledged by all others, and her sons stood in line to inherit the kingdom. And that's where the trouble came, for in Zululand princes killed kings.

So as soon as the Female Elephant announced that she had selected Thetiwe to be this Paramount Wife, Shaka bowed, backed out the door of his mother's kraal, and had Nxumalo summoned: 'Didn't you tell me that you fancied the girl Thetiwe, of the women's regiment?'

'I did.'

'You're to marry her this afternoon.'

'Mighty Lion, I haven't cattle enough to pay lobola for such a woman.'

'I give you three hundred cattle.'

'But her family . . .'

'I will command her family to approve. Now!'

Hasty and flimsy arrangements were made on the spot, and before the Female Elephant could protest, a wedding was arranged. The king himself officiated, and when the witch doctors had shaken their matted locks and rattled their dried gall bladders, blessings were said and the surprised couple were married. Then, to spirit them away from Nandi's wrath, they were sent north to conduct a negotiation which would determine the future course of their lives.

Their quarry was Mzilikazi of the Kumalo clan, an extraordinary young commander who even now, at the youthful age of twenty-seven, was betraying signs of challenging Shaka. This Mzilikazi had refused to send Shaka three thousand cattle captured in his raids, and twice he had rebuffed emissaries sent to collect them. Now Nxumalo and Thetiwe, armed with plenipotentiary powers and one hundred warriors, went to recover the cattle.

They found Mzilikazi at his unpretentious kraal in the northern forests, and when they saw him they simply could not believe that this reticent, whisper-speaking young warrior would dare antagonize the King of the Zulu. But that was the case. Bowing in servility, the young leader extended every hospitality to his guests, but no cattle. Whenever Nxumalo raised the question of the cattle—'The lion grows impatient, Mzilikazi, and he wants to eat'—the young leader smiled, blinked his hooded eyes, and did nothing.

They stayed with him for two weeks, and the more they saw, the more impressed they became. One night, upon retiring, Nxumalo made a final threat—'If we don't take the cattle home with us, Mzilikazi, the regiments will come north'—and when he wakened next morning he found that all his men had been surrounded by the commander's warriors and were immobilized.

Mzilikazi ruled wisely and with a minimum of passion. He was so considerate of his subjects that he kept about him no gang of assassins to inflict his will. No rhinoceros whips were allowed to sting his cattle; supple reeds from the river had to be used. In all things he was gentle: speech, movement, the giving of orders, his manner of dress, his love of singing. He was so utterly different from Shaka that whenever Nxumalo looked at him he thought: How pleasant it would be for a warrior to serve in the retinue of this noble man.

But in the end Nxumalo and Thetiwe returned home without a single cow. At the final meeting Mzilikazi said in his silken way, 'Tell Shaka not to waste his energies sending for the cattle. They will never be released.'

Nxumalo knew that he was obligated to resist such arrogance, but he said, without raising his voice, 'Then you must build high fences of thorn to protect them.'

And Mzilikazi replied, 'The love my people bear me is my fence of thorn.'

When Shaka heard of this insolence he ordered his regiments to assemble, and within the week Nxumalo was at the head of his iziCwe marching right back to Mzilikazi's kraals. The siege was short . . . and bloody, but the boy-general with the quiet manners escaped in some safe direction that could not be detected.

Now the beneficial results of Shaka's approach to government manifested themselves. An area larger than many European nations, which had festered for centuries in petty anarchy, became a unit, orderly and prosperous. The two hundred tribal loyalties which had previously rendered sensible action impossible were now melded into one, and families that two decades ago had not even heard the word Zulu now proudly proclaimed themselves as such. Whatever new triumph Shaka attained brought a shared glory to them, so that what had begun as a small clan of thirteen hundred Zulu was magically transformed by his genius into a powerful nation of half a million.

Order reigned in the land, and advancement was open to even the latest convert to the Zulu cause. A boy from the Sixolobo tribe entering his Zulu regiment at fourteen had just as fair a chance of becoming its commander as did any son of a distinguished Zulu family. In fact, by the time he was fifteen, with a year's training behind him, he was a Zulu, and no one ever again referred to him as a Sixolobo. And such citizenship was not reserved for the young; this boy's parents could come into Shaka's court and demand justice the same as anyone else, and his sisters could enter the kraals as wives to men who were born Zulu.

Peace also prevailed, and the central kraals along the Umfolozi River would pass years without experiencing attack, so that Shaka's name became revered throughout his kingdom. Citizens cheered when he appeared, waited on his commands, and were gratified with the benefits he brought them.

Nxumalo, for example, had scores of reasons for loving his powerful friend. He had already served as general of the finest regiment and as plenipotentiary in arranging peace with outlying clans. In 1826 Shaka gave further proof of his affection for the man who served him so well.

'Nxumalo, you must come to my kraal,' the king said, and when they reached the sacred area two beautiful Zulu girls were waiting. 'These are your brides,' Shaka said, ordering the seventeen-year-old girls forward.

'This time, Mighty Lion, I have the cattle to pay for them.'

'Their parents have already received their lobola . . . from me.'

'I am most grateful.' It was a considerate thing Shaka had done, for in Zulu custom a husband was not permitted to go near his first wife, or any other for that matter, so long as she was pregnant or nursing a baby, and since she continued to nurse till the child was four and a half, this meant that the man was without sexual affection for about five years at a stretch. The problem was solved by allowing the man to take multiple wives, always supposing that he could pay for them in cattle, because this meant that as one wife after another became pregnant, there would be replacements, and one of the standard jokes in Zulu regiments dealt with the fiery commander who had seven wives, all pregnant at the same time: 'He might as well have been unmarried.' Now that Thetiwe had a baby, it was helpful to her for Nxumalo to take additional wives; Nxumalo, on his part, was made additionally beholden to his king.

But in a wonderfully subtle and corrective way Nxumalo's good fortune was beginning to produce its own penalties, for an ancient black tradition had been amended to provide a clever strategy for leveling society and cutting off any upstart whose popularity and power might begin to threaten the king's. This was the smelling-out ritual; now when witch-seekers coursed through the crowd, they were identifying those subversive persons whose removal would purify the tribe.

A smelling-out was conducted on sound psychological principles: as the witch-seekers with their gall bladders, snake skeletons and wildebeest tails dashed through the assembly, the crowd uttered the low, throbbing sound of a thousand voices moaning. If the seekers approached someone who by common consent ought to be removed from society, the humming increased to an audible roar, assuring the seekers that this man's death would be popular. In this way Zulu society cleansed itself. With subtle tactic it announced a consensus that was immediately enforced, for as soon as the witch-seekers nominated a man by waving their wildebeest tails in his face, he was grabbed, bent double, and destroyed with four bamboo skewers.

Nxumalo, as he accumulated fresh proofs of the king's favor, realized that he was moving into the realm of danger when the witch-seekers could mysteriously decide that the Zulu had had just about enough of him. Rumors were already circulating: 'Nxumalo? He came from nowhere. Connived against better men to win leadership of the iziCwe. Failed in his mission to Mzilikazi. Now has more cattle than a man should dream of owning. Nxumalo, like the white stork, flies too high.' So now whenever the Zulu were summoned for the next batch of removals, he began to sweat, appreciating like an ancient philosopher the transient nature of human glory.

In spite of this encroaching danger, he was needed by the Zulu, for although Shaka's system was well-nigh perfect, it had one self-destroying weakness: if a nation is totally geared to the waging of war, it had better ensure that war keeps occurring somewhere; and if incessant warfare is the rule, then trusted leaders like Nxumalo are essential. Every improvement that Shaka made obligated him to seek opponents against whom to test it, for he dared not allow his war machine to rest. It had to be housed and fed and armed with iron-tipped assegais: whole communities did nothing but forge iron; others spent their days fabricating stinkwood shafts.

So, like the emperors of Rome dispatching their legions to the far frontiers in search of new enemies, Shaka sent his regiments to distant valleys, where tribes that had committed no offense found themselves surrounded. And because Zulu warriors needed constant practice with their stabbing assegais, they collected few prisoners, but many cattle and women. This increased the wealth of the victors but not their stability, and many men discovered that as they acquired more cattle and wives, they also acquired the enmity of their friends. Many a prospering Zulu who was nominated by the witch-seekers wondered as he died in skewered agony how it all happened. War threw men upward, but the moaning of the populace dragged them back down.

It was in 1826, when Hilary and Emma Saltwood were entering Salisbury to visit his mother, that Shaka became acutely aware that he, too, formed part of this vast, impersonal process of advance and decline. He did not have to fear the diviners, for they were his agents; by subtle means he indicated whom he wanted them to remove, so that the leadership of the kingdom would always remain at a dead level, with no new heads rising suddenly above the multitude. What did threaten him, and all men, was the inexorable passing of time, the loss of a tooth now and then, the death of an uncle, the sad, sad wasting away of a man's life. Diviners were the enemy of Nxumalo; time, the enemy of Shaka.

By now a set of daring British traders had settled on the coast well to the south of Zululand, and among them was a tough, ingratiating Irish-Englishman named Henry Francis Fynn, a man whose personal courage equaled his brazen ingenuity. He introduced Shaka to Western ways, instructed him regarding the powers of the English king, and doctored his sick followers in the kraals. The extraordinary details of Shaka's final years might never have been known to the world at large had it not been for the recollections of Fynn, and the colorful journal of an imaginative eighteen-year-old, Nathaniel Isaacs, who had also made his way into the area.

No one will ever know what really went on in the minds of these traders as they observed customs and ancient traditions so utterly alien; their remembered response was clear, though, and in their writings they created the portrait of Shaka, the monster, driven by an unconquerable lust for slaughter:

> His eyes evinced his pleasure, his iron heart exulted, his whole frame seemed as if it felt a joyous impulse at seeing the blood of innocent creatures flowing at his feet; his hands grasped, his herculean and muscular limbs exhibiting by their motion a desire to aid in the execution of the victims of his vengeance; in short, he seemed a being in human form with more than the physical capabilities of a man; a giant without reason, a monster created with more than ordinary power and disposition for doing mischief, and from whom we recoil as we would at the serpent's hiss or the lion's growl.

Confronted by such a horror, Fynn, Isaacs and the other Europeans who joined them were nevertheless to stay in Shaka's domain up to four years, unharmed, desperately trying to make money, and conniving constantly to have the British Colonial Office bail them out.

If Fynn and Isaacs were horrified by Shaka's killings, he was appalled to learn that the British imprisoned their offenders: 'Nothing could be more cruel than to keep a man lingering, when one swift blow would free him forever.'

But Fynn was a clever man, seeking any chance to gain the approval of the Zulu ruler, and after studying the man, he came up with a brilliant approach: a promise of liquid which prevented hair from turning gray.

'Yes,' said Fynn, 'you rub this magic liquid in your hair, and it never becomes white.'

'Immortality!' Shaka cried, demanding to know what this elixir was called.

'Rowland's Macassar Oil,' Fynn said.

'Have you any?'

'No, but a year from now, when the trading ship comes in . . .'

It was a year of anxiety. To all parts of his realm Shaka sent messengers seeking to learn if anyone had Rowland's Macassar Oil, and his tragic countenance when none was produced alerted Nxumalo to the king's confused state of mind: 'If I could live another twenty years . . . forty . . . I could have all the land ever seen under my control. Nxumalo, we must find the oil that prevents a man from growing old.'

'Do you really think there is such a thing?'

'Yes. The white men know of it. That's why they have guns and horses. The oil!'

When the oil did not arrive and gray hairs multiplied, Shaka had to face the problem of a successor. He was only forty, with death far off, but as he said to Nxumalo, 'Look at my mother, how she fades. I don't want the magic oil for myself. I want it to save her life.'

'She's old—' Nxumalo started to say, hoping to prepare the king for his mother's eventual death, but Shaka would hear no such words.

In terrible rage he shouted at his aide, 'Go—leave me! You spoke against the Female Elephant! I'll kill you with my own hands.'

But two days later Nxumalo was summoned back: 'Trusted friend, no man can rule forever.' As Shaka uttered these bitter words tears filled his eyes and he sat with his shoulders heaving, finally regaining enough control to add, 'If you and I could have another twenty years, we'd bring order to all the lands. We'd even bring the Xhosa into our fold.' With bitter regret he shook his head, then seemed to discharge his apprehensions: 'Nxumalo, you must go north again. Find Mzilikazi.'

'My King, I've seen your hatred for this traitor who stole your cattle.'

'It is so, Nxumalo, but you will take ten men and find him. Bring him to me. For if he rules the north and I the south, together we can protect this land from strangers.'

'What strangers?'

'Strangers will always come,' Shaka said.

Nxumalo's secret mission involved a long trip into land that no Zulu had ever entered, but they were guided toward Mzilikazi by the battered clans who trembled in the wake of the fleeing Kumalo commander, and at the end of a most tiring journey the kraal was located, and in it waited not a regimental commander but a self-proclaimed king.

'King of what?' Nxumalo asked.

'King-of-All-He-Will-See. Is that not enough?'

Nxumalo looked at the eyes still hooded, the face still handsome and delicately brown, but it was the voice that haunted—soft, whispery, extremely gentle, like the man himself: 'Why would Shaka invite me, an enemy, to his kraal?'

'Because he needs you. He knows you are the greatest king in the north, as he is in the south.'

'If I stay here, I'm safe. If I go there . . .' He indicated an assegai in his side.

'No, Shaka needs you.'

'But I hate battle. I want no more of killing.' He spoke with such intensity, in that silken voice, that Nxumalo had to believe him, and at the end of six days' talking it was apparent that Mzilikazi, in many ways as able a king as Shaka, was not going to combine forces with the Zulu.

'This time, Mzilikazi, no threats from me,' Nxumalo said.

'Friends don't threaten each other. But because I know that you will listen to my reasoning I have a gift for you. Look!' And when the lion skins decorating his kraal—an indulgence Shaka would never have permitted—were parted, there stood a lissome girl of twenty prepared to go with Nxumalo as a gift.

'Shaka will think that you gave me the present because I did not argue diligently.'

'Shaka knew I would not join the Zulu. He'll understand the gift,' said Mzilikazi, and while Nxumalo stood next to the attractive girl he studied this strange king, so different from his own. Shaka was tall, iron-hard and lean; Mzilikazi seemed to be getting fat and soft. When Shaka spoke the earth seemed to cringe in obedience, but Mzilikazi smiled much more than he frowned and his voice never rose in anger. Furthermore, Shaka was a brilliant but violent man, somewhat distant even to his friends, while Mzilikazi was frank and open to all, a man who seemed always to do the right thing. He was much too clever to be trapped by the great King of the Zulu, and told Nxumalo, as the latter started south with his fourth bride, Nonsizi, 'We shall not meet again, Nxumalo. But I shall always remember you as a man of good heart. Tell Shaka that the conversations are ended. I shall move far from his reach.'

The pudgy king was right; Nxumalo never saw him again, but remembered him often and with the warmest feelings, for he commanded respect. As Nxumalo told his new bride, 'I can't understand it. Mzilikazi started out with his people like a band of brigands on the run. Now he's forming a kingdom.' Among the clans Mzilikazi's followers touched in their wild movement they became known as the fugitives—the Matabele—and under that name they would flame through the generations, the tribe that outsmarted Shaka of the Zulu.

When Nxumalo crossed the Umfolozi River in the spring of 1827 he found the Zulu tense and frightened, for the Female Elephant had fallen ill, and her son was dispatching messengers to all parts of the kingdom to see if anyone had found a bottle of Rowland's Macassar Oil which would darken her hair and prolong her life. A member of Nxumalo's kraal, seeing the master returning with a new wife, hurried to him with a warning: 'Three messengers who returned without the oil have been strangled. If you say you have none, you may be killed. So tell him immediately that you heard of a source at the north.'

'But I didn't.'

'Nxumalo, if the Female Elephant dies, we'll be in great trouble.'

'But why should I lie to him? He will soon learn the truth.'

The matter was solved by the grieving king; he did not ask for Fynn's magic liquid. What he wanted was news of Mzilikazi. 'He has fled,' Nxumalo said bluntly. 'He feared you as the king and knew that he could not stand against you in battle.'

'I didn't want to fight him, Nxumalo. I wanted to enlist him as our ally.'

He had much more to say; with his mother's illness reminding him of his own mortality, the succession to his throne was uppermost in his plans, but at midafternoon all this was swept aside when a trembling messenger came with the awful news: 'The Female Elephant has died.'

'My mother? Dead?'

Shaka withdrew into his hut, and when he walked out an hour later he was in full battle dress. His circle of generals and the nation's elders watched anxiously, but he betrayed no sign of the titanic grief welling up inside him. For half an hour the great leader rested his head on his tall oxhide shield, keeping his eyes on the ground, where his tears fell in the dust. Finally he looked up, wild-eyed, to utter one piercing scream, as if he had been mortally wounded. That scream would later echo to the farthest reaches of his kingdom.

With Nxumalo and three generals close behind, he went to his mother's kraal, and when he saw her dead body, with one sweep of his arm he ordered every serving woman to be readied for her final journey: 'You could have saved her, but you didn't.'

When Nxumalo saw that his beloved wife Thetiwe was among those pinioned by the knobkerrie team he shouted, 'Mighty King! Do not take my wife.' But Shaka merely looked at him as if he were a stranger.

'They could have saved her,' he mumbled.

'Mercy, Companion-in-the-Battles.'

With a powerful hand Shaka gripped his advisor by the throat: 'Your wife cured my mother's eye. Why could she not cure her now?' And Nxumalo had to stand silent as lovely Thetiwe was dragged away. With nine others she would share Nandi's grave, but only after all the bones in her body were broken in such a way as to keep her skin intact, since the Female Elephant demanded perfection in her dark place.

Now word flashed along the riverbanks that Shaka's mother was dead, and almost as if they were being driven by unseen herdsmen, the Zulu came out to mourn. Wailings pierced the air, and lamentations filled the valleys. People threw away their bead adornments and tore their clothes, and looked askance at anyone whose eyes did not flow with tears. The world was in torment.

All the rest of that day and through the night the wailing continued until the earth itself seemed to be in anguish. Some men stood transfixed, their faces upturned, repeating over and over the shrieking dirges, and others spread dust over themselves, screaming all the while.

At noon next day, 11 October 1827, the awful thing began. It was never known exactly how it started, but one man, crazed by thirst and lack of sleep, seems to have stared at his neighbor and cried, 'Look at him. He isn't weeping,' and in a flash of hands the indifferent one was torn apart.

A man who sneezed was charged with disrespect for the great mother and was slain.

A woman coughed twice and was strangled by her own friends.

The madness spread, and whoever behaved in any conspicuous manner was set upon and killed by the mob. A woman who looked like old Nandi was accused of having stolen her countenance, and she perished. A man moaned his grief, but not loudly enough, and was clubbed.

On and on, throughout all that long afternoon, the grief-stricken citizens wailed their laments and watched their neighbors. Five hundred died near the hut of the Female Elephant. The footpaths were strewn with bodies, and as the late-afternoon sun struck the maddened faces, spies looked to see whether the eyes held tears, and if they did not, the owner was strangled: 'He wasn't weeping for the mother.' Soon a thousand lay dead, then four thousand.

In sheer exhaustion some finally had to sit down, and when they did so, they were slain for lack of veneration. Heat of day caused some to faint from lack of water, and they were stabbed with assegais as they lay. Others wandered to the Umfolozi for a drink, and as they bent to reach it they were stabbed. Two unfortunate old men with weak kidneys had to urinate and were pierced with spears for their irreverence.

Gangs raged through the area, peering into every kraal to see if any had failed to honor the dead woman, and when recalcitrants were found, the huts were set afire and the occupants roasted. A mother suckled her child, whereupon the crowd roared, 'She feeds when the great mother lies dead,' and the pair were slain.

Through the day Shaka remained in the royal kraal, unaware of the killings as he received a file of mourners who tried to console him with chants honoring the Female Elephant. Their bodies trembled with fever; they fell to the ground and tore at the earth; and each expressed an honest grief, for Nandi had indeed been the mother of the nation. Beyond the kraal the hills rang with cries, and toward sunset Shaka rose: 'It is finished. The great mother has heard her children.'

When he left the kraal he saw for the first time the extent of the madness, and as he passed over bloodstained earth he muttered, barely coherently, 'It is finished.' He ordered two regiments to put an end to the mass killings, but undisciplined bands now rampaged far into the countryside, acting on their own and killing anyone who showed inadequate remorse, even in distant villages where news of Nandi's death could not have penetrated. 'You should have known,' the fanatics cried as they wielded their assegais.

Shaka's Dark Time the Zulu named these last three months of 1827, and the outside world would never have known the extent of the tragedy had not Henry Francis Fynn been visiting with Shaka on the day Nandi died. He would report seeing seven thousand dead himself, and from the distant countryside he received additional reports.

When the first spasm ended Shaka turned to the normal procedures for national mourning, and Nandi was accorded the full rites given a great chief: 'For one year no man may touch a woman, and if any woman appears pregnant, having made love when my mother lay dead, she and the child and her man shall be strangled. From all the herds in this kingdom no milk shall be drunk; it shall be spilled upon the ground. No crops shall be planted. For one year a regiment shall guard her grave, twelve thousand in constant attendance.' Initial hysteria was forcefully channeled into absolute obedience, and now additional people were killed if they drank milk or lay together.

At the end of three awful months those closest to Shaka convinced him that the nation he had worked so diligently to construct was imperiled by these excesses, and he terminated all prohibitions except the one against pregnancy, for he could never comprehend the need for sex. At a vast ceremony ending the Dark Time, herdsmen were ordered to bring their beasts, one hundred thousand in all; their bellowing would be the final salute to the Female Elephant. When they were assembled, Shaka demanded that forty of the finest calves be brought for sacrifice, and as the little creatures stood before him, their gall bladders were ripped out and they were left to die. 'Weep! Weep!' he shouted. 'Let even animals know what sorrow is.' Then he bowed his head as the contents of the forty gall bladders were poured over him, purifying him at last of the evil forces that had hastened the death of his mother.

The diviners and witch doctors, seeing a chance to reestablish their authority, seized upon Nandi's death as a way to chasten the king: 'We know what caused her death, Mighty Lion. A cat walked past her hut.'

Shaka listened avidly as the diviners revealed what dark spells had been cast by women who owned cats, and when the indictment was complete he roared, 'Let all with cats be found!' And when these women were assembled, including one of Nxumalo's wives, he screamed at them, demanding to know the poisons they had disseminated through their cats. When the terrified and bewildered women, three hundred and twenty-six of them, could make no sensible reply, he ordered them slain, and they were.

One morning Shaka took Nxumalo aside, seeking to recapture the friendship he knew he needed: 'I'm sorry, trusted guide, that Thetiwe and the other died. It was necessary.' When Nxumalo nodded, acknowledging the king's power, Shaka pointed out: 'I gave you the women. I had a right to take them away.' Again Nxumalo assented, and Shaka said, 'I wanted the world to see how much a son could love his mother.'

And that speech was the beginning of the final tragedy, for when the king endeavored to assure Nxumalo that all was again well between them, the latter thought not of his words but of a gentler king far to the north with whom sanctuary might be found. Shaka noticed his lack of response, and his dissatisfaction with the one man who might have saved him was launched.

Ironically, Shaka decided to cast Nxumalo aside at the precise moment when he was needed most, for the Zulu were beginning to see that the welfare of their recently established nation depended upon a man subject to irrational behavior; they also saw that since he had no sons, he had no direct heirs, and that if he died in one of his paroxysms, the kingdom would be adrift.

Unlucky chance also worked against him, for if the Female Elephant had pushed him to glory, another woman of equal determination was now ready to destroy him. Mkabayi, his father's sister—whose name meant Wild Cat, an ominous portent—had nursed a smoldering resentment against Shaka from the moment he usurped the Zulu leadership, and now, seeing the disarray of the kingdom, she infected two of Shaka's half brothers with her poison. Dingane and Mhlangana began to meet secretly with her, and after a few tentative discussions, realized that they must enlist the support of some military leader. The fact that Nxumalo had lost two wives—killed by Shaka's orders—made him a likely candidate.

The brothers had to approach him with caution, for if he betrayed a single intimation, Shaka would kill them all. So Dingane, a clever, conniving man, asked, 'Nxumalo, has it ever occurred to you that the king might be mad?'

He had been expecting just such an opening from someone, but he, too, had to be cautious, not knowing the true temper of the brothers. 'You saw him at the punishment of the Langeni,' he said. 'He forgot who I was.'

'Advise us straight. If anything happened to the king—his biliousness, I mean—would the iziCwe run violent?'

'My men love their king.'

'Were . . . two of your wives . . . slain?'

He did not like the devious way Dingane asked his questions, so once more he was evasive: 'Shaka gave me three women. He said he had a right to take two of them back.'

The brothers were satisfied that Nxumalo wanted to join them but was fending them off, so Dingane said bluntly, 'You must know you're to be smelled-out at the next gathering.' Nxumalo only looked at him, unbelieving, so Dingane whispered, 'One witch-seeker said to me, "That Nxumalo, two wives dead. It must be an omen." Your bamboo skewers are being hardened. Before this year is out, you'll hang screaming in the tree.'

Nxumalo properly interpreted this as a suggestion that he take up arms against the king, but even though his allegiance to Shaka the man had begun to erode, his tradition of obedience to the concept of kingship remained, and he could not at this first meeting abandon it, so with great daring, well aware that the brothers might feel they must kill him to preserve their secret, he said, 'Dingane, I know what you're plotting. And I understand. My heart is broken by what Shaka has done to me, and I hate his madness. But I'm his general and I can't . . .'

It was a fearful moment, with lives in balance, but the brothers had to risk it, for to succeed in their conspiracy, they must have this general: 'Would you be able to forget that we have spoken to you?'

'As a soldier I cannot act against my king, but I know he is destroying the nation. I will remain silent.'

When he left, the brothers smiled, for they were certain that Shaka would do some additional outrageous thing that would alienate even Nxumalo. The king was marked for murder.

Shaka sensed that the dynamics of the situation required him to keep his army on the move, so he advanced into new territories, well to the south toward the Xhosa, and for the first time his regiments gained only a modified success; he executed more warriors than ever before for cowardice. He allowed his regiments no rest, but sent them feverishly to new lands in the north, and again they encountered disaster.

'Where's Nxumalo?' the king cried in anguish one afternoon.

'He's with his regiment,' a knobkerrie said, not wanting to irritate Shaka further by reminding him that he had ordered Nxumalo to be confined.

'Never here when I need him. And Fynn fails to bring me the magic oil.' He almost whimpered. 'So much work remains, I must not die.'

And the executioners wailed, 'Deathless-Stomper-of-the-Rhinoceros, Fearless-Slayer-of-the-Leopard, you will never die.'

'What is death?' the tormented king asked. 'And before you answer that, what is life?'

Four attendants who were accustomed to nod gravely at everything he said were suddenly seized by the knobkerrie gang, and two were stood to the left of the king, two to the right. 'Kill those,' Shaka said, and the two on the left were slain. 'They are death,' the king said, 'and these are life. Tell me—what is the difference?' And he kept this grim tableau in place for three hours, staring and pondering.

Then with a leap high into the air he roared, 'Fetch me the women who were pregnant before my edict,' and more than a hundred women in all stages of pregnancy were dragged before him. With sharp knives he began to slice open their bellies to see for himself how life progressed, and as he continued his studies with the later women, the first ones lay dying in a corner.

When word of this hideous experiment flashed through the kraals, disseminated by men whose wives had been taken, Dingane exulted: 'Now we'll have Nxumalo with us!' And he took his brother to the kraal where Nxumalo was being held and told him, 'Shaka has taken Nonsizi. He's going to cut her apart.'

'What!' Like a bull elephant crashing through trees, Nxumalo burst out of the kraal to save the lovely girl Mzilikazi had given him, and when he ran in maddened circles, Dingane said, 'Over there!' pointing to Shaka's kraal.

Nxumalo arrived in time to see the knobkerrie men pulling the hundred and sixth woman to Shaka's table, and it was as Dingane had warned —Nonsizi of the Matabele. 'Shaka—she is my wife!' he cried, but with an impatient shake of his head the king indicated that his helpers were to remove this interruption.

'Shaka!' Nxumalo repeated. 'That's Nonsizi, my wife.'

In a kind of stupor, the king looked up, failed to recognize his general, and said, 'She cannot be your wife. All women belong to me.' And while Nxumalo was pinioned, the king dissected Nonsizi, then hurried to the last three women, crying, 'Now I will know. I won't need the hair oil!'

In that awful scream-filled moment any vestige of allegiance or obedience vanished, and as soon as Nxumalo could break away, he sought the brothers and said, 'Shaka must be killed.'

'We knew you'd join us,' the king's brothers said, and they took him to their aunt, Mkabayi the Wild Cat, who said grimly, 'We must strike the tyrant now.' And it was her force of character, allied with Nxumalo's, that sealed the king's fate.

Had the plotting been left to Dingane, Shaka might have escaped, for when that shifty fellow realized that he might actually have to stab the king, he began to vacillate, until one night Nxumalo grabbed him by the strands about his neck and whispered, 'We shall kill him together—the three of us. He must be removed.' Forever obedient, he was now obedient to the needs of the Zulu.

But he had still to face two extreme tests, in one of which lay a bitter irony. In a kraal near his, in which the king kept some four hundred of his wives, there was a girl named Thandi, who had served briefly in a women's regiment before the king selected her to be his wife. Once during a lull in maneuvers Nxumalo had encountered her while she was resting beside the Umfolozi, and they had invited each other to enjoy the pleasures of the road, and several times after that Thandi had contrived to be in the vicinity of the iziCwe, and on two different nights they had run a terrible risk by making real love, with the possibility that she might become pregnant.

He found her so delightful, so fresh in her attitudes, that he had started accumulating cattle to pay her lobola, when the king abruptly chose her for his own. True to his custom, Shaka rarely came near her; once during their years of marriage he had spent part of an evening talking with her, boasting of his prowess in battle, but even though she had listened attentively and said several times, 'How brave you must have been,' she never saw him again. That brief encounter was supposed to suffice for the fifty remaining years she would spend in the royal kraal.

Now, through the agency of servants, she let Nxumalo know that she would brave any death if he were willing to run with her to find some home less pitiful, and one night while Nxumalo was brooding upon this matter, it occurred to him that one of the worst things his king had done was this imprisonment of so many beautiful girls, thus keeping them in fruitless bondage till their years were wasted, and he decided that if with the others he must kill the king, he would at the same time put his life in triple jeopardy by stealing one of the king's wives. In great secrecy he drafted plans, and felt as if life were starting anew when Thandi came boldly to the kraal fence to smile at him, indicating her assent.

Next day came the severest test, for the king abruptly summoned him, and as Nxumalo entered the royal kraal, came toward him with tears in his eyes, and confessed: 'Oh, Nxumalo! In my madness I thought of sending the witch-seekers after you, but now I see that you're my only friend. I need you.'

Before Nxumalo could reply, the king led him to a cool spot and shared a gourd of beer. Then, taking Nxumalo's two hands in his, he said, 'My brothers are plotting against me.'

'Not likely.'

'Oh, but they are. I dreamed I was dead. It's Dingane. I see him whispering. Mark my words, he's not a trustful man.'

'He's of royal blood. He's your brother.'

'But can I trust him?' And without awaiting a reply, Shaka sighed. 'I am cursed. I have no son. No one to trust. I'm growing old, and still the magic oil fails to arrive.'

Nxumalo could feel no sympathy for this slayer of women, and a response too dangerous to utter leaped to his mind: Shaka, you could have had a score of sons. Nine years ago, if you had accepted Thetiwe instead of throwing her at me, you could have had six sons.

Again Shaka gripped Nxumalo's hands. 'You're the one honest man in this nation. Promise me you'll watch over me.'

With a lingering pity Nxumalo looked at the stricken man, this violent giant whose leadership had been corrupted by madness, and as he tried to formulate words that would allow him to depart, the king cried with deep remorse, 'Oh, Nxumalo, it was wrong of me to kill your wives. Forgive me, old friend. I killed them all, and learned nothing.'

'You are forgiven,' Nxumalo said grimly, and with a deep bow he left the royal kraal, marched, ostensibly, back to his own, then slipped away to join the Wild Cat, who was instructing her nephews for the kill. 'Shaka knows your intentions!' he cried. 'He will kill you soon.'

Dingane, although of royal blood, was no Shaka. He lacked courage, and, as the king had said, he could not be trusted. 'What shall we do?'

'Slay him now.'

'Now?' Dingane asked, looking at his brother.

'Now,' Nxumalo repeated.

They would strike at dusk—all three of them—when the king was more or less detached from his knobkerrie guards. 'I'll fetch my assegai,' Nxumalo said, and as he went toward his kraal he realized that Dingane had modified the plan so that only he, Nxumalo, would be seen by anyone watching. This meant that when the tumult erupted, he as a commoner could be thrown to the maddened crowd. 'We'll have none of that, Dingane,' he muttered, and he diverted his course to the wives' kraal, where Thandi was waiting for his signal, and he told her that within the hour she must try to escape, prepared to flee north.

He then went back and told his remaining wife, 'Be ready to leave at dusk.' She did not ask why or where, for, like the others, she had deduced that he was soon to be impaled. His survival was hers, and to be saved she must trust him.

As the sun started its descent on 22 September 1828, the three untrusting conspirators met casually, checked one another to be sure the stabbing assegais were ready, then walked like supplicants with a petition for their king and brother.

'Mhlangana, what do you seek?'

The answer, a lunging assegai under the heart.

'Dingane! From you I expected treachery . . .'

Another leaping assegai.

And then Nxumalo, trusted advisor, driving his assegai deep into Shaka's side.

'Mother! Mother!' the great king cried. Clutching at air, he tried to steady himself, went dizzy, and stumbled to his knees. 'Nandi!' he wept. 'My father's children have come to kill me.' But when he saw the blood come spouting from his wounds he lost all strength and toppled forward, crying, 'Mother!' for love of whom he had erected a mighty kingdom.

In the mad confusion following the assassination, Nxumalo, accompanied by one wife, the gift of Shaka, and the lovely Thandi, scrambled across the Umfolozi River and headed northwest. They hoped to overtake their friend Mzilikazi, rumored to be building a new sanctuary there for his fugitive Matabele.

With them they had four children, two by Thetiwe, the first wife, and two by number two, who had died because she owned a cat. They had with them a small herd of cattle, some cooking utensils, and not much else. Four other fugitives joined them, and this complement of eleven were prepared to live or die as accidents and hard work determined.

By the end of the first week they had become a resolute band, skilled in improvising the weapons and tools needed for the endless journeys ahead. They traveled slowly, stopping at likely refuges, and they foraged brilliantly. Thandi, the youngest, was especially good at thievery from kraals they passed, and kept the family in a reasonable supply of food.

They ate everything, killing such animals as they could and gathering berries and roots like grubbing creatures in a forest. At the end of the first month they were a tight, dangerous group of travelers, and when one of the men caught himself a wife from a small village, they became twelve.

Like thousands of homeless blacks in this period, they had but two ideas, to escape what they knew and to grasp at anything that would enable them to exist. Nxumalo hoped to overtake Mzilikazi and take service in some capacity with a king who promised in almost every respect to be superior to Shaka. 'Not as handsome,' he told his wives, 'and not as brave in battle, but in everything else a notable king.'

From time to time the little family stopped at some kraal, risking the dangers involved, and by so doing they discovered that Mzilikazi had moved far to the west, so they set out in serious pursuit.

And then they learned the meaning of the word Mfecane—the crushing, the sad migrations, for they came upon an area, fifteen miles wide and stretching endlessly, in which every living thing had been destroyed. There were no kraals, no walls, no cattle, no animals, and certainly no human beings. Few armies in history had created such total desolation, and if Nxumalo and his family had not brought food with them, they would have perished.

As it was, they began to see signs indicating that hundreds of people had been slain, their bodies left to rot; for mile after mile there would be strands of human bones. Nxumalo thought: Even the worst destruction wreaked by Shaka could not compare with such desolation. And he began to wonder what kind of all-consuming monster had wrought this ravishment.

It was half a year before he found out. With an instinct for preservation, he led his family back to the east, and after a hurried march, went beyond the swath of total destruction; here in the wooded area where streams ran, only the kraals had been destroyed, not the land itself, and one afternoon they came upon the first surviving humans. They were a family of three living in trees, for they had no weapons to defend themselves against the numerous wild animals that prowled their vicinity at night. They were so wasted they could hardly speak, but they did utter one word that perplexed the travelers: 'Mzilikazi.'

'Who was pursuing him?' Nxumalo asked.

'No one. He was pursuing us.'

'Mzilikazi?'

'A monster. A life-eating monster.'

'Feed them,' Thandi said. 'Don't question them when they're starving.'

So Nxumalo's men caught antelope for the wretched ones; they ate like beasts, the boy gulping the raw meat while he protected his portion by covering it with arms and legs. When the family slowly returned to human condition Thandi allowed Nxumalo to query them again, and he said, 'Surely Mzilikazi did not do this.'

'He slaughtered everything—trees, dogs, lions, even water lilies.'

'But why?' Nxumalo asked, unable to comprehend what he was hearing.

'He summoned our group of kraals . . . told us he wanted our cattle. We refused . . . and he started the killing.'

'But why slay everyone?'

'We didn't want to join his army. When we ran away he didn't even send his soldiers after us. They didn't care. They had enough to do killing those at hand.'

'But what was his purpose?'

'No purpose. We weren't useful to his moving army. In his rear we might cause trouble.'

'Where was he marching?'

'He didn't know, his soldiers said—they were just marching.'

After long consultation with the men in his group, and also with his wives, it was agreed that the family should be allowed to join them; the man could help with the hunting and the boy could prove useful later on, but when the enlarged group had been on the road three days, the new man died. Nxumalo assumed that one of his own men had killed him, for immediately the wife was taken into that man's care, without much protest from her.

When they had traveled as a unit for several weeks, they came upon the ultimate horror. They had been traversing mile after mile of total desolation—fifteen kraals without a sign of life, not even a guinea hen—when they came upon a small group of people living in a half-destroyed hut, and after a cursory inspection Thandi came to Nxumalo, trembling: 'They have been eating one another.'

The miserable clan was so desperate that they had resorted to cannibalism, and each wondered when the next would die, and at whose hand.

For these people there was no hope. Nxumalo would have nothing to do with them—they were untouchable. And he was about to leave them to their misery when Thandi said, 'We must stay and make them some weapons so they can kill animals. And our men must bring back some antelope to give them fair food.'

So at her insistence the group halted, and the men did go hunting, and after a while the cannibals, fourteen of them, began to fill out from their eating of antelope, and with their spears they now had a chance of fending for themselves. But despite Thandi's pleading, Nxumalo would not permit this group to join his, and when the family moved north the former cannibals stood at the edge of their desolate village, looking after them with strange expressions.

After a long time the signs of destruction diminished, and then stopped. Mzilikazi's armies had moved sharply westward, and for this Nxumalo was grateful, for it meant that he could now proceed northward without running the risk of overtaking the dreadful devastators or being caught in one of their chance sweeps to the rear. Of course, even this new land contained no people, for Mzilikazi had slain them all—hundreds upon hundreds—but there had been no general devastation, and the wild animals had returned.

Finally, after more than a year of this wandering, with two additional children being born to Nxumalo's wives and two to the other women, they came to a chain of low hills that looked much like the lovelier parts of Zululand, except that rivers did not flow through them. There were small streams, and Nxumalo began to think that beside one of them he might stop and build his kraal, and then one day as he came out of a valley he saw a pair of hills shaped like a woman's breasts, and they seemed a symbol of all the joys of the past and his dreams for the future: the deep love he had borne Thetiwe, his first wife; the tenderness he felt for his second, killed because of her cat; the passion he had known with Nonsizi of the Matabele; and the delight found in his two surviving wives, who had accepted the hardships of this journey without complaint. His six children were prospering and the men who had joined him in the flight had made themselves indispensable. The family deserved a halting place; it was with hope that he ascended the pass between the two hills, and when he reached the high point he looked down upon a lake and saw beside it the marked grave of the Hottentot Dikkop, buried there sixty years before by that wanderer Adriaan van Doorn.

'This has been the living place of men,' Nxumalo said, and with joy he led his people down the hill to take possession.

The Mfecane that raged through southeast Africa in the early decades of the nineteenth century produced excesses which went far in determining the development of an immense area.

The rampaging of the two kings, Shaka of the Zulu and Mzilikazi of the Matabele, set in motion sweeping forces which caused the death within a short period of time of huge numbers of people; chronicles unfavorable to blacks estimate two million dead within a decade, but considering the probable population of the area in those years, this seems grotesquely high. Whatever the loss, and it must have been more than a million, it was irremediable and accounted in part for the relatively weak defenses the surviving blacks would put up within a few short years when white men, armed with guns, began invading their territory. Starvation, cannibalism and death followed the devastation of the armies, while roving bands of renegades made orderly life impossible. Entire clans, which had known peaceful and productive histories, were eliminated.

The principal contributor to this desolation was not Shaka, whose victories tended to be military in the old sense, with understandable loss of life, but Mzilikazi, who invented the scorched-earth policy and applied it remorselessly. Why he slaughtered so incessantly cannot be explained. Nothing in his visible personality indicated that he would follow such a hideous course, and there seems to have been no military necessity for it. He killed, perhaps, because he sought to protect his small band, and the surest way to do so was to eliminate any potential opposition. Young men and male children became targets lest when they matured they seek revenge against the Matabele.

The widespread slaughter did not seem to alter Mzilikazi personally. His manners did not become rough, nor did he raise his voice or display anger. The young English clergyman who came out to Golan Mission in 1829 to replace Hilary Saltwood stayed there briefly, then, like his predecessor, felt obligated to move into the more dangerous northern territories, where he became a permanent friend to Mzilikazi; of him he wrote admiringly after the Mfecane had run itself out:

> The king is a likable man of only medium height, fat and jolly, with a countenance so serene that it seems never to have known vigorous events or dangers. He speaks always in a low voice, is considerate of everyone, and has proved himself most eager to cooperate with white men. He told me himself that he wanted missionaries to come into his domains because he felt that at heart he had always been a Christian, even though as a boy he could have known nothing of our religion. Indeed, he gave me for our mission one of the finest pieces of land in his capital city and sent his own soldiers to help me build it. Detractors have tried to warn me that I must be on guard, because Mzilikazi's soft ways hide a cruel heart, but I cannot believe this. He has known battle, certainly, but in it, so far as I can learn, has always conducted himself with propriety, and I consider him the finest man I have met in Africa, whether Englishman, Boer or Kaffir.

It must not be supposed that Mzilikazi and Shaka were personally responsible for all the Mfecane deaths. In many instances they merely set in motion vast dislocations of people whose ultimate exterminations of minor tribes occurred at distances far from Zululand. If ever the domino theory of inter-tribe and inter-nation response to stimulus functioned, it was during the Mfecane. A few hundred Zulu started to expand in all directions, and when they moved south they disturbed the Qwabe, who themselves moved farther south to disrupt the Tembu, who moved on to dislocate the Tuli, who encroached upon the Pondo, who pressured the Fingo, who impinged upon the secure and long-established Xhosa. At that moment in history the land-hungry trekboers were beginning to encroach upon territory which the Xhosa had long used as pasture; and caught between two grinding stones, the Xhosa sought relief by attacking kraals like Tjaart van Doorn's, whose owners brought pressure on Cape Town, which caused questions to be asked in London. Similar chains of dominoes collapsed in other directions as tribes moving outward dispossessed their neighbors of ancestral lands.

That Shaka slew hundreds with merciless ferocity is historical fact. That the Mfecane set in motion by Shaka and Mzilikazi caused the death of multitudes is also fact. But the behavior of these kings must be judged against the excesses which others, sometimes better educated and Christian, had perpetrated along the shores of the Indian Ocean. In 1502, when Vasco da Gama, the enshrined hero of Portugal, was angered by the officials of Calicut, he slaughtered a shipload of thirty-eight inoffensive Indian fishermen, dismembered their bodies, packed heads, arms and legs into a boat and sent it drifting ashore with the suggestion that the ruler 'boil the lot into a curry hash.'

The results of the Mfecane were by no means all negative. When it ended, vast areas which had formerly known only petty anarchy were organized. The superior culture of the Zulu replaced less-dynamic old traditions. Those who survived developed an enthusiasm they had not known before and a trust in their own capacities. In widely separated regions, deep loyalties were generated upon which important nation-states could be erected.

For example, the Sotho, who were never attacked by Shaka, consolidated a mountain kingdom first known as Basutoland and then Lesotho. The Swazi anchored themselves in a defendable redoubt, where they built their nation of Swaziland. One tribe, under terrible pressure from both Shaka and Mzilikazi, fled north into Moçambique, and helped form the basis of a state that would attain its freedom in 1975.

Even in that year the lasting effect of the Mfecane could not be determined, since the vast movement was still having its repercussions, but perhaps the principal result was the forging of the Zulu nation under Shaka, who took a small tribe with only three hundred real soldiers and about two hundred apprentices and within a decade expanded it with such demonic force that it conquered a significant part of a continent. In area the Zulu kingdom magnified itself a thousand times; in population, two thousand; but in significance and moral power, more like a million.

Had Shaka died before his mother, he would be remembered in history only as another inspired leader who, in accordance with the harsh customs of his time, had brought discipline to an unruly region; his accomplishments would have been respected. But he died after his mother, and the savage excesses of his Dark Time, plus the heroic manner of his death, elevated him beyond mere remembrance and into the realm of legend.

In the most remote corners of southern Africa huddling blacks would dream of the day when mighty Shaka would return to lead them into their heritage. His military prowess was magnified; his prudence as a ruler exalted. Out of his personal tragedy Shaka offered his people a vision.

At Vrijmeer, well north of Zulu power and safely south of Mzilikazi's burgeoning kingdom, Nxumalo, one of the few men who had known both kings intimately, came to realize as he grew older that the really glorious time of his life had been when he led Shaka's iziCwe into battle in its new formation of body-arms-head. Then he and his men, held in vital reserve with their backs to the fray, waited for the imperial command to storm forth. 'What a moment!' he told his children as they sat beside the lake, watching the animals come down to drink. 'Spears flying, men hissing as they killed the enemy, consternation, turmoil, then the calm voice of Shaka: "Nxumalo, support the left flank." That's all he said. And with a cry we leaped to our feet, turned to face the battle, and sped like springboks to destroy the enemy.'

The children were ordered to forget the rest: Shaka's murder of their mothers; the savagery of the Dark Time; the terrible denouement when assassins stalked the king in order to save the nation.

'The thing to remember,' Nxumalo said one evening in 1841, when he had white hair and his children were older, 'is that Shaka was the noblest man who ever lived. The wisest. The kindest. And never forget, Mbengu. Carry yourself tall, because Shaka himself was once married to your mother Thandi.'

When the children asked why, if he loved Shaka, he had not returned to Zululand, he explained: 'You've heard the old rumors. Dingane murdering his own brother Mhlangana, who had helped him gain the throne. If we had gone back, Dingane would have murdered us, all of us. He was always treacherous.'

He preferred nobler thoughts: 'When our nation falls into trouble, Shaka will return to save us, and we'll shout "Bayete!" and if you are men and women of character, you'll respond and Zululand will throb with marching feet, for he will always be our great leader.'

'But didn't you kill him?' a grandson asked.

There are some questions that cannot be answered intelligently, and Nxumalo did not try.

Glossary and Genealogical Charts

In writing of a people with a language as evocative as Afrikaans, the temptation is to lard the narrative with a spate of colorful short words like *kloof* (ravine) or astonishing compounds like *onderwyskollegesportsterreine* (education college sports fields). I try to avoid this device, judging it to be exhibitionism which does not aid the reader. However, to write of the Afrikaner without a seasoning of his language would be an injustice. I have, therefore, used those few words without which the narrative would lack verisimilitude, and in this glossary have marked with an asterisk those which can be found in our larger dictionaries as English adoptions.

*ASSEGAI	slender hardwood spear *Arabic*
BAAS	master; boss
*BAOBAB	tree with swollen trunk *Bantu*
BAYETE	royal salute *Zulu*
*BILTONG	strips of sun-dried, salted meat (jerky)
*BOBOTIE	ground meat, curry, custard *Malay*
*BOER	farmer (capitalized: South African of Dutch or Huguenot descent)
*COMMANDO	Boer military unit (member of such unit)
*DAGGA	marijuana *Hottentot*
DANKIE	thanks
*DISSELBOOM	main shaft of ox wagon
*DOMINEE	minister of Afrikaner churches
FONTEIN	natural spring (fountain)
HARTEBEEST HUT	wattle-and-daub hut with low walls, no windows
*IMPI	regiment of Zulu warriors *Bantu*
*INSPAN	harness draft animals
JA	yes
*KNOBKERRIE	club with knobbed head *Hottentot*
*KOPJE	small hill, often flat-topped

*KRAAL	African village; enclosure for livestock *Portuguese*
*LAAGER	defensive camp encircled by wagons
*LOBOLA	cattle paid for bride *Bantu*
*MEALIES	British maize; American corn (hominy grits)
*MEERKAT	small mammal (resembles prairie dog)
MEJUFFROUW	Miss; young unmarried lady
MEVROUW	Mrs.; becomes Mevrou
*MFECANE	the crushing (forced migration following Zulu consolidation) *Bantu*
MIJNHEER	Mr.; becomes Mynheer and Meneer
*MORGEN	land measure (about two acres)
NACHTMAAL	night meal (Holy Communion) (becomes Nagmaal in Afrikaans)
OUBAAS	old boss (old fellow; grandfather)
OUMA	grandmother
*OUTSPAN	unharness draft animals
*PREDIKANT	clergyman (especially of Dutch Reformed churches)
*RAND	unit of currency worth about one dollar (abbreviation of Witwatersrand)
*RONDAVEL	hut with circular floor plan
*SJAMBOK	short whip of rhinoceros or hippopotamus hide *Malay* from *Persian*
SKOLLIE	hooligan (especially Cape Coloured)
*SLIM	clever; crafty; cunning; shrewd (the original English meaning of this word)
*SMOUS	itinerant merchant (peddler) *German*
*SPOOR	track or trail of man or beast
*STOEP	stoop (porch)
*TREK	arduous migration (especially by ox wagon)
TREKBOER	nomadic grazier
TSOTSI	member of street gang *Bantu*
*UITLANDER	outlander (capitalized: foreigner, especially on the gold fields)
*VELD	open grassland with scattered shrubs and trees (veldt is archaic)
*VELDKORNET	minor district official (in military: lieutenant)
*VELDSKOEN	rawhide homemade shoe (also veldtskoen)
VERDOMDE	damned; cursed
V.O.C.	Vereenigde Oostindische Compagnie (United East India Company)
*VOLK	nation; people
VOORTREKKER	forward trekker (member of the 1834–1837 Great Trek)
VRYMEER	Freedom Lake (in Dutch: Vrijmeer)

Pronunciation: In general, words are pronounced as they look, except that J = Y; V = F; W = V; OE = U. The name Van Wyk = Fan Vake; and for no reason that can be explained, Uys = Ace. Vrymeer, of course, is Fraymeer.

The Van Doorns

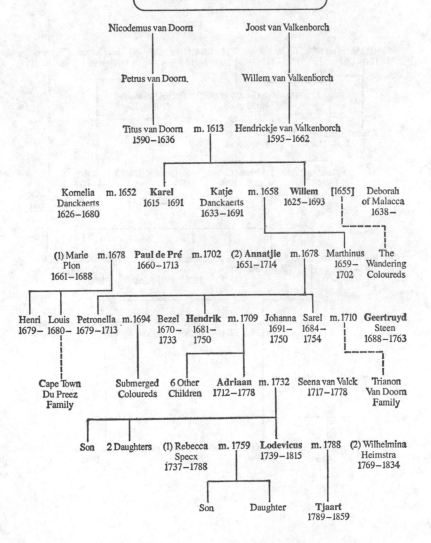

Nicodemus van Doorn   Joost van Valkenborch

Petrus van Doorn.   Willem van Valkenborch

Titus van Doorn   m. 1613   Hendrickje van Valkenborch
1590–1636   1595–1662

Kornelia   m. 1652   **Karel**   Katje   m. 1658   **Willem**   [1655]   Deborah
Danckaerts   1615 1691   Danckaerts   1625–1693   of Malacca
1626–1680   1633–1691   1638–

(1) Marie   m. 1678   **Paul de Pré**   m. 1702   **(2) Annatjie**   m. 1678.   Marthinus   The
Plon   1660–1713   1651–1714   1659–   Wandering
1661–1688   1702   Coloureds

Henri   Louis   Petronella   m. 1694   Bezel   **Hendrik**   m. 1709   Johanna   Sarel   m. 1710   **Geertruyd**
1679–   1680–   1679–1713   1670–   1681–   1691–   1684–   Steen
                                 1733   1750   1750   1754   1688–1763

Cape Town   Submerged   6 Other   **Adriaan**   m. 1732   Seena van Valck   Trianon
Du Preez   Coloureds   Children   1712–1778   1717–1778   Van Doorn
Family   Family

Son   2 Daughters   **(1)** Rebecca   m. 1759   **Lodevicus**   m. 1788   **(2)** Wilhelmina
                  Specx   1739–1815   Heimstra
                  1737–1788   1769–1834

Son   Daughter   **Tjaart**
                            1789–1859

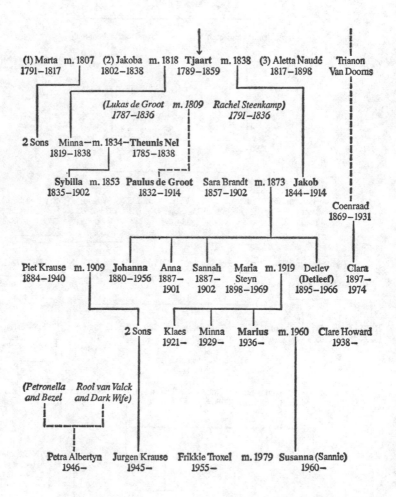

(1) Marta m. 1807 (2) Jakoba m. 1818 **Tjaart** m. 1838 (3) Aletta Naudé Trianon
1791–1817 1802–1838 1789–1859 1817–1898 Van Doorns

(Lukas de Groot m. 1809 Rachel Steenkamp)
1787–1836 *1791–1836*

2 Sons Minna—m. 1834—**Theunis Nel**
1819–1838 1785–1838

Sybilla m. 1853 **Paulus de Groot** Sara Brandt m. 1873 Jakob
1835–1902 1832–1914 1857–1902 1844–1914

Coenraad
1869–1931

Piet Krause m. 1909 **Johanna** Anna Sannah Maria m. 1919 Detlev Clara
1884–1940 1880–1956 1887– 1887– Steyn **(Detleef)** 1897–
1901 1902 1898–1969 1895–1966 1974

2 Sons Klaes Minna **Marius** m. 1960 Clare Howard
1921– 1929– 1936– 1938–

(Petronella Rooi van Valck
and Bezel and Dark Wife)

Petra Albertyn Jurgen Krause Frikkie Troxel m. 1979 Susanna (Sannie)
1946– 1945– 1955– 1960–

The Nxumalos

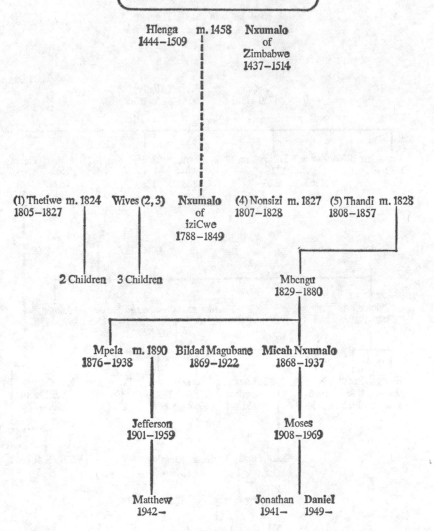

Hlenga
1444–1509

m. 1458

Nxumalo
of
Zimbabwe
1437–1514

(1) Thetiwe m. 1824
1805–1827

Wives (2, 3)

Nxumalo
of
iziCwe
1788–1849

(4) Nonsizi m. 1827
1807–1828

(5) Thandi m. 1828
1808–1857

2 Children

3 Children

Mbcngu
1829–1880

Mpela m. 1890
1876–1938

Bildad Magubane
1869–1922

Micah Nxumalo
1868–1937

Jefferson
1901–1959

Moses
1908–1969

Matthew
1942–

Jonathan
1941–

Daniel
1949–

The Saltwoods

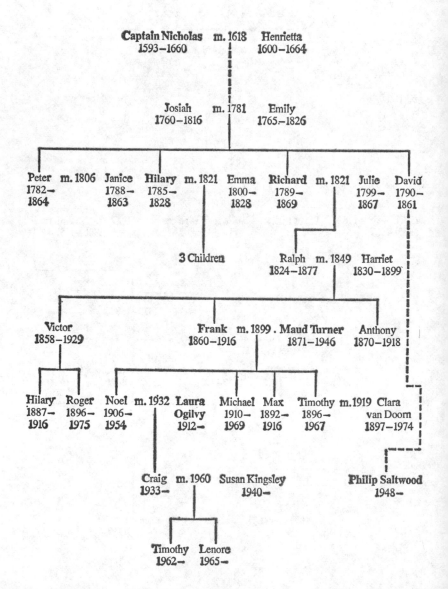

Captain Nicholas m. 1618 Henrietta
1593–1660 1600–1664

Josiah m. 1781 Emily
1760–1816 1765–1826

Peter m. 1806 Janice Hilary m. 1821 Emma Richard m. 1821 Julie David
1782– 1788– 1785– 1800– 1789– 1799– 1790–
1864 1863 1828 1828 1869 1867 1861

3 Children

Ralph m. 1849 Harriet
1824–1877 1830–1899

Victor Frank m. 1899 . Maud Turner Anthony
1858–1929 1860–1916 1871–1946 1870–1918

Hilary Roger Noel m. 1932 Laura Michael Max Timothy m. 1919 Clara
1887– 1896– 1906– Ogilvy 1910– 1892– 1896– van Doorn
1916 1975 1954 1912– 1969 1916 1967 1897–1974

Craig m. 1960 Susan Kingsley Philip Saltwood
1933– 1940– 1948–

Timothy Lenore
1962– 1965–

Travels and Treks

0   200 miles

0   200 kilometers

DEATH OF
GUMSTO ×

Orange River

Vaal R.

Orange River

Rooi van Valck's ×

A T L A N T I C

O C E A N

Gra

1751
×

1742
×

Golan

Cape Town ●
1648   × 1662

× 1692

1724 ×

Jean Paul Tremblay